Also by Chelsea Quinn Yarbro

Hôtel Transylvania

Available from Warner Books

Chelsea Quinn Yarbro

Night Blooming

*From the
Chronicles of
Saint-Germain*

ASPECT®

WARNER BOOKS

An AOL Time Warner Company

Aspect® name and logo are registered trademarks of Warner Books, Inc.

Warner Books, Inc., 1271 Avenue of the Americas, New York, NY 10020
Visit our Web site at www.twbookmark.com.

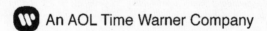 An AOL Time Warner Company

Printed in the United States of America
First Printing: October 2002
10 9 8 7 6 5 4 3 2 1

Library of Congress Cataloging-in-Publication Data
Yarbro, Chelsea Quinn
　　Night blooming / Chelsea Quinn Yarbro.
　　p. cm.
　　ISBN 0-446-52981-8
　　1. Saint-Germain, comte de, d. 1784—Fiction. 2. Charlemagne,
Emperor, 742–814—Fiction. 3. France—History—To 987—Fiction.
4. Alcuin, 735–804—Fiction. 5. Vampires—Fiction. I. Title.

PS3575.A7 N54 2002
813'.54—dc21   2002016876

Book design by Mada Design, Inc. / NYC

for Wiley Saichek

franksland **800** A.D.

author's note

The rise of the Frankish chieftain known to history as Charlemagne has become so cloaked in legend that the real man is hard to find in the myth. Probably the most obvious difference between the historical and fabled man was that Frankish he may have been, but French he was not. The Franks were a powerful Germanic tribe occupying, among other territory, that part of Gaul called Francia that includes modern-day France. Their language was Teutonic, and their customs were based on German tribal structures. In the words of the late-Empire Romans and Byzantine Greeks, the Franks were barbarians; Charlemagne, being a good Frank, spelled his name Karlus, or Karl, as his sigil clearly shows. He also stood over six feet four inches in a time when the average nobleman was about five feet two inches. No wonder he was called The Large, or The Great (lo Magne).

When Pepin the Short became King of the Franks in 754, he ended the Merovingian dynasty that preceded his rulership. He also gave his support to the Roman Catholic Church and in exchange for Church recognition of his claims, promised to hold the western territory of the Roman Empire for the Church. Pepin conferred the region of Italy known as the Papal States on the Church by claiming Byzantine lands in Italy and declaring that these territories now belonged to the Pope. Known as the Donation of Pepin, it marked the beginning of Papal politico-temporal power in Europe, and guaranteed Church support of Pepin's claims on the Frankish throne. Upon Pepin's death in 768, his two sons, Karl and Karloman, were bequeathed Pepin's divided kingdom. After Karloman's death in 771—rumored to be by poison but possibly from appendicitis—Karl-lo-Magne, then about twenty-nine years old, became King of all the Franks and began an ambitious program of empire building. He also reconfirmed the Donation of Pepin, thus uniting his efforts with the interests of the Catholic Church.

With the Christian world divided and emotions running high on both sides, one might suppose that the position of Jews would be problematic. In Karl-lo-Magne's territories, Jews were highly regarded members of the community. It was not uncommon for Christians to attend Jewish services, and for Jews to go to Mass and be entertained by Bishops and regional nobility. A few Jews were elevated to positions of considerable power in Karl-lo-Magne's court, and Jewish scholars were often consulted on Old Testament doctrinal issues. In the Roman Church, Jews held important posts as scholars, secretaries, and legal advisors. Certain regions of Karl-lo-Magne's kingdom were anti-Jewish, but those regions tended to general xenophobia, and their unsympathetic attitudes were not limited to Jews alone, but to all manner of outsiders.

The world of Charlemagne was a precarious place, existing amid the remnants of the western half of the Roman Empire, trying to keep the powerful Byzantine Empire (the Eastern Roman Empire) at bay, battling other barbarian tribes, and oftentimes fending off insurrections within their own ranks. The lofty goals of ordered peace under the restoration of Roman law often seemed not only unattainable but absurd. Karl-lo-Magne included scholarship and, to a lesser degree, arts among the various talents he sought out for his Court, a decision that was to shine a bright light on his reign that is mostly lacking in the backwater of Europe during that period called the Dark Ages. By having men of letters as well as soldiers around him, Karl-lo-Magne guaranteed he would be remembered, for much of the work of the intellectual community was to document Karl-lo-Magne's activities.

And what a lot of activities there were: Karl-lo-Magne was on campaign for most of his reign—campaigns against the Moors and the Saxons and the Longobards (Lombards—Germanic peoples living in northern Italy) were undertaken regularly, Karl-lo-Magne leading his forces on campaign. Most of Frankish society was predicated on war, something Karl-lo-Magne tried to modify to some extent even while exploiting the Franks' capacity for it. He not only strove to achieve a single code of laws for his subjects and to make education available—if not compulsory—for all upper-class children, he tried to establish a sense of what today would be called national identity. He, himself, spoke German, Latin, and a little Greek, but could not read nor write beyond signing his name and sigil; most of his military supporters were also illiterate, employing clerks and scribes to handle any reading or writing, which bound the military class to the Church ever more closely, since monks were the largest generally literate class in all Frankish territory. Karl-lo-Magne put money into the development of canals for merchants' traffic, into building fortresses and castles, into establishing centers of learning, into creating an ongoing political tie with the Church, and into expanding the system of roads in his empire, any one of which would have been a major achievement for a ruler of the period, and were all the more remarkable in that his efforts, for the most part, paid off, at least during his reign. By the time of his death in January of 814 at the seriously advanced age of seventy-one or -two, Karl-lo-Magne had dramatically changed the face of Europe. By becoming the military head of the Roman Empire in the West—as compared to the Roman Empire in the East as the Byzantine Empire styled itself—he laid the foundation of the Holy Roman Empire, which, though neither holy nor Roman nor an Empire, still shaped European politics for the next eight hundred years.

In his efforts to create unity among his people, Karl-lo-Magne banned the speaking of Celtic, destroyed major pagan shrines, broke the hold of minor princes and regional warlords, pushed back the Moors in the southwest, the Longobards in the south, the Avars in the southeast, and the Saxons in the northeast, and generally drew all power under his wing, extending his control to all aspects of his empire. This usually also included certain Church privileges that Karl-lo-Magne took upon himself, particularly the appointment of Bishops, who not only had the authority of the Church but generally had rich revenues from their bishoprics not unlike the revenues that the lay authorities had from their fiscs, counties, and duchies. Bishoprics were valuable prizes and were far more secular in their character than they are in modern times—although it is as well to keep in mind that for Karl-lo-Magne and his contemporaries, the eighth and ninth centuries *were* modern times—and were sought after by high-ranking families to add to their material and territorial wealth. Bishops hunted, banqueted, drank, whored, kept slaves and musicians and mistresses, had bastards to whom they bequeathed Church property, were touchy about their prestige, and tended to behave very much the way the military nobles did.

In spite of Karl-lo-Magne's efforts, the languages of his subjects remained fairly chaotic once the Royal Court and the upper echelons of the Church were left behind; even at that level of society, the language was an amalgam of German and Latin, with little formality and fewer rules; certainly the formal structure of Classical Latin was gone, and had been replaced by a haphazard application of Latinate rules on German vocabulary that occasionally bangs its linguistic shins on present-day academic training. Also the Latin itself had worn down over time—for example, the Classical Latin *caldarium* (heated bath) had become *caladarium* the century before. Because of that, I have used the terms of the period when they are regularized enough to be correctly consistent. When that consistency is lacking, I have used the modern terms for the sake of comprehensibility. For example, I used the modern title Bishop instead of the nine different regional versions of that title used in Frankish territory during Karl-lo-Magne's reign, and the modern names of cities and towns when there were multiple names for the places in question. There are a few terms and offices that are peculiar to the period—for example: *magnatus-i* (high-ranking non-military functionary), *missi dominici* (Carolingian Inspectors General and couriers), *mariscalcus-i* (masters of horses and stables), *buticularius-ii* (butler: in charge of household economy, particularly provisioning the kitchen)—that are precise and consistent, and those I have used in their original forms. Items of clothing have their period names, as do units of measure, although these often varied from place to place. There were also Frankish names for all the months, as well as Roman ones, but I have used their contemporary names for clarity's sake. At the time, few persons had last names in the sense that modern persons do; compound names were fairly rare but not unheard-of, but lacked the connecting hyphen that such names have today: Gynethe Mehaut is like Marie-Louise, not like Mary Smith. Merchants were generally known by their city of principal business, such as Gerardius of Arles; artisans were identified by the trades: Clovis the Joiner, Irmold the Fletcher, etc. The military upper class were known usually by the land they controlled, and while most had clan or family names as well as personal name, they were more indicative of lineage than many last names are now.

Although Karl-lo-Magne's capitol was at Aachen, he maintained a number of Royal Residences throughout his realm, such as Paderborn—once he conquered the Saxons whose capital it was—and often traveled to them, taking his entire household, including his widowed mother, Bertrada (Bertha), called Big-Foot, until her death, and most of his daughters with him, along with dozens of courtiers, soldiers, nobles, petitioners, monks, scribes, women, entertainers, servants, and slaves. This formidable company traveled much as an army of the period did, moving across the land slowly and commandeering food and shelter everywhere they went. His residences had permanent staffs whose job it was to keep the residence ready for Karl-lo-Magne's visits. A small group of officials had the duty of notifying and supervising preparations for Karl-lo-Magne's—and his Court's—arrival. Other high-ranking nobles were sometimes ordered to receive all of Karl-lo-Magne's retinue, which, while an honor and a sign of favor, could also prove costly for the appointed host, who had to feed, house, and entertain the visitors in as grand a style as courtesy (meaning courtly standards, not good behavior) demanded. Even religious institutions, such as monasteries and the households of Bishops, could be required to host Karl-lo-Magne's entourage, for the political reality of the time established a quid-pro-quo arrangement between the Franks and the Church in Frankish territories.

The Church contributed to the life of the empire in many ways, perhaps none so significant as the establishment of major monasteries and convents throughout Karl-lo-Magne's realm. Not only did these thriving communities contribute to the local economy, they served as learning centers and safe havens. The vast, forested expanse of the central Frankish lands was peppered with religious communities offering hospitality to travelers and refuge for those driven from their farms by war or plague or famine. Since priests were not yet forbidden to marry, many of them maintained private households in towns and villages, fairly isolated in their work, and as such did not have the powerful community presence of (technically celibate) monks, whose monasteries were often villages in themselves, where God's Work dictated the behavior of the occupants—at least in theory. In many ways the monasteries actually served as a substitute for towns, which were small, dangerous, and disease-ridden. Most monasteries and convents were dedicated to maintaining the prestige of their patron saints, and not only because it added to their importance but because the reputation of a saint was often all that stood between the non-military religious and the greedy military elite, who were disinclined to attack a monastery or convent if the patron saint was considered a powerful one, who could be counted upon to exact supernatural revenge for any abuse of his or her monks.

Alcuin of York's administration of the major monasteries helped in cementing the goals and policies of Karl-lo-Magne; he also protected Church interests by encouraging mutual support among regional military and religious institutions. By maintaining a standard of performance for scholarship, Alcuin made it possible for the monasteries to provide a dependable recording service to the ruling class, which inclined the nobles to value—and therefore protect—the monasteries. The work of the clerical scholars done during Karl-lo-Magne's reign proved invaluable to Karl-lo-Magne as well as to later centuries through the compilation of *descriptiones* and *itineraries*—comprehensive lists and catalogs of the world around them; they also reformed writing through the invention of the Carolingian minuscule, or what we call lowercase letters, such as the ones you are reading right now.

Until the thirteenth century, the Church had no policy on stigmata, leaving it up to local religious authorities to decide if the wounds were holy or damnable in their implication. Rare though it was, the stigmata did occur from time to time, and response to it varied from veneration to persecution, depending on the prevailing superstition of the era. St. Francis of Assisi was the first stigmatic to have his injuries officially recognized as spiritually favorable, a perception that has carried on to the present day. At the time of Karl-lo-Magne, the stigmata phenomenon was considered dangerous, whether good or bad in its interpretation, and for that reason, stigmatics were carefully watched by Church authorities.

During Karl-lo-Magne's reign, two major agrarian developments—the three-field rotation system of farming, and the standardized horseshoe—significantly changed agriculture and travel. For the first time since the Roman Empire in the West fell, crop surpluses became possible, for the three-field rotation, planting two fields and leaving one fallow for grazing each year, reduced the catastrophic impact of crop failure by having two crops each harvest season instead of one. Famine still occurred but less regularly than before, and was more quickly recovered from. The innovation of the standardized horseshoe simplified military campaigns and farming alike and made travel a bit less precarious by ensuring shoes for horses that were readily and relatively inexpensively available. Another Frankish innovation that came shortly after Karl-lo-Magne's death was the invention of a heavy, wheeled plow that allowed for a deep, turned furrow rather than a shallow scratch in the topsoil; this allowed for tathing—covering the fields in dung and straw during the winter—which could be plowed back into the earth in the spring, replenishing the earth with fertilizer as well as supporting the crop rotation. In the gradual disintegration that followed Karl-lo-Magne's death, farming continued to flourish in western Europe.

These improvements would not have been possible without the increase in iron mining in German territories. This, along with silver mining in what is now western Poland, made the Franks rich and powerful, providing the raw material of wealth and the means to control the market. Frankish iron made the heavy plow and standardized horseshoe possible by producing a supply of ore that was more than adequate to military needs; it allowed for horses to carry and pull heavier loads, and for larger, heavier horses to be bred—both unlikely without the standardized shoe, made possible by the increased supply of iron. Suddenly scissors, shears, sickles, knives, spades, and other iron utensils were also being made for a much more general market than had been possible since the fourth century. Because the Franks controlled the silver mines, the Carolingian monetary system—such as it was—was silver-based, not gold. Money was in short supply in any case, no matter of what metal; most commerce was based on trade of goods and services. A further problem with gold was that it had to be got from other governments, and could be costly in more ways than one. Rather than burden himself with gold-based obligations, Karl-lo-Magne saved his gold for royal ornaments and ceremonial objects and minted almost all his coins in silver.

The population of Europe during Karl-lo-Magne's reign—and for almost a thousand years thereafter—was about 80 percent peasant, 10 percent military and clergy, 8 percent artisan (predominantly masons, smiths, potters, weavers, leather-workers, millers, and all manner of wrights), and 2 percent merchant classes. In this population, days and seasons were more important than specific dates, and the society reflected that: the calendar had not been regularized, and though Karl-lo-Magne used the Pope's calendar for state documents, many of his subjects did not, resulting in a level of official confusion that lasted well into the Medieval period. Karl-lo-Magne also had his own system of months, which he used generally. Time was reckoned by sundials and canonical Hours, and not by any agreed-upon discrete measurement of minutes. Sunrise and sunset established the limits of the peasants' and artisans' day, the religious lived by the eight Hours of the Divine Office (with an optional observation of Nocturne or Vigil), which was a round-the-clock schedule of prayers and chanting, keeping a somewhat different schedule in the eighth century than they do now; the military lived by the pragmatic demands of campaigning.

As always, there are a number of people to thank for various kinds of help in researching this novel: Barry Carlton for campaign maps of Karl-lo-Magne's conquests and expansions; Louise Sagan for information on languages and dialects in Karl-lo-Magne's territories; J. K. Grunning for information on the religious institutions and structures of the Carolingian epoch; Desmond Creary for references on Carolingian art and manuscripts; Raymond Vassar for untangling the ninth-century political interaction of Byzantium and Rome; Philippe Cartier for information on Frankish social history; Hudson Scarpard for his knowledge of the state of learning and education in Carolingian times; Leonard Pasterman for information on Karl-lo-Magne's movements, with apologies for occasionally putting him fictionally where he was not actually; Angelica Wilson for her information about domestic production and village-level sufficiency in Frankish territories; and Lorinda Nohl for access to her material on Frankish domestic and agricultural innovation. Any errors in historicity are mine, and none of these good people's.

On the other end of the process, thanks to my agent, Irene Kraas, for all the hard work; to my editor Betsy Mitchell, Larissa Rivera, and the good people at Warner Books, especially Laurence Kirshbaum; and with a nod to Stealth Press for their fine editions of the early Saint-Germain titles—and the handsome covers by Muran Kim. Other thanks are due to Lindig Harris for book searches and the newsletter, *Yclept Yarbro* (lindig@mindspring.com); to Sharon Russell, Stephanie Moss, Elizabeth Miller, and Katie Harse for their continuing enthusiasm; to accuracy readers Joel Weissberg, Libba Campbell, and Ernestine Maxwell; to clarity readers Imelda Veasy, David Green, and Susanne Lyleson; to regular readers Maureen Kelly, Jim Watkins, and Megan Kincaid; to Bowling Green University for archiving my manuscripts; to Robin Dubner, my attorney, who looks after Saint-Germain's interests; to George Meckel for some excellent advice; to Tyrrell Morris for maintaining my computers in the face of viruses and worms, as well as my Web site (www.ChelseaQuinnYarbro.com); and to the bookstore owners and readers who continue to support this series—without you, this might all be an exercise in futility.

Chelsea Quinn Yarbro
Berkeley, June 2001

part one

KARL-LO-MAGNE

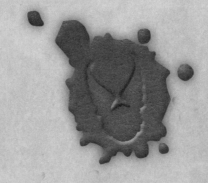

The greetings of Alcuin of York, to the magnatus Hiernom Rakoczy, de Santus Germainius of Torun, on behalf of Karlus, King of the Franks, at the behest of whom I request that you come to Sant' Martin at Tours where eminent grammarians, calligraphers, and geographers have gathered to aid in the work of various itineraries on the order of the King's Will. This must serve as a summons to you to join our efforts, as I shall delineate further.

Your fame has reached us from even so far as the territories where you have come to live. We have been told that you have been much about the world, even as far as the lands of the Great Khan, and can add to our geographic exercises, as well as our efforts to expand our description of the greater realms of the earth. Your knowledge, therefore, would receive the utmost respect and attention, and in time you may earn the regard of Great Karl himself, as well as the gratitude of Holy Church.

It is also said that you have skills in mathematics which rival the Arabs for subtlety and potency, the which you may be persuaded to include in your instruction of us. It is known that the use of numbers is a most erudite talent, and one that would benefit our King most truly. If you will agree to teach us what you know, the value of your presence here will exceed that of any other single scholar. If this distinction can add to any argument I might put forth to bring you into Frankish lands, then consider it and let it be the final factor in your deliberations.

The missi dominici who carry this letter will provide you escort to Sant' Martin at Tours. They are proven men, worthy of the King's trust, and stalwart in their purpose. Otfrid of Hersfeld and Fratre Angelomus have served Great Karlus for many years, and you may trust them as you trust in the King. They have the right of paravareda, allowing them to requisition horses on your journey once you have crossed into Frankish lands. Until that time, you will need to provide horses for your own travel, as well as all provisions, for as great as his power is, Karlus cannot command beyond his own borders.

You will be permitted to bring four servants and three soldiers with you, but no more than that. You will be allocated housing here until Karlus makes other

provisions for your keep. If you can afford to provide for your own maintenance, then you may apply for such grants as the King may wish to accord you.

This travel will bring you into Great Karl's lands in the month of
September if God is good and your passage is swift, and you meet with no
misfortunes in your travels. Your place will be ready for you at the Feast of
Moses, and for every day thereafter to the Nativity, when, if we have no
word of you or of your escort, we will command a Mass of Remembrance for
the repose of your souls, and your names will be enrolled among those to be
prayed for, as an acknowledgment of your service to Karlus.

It would be most ungracious of you to refuse this generous offer from
Karlus, who only extends such invitations as this one to the most worthy of
foreigners. Karlus has a long memory and a longer arm, and would not be
pleased to learn that you returned his kindness with impertinence. Consider
the advantages our King may offer you, and come with the missi dominici
willingly. You will not regret accommodating our King, but you may well rue
refusing him.

May God speed you here, and may you rejoice in the favor of Karlus.
Written by my own hand on the Feast of Barnabas the Apostle in the 796th
Year of Grace as proclaimed by the Pope in Rome.

Alcuin of York
Abbott, and Bishop, Sant' Martin at Tours,
and of Cormery, Ferrieres, Sant' Loup, Sens,
Flavigny, and Sant' Josse

∽

chapter one

NUDGING ONE OF HIS SLAVES with the toe of his boot, Bishop Freculf waited for him to bring a stool so he could dismount with the dignity of his
station. He was dressed for summer hunting, his russet gonelle of heavy linen just
now wrinkled, pulling out of his girdle, torn at the shoulder, and stained with the

blood of deer. His femoralia were covered with tibialia over which the broad bands of his high brodequins were laced, and all were spattered with mud. His only sign of rank was his massive pectoral crucifix on a collar of crosslets, which he had wiped clean of dust and mire. He rose in his stirrups and looked at the Priora of the convent. "What was it you wanted me to see?" he asked, his aristocratic accent giving him added authority beyond his powerful position. "I have left my escort outside. They will wait for me."

The slave put a mounting stool in place and knelt, holding it in position, while Bishop Freculf came out of his saddle.

Priora Iditha dropped to her knees before the Bishop. "You cannot imagine, Sublime, what has been put upon us."

Bishop Freculf laid his hand on the Priora's head. "Then you must show me, Sorra. That is why you summoned me." He motioned her to rise, and added to his slave, "Hold my horse. And better harm should come to you than to him."

The Wendish slave nodded to show his devotion, got to his feet, and took the big roan gelding's reins in his hands. He did not look directly at the Bishop, for that affront would earn him a beating.

The convent of Santa Albegunda was a relatively small establishment on the road between Stavelot and Reims, housing 118 nuns, their 149 servants, and 175 slaves. Famous for its miraculous cures of bodily malformations, it was handsomely endowed and maintained a fisc larger than many other similar establishments. It was comprised of eleven buildings, including a barn and a stable, in addition to an herb garden, two orchards, four fields, a vineyard, and a pond, all enclosed within its stout outer walls. The Abba, Sunifred, was the daughter of the local Potente, a petty noble called Hilduin, and as such was able to command more support from the people of the region.

The Priora led the Bishop through the courtyard toward the smaller chapel, saying as she went, "We have had no guidance in this situation. We must rely on you to tell us how to proceed."

"Of course," said Bishop Freculf, tapping his short whip against his thigh as he walked. It had been a hot afternoon that was now turning to a warm night, and he was still sweating freely. "Do you think this will take long?"

"I cannot tell," said Priora Iditha, and stepped into the narthex of the chapel. "Look for yourself."

"What am I to see?" asked the Bishop, crossing himself as he glanced along the narrow aisle toward the altar.

"She is praying," said the Priora, lowering her voice slightly.

"Prostrate?" The Bishop was mildly surprised. "Is she a penitent?"

"That isn't for me to say," Priora Iditha answered. "We are in something of a quandary about her. Abba Sunifred has not been able to determine what to do about her. She has proven a difficult case, as you can understand she might. Her father—a tanner and seller of hides—brought her to us when their village priest said he could not deal with her any longer."

"Is she willful?" Bishop Freculf asked, perplexed by this continued evasion.

"Not that we can discover. Come speak to her; determine her demeanor for yourself," said the Priora, motioning to the Bishop to follow her.

The Bishop hesitated. "Should we interrupt her praying?"

"If we wait for her to finish, we may be here well past nightfall, and you will not have the banquet that your cooks are preparing for you even now," said the Priora, who knew enough about the Bishop to be certain of his evening plans. "You have musicians and jugglers at your villa, have you not?"

Bishop Freculf smiled. "I am a most fortunate man."

"May God be thanked," said the Priora.

"I do thank Him, Sorra, every morning and every night in my prayers." He smiled wolfishly. "Come, then. Let us see what has caused such an uproar in this holy place."

The Priora led him down the aisle, her attention on the figure lying prone with arms outstretched before the altar. "Gynethe Mehaut," she called. "Rise. Bishop Freculf is here."

For a moment nothing happened, and then a figure materialized in the swath of a dust-colored linen stolla belted with rope. She was pale as new curds, thin to the point of gauntness, and somewhat less than average height. Her hair was the color of ivory in a single braid down her back. She might have been a ten-year-old child if not for the rise of her breasts. As she looked up, Bishop Freculf gasped, for her eyes were red as garnets. "Sublime," she said.

Bishop Freculf stared at the young woman, then turned to the Priora. "This is most . . . unusual." He contemplated the young woman, assessing her oddities and trying to determine what they might portend. "Most unusual," he added. He stroked his beard and stared at her. "Are you ill?"

"Not that I am aware of, Sublime," said Gynethe Mehaut.

"This is not the whole of it. Gynethe Mehaut, hold out your hands," the Priora said.

Turning her red eyes away, she lifted her hands, palms up, her manner suggesting distress and shame. There, against the white flesh, was blood in the center of both palms, sluggishly wet.

The Bishop stared. "What have you done?" he demanded, his face flushing with outrage. "How dare you do this?"

"I have done nothing," said Gynethe Mehaut, her voice just above a whisper. "I pray and this happens."

"How?" he demanded. "What do you do to yourself?"

"Nothing," she insisted. "I do nothing. I pray."

"Then why should you have hurts like that? They are blasphemous!" The Bishop strove to contain his growing sense of outrage.

"I don't know how I come to have the marks, Sublime, and I have prayed deeply in the hope of learning the reason for them," Gynethe Mehaut whispered, about to hide her hands in the capacious sleeves of her stolla. "God has not revealed that to me, no matter how I supplicate."

"They began when she achieved womanhood," said the Priora. "She bleeds, and not just woman's blood."

He caught her hands in his own. "You have cut yourself."

"I haven't," she murmured.

"You *must* have," the Bishop insisted. He glared at her, then averted his gaze, his brow knit; he was badly shaken.

"We have watched her, Sublime," said the Priora. "She has not cut herself that we have seen, and yet she bleeds."

The Bishop shook his head vehemently. "No. No. Those wounds are only found in Christ Jesus. No other may have them."

"Unless they are inflicted as a punishment, when the hands are nailed so that sins may be expiated," said Priora Iditha. "But this woman has not been punished."

"Perhaps she was punished before she came here," suggested the Bishop, his indignation barely controlled.

"She has been here for many months. The marks haven't changed in all that time," said the Priora. "Tell him, Gynethe Mehaut."

"I have had them for more than five years," said the pale young woman. "I was sent here to be cured of them. I have prayed I would be cured."

Bishop Freculf shook his head. "There is something very wrong here. The prayers of the Sorrae and the water from the well should have salved your . . . injuries." His eyes narrowed. "Unless you are not a child of the Church, but are sworn to old gods or to the Devil Himself."

Gynethe Mehaut drew back in horror. "No, no, Sublime. Nothing like that. I have lived within the care of the Church all my life. I have always been faithful to Christ and the King."

"It's true," said Priora Iditha. "She was taken by the Sorrae at Sant' Osmer in Rennes, just a babe. They cared for her until she was a woman, and then the Sorrae sent her back to her parents and the care of their priest. I have the account from the Abba, Serilda of Nerithe, if you wish to review it. She has a most excellent reputation for piety, and she gives a good account of Gynethe Mehaut."

"Indeed I do want to see this," said Bishop Freculf. "I will examine it at once."

"It will be given to you, along with what Patre Ermold wrote about her. We have both to show you," said Priora Iditha. "And a letter from the Bishop of Rennes, telling of his agreement in sending her here."

"And I will look at them closely, never fear," said the Bishop. "Where is Abba Sunifred? I would like to have a word with her."

"She is out hunting, Sublime, as I told you," said the Priora apologetically. "I do not expect her until sunset."

"She's with her father, no doubt," said the Bishop. "Very well. I will see these accounts; then, when the Abba is back, she and I must talk." He let go of Gynethe Mehaut. "I should have been told about this before now. Why did you wait so long?"

"We were praying for a cure for her, Sublime. That's why Patre Ermold sent her here, with his blessing, the blessings of her parents, and her Bishop. Abba Sunifred said we could not stop our prayers—"

"She wanted the glory for this convent," said the Bishop. "As well she might. Santa Albegunda is a most puissant patroness."

"I am grateful that you understand," said the Priora, turning her back on Gynethe Mehaut, who had prostrated herself before the altar once again. "Remain here. If we need you, we will summon you."

"Yes, Priora," said Gynethe Mehaut, her voice muffled by the sleeve of her stolla.

"She seems obedient," said the Bishop as he and the Priora left Gynethe Mehaut alone in the chapel.

"That she is. And devout as well. I have no doubt that she is sincere in her faith. She fasts on Sunday and Wednesday, and attends Vigil faithfully. She keeps herself before the altar for most of the night and half of the day. She claims that she has to do this for the sins of the world." Priora Iditha shook her head vehemently. "It is most troublesome to see her hands as they are."

"She is a woman, and as such, heir to all the sins of the flesh in this sinful world. It is not fitting that she should have the marks of Our Savior on her flesh, but that she does so to profane the wounds. What woman can have this honor?" The Bishop entered the largest building, the one that housed the nuns and their servants. "Where are these records?"

"If you will go to the church, I will bring them to you there. Or you may remain here, Sublime. The Sorrae are preparing for the evening meal, and so it would not be fitting for you to come any deeper into the convent." Although the Priora said it subserviently enough, it was clear that she would require the Bishop to stay in the public portions of the building.

"Perhaps I should await you in the courtyard," the Bishop murmured. "The Sorrae are not to be compromised, particularly not by a Bishop."

"No, most surely not," said the Priora with feeling.

With a gesture of dismissal, Bishop Freculf returned to the courtyard, where he ordered one of the convent's slaves to bring him a cup of wine. "Use one of those from your own kitchen," he added. "My cup is packed in my saddlebag and I do not wish to get it out."

The slave abased herself and went to do as he ordered.

Left to his own devices, Bishop Freculf drew a knife from the scabbard on his belt and began to pare his fingernails, taking care to collect all the bits when he was done so that no one could use the parings against him. He was just finishing up when the slave returned with a cup of wine, which she held up to him as she knelt before him. He dropped the bits of his nails into the wine and took the cup from her, swirling the wine in the cup and gesturing to her to leave him. He was half-finished with the wine when Priora Iditha returned, three rolled scrolls in her hand.

"Here. You may read them now, if you wish, Sublime. The Superiora would not like these reports to leave the convent, in case she may have use for them in days to come." This was more emphatic than it was proper for a nun to be, but the Priora was used to exercising her authority and did so now.

"Would the Abba allow me to take these?" Bishop Freculf asked. He knew the answer would be yes, for Sunifred was his second cousin and was bound to help her kinsman who was also her most immediate Church authority.

"No doubt she would," said Priora Iditha. "If you care to wait to ask her, I will have the slaves bring you bread and cheese. It is not as fine as what you will have at your banquet, but it will be what the Sorrae are having." It was an obvious ploy, yet it worked.

"No. I do not want to wait so long, or to impose upon you." He did not have to add that he much preferred the banquet awaiting him at his villa than the simple fare of the nuns.

"As you wish, Sublime. I will have a brazier brought, to give you better light," she said, and clapped to summon a slave. "The Bishop would like some light."

The slave pulled at her forelock and hurried away.

"Do you have to beat her much? She's very obedient," said the Bishop.

"Not too much. She is devoted," said the Priora. "Why would we keep a disobedient slave?"

There was a silence between them; then the Bishop said, "You have been diligent in maintaining the convent. I hope the Superiora is as careful in supervising the nuns."

"With God's Grace," said the Priora. She prepared to leave, but she stopped. "How long will you need to read?"

"I'll summon you when I am finished. It will not be long," said the Bishop, and sat down on the widest bench along the wall. When the slave brought a brazier, set it near him, and lit it, he unrolled the largest scroll and scanned its contents, murmuring as he read.

The Vespers bell was ringing when Bishop Freculf rolled the second scroll closed and called for a slave. "Bring the Priora," he ordered, and paced the courtyard until Priora Iditha returned. "I have read two of these," he told her, holding out the scrolls to her. "A most interesting account, both of them. One day I will read the third. I will consider what they say, and I'll let you know my judgment on this matter." He put his empty cup aside.

"I will tell the Abba when she returns," said the Priora. "And we will pray for you."

Knowing he was entitled to this, the Bishop merely nodded. "I'll address her on the matter shortly. No more than a week." He held out his hand so that the Priora could kiss his episcopal ring.

"Very good, Sublime," said Priora Iditha, kneeling to kiss the ring, then rose. "We will guard her."

Bishop Freculf knew that she meant Gynethe Mehaut. "Do so. But bear in mind, you may have a ravening wolf in your midst. Keep her close, and do not hesitate to confine her if she requires it. It would not be prudent to have such a one as she walking abroad."

"We will take care of her, Sublime," said the Priora, moving away from the Bishop to answer the bell's summons to prayer.

The Bishop left the courtyard, going toward the stable, calling for his horse. He waited while a slave led the animal out to him, brought a mounting stool, and knelt to hold it in position. He swung up into the saddle and started his strawberry roan toward the door. "I am leaving," he announced, and watched the servants scurry to pull the brace from the brackets. The gates creaked open; the Bishop rode through to the opening and signaled his armed escort to fall in around him. Behind him, the gates closed. The Bishop glanced back over his shoulder, pleased at how well he had handled this most difficult situation.

Inside the convent the Superiora and Priora met in the narthex of the chapel while the gathered nuns began to chant the salutation of the Angel to the Blessed Virgin. "What did he say?" Superiora Gundrada whispered.

"He will consider the reports," said Priora Iditha.

"But he has made no decision?" Superiora Gundrada persisted.

"Not that he imparted to me." The Priora frowned. "I don't know what we'll say to the Abba when she returns."

The Superiora shook her head. "She will not be pleased."

"Then let her pursue the matter—he is her kinsman." The Priora was annoyed.

"If he will not tell her what he thinks, then we will have to continue to house her, and who knows what that may do. Once word gets out about her—"

"Will that happen?" the Superiora asked.

"The servants talk, the slaves talk. How are we to deal with that?" Priora Iditha looked long and steadily at the Superiora. "I haven't satisfied myself that we should keep her here. There must be somewhere she can be sent, where she will be away from danger, and we need not fear her."

"You do fear her, then?" the Superiora inquired distantly, as if none of this had anything to do with her. "She is such a submissive child."

"Anyone would, seeing her. Her eyes alone are enough to set sensible men into a frenzy." Priora Iditha folded her arms. "I cannot think that the Abba would want us to have the risk Gynethe Mehaut entails for us."

"That's as may be," said the Superiora. "The Bishop will decide." She held up her hands, extending them in prayer.

"Your piety is beyond question," said Priora Iditha rather dryly. "But not all the Sorrae are as diligent as you are. Some are not here in the full flower of faith, but for other reasons."

"True. And we keep safe custody of them," said the Superiora with a touch of unpious pride.

Priora Iditha decided not to pursue the matter. She moved away from the Superiora, going into the chapel to join in the chants of the nuns; after a dozen heartbeats, Superiora Gundrada followed after her.

Midway through the next morning Abba Sunifred returned to the convent, escorted by six of her father's mounted comrades, who led two mules carrying two boars and three deer ready for the spits in the kitchens. The soldiers saw her into the outer courtyard, handed the mules over to the convent slaves, and departed without dismounting. The Abba watched them leave with a wistful look in her ruddy face. Then she signaled to the slaves. "We will have venison tonight. The pork will go into salt and smoke, against lean times."

"Yes, Abba," said the head slave, having the right to speak to her.

"And summon the Priora to me. I will be in my apartments." She strode off, her step energetic, her meaty cheeks flushed, and not from the warmth of the day but from the fading exhilaration of the hunt. She hummed as she went, the melody one she had heard the soldiers sing.

One of the slaves hurried off to do her bidding, while three others took the fresh-killed game from the baskets on the mules, and a remaining slave led the mules into the stable; four novices bearing short sticks followed the slaves to be sure they did their work as they should.

A short while later, Priora Iditha stood outside Abba Sunifred's door, asking humbly to be admitted; the Abba's maidservant opened the door for her. "She is in her reception room."

"Very good," said Priora Iditha, knowing the Abba's apartments had only three rooms and the Abba only received visitors in the reception room. She followed the maidservant into that chamber and knelt to the Abba. "May God show you favor."

"And you, Priora," said the Abba. "Take a seat and tell me what has happened since I have been gone."

Although this report was customary, Priora Iditha hesitated before giving it. "One of the slaves ran off," she began when she had gathered her thoughts. "Sorra Atula has put more hives in the apple orchard. Sorrae Eldalinda and Richilda have taken over the milking of the ewes since Sorrae Madelgard and Ercangarea have taken fevers and are laid in their cells to recover; Superiora Gundrada will report to you on their condition. And your kinsman, Bishop Freculf, came to see Gynethe Mehaut. He read two of the accounts we have of her and said he will make a decision about her in the next days."

"Good, good," said Abba Sunifred. "May God guide him aright."

"Amen," said Priora Iditha. She knelt and kissed the Abba's hand. "May God keep you to be our male mother, as the Apostles proclaim."

"Amen," said Abba Sunifred, then added, "And the sooner we are shut of her, the better."

Priora Iditha was shocked. "She came to us for succor and the protection of her soul."

"Perhaps. My kinsman shall decide that." Abba Sunifred crossed her arms. "She is too . . . too perplexing a presence. She should be with those who are better prepared to deal with her than we are."

"If the Bishop decides she must remain here, what will you do?" the Priora asked, an edge in her voice as she rose to her feet.

"I will obey him, of course, as a dutiful Abba must." There was a glint in her blue eyes that suggested the Bishop would be wise to order Gynethe Mehaut removed from Santa Albegunda. "We have already had pilgrims ask to see her, and this is not beneficial for this convent or for the maid herself."

"That is true," the Priora agreed, for she had been troubled by the rumors that were already flying about the white-skinned, red-eyed woman who had been taken into the convent; in time this would only get worse.

"Then you will speak with my kinsman when he comes again, to remind him of the danger we may face in regard to this woman," said Abba Sunifred. "He will deal with her for her good, and for ours." This time she signaled to Priora Iditha to leave her.

The Priora abased herself and left the apartments, apprehension growing with every step on behalf of Gynethe Mehaut, who had come to them for their guardianship and was becoming a piece in a game. She turned toward the chapel, gathering her thoughts and praying for the wisdom to tell the young woman to prepare for changes in her life without causing her distress; the nearer she got to the chapel, the more futile her prayers became, so that, in the end, she dared not speak with Gynethe Mehaut at all, postponing the conversation until Compline, after which Gynethe Mehaut would walk in the herb garden, among the night-blooming flowers, where Priora Iditha could meet her and be assured of their privacy.

TEXT OF A LETTER FROM THE SCRIBE ARDULF ON BEHALF OF HARTGAR, GRAV OF SOLIGNAC, TO BISHOP WOLVINUS AT BOURGES, CARRIED BY COURIER UNDER ARMED ESCORT.

To the most puissant, most pious Bishop Wolvinus at Bourges, the greetings of the Grav of Solignac, Hartgar by name, advanced by the mandate of Karl-lo-Magne to the position left vacant by the death of Rihwin from fever. I take leave to address myself to the missive you had carried to Rihwin on behalf of the people of Bourges.

I regret to tell you that although the famine that has struck so much of Karl-lo-Magne's lands is passing at last, in this region, at least, it is not yet over. Farmsteads stand abandoned, and many fields lie fallow out of their season. Pigs and cattle are scattered in the woods, and sheep are gathered into flocks by anyone with purpose enough to venture into the deep meadows and higher peaks. I say this in preparation for my necessary denial of the aid you request of this region. Perhaps one of the Abbotts will have food to spare from monastery fields, but I must tell you, though I take no pleasure in it, that we, here, do not have enough to feed ourselves, let alone your people.

Further, I must ask you for your prayers on behalf of those still living. The fields will not support us again for at least a year, and in the meantime, fever has come into the region, scything down those that famine has spared. Every day the funeral bells toll, and families are consumed with new grief. Surely your supplication to Heaven will bring us surcease of the suffering we have endured. This may appear a poor exchange, for we ask prayers of you when we cannot do anything to relieve your hunger, but I fear that without the prayers of such mighty men as you, Heaven will remain deaf to our cries and this region will be lost to the King and the Church. Since neither of us wants that, I beseech you to do your utmost to petition God for an end to our plight.

It is no easy thing, Sublime Bishop, for a Grav to admit so much to anyone but the King Himself, and in doing this, I rely upon you to guard what I have said from the eyes of the world, as I would do for you, should you make such a request of me. It is mete that you and I share confidences, as is the Right of our place in life, but few are entitled to know these things, and we must be mindful of this at all times. There are enemies of the King who would use this against his rule, inciting the farmers and artisans to rise up against travelers and the Potenti who govern them, which you can desire no more than I do.

Until such time as our hardships are lessened, I must continue to withhold aid to you, for we cannot give what we do not have. In time, as the conditions here improve, I will strive to see that you are provided with grain and wine and oil. Once the flocks are flourishing again, I will order that you be provided with cheese, salt-meat, and leather, but that is at least a year away, if God is good to us once more. I swear on my sword, Greytooth, that I will do this in spite of all Hell has to throw at me.

The courier who carries this and his escort will return to me when they have presented this to you. I have told them to wait upon you for no more than two days, so if you wish to send a response with them, you must attend to it promptly or entrust it to another courier. If you decide to postpone your answer to me, I ask that you tell my courier so that he may depart without failing in his duty to me. I await your reply in the full certainty that you will uphold my decision and will support our labors with your prayers.

At midsummer, the Feast of Apostle Thomas, in the Pope's Year 796.

Hartgar de Solignac
By the hand of Ardulf, scribe,
monk of Sant' Ambrose

◡

chapter two

UNDER THE TREES THE MID-DAY HEAT was less smothering than it had been in the open, but the horses and mules were lathered and plodded along the rutted, dusty road as if they had spent the morning in a hard canter instead of at the same steady walk; the armed soldiers who had joined the missi dominici and the two men with them only three days ago were drooping in their saddles. Four mounted Wendish soldiers had been turned back at Erfurt, and just now the new escort of six could envy those soldiers, who undoubtedly had sheltered for the worst of the day. Even the breeze moved in a desultory way, hardly doing more than tweaking the leaves as it passed on in an exhausted breath.

Hiernom Rakoczy showed no sign of discomfort, although he was glad to be out of the direct sunlight; not even a hint of sweat on his upper lip or forehead marred his neat appearance, from his black linen gonelle to his thick-heeled Avar stirrup-boots in red-tooled leather. He might have entered the presence of the Pope Himself without offending. He was an impressive figure in the saddle: slightly taller than the soldiers and Otfrid, he had a presence about him that did more than his height to invest him with quiet authority. Just behind Rakoczy rode his body-servant, called Rorthger, a straight-backed man of middle years with tawny hair going to grey, and eyes of ice-blue. His garments were nearly as fine as his master's, and his dun horse was of equal quality to Rakoczy's grey.

"We must be careful here," said the leader of the escort. "There are robbers in these woods. We must be wary."

"Should we draw our swords?" Rakoczy asked, apparently untroubled by this announcement.

"Not yet," said Otfrid, the military man of the missi dominici who accompanied Rakoczy. "If we have them in our hands, we may become lax, and then we can be more easily surprised. It has happened before." He indicated Fratre Angelomus, his comrade. "Let us hope his prayers can shield us. His patron is Sant' Michaell, the Archangel, God's Warrior."

"Of course; I do not count anything to Sant' Michaell's discredit, for he is a most puissant force," said Rakoczy quietly, aware that everything he said would be repeated and scrutinized. "But in addition, let us be ready to do what we may to protect ourselves, to be worthy of such a patron." He reached up to his shoulder to touch the hilt of the long Byzantine sword slung across his back. He had a short-sword hanging from his wide leather girdle that also carried a dagger, a wallet, and small sack of Roman stars of bent, sharpened iron that could be scattered on the road to cripple any charging animal or man.

"The soldiers know their work," said Otfrid. "Let them do it."

"So long as we can fight together," said Rakoczy, his judgment reserved for the time being. "It would do no good for any of us if they are unwilling to stand with us."

"These men are fine fighters," said Otfrid a bit stiffly, as if he felt he had to defend his Franks. "As fine as any under Karlus."

"Then I rejoice for him," said Rakoczy dryly. He thought back to the Emir's son, who had sent his finest soldiers after him and had failed to run him to earth in spite of all their efforts. There were other soldiers he had seen and had fought with and against over the centuries, including his own men, nearly three thousand years ago, and the memories of their valor, pride, and fear held him for several long moments. He had long since stopped thinking of soldiers as glorious; he now regarded them with a combination of dismay and sympathy. Shaking off the images that filled his memory, he forced himself to concentrate on the wood around them, on the oak and larch and yew, on the brush and thickets among the trees. The smell of green growing things filled the air, along with the occasional perfume of ripening fruit. He gathered his reins more firmly into his left hand, leaving his right free. He might have done the same with the left, but soldiers were often superstitious about left-handedness.

"There is an inn farther along this road; a village runs it, not a monastery. They give shelter to merchants and soldiers and the King's Guests," said Otfrid a bit later as they passed through a small clearing. "There is water and fodder for the animals and food and a bed for all of us. We should reach it well before sundown; we need not camp in the open tonight."

"Just as well. The animals are worn out by the heat," said Rakoczy.

"We should arrive by late afternoon," said Fratre Angelomus, with an emphasis that showed he was trying to summon up confidence in his statement. "If nothing impedes our progress."

"The animals aren't the only ones needing food and drink. We could do with a meal, as well," said the leader of their soldiers. "It has been a long morning."

"It is summer," said Rakoczy, his half-smile enigmatic. "The days are long and the nights are short."

"And the Angels watch over us. Amen," said Fratre Angelomus, clearly on edge as they moved deeper into the trees. He knew how dangerous the forests could be, and summer was slightly less risky than winter, if only because the animals of the forest were not as hungry.

Beyond the little glen, the road was narrowing, now hardly more than a goat-track; the trees crowded in around them, and the sounds of birds became unnaturally loud. The horses and mules continued on steadily, making their way at the same pace as they had traveled since dawn, but now the men riding and leading them chafed at their slow progress, as if afraid of interlopers, or the many denizens of the forest.

"There may be bison ahead," said one of the soldiers. "There's dung on the trail, and we're not prepared for hunting them."

"Then let us be wary. They often rest through the heat of the day. It would be unwise to surprise them," said Otfrid. "They have charged larger groups than this one, and, as we're not equipped to kill and dress them, it's best to avoid them, and the elk."

"We'll be careful," said the soldier who was second to the lead.

The shrill cry of a hawk came from beyond the treetops and was met with a flurry of activity in the undergrowth, and a badger bustled across the road a short distance ahead.

"Out in the daylight—an ill-omen," said Otfrid, watching the animal vanish into the undergrowth.

The birds went silent, except for one high, piping cry of alarm.

"How many rivers do we have to cross before we reach the inn?" asked the soldier at the rear.

"Only four streams and a rill or two," said Otfrid. "The widest of the rivers is bridged; the others can be forded, but one not so easily as the rest." He glanced at the mules and the packs they carried. "It may be difficult for those creatures; the ford at Sant' Wigbod is deep in summer, when the melting snows from the mountains feed it. Three mules. They may be a problem."

"How soon do we reach that ford?" Rakoczy asked, as if he were merely curious. The thought of going through running water in daylight made him feel a bit queasy, and he knew he would have to prepare himself for the ordeal. At least his soles were generously lined with his native earth, which would afford him some protection, but with the combination of sun and running water, he would be uncomfortable, although not as miserable as he had been the first time he had gone to Britannia, when he had been all but incapacitated by the combination of tide and daylight and had been ordered back to Gaul to recover.

"We will come upon it by mid-afternoon, shortly before we arrive at the inn. It will be our last crossing today," said Otfrid. "There are peasants nearby, and they might ferry your chests over the river on rafts if you can recompense them. They will not give their time for love of God or of Karlus." He almost sneered. "They are lazy in summer, and may not want to be of use to us."

"It would be prudent to carry the chests on rafts," said Rakoczy, knowing that water could leech the potency of his native earth contained in the chests more quickly than anything else. "I will pay them in silver or gold for their service."

"Pay them in any way you can," Fratre Angelomus said forcefully. "You come on Great Karl's order, and they must honor his summons even as you have done."

The lead soldier held up his hand to signal the company to halt. "A bear is near-by," he announced, his warning punctuated by a chorus of uneasy whinnies from the horses.

"If we make noise, that should be enough to get the animal to move off," said Otfrid, and began to clap his dagger on the rim of his oblong shield.

"Unless it is a sow with cubs," said Rakoczy. "Noise is a good tool, but let us not rush. That could startle the animals we would rather not disturb."

There was an uneasy moment, and then two of the soldiers began to sing rau-cously, about the women of Italy. The others, including Fratre Angelomus, joined in. Rakoczy, who did not know the couplets, did not sing with the rest, though he was glad to hear the others. He gave added attention to the brush ahead, and was relieved to hear the crash of animals clambering through the undergrowth. He looked about, knowing that the trees provided an impenetrable barrier beyond ten strides; he saw shadows moving at the limit of visibility and identified them as a herd of elk. At another time he would have encouraged the men to hunt in order to bring meat to the table of whomever would be compelled to play host to them at the end of the day—innkeeper or local Potente—but it would take too long and be too exhausting in this heat.

The first two streams were so shallow their water hardly rose higher than the pasterns of the horses and mules, but the one after was deep enough to be bridged; the stone pediments on either side of the stream supported heavy oaken beams with rough planking for a road surface. The little party had to cross one at a time so as not to overload the bridge.

"They say there was a stone bridge here, in the days of the Romans, and that the Legions crossed it many times," Otfrid informed them as Rakoczy came over to the western bank. "All of it was stone, and it arched, as the great bridges do."

"It certainly looks like it," said Rakoczy, who had seen many of these bridges built, six and seven centuries ago. Now there were only cobbled-together rem-nants of what had been left behind, no longer the structures the Romans had made—although Karlus was known for his ambition to re-create what had been lost, and had devoted much of his time and fortune to improving the roads in his territories. "It is never easy to keep up bridges."

Rakoczy and his manservant were fourth and fifth over the bridge, and when they had reached the other side, Rakoczy put one hand to his brow, the last vestiges of the vertigo that seized him when crossing running water fading. "That stream is quite deep," he observed.

"Yes. It comes fast from the mountains," said Otfrid. "The peasants avoid it, saying it likes drowning them." He shrugged. "Peasants always believe such things. They pray to Christ and they pray to the gods of the fields and mountains, as if they were equal."

"We have tried to show them how powerful patron saints are, and how they favor those who do them honor," said Fratre Angelomus, "but they will persist in their errors." He pointed to a cluster of huts a short distance from the road. "You may be sure that the men who live there give as much to the forest spirits as they do to the monastery that protects them."

"Old ways die hard," said Rakoczy, remembering the chalices of blood in the mountains of Spain.

"Old ways endanger salvation," said Fratre Angelomus austerely, crossing himself and waiting for Rakoczy to do the same, nodding his approval when Rakoczy did.

The last of their escort came over the bridge, and they continued on. Now they had taken out small fans to keep off the swarms of flying insects that gathered around them, buzzing and eager. At first none of the party noticed that the gnats and midges and mosquitos avoided Rakoczy and his manservant, but when they did, they were filled with curiosity and alarm.

"How do you manage it?" Otfrid asked, making no excuse for the envy in his voice. "Nothing has bitten you."

Rakoczy had an answer ready. "I have a preparation that keeps them away," he told them, which was true enough, but was not the reason the pests would not bother him; those of his blood were never troubled by biting insects. "If you would like some, I'll be honored to provide it when we leave tomorrow morning. It should protect you all day."

Otfrid signaled his acceptance by touching his palms together in a gesture of supplication. "I and my men would be grateful."

"Then you shall have some ointment to rub on your face and arms," said Rakoczy, glancing at Fratre Angelomus as he spoke.

"No," said the monk. "I do not refuse what God sends us to test our flesh. That is our sin remembered." He regarded the others with narrowed eyes.

"May God send you lice, then, Fratre," said one of the soldiers, "to add to your sanctity."

"Amen," said the monk, briefly bowing his head before he took his place in their group once more.

When they reached the ford of Sant' Wigbod, the river was high, and the current was swift; part of the gravel bar that had marked the eastern side of the ford was gone, and two heavy guy-ropes bore mute testimony that the ford now had to be ferried across. The bank on the far side rose more steeply than the arm of the bar on this, indicating that getting back on the road once they were across would be a serious task, requiring extra effort and planning to do the task properly.

"Find the men who tend this place, and bring them here at once," Otfrid ordered two of the soldiers who accompanied them. "We must get over shortly, or darkness will overtake us before we reach the inn." He pointed to the south. "There is a meadow not far from here, where they graze their goats and cattle. You should be able to find four men to aid us."

"Tell them they'll have silver for their troubles," Rakoczy added. "Silver with Karlus' name upon it."

The soldiers obeyed at once, forcing their hot, tired horses to a bone-jarring trot as they sought out the men who kept their animals in this part of the forest.

While the two soldiers were gone, Fratre Angelomus dismounted and recited the mid-afternoon prayers his calling required. The rest of the group echoed his *Amen* and tried to do their best to seem devout out of respect for Karlus, who insisted that all men in religious Orders be given the same respect his Potenti received. When the monk was finished, he got back on his horse and continued to wait with the rest.

When the two soldiers returned a while later, they brought with them five roughly dressed louts whose language was a strange amalgam of Frankish and Celtic, barely comprehendible and hard on the ear.

"They all insisted on coming," said Rotgaud, the older of the two soldiers. "Each wants a coin." He glanced at Rakoczy. "Well?"

"They shall have them," said Rakoczy, opening the leather wallet that hung from his belt and removing half-a-dozen silver coins. "Here," he said, holding out his gloved hand with the coins shining against the black leather.

The peasants exchanged glances, and one of them made a gesture that seemed to convey consent; two of the men went off to fetch the raft they used for ferrying while the other three began to assess the loads to be carried, taking obvious precautions to touch nothing until Otfrid signaled them it was all right to do so.

"What do you think?" Fratre Angelomus said to Rakoczy.

"About what?"

"These men—do they know the worth of those coins, or are they only fascinated by their shine? Men like this"—he smiled slightly—"you could probably give them a small amount and they would be as satisfied as they would be with a larger one, so long as the silver is untarnished."

"I have found," Rakoczy said with a cordiality that was belied by his enigmatic gaze, "that men who labor know the value of what they do. If they do not know the worth of their work, I should do, and give them payment commensurate with their moil, as I expect to have from these men." He took the largest coins from his wallet and slipped them inside his glove where he could be sure of having them ready when they were needed. "I have also found that I am better served in this world if I give full value for effort."

Fratre Angelomus cocked his head. "Is it so," he murmured. "Well, so long as the Church receives her due, and Karl-lo-Magne, you may do as you wish, I suppose."

Rakoczy said nothing more to the monk; there was a silence between them that was heavier than the heat.

"The men are coming back," said Rotgaud, pointing toward the peasants pulling a broad, runnered sledge behind them, a sturdy square, equal to a tall man's height, of thick oaken planks with a lip around the edge and a place to attach a rudder. The man in the lead was red-faced and panting, his loose mantel clinging to him, darkened by sweat.

The peasants approached the ferrying ropes, going as far out on the gravel bar as was prudent, the sun falling full upon them and a swath of the river, making it shine like polished metal. The leader signaled his fellows to begin loading the sledge. His orders, although largely incomprehensible, resulted in the pack-saddles on the mules being unloaded and the crates and chests they had carried stacked on the sledge; then the laden sledge was shoved down to the edge of the river. The leader looked at Otfrid, and said, in poor Frankish, "Three of you cross, and get ready to pull the load out of the water."

Otfrid bristled at the effrontery of the man, but Rakoczy said, "A very good idea. My man will lead the mules across, and I'll come after the ferry. This way we will be able to help if anything goes awry, and need not depend wholly on you to guard my goods. The Fratre can go with whichever group suits him, but it would probably be best if you, Otfrid, went with Rorthger, to supervise the retrieval of the sledge." He coughed once and made a self-deprecating gesture. "I will do all I can to help the men handle the ferry; these are my things, and I should be responsible for them."

This last concession gave the missi dominici an acceptable reason to accept Rakoczy's proposal; Otfrid nodded and signaled to Rotgaud. "You and I will go with the manservant. Adalgis and Stracholf, you stay on either side of the ferry; if it needs steadying, you are to do it. If any of the Magnatus' chests are lost, you will be accountable. The rest can bring up the rear with Magnatus Rakoczy. Keep to the downstream side, in case any of the chests should slip into the water. I don't want to have to chase them down the river." He urged his horse into the water, letting her drink before using his heels to move her on across; behind him, Rorthger tugged the lead-ropes to pony the mules into the water.

"We're ready," said the head of the peasants, and stepped aboard the ferry, putting the rudder in place to swing it down once the ferry was fully in the river. Beside him, two of the soldiers set their horses splashing into the current, Adalgis whooping at the relief from the heat.

The smallest of the mules balked just before he began to swim across the deepest stretch of river; he craned his neck as high as he could and angled his ears back in disapproval of what he had to do. Rorthger clicked his tongue and tugged on the lead, and the mule finally caught up with his fellows just as Rorthger's dun gelding began to scramble up the bank, water streaming off his now-mud-colored coat. The mules came after him, far more surefooted than the horse, and tried to shake themselves off—they succeeded only in loosening the girths of their packsaddles. Rorthger led them to the side of the road, leaving a clear path for the ferry, which was now almost at mid-stream, holding its course precariously as the three peasants aboard it struggled to pull it along the guy-ropes while their leader held onto the rudder for dear life and his companion held the guy-ropes steady.

Rakoczy tapped his grey with his heels; the horse moved into the sunlight and the river behind the ferry, bringing his head up as the water rose above his chest; Rakoczy wrapped one hand around the high pommel of the saddle to keep from swaying with vertigo. He kept his hand on the reins but relied on the horse to choose the most direct crossing, for weakness overwhelmed him as he strove to maintain his seat. The pull of the current insidiously sapped his strength, his vision wobbled, and he felt his skin start to burn. Pressing his lips firmly together, he concentrated on reaching the far bank. He could feel the grey swimming, and that added to his discomfort, for even that tenuous connection to the earth was gone now. When the horse's front hooves struck the first rise of the bank on the far side, a little of his misery abated.

The peasants were busy struggling to haul the ferry out of the river and up the bank. They shouted to one another and gave terse commands; Otfrid ordered Rorthger to bring the mules to help, which Rorthger did at once, moving them into position with the ease of long experience, setting the draw-lines across the mules' chests and starting them pulling. The sledge lurched forward, then slid up the bank, coming to a stop ten strides from the river, the peasants leaping off to unload the sledge.

"Come on, then!" Otfrid called out to Rakoczy and the men still in the river.

Rakoczy sighed as his horse clambered up the bank to stand next to the sledge.

He did his best to conceal his discomfort, but he also took the time to press as much water out of his clothes as he could.

"Don't worry, Magnatus," said Fratre Angelomus. "On such a day as this, you'll soon be dry."

"That will please me very well." Rakoczy watched while the peasants put his crates and chests back on the mules' packsaddles under Rorthger's supervision.

"You dislike swimming?" Fratre Angelomus inquired with false concern.

"I am not comfortable in running water," Rakoczy allowed, knowing that the monk had watched him in the river.

"You fear drowning; many do, for they do not put their faith in Christ and His Mercy," said Fratre Angelomus. "A pity. Karlus himself is a great swimmer. He has a pool, such as the Romans of old enjoyed. He expects his companions to swim with him."

"I shall keep that in mind," said Rakoczy. "Thank you, Fratre, for telling me." He did not mention that he had heard of this swimming pool some years ago, when the project was first begun.

"If he calls you to his Court at Aachen, you will have to swim; all his Majori, Potenti, Primori, Illustri, and Magnati are required to swim with him," Fratre Angelomus said, clearly enjoying himself.

"And so I shall," said Rakoczy, and peeled back his glove to get the silver coins he had placed there. He counted out the six of them and held them out to the leader of the peasants. "One for each of you, and an extra for your patron saint. You have served us well." He wondered where the shrine of Sant' Wigbod was, for he saw no sign of it at the ford.

The leader took the coins and uttered a string of garbled phrases, the gist of which seemed to be gratitude for such payment. He handed out the coins to his fellows, holding the sixth aloft in what appeared to be a dedication. Then they made their way down the bank, eased the sledge into the water, and worked it across the river, using the ropes far more easily than before. One of the men began to sing a vigorous song, and the others joined in.

"They sound like howling wolves, and they think such howling will please their patron," Fratre Angelomus complained, looking over his shoulder at the peasants. "Hardly more than beasts," he declared, then swung round to confront Rakoczy. "You should not have given them so much."

"I provided money for Sant' Wigbod, so the Church is not deprived; how can you disapprove of that?" Rakoczy said brusquely; the water left him enervated, the sun was adding to his discomfort, and his tongue was sharper than he usually allowed it to be. "Let us move on. The day will wane in a while."

Otfrid raised his hand to order them on. "The inn is not far away now. Be glad of that," he said. "We should all be dry by then."

"We will have to wax the saddles," complained Stracholf. "And all our leather." He put his hand to his metal-studded leather hauberk, his face set in disapproval.

Rakoczy knew what was expected of him. "I can give you more of the oil I offered you before," he said to all the men. "It will restore your leather quickly, without cracking it."

Otfrid grinned. "Thank you for not making us ask," he said, for asking would have imposed an obligation he was reluctant to establish with anyone to whom he was not related. "I will tell Great Karl that you have been generous with your supplies. It will please him to hear this."

"That is good of you," said Rakoczy, mastering his discomfort sufficiently to continue in courtly form. "I will tell him that I had good attention from you."

Fratre Angelomus regarded the others with an air of superiority. "When I write my account of this journey, I will say that Magnatus Rakoczy came well-prepared." He knew the advantage his literacy gave him, and he enjoyed exercising it.

"And I look forward to reading it," said Rakoczy, adding gently, "I take great pleasure in reading."

The group rode along in silence as the shadows began to lengthen and a breeze, warmed from the fields, strummed the leaves of the trees, lending a persistent sigh to the afternoon. Gradually the light began to change, becoming softer, more ruddy, the shadows longer and of a purple-blue that made the patches of sunlight seem brighter by contrast. The wind was brisker now, and not as warm, no longer as fragrant with flowers and growing things as it had been earlier in the day. Hawks and falcons and kites surrendered the air to owls and bats as birds came back to the forest to roost; the day creatures returned to their lairs and lays while the night-dwellers began to stir.

"There!" Otfrid cried out, rising in his stirrups and pointing. "The inn!"

It was a three-story wooden building surrounded by a stout wooden stockade; a glowing lantern built above the eaves announced there was room inside for guests; there were no visible windows, a discouragement to robbers and brigands alike. Little as most of the men in the party would be willing to admit it, they were relieved to arrive here at last, and to see the lantern burning in welcome. Otfrid rode up to the gate and pulled on the bell-rope to summon assistance, shouting, "We come in the name of Karlus-lo-Magne! Open to us, as you would serve him!" He tugged the bell-rope again, and the unmelodious clang sounded through the gathering dusk.

The wicket-gate, a short distance from the main entrance, opened, and a large-bellied man peered out. "Great Karl's men, are you? How do I know you're not outlaws, or worse?" He held a cudgel in his hand, and he regarded the men skeptically.

"We—Fratre Angelomus and I—are missi dominici, and we are escorting Magnatus Rakoczy and his manservant to Sant' Martin's, at the pleasure of the King," said Otfrid. "Fratre Angelomus will tell you the same."

The man laughed his scorn. "As if no monk has ever robbed anyone. Get down and bring me your staff."

Otfrid dismounted and took his staff of office from his saddlebag, then carried it to the innkeeper. "Here. If you have seen one of these, you will know this is genuine. We have the right of tractoriae, and can command food and lodging from you, and fodder and water for our animals. If you refuse us, you can be killed for your failure to do the King's Will."

The innkeeper examined the staff, peering through the waning light for a short while, turning it over and over, examining it meticulously. Then he handed the staff back to Otfrid. "It appears genuine, so you are either what you claim to be, or you have killed the real missi and are raiding the places along the road. You know it has happened before." He sighed.

"And there have been men who posed as honest landlords who have robbed and murdered those who put themselves into their protection," said Otfrid. "We must each of us extend our trust to the other, or you will lose our patronage and we will have to make camp quickly."

"I'll open the gate for you," said the landlord, stepping back inside the wicket-gate and setting its bolt in place loudly. A long moment later, the main gate was unbraced and the two doors swung open. "Enter, Majori." His greeting lacked warmth, but he reverenced the men as they rode through, and he clapped his hands to summon his few slaves to take charge of the horses and mules. "I suppose you want a meal?"

Otfrid coughed. "For ourselves and our mounts," he said. "Fratre Angelomus eats no meat, so bread and fish will suffice him, or cheese. My men and I would like more substantial fare."

The landlord made a gesture of compliance. "I have a goat on the spit and I can roast geese for you, if you don't mind having to wait a bit."

"If you can give us wine and cheese, we'll be glad to wait," said Otfrid with a warning glance at the men accompanying him. "Magnatus Rakoczy has taken care of food for himself since we began this journey. I don't suppose he'll impose on you for his repast." He looked at Rakoczy, who was still mounted, ducking his head. "Not that I mean to speak for you."

"You are quite right," said Rakoczy. "Good landlord, is there provision in your stable for my man and me to sleep tonight?"

The landlord regarded the stranger with shock. "Surely your man would—"

Rakoczy interrupted him. "I am traveling with valuable materials, some of which are part of the work Great Karlus has summoned me to do. I would prefer to guard them myself, than entrust them to others who do not understand their worth." He did not add that he far preferred sleeping in a stable than in the cramped, windowless confines of the inn.

Fratre Angelomus interjected his own remark before the landlord could speak. "Do permit it, I ask you in the Name of Our Savior. He has done this all the way from the Wendish lands." He sounded tired and annoyed. "It is better to let him do as he wishes."

The landlord stared at Rakoczy, but knew better than to set himself against so august a guest. He reverenced the man again and pointed in the direction of the stable; the peculiarities of the Illustri were not his to question, and it was not worth the loss of his inn to argue. "My slaves will show you what you ask for." He stepped back to give room to the soldiers and monk as they dismounted and surrendered their reins to the three slaves who had answered the landlord's summons.

One of the slaves had brought an oil-lamp, and holding it aloft, he led the way back to the rear of the inn-yard to the stable. "There is water in the trough, hay in the loft, saddle pegs on the end-wall, storage in the aisles, and a smithy behind all." He recited this as he had done many times in the past, without inflection or emphasis of any kind; he did not look directly at Rakoczy or Rorthger.

"Do you have grain for the horses?" Rakoczy asked as he led his grey to the long manger that reached the length of the stalls.

"That is extra. You will have to pay my master." He bent double, then took up the task of unsaddling and brushing the horses the escort had been riding, taking care to check their legs and feet for cuts, strains, and stones. He worked slowly and with care, knowing any unreported hurt would result in a beating.

Rakoczy and Rorthger tended to their horses and mules, their work quick and easy, made so by long practice. The mules were the most tired, hardy though they were, and therefore in obstreperous states of mind. The largest mule attempted to nip Rakoczy and received a slap on the nose for his trouble. "Mars is in a bad mood," Rakoczy remarked in the Latin of Imperial Rome as he went on unloading the packsaddle.

"He has been for the last few days," Rorthger agreed in the same language. "But he's eating well."

"It's probably the heat. I'll add some salt to his hay. I'll do it for all of them." He piled the last of the crates in the aisle that ran down the center of the stable. "Break out my mattress, will you? Before I pile more chests on top of it."

"Of course," said Rorthger, going to do as he had been asked. "How much longer do you think we will need to get to Sant' Martin?"

"Twenty days, probably, if there are no serious delays, and if all our animals remain sound, and we encounter no more hazards than we did at Sant' Wigbod," said Rakoczy, his manner detached. "But that may be asking for too much. The roads are poor, though they're better than what the Wends have. The bridges are . . . well, you've seen them as well as I have. Some may be in better repair, but we can't assume they will be. And we have more deep rivers to cross before we reach Sant' Martin."

"They're not Roman-made roads, most of them," said Rorthger. "Unfortunately." He pulled the lid off one of the crates and unrolled a thin mattress.

"No, they're not," Rakoczy agreed. "If you'll put that next to the—"

"Crates and chests. I know," Rorthger said.

Rakoczy shook his head. "Pardon me, old friend. I am well-aware you are able to do all your tasks without a word from me."

"It doesn't bother me, my master," said Rorthger. "I find it comforting."

"Just as well," Rakoczy murmured. "Hand me the stiff brush, will you? Mars has mud in his coat."

"So do they all," said Rorthger. "Are you planning to stay in tonight?"

"Probably," said Rakoczy. "I don't want to have to hunt livestock—these people have none to spare, and perhaps they keep them in pens with guards."

"You will need sustenance soon," Rorthger said carefully.

"Yes," said Rakoczy, continuing to brush the mule. "I know."

TEXT OF A DISPATCH FROM PATRE LUPUS OF SANT' BERTIN, COELONI, PRAXTA, AND SATTO RIVA TO COMES HARTMUT OF SPEYER.

To the most illustrious Comes Hartmut, in my duty to Karl-lo-Magne and my devotion to the Church, I send this report on the current state of affairs in my district, in the sure knowledge that it will serve both the King and the Pope to do this.

I have been assigned to these four villages, as Church records reveal, and I do my utmost to see to the souls of all those who live in these villages. In humility and obedience, I have prepared this account for you:

Coeloni has recently been visited by a pestilence that brings cough and fever. We have petitioned Christ to succor those who have taken ill, and most have recovered. The pestilence has not yet spread to the other villages, and to that end, we offer up thanks for the preservation Our Lord has given to us.

In Sant' Bertin, the peasant Adalung, who has prospered in recent years, has died suddenly and terribly. His widow has taken a man into her house and she has said she must have him there to protect him from Adalung's kin, who have sworn to claim Adalung's goods, lands, and chattel in spite of anything she may do. They say that Adalung died by her hand, and that vengeance is required of them. If it is true that she brought about his death, she should suffer for it, and the family gain all they seek, but if she is innocent, they defame her by their claims. I earnestly entreat you to put this matter in the hands of Bishop Fridugis for judgment.

Also there was a sheep born with what appeared to be a second pair of eyes and a part of a nose beside its proper head. The animal was left in the forest for the cats and wolves to fight over, for no one was willing to bring curses on their knives and axes by killing anything so unnatural. The ewe that brought forth this dreadful creature has been butchered and her meat given to the slaves. I have prayed for the end of these horrible occurrences, and I have sworn to rid the village of any such monstrosity should one be found again.

In Praxta an escort of missi dominici and soldiers passed two days along with the Magnatus they were taking to Sant' Martin at Tours. They were generous with the people, and sponsored a feast in honor of the Apostles, which was a grand occasion, but did not become too festive, so that the Apostles would not be shamed by what transpired.

Also at Praxta, there was a mad dog, and the men clubbed it to death, but only after it had bitten four people of the village, including, I regret to tell you, my wife. All have been laid to rest at the side of the road with crosses to mark them, so that other mad animals will be warned away. I have kept watch for my wife, to be sure that her ghost does not wander, unsaved, but I have not seen her, so I thank Our Savior for preserving her and bearing her to Paradise.

In Satto Riva the orchards have been struck with a blight, so that the apples form but do not increase, leaving only small, hard lumps hanging on the trees. Some wish to cut down the orchards and burn the wood, but others believe that the bad fruit should be removed and new grafts made. No final decision has been made, but with famine only a year behind us, I cannot think that anyone would decide to take down trees. It is only the apples that have been stricken: lemons, peaches, and berries continue to thrive, and so the specter of hunger does not loom over us as it did two years ago. I have asked the monks of Sant' Luchas to pray for us, and the Abbott has said that they would, for their orchards have also seen apples fail them this year.

At Harmut the shepherd with the largest flocks has been accused of using his daughters as his wife. This has angered his wife's family, for they fear he will not honor her in age, and will send her back to them while he has his daughters to pleasure him and give him sons, which his wife has failed to do. We are taught that this is wrong, but in these villages, it is not so uncommon that the people understand why a man might do this. I cannot bring him to the Bishop because the villagers would rise against the Church if I did. So I must pray for his deliverance and the delivery of his wife, who may yet suffer. Perhaps if I find husbands for the daughters, all this will pass and the village will not be shamed by his actions. I have urged him to Confess to God all he has done, but he sees no error in the urges of his flesh, for he says that he is guarding himself against lust—without his daughters to assuage him he might be tempted to impose on women who are not entitled to his protection. He says that Karlus himself keeps his daughters with him, and all the world accepts it. Nothing I say can change his view of that. I know many in the village share his sentiments, and so I cannot confront him, or ask for more concessions to the expectations of the Church.

Submitted in duty on this day, the Feast of Sant' Evurtius, Bishop of Orleanus, for your considera-tion and your contemplation, by

Patre Lupus,

witnessed by Fratre Boddulf of Sant' Luchas.

∾

chapter three

SANT' MARTIN'S DOMINATED TOURS, although it was a short distance from the town itself, connected by a road that bristled with impromptu businesses, like a traders' carnival that had set down for a short while, though it had been there for decades. People traveled between the monastery and the town in ox-drawn carts, on donkeys, horses, mules, and on foot, many of them with their trades on their backs, some hoping for sanctuary, a few preying on all the rest.

The abbey was a sprawling cluster of buildings surrounded by high walls that enclosed all the amenities of a small town: dormitories; dining halls; stables; barns; pigstys; a goat shed; a sheepfold; a brewery; a creamery; a bakery; a mill; an oil-press; a winepress; a tannery; a grainery; a smithy; a workshop for turners and coopers; a weavery; two bathhouses; rabbit coops; chicken coops; beehives; an infirmary; a hostel for travelers and another for refugees seeking sanctuary; four latrines; a laundry; a school; a library; an herb garden; a vegetable garden; a night garden; four ambulatories; a muniment hall; a scriptorium; a petitioners' court; and a collegium where manuscripts and maps were copied, studied, and stored; and rising above it all, the Cathedral of Sant' Martin itself, a strong, impressive structure with clerestory alabaster windows, a lantern that rose four stories, and chapels huddled around it like its nursing young.

Otfrid led the way through the town toward the monastery, avoiding the two big markets where many peasants and merchants gathered with their animals and families to trade or, more rarely, sell their produce and goods. The excitement today was a bit feverish, as if the weather had infected everyone; it was a hot, overcast afternoon at the end of August, hazy and strength-sapping. The city and the road buzzed and stank, the shimmering air like water about to boil.

"That is the swine-market," Otfrid explained unnecessarily, pointing off to his right. "The cattle-market is just beyond."

"Away from the central wells, I see," said Rakoczy, approving of that precaution.

"The best wells are inside the monastery walls," said Fratre Angelomus, a bit smugly. "They are pure and flow all year around. They are the blessing of Sant' Martin himself."

"That's why the monastery was built there," said Rakoczy, recalling how the Church had come to control wells and streams as part of its vigorous expansion; this served a double purpose, for it made the monasteries relatively safe from siege, as well as taking over many sites of traditional pagan worship. "A wise choice." His smile was not entirely pleasant, for his face was reddened by his prolonged exposure to the sun; he longed for a quiet, dark cell where he could recover from his reaction to sunlight that not even his native earth in the soles of his heeled Persian boots and padding his saddle could entirely counteract, particularly in these bright days of the waning summer.

"It was the inspiration of the founder that put Sant' Martin's where it is," said Fratre Angelomus, offended by Rakoczy's too-worldly explanation.

"That was my meaning. Do you think the wells weren't inspiring?" Rakoczy said without a trace of umbrage. "Wouldn't God rather have His monastery be as safe as possible? And wouldn't those wells make the monastery the safe haven it was intended to be?"

Fratre Angelomus scowled. "Don't you accept the doctrine of divine inspiration?"

"I would not presume to comprehend the purpose of God," said Rakoczy.

"At least you are willing to admit that," said the monk.

"There is no reason to wrangle," said Otfrid. During their travels, he had grown weary of Fratre Angelomus' constant challenging of Rakoczy; it was not for them to interrogate the foreigner, only to deliver him to Alcuin, no matter what the monk thought. At first their disputes had been mildly entertaining, but now, after two months of daily exchanges, Otfrid was heartily jaded. "Our journey is almost over." They had gone out of the town and were now on the road to the abbey, a busy thoroughfare lined with stalls filled with livestock. Among these stalls were other, more permanent buildings: inns, taverns, and brothels.

Fratre Angelomus managed to smile. "For which we must thank God and the Will of Great Karl."

"Amen," said Rakoczy, aware that if he failed to endorse Fratre Angelomus' faith, he would increase the suspicion the monk already harbored toward him.

Rotgaud pointed toward the massive gates of Sant' Martin's, now standing open, guarded by monks holding thick wooden staves that could be used as weapons as well as walking sticks. "There is the place we must leave you, for armed men cannot enter the monastery precincts." He motioned to the soldiers with them. "We turn back here."

The others drew rein, almost surprised that their wayfaring was over and that they had at last come to the end of their time together. Two of the men regarded Otfrid with the respect his position demanded, but the other two did not. "We are now without work," Adalgis complained just loudly enough to be heard over the babble from the street and the market beyond, his young face marked by dust and ambition. "We have served you well, haven't we?"

Rakoczy, who had been expecting this, opened his wallet and pulled out twelve silver coins. "Let this hold you for a while, so that you may find suitable advancement in your next employment, and not be compelled to accept the employ of anyone with a few coins to give you. Find a lord worthy of your service." It was more than generous, and all the soldiers knew it. Before Adalgis could snatch the money, Rotgaud motioned to them to receive the silver humbly; he took the first place in line for the largesse. "You have all done all you were asked to do, and more," Rakoczy went on. "I thank you."

"Very well," said Adalgis, who had never had so much money at one time in his life. "You have used us honorably, and we are obliged to you."

"I am not your lord, nor am I apt to be in future," said Rakoczy as he passed out the coins. "I am a foreigner here at the behest of Karlus the King. You have ensured that I may do as he bade me." This was the correct response, and all of them knew it.

The four soldiers reverenced Rakoczy, then pulled their mounts away from the gates of Sant' Martin's, urging their horses through the market throng toward the largest of the taverns.

"They may not have their coins by morning, between drink and dice and women," said Otfrid. "But you did well by them."

Rakoczy shrugged. "They deserved my gratitude, yet I have few means to express it: as a stranger without lands or honors to bestow, I cannot offer much more than coins for their efforts, which I have done."

"You gave coins to peasants," Fratre Angelomus said, as if to cheapen Rakoczy's gift to the soldiers.

"They worked when I bade them. What more could I do?" He inclined his head toward his manservant. "I also pay him."

Fratre Angelomus shook his head. "Not what a man of rank would do."

There was a subtle shift in Rakoczy's stance, a different light in his dark eyes; his compelling gaze rested on the monk. "Perhaps," he allowed in a gentle voice that carried more authority than a shout would have; Fratre Angelomus moved back, masking his reaction by dismounting and tugging experimentally on the billets beneath the wide skirt of his saddle.

"If you tell the warder you have arrived, you will be taken to your assigned quarters," said Otfrid. "Fratre Angelomus and I will find proper lodging in the city. In the morning we leave for Aachen, to report on our errand."

"Then I will thank you now," said Rakoczy, paying no heed to the monk. "You have done well, and so I will inform Alcuin."

"You offer us no money," said Fratre Angelomus, his features expressing his scorn more than his tone. "Yet you paid the soldiers lavishly."

"Of course: it would disgrace Karl-lo-Magne to pay you, who are his sworn men, and I have no wish to do that. It would be a most unfortunate beginning to my stay here." Rakoczy turned to regard Fratre Angelomus. "I will give a donation to Sant' Martin in your name, if that would please you."

"You will do as you must," said Fratre Angelomus, busying himself with the girths of his saddle before remounting.

"And you, good Fratre, will do as you must, as well," said Rakoczy, nodding to Rorthger and indicating the gates. "We part here, good missi. My thanks to you for bringing me here; I wish you a swift and safe journey to Aachen."

"Amen," said Fratre Angelomus.

"Godspeed," said Otfrid, and set his horse trotting away from the monastery.

Rakoczy raised his hand in farewell, then said to Rorthger, "Well, shall we go in?"

Rorthger tugged on the mules' leads and fell in behind Rakoczy. "I am ready."

"I wonder if I am," said Rakoczy in Greek. "What if we should follow after Otfrid, leave Sant' Martin's, and return to the Wendish marshes?"

"We would have made a long journey to no purpose," said Rorthger in the same language. "And you would disappoint Karlus without good reason."

"Yes. But it is temp—" He broke off as he came up to the monks guarding the gate. "I am Hiernom Rakoczy; your Abbott, Alcuin of York, sent for me." He spoke in Latin and repeated himself in Frankish.

"I am Fratre Berengarius," said the man with a silver crucifix hanging from a thong around his neck. "Our Abbott is expecting you. If you will come with me?"

Rakoczy inclined his head. "Of course." He gestured to Rorthger to come with him.

"Your mounts and pack animals will go to the stable." Fratre Berengarius pointed off to his right. "Your manservant may deal with settling them. He will have stalling provided for your horses and mules. When that is done, have the slaves bring your chests and crates to the collegium where rooms have been set aside for your use." He stood still while Rakoczy dismounted and handed his reins to Rorthger. "The slaves will know where to take your things."

"Fine," said Rakoczy, and gestured compliance to Rorthger. "I will join you in a while, I must suppose. I don't know how long the Abbott will keep me in attendance on him."

"As you say, my master," said Rorthger. "You must suppose." He did not quite smile, but there was a quirk at the corner of his mouth that told Rakoczy that Rorthger was amused.

"Exactly," Rakoczy responded, and went to the monk. "Lead on, Fratre Berengarius."

The Fratre did not like Rakoczy's lack of what he considered appropriate reverence for the monastery; his lips were set in a thin, disapproving line as he nodded toward a large building on the west side of the Cathedral. "That is the way to the collegium. I will escort you to Abbott Alcuin, who will receive you as soon as he can. He has many duties that require his attention."

"And my arrival is the least of them," said Rakoczy patiently. "I am aware of it, and I am wholly at his service."

They went off through a group of people huddled together, their clothes unlike the costume of this region; one of the men leaned on a pair of stout walking sticks, trying to favor a grotesquely swollen ankle.

"They are from the Pyrenees," Fratre Berengarius said. "They have come here for succor and the hope of getting land to work."

Rakoczy had a fleeting image of Csimenae and her unholy tribe in their self-made mountain fisc; then it was gone, and he remarked, "The monastery must take in hundreds of refugees in the course of a year."

"That we do. It is worst now, with the harvest coming, but all year, even in winter, they seek us out, from all over Karl-lo-Magne's lands, and beyond." He was unabashedly pleased to announce this. "Sant' Martin is a powerful patron."

"No doubt the presence of Great Karl's chief advisor is not a disadvantage," Rakoczy said.

Fratre Berengarius shook his head. "Christ leads them to us, for the salvation of their souls. We must protect them in the Name of Christ or disgrace our vows."

Rakoczy looked up at the shoulder of the Cathedral, the transept that bulged with chapels and oratories. "A most remarkable building, this Cathedral. Indeed, the whole monastery is impressive, so well laid out and carefully kept."

"The Prior is strict, and so is the Superior. The Rule is upheld here." He pointed to a group of monks rolling newly made barrels toward the monastery brewery. "There is labor for all of us, and we know we must do it for the Glory of God."

"How many monks live here?" Rakoczy asked, doing his own calculations.

"Two hundred twenty-six at present, forty-three novices, three hundred thirty-nine slaves, and sixty-one lay-Fratres, most of them one-time soldiers who have left the field of battle forever, and have given themselves to God instead of the King." He was proud of these numbers and carried himself a bit straighter as he led Rakoczy past the brewers.

Rakoczy interpreted the vocation of the former soldiers as being the result of some disabling injury rather than a sudden awakening of fervor, but he said, "A great credit to Sant' Martin."

"Amen," said Fratre Berengarius. "That passage to your right—take it."

Rakoczy suspected that he was being taken the long way around to his destination, and assumed that Fratre Berengarius had been asked to do this, either to delay his arrival, or to show him the extent of the monastery. This right-turning path led past a cloister and a chapter house, then along the flank of the Cathedral toward a two-story building with a Roman arch over the center entrance. Rakoczy went toward the entrance, Fratre Berengarius immediately behind him. "Is this the collegium?"

"It's the scriptorium; the collegium is behind it, facing the petitioners' court. Go through the arch and across the courtyard. The next building is the collegium. It is larger and has more rooms than the scriptorium. Two or three will be assigned to you. Your manservant will be taken there with your belongings. A bed will be prepared for him in the corridor, to guard you." Fratre Berengarius made this sound like an unearned honor. "He *is* a servant, isn't he—not a slave?"

"I have no slaves," said Rakoczy with utter finality. "And he will occupy my rooms with me. He can guard me better from inside than from the hallway."

Fratre Berengarius had no answer for this idiosyncracy, attributing it to Rakoczy's foreignness; he took advantage of their entry into the courtyard to change the subject. "You will see there are three passages. The one on the left is for Fratres, the others are for Magnati, Illustri, Sublimi, and Potenti. Bellatori are housed in the dormitory, when they are admitted here at all."

Rakoczy smiled. "Which am I to use?"

Fratre Berengarius stared at him. "Which—?"

"Passage," Rakoczy said patiently.

"The central one, at least today. The Abbott will say which you are to use in future." He indicated a staircase. "Your quarters are that way. I'll show you where when the Abbott is done with you."

"Thank you," said Rakoczy, making note of the narrowness of the flight, and the steepness. "You must go single file up and down those stairs."

"As our Rule requires," Fratre Berengarius agreed.

Rakoczy nodded. "Sant' Benedict said little about staircases."

"Our Rule enlarges his dicta," said the monk, pointing to a corridor on their left. "If you will turn here?"

"Of course," said Rakoczy, doing it. The long passage was two stories high, the upper level galleried with a series of small arches. The sounds of many hushed voices made the air rush and whisper like the waves of the sea.

"There is an alcove ahead. Enter it," said Fratre Berengarius.

The alcove proved to be large, the size of a reception room, but lacking a fourth wall and a door. There was a long trestle table set up across it, and half-a-dozen men in habits stood around it, frowning down on a swath of silk marked with red dye; Rakoczy recognized the object of their scrutiny as an Imperial map from the Court of the Emperor of China. It was at least two hundred years old; age made it fragile, something the monks took into consideration in their handling of it.

"Sublime Abbott," said Fratre Berengarius in a respectfully lowered voice.

A white-haired man whose tonsure no longer needed the barber's efforts to maintain looked up, blinking as those with short sight were inclined to do; he approached Rakoczy in a friendly manner, not overly familiar, but genial enough. He stopped an arm's length from the new arrival. "So you're Rakoczy. Your reputation precedes you." He came up to Rakoczy's chin, an angular man with snapping blue-green eyes, a large nose, and hairy ears.

"And you are Alcuin of York?" Rakoczy inquired, knowing it was possible that this man could be his deputy. "Your reputation is known far beyond the territories of Great Karl."

"I am he," he said with a modest ducking of his head. "You came in good time. I hadn't thought you would arrive for another two weeks at least."

"The missi dominici and the escort who brought me urged us to travel with dispatch," said Rakoczy, then took a chance and added, "I see you have a map from China."

"We think so," said Alcuin. "Perhaps you can assist us on this point."

"Certainly," said Rakoczy, and stepped up to the table. "It is an old map, as I'm sure you know."

"Yes," said Alcuin. "I thought so, too."

Rakoczy had the uneasy feeling that this was some kind of test, and that the whole encounter had been staged for his benefit. He reverenced the monks around the table, then bent over the silk. He read the names of rivers and cities, but decided not to say too much of this, for he did not know what the monks had already been told about the map, or what they had decided on their own about it. "This is of the northern part of China, from the ocean to the far end of the Chinese lands, near the Celestial Mountains, from the lands of the Mongols on the north to the edge of the Land of Snows on the south, a considerable area to cover," he told them. "Those mountains are extremely high, and they cannot be easily crossed, so the route is an important one, and also vulnerable. The trade routes go along the northern side of their foothills, where the lands are long, empty plains and arid wastes." The last time he had traveled the Old Silk Road had been in the Year of Yellow Snow, when the cold never released its grip on the land at any part of the year, and the skies had dulled and darkened. "There is a city here." He touched the silk lightly. "Kara-khorum. Many caravans go through it, from Byzantium and the peoples north of the Caspian Sea, the inland sea beyond the Black Sea."

"There is no such sea," one of the monks said scornfully.

"But there is," Rakoczy countered mildly. "I have seen it."

"A man may claim anything when no one can challenge him," the monk persisted, his demeanor resistive. "You could tell us anything and expect us to believe you."

"Fratre Roewin," Alcuin admonished him gently. "Let the Magnatus tell us what he knows."

"But he takes us for fools, Sublime Abbott," Fratre Roewin protested. "He is repeating fables for credulous imbeciles."

"Which we may be, and ignorant as well," said Alcuin. "Therefore it behooves us to listen. We will judge what he says later, when we have had time to discuss it."

Rakoczy was now certain that this was a test and that it had been prepared for him. He studied the map, choosing what to tell them about it, cognizant of the fact that the monks had already received some information about this treasure that they were measuring against what he told them. "This map is old, good Fratres, more than a hundred years, by the look of it, and you ask me to tell you what I know about it, though it is ancient. How long have you had it?"

"Is that important?" asked the young monk.

"Not particularly, but I know that from time to time spies smuggle maps out to the Mongols, who want to raid in China." Rakoczy lifted his fine brows inquiringly. "Consider the use such a map could have, how misleading it could be. A foe, with such incorrect information, might make crucial errors, which the Emperor of China would turn to his advantage. And regional warlords could have a misleading map prepared that would give his men the advantage against their rivals. This does not appear to be one such, but if it is a successful ruse, it should not appear deceptive in any way. Such maps are more readily to be had, and they are often sold to the credulous, and such maps are occasionally and deliberately smuggled out of China, intentionally deceitful, to confound the Mongols, and other enemies beyond the borders of China; this may be one such."

"It came into our hands a decade ago," said Alcuin, waiting expectantly.

"From what source? Can you tell me?" Rakoczy said.

"There was a delegation from Byzantium, and this was among the gifts they brought to Great Karl," said Alcuin. "More than that, we do not know."

"Well, it is from China, that is beyond question; it is authentic, not a copy, so you may rely on what it depicts, unless it was designed to cozen the enemies of China. It is accurate as far as I can tell, but that may be part of its usefulness," said Rakoczy, who was certain this was not the case; he was certain the map was authentic, but he did not want to speak against the group wisdom. "The Emperor of China has many maps, but whether this is one of them, I cannot tell." In fact, he had read the characters on the side of the map that said it had been commissioned by the Governor of Kuan-Nei Province for the use of his couriers; he decided to keep that information to himself. "It marks fortresses and towns, and merchants' roads. It also shows rivers and lakes, with information about how to cross." He indicated two of them, then pointed to the next features on the silk. "These towers are the fortresses, and this walled house means a village."

"How can you be sure?" The monk who asked was young, perhaps no more than twenty. "Couldn't they be something else?"

Rakoczy wondered what the monks had been told, and by whom. "I have seen other Chinese maps," he said. "That is their tradition. They distinguish such buildings in that manner."

"How do we know you are reporting aright?" The young monk folded his arms into the sleeves of his habit.

"You invited me here so that you could ask these questions of me, and I have come. Why would I lie to you, or mislead you—particularly now, when I have only just arrived?" Rakoczy fixed the young man with his dark eyes, waiting until the monk lowered his eyes. "I have no reason to—"

Alcuin made a gesture that stopped the rankling. "I think we must accept Magnatus Rakoczy's good-will and just intentions until we find otherwise."

"He comes from the East," said the shortsighted monk. "The Byzantines rule in the East."

"So they do," said Rakoczy. "And the Bulgars. Beyond them is the Khazar Empire, and dry realms of the Turks and Mongols. Finally there is the vast land of China, that reaches to the Unknown Sea." He recalled his cold journey again, and said, "Byzantium is only a small part of the world, Fratres, and great though it may be, there are greater still to be found."

"And whom do you serve?" the young monk demanded.

"Fratre Theodo," Alcuin said mildly, although this was clearly a rebuke.

Rakoczy held up his small hand. "No; I'll answer him. For the time being, I serve Karl-lo-Magne, until it suits him to dismiss me, or I am called away by relatives of my blood." It was an acceptable response and delivered with conviction; the young monk colored and looked away toward the end of the table as if he had not seen it before; he would not look in Rakoczy's direction.

"You have seen these places?" Alcuin asked, waving his hand at the silken map. "With your own eyes?"

"Some of the places," Rakoczy answered truthfully.

"It must have been the journey of years," said Alcuin.

"I was gone for some time," Rakoczy responded. "On the journey home, we traveled quickly. It took slightly more than a year to come from Ch'ang-an to my homeland in the Carpathian Mountains. There was famine in the land, and speed was required." Famine had been the least of it, but it was something these men would understand, having come through just such a calamity two years ago. "But that was an extraordinary passage, driven by necessity."

"As is much travel," said Alcuin. "Consider those wretches who come here for sanctuary. They come for dire reasons, and we, in the Name of Christ and Great Karl, take them in."

"I was not so fortunate in my trek," said Rakoczy.

"The Church does not extend much beyond Karlus' borders," said Alcuin. "I am not astonished that you found no succor in those wild lands."

Rakoczy kept his thoughts to himself, saying only, "It was a difficult time."

There was a long silence, and then Fratre Roewin said, "As much as you can tell us, we will add to our itineraries and descriptions of the world, and if it proves incorrect, Great Karl will decide what is to be done."

"I am on my mettle, then," Rakoczy said with an ironic lilt to his voice.

"Karlus requires true service," said Fratre Roewin. "If you fail to give it, you will face exile, and worse."

"That is acceptable," said Rakoczy, seeing Alcuin's slight nod of approval.

"This place," said Fratre Theodo, pointing at a character at the end of the map. "What is it? What can you tell us about it?"

"The place is Talas. It is in the far west of the Chinese Empire, in a small valley between great mountains. It is on the northern trade route, which brings fur and amber into China. The river bears that name. A battle was fought there about fifty years ago." Rakoczy rubbed his clean-shaven chin; he suspected he had been asked about this place because these monks had heard of it.

"You don't know what lies north of it, do you?" asked Fratre Roewin.

"Mountains, a large, long, hooked lake, and Turks." Rakoczy faltered, "Or so I was told by my guides. I didn't travel there myself."

"Did you trust your guides?" The Fratre who asked was blind in one eye, and scarred from brow to cheek.

"Yes. They kept me alive," said Rakoczy.

"Then you were a fortunate man," said the scarred Fratre.

"Fratre Isembard has reason to distrust guides; you must pardon him for questioning you," said Alcuin, making a gesture to Rakoczy. "You may sit; so may we all."

All but one of the seats were short, plank benches; the X-shaped chair at the head of the table was reserved for Alcuin, who sank onto it while the others jockeyed their way onto the benches, which were each designed for two men. Rakoczy was permitted to occupy a two-man bench alone. Once everyone was in place, Alcuin nodded to Fratre Roewin.

"We were told by a merchant from Tana that this map belonged to the Emperor of China himself." Fratre Roewin could not keep the satisfaction out of his voice.

"It is an official map," Rakoczy agreed. "But all the Emperor's personal records are done in red, and this is in black."

"Are you saying it is not the Emperor's?" Alcuin inquired.

"I am saying that it isn't in red ink." Rakoczy shrugged. "I would suppose it could be a copy of one such map, but it isn't the map itself."

"An astute response," said Fratre Theodo in a slightly condescending tone.

"It is all I can say," Rakoczy responded. "Anything else would be speculation."

"You've seen the trade road, though," said Fratre Isembard, satisfying himself on that point.

"Yes, I have," said Rakoczy. "I will be pleased to tell you as much as I can recall of the way."

Alcuin nodded. "It is true that will be most helpful in compiling our descriptiones and itineraries, and for that alone, I am certain that we were well-advised to bring you here. No doubt there will be many other uses to which your knowledge can be put; we will determine them all in time." He paused as a loud but unmusical bell rang from the Cathedral. "It is the hour for prayer."

The monks rose and formed a line, the oldest at the front, the youngest at the rear; Alcuin blessed himself and the monks and prepared to leave from the collegium, but he paused, looking directly at Rakoczy. "The slaves will have your chests and crates in your chambers. One of them will lead you there. You will not be asked to observe our Hours today, but tomorrow we will expect you to join us in worship." He inclined his head as a sign of welcome. "There will be a meal served in two hours."

"I believe I will rest this afternoon; I thank you for your graciousness," said Rakoczy. "And I thank you for your hospitality."

"It is what Our Lord commands us," said Alcuin. "Those who stop with us are given a haven in His Name."

"I thank you, as His servant, for so carefully fulfilling His bidding," said Rakoczy, staying with the forms of custom among the Franks. "You honor me with your kindness."

"As you honor us with your presence." He clapped his hands, and a slave hurried up in response. "Take the Magnatus to his appointed chambers."

The slave lowered his head and averted his eyes as the monks filed out, and the sound of chanting arose, a repetition of prayers on a cycle of five notes.

Rakoczy looked at the slave. "Thank you," he said, and saw the man start in surprise at such recognition; belatedly he remembered that the Franks' desire to emulate the Romans of old did not extend to acknowledging the service of slaves. He realized he would have to go on carefully. "It is the custom of my people to show gratitude for service, no matter who gives it." This was stretching the truth a bit, for Rakoczy had not come to that habit until he, himself, had been a slave.

"Foreign," said the slave, accepting this as an explanation. "Come with me."

With a gesture of acquiescence, he followed the slave out into the narrow corridor, which now echoed the chants of the monks. Passing through the central archway, they entered a steep, narrow staircase that led upward to the second floor of the collegium, where they entered a gallery that overlooked the grounds of the petitioners' court on one side and faced a wall interspersed with ironbanded doors on the other; it ran the length of the building and ended at another staircase. The slave stopped in front of one of the iron-banded doors, reverencing Rakoczy.

"I take it this is mine?" Rakoczy inquired.

"The next door is for your manservant, since you have ordered that he will sleep inside your door and not in front of it." The slave was curious about this arrangement, but would not ask any questions, for such impertinence would earn him a beating.

"That is correct. It is another of my foreign habits." Rakoczy drew back the latch, and the door swung outward, revealing a small study with a worktable and a stand for books. There were three oil lamps providing as much smoke as illumination, and on the table, a sheet of precious parchment from which an old text had been meticulously scrubbed and scraped. In the middle of all this was an untidy stack of crates and chests—Rakoczy's belongings, ready to be opened and emptied. "How orderly it all is. Alcuin is an excellent host."

The slave said nothing.

"And my man-servant—where is he?" Rakoczy went on.

"He has gone to the kitchens, to make arrangements for your food. He says only he prepares it for you." The slave waited for a response. "They say he wants to kill the fowl and shoats himself, and do all the preparation."

"A man who has enemies must be careful to dine only with friends," said Rakoczy, paraphrasing the old Roman aphorism with a smile.

"Yes," said the slave, who abased himself and withdrew, leaving Rakoczy to deal with the stack of his trunks and chests. He moved aside those with clothing, books, weapons, and medicinal supplies, and took the largest crates into the small chamber beyond, where a makeshift bed had been set up. Rakoczy moved this, dismantling it quickly and efficiently, then putting two chests in its stead, for they contained his native earth and would provide him rest that nothing else could give.

Rorthger arrived a short while later, a fresh-killed and newly plucked goose in his hands. He looked about, noticing that the crates and chests had been dealt with. "I hope no one saw you do this. There is speculation enough about you already. If they knew you do the work of servants, their curiosity would increase tenfold." He spoke in the Latin of his youth.

"Of course I was not seen; the door was closed while I worked," said Rakoczy, also in Imperial Latin, and nodded to the goose. "I take it that's supposed to be my evening meal?"

"Yes. I trust you don't mind." Rorthger gave a slight smile. "I have much less to explain if I am acting on your orders. I'm sorry I could not bring you a live one. I thought this was the more prudent thing to do."

Rakoczy nodded. "Yes, yes. I concur. I'll manage, later tonight." He put his hand up. "Were you followed?"

"I don't think so. They're all either praying or getting ready for their supper."

He looked about and shrugged. "I have a bench in my quarters. I'll cut this up in there."

"Go ahead. You've waited long enough for a decent dinner." Rakoczy took a long moment to listen, assessing all the sounds he heard through the stout door and thick stone walls. "This is a substantial place."

"Yes, it is," said Rorthger. "I have studied it superficially, and I think it is about the most formidable building I have seen since we left China."

"The Franks are an industrious people," said Rakoczy, and gestured to the door. "Best put a crucifix on it, and over our beds. These monks expect it."

"I will tend to it. Which shall I use?" Rorthger continued to work on the goose, preparing to joint it.

"Not the Byzantine, I think," said Rakoczy with a wry smile. "They're suspicious enough of us without that. No, use the old ones, the Gothic ones, from Caesaraugusta."

"All right. Anything more?" Rorthger kept a somber expression, but his light-blue eyes shone with private nostalgia.

"Choose some bit of art—religious enough, not the dancing dwarf with the huge phallus—and make sure it is where the slaves will see it," Rakoczy said. "Alcuin may be pleased to have me here, but not all the monks share his view."

Rorthger sighed his agreement. "That's my impression, too. Listening to the kitchen slaves, I gleaned a fair amount."

"Did anyone notice you listening?" Rakoczy asked, a bit more sharply than he had intended.

"Of course not," said Rorthger, dismissing the notion with a wave of his hand. "I wouldn't do anything sloppy, my master."

"I know, old friend," said Rakoczy, chastened. "I must be more on edge than I thought." He took a turn about the confines of the room. "Well, we're here now. We ought to make the best of it."

Rorthger nodded. "I'll put up the crucifixes as soon as I eat," he promised as he opened the interior door connecting his chamber with Rakoczy's. "As you say, we ought to make the best of this."

TEXT OF A LETTER FROM ABBA SUNIFRED OF SANTA ALBEGUNDA TO BISHOP ISO OF SANT' AUDOENUS IN STAVELOT; CARRIED BY FRATRE OSWIN AT THE ORDER OF BISHOP FRECULF.

Amen. Benedicamus Domino. Amen.

To the most esteemed and reverend Bishop, Iso of Sant' Audoenus, the greetings in God of Abba Sunifred, of Santa Albegunda and daughter of Potente Hilduin.

Sublime Iso, I come to you with the petition that you receive at your monastery one Gynethe Mehaut, who has been given into our care, for we find we cannot tend to her as devoted nuns should. She requires more learned supervision than we offer here. So I now implore you to say you will do as Our Lord commands, and receive into your protection one who needs your prayers and guidance as few others in this afflicted world.

She does not bring disease with her, so you may put your thoughts to rest on that point, nor is she mad, or not in the conventional sense of raving. She occasionally displays wounds in her hands and feet, and no one can tell how they came to be there. Her blood flows for as long as a month, and then, for a time, her hands and feet heal, only to bleed again, at a later day. This has caused such dismay among the women here that I cannot continue to vouch for her safety, and thus I send you this petition in the fervent hope that you will be better able to minister to her; if not at Sant' Audoenus, then at some other monastery or nunnery under your protection.

It is my most ardent prayer that you, and your Sublime colleagues may determine the cause of these wounds she has, be they signs of blessing or damnation. You, being nearer to Aachen, may draw upon the counsel of many learned men to consider her case, and that would be most laudable in you, for we have been unable to establish for a certainty if this young woman comes among us, white as a lamb, or ravening as a red-eyed wolf. Imploring your wisdom be turned to Gynethe Mehaut, we ask you to accept her into your care, for the good of her soul and the protection of her body.

I am prepared to send her under guard and accompanied by Priora Iditha, who has cared for Gynethe Mehaut for some time, and has learned to deal with the wounds as well as to protect her from the sun. Priora Iditha can instruct you on the case of Gynethe Mehaut, including advising how she is to be housed and cared for. Gynethe Mehaut, as her name suggests, is of a most pale skin, and I should warn you, as I have already implied, her eyes are red. This, too, has added to the consternation her presence has excited here. She cannot easily go abroad in sunlight, which quickly burns her and makes her ill. I have no doubt your monks, tending as they do to the simple, the dumb, and the mad, will be less distressed by Gynethe Mehaut than my nuns are.

Prayerfully I await your answer, and I beseech you to agree to give succor to this unfortunate young woman. As Bishop Freculf will vouch, she is not marked by secret sin, nor has she been wayward in her faith; she prays many hours daily, and keeps watch in the night garden for all of us at Santa Albegunda. She is not a foolish woman, and you need not fear she will conduct herself impiously or bring discredit upon your monasteries. For the sake of Our Lord, I ask you to agree to take her at Sant' Audoenus; on behalf of Gynethe Mehaut, I implore you to honor the Virtue that shelters the homeless and protects the helpless.

I will be forever grateful to you, Bishop Iso, and will remember you in prayers day and night for the rest of my life. My father, also, will provide you with four fat pigs and a dozen geese each year for the kindness you extend now to this young woman who bears so many afflictions from the Hand of God.

I prayerfully await your answer on this, the Pope's Feast of Sant' Leodegar of Autun, in the Church's Year 796, at Santa Albegunda.

Abba Sunifred

chapter four

A SLOW DRIZZLE IMPEDED THE PROGRESS of the small company of monks and their escort of three pair of missi dominici, four servants, and two men-at-arms as they made their way along the road toward Aachen. The road was covered with fallen leaves, muffling the sound of the horses, the oxen, and carpenta wheels as they made their way north and east. This was their tenth day of travel, and the demands of the road were telling on all the party. Alcuin of York rode in the van of the company, with Hiernom Rakoczy beside him this afternoon. "My old bones don't do well in this weather," he complained, rubbing at his knee. "You don't know yet—you're still a man of good years."

"You could ride in one of the carpenta," Rakoczy pointed out, indicating the three large, ox-drawn wagons in the center of their traveling group; he had no wish to discuss his age.

"Alcuin of York? In a carpentum? Behind two oxen? How could I hold up my head if I rode like a woman, or an ancient? Or one of those old pagan priests?" the monk exclaimed in false indignation. "I am not doddering yet, thank you, that I need to be tended by slaves. The Merovingians may have been satisfied with riding in a carpentum, and they may have reserved that honor for warlords and sacerdotal nobles, but I take my example from Karlus, and will stick to my horse in spite of all." He shook his head and said more calmly as he patted his mare's neck, "Besides, those wheels rattle worse than the hardest trot."

"True enough," said Rakoczy. "How much farther do we go today?"

"We will reach Santi Raffaell and Gabraell the Archangels in time for Vespers," said Alcuin. "Then another day and we will be with Great Karl at Aachen by the end of it, praise be to God for it! The road will be better tomorrow."

"Because we'll be approaching Aachen?" Rakoczy suggested.

"That, and because at the end of harvest, he has the local peasants drag logs over the road, to lessen the ruts. The logs then go toward building his palace." Alcuin smiled stiffly. "Karlus doesn't like waste."

"You mean the logs," Rakoczy said.

"Logs, or anything else. He says the Greeks waste everything in vain display and will suffer for it. The Romans are almost as bad." Alcuin pulled at the hood of his pluvial. "It will be good to be warm again."

"Does he often send for you after harvest?" Rakoczy asked, who had heard mutterings about this at Sant' Martin, not all of them favorable to such travel, for the dark days at the end of autumn were known to be especially dangerous, short hours of light and treacherous weather adding to the ever-present hazards of bandits and fever.

"He has before," said Alcuin, a hint of resignation in his remark. "I wasn't surprised to be summoned this year. There was famine in the country just two years ago, and it is important for Karlus to have all the information we may offer him, against the possibility of greater starvation." He glanced back at the leader of the missi dominici. "Comes Gutiger is not pleased at the favor I show you."

"Nor should he be," said Rakoczy. "I trust you will let him ride with you for a time, or I will have him for my enemy."

Alcuin sighed. "I suppose you're right. A man has enemies enough in this world without seeking to make more for himself." He motioned to the Comes, who was one rank behind them. "My son. Come join us." He indicated his left, for Rakoczy already rode on his right.

Comes Gutiger looked about suspiciously, as if expecting to be the butt of a jest. "Why do you want me?" He carried the hanging banner displaying Karl-lo-Magne's sigil, ensuring their preferential passage on all roads in Franksland.

"To help pass the time. This is a dull day to be abroad, and the road is wearisome. Magnatus Rakoczy has been telling me tales of foreign climes, so that I need not dwell on what we endure now, although I do not doubt that such places as the one with mountains to the sky too high for men to climb, and forests filled with monkeys, tigers, and elephants may be a trifle fanciful; no other traveler in the East has told us of such wonders." Alcuin cocked his head in Comes Gutiger's direction. "You have campaigned in the land of the Longobards, haven't you? Surely you must have seen strange sights there, and done things that you can boast of with honor. You have gone into the mountains at the north and east of the Longobards' land."

"Not as strange as you might think: trees, rocks, rivers, poor roads, small hamlets, fortresses, monasteries, pagan groves, merchants, and pilgrims. Where there were unbelievers, Great Karl tore down the old shrines and built monasteries and churches instead. Where there were Celts, he ordered that Frankish should be the tongue they speak, or Latin. Where there were fortifications, he seized them and garrisoned them with his own men. Longobardia is much like other places Great Karl has subdued," said the Comes, who was a russet-haired, square-faced, bellicose man of twenty-nine. "The people there are stiff-necked and treacherous. And the air of Longobardia is very bad. Many die of fevers from it."

"All of Italy has bad air," said Alcuin. "Not even the Pope can escape it."

"And the Longobards suffer from it, too," said Comes Gutiger. "As many of their soldiers die as ours. It is a great misfortune."

Rakoczy nodded; he had seen the ravages of the bad air—the mal aria—from the shores of the Adriatic and Aegean Seas to the western reaches of Spain. He made a gesture to ward off misfortune. "Who can escape the dangers of pestilence?"

"The man with a fast horse," said Comes Gutiger.

Alcuin shook his head. "No. When a man's hour is come, nothing will avail to save him. The end comes for all of us, and it is beyond our reckoning to know the hour. Who shall live and who shall die is in the Hands of God." He touched his pectoral crucifix through his pluvial. "Let the physicians do their best, it is God Who will decide."

"Amen," said the Comes.

"Amen," Rakoczy echoed.

"You must see that there is Heavenly favor in age," said Comes Gutiger, determined to make the most of his opportunity. "God has given Great Karl many,

many years and kept him hale. And you, Bishop Alcuin, you have lived long. This is surely a sign of God's love of you."

"Today I am not so certain as I am on days when my joints don't hurt," said Alcuin, and laughed at himself. "But I think where life is long, God is good."

Rakoczy thought back to his centuries in the Temple of Imhotep and the thousands upon thousands he had watched live and die there, and found himself now, as he had become then, unable to turn away from pain he could alleviate. He took a deep breath. "I do not offer this for any reason more than it is fitting to alleviate suffering where it is possible: I have among my things an unguent that may ease your hurts. When we stop for the evening, I will give you a vial of it."

"After prayers, I will thank you," said Alcuin. He looked over at Comes Gutiger. "It is a hard day when the leagues are so long in passing."

"It would be harder still if this company were larger." He nodded to the carpenta. "We can go no faster than the oxen."

"It is the way of traveling," said Rakoczy.

"For many," said Comes Gutiger. "It is the plan of Great Karl to have all his army's carpenta, plaustera, and carruca drawn by horses. They will speed the march of his forces."

"Horses will need more food than oxen. And better food than oxen require: horses cannot subsist on thistles and dry grass; that could make your campaigns more difficult. You may have to carry your own grain and hay," Rakoczy pointed out. In the Year of Yellow Snow, when the frost had killed all the spring grass, the Avars had lost more than half their herds for that reason.

"There is truth in what you say," Comes Gutiger admitted. "But it is fitting that the army move more quickly than the enemies of Great Karl. Horses are faster than oxen." He glared at Rakoczy, daring him to contradict this military truth.

"Oh, I have no disagreement with you on that point," said Rakoczy, his voice level. "I only observe that there is a risk to such strategy."

"Um," said Comes Gutiger.

"Let us have no discord," Alcuin interjected. "We all travel at the Will of Karlus, and it is mete that we do so in comity and good-fellowship."

Rakoczy ducked his head compliantly. "I have no desire to incite ill-will, good Comes," he said, and added, "Being foreign, I may sometimes transgress, but that is not my intention, and I ask your help in rectifying my errors. Should I do anything that offends you, tell me at once, that I may offer you an apology. I have been shown only cordiality since I came into Franksland, and I would be ungrateful to return that with anything but couthy ecomania."

"So you tell me," Comes Gutiger said curtly, inwardly dismayed by Rakoczy's concessions. He had anticipated a sharp defense, not this smooth talk.

"A most elegant sentiment," Alcuin approved.

"A sincere one, in any case," said Rakoczy, more for Comes Gutiger's benefit than Alcuin's.

"Demeanor is always important," approved Alcuin. "As a traveler, you must know that better than most others do."

"It does seem so to me, and has served me in good stead," Rakoczy assured him. "Particularly as I am no longer young."

Alcuin swung around as far as his saddle would permit. "You are hardly doddering, Magnatus. You are sound in limb and wind. Your wits are not addled. What does it matter that you will not see twenty again? Who among us will?" He laughed aloud, startling his mare.

Comes Gutiger snorted, his face showing the disgust he dared not speak aloud. "Age touches all who do not fall in youth."

There was a party of travelers ahead of them, moving more slowly than the travelers from Sant' Martin; it consisted of an escort of three armed men and two enclosed carruca, the curtains drawn over the frame of the vehicles painted with illustrations of a female saint.

Alcuin signaled his party to slow down and said to Comes Gutiger, "You, and Magnatus Rakoczy, come with me." He put his mare to the trot; he did not bother to see if the two others accompanied him.

At the sight of the banner Comes Gutiger carried, the leader of the travelers ahead of them brought the party to a halt, and the men-at-arms lifted their right hands to show them empty. "Victory to Karlus!" they cried in ragged chorus.

"Very good," said Alcuin. "We must ask you to keep to the side of the road while we pass you. I hope you will not be inconvenienced."

"We are bound for Sant' Audoenus," said the leader of the three armed men. "At the order of Bishop Freculf and the Abba Sunifred of Santa Albegunda. We will reach our destination tomorrow."

"Sant Audoenus," said Alcuin in some surprise, for he knew Sant' Audoenus' reputation as a haven for the ill and the tormented. "Are your charges afflicted?"

"One is . . ." The leader fell silent as the curtain over the carrucum lifted and a habited nun emerged.

"I am Priora Iditha, and I am attending a woman in the charge of my Order. She rides with me to Sant' Audoenus, at the pleasure of our Abba and Bishop Freculf. Two other Sorrae ride in the other carrucum. They will return to our convent with me, or without me, when Bishop Iso decides what is to be done with our—" She indicated the curtain concealing the other passenger. "I am prepared to remain with her, should the Prior and Abbott of Sant' Audoenus deem it best, and have leave to do so."

"Very good; your Bishop and Abba are wise," said Alcuin, then changed his tone. "We will not keep you long, and we will wish you Godspeed on your journey." He was about to swing his mare around, but faltered, and turned back. "Why do you take this woman to Sant' Audoenus?"

Priora Iditha was clearly torn, for she knew she should say nothing of the duty entrusted to her, yet she could not refuse the order of someone traveling under the King's banner. "She has need of the care and the prayers of the monks."

"Of course she does," said Alcuin bluntly. "Why would you take her there if she did not." He waited with ill-concealed impatience.

There was a gentle cough from inside the carrucum. "I will step out," said a pleasant voice, and a moment later, Gynethe Mehaut stood beside Priora Iditha. She was habited like Priora Iditha, and her hands were swathed in strips of linen.

Comes Gutiger swore and backed his horse away half-a-dozen paces. Alcuin stared, transfixed. Only Hiernom Rakoczy leaned forward, unafraid and unalarmed.

"Our Abba has asked the Sublime Iso to take her in," said Priora Iditha as calmly as she could.

"May God give her peace," said Alcuin hurriedly, and tugged on his mare's rein to turn her around.

"Red eyes. It cannot be good to have red—" Comes Gutiger broke off and followed after Alcuin.

"Take care to stay out of the sun," Rakoczy said kindly, addressing Gynethe Mehaut directly. "And bathe often: skin such as yours can become injured when it isn't clean. Do not worry about vanity: there is none in saving your body from damage. You have a most exceptional condition, and it imposes its burden upon you. Do not be frightened or ashamed: you are a singular woman; that is the whole of it." He nodded once to Priora Iditha. "Watch after her, Priora. Care for her. She is a most delicate blossom, like the jasmine; she cannot easily sustain the blows of the world." With that, he made a little reverence, then nudged his grey with his calf and went back to the Sant' Martin group.

While they watched the Santa Albegunda travelers move to the side of the road, Alcuin whispered to Rakoczy. "In all your travels, have you ever seen anyone like that?"

"Yes, I have," said Rakoczy. "Very rarely," he added.

"I should hope so," exclaimed the monk. "What a most terrible affliction! God visits strange suffering upon His children."

"Is she a leper? So white?" the Comes asked, his voice raised half an octave in fear.

"No," said Rakoczy before Alcuin could answer. "There is no rotting of her flesh, and no thickening of her features. The whiteness was on her when she was born, or I know nothing of the matter."

"It may be a sign of great blessing, to be white as a newborn lamb. How remarkable." Alcuin made a gesture of protection, just in case.

"No doubt," said Rakoczy, a sardonic note creeping into his voice. "And that, as you say, good Alcuin, does not, perforce, mean un-Godly. Sometimes such singularity is a mark of favor."

Alcuin nodded. "Yes. It could be so."

Comes Gutiger shook his head emphatically. "Nothing so pale—she is whiter than a bled corpse!—can be—"

"The Lamb is white as fresh-fallen snow," said Alcuin thoughtfully, pursuing his own ruminations. He made a gesture, and his party moved forward again. "The garments of the Angels are white."

"But red eyes!" Comes Gutiger protested.

"Yes. That is troubling," said Alcuin. "Well, let us pray for her preservation from all harm, and her deliverance from sin." They were almost abreast of the carruca, and the monk averted his eyes. "How long will she remain like that?"

Rakoczy reminded himself that for Alcuin, the miraculous was an expectation of faith. "All her life, Sublime. I have never known of anyone born as she was to become as other humankind are."

"How can that be? May not God intercede and transform her?" Alcuin asked. They were past the carruca now, and the leader of the men-at-arms held out his empty right hand in salutation; Alcuin sketched a blessing in his direction. "Surely God or one of His powerful Saints may bring about a change in her, so that she would be made like you and me."

This was precarious ground, and required a careful answer. "Say rather how could any change come, since God has been pleased to make her in this wise," Rakoczy corrected him gently. "I should worry for the health of anyone whose skin suddenly changed color, particularly for one born so pale. It could mean that she would have more to suffer than she has now."

"Well, you have cared for the sick in many lands; I will suppose you have learned much." The dubiety in his voice warned Rakoczy to change the subject shortly. "You have learned a great deal, haven't you?" It was clearly a challenge.

"Not nearly enough," said Rakoczy with genuine feeling, unwilling to dispute the matter. "I cannot tell when a man ails and nothing will avail him, why it has been so."

The Comes snorted and tried not to laugh. "You aim high, foreigner."

"Certainly. What else is worth my time, or the time of any man?" Rakoczy put a slight emphasis on the last word, and almost at once regretted it, for he was worried that this might be noticed and attributed to something more than his awkwardness with the language.

Alcuin chuckled, a sound like falling pebbles. "I should not like to debate you, Magnatus," he declared, and ended on a cough. "And not while riding on such a dreary day as this one, for what inspiration is there in such lowering skies?"

"I should not enter into such a dispute; it would be churlish of me to compel such a contest upon you after the courtesy you have shown me," said Rakoczy, and stared along the road so that he need not continue his attempts to avert more discord. He wished he could bring Rorthger up from his place behind the carpenta, but he knew it would not be tolerated; he settled back in his earth-lined saddle and listened to Alcuin discourse on the nature of the season while Comes Gutiger did his best to assume the look of someone interested in the subject, for it was prudent to humor Alcuin, who enjoyed Great Karl's trust and favor.

It was growing dark and the rain had turned to a persistent, clammy mist when they arrived at Santi Raffaell and Gabraell; the warder who answered their summons on the bell outside the gate—a tertiary Fratre with a missing eye and scars on his face and hands—let them in with something approaching a flourish; the sound of chanting accompanied his welcome. "They are at Vespers, but as soon as they are finished, the Abbott will come to greet you, and the Prior. Come in, and dismount. I will summon slaves to tend your animals." He clapped his hands excitedly. "Hurry! The Sublime Alcuin of York is here!"

Alcuin climbed out of his saddle with the slow care of a man whose knees and back were stiff. He tried to stretch and gave up the attempt, blessing himself instead. "God reward you," he said automatically to the tertiary Fratre.

"And bring you peace," the tertiary responded. He reached to take control of Alcuin's mare's reins. "You must be tired. Be welcome to this monastery, in the Name of God. There will be hot honied wine in the refectory; one of the slaves will show you the way." He motioned to the nearest of them. "Bolbo, take these worthy travelers to the refectory and build up the fire."

Bolbo nodded and tugged at his forelock; he would not look at any of the exalted company directly, but motioned with his arm as a sign that they should follow him.

"I'll see your horses are stalled and cared for, and your oxen," said the tertiary Fratre. "You have nothing to fear now you have arrived. Raffaell and Gabraell are powerful, and they protect those who come to them."

"Of course," said Alcuin, rubbing his hands together briskly and bringing them up to his lips to blow on them. "We will follow your slave."

"Yes. Yes. Certainly. I will tell Abbott Ansigus that you are come shortly."

The tertiary Fratre did his utmost to smile encouragement and reverenced the group repeatedly.

"I know that man," Comes Gutiger muttered as he fell in slightly behind Alcuin.

"What man?" Alcuin asked.

"The warder, the one with the scars." He scowled and sneezed.

"How do you know him?" Alcuin inquired, not particularly interested.

"I think he was a soldier once," said the Comes, his face set in hard lines.

"I should think so, by the look of him." Alcuin ducked under the eaves of the building to which the slave had led them. "Is this the refectory?"

The slave reverenced them and went through the stout door into a vestibule with a small reception room beyond, and the dining room to one side. He pointed to the reception room, where a smoldering fire provided a modicum of heat and a group of padded benches provided easier seating than the saddles had done. There were torches and braziers to augment the fire's light.

"Not much for talking, is he?" said the Comes.

"The slaves here are not supposed to address their betters," said Alcuin as he removed his pluvial and hung it on a peg on the wall. "There. You see? He is putting logs on the fire. We should be cozy in a little while."

Rakoczy, who had had little to say during the last part of their day's journey, now tugged off his thick woolen mantellum and said, "It's going to be a miserable night."

His remark proved to be the truth; the monks emerged from their chapel Vespers to offer a lively banquet of roast boar and pickled beef stuffed with onions, after which all the travelers retired to a number of small, unheated dormitories, each containing four cots, for a night's sleep made easy by fatigue; not even the predawn Matins and Lauds could disturb them. Slaves awakened them at Prime to prayers and the milky morning light diffusing through thick, dank fog that sapped warmth from their bones and cut through their garments with the keenness of Damascus steel and made ghosts of breath.

Rorthger met Rakoczy in the stable while most of the party lingered over a spartan breakfast of bread, cheese, and beer. "How are the horses?" He spoke in Persian.

"Cold," Rakoczy answered in the same tongue. "We'll have to resist the impulse to let them run to warm them, for they will take true chills if we do. A pity we don't have some of those Avar trappings." He laid his arm on the rump of his grey.

"The large triple sheepskins they put on their horses in snow?" Rorthger asked, and answered his own question. "Yes. That would be useful. For now, we could take our mantella and put them over their backs and flanks."

"And may do so," Rakoczy agreed. "Do you have my woolen capa readily to hand? If you do, I'll put my mantellum from his shoulder to his tail, and wrap myself in the capa." He reached for one of the stiff brushes and began to groom his gelding, starting on the neck and working down and back. "His winter coat is thick, that's something."

"But in this cold—" Rorthger said, and stopped. "It isn't as severe as the Year of Yellow Snow, I'll grant you that. But it is bad enough."

"I agree," said Rakoczy mildly. "It has been more than three centuries, yet every cold winter makes me remember it in appalling detail."

"Do you think it will come again, such a winter as that was, lasting more than the year around?" Rorthger asked, his voice carefully neutral.

"Eventually, but not, I would guess, for many years. I have lived a very long time, and I have seen only that one instance of such all-encompassing cold; I do not suppose another such will come in the next several centuries," said Rakoczy. He looked away toward the open door, but seeing his twenty-eight centuries of life, not the drift of fog that blurred everything with its gelid gauzery.

Rorthger opened one of the cases that lay near the stall. "Yes: you are right, of course. Here is your capa. The one with the badger-fur lining in the hood. The wool is double-thickness."

"Fine," said Rakoczy, and took off his mantel, exchanging it for the capa and draping the long mantellum along the grey's back. "The saddle-pad, if you will."

Rorthger handed it to him, and Rakoczy put it in place, the fleece side down. Then he lifted the saddle from where it rested on the support just outside the stall and settled it on the gelding's back and reached for the girth under the horse's belly, drawing it up to the single, large buckle at the edge of the tooled-leather skirt of the saddle. He flipped the stirrup-leathers and they dropped down into position, their large, triangular metal stirrups swinging a little. Then he took the breast-collar and buckled that across the grey's chest. "I'll be ready to ride as soon as the rest are. Sooner."

From where he had just finished grooming his dun, Rorthger laughed a little. "What will you tell them if they ask you about how you have used your mantellum?"

"I will say it is a custom of my people," Rakoczy answered. "You had best use your mantellum the same way, or they may become suspicious."

They had just bridled their horses when Comes Gutiger came into the stable, wiping crumbs from his mustache. "There you are! You didn't join us at table."

Rakoczy did his best to offer an ingratiating smile. "Those of my blood dine in privacy."

"So you've said, so you've said," the Comes agreed, looking around. "Where are the stable-hands?"

"I should imagine that they're at morning prayers with the rest of the inmates," said Rakoczy. "Even slaves must pray."

Comes Gutiger made an impatient slap at his thighs. "So you won't entrust your horses even to monks, or the slaves of monks! It's one thing to distrust Illustri and innkeepers, but monks!"

"The habits of a long-time traveler," Rakoczy said apologetically as he buckled the throat-latch of the bridle in place.

"Great Karl won't like it," the Comes predicted with something akin to smugness.

"You may be right," Rakoczy conceded as he backed his grey out of the stall. "But this way, if anything goes awry, I can blame no one but myself."

"They are your horses," Comes Gutiger conceded, and went to summon slaves to groom and saddle his mount, moving away as the stable-slaves answered his summons.

"Have you broken your fast?" Alcuin asked as he came into the stable. He cocked his head at Rakoczy, adding, "Of course not." He tapped his first finger to his chin. "You seem never to eat, and yet you maintain good flesh on your bones."

"I am nourished, as I told you," said Rakoczy, securing his grey's reins to the rail near the double doors.

"Yes," Alcuin mused. "That is apparent. And yet, I am astonished when you do not join us at table. No matter how your people do such things, all men must eat."

"So they must. My kin have our customs, as you have yours, and I honor them no matter where I am, or in what company." Rakoczy stepped aside as Rorthger led out his dun. "I will groom our remounts, and then we will be ready to leave."

"Excellent," Alcuin approved. "You set a fine example for all our party." This last seemed to be an oblique apology for his remarks about Rakoczy's unfamiliar dining habits.

"I have traveled a great deal," said Rakoczy, patting his grey.

"Using your mantellum to keep off the chill is a fine notion. Sant' Martin would approve, lending your garment to a lesser creature. Will you also cover your remount?" Alcuin was paying close attention to everything Rakoczy did.

"Much as I want to, it would not be practical. But I will hitch him to the second carpentum, and let the heat from the oxen help to keep our horses warm." Rakoczy went to the stall where his second grey was tied and began to brush the bits of mud and other debris from his heavy winter coat. "Do we remount at mid-day?"

"I suppose we will," said Alcuin, stretching, his joints snapping and squeaking. "That ointment you gave me has eased the worst of my discomfort."

"Then I am well-satisfied," said Rakoczy, continuing his task.

"I thank you for providing it, and I thank God for giving you the knowledge of such simples." He folded his hands and did his best to smile. "The journey will soon be over."

"I pray so," said Rakoczy, bending to brush off the mud around the grey's pasterns.

Alcuin studied the foreigner for a long moment. "Well, I must tell the rest to hasten." With that, he left the stable, only to return shortly with the rest of the traveling party. "Look," he said, pointing to Rakoczy, "the foreigner once again gives the blush to us all."

One of the men-at-arms cursed and was immediately hushed by a monk. Comes Gutiger was already hectoring the stable-slaves to redouble their efforts. "It will be mid-morning before we leave at this rate!"

"Speak lightly," Alcuin admonished. "It is not your place to hound these slaves."

Comes Gutiger kicked at the ankle of one of the slaves. "Hurry!"

"Comes!" Alcuin said sharply. "If the slave must be beaten, it is for the Prior to do it, not you." He went to supervise the yoking of the oxen, checking the carpenta at the same time, urging everyone to work with dispatch. "Do not be laggard. We are to reach the court of Karlus today. We do not want to arrive at an unseemly hour."

The slaves redoubled their efforts and worked in determined silence while the rest of the company came from the refectory and made the habitual inspection of their tack before instructing the slaves which horses to saddle and which to tie to the carpenta. The oxen shuffled and were given handfuls of grass for cuds, then led out into the narrow courtyard in front of the stable; shortly thereafter, the horses were ready and the missi dominici ordered the riders to mount and the drovers to take their places in the carpenta.

The party left the monastery as the monks were beginning Terce, their prayers preparing them for their day's labors. The chanting followed Alcuin's company a short way down the road, and then the fog muffled even that reassuring sound as they proceeded on toward Aachen.

It was approaching mid-day when there was the first intrusion on their journey: somewhere deep in the trees came the sound of galloping horses, the breaking of branches, and the baying of hounds.

"The hunt is out," said Alcuin, and said to Comes Gutiger, who rode on his right side, "A pity that we cannot join them."

"It is, it is," said the Comes, his rough features brightening at the sound of the chase.

"What do they hunt, do you think? Stag? Boar? Bear?" Alcuin grinned. "If they find game, we will have a feast tomorrow!"

"And sport today," said Comes Gutiger, clearly disappointed that he could not join the hunters.

Riding behind Alcuin and the Comes, Rakoczy looked about uneasily; he could hear something not a horse running near-by, and that troubled him. He reined in and let Rorthger catch up with him. "Is my spear ready to hand?"

"Which one?" Rorthger asked.

"Make it the heavy one. Can you take it from our supplies? It may be unreachable, but I hope it is not." He paused, paying keen attention to the noises coming from beyond the trees. The hounds were nearer; but the mist was still thick, and he could not make out precisely where they were, for the woods echoed and distorted sound.

"I'll try," said Rorthger. "I can get your Byzantine long-sword."

"Better than nothing," said Rakoczy. "If you will fetch it?"

"At once," Rorthger declared, and rode to the third carpentum, signaling the drover to let him climb aboard. After a nod from the drover, Rorthger swung out of the saddle and onto the narrow rear platform of the carpentum, secured his dun's reins to the square-bodied wagon, and climbed through the rear door, to emerge a few moments later with a Byzantine long-sword in his hand. He loosened his horse's reins, mounted up again, and rode up to where Rakoczy was, at the edge of the roadway. "Your sword, my master," he said, and handed it to him by the quillons.

"Thank you, old friend," said Rakoczy, and gave the sword an experimental swing, reminding his hand of its heft.

"It's just the hunt," said Rorthger, puzzled by Rakoczy's edginess.

"It is the hunted that concerns me," Rakoczy countered. "I am certain that whatever they're chasing could break onto the road at any time."

"And you want to be prepared," said Rorthger. "Do you think it is boar?"

"Possibly," said Rakoczy, and noticed the men-at-arms exchanging suspicious glances. "They're troubled, too."

"About the game or about your sword?" Rorthger asked, his tone sharp.

"Both, I would guess," said Rakoczy, holding his grey at the edge of the track.

"Magnatus," called out Acuin, "what are you doing?"

"I am keeping watch, in case the game they are chasing should come this way," Rakoczy answered. "It would cause much disorder to have a stag run into our midst, or a boar."

"The missi dominici can do this," Alcuin reminded him.

"So can the men-at-arms, but they need not; I have some experience in dealing with hunts," he said, and thought that often as not he had been the prey, not the hunter. He continued to listen, aware that the hunt was coming closer.

"Very well," said Alcuin, a querulous note in his voice. "In such fog we need all the eyes we have."

"Amen," said Rakoczy.

Rorthger swung his dun back toward the rear of the party, where the other servants rode. He brought his horse into line with the others and said, "My master has need of my assistance."

"So it seems," said one of the other servants, and added, "Foreign ways."

"That they are," Rorthger agreed, unwilling to be offended by the remark.

The noise in the forest increased, and the horses became fretful, tossing their heads and sidling, needing to be urged forward with spurs and the pressure of legs.

Rakoczy, who was nearer to the screen of brush and trees than the rest, held his grey firmly, ready to pull the gelding's nose down to his toe if the horse should try to bolt. The grey minced along, eyes rolling and sweat frothing around the breast-collar.

Suddenly the sounds became loud, and a moment later, a bear came running out of the misty trees, its tongue lolling, panting heavily. At the sight of the travelers, it stood upright and advanced on the group, its forepaws swiping the air in front of it; the party on the road was thrown into disorder: horses reared, squealing in fright, and even the stolid oxen broke into a lumbering run, pulling the carpenta bounding behind them.

Holding his grey as steady as he could, Rakoczy set the gelding running at the bear, his Byzantine sword swinging up from beneath as he passed dangerously close to the infuriated creature. The long, blue blade caught the bear just below the ribs and sank deeply in. Rakoczy wheeled his gelding and rode a short distance away while the bear staggered, bellowed, and fell forward, forcing the sword through its body and out its back.

Alcuin managed to halt his mare and bring her back toward the dying bear. "Very impressive," he said to Rakoczy, wheezing a little from his unexpected tussle with his mount.

Whatever response Rakoczy might have made was silenced as the brush at the side of the road was trampled down; a huge bay stallion rushed onto the road, his rider whooping and laughing, brandishing a long hunting spear and swearing merrily. Almost immediately there were a dozen more huntsmen around him, paying little heed to Alcuin's party.

The man on the bay stallion was proportionally as large as his horse: tall, broad-shouldered, big-bellied, with white hair and beard, he swung his horse around and went to look at the fallen bear. "With a sword!" he exclaimed in a high voice. "Who has done this?"

Alcuin maneuvered his mare through the crush and reverenced the big man from his saddle. "It was the foreigner, Rakoczy, there on the grey, Optime Karlus," he said.

"Rakoczy!" the King summoned. "You did this?" He pointed to the bear.

Rakoczy dismounted and reverenced the King. "I did," he said.

"Fine sport! A true eye!" Karl-lo-Magne swung out of his saddle and strode over to the bear: Rakoczy stared, for although he had been told the man was tall, he had not expected someone who was head and shoulders above him. "It may be you are wasted on the clerics," he said, and laughed at his own remark; the huntsmen with him joined in his laughter.

Alcuin spoke up at once. "Wherever you need this foreigner to be, that too, shall be my desire. I will relinquish my claim upon his talents at a word from you."

"Generous, Flaccus," said Karl-lo-Magne, using one of his court nicknames for the Bishop. He looked at his companions. "Have the carcase fetched and dressed. We dine on bear tomorrow. And see that the foreigner gets his sword back." With that he got into the saddle again. "I will receive you as soon as you reach Aachen," he said to Alcuin. "Make sure the foreigner is with you." He did not wait for an answer or a reverence; he set his bay stallion bounding down the road, his companions trailing after him.

Alcuin rode up to Rakoczy. "You have impressed Great Karl—not an easy thing to do."

"It wasn't my intention," said Rakoczy, looking down at the dead bear.

"Don't tell him that," Alcuin recommended as he began to restore order to his missi dominici and the rest of his escort.

Rakoczy nodded his acknowledgment as he once again took his place in the group, all the while listening to the fading hoofbeats of Karl-lo-Magne and his huntsmen.

Text of a letter from Fratre Berahtram to the Comes Gosbert.

To the most illustrious Comes Gosbert, currently attending on King Karl-lo-Magne at Aachen, the most respectful greetings of Fratre Berahtram of Sant' Zaccharius monastery near Sachenwasser.

Great Illustre, I make bold to send this to you, in the hope that I may recommend myself to your service. I have been a monk since the age of seven, and my Abbott will tell you that I have carried out my duties and submitted myself to the Rule in an exemplary fashion. I have learned to read Scripture in Latin and Greek, and I am able to frame letters in Latin, Greek, Frankish, and the vulgate of Longobardia. Also, I have been taught to draw and interpret maps, which may add to my usefulness.

I will not dissemble: though I am a poor monk, with no family to prosecute my interests, I still seek to achieve a good place for myself in the Church, and to that end I hope one day to become a Bishop. Working for you would increase my notice, and would make it more likely that the King would secure such an appointment for me. Many worthy monks have hoped that their reputations would be enough to advance them, but they are still at their labors, with no likelihood of change.

If I could place myself in your service, my Abbott, Rokinard, your cousin, believes I might find the avenue to the goal I seek. Therefore I have dispatched this to you, along with samples of my writing and translating so that you and your clerks might decide if I have enough to offer you.

I pray God sends you to know the right,

Fratre Berahtram

At Sant' Zaccharius, the 10th day of November in the 796th Year of Salvation by the Pope's calendar

chapter five

IT WAS ALMOST MIDNIGHT when the banquet finally came to an end. Karl-lo-Magne rose from his elevated chair and lifted his cup one more time, his threadbare velvet mantellum glistening where the light from the braziers struck the gold thread shot through it. "God send you safe sleep and salvation," he intoned, and drank a single mouthful; unlike most of his court, the King was rarely drunk, and never at such large and volatile gatherings as this one, which was to mark the beginning of the Holy Days of Nativity, and which was a solemn occasion at Court: Bishops and Bellatori, scholars and Illustri, Comesi and

Magnati gathered together for the feast at the dark of the year at the behest of Karl-lo-Magne, who wanted his vassals to renew their oaths of fealty on the Holy Nativity that also began the Pope's New Year. "Thank you for your attendance. The slaves will light you to your beds." Obediently the courtiers got to their feet—some more steadily than others—and made their way toward the several doors that gave onto the dining hall, where slaves with rush-lights stood; other slaves began the tedious chore of cleaning up the debris left behind, one of them being bold enough to mutter a profanity under his breath.

Outside a cold wind slapped at the buildings, dispersing the smoke from the myriad chimney-pots toward the stars in the south. Guardsmen patrolled the walls and manned the gates, wrapped in mantella lined in fur, and shivered still. The shouts of the guests calling for rush-lights and slaves echoed along the stone corridors; from the chapel came the droning prayers of Nocturnes.

"Rakoczy," said the King as he caught up with the foreigner on the gallery above the main courtyard, "I didn't see you eating tonight."

The foreigner set his stride to suit Karl-lo-Magne's, although he did this as inconspicuously as possible, not an easy thing with such a disparity of height. "As I told you, Optime, I eat in private. Among my people anything else is . . . insulting." He pulled his black wool, ermine-lined mantellum more tightly around him. "I mean you no disrespect."

"No doubt the custom prevents poisoning," said Karl-lo-Magne, nodding to himself. "You also had none of the wine."

Rakoczy reverenced the King. "Your pardon, Optime: I do not drink wine."

"So prudent," Karl-lo-Magne marveled. "Would that more of my Court shared your aversion." He strolled along, seemingly content to remain in Rakoczy's company a while. As they reached the junction of two corridors, he halted and turned to the foreigner. "You have been here six weeks—time enough to have formed an opinion. What do you think of Aachen?"

"It is a most impressive place," said Rakoczy, knowing this was the answer the King sought.

"But not the most impressive you have seen," Karl-lo-Magne remarked a bit too casually.

Rakoczy had seen pyramids and temples, palaces and China's Great Wall, Rome at its most glorious and the pantheon of Athens when Socrates taught there, the stupas of Burma and the ruins of Carthage. He considered his answer carefully. "In this part of the world, only the mountains are grander."

Karl-lo-Magne tapped his nose. "A very canny response. You are a fellow to reckon with." Mulling this over, he went a short distance in silence; as he reached the end of the gallery, he stopped. "Now that you have seen my Court here, are you content to remain at Tours, or would you be willing to take up your work for me, to assist me in all I may need of such a learned man as you are?"

"Optime, a most gracious offer," Rakoczy said carefully, "but it was Bishop Alcuin who summoned me, and I believe my first obligation must be to him."

"Alcuin is my most trusted advisor. As such, he would be the first to recommend that I avail myself of the most useful men in Franksland. He will not refuse my request if I ask him to send you to me. He knows that I make no frivolous demands." Karl-lo-Magne said it confidently, almost smugly.

Rakoczy could not keep from a wry smile. "You are fortunate indeed to be secure in the devotion of your subjects."

"It is because I have done much to aid them all, and they are grateful," said Karl-lo-Magne, so complacently that Rakoczy knew the King had not noticed the irony in his remark. "I have claimed half the world, and all those loyal to me have been enriched by it. It is not the last of what I shall do, and my faithful know that as well."

"More spoils?" Rakoczy suggested, his amusement masking a somber intent.

"That is the least of it. I can offer more holdings, and greater advancements." His stern tone warned Rakoczy that the King would not countenance more such observations from him.

"You have done much," Rakoczy echoed carefully.

"As much as the Great Khan?" Karl-lo-Magne challenged.

"The present Emperor of China holds sway over vast lands, but he himself did not subdue them: that was accomplished many generations ago, by ancestors he holds in the same high regard you hold the Saints and Martyrs." Rakoczy put the tips of his fingers together. "At least, that is my understanding. Others may give different accounts."

"Ah!" Karl-lo-Magne exclaimed. "Then you do allow for differences in reports."

"That I do; what sensible man does not?" said Rakoczy, whose long centuries of experience had taught him that there was little worthwhile in disputing varying accounts of events. "So must you, to continue to expand your borders as you do, for I would suppose you have often been told that advance and conquest were impossible, and yet you have done both. Anyone who seeks to go beyond old limits must question accounts."

"Another canny answer," Karl-lo-Magne approved. "You are a most scrupulous man, Magnatus."

"Surely you comprehend the need for that," said Rakoczy, his manner deferential.

"I have long known the worth of such meticulousness," said the King. "And to value it more with every passing year."

Rakoczy ducked his head as a sign of respect. "Every passing year, you add to your accomplishments." It was a courtesy to say so, and both of them knew it.

"Yet I am growing older and I must set my seal firmly if all I have done is to last beyond me," Karl-lo-Magne grumbled. "There are men at Court who come to enrich themselves and who hope to reap a fine harvest when I die. They think to put an end to the might of my family, to usurp the power I will rightly bestow on my sons. This isn't going to happen."

"No, Optime," said Rakoczy.

"How can you know my concerns? You have no children and your family is lost. Nor are you ancient yet—your hair is still dark and you walk with strong legs and a straight back—but you have been about the world. You have seen more than most of those around me, and you have struggled to preserve yourself in faraway climes, as you yourself admit."

Rakoczy wondered what Karl-lo-Magne intended, and supposed the King was once again thinking aloud. "It is true that I have traveled far."

Karl-lo-Magne made up his mind, saying with certainty, "I will rely upon you to tell me what your experience has taught." He regarded the foreigner with narrowed eyes.

"Then perhaps I should tell you I am older than I appear," said Rakoczy, and added, "As to advising you, you may not like what I say."

"But I will listen. You may be certain of that. And I will not upbraid you so long as you are honest. So many of my courtiers protest their honesty, but they lie with full deliberation." Karl-lo-Magne scowled down at his feet, wrapped now in heavy sheepskin tibialia that were held in place by the straps on his brodequins. "I would ask you to err on the side of truth."

"Truth? If I do, will you believe me?" Rakoczy inquired. "I am not a Frank, and that could create uncertainty in your mind."

Karl-lo-Magne laughed hugely. "So!" He clapped his big, hard hand on Rakoczy's shoulder. "I like you, foreigner. I know you for a courageous fellow— killing that bear with your sword!—and not given to idle boasting. Your conduct is beyond reproach—I could wish that more of my own courtiers behaved as well as you do. You have asked me for no advancement, although I have offered you distinction. If you are greedy or false, you have concealed it well."

"I have gold enough to meet my needs, and I am a stranger here; it would be folly to betray your hospitality," said Rakoczy, watching the King out of the tail of his eye.

"Gold!" Karl-lo-Magne scoffed. "Shiny trinkets and festive clothing and crucifixes are made from it, and the Greeks love it as a starving man loves fat geese. Here, our wealth is silver. Still, gold is useful in its way." He cocked his head.

"Enough gold. A curious remark. What is enough gold? Can you tell me?" He stopped beside a torch-bracket in the wall, where a pitch-soaked branch was burning. "How have you determined enough?"

"Enough is sufficient for me to live well at cost to no other man for at least five years," Rakoczy said, glad it was essentially the truth. "I have brought that much with me."

"Do you not think it's risky to admit so much to me? I might order all of it confiscated." The light in his bright-blue eyes suggested that he was considering just such an action.

Rakoczy gave a calculatedly brash answer. "You would do it if I carried silver. Gold, as you say, is for Greeks, and other foreigners. The Church is fond of gold."

"And I must deal with them all. Byzantium may think me a barbarian chieftain, but they have a high regard for any gold I may have, and they do not scorn my silver. They offer their gold to me at un-Christian rates, thinking to embarrass me. It is they who are shamed. No man who worships the Risen Christ should demand so much from those who share his faith." He had been pulling at his beard immediately beneath his lower lip, recalling past insults from the Byzantines. With a shake of his head he recalled himself. "Still, you are—as you say—a foreigner, and what you have can be useful to me." His glance toward Rakoczy was speculative.

Taking advantage of the moment, Rakoczy said, "I will gladly pay you in gold for two or three fiscs, in the place you choose. You will have gold, which you can use to deal with Byzantium; I will be able to make my way in the world from what the fiscs produce." It was a bargain beneficial to Karl-lo-Magne, and both men knew it.

"Very well. I will authorize four contiguous fiscs to your usage. I will choose them in a place that isn't too remote from Aachen so you may attend upon me when I am resident here. For that you will have to supply me with one mounted soldier, with all his equipment, and provide for his maintenance. In addition to the money for the use of the fiscs, of course." Karl-lo-Magne smiled broadly, revealing a few missing teeth.

"Of course," Rakoczy agreed, relieved. He reverenced the King. "It will be my honor. You will have me at your call whenever it suits you, and I will not be a charge upon you."

"Truly," Karl-lo-Magne said, his eyes hardening. "Some of my Potenti will not like this."

"Because I am a foreigner?" Rakoczy suggested.

"That, and other things." Karl-lo-Magne was becoming caught up in imagined complications. "You do not know how jealous some of my kinsmen can be."

"It is true I am a foreigner without blood relatives in this land," Rakoczy said in agreement. "No feuds compel me to be any man's enemy; my father and uncles are long dead; my mother as well; no brothers seek to lay claim to what I am granted; I have no sons to provide a share of my property upon my death, no daughters or orphaned sisters requiring dowries. Surely this must mitigate my foreignness a little."

"Dowries," Karl-lo-Magne muttered, glowering down the dark corridor beyond the glare of the torchlight. "The fate of a man with daughters. Sons are bad enough—the clever ones may be treacherous, the foolish ones are tools of treacherous men—but daughters! Let no man have daughters, lest he give away all his holdings to provide for daughters, whose husbands will turn them against you and try to seize more than you have already given. Females are the very devil for a man with territory and wealth." He coughed suddenly, as if he had just realized he had spoken aloud: he had never allowed his own daughters to marry, and now Rakoczy had a fair idea why.

"I may have disadvantages, Optime, but I also am unencumbered," Rakoczy said at his most mild.

"Yes. Yes." Karl-lo-Magne continued to stare at the torch, his gaze on something far away.

"And I am capable of doing your will without creating difficulties in obligations," he went on.

Karl-lo-Magne nodded slowly. "At the Resurrection Mass, before all my Court I will grant you the fiscs—contiguous, near Aachen—for a year, without let or lien upon them in return for your gift of two Roman measures of gold from your stores. If at the end of that time I am satisfied that you have not brought any claims against me, and that you have kept your Word, and provided me with an equipped fighting man, I will extend your tenancy for five years, for eight Roman measures of gold. If you remain in Franksland beyond that time, we will treat again of the matter."

"Optime is most gracious," said Rakoczy, reverencing him again.

"Optime is nothing of the sort," Karl-lo-Magne growled, but his blue eyes glinted with pleasure. "You have skills and knowledge I must have if I am to press eastward." He held up his hand. "Say nothing of what we discuss to anyone, not even your Confessor, for surely he must inform his Bishop of anything you reveal, and the Bishop will impart his knowledge to the Pope."

"You and His Holiness are allies," Rakoczy reminded the King.

"Of course we are; of course." He blinked twice, recalling himself to his present situation. "But a prudent man must always keep certain things to himself."

"Does the Pope not want you to expand your holdings to the east?"

"He wants the Moors gone from Hispania, and he doesn't want to give the Greeks anything to complain of; the Papal Court is riddled with spies for Constantinople, and everything the Pope says is heard by the Patriarch. It would please the Patriarch to be able to depose the Pope and put his own clerics on Sant' Pier's Seat. More than that, Byzantium has intentions for Wendish lands as much as I do, and on Moravia, if they can subdue the Avars long enough to get there." He glared at Rakoczy. "That you must not repeat."

"I will not," Rakoczy assured him; he had decided that Karl-lo-Magne was testing him, telling him fairly important things that could be traced back to him if they became known.

"About the Wends," said Karl-lo-Magne in a speculative voice. "Do you think they are strong enough to put up a defense against me?"

"Whether they are or not, they will not let you into their territory unchallenged," said Rakoczy. "As you must know already."

Karl-lo-Magne nodded. "Yes. I have some sense of this." He stretched suddenly, and his shadow all but blotted out the light from the torch. "But, as you have said, there are more ways to view any report than simply on its own merits."

Rakoczy managed a one-sided smile. "I have my own again."

"You would do well to remember that, and to hold what I say in high regard, more than my other courtiers, for they have established themselves in my affection," said the King, almost preening. "Another thing: I have also noticed that you keep no woman, or boy, for your pleasure." He said it so nonchalantly that Rakoczy was immediately on guard.

"I am a foreigner and new to your Court," said Rakoczy with an inclination of his head. "You have made me welcome, but I am not one of you, nor will I ever be. This does not commend me to those seeking alliance." He said nothing of the women he had visited in their sleep, taking what he needed and leaving a sweet, sensual dream behind.

Karl-lo-Magne chuckled. "Adroit. You're very adroit." He made a gesture. "There are widows at my Court, women whose husbands bound them to them in life and death. They cannot marry again, or they will lose all support granted to them. If one of them should please you, I would be willing to countenance the union, short of permitting marriage."

"I am in no position to seek a wife," said Rakoczy, his manner respectful but firm. "And I am not one who takes pleasure in male flesh."

"The Church will be glad of that—often though the clerics may choose such for themselves," said Karl-lo-Magne. He thumped Rakoczy on the back. "Then it's settled. You'll get your four fiscs, you will maintain a fighting man—"

"I will maintain two," Rakoczy corrected him. "That should still any quibbling from your kinsmen, who may believe that they are more entitled to the fiscs than I."

"Two. Very good," said Karl-lo-Magne. "And you will select your mistress from among the widows I will recommend to you."

"As you wish, Optime," said Rakoczy, offering another reverence.

"How can you say so little and mean so much?" Karl-lo-Magne marveled. "I am astonished at how well you contain yourself."

"When a man is an exile, he learns such methods," said Rakoczy.

"Yes. Exile exacts a price. Alcuin told me that you come from what is now Avar territory." He yawned abruptly.

"My father ruled there," said Rakoczy, not adding that that had been more than twenty-seven centuries in the past.

"I must assume he is dead," said Karl-lo-Magne.

"Long ago," said Rakoczy.

"How fortunate that you are still alive," Karl-lo-Magne remarked in his offhanded way.

Rakoczy's expression was bleak. "I am the only one."

"Such is the fate of failed Kings," said Karl-lo-Magne, then he cleared his throat and spat to keep a similar fate from befalling him.

"Amen," Rakoczy made himself say.

There was a brief silence between them; then Karl-lo-Magne patted Rakoczy on the shoulder again. "Well, you have made a life for yourself."

"In my way," said Rakoczy, with a quick, enigmatic smile.

"Well and good," said the King, and shoved the foreigner gently. "Get you to bed. Almost everyone is asleep, and we should be among them. Morning comes too early even in the dark of the year." He gave a crack of laughter at his own mild joke. "Tomorrow is the New Year and the day of Christ's birth. Fortunate is the man who has such a birth for a blessing."

Rakoczy shook his head. "Not always a blessing, Optime. Today is the day of my birth; some of the Church have called that blasphemy," he said lightly, remembering how the accident of being born at the Winter Solstice had marked him for the priesthood of his people, and his long, vampiric life.

"Every man has that day, and God Himself determines it," said Karl-lo-Magne. "If this is truly the anniversary of your birth, it must be a sign of distinction." He waved Rakoczy away. "God send you good sleep, Magnatus."

"Thank you, Optime. And God guard you and yours." He continued down the corridor, his night-keen eyes having no need for torches or rush-lights.

Rorthger waited for him in his chamber, an L-shaped room with two clerestory windows and a single cot; Rakoczy's chests were stacked against the far wall, and Rorthger had opened two of them and had rolled a mattress on top of the largest of them. "You seem pensive, my master," he observed as he took Rakoczy's black wool mantellum from his shoulders.

"I am more than that, old friend," said Rakoczy, reaching for his capa and pulling it on. "I will not be gone long; but I need to get some sustenance." He managed a quick, self-deprecating smile. "I fear I cannot go to the larder, as you do; I must seek out other sources."

"Have you chosen a woman to visit?" Rorthger asked, more out of habit than doubt.

"Yes. She is the daughter of one of the Potenti, sixteen and not yet married. She's restless in her soul, and she will want such a dream as I provide." He held up his hand to forestall any other observation Rorthger might make. "She isn't another Csimenae; she is more like Nicoris was at first—full of longing and eager for more in life than what she thought was before her, though she does not know it." A frown flicked between his brows at the recollection of the two women.

"Two different pains," said Rorthger neutrally. "I cannot argue with your plan; I have raided the larder, as you said."

"I should be back well before Matins," said Rakoczy as he reached for the door; here Matins was sung between midnight and dawn, followed by Lauds. "Oh, by the way, the King is willing to grant me four fiscs in exchange for gold."

"And do you want those fiscs?" Rorthger asked, keeping all color out of his question.

"It will depend on where they are," said Rakoczy. "But I believe Great Karl was in earnest when he said he would like to keep me at summoning distance."

"Then you are minded to accept his grant," said Rorthger with a hint of a sigh.

"I was hoping for it," said Rakoczy with a hint of amusement. "It will keep us within the scope of Karl-lo-Magne's Court without having to be part of it."

"Do you suppose you will need it?" Rorthger asked. "The grant, I mean."

"Do you suppose we will not?" Rakoczy countered. "These Franks do not love foreigners, and they don't trust those who are not connected to them by blood or marriage. This is a dangerous Court, and no matter what Great Karl says, he is mercurial; he turned away the Comes Althuhard because of something he saw in a dream. He might well do the same for me, with less incentive. If I have a grant of land, he will be more likely to keep to his bargain with me because of the soldiers I will have to maintain for him."

"He is loyal to Alcuin," Rorthger reminded him. "The Bishop may not be willing to part with you."

"Yes, he will. Alcuin is faithful to the Church and defends Karl-lo-Magne, and his clerics report on everything. He will not risk that because of one foreigner." Rakoczy slipped out into the corridor. "At least the Court sleeps. The monks will doze between Nocturnes and Matins."

Rorthger gave a single chuckle. "Do not be too long. The Court may sleep, but there are Guards awake, and slaves."

"I will avoid them," Rakoczy said, and stepped away into darkness. He moved quickly and silently along the stone passageway, going along toward the main part of the palace, where Karl-lo-Magne housed his Frankish guests. He found the place he was seeking easily enough and stopped at the door to the young woman's chamber—a slave lay across the doorway, stretched out on a sheepskin and snoring. Rakoczy had encountered such barriers before and had learned to regard them with respect. Moving through the gloom with care, he leaned over the slave and very slowly eased the door open. The moan of the hinges was almost enough to persuade him to abandon his efforts; but the slave remained asleep, and after a long moment, Rakoczy resumed his gentle pressure on the door until it provided him room enough to slip into the chamber.

The cubiculum was hardly more than a cell, with a single, narrow window. The bed was good-sized and took up most of the apartment, leaving just enough space for a trunk. His vision unhampered by darkness, Rakoczy made his way toward the bed, looking down at the young woman who lay there, sleeping, beneath a linen coverlet and a bearskin, her braided hair lying like ropes around her head, her young face already marked by discontent. There was a bruise on her cheek, the token of her father's disapproval.

"You are dreaming, Aelis, dreaming in the deepest, sweetest sleep," Rakoczy said just above a whisper. "All your delight is in your dream. You have no fear, no wish unfulfilled. You are free of all fetters, and nothing you desire is withheld from you." He sank onto the bed beside her, his soft, musical words continuing as if with a song. "Let your dreams take you wherever you wish to go. You are able to have the things you seek, and you are content with what you choose for yourself. Let your dreams carry you, let them lift you up, let them become all your joy." Lightly he touched her face, and more lightly he moved aside the coverlet and bearskin, revealing her breasts and belly. "Your body is your dream, Aelis. Your skin is like a harp: it awakens to the touch." His fingers grazed the swell of her breasts; she sighed and her face softened. "Be filled with music, Aelis. Let yourself be the melody."

She rolled away from him, languorous in her readiness; she stretched out one arm, revealing more bruises.

Rakoczy shifted his position gingerly, taking care not to do anything to lessen her sleep. As he stroked her side and back with the feather-touch he had learned so long ago, he felt her respond. "You are consumed with delight, Aelis," he murmured. "You are all pleasure, all joy." He continued his discovery of her body, and as she became more aroused, he whispered, "Take your pleasure. Fill your hands with it. Fill your flesh with it. Be the music that rings in your soul, Aelis."

She spasmed, and his lips brushed her neck as she gave herself up to her release and her dream. As the last delicious convulsion shook her, she said "Monchriet," with such longing that Rakoczy felt an instant of envy for the man who had been in her dreams.

"Fortunate Monchriet, whoever you are," he whispered, and saw the edge of her smile. He shifted one of her pillows to support her shoulders, and then he slid out of the bed, gratified and unassuaged at once. He eased the door open and stepped over the slave; he told himself it was just as well that Aelis would have Monchriet in her dream and not him, but this realization sharpened his longing to be known, to have a lover once again who would not be repelled by his true nature. That had happened so rarely in his centuries of life that he regarded such recognition as a treasure—to have a lover who would not only accept him for what he was but would desire it as well, that was a dream beyond hoping for, though he yearned for it. Feeling somewhat restored, he took the most direct route back toward his quarters, not wanting to have to make his way through the warren of corridors twice in one night. He had almost reached the stairs to the gallery he sought when a fatigue-roughened voice stopped him.

"Halt, in the Name of the King."

Rakoczy went still; inwardly he chastised himself for failing to observe the Guard in the atrium. He put his hand on the hilt of his poignard, which lay along his back under his capa. "I have halted."

The soldier who approached Rakoczy was a man of middle years, his face lined and pitted, his expression a pugnacious sneer. "Where are you bound?" he demanded, and pointed along another corridor. "The latrines are that way."

"I do not seek the latrines," said Rakoczy haughtily, suspecting that arrogance would succeed with this Guard better than concession. "I have been asked to meet—"

"Not on the Eve of the Mass of Christ's Birth," said the Guard. "The Pope has said that men are to keep themselves chaste in honor of the night." The Guard apparently had a poor opinion of this order, for he spat to show his disgust.

"I didn't say that the meeting was for pleasure," Rakoczy declared, and offered the Guard nothing more.

"Go back to your quarters," the Guard ordered. "If I have erred in keeping the King's Peace, then I will accept my punishment."

Rakoczy shrugged. "What is your name, Guard?"

"I am Usuard, son of Ansgar." He glowered at Rakoczy.

"I will remember you," said Rakoczy, and turned on his heel, going back the way he came.

The Guard swore, watching Rakoczy until he vanished in the darkness of the hallway.

Text of a letter from Atta Olivia Clemens in Rome, written in the Latin of Imperial Rome and carried by the Pope's messenger.

To the renowned foreigner Hiernom Rakoczy de Sant' Germainius currently in attendance on the Frankish King Karl-lo-Magne at Aachen, the greetings of Atta Olivia Clemens near Roma.

You cannot imagine how pleased I was to have your letter, for it has been some time since I had the pleasure of reading of your venture. It is a fine thing to know you are so near to me, and that you are not in lands that are at war. How good to know you are no longer off in the Wendish marshes in that dismal castle you had built for yourself, but have come into Franksland, where I can send letters and have some hope that they may eventually reach you. I was also pleased to learn that you have come to give service to a King who has allied himself with the Church. I have long known the advantage of serving the Papal Court, and accommodating the occasional requests of the Pope for a private place for discreet meetings. You may want to encourage the same for Karl-lo-Magne. You must surely know the advantage of having the most important man in the region in your debt.

Roma is a sad place these days: it is no longer the way you remember it, for much of it is falling to ruin, even greater than what you witnessed when last you came here. It has been sacked and portions rebuilt from the wreckage left behind so often that it is now a kind of parody of the city it was. Villa Ragoczy still stands, but it is in poor repair, and I have not been able to get the needed permissions to set it to rights. There is a wall around the main building, to protect it—that, I have been able to do. It is much the same at my estate, except that the wall encloses the stables as well. Not that I have been able to keep the horses. I have had to give up mares and stallions to all manner of lords and Churchmen. I do not want to discourage you, but this is no longer the capital of the greatest Empire in the world, it is a battered town

with less than a quarter of the population of Nero's day, a poor relation to
the splendor of Byzantium.

Still, it is Roma, and my native earth. I cannot help but love every worn
stone of it; I have done all I can to keep my estate intact, which has proven
to be more difficult than I thought it could be. Yes, making myself useful to
the Pope has helped to stave off the most outrageous depredation, but as I am
determined to stay here for another eight years at least, which will make a
total of twelve, I must make myself valuable to the Pope or risk official disapproval of a sort that would be more than inconvenient. I have not yet
decided where I should go next when the twelve years are done, except that I
have no desire to return to Constantinople. One stay there was more than
enough to persuade me that I have no wish to live there.

I will, of course, supply you with horses. I have half-a-dozen yearlings that
would suit you, and a good number of three- and four-year-olds; the latter are
ready to ride, and schooled to the saddle and the rigors of the road. Do you
want any mares, and if you do, do you want them in foal? I can provide you
as many as four. I will send along one of my chief grooms and Niklos
Aulirios, if you like. I would feel more comfortable if he were to bring the
horses to you. I await your answer most eagerly, for I know the Pope's courier is as speedy a messenger as any in the world today; he can go from Roma
to Aachen in just over six weeks, remarkable speed for these times, and possible because of King Karlus.

While we are on the subject of travel, do you think you might come here
to visit? I confess I would be delighted for your company. You would be welcome at any time, and no one could question a respectable widow like me
entertaining my blood relative. I can bring a nun to share my villa if the Pope
is displeased. You and I haven't had an opportunity to spend time together
for more years than I like to think. No doubt we have much to learn from
one another. I have those around me who claim to be my friends, and perhaps a few of them are sincere. But, as you know, courtiers of any stripe
cannot be trusted, particularly not with great secrets, such as the one you and
I share. It would give me much happiness to see you again, for it has been a
long, long time.

Niklos Aulirios, as I have said, is busy seeing to the breeding of my mares
and is doing so with more optimism than he has in the last five years. I have
had the good fortune to purchase two fine stallions, one from an Avar, and
one from an Egyptian. I am certain that the foals of their get will be fine animals, and that, in turn, will make the Pope inclined to continue to allow me

to carry on in this place, for Leo III considers himself a fine judge of horse-flesh, and it would be impertinent of me not to agree with the Pope. I have told Niklos to make His Holiness a gift of the second-best filly foaled this spring, and, after some reluctance, he has agreed to do it. He wants to have another generation before making such gestures, but the fillies foaled this spring will not be bred for another five years, and by then I will be in another part of the world, and any advantage I may have gained from such a present will be lost. So for the time being, Niklos is willing to accommodate my demands. He will not be so recalcitrant in regard to the horses he chooses for you: he is well-aware that you taught me all I know about these animals, and his respect for you is very great.

The winter has been a wet one, but I have hope of an early spring, which will mean fewer dreary days, but could also bring trouble to Roma, for once the rains are stopped, armies and other bands take to the roads, and, as the old saying has it, all roads lead to Roma. Not that that is any great achievement, for the roads have served only to ease the way of conquerors to Roma's gates. The city has not been sacked in several years, so it is not impossible that one group of barbarians or another may take it upon itself to remedy that lack.

Magna Mater! Will you look at how cynical I have become! And I am cynical enough to say that this is more realism than cynicism. Still, anyone having so long a life as those of our blood have must occasionally remark on the nature of the world, and the many ways that the worst of man's nature is made to supercede the best. Heretical as that notion may be, I have seen nothing to suggest that I am in error. Should I mention it to my Confessor, I wonder, or keep it to myself and risk perpetual damnation? There are those who would say that damnation is already assured for me.

I am rambling, and before I say something truly foolish, I will say farewell to you, and ask you to write to me when you have the opportunity to do so. Be sure that this brings you my undying friendship and the full measure of our blood bond,

Olivia,
At Roma, the beginning of February,
in the Pope's Year 797

~

chapter six

TWO CARPENTA CAME LUMBERING down the muddy track that served as the road to the walled villa Karl-lo-Magne had granted Magnatus Rakoczy, one of them laden with furniture, the other with crates of fabrics, furs, and household goods that would be needed here in the days ahead. The carpenta were accompanied by four armed men and a clerk who was under orders to make an inventory of everything Rakoczy brought to the villa. It was the first warm day of spring, and in accord with this promising change in the weather, the place now seemed more hospitable than forbidding; the woods were bustling with squirrels and birds, and in the small, newly fenced pastures, ewes and nannies were nearing the birth of their young.

"God give you good day, Magnatus!" called out the leader of the armed men, addressing the closed gate. He looked as rugged and raw-boned as the clay-colored horse he rode; his manner suggested he had more experience of battle than courtesy. He signaled the company to halt a short distance from the gates, from which position he called out again. "Magnatus Rakoczy!"

"God give you good day," said a pleasant voice not half-a-dozen steps away from him as Rakoczy emerged from the thick underbrush that flanked the approach to the villa. "You come in good time. My household has just completed their prandium, and it will be an easy thing to prepare such a meal for you, for you must be ready to eat."

"I have the honor to bring you—" the leader began only to be interrupted by Rakoczy.

"My goods and supplies; yes, I can see that. You and your cargo are most welcome." He walked past the carpenta to the gates and slapped his palm on one of them. "Rorthger. Open up!" He turned back to the men behind him. "I haven't had time to install a warder-bell yet. The old one had been removed when the former tenant left, three years ago."

A muffled response was followed by the unmistakable sound of a bolt being drawn back, followed at once by the grumble of hinges as the gates swung wide. "Enter in the name of Karl-lo-Magne," said Rorthger as he stepped out of the opening. "There will be food and drink for you in the dining hall. The stables are to your left, and the keep—" He pointed to the main building within the walls.

"Summon your slaves," said the leader of the armed men.

"I keep no slaves," said Rakoczy calmly. "My mansionarii will tend to your needs." He indicated a small group of housemen. "They, the mariscalcus and his grooms, will carry out your orders."

The leader of the armed men shook his head at this irregularity. "Very well. You!" He pointed to the housemen. "Unload these carpenta, and stow the items as you are ordered."

"I'll direct the work," Rorthger said before the men could move. "I am camerarius here."

"Thank you," Rakoczy said softly, then raised his voice. "My cook stands ready to put geese on a spit for your meal."

It was better fare than the men had expected, and they quickly turned the labor over to the housemen, moving with the determination of hunger.

As he reached Rakoczy, the leader of the armed men paused. "I am Heric, son of Heric. These soldiers and I are all Comes Giralt's men."

"Welcome, Heric, and your company." Rakoczy indicated the largely empty building around them. "As you see, the goods you bring are needed here."

The men nodded, two of them looking a bit apprehensive, for in so empty a house, where were they to eat?

"My mansionarii have made a rough table and benches," Rakoczy went on as if he knew the men's concern. "You may use them if you don't find it too much beneath you."

Heric laughed. "We are used to campaigning. A plank between two rocks is table enough for us." As he entered the dining hall, he slapped his hands together. "Why, this is excellent," he exclaimed, looking at the table and the huge maw of the fireplace beyond where four geese were just beginning to brown on a spit.

"My cook has cheese and bread for you, and I purchased a tun of beer from the monks at Sant' Cyricus, which is only two Roman leagues to the east of here," said Rakoczy; then, turning to one of the two scullions tending to the spit, he said, "Go fetch bread and drink for these good men."

The older scullion pulled his forelock and hastened away.

"Will the geese burn?" one of the two drivers of the carpenta asked.

"Not so long as the scullion continues to apply olive oil from time to time," said Rakoczy, his dark eyes fixed on the youngster manning the spit. "Do not fear that I will complain if you use all the oil. There is a cask of it in the kitchen."

The scullion ducked his head and continued to work the chain that rotated the spit.

"Sant' Cyricus," said Heric. "A most illustrious monastery. And Santa Julitta is next to it, is it not?"

"Yes. They remain together as they were in life—mother and son; the nuns were there first." Rakoczy paused. "Santa Julitta's nuns are renowned for their hives and honey-wine."

"So I have heard," Heric said, trying to appear interested; he was clearly anxious to eat. "We broke our fast before Prime," he explained.

"No doubt you will be glad of a proper meal," said Rakoczy. "Well, take your places at the table and rest assured you will not have long to wait. There is new bread in the bake-house."

The men did as they were bade, two of them almost coming to blows over the right to sit at the foot of the table, since Heric had clear claim to the head. While they were jostling, three mansionarii came in bearing trays piled with fresh-baked trenchers that they distributed to all the men at the table; a fourth mansionarius brought fine earthenware cups, setting them down for the diners. A long moment later, the scullion returned pushing a cauldron on wheels, the handle of a ladle rising up from the thick soup in the large vessel. He set about serving this, pouring the soup into the bread trenchers, giving generous portions to all the men. The aroma of cooked venison, cabbage, and onions was a palpable presence in the dining hall, and the men drummed their knife-handles on the table in approval. Another mansionarius brought a tray laden with cheese and a tub of new-churned butter; this he placed half-way along the table, then departed for the kitchen and his own meal. Then the buticularius came with a great pitcher of beer, pouring Heric's cup full first, and then making his round of the table.

"Karl-lo-Magne himself could not offer better," Heric enthused as he saw the extra bread and quantity of butter, two luxuries he rarely encountered from Magnati. The food was of a quality usually reserved for men of higher rank than he; he decided Rakoczy's foreignness was not entirely a bad thing.

"There is more beer for those who want it," said Amolon, the buticularius, as he put the pitcher on the table; it was still half-full.

"You may begin, Heric. As soon as you are done with this, the geese will be ready, and you will be served them, with mustard-seed sauce and a cream of saffron." Rakoczy inclined his head. "I haven't engaged a senescalus yet, so you may give your requests to my buticularius." He indicated Amolon. "Enjoy your food, and may you have good appetites." Saying this, he turned away, leaving the men to eat and drink. As he went out of the dining hall, he signaled to Amolon. "See that they do not lack for anything we can provide, and do not grudge them a whim or two if we can supply their wants. Their report of their reception here will ring loud in Great Karl's Court."

Amolon reverenced Rakoczy. "Truly, Magnatus." He cocked his head toward the lively gathering, his lip curling slightly in disdain for them. "Such men may gorge themselves if given the chance."

"Then let this be one such," said Rakoczy. "And let us be glad that they are satisfied."

The buticularius shrugged. "That's as may be." He had been born to house-service and had acquired all the prejudices of his position before he could count. Now, at twenty-nine, he had achieved the advancement he had long sought in life and was determined to make the most of it.

"Think of how it will reflect on all of us, that these men are treated well." Rakoczy left Amolon to supervise the meal, strolling out to the courtyard again to watch the progress being made. "My red lacquer chest," he approved as Rorthger helped one of the mansionarii take it out of the carpentum. "See that is put in my upper room."

"Where we have put your books," Rorthger confirmed, and kept on with his work.

"That is the place," Rakoczy agreed, and passed on toward the stables where Hradbert, the mariscalcus, was finishing up with bedding the stalls for the horses. "The horses will need time in the pasture before sunset," he said to Hradbert.

The mariscalcus nodded. "We have put the oxen in the pen behind the next barn," he informed Rakoczy in a tone that implied working with such animals was beneath him.

"Fine. See that they are fed this evening and tomorrow morning, with sweet hay," said Rakoczy. "Are the horses well?"

"The smith will have to replace the shoes on one—the hooves are grown out so far that the poor beast is walking badly." Hradbert frowned. "You would think that the King's mariscalci would take better care of his horses."

"His best have probably accompanied him to Paderborn," Rakoczy suggested, recalling that the Court had withdrawn from Aachen a week ago, leaving workers and mansionarii to bring Aachen to rights in the King's absence.

Hradbert spat. "A poor excuse. The horse could go lame, or cast a splint with such hooves, and what would happen then?" He gave his own answer. "The mariscalcus would be blamed, and he would suffer the consequences."

"Well, see to it, if you would," said Rakoczy.

"There is no smith in the next village," Hradbert told him, annoyance and dismay making him brusque.

"Then fire the smithy and I will do the work," said Rakoczy, so calmly that Hradbert stared in amazement.

"You? A Magnatus?" Hradbert coughed out the words.

"Certainly," said Rakoczy with all the ease he could muster. "I have traveled, and I find no shame in being able to shoe my own horses, or mend my own spear, or sword."

This novel view still did not sit well with the mariscalcus. "You have a camer-arius; if one must labor, let it be him."

"Rorthger has many skills and I prize all of them. It is fitting that I have some value beyond the heritage of my blood." His wry smile was lost on Hradbert. "If you do not want to fire the smithy, I will tend to it myself."

This was too much for the mariscalcus, who held up his hands in appeal to Heaven. "No, no, Magnatus. If you insist on doing such lowly work, I will see that my grooms lay the fire, at least." He looked around the stable. "When do you want to do this?"

"Tonight, when the household is at comestus. No one need see me then," said Rakoczy, and decided that the evening meal would be as generous as the prandi-um his mansionarii had just served in the dining hall.

Hradbert sighed in relief. "That would be as well. But when will you eat?"

"I will take sustenance in private, after the custom of my kith; it will not keep me from the smithy," said Rakoczy, and made a gesture of encouragement. "Fear not, Hradbert: by summer you will be accustomed to my strange ways, and I will understand yours better. Neither of us will be puzzled by the other, and what you now find foreign will be only eccentricity."

"The King will return at the beginning of harvest, when Aachen is once again stocked and more building has been completed." Hradbert sounded a bit wist-ful, for he had been an under-mariscalcus at Aachen, and although his present position was an advancement, it also took him away from the Court of Karl-lo-Magne, which irked him. "While he is at Paderborn, the Illustri will want to be near him; he keeps many of those he favors near at hand."

"Perhaps I will be summoned to Paderborn," Rakoczy said. "Then you could accompany me to care for my horses in the King's stable." He saw the eagerness in Hradbert's face, and added, "I have more horses coming; they should be here before the early harvest."

"So you said when you brought me here," said Hradbert. "Not that I protest," he added hastily.

"I understand," said Rakoczy. "You would rather have your advancement through Karl-lo-Magne, not a foreigner like me."

The mariscalcus shrugged, reluctant to admit something that would discred-it him. "I know the way of the King's stables."

It was a feeble recovery, but Rakoczy accepted it. "Well, for the time being, tend to these six horses for me, take care of my five horses, and supervise the building of more stalls; by the end of summer, you will need another two or three grooms to keep up with all that must be done; I rely on you to hire the best when the time comes." He turned toward the door. "Remember, I want the smithy fired before comestus."

"It will be done, Magnatus," said Hradbert, reverencing his employer.

Rakoczy went out of the stable toward the bake-house, making a mental note to approach the local miller in the hope of finding one of his sons to operate the mill half-a-Roman-league distant from his villa. That would reassure the cook and lessen the worries of the mansionarii, most of whom feared being starved out of this foreigner's service; it had happened in other places, and without plans to avoid such a fate, it could happen here. He went past the creamery, which still lacked a door—that would be a task for the next few days. He was about to enter the villa through the kitchen door when he heard a minor commotion beyond the herb-garden. He listened a moment, then started toward the voices.

Just beyond the garden wall, one of Rakoczy's mansionarii was in a heated argument with a local peasant. They were so intent on their dispute that neither of them heard Rakoczy approach, and when he spoke, they both jumped and immediately fell silent.

"I haven't a very good command of the regional dialect," Rakoczy said politely, "but I gather one of you believes I have wronged you in some way."

This mannerly interjection did nothing to induce either man to talk; the peasant began to back away.

"What is the trouble here?" Rakoczy said a bit more firmly. "If you will tell me, I will try to redress any wrong I may have done."

The peasant let forth a torrent of words, so rough and fast that Rakoczy had trouble following them. Finally the peasant made a sign to ward off the Evil Eye and began to move away from the garden wall. "Foreigner!" he accused; he pulled his cuculla of rough-woven wool close around him as if to block out the world, and his goat-skin hood hid his features in its shadow.

"Wait!" Rakoczy ordered, and saw the peasant halt in his tracks. "What is the matter?"

"My uncle says you have put a spell on this place," the mansionarius admitted in an abashed voice. "I have tried to tell him you have not, but he—"

"A spell?" Rakoczy watched the peasant, trying to understand his fear. "What kind of spell does he think I have cast?"

"He thinks you have come to make all the peasants your slaves, the way Comes Udofrid did by force of arms," the mansionarius explained nervously, afraid to look either at his master or his uncle. "He says all foreigners are bound to do us harm."

"I am not Comes Udofrid," said Rakoczy, trying to recall what he had been told about the previous tenant of this villa and the fiscs it commanded; he had heard that the man was impetuous and irascible, but neither of those characteristics was unusual or frowned upon among the Frankish nobles. "If some wrong was done on his authority, I will do all that I can to put that to rights, though nothing of him or his attaches to my blood. I do this in the name of accord."

"Ha!" The peasant pointed to Rakoczy, and said in a reasonably clear accent, "You are as bad as any of them."

"Comes Udofrid was murdered by his wife's brother, who was said also to be her lover, and the Church spoke against them for their crimes," said the mansionarius. "Comes Udofrid demanded rents beyond what the peasants in the village could pay, and so they didn't warn him about his wife's brother, though they knew what was going to happen. Four leaders in the village had their eyes plucked out for not warning Comes Udofrid of the treachery of his wife." The mansionarius stared down at his feet. "My father was one of them. Now my uncle is afraid that I will suffer the same fate."

"Not on my account," said Rakoczy. "I am not married, so no wife can betray me—"

"Worse, then," the peasant exclaimed. "You will command our daughters for your pleasure. One of the women of our village has a daughter of the King's get." He was speaking slowly and with great care so Rakoczy would understand him.

Karl-lo-Magne had bastards everywhere, and Rakoczy knew this as well as anyone in Franksland. "She is not alone," he said, not wanting to be drawn into speaking against the King.

"It is one thing to have a King's bastard," said the peasant. "It is another to have one by a foreigner who puts spells on things."

The mansionarius caught his lower lip in his teeth. "Forgive my uncle."

Rakoczy shook his head. "I have no reason to forgive him; he is seeking to protect his own, which any man must do." He paused, then said, "If I give you my Word that I will not impose on your women, will that assure you?"

The peasant rubbed the back of his neck. "An oath to a peasant has nothing to bind it. You may say anything that pleases you and no one will expect you to honor it."

"My Word to anyone is bond to me," said Rakoczy in a quiet voice that stilled all protest.

"Until it is inconvenient," the peasant declared. "Foreigners cannot be held to account."

Rakoczy stiffened. "I am not used to being mistrusted. You have my Word, and that is sufficient."

The peasant held up his finger. "If any woman should come to me and say that you have got her with child—" It was daring of him to challenge Rakoczy so openly.

"No woman has had child of me before," Rakoczy said bluntly. "And I will not demand of a woman what she will not give willingly."

"Fine pledges! You wear silks and have jewels on your weapons, and you have the regard of the King—do you think any woman would be fool enough to deny you?" the peasant scoffed. "Swear as you will, I'll not—"

"Uncle!" The mansionarius had blanched in shock. "Foreigner or not, his tenancy is a grant from the King himself, and you risk all my father lost."

"So!" the peasant burst out. "It comes to that!"

The mansionarius gave the peasant a pleading look. "Uncle, leave me, I beg you. You may scorn this Magnatus, but I cannot."

"You can, if you want to come back to the village again. Doubarth the sawyer will have you as his apprentice and heir if you return." The peasant pointedly ignored Rakoczy.

"Doubarth has two apprentices already, and I have the joiner's trade my father taught me while he lived," said the mansionarius. "Go, Uncle. Please."

"I will, but do not ask me to come again," the peasant grumbled, and turned his back on his nephew.

Watching him go, the mansionarius sniffed back tears. "He didn't mean anything, Magnatus. He is not always wise."

"He seems frightened to me, and fear rarely imparts wisdom," said Rakoczy. "Are the rest of the villagers like him?"

"Some are," the mansionarius admitted. "The Priest has said that the King would not send such misfortune to us twice."

"So there is a Priest in the village, even with a monastery and a nunnery so near." Rakoczy frowned. "Why is that?"

"The village is the other direction from Sant' Cyricus and Santa Julitta," the mansionarius reminded him. "This villa is half-way between them."

"Ah," said Rakoczy, thinking again that the maps Karl-lo-Magne's clerks had provided him were far from accurate.

"My uncle . . . You will not . . ." The mansionarius looked at Rakoczy. "He didn't mean . . ."

"Your uncle is safe, for the time being. I will not allow him to encourage insurrection, for that would be against the King," said Rakoczy, and studied the young man. "What is your name?"

It was a most unusual question, for those of high rank rarely bothered to know the names of their lesser servants. The mansionarius almost choked. "Bufilio, I am Bufilio," he said.

"Well, Bufilio, I am grateful for what you have shown me, however inadvertently." Rakoczy glanced after the retreating peasant. "You would do well to be careful around your uncle."

"I doubt he will speak to me again," said Bufilio. "He is a hard man. He has sent three of his children away from the village because they would not do as he commanded them. He has just two left, and neither would defy him in anything, lest he send them away as well."

"Truly a hard man," Rakoczy agreed. "But if you do find yourself in his company, caution him. I can give him my Word, but no other man of rank need abide by it."

"I'll tell him, Magnatus." Bufilio coughed twice and ducked his head. "I should not stand here talking to you. It isn't fitting."

"Before you go, tell me your uncle's name and his occupation." It was an unusual request, but there was nothing frightening in the Magnatus' manner. "In case I should need to address him again."

"He is Marbonet, the village skinner. His cousin is the tanner. Both are leaders among the people." Bufilio coughed. "I have duties to attend to."

"Then leave, if you must." Rakoczy stepped aside, causing Bufilio acute embarrassment at this very minor courtesy. As the young mansionarius rushed off, Rakoczy started back toward the villa, where he could hear the men in the dining hall singing raucously. He realized it was going to be a demanding afternoon.

The cook was in the kitchen garden cutting the last remaining winter kohlrabi out of the vegetable patch, muttering to himself and glaring at the various empty sections in the beds. He reverenced Rakoczy as the Magnatus approached. "God give you good day."

"And you, Wolkind," said Rakoczy. "I see you are getting ready for comestus."

"They are gluttons, every one of them. Their prandium should have contented them through the night," the cook grumbled. "You do not have to give them more than what you have already provided."

"Perhaps. But we do not want it said that the new Magnatus keeps a stingy board, do we?" Rakoczy let this hang in the air between them. "You have a fine reputation—why discredit it?" His smile was fleeting. "Well? What do you say, Wolkind?"

The cook nodded. "You have the right," he admitted. "But this garden is neglected and many of the plants have been taken away, probably by the peasants. I must have seeds in the ground, and soon, if I am to do anything beyond peas-porridge for the household."

"Purchase cheese and milk, and cabbages, from the peasants," Rakoczy recommended.

"But they owe you that in rents, as tenants of the fisc on which they live," Wolkind protested. "You can claim it as your right."

Rakoczy shook his head. "If I were a Frank, perhaps, but I know none of them trust foreigners, and will resent every claim I make on them. So I will give you silver and you will give good value to them."

"They will not be persuaded with money," Wolkind warned him.

"No, but that will lessen their anger," said Rakoczy, a world-weary note in his voice. "For the time being, this will be enough."

The cook could not keep the shock out of his face. "They are peasants! They deserve whatever you demand of them. If you accommodate them, they will become unmanageable. Make them submit to your will and that will keep them well in hand."

Rakoczy changed the subject. "When is the first spring market?"

"In the village, or in Stavelot?" Wolkind asked, knowing it was unwise to force any Magnatus to discuss anything with a lesser person.

"Either."

"The village will have a market in six or seven weeks, when the sows have given birth and the piglets can be taken from their mothers. Stavelot has a market the week following the Resurrection Mass, and many come from leagues and leagues away." The cook dropped the last kohlrabi into his basket and said, "It lasts for four days, and if you will permit, I will attend the first two days, to restock my larder and my garden. I will also want to buy chicks, and ducklings, and goslings." He hesitated. "You will have to give me silver, for the land hasn't been harvested here in more than a year."

"So I surmise," Rakoczy said. "You shall have a purse of silver coins. All I ask is you spend wisely." He saw the cook blink. "You may use the carrucum for your travels, and yoke an ox to pull it."

"You have no oxen, Magnatus," Wolkind reminded him.

"I will have. I will purchase oxen and a mule, if I can find one." He started toward the kitchen, wanting to get out of the sun, which, in spite of his soles being lined in his native earth, was beginning to pain him. "See that my guests are well-fed and I will be pleased. You are not to fret about your supplies, or the cost: I will see that you are not skimped."

Wolkind reverenced Rakoczy. "It is as you wish, Magnatus."

The kitchen was uncomfortably hot, for a gutted and dressed pig was being turned on the main spit in the open hearth, the first effort that would become comestus at sundown. Two scullions pricked the flesh to let the fat run, and then poured beer mixed with garlic over it. The smell was just beginning to fill the room, but it would soon be overwhelming and the scullions would be drinking as much of the beer as they were slathering on the pig. Two of the mansionarii were finishing their comestus at the old table in the corner near the window; they had a loaf of black bread split between them, and each used his portion to sop up the last goose grease from the skeleton splayed on the tray they shared.

Rakoczy went through the kitchen and climbed the narrow stairs to the second floor. The songs of the men in the dining hall roared their echoes along the stone walls, turning into a chaos of sound in which all words and melody were lost. The noise followed him all the way to the next staircase, which led to the top of the villa and two sloped-ceilinged rooms that Rakoczy had chosen for his private use. He saw with satisfaction that his red lacquer chest had already been brought to the larger of the two rooms. Entering the smaller room, he saw the chest containing his native earth set up with a thin mattress atop it. He laid his hand upon it and felt the annealing presence it provided. Sighing with relief, he stood for a while, then stepped back into the larger room as he heard men coming up the stairs.

"This is heavy," one of the mansionarii protested.

"It isn't our right to question the Magnatus," said the other.

"What is this thing?" the mansionarius asked.

"A stone beehive, as the camerarius said," the second man answered, and grunted with the effort of raising the athanor up another tread. "Don't talk so loudly. Someone will overhear us." He steadied himself on the stair.

"A beehive? Or an oven," the first said, guessing more accurately than the second.

"What would a Magnatus bake?" the second asked, chuckling even as he groaned. "He isn't a baker, is he? What would he use an oven for?"

"Only three more steps," said the first. "Hold tight."

"What do you think I'm doing?" the second demanded. "You have to turn a little to the left."

"I remember," said the first, and his wooden shoes scraped on the stairs. "To the left."

The first man appeared, moving backward, the larger end of the athanor in his hands. He swayed as if his back hurt, and his arms were trembling with strain. "You have three more steps to go," he said, and nearly dropped the athanor as he caught sight of Rakoczy. "Magnatus!" He ducked his head without being able to reverence him.

"Put it in the center of the room, if you will," Rakoczy said evenly.

"If that is what you want," said the mansionarius. He continued to back up, doing his best to look as if this were easy.

The second mansionarius came into sight and looked toward Rakoczy as if expecting a rebuke. "The middle of the room?"

"If you would," said Rakoczy. He indicated the place. "Here."

The two mansionarii made a last struggle and brought the athanor to where Rakoczy wanted it, and set it down with a thump. They turned toward Rakoczy uneasily, expecting a blow for their clumsiness.

"You have done well," said Rakoczy, and motioned to them to leave.

"We have two more chests to bring up, Magnatus," said the mansionarius who had backed up the stairs; he was ruddy-haired, perhaps thirty years old, and was missing two fingers on his right hand.

"Then do it," said Rakoczy. "When you are done, go to the kitchen and have a cup of beer. You may tell the cook you have my permission." No one in the household would make such a claim if it were not true, for that could result in expulsion from the household with a brand for treason on the shoulder.

"That is generous of you, Magnatus," said the red-haired mansionarius, and glanced at his younger companion. "Let's get back down."

"You are in a hurry," said the second.

"For a cup of beer? Yes, I am," said the first. He reverenced Rakoczy, then hurried off down the stairs.

The second ducked his head, then reverenced the Magnatus. "What do you want us to do here?" As soon as he said it, he fled.

Rakoczy watched the youngster go, and he wondered what the mansionarii would say to their fellows when they went to dine at sunset. He went to open his red lacquer chest and removed two vials of tincture of willow; he would offer them to the mansionarii, and hoped that the lessening of their hurts it would provide would be enough to incline the men to be less apprehensive about his foreignness than they were now. Determined not to be discouraged, he assumed all his household servants would eventually accept him, but though he argued inwardly at his most cogent, he could not convince himself this would ever be the case, especially once he began to work in the smithy, doing work no man of rank should do.

TEXT OF A REPORT FROM FRATRE ANGELOMUS, WITH OTFRID, MISSI DOMINICI TO KARL-LO-MAGNE.

To the most excellent ruler, Karl-lo-Magne, Otfrid and Fratre Angelomus tender their account of their recent escort of the Magnatus Hiernom Rakoczy, of Sanct' Germainius, from his fiscs to Paderborn, according to your stated Will.

The Magnatus received us at his villa, serving us fine meals and having our horses stabled as well as his own, and they were groomed as if for a procession. This attention is evident in all his holdings. His fiscs are in good heart and many of the buildings are being rebuilt and repaired from the damage of the former tenant to whom you were magnanimous enough to present the fiscs now held by Rakoczy.

We were presented to the two fully armed and mounted men Rakoczy has provided as part of his vassalage to you. One is a former Guard from Aachen who is grateful to the advancement Rakoczy has afforded him: a fel-

low named Usuard, son of Ansgar. The other is a local fighting man, Theubert of Sant' Cyricus; he has been a Watchman at the monastery of that name and was trained by the Abbott himself, who was once a famous Comes and retired from the world when he lost his arm to the perfidious Moors in Hispania.

We brought him as directly as we could to your Court as you commanded we do. It took us just under two weeks, riding from dawn until dusk, and with the lengthening days, this has let us make good speed on the road. There was hardly any mud encountered, and, as we have ridden horses rather than been paced by oxen, we have been able to progress rapidly.

The Magnatus has been installed at the house of Maurus the merchant, where he has been given a good reception by the men of the household and provided the largest bedchamber and two large basins made of copper for his use in token of his favored position with the King. The Magnatus has returned this kindness to Maurus by presenting him with a cask of new wine and a cup of gold ornamented by fine stones he claims are rubies from the East. This has pleased Maurus, and he has said that his entire household is in the debt of the Magnatus, and it may be that the Magnatus will sponsor a journey for Maurus, who has of late wanted to enter Wendish lands to purchase amber and furs.

The armed men who accompanied us in their duty to Great Karl have said that they have been treated well by Rakoczy, who, they say, tempered the weapons he provided them himself. While I do not entirely believe this, I did hear his mansionarii say that the Magnatus works his own forge in the smithy, so it may be true. It is also said of him that he has provided tinctures and unguents to treat the ills of the household, and these treatments have helped to end their pains and fevers. If this is a genuine skill, it could be of use in the King's service when next Great Karl campaigns.

It is useful to know that the Magnatus has been able to learn the tongue of his peasants well enough to listen to their complaints without the aid of a clerk, and this may become to his advantage if he is to remain at the fiscs Optime has granted him.

By my own hand on the Pope's Feast of Sant' Epiphanius of Salamis, on the Mass of Mid-May, the Church's Year 797.

Fratre Angelomus

chapter seven

O NLY THOSE KEEPING VIGIL were in the chapel at Sant' Audoemus; most of the monks were asleep in their dormitories, dreading the sound of the Matins-bell that would ring well before dawn. In the two other dormitories of the monastery, the maimed, the crippled, and the mad kept their own watches, some of them chained to the walls, others on cots, still others in places of their own choosing.

"I don't belong here," said Gynethe Mehaut to Priora Iditha as they walked in the night garden of the monastery, making the most of the warm June night; it was unusual for the two of them to have much time together, and Gynethe Mehaut wanted to make the most of it.

"I know," said Priora Iditha kindly. "But I believe there is little I can do to change your situation. Do not repine. Your welfare is being considered by Sublime Iso, or it will be as soon as he comes and I am permitted to speak to him on your behalf."

Gynethe Mehaut sighed. "I realize that. And I understand that I must accept what is provided me." She gestured toward the infirmary and the confinement cells, at either end of a stark building set against the highest part of the wall. "I am not like the others: I am not mad, and I am sound of body, although my body is strange. My bleeding is not like other sorts of wounds. It isn't like women's bleeding. What these monks offer can avail me nothing. They might as well send me to the remotest island in the Western Sea." She stopped to bend down to an open, white blossom that released a sweet fragrance onto the night air. "Sometimes I think I am like these flowers—of my own nature, as God made me."

"I agree," said Priora Iditha. "But Bishop Iso has said you must remain here until he can decide about your case. You know he is to come here soon, and at that time he will learn that there is more to your condition than white skin and red eyes. If only your hands didn't bleed. More than your skin and your eyes, that is what troubles everyone. That is what the Sublimi must decide about, on Bishop Iso's advice. Be obedient to the wishes of the Sublimi, and the time will pass quickly."

"They expected the Bishop yesterday, and still he isn't here," said Gynethe Mehaut, doing her best not to fret. "What if he has met with trouble?"

"We will hear of it if he has. He may come tomorrow, or the day after," Priora Iditha offered, sharing her apprehension. In the silence that followed, Priora Iditha watched her charge carefully.

"They say the Saxons have submitted to Great Karl," said Gynethe Mehaut, making it clear she wished to speak of other things.

"So they do," said Priora Iditha. "It is a great victory for the King."

"Truly it is," said Gynethe Mehaut. "Then the Wends will fall, and the Emperor in Constantinople will tremble. The Golden City of the Greeks will not shine so brightly." She shoved her bandaged hands into the capacious sleeves of her gonella and stared up at the waxing moon. "I wish I could see these wonders: Constantinople, the castles of the Saxons, Roma."

"Perhaps one day you will," said Priora Iditha, not believing it for an instant.

"It all rests with Bishop Iso and his fellows; if they decide I must become cloistered, then I will see nothing but nunnery walls until I die," said Gynethe Mehaut, reminding them both of the obvious.

"And, because you are faithful to the Church and the King, you will abide by the Sublimi's decision, even if it means you're to remain here the rest of your days," said Priora Iditha, a bit more sternly than before.

"I must," said Gynethe Mehaut simply. "My father gave me to the Church and I am bound to obey its strictures. I accept my place as my father's bond, though it is more his desire than mine. I pray for a true vocation, but I haven't received it." She sighed again. "Sometimes I wish I could leave here, and live like everyone else."

"You?" Priora Iditha looked shocked, and spoke sharply. "You cannot live as others do, not as you are, and well you know it."

Gynethe Mehaut took a long, slow breath. "Perhaps not. Yet I would be glad of it, if I could. It would be pleasant, not to have to be regarded with dread wherever I go, and to be confined with the infirm and mad. It would be sweet to walk in the sun without fearing burns and worse."

"Your domicile may change," said Priora Iditha, doing her best to shore up her charge's flagging confidence. She made her voice more heartening. "Have faith in the Bishop. He will decide where it is best for you to live."

"In another prison, perhaps more comfortable, perhaps less, but still a confinement, hemmed in by monks and nuns as good as armed guards. I fear I will not be in the world again now I am gone from it." Gynethe Mehaut looked up at the moon. "You entered Orders willingly; I have been given no opportunity to go about in the world before entering the care of the Church, though I wish I could. I cannot even become a nun, not while the Bishops are uncertain about me. So I am between the world and the Church, and neither will have me."

"The world is not such a place as you should wish to enter," said Priora Iditha. "Here, at least, the Saints and God protect us."

"Must protection be all? Isn't there more to the world than danger?" Silent tears slid from Gynethe Mehaut's ruby-dark eyes down her white cheeks. She did not bother to wipe them away; she pressed her lips together to keep from sobbing.

Priora Iditha shook her head. "For you, danger is your lot in life. You are not alone in your travail. In the world, aren't women prey to every dangerous or foolish man? Aren't women valued because they give birth to sons, and make alliances possible? Is that what you want for yourself? You cannot hope to marry— no one would have you as anything but a mistress, or a whore."

"With these hands?" Gynethe Mehaut laughed miserably. "They would fear damnation or they would be afraid to offend the honor of God."

At this, Priora Iditha relented. "Yes. Your hands are as much a problem as your skin. And your eyes," she added, glad the moonlight turned the red to an unearthly shade of violet.

"If God would only inspire the Bishop with an understanding of what I am, I should be thankful beyond all reckoning." Gynethe Mehaut pulled her hands from her sleeves and looked at the bandages that were already showing patches of blood on the palms. "I have prayed and prayed and prayed. God does not hear me, nor Virgine Maria, nor any Saint. I have no answer."

"God and the Hosts of Heaven don't often speak to women," Priora Iditha reminded her. "You must hope that the Bishop will be given an answer." She regarded Gynethe Mehaut with sympathy. "It is a burden to be patient, but it is also the lot of women. We are here to wait upon the wants of others, whether father or husband or God."

"So I am told, very often." She walked away from the night-blooming plants into the beds of herbs. "I wish I could do something useful. I would feel less at the mercy of . . ." She could find no word to describe her vulnerability. "I would like to prepare medicaments and medicinal pomanders. I have studied the art, and I know I could do it. But because of this"—she held up her hands—"I am ordered to touch nothing that might take malign influences from the blood."

"Then you must abide by what you have been told, or be thrown on the world to beg. This would be your fate, to have to stand at the side of the road and implore charity from those who pass," said Priora Iditha, who had plucked a spray of fragrant blossoms to tuck into her long braid, then thought better of it and dropped the flowers.

"Where I should die quickly," said Gynethe Mehaut with utter conviction. "Who would give food to me, or shelter, but the Church?" There was no trace of pity for herself in her tone, only a stark expression of what she knew.

Priora Iditha said nothing; she continued along with her pale-skinned charge for a short way, then stopped. "You should be at prayers soon. Vigil is almost over."

"Yes," said Gynethe Mehaut.

"And you must give thanks for your deliverance."

"From what?" Gynethe Mehaut asked, a hint of bitterness in her voice. "From what have I been delivered that I should thank God for it?"

"From beggary and worse," said Priora Iditha at once. "The Church has given you a haven, for which you must be grateful. You might well be stoned or scourged if you were among the people."

"I suppose I might," Gynethe Mehaut said after a long moment of consideration. "Still, it is not always an easy thing to be thankful for such blessings as I have." She began to walk faster.

"That is the test of our vassalage to God, and a demonstration of our devotion," said Priora Iditha, wondering if she would be as certain if she were in Gynethe Mehaut's position. She kept up with her charge, going toward the chapel. "Once you have begun your prayers, I will leave you. There will be new bread and cheese in your cell when you are done."

"As there is every morning," said Gynethe Mehaut fatalistically.

"As there is every morning," Priora Iditha agreed. They had almost reached the chapel now, and the last chanting was coming to an end. The drone of the Vigil blessing confirmed that the Hour was over, and a short while later, a dozen monks came wearily out of the chapel, most of them bleary-eyed with want of sleep.

When the chapel was empty, Gynethe Mehaut entered it, her head lowered and her manner entirely acquiescent to the demands made on her. She knelt, held up her hands, and began her first prayers, then stretched out on the stones to continue her devotions.

From the chapel door, Priora Iditha saw that Gynethe Mehaut was compliant with her regimen of penitential prayers, then went off toward the kitchen to secure the bread and cheese she would put in her charge's cell before going off to her own bed in the nuns' dormitory, for Gynethe Mehaut was forbidden to eat with the monks and nuns, for fear of contamination. She walked quickly, her attention on the narrow path, and so did not at first notice what seemed to be stable-slaves lying together under an apple tree; gradually she became aware of their whispered voices, and in spite of all her proper intentions, she stopped to listen.

". . . the Sublime arrived so late?" said one, his voice sounding tired.

"He came from Sant' Martin at Tours," said the other, grunting at the end with a kind of rough pleasure.

"From the Great Alcuin," said the first, beginning to pant.

"So he told the Superiora," said the second.

"Will he go on tomorrow? Does he—" He broke off with a sensual moan. The two continued their rutting, wholly unaware that they were overheard. Finally both young men moaned, shuddered, and sighed. "About Bishop Iso?"

"Tomorrow he will rest here; he will hold Court," said the second, sounding half-asleep. "Then he and his retinue will travel on to Paderborn."

The first sighed. "Then we will have tomorrow night as well."

The second murmured bits of words, but was clearly drifting off. "Meet again? Tomorrow night?" His voice was muzzy, and he yawned at the end.

"If it is possible." The second rose to his feet unsteadily, tugging down his camisa and using its hem to wipe himself before starting toward the stable and his bed in the hayloft.

Priora Iditha made herself continue walking as if she had just come along; she paid no attention to the slave as he slunk through the shadows. She kept on at the same steady pace until she reached the kitchen door, which she struck with the flat of her hand to summon the pantry scullion.

The door opened and the scullion held out a wedge of cheese and a half-loaf of bread. He was about to turn and go back to the pantry when Priora Iditha stopped him.

"I am told Bishop Iso is here," she said.

"That he is," said the scullion. "He came shortly before sunset with a retinue of fourteen. They have been given the whole of the travelers' dormitory, and the bison haunch that hung in the smoke-house was served to them." He smiled. "There was meat left over." This was obviously a happy treat for the scullion.

"Why have I been told nothing of his coming?" asked Priora Iditha, who expected no answer from this kitchen slave.

"Why should anyone tell you? You are not from here. You are only a protector for the White One," he said, and slammed the door.

Making her way toward the three dormitories, Priora Iditha tried to tell herself that this could have nothing to do with her, or with Gynethe Mehaut, and could not convince herself of it. The more she thought on it, the more ominous the Bishop's presence became. She continued to walk faster until she was almost running. She had to do something—but what? and why? How was she to fulfill her duty if the Bishop would not agree to see her? Fighting off panic, she entered the nuns' dormitory and went up to the second level, where the individual cells were. Gynethe Mehaut's was the fourth door along, and Priora Iditha slipped into it, putting the bread and cheese down on the single chest at the foot of the narrow bed. Then she left and descended to the first floor, where the sleeping accommodations were more communal—four to a room, although Priora Iditha shared her allotted chamber with only one other woman, an elderly nun from the lowlands to the north, Sorra Wandrilla, who was all but crippled by painful knots in her joints.

As was often the case, discomfort had kept Sorra Wandrilla awake, and she regarded Priora Iditha's arrival with grateful interest. "So your charge is once again at prayers."

"The Sublime ordered her to do, and she obeys him," said Priora Iditha, saying much the same thing as she did most nights.

Sorra Wandrilla shifted a bit on her bed. "The Bishop is here." She announced this as if hoping to give startling news, and so was disappointed by Priora Iditha's answer.

"So I have heard. He and his retinue will be here until day after tomorrow." She lay down and stared at the ceiling, vaguely visible in the gloom. Little as she wanted to admit it, she was worried for Gynethe Mehaut.

"Tell me, has he reached a decision about the White One?" Sorra Wandrilla asked.

"I hope so," said Priora Iditha, and tried to will herself asleep. She quietly recited her prayers, taking comfort in the familiar Latin cadences. She tried to make herself believe that she would have no difficulty in presenting her petition to Bishop Iso, but the more she dwelt upon the possibilities, the more unlikely it seemed that he would seek her opinion.

"This is a great burden for the Bishop," said Sorra Wandrilla, her tone quarrelsome.

"It is a great burden for Gynethe Mehaut," Priora Iditha countered, and resumed her orisons.

"God made her as she is. It is her burden to bear," said Sorra Wandrilla, as if this settled the matter.

"The Bishop should realize that better than you or I do," said Priora Iditha. She had lost her place in her prayers and so started again from the beginning.

"The Pope may have to settle this," said Sorra Wandrilla. "Only he has the puissance to know what God's Will may be."

"Then the Bishop will handle the matter, and present it to the Pope when he is next in Roma," said Priora Iditha, becoming exasperated.

"The other Sorrae want her gone from here," said Sorra Wandrilla. "They prefer the mad to her. The mad are addled in their wits; your charge is dangerous."

"Then tell the Bishop so when he holds Court after Prime," said Priora Iditha, raising her voice a bit. "I shall ask him to hear me then, too."

"I will, and I will pray for eloquence, to make it known how perilous the White One is to our souls." The old nun shifted onto her side, groaning a little from the nagging pain of her joints.

"Be sure that God will hear us, and Sant' Audoenus, as well. See you devote yourself to truth, not only to your fear." Priora Iditha's tone was sharp, and she tried to soften it. "I will pray for wisdom."

"See that you do," snapped Sorra Wandrilla, pulling her rough blanket more securely around her.

It was tempting to try to have the end of their wrangle for herself, but Priora Iditha held her tongue. She returned to her prayers and was soon fast asleep, only to be wakened far too early to the summons to Matins and Lauds. Rising and adjusting her gonella, she clapped a veil over her hair before starting down to the chapel. Although she was painfully aware of Sorra Wandrilla's condemning gaze, she ignored it as she made her way down the steep, narrow stairs.

Thirty-seven nuns—three more than was their usual number—formed an ill-defined line bound for the chapel, most of them barely awake, a few of them caught up in their Office already. The call of night-birds accompanied their whispered prayers as they crossed the open courtyard in their march to the chapel. Half-way there they were joined by the monks, their company swelling to 116 before they went into the narthex and formed lines to begin Matins. There was a bit of a stir as Bishop Iso appeared, very imposing in his silken gonelle and brocaded femoralia; his pectoral cross was gold-and-silver set with polished gems, a reminder that the Bishop came from a wealthy family, the son of a true Illustre. He uttered the prayers in a penetrating voice that commanded the others to equally fervent expression.

Off to the side of the altar, Gynethe Mehaut remained prostrate, imploring every Saint she could think of to intercede for her. Most of the monks and nuns ignored her, although she noticed that the Bishop occasionally glanced toward her uneasily. She kept on with her devotions, wanting to give him no cause to think her lax in her duty to God, and soon Lauds was ended.

At Sant' Audoenus, the monks and nuns broke their fasts after Lauds and before Prime, so as the sky streamed pink with the coming dawn, the refectory bristled with activity as the novices and slaves brought out bread, cheese, and watered wine for the more senior members of the community, extra portions being served today in celebration of Bishop Iso's visit. This morning conversation was subdued, for the presence of the Bishop impressed most of the nuns and monks, and none of them wanted to do anything that might give the Bishop cause to be displeased with them, for such displeasure could bring terrible consequences upon them, which none of them wanted.

"I will hold Court in the reception room immediately after Prime," Bishop Iso announced. "Those having questions to lay before me, present yourself to my slave Conwoin." He indicated the man at his side, a well-built fellow in his twenties with a mass of chestnut hair and a supercilious expression. "Tell him your cause, and he will arrange matters." He folded his hands before pulling his full loaf of bread apart into three sections in honor of the Trinity. "May God send all bread to our needs, and may we thank Him for his generosity."

The others repeated this blessing and fell to eating, making the most of the luxury of butter that was served in the Bishop's honor. A final extravagance was ordered by the Abbott: trays of dried plums, pears, and apples were set out on the long plank tables, which brought a general cry of approval from those seated on the benches, and exclamations of thanks to the Bishop.

Abbott Bosoharht stood to deliver the morning reading, choosing from the Prophecies of Jeremiah the Lamentations for Jerusalem. "*The King of Babylon the Golden, the great city of the East, came to Jerusalem, and by force of siege took the city as his own. So that when the King of the city fled with his nobles and his warriors, he was pursued and captured, and all those near to him were slaughtered and the King taken away in chains, and others who had not been killed also went with him into slavery and exile. Among them, I, Jeremiah, went, and when God spoke from my mouth, he vowed that evil would befall Golden Babylon, and that Jerusalem should be delivered from all enemies, for I have kept my trust in God, and I have prayed for salvation even in the depths of despair.*' "

Bishop Iso studied Abbott Bosoharht for a long moment when the old man sat down again. "Yes," he said, drawing the word out. "Just so."

There was an exchange of whispers along the benches as the monks and nuns considered what the Abbott had said to them.

Fratre Nordhold, who was somewhat foolish, suddenly exclaimed aloud. "It isn't Babylon at all. It is Byzantium. It is Roma. We Frankish monks are the warriors of the Pope. The Greeks want to bring down Roma and all those faithful to her."

The monk beside him, chagrined by this outburst, patted Fratre Nordhold on the arm and urged him to eat.

"We must keep the faith," said Fratre Nordhold, purpose making his voice louder than before. "I see what it is: we must be the salvation of Roma and the Church."

Bishop Iso stared at Fratre Nordhold. "If you must speak, Fratre, lower your voice, at least, and remember that there are many who are not so devoted as you are." There was no misunderstanding his tone of command; Fratre Nordhold ducked his head and stuffed a wad of bread into his mouth. The Bishop looked toward the Abbott. "Have you anything more to add?"

Flustered, Abbott Bosoharht shook his head and picked up a dried plum from his shallow plate. He ate, but he seemed to have difficulty swallowing.

Watching all this, Priora Iditha felt a tide of dismay run through her. The Abbott would do nothing now that did not suit the Bishop, not after such an embarrassing incident. She thought about Gynethe Mehaut and was glad that the pale-skinned woman had not been asked to join in this meal; it had been awkward enough to show honor to the Bishop without including so remarkable a woman as Gynethe Mehaut in the occasion. There was too much uneasiness in the refectory as it was—with Gynethe Mehaut present the air would be charged even more. When the butter was passed to her, she used her knife to pare off a long curl of it, and then to smear it on her half-loaf of bread as the nun next to her claimed the tub for herself. While she nibbled on the delicious combination of bread and butter, the Priora did her best to organize her thoughts, preparing for her appeal to the Bishop. For her, breakfast was over all too soon. As the monks and nuns rose to their feet, the bell rang for Prime, and all the company grew silent, making their way out of the refectory to their places of private prayer. For Priora Iditha, this meant the corridor outside Gynethe Mehaut's cell, where a century-old crucifix hung on the wall, the corpus stained with the blood of faithful Christians. After making sure that Gynethe Mehaut was asleep, Priora Iditha knelt, raised her hands, and began to recite the prayers she had learned so long ago.

When Prime was over, Priora Iditha hoped she was ready for what she had to do: she hurried down to the reception room and saw to her dismay that five others were there ahead of her. She found it difficult to conceal her distress, but strove to maintain a proper demeanor while she went to the Bishop's slave, Conwoin, and said, "I am Priora Iditha of Santa Albegunda, and I wish to speak to the Sublime Iso regarding my charge, the woman called—"

"The Pale Woman," said Conwoin, nodding. "Yes. Sublime is expecting to speak with you as soon as the Abbott is finished with his report."

Somewhat startled, Priora Iditha gestured her gratitude. "I wait upon the Bishop's pleasure."

"Most certainly you do," said Conwoin, lifting his head enough to make it plain that he was still in charge of the audiences.

To her astonishment, Priora Iditha recognized the voice of one of the slaves she had inadvertently eavesdropped upon the night before. She was nonplussed enough to find it difficult to muster her thoughts, but managed to say, "I pray he will hear me."

"May God please," said Conwoin. He left Priora Iditha standing in the doorway of the antechamber, her dignity failing to conceal her confusion.

Unable to think of anything to say, Priora Iditha went to the bench under the single, narrow window, her hands tucked into her sleeves, neat as a cat, keeping the appearance of someone who was as confident as she was self-possessed.

Contemplating the painting on the far wall, she wanted to ask questions about the events in the life of Sant' Audoenus, but held her peace, afraid that she would give offense for making such inquiry. She gave herself over to unscheduled prayer in the hope of quieting her apprehension. Half-way through the Penitential Psalms, she became aware of Conwoin standing before her. "Yes?"

"Bishop Iso will see you now," said Conwoin, an unctuous smirk on his handsome face.

"Very good," said Priora Iditha, rising and summoning all her good sense.

The reception room had been arranged to the Bishop's liking, with an X-shaped chair on the raised platform that the Bishop occupied with the same hauteur as a Potente or an Illustre would for Court. He held his crook of office negligently in his left hand; he used it to gesture to Priora Iditha that she might approach him. There was a nun standing behind Bishop Iso, a soft-faced young woman who held a basin and cloth for the Bishop's use.

After reverencing Bishop Iso, Priora Iditha came within ten steps of him and contemplated his face, looking for some sign of his state of mind. "Sublime, I must speak to you about Gynethe Mehaut."

"The White One," said the Bishop. "She was brought here some time ago. I have been told she remains in your care."

"Yes," said Priora Iditha, somewhat startled by all the information the Bishop had at his disposal. "She has been living a penitent's life here, and that is what troubles me."

"Are you saying her penitence isn't genuine?" Bishop Iso looked disapproving at this suggestion.

Priora Iditha answered hastily, "No, no," holding up her hands in protest at this idea as she rushed on. "She keeps to her prayers devoutly and she doesn't ask to be spared. She is in the chapel from the end of Vigil until Prime, and she rests through the day until Vespers, because she cannot endure the sun. It is true that she has ills that demand she live an unusual life, but this monastery is dedicated to the treatment of the crippled and the mad, and she is neither, and cannot use the purpose of Sant' Audoenus to bring Glory to God."

"She bleeds from the hands, and she cannot walk abroad in the day," said Bishop Iso, making the statement a denouncement. "Do you deny these things?"

"No, I do not," said Priora Iditha, and reeled under a sharp blow from the Bishop's crook. "You have no reason to beat me, Sublime." She could see the nun watching her, and that shamed her more than the impact of the crook had done.

"I am your Bishop," he reminded her. "If I believe you should be beaten, that is sufficient." To prove his right, he struck her again. "See that you do not contradict me."

Under the sudden numbness in her shoulders, Priora Iditha could sense pain; she bit her lower lip to keep from crying out. "I have not contradicted you, Sublime," she dared to say, and flinched as the crook descended again. "No, Sublime. I pray you, do not."

Bishop Iso smiled. "Prostrate yourself, Priora. You may address me from the floor."

Priora Iditha did as she was told, almost collapsing as she leaned onto her arms. "I obey you, Sublime."

"Very good," said Bishop Iso. "Now, tell me what you wish me to know of the White One."

Priora Iditha took a deep breath. "Gynethe Mehaut is a pious woman. Her pale skin marks her with purity. Her hands bleed in reverence to the Christ." She heard the nun whisper something but could not make out the words she spoke.

"You don't know that," said the Bishop.

"I pray, and I supervise Gynethe Mehaut's prayers—" Priora Iditha began, only to be interrupted.

"I wasn't talking to you," said Bishop Iso, and went on in a lowered voice to the nun, "If she is diabolical, you could be in grave danger."

"God will protect me, and Santa Maria," said the nun.

Bishop Iso coughed and said something under his breath, then spoke up. "Sorra Celinde has offered to serve as guardian for Gynethe Mehaut. You will be able to return to your duties at Santa Albegunda, and Gynethe Mehaut will be able to leave this monastery. I have decided that she must be presented to Great Karl, who will judge what is to become of her." He rapped the floor with his crook and held out his hands; Sorra Celinde brought him the basin so he could wash his hands, signifying he had completed his decree in the matter.

"But," said Priora Iditha, starting to rise, "what is to become of her?"

"You are not to move," said the Bishop as she dried his hands.

Startled, Priora Iditha dropped back onto the flagstones; feeling was returning to her shoulder, spurting hurt through her body as she obeyed Bishop Iso. "Is there more, Sublime?"

"There may be." He considered. "You may repose confidence in Sorra Celinde. She has raised six of my bastards for me, and only one has died. She will care for the White One as well as anyone could." He leaned onto his right arm. "You may think that only you are capable of dealing with her as she requires, but you would err. After I have concluded Court here, I want you to meet with Sorra Celinde and tell her all that you believe she must understand to protect the White One. That done, you will take your leave of your charge and prepare to return to Santa Albegunda. I will order a letter for Abba Sunifred, commending your service." He motioned her to rise. "If you do not accept this, you will remain here, with the madwomen."

It was an effort to rise, but Priora Iditha gritted her teeth and managed to stand without making a sound. "I will do as you command, Sublime," she said, a touch of nausea making the words difficult to speak.

"Very good," Bishop Iso said, dismissing her with a wave of his crook. "Wait in the antechamber for Sorra Celinde."

"May I speak with Gynethe Mehaut? She should be allowed to prepare for this change." Even as she implored Bishop Iso, Priora Iditha knew it was useless: Gynethe Mehaut would learn of this only when everything was in place.

"Stay in the antechamber," said the Bishop. "If you leave, I will know you for a dishonored nun, and you will be confined for your apostasy."

Priora Iditha lowered her head. "As you say, Sublime. I am here to serve you and God. I ask for nothing more in life but that I please God, and His servants." It was a worthy speech, and she could see that Bishop Iso was satisfied for the moment. She backed out of the reception room, hoping she would not weep until the door closed. She almost succeeded in her attempt, the first traitorous tear sliding down her cheek as she made her reverence to Bishop Iso; she let it fall, knowing that wiping it away would acknowledge her distress. Once out of the reception room, she took her seat on the bench she had occupied before. Here she waited while Terce came and went and the Bishop continued to hear the petitions of the waiting monks.

It was well past mid-day when Sorra Celinde appeared, her face showing a fresh bruise. "The Bishop has gone for prandium, and I have until he returns to arrange matters. I must not speak with you too long, so I ask you not to bother with anything that is unimportant to her."

This daunting request finally brought Priora Iditha's temper to the fore. "I am not telling you the habits of a young mare," she snapped.

Sorra Celinde managed an apologetic smile. "I mean no disrespect," she said in a conciliatory tone. "But the Bishop is impatient, and, like you, I would prefer not to be struck again."

Priora Iditha schooled herself to a mild answer. "I will do what I can to speed your instruction." She looked up at the other nun. "What do you need to know?"

"I rely upon you to tell me," said Sorra Celinde, sitting down next to Priora Iditha. "I haven't seen the White One. You must begin with what I will see."

Priora Iditha coughed. "She is pale as ivory," she began. "Her hair is white, her eyes are red, and she cannot abide the sun. She is very thin, and does not put on flesh readily. She bleeds from the palms of her hands but without any apparent wound."

"The Devil!" Sorra Celinde exclaimed.

"Or God, or some other cause unknown to any of us," said Priora Iditha. "She is well-spoken, having been in the care of the Church most of her life, and she is able to read and write a little. She is fond of gardening, and at Santa Albegunda tended the night-blooming garden. Here, she often walks among the herbs and flowers before attending to her devotions. She prays from Vigil through Prime every night, and sleeps from dawn until late in the afternoon. Her bandages on her hands must be changed daily. She bathes every other day—"

"Why?" Sorra Celinde asked, shocked.

"Her white skin is given to rashes. If she fails to bathe, the rashes become terrible and she develops open sores on much of her body." Priora Iditha saw the doubt in Sorra Celinde's face. "She has to be cared for, or, like an infant, she will suffer. She must not be denied bathing. She must be kept out of the sunlight. She must have her bandages changed daily."

"I'll remember," said Sorra Celinde with another of her smiles. "She must be grateful to you for all you've done."

"She has no reason to be. I accepted the responsibility for her care most willingly," said Priora Iditha, trying to keep from believing she was betraying Gynethe Mehaut with every word.

"Then she is doubly fortunate," said Sorra Celinde. "I will present myself to her at the end of the day, when you will be ready to depart from this place."

As much as Priora Iditha longed to protest this high-handed decision, she could not bring herself to face another beating from Bishop Iso. She made a little reverence, and said, "See you are diligent in your care of her."

Sorra Celinde's smile brightened, showing more of her teeth. "Oh, I will, Priora. Do not fear: I will."

TEXT OF A LETTER FROM FRATRE GRIMHOLD IN ROMA TO BISHOP FRECULF AT SANT' POTHINUS OF LYONS IN NIVELLES; THE MESSENGER CARRYING THE LETTER WAS MURDERED IN LONGOBARDIA AND THE LETTER WAS TURNED OVER TO ARDO PICCOMINUS OF RAVENNA.

To the most illustrious Sublime Freculf, the heartfelt greetings of Fratre Grimhold, your devoted cousin and fellow-religious on this, the middle of May in the Pope's Year 797.

I have been staying close to Leo III, as you ordered me to, and I have had the opportunity to advance our House in his esteem. I have also become aware of all the efforts being made on behalf of the Byzantines to subvert the True Church and bring it to the Greek Church as a vassal. Your cautions are well-taken, and I have made it my goal to preserve the True Church. This is going to be a difficult task, for in all the city of Roma there must be a hundred spies for the Greeks. Servants and slaves are regularly suborned by the agents of Constantinople; no one may think himself safe from them, not even Pope Leo. Or perhaps I should say, most especially him, as he is often the target for spite and anger. You may tell me to remain near His Holiness, which I will do, but I cannot promise to preserve him from all the mischief of the Greeks. There is too much to guard against, and too many near the Pope whose devotion is not certain for me to vow that I can provide protection against all danger.

This year the mal aria has been severe. I have seen bodies of the dead left in the street for the monks to bury for charity, and I am told that those who have studied such things believe that the summer will bring more deaths. Many of those living within the walls have been taken with fever from the bad air. Some of the Guards have been too ill to keep to their duties and it may be many weeks before a full force can be mounted on the walls. In the meantime, various Churchmen have provided soldiers from their own households to keep watch. There have been rivalries among those soldiers, and because of that, the walls are more often the site of small battles among the Guards than the place where the city has its first protection.

During these hard days there have been many rumors that the Byzantines are doing their utmost to prey upon the Pope. I have been told by those who are well-informed that many bribes are paid to subvert the Church and bring its purposes to serve the Patriarch in Byzantium. Some go so far as to say that there is a plot in place to waylay and kill the Pope so that one of their own Bishops may be advanced to Sant' Pier's Seat, and thereby surrender the Church to the Empire in the East. While I cannot find any confirmation of this beyond persistent rumors, I do know that it is possible that such a plan could be put forth and that, having been put forth, it could succeed.

I have removed from Sant' Ioannes to private quarters since two of the Fratres were murdered in their beds. They were Frankish monks and I, for one, fear that I might be among those intended to die. I have taken private rooms in a house not far from Sant' Pier's. I am able to bar my door at night, and my slave tastes all my food so that I am safe from the most direct dangers to my safety. My slave has pledged that he will guard me for the honor of the Pope, and I am minded to believe him, for he was raised by monks and has spent all his life inside the walls of Roma.

There have been better markets in the last month, and there is hope that this year will finally bring an end to the shortages after the famine of three years ago. There are more swine and lambs for slaughter, and they say that there will be a good wine harvest, so that in two years all the casks will be filled again. Grain is still in short supply, but by August there ought to be enough to feed the city properly. If your holdings in Longobardia are in good heart, you may plan to sell grain in Roma to your advantage. It is worthwhile for you to bring your grain as late as you can, for there will be grain from the south early in the harvest, and it will soon be gone. Later in the harvest, grain will be rare again, and that from the north will be sought eagerly. If you allocate two fiscs for sale in Roma, you will be pleased with the profit, and you will serve the Pope's cause, as well. Be prudent and keep your plans to yourself, for if others bring much grain to market, you will not be able to command the price that you can now.

Let me urge you to come to Roma as soon as you can. The Greeks must be checked or the Pope and the Church will suffer. When you come, bring soldiers, for they may be needed. If you send me word when you depart, I will make arrangements for your stay, so that you will be housed and fed in the manner you deserve. Do not assume the Church can do this, for it may be too hazardous to entrust your welfare to the Church.

I am always devoted to you, your family, and the Church, and so I swear before the altar of God, and set my hand:

Fratre Grimhold
∽

chapter eight

THERE WERE FOUR WOMEN sitting before the hearth in the private reception room, one of them carding wool, the others pretending to admire her work. All four were widows, their ages ranging from nineteen to forty-one. They were vaguely aware that they were being watched, and they were determined to make the most of this opportunity, for Paderborn had proven far more dull than they had hoped it might be when Great Karl had ordered them to accompany him. It was a drowsy afternoon, heavy with summer warmth and the ripe odors of the busy city; the shadowy interior of the room provided shade without much coolness, for the two narrow windows were high up the wall and faced east, away from the desultory breeze.

"Have you seen anyone, aside from servants?" asked Hathumod, the youngest of the four, whose girlish prettiness had recently started to fade, leaving behind soft features without much character to shape them; she was dressed in dark red to show she was still in mourning.

"Not today," said Odile, at thirty-six, the second-oldest of the four; she had been a widow for nearly three years and no longer wore official mourning, but braided wine-colored bands into her chestnut-colored hair to show her status. "The Court has been off to some kind of market—horses, I think."

"The King and his search for a proper horse," said Ermentrude, the oldest; her hands were crabbed and her hair was the color of frost; she wore deep blue as the King's mother Bertrada had done during her long widowhood. "He is as bad as a boy."

Hathumod laughed aloud. "He is a giant. He must find strong horses, with long legs, or they will drop from under him."

Leoba Baldhilde, who was carding, shook her head. "It is right for a King to have the finest horse. It would insult his dignity to have less than the finest." She was a purposeful woman, needing to be busy all the time; her sister was a distinguished nun and had been encouraging Leoba to take the veil. "What Frank would want to see the King on an inferior mount? Not one, I suppose."

There were murmurs of endorsement, and finally Ermentrude raised her hand to quiet them. "You cannot know who's listening. We should not make light of the King."

"Probably not," said Hathumod, "but what else is there to do?"

"Odile could read to us," Ermentrude suggested.

"The only books here are a *Rerum Naturae* and a book of *Descriptiones.* I don't think either would interest you," said Odile apologetically. "When Karlus returns, then we can ask for something else to read."

From the gallery where he was watching behind a carved screen with Karl-lo-Magne, Rakoczy said just above a whisper, "Is she the only one who reads?"

"Odile, widow of Aistulf of Sens who died at Paris during the famine three years ago, along with most of their children," said Karl-lo-Magne, nodding and keeping his high-pitched voice low. "Yes. She reads. Hathumod knows her numbers, but she reads very little."

"Hathumod is little more than a child," said Rakoczy.

"She has already borne three sons. Her husband died last year of a fever. She is willing to have a lover if he will honor any children she produces." Karl-lo-Magne smiled.

"But she cannot marry again or she will not be supported by his family—do I understand that aright?" Rakoczy asked. "None of these women can."

"It is true. Consider Hathumod: she is biddable, and she will not demand more of you than you are willing to give." Karl-lo-Magne raised a single brow. "Well?"

"Does Odile have any children still alive?" Rakoczy inquired. "For it appears to me, Optime, that you are eager for Hathumod yourself."

"She is a tempting morsel, and her youth can warm my cold, old bones." The King licked his lips. "I can show her children honor, those of her husband and mine as well."

"Then tell me about Odile," Rakoczy pursued.

"I will," said Karl-lo-Magne, and spoke a little louder. "She has a son, named for his father, who is in service to a Longobard noble who is faithful to me. He has been there two years. It is a good arrangement for the lad, and his mother, as well, since she has only her widow's portion to keep herself. The boy is eleven now, as I recall, and will one day enter the ranks of my fighting men, if God spares him fevers and broken bones. There were other sons, and a daughter, I think, but none lived through the famine." He studied Rakoczy's face. "Are you certain about Odile? She is said to be somewhat willful. I can understand why you might not like Ermentrude, but Leoba Baldhilde is pleasing and industrious, and aside from her convented sister is unencumbered, but for her husband's family."

"She doesn't read," Rakoczy reminded the King. "I have a great many books."

Karl-lo-Magne clapped his hands and paid no attention as the four women looked up. "I have been told that you do, by Alcuin. He remarked upon your books, in number and in quality. He was impressed with your Greek texts in particular. How many books do you own?"

"I have seventy-three with me in your Kingdom; twenty-two are part of the property I brought here when you summoned me," said Rakoczy, fairly certain that Karl-lo-Magne knew that already; he said nothing of the hundreds he owned and kept in other places, and for a moment longed for the hundreds more he had lost over the centuries.

"So many!" Karl-lo-Magne marveled. "You must have spent a fortune on them." Rakoczy shrugged. "Books are a wealth of their own."

"But seventy-three! Most men—if they must read—would be content with ten, or fifteen." Karl-lo-Magne did not wait for any comment Rakoczy might offer; he leaned forward so that he could speak to the women below. "You will join us at comestus."

The women all looked up sharply, and Leoba Baldhilde inhaled sharply, the color mounting in her face. All four women reverenced the King.

"Optime distinguishes us too much," said Ermentrude, recovering enough to be gracious for all of them.

"Optime seeks a little relief from the rigors of the day," said Karl-lo-Magne, and chuckled. "You good ladies will succor me." He indicated the man in the black gonelle and femoralia beside him. "Magnatus Rakoczy will join us, although, unless I am mistaken, he will not eat with us. It is a custom among his people to dine privately, and there is wisdom in such practices."

Rakoczy whispered an apology and prepared to leave the gallery.

"Optime," called out Odile, "have you a book you could spare us? Your clerks must have some they have brought with them."

"You are bold in your request," said Karl-lo-Magne, not entirely pleased with her forwardness.

"We are bored, Optime," said Odile, reverencing him again. "If we must spend hours alone, at least spare us a book, or a music-maker."

Karl-lo-Magne stared at her for a long moment, then said, "Rakoczy has books, a great many books. Direct your pleas to him." He turned toward the stairs that led down to the main level of the castle. "Do you have a book with you that you could allow the women to use for a day or two that it would not trouble you to lend? Something that would entertain them?"

"I have some poems, Roman poems in Latin, from many centuries past," he said, thinking that Publius Ovidius Naso's *Metamorphoses* would make strange reading for these women.

"Good. Excellent. The Romans always provide edifying texts," Karl-lo-Magne approved. "If you will be willing to let them have the volume? If they harm it, I will command a copy be made for you."

"It is my honor, Optime," said Rakoczy, aware that the King-would be annoyed if Rakoczy failed to comply with his request, yet certain that few monks would be willing to copy such a work as *Metamorphoses;* he decided it was a necessary risk.

"Very well, then," said Karl-lo-Magne as he reached the bottom step. "You may use the book as a reason to spend time with Odile, if that suits you." He waved his hand. "Since you will have a woman who reads."

"I believe she would find me a better companion for that reason as well, for she would have, beyond the joys of the flesh, the additional pleasure of reading," said Rakoczy. "She will share my high regard for books."

Karl-lo-Magne sighed. "It is a fine thing, to be able to read. I always sleep with a tablet and stylus, in case God should bless me with the ability to read and write while I sleep, as He bestows so many other favors through the agency of dreams and visions."

Rakoczy had been told about this habit of the King's, and so said nothing disparaging of the practice. He reverenced Karl-lo-Magne, saying, "You have those who can read for you, Optime, which is a great gift. If God should inspire you, so much the better, but you still have the written word within your ken. Many have not the gift of reading, nor the clerk to read for them, a sad thing indeed."

"You speak truly enough, foreigner," said Karl-lo-Magne. "Well, come along with me. The mansionarii will have a place prepared for us shortly. I will not ask for any food for you, but I would like your company. It is a pleasurable thing to have a simple meal upon occasion, and in such company. Most of my Court will not dine until later, and I must sit at the High Table in the Great Hall then, but just now, you and the ladies are sufficient companions for me, delightful and undemanding. And the High Table need be nothing more than two steps above the company."

"Optime honors us beyond our deserts," said Rakoczy, knowing many of the courtiers would be jealous of this sign of favor.

"Nothing of the sort. You have brought me two armed men, as you said you would do, and I would be lax if I made no show of approval. It would also incline my courtiers who are less diligent in their duty to me than you have been to honor their pledges. For that alone I am grateful; know that you give me occasion to remind them of the benefits in not shirking their obligations." He ambled along the broad corridor, the narrow circlet of gold on his brow his only sign of rank. "You have behaved well, especially for a foreigner. I will acknowledge your service, and so others will be taught to fulfill their vassalage."

"If Optime wishes," Rakoczy said, keeping half-a-step behind Karl-lo-Magne.

"I do wish," said the King. "Do not question me." The warning was plain, without apology, and determined. He paused in the archway of the Great Hall of Paderborn Castle. "There. You see? My Court will dine here tonight. The mansionarii will make it splendid with flowers and boughs, and a rhymer will tell of the exploits of Saints and heros. But that is for later. Shortly you and I will go to the women's dining hall and sit with the ladies."

"I look forward to such an opportunity," said Rakoczy, and almost meant it.

"Be careful that you do not choke on a lie, Magnatus," Karl-lo-Magne recommended with a wag of his finger. "You are troubled because you fear the jealousy of my Court. I will tell them what will happen if they do anything to harm or disaccomodate you. None of them will risk my displeasure for the sake of a foreigner without blood ties in Franksland." He clicked his tongue. "It is your lack of relatives that inclines me to listen to you and to believe what you say: you have no good reason to lie to me, and many reasons to be truthful."

"I am relieved to hear you say so, Optime," said Rakoczy.

"If you should fail me, you know I will exact retribution from you, but if you continue to behave in this exemplary way, I will honor you, and be glad that I need not also show favor to your family." Karl-lo-Magne touched his shoulder in salute. "You are worthy of my high regard, at least thus far."

Inwardly, Rakoczy was sure this distinction would only serve to make the jealousy of the Court worse, but he reverenced Karl-lo-Magne, saying, "I am here to serve you, Optime."

Karl-lo-Magne chuckled. "You are, foreigner; you are." He strolled away, still chuckling, leaving Rakoczy alone in the gallery.

They did not meet again until shortly after the start of comestus, when Rakoczy entered the women's dining hall that Karl-lo-Magne reserved for his more intimate meals. The King was seated at the High Table with three of his daughters, the four widows occupying a single table two steps below his; the intimacy of this arrangement was high tribute to the four women, and all of them were aware of it. Slaves and scullions were bustling in with spits laden with broiled pheasants and ribs of lamb, working the meat off the hot iron rods and into the fresh-baked trenchers set in front of all the diners. The odor of the food was strong and greasy.

"You are late!" Karl-lo-Magne bellowed, frowning angrily. "You should not be late."

"I apologize, Optime," said Rakoczy, reverencing the King and remaining standing in a show of respect. "One of the fighting men I have provisioned on your behalf had a serious chink in his sword. I have repaired it and now he is fully armed again." He had actually replaced the damaged blade with one of his own making, but kept that to himself.

"Work for a slave to do," Karl-lo-Magne said, determined to insult his guest.

"Not if I am certain my work will provide the soldier with a stronger weapon than your smiths can," Rakoczy rejoined, knowing that concession now would be an invitation to trouble. "You charged me with furnishing the armed men I sponsor with the finest weapons I can. I was fulfilling my obligation to do so." He reverenced Karl-lo-Magne again. "Besides, Optime, since I dine in private, as you are aware, what does it matter if I miss half the meal? There is no occasion that demands my attendance." He gestured to indicate the women at the lower table. "You have enjoyed the full attention of these gracious ladies and I will not starve simply because I didn't arrive as the first dish was brought out. If this were a formal banquet, then I would be lax indeed, but for such an occasion as you have here? You have new bread trenchers out before you, but nothing is in them yet, so I must assume your meal is not a hasty one, and you haven't passed beyond the pickled eggs yet." It was a calculated risk, talking to the King in this way, but Rakoczy hoped to deflect the worst of the King's displeasure by pointing out his own oddity.

Karl-lo-Magne gave a sour grin. "All right, Magnatus. I cannot dispute that. Have a seat with the ladies. They will make a place for you on the bench." It was a subtle punishment, and both men knew it.

Rakoczy reverenced Karl-lo-Magne and took a seat between Odile and Ermentrude, straddling the bench gracefully before swinging both legs under the table. He showed no sign of distress at this slight, and instead of sulking as many another might, he took advantage of his situation, directing his attention to Odile, asking how she was enjoying her stay in Paderborn. To encourage her, he said, "I have not been here in some time, and I see the city is much changed. The King is making it a finer town than it was of old."

Odile smiled slightly and reached for her cup of beer. "I have only been here this once, and we don't go about the city, for it is still deemed unsafe for women to walk abroad alone, and there are no soldiers to spare as escorts. I can speak only of this castle and its immediate neighbors." She glanced at him speculatively, her expression a combination of seductiveness and caution.

"Perhaps, then, Optime might allow me to escort you about the markets when it suits him," Rakoczy suggested. "It would be my pleasure to revisit this place with the benefit of new eyes."

"Perhaps," said Odile, with a quick glance in Karl-lo-Magne's direction. "If it suits the King."

"Of course," Rakoczy said at once. "You and I attend on him at his pleasure, and it would be the height of ingratitude to do anything against his Will."

Ermentrude laughed a little. "This is a most soft-tongued fellow," she said to Odile, looking past Rakoczy as if he could not understand her.

Odile shook her head. "A flattering word isn't enough to entice me any longer; I heard too many of them from my husband, when he cajoled me or returned from whoring." She looked directly at Rakoczy, a challenge in her pale-blue eyes. "You have a bearing about you, a presence, Magnatus, and that is more to my liking than compliments and persiflage."

"Then I shall seek to address you in a more dignified manner," said Rakoczy, and went on with only a trace of a smile in the back of his dark eyes. "I am told you read. What are your preferences?"

Somewhat startled by the question, Odile had another mouthful of beer. "I . . . I do not know that I have any preferences. To read is a blessing in itself, that I am obliged to anyone for allowing me to peruse something I have not seen before, whatever it may be."

From his place at the High Table, Karl-lo-Magne laughed. "Listen to her. Who is bantering now, Odile?"

Color mounted in her cheeks and she coughed. "I did not mean anything—" She gestured with her cup to finish her remark. After swallowing, she said to Rakoczy in an undervoice, "I understand why you are here, Magnatus, and why you are talking to me."

"How do you mean?" Rakoczy asked quietly.

"The King has told you to choose one among us. We all understand that." She could not quite look at him, so instead stared at the space over his right shoulder.

"Oh," said Rakoczy, troubled that she had been ordered to make herself available.

"I am willing to do as the King wishes, if you should choose me. You wouldn't have to force me," she assured him with a slight smile.

"I would not want to force you, in any way. If you are willing, I will not ask you to say so now, unless it pleases you to do so. I will not demand an answer before you are ready to give it," said Rakoczy, wanting to spare her embarrassment. He gave her a long moment to respond, and when she remained silent, he went on. "Idle conversation is not to your taste. Very well, I shall not foist too much upon you: let me, instead, supply you with a list of books I have with me, and you shall choose which you would like to read." That would spare her the potential embarrassment of the *Metamorphoses*. He reached out for the pitcher and poured more beer into her cup, and then into the cups of the other widows.

"He's dainty as a Roman," said Ermentrude, not quite approving. "Have you been there, Magnatus?" She asked this graciously, but with the air of one who expects a denial.

"Not recently," said Rakoczy, recalling his villa on the northeast side of the old walls; it had been built during Claudius' reign and although in disrepair, was currently being managed by Atta Olivia Clemens, an arrangement that gave him a sense of continuity he did not often experience over the centuries.

"But you have been there," said Ermentrude with a sigh. She drank more beer. "I know I will never see it, but I long to go there."

"It is not so fine as it once was," warned Rakoczy, recalling the magnificence of the city when the Caesars ruled there.

"Roma is a splendid place!" Karl-lo-Magne boomed. "The Pope maintains his Court there, and we of the West still honor it as the center of the world, no matter what the Emperor Constantininus VI and his mother Irene in Constantinople may say. It is only their envy that makes them slight Roma." He looked around at his daughters and smiled as they seconded his utterance. "One day, Roma will be the Empire it was before, only vaster and more rich, and more highly esteemed than ever before. Roma will reclaim her place in the world, and Byzantium will bow to her again, as she did at the beginning."

"Is that what you intend, Optime?" Rakoczy asked in a respectful tone, all the while aware of what an impossible task Karl-lo-Magne had set himself.

"It is, although my good advisor Alcuin is against such ambitions, telling me I am tempting God to bring me down for pride. But it isn't pride that drives me, it is yearning for the might that the West once had, and I am determined we will have restored to us. When we can drive the Moors out of Hispania, and then push back the Wends and the Moravians as we have the Avars, then we might bring the proud Byzantines to submission, as they ought to—" He stopped as the Paderborn senescalus came to the entrance to the small dining hall and reverenced him. "What is it?"

"There is a messenger from Roma. He has arrived but a moment ago, seeking audience with you. He says it is of crucial importance." The senescalus stood very straight, anticipating a reprimand for interrupting so private a comestus.

Karl-lo-Magne looked about as if he expected to be overheard, and kept his tone low. "What is his purpose?"

"He didn't tell me, Optime," said the senescalus. "I cannot force him to reveal anything to me. He says it is for your ears alone."

Sighing, Karl-lo-Magne shoved himself out of his chair. "I think I should probably speak to him, then, although it is insolent of him to present himself in this manner. It offends me to be summoned like a servant. Still, it may be that he is ordered by His Holiness to demand an immediate audience, and to refuse it would traduce the honor of the Pope. . . ." He picked up his knife and tucked it back in his belt. "You need not wait for me if the food is getting cold. Otherwise, assume I will be with you in a short while." With an abrupt movement he swung around to leave the room.

"Cherished father," said Gisela, "we will wait for you before we continue to eat." She slipped out of her chair and knelt while Karl-lo-Magne strode to the door. "Bring more beer," she ordered as soon as her father was gone. "If we cannot eat, at least we can drink."

There was an awkward silence among the women and Rakoczy as all tried to fill the moment without slighting the King. Finally Rotruda nudged her half-sister and clapped her hands. "Where is the beer?" she demanded, and leaned forward, her arms on the table-plank.

One of the scullions almost dropped his end of the spit he was carrying with another scullion. He ducked his head, confusion making him clumsy, and looked about for some means to support the spit while he hurried to carry out the King's daughters' orders. His distress made the women laugh, and one of them pointed to the unfortunate scullion and made a scandalous suggestion about the state of his femoralia and his buttocks; the youngster turned scarlet and fled.

"He'd better bring the beer," said Rotruda, scowling at the scullion as he bolted from the room, leaving his fellow to struggle with the hot, laden spit. "I have a great thirst upon me. Hurry! If you do not, I'll have you beaten!"

"Father does not like drunkenness," said Gisela with a sigh. "He doesn't like to fuddle his wits. He doesn't mind if the rest of us drink, thank all the Saints."

"Well, I do like drinking," said Rotruda, petulantly. "I am ready to fetch our beer myself if someone doesn't bring it, and quickly."

"Someone will," said Bertrada, named for her grandmother and inclined to take on grand airs because of it. "Else they'll be whipped."

"They may be whipped anyway," said Gisela. "The buttocks on that scullion almost demand whipping."

Rotruda laughed, her good-will restored. "Optime does not want us neglected. You must see that." She giggled and looked down at the four widows and Rakoczy. "We know his favor will never falter. You cannot be so certain."

Ermentrude sniffed. "At least we have been allowed to marry."

The three women at the High Table exchanged looks. "Our father does not want to part with us. He doesn't forbid us to have our pleasures. He only forbids us husbands."

"It isn't the same thing," said Ermentrude smugly, and drank the last of her beer, "having lovers. We have the protection of our husbands' family."

"And we the protection of our father," said Rotruda smugly.

Three scullions—none of them the chagrined lad who had scurried from the room—came from the kitchen, each with a pitcher of new wheaten beer in his hands. They bustled about the tables, taking care not to brush their greasy camisae against the gonellae of the women. In a short time they had refilled all the cups and left the pitchers on the table for further servings. Immediately Bertrada reached for the pitcher nearest her and claimed it for her own use.

"We will want more, by and by," she warned the scullions.

The scullions exchanged uneasy glances, and one of them, staring down at his feet, dared to say, "We are told to keep the rest for the banquet tonight."

Bertrada glowered at him. "Set aside three more pitchers for our use or it will be the worse for you."

"There is wine, Illustra. Let us bring you wine." The desperation in his voice intrigued Gisela, who leaned forward.

"I didn't think we had much wine," she said with exaggerated sweetness. "I was under the impression that all we could drink is beer."

"There is enough wine to meet your needs," said the scullion, increasingly anxious under this continuing scrutiny of the King's daughters. "There isn't enough to serve all the guests at a banquet."

Bertrada decided for them all. "Wine will do. See you bring it at once. Bottles for each of us. That means seven of them, since the foreigner doesn't drink." She looked directly at Rakoczy. "Or eat, at least not in company, after the custom of his people, strange though it is."

Taking advantage of this shift in attention, the scullion bustled off toward the kitchen.

"Beer first, then wine," said Gisela, nudging Rotruda with her elbow.

"It is acceptable," said Rotruda, drinking down her beer and holding out her cup for more. "We'll be drunk as Bishops."

All the women laughed and tossed off the contents of their cups; Rakoczy noticed that Odile was less eager than the rest to become intoxicated, which intrigued him. He studied her profile and noticed she was aware of his interest, for she smoothed back a wayward tendril from her face and smiled uncertainly.

"What are you thinking, Magnatus?" she asked in an attempt at boldness.

"I was thinking that you are an interesting woman, Good Widow," he replied, determined to end any awkwardness between them. "And I am trying to decide which of my books you might find most engaging to read."

Her smile became more genuine. "Optime told me you have books with you. How fortunate for you, that you can keep books. I have two of my own, and would have more, but I cannot read Greek; I learned Latin when I was with the nuns of Santa Burgundofara."

"You were taught there?" Rakoczy asked, encouraging her to talk.

"I was a novice for three years, when I was younger." She glanced at him, then went on. "I was a third daughter and my father gave me to the Church. But then my oldest sister died in childbirth and my other sister took a fever and became an invalid." She reached out for her cup of beer and drank. "So I was recalled from the nunnery and married."

Rakoczy heard this out with a mixture of sympathy and resignation. "Your father required it of you?"

"All my family," she answered. "With my only living sister unable to marry, it was left to me to make sure our House was not extinguished, although our name may be lost."

"A heavy burden for you to bear," said Rakoczy.

"Possibly, but it is mine," said Odile with a touch of pride. "My husband was a fine man, of good rank and excellent reputation, and I was proud to give him children, although God wasn't willing to allow me to keep most of them. With just one son left alive, I am thankful to God for preserving our House, for we might have lost the whole of it."

Rakoczy heard her out, paying close attention to her nuances of tone. "Still, you have lost much, and such losses demand a toll in grief."

Odile looked away in confusion. "I wouldn't have said so."

"Perhaps not," said Rakoczy. "But it remains with you, however you name it."

Four scullions bearing spits came into the hall, with knives in their hands, ready to cut meat to serve the diners. The most senior of them had a platter balanced on his head, and this he held out to be filled once the spits were set on trestles.

"Boar, bison, goose, and lamb," said the senior scullion, pointing to the meats on the spits. "Tell me which you will have."

Bertrada got to her feet and made an inclusive gesture. "Cut from all of them, and we'll take what's to our taste." Her color was high and there was a certain recklessness about her that alarmed her sisters; Gisela nodded to Rotruda, and both women motioned to Bertrada to sit down.

The senior scullion did as the King's daughters wished, slicing generous portions from the meat on the spits. When the platter was well-laden, he summoned two of the scullions to carry the platter to the High Table, where Karl-lo-Magne's three daughters stuck the cuts they wanted with their knives to carry the meat to their trenchers.

"The aroma is very good," said Rotruda, pulling a bit of the boar off the rib with her fingers. "And it is tender, for a change."

"We rubbed the meat with butter and honey," said the senior scullion, going well beyond what was permitted of servants.

Rotruda scowled at him. "If I wish to know this, I will ask the kitchen staff." She lowered her eyes. "You forget yourself."

"My father will order you beaten if you forget yourself," said Gisela sternly. "Servants think they're better than they are."

The senior scullion reverenced the women at the High Table and retreated into silence. As he served the low table, he refused to speak, communicating by gesture alone and doing what he was called upon to do with as much dispatch as he could manage.

"I will have bison and goose," said Odile when the senior scullion came up to her. She poured wine into her cup and watched as the scullion offered the platter. When she had retrieved the meat she wanted, she set to work with her knife, trying to cut her portion into smaller sections.

"The food is getting cold," said Bertrada from the High Table. "We should eat."

At that the seven women fell to, eating rapidly and with gusto, washing down their mouthfuls with wine. For a short while the small dining hall was silent but for the sounds of chewing. Then there was an impatient step in the corridor, and Karl-lo-Magne strode back into the hall, glowering fiercely. He stepped onto the dais and back to his chair at the High Table. All the women stopped eating and watched him attentively.

"Magnatus," said the King. "Come up to me."

Rakoczy obeyed promptly, wondering what had so distressed Karl-lo-Magne that he should have lost all trace of joviality. He concealed his apprehension with an expression of cordial interest, his bearing respectful. "What may I have the honor of doing for you, Optime?"

"The messenger from Roma brings most troubling news," Karl-lo-Magne muttered. He got out of his chair again and tugged on the black sleeve of Rakoczy's gonelle, drawing him into a corner of the room. "There is a plot against the Pope."

"Surely more than one," said Rakoczy, recalling all the rumors he had heard.

"This one is more serious, and more treacherous. It is driven by ambition and apostasy," said Karl-lo-Magne. "There are bands of scoff-laws in Roma who can be bought for all manner of mischief. It is said that money has changed hands, to secure the services of these marauders: there is an indication that two of the bands have been paid to waylay and murder Leo, or at least it is what His Holiness fears."

"Is there any reason to think this more likely to happen than any of the other plots against His Holiness? Is there some reason to fear this present threat more than any other? Why should you think so?" Rakoczy asked, wanting to provide Karl-lo-Magne with as many options as he could. He wished he had been allowed to bring Rorthger with him, for now he wanted as much information as he could gain; Rorthger was always alert to the talking among servants, often more reliable than the rumors spread in Courts. But the missi dominici who had escorted Rakoczy to Paderborn had had no provision for including a servant for the Magnatus, and so Rorthger remained at the fiscs, in charge of the walled villa and the lands around it.

"I wouldn't think so, but for the urgency and the source of the message: it came from one of my Bishops, and under Church seal." Karl-lo-Magne pulled on his beard. "I cannot ignore this appeal for protection. Much as it would be difficult to arrange to protect the Pope, it is preferable to being forced to accept a Byzantine tool as Pontiff. If Leo is killed, who knows who will sit on Sant' Pier's Seat?"

"Then what do you plan?" Rakoczy asked, aware that Karl-lo-Magne expected the question.

"I suppose I must be prepared to send a company of soldiers to Roma to be guards for the Pope, and I must authorize the arming of monks faithful to Leo himself, if it comes to that." He tugged on his beard again, his scowl directed at a place on the floor. "This must be settled within the year, or Constantininus and his mother in Constantinople will have the advantage, and the Papacy will be lost to the Greeks."

"What do you want me to do?" Rakoczy inquired with a minor reverence.

"I don't know yet, but I want you to stay near at hand. I may have use for you, and when I do, you must not be away from my Court." He laid his hand on the hilt of his dagger. "If the Pope falls, then we will be at war with the Byzantines."

"It would seem urgent, then, to be sure Leo lives," said Rakoczy.

"That is why I must ready soldiers to go to Roma. I hope I will not have to send them, for it would provoke all manner of trouble." Karl-lo-Magne looked directly at Rakoczy. "There are many peoples who may want to take advantage of the change in Roma. I will have to be ready to hold my borders here in Saxony and in Longobardia and in other places. This will be a demanding time, no matter what I must do to protect the Church. But if I lose what I have gained in maintaining the Church, I will forfeit the strength that the Church depends upon me to provide."

Rakoczy heard him out. "You will have to decide how to balance these matters, Optime. And, as I am a foreigner, I can only tell you that your Kingdom is a rich prize and you have enemies beyond those you share with the Pope."

Karl-lo-Magne uttered a single, angry laugh. "Of course I have enemies. All men have enemies." He folded his arms. "I cannot let it be known that I have received this message, or my enemies will act at once to align themselves with the Moors in Hispania or the Greeks in Byzantium."

"That is nothing new, Optime, and so far no such alliance has survived long enough to damage anything you have achieved." Rakoczy looked over his shoulder. "Your daughters are listening."

"Let them," said Karl-lo-Magne. "They will hear about the whole of it soon enough." He shrugged. "So will all the Court. I must be prepared before any word gets out."

"Cherished father," called Rotruda. "Our meal is getting cold and our wine is getting hot."

"Then eat and drink," said Karl-lo-Magne testily. He put his hand on Rakoczy's shoulder. "Stay near, mind. I may have need of you, and I don't want to wait upon your arrival. For now, return to your place."

"I will," said Rakoczy, reverenced the King, and went back to the lower table where he once again sat beside Odile.

"Optime shows you distinction," Odile remarked.

"I am much honored," said Rakoczy.

Odile smiled. "How very well you keep his confidences." She reached out for another helping of meat—lamb this time—and dropped it into her trencher.

Ermentrude reached across Rakoczy to secure another portion of bison for herself. "There are men who will watch you, Magnatus. Not all of them are your sup-porters."

"I am aware of that," said Rakoczy as graciously as he could.

"And you must realize that you are watched in suspicion," Ermentrude added, reaching for her cup of wine for another long drink, as did Leoba Baldhilde.

Rakoczy did not bother to answer her; he could see she was feeling her beer and wine, and therefore could not be held accountable for anything she said. He reached for the platter of meat and offered it to Ermentrude, and when she had helped her-self to another slab of boar, he held the platter out to Odile. "What would you like?"

"Nothing more," said Odile, suddenly looking bashful.

"Don't refuse food on my account," said Rakoczy. "If you are hungry, eat."

"And you?" Odile asked, pulling a bit of bread off her trencher and eating. "Do you deny yourself?"

"From time to time," Rakoczy replied. "As all men must."

Odile shuddered. "Yes." She made a sign to ward off bad fortune.

Rakoczy thought of her husband and children dead of famine, and told her, "You have had great losses; I am sorry that cannot be changed."

She shrugged and said in a rush of candor, "If I am to be your mistress, I must also be Optime's spy." Then she clapped her hand to her mouth as if to keep more words from escaping.

Very gently he touched her cheek. "I know," he said.

Text of a letter from Rorthger to Hiernom Rakoczy at Paderborn, written in the Latin of Imperial Rome, and carried by missi dominici to Paderborn.

To my most esteemed master, Hiernom Rakoczy, Comes Sant' Germainius, the greetings of Rorthger at his master's fiscs at the longest day of the year.

Most puissant Magnatus, I am pleased to report that the crops are flour-ishing and it is likely that you will return to a good harvest. I am relieved that this has been a good spring, and that the summer bids fair to continuing along fruitful lines. I have also taken the first of the spring lambs to market, as well as five shoats, and traded them with local peasants slightly to the peasants' advantage, but not so much that they will seek to dupe you in future. I have secured beer for the mansionarii and the masons I have engaged to restore the walls of the villa, in accordance with your instruc-tions. The two brewers in the village have agreed to keep the villa supplied so long as we provide fruit and berries, along with a few silver coins, which is reasonable enough.

In order to keep on good terms with the Church, I have arranged to purchase wine and mead from the nunnery of Santa Julitta, and from the monastery of Sant' Cyricus I have asked to purchase parchment and ink; I have made donations to both communities in your name, with the assurance that you will continue to support a portion of their endeavors on a yearly basis, an arrangement which the Abbott and Abba have accepted, at least for the time being. I have also promised the nuns of Santa Julitta that you will send medicaments to their infirmary when you return from your service to the King, which the Superiora has welcomed.

I have bred two of your mares to the stallion Atta Olivia Clemens has sent to you: he is a fine creature, deep-chested and sturdy with a fine, arched neck and a good manner. Niklos Aulirios vouches for the horse, saying he has responded well to his training, and his get will be as strengthy as he is. He is a blue roan, which Bonna Dama Clemens informs me you will understand and appreciate. The mares have settled, so next May there should be foals in the pasture as well as calves and lambs.

In addition to the stallion, Bonna Dama Olivia tells me news of Roma, some of it most distressing. She informs me that the Pope was attacked by roughians, and was feared to be near death, only he has vanished from Roma, and it is not known where he has gone. Some speculate he has died and been secretly buried, so as to delay the next Papal election. Some say he has been kidnapped by the Byzantines, and is even now in a cell in Constantinople. Some say he has fled to Karl-lo-Magne for protection. Some say that the Church has sent him to a monastery in Longobardia, where he can recover from his injuries under the protection of the Church. Whatever may be true, from what Bonna Dama Olivia tells me, Roma is in disarray over these events, and the confusion is likely to spread outward from Roma into all the Roman churches and monasteries. If this were the case, you would need to be very careful, for until the fate of the Pope is known, there is likely to be a great deal of bickering and discord throughout the Church, and you may find yourself under scrutiny, for many of these Franks are wary of foreigners, as you are already cognizant. I mention this only to keep your precarious circumstances uppermost in your mind. She also writes that most of this incident, very widely reported and believed, is generally false, for although the Pope was waylaid, his Guard extricated him from the miscreants and have generally confined him to the Lateran Palace for his safety, and that the Pope is truly still in Roma, no matter what tales are spread abroad, most of which are intended to undermine Leo's authority and make him seem incapable of continuing to lead the Church. And if he is long a prisoner of his own Guard, what they say may become true, and he will not be able to maintain his position. Bonna Dona Clemens also believes this has been an attempt to force Karl-lo-Magne to reckless action on the Pope's behalf, which could lead him to a confrontation with the Byzantines that could be Pyrrhic in cost.

I hope you will return before harvest. It will do much to please the people of this region to see you at their festivities, particularly if you will hold a Court, so that their various grievances may be addressed in a way that will stand up to the scrutiny of the missi dominici, who come here four times a year in the King's name to see that his Will is carried out everywhere. I am continuing to administer the fiscs along the lines of your instructions, and I am pleased to report that there has been a softening of the attitude of the peasants in the villages near-by, to the point that they no longer refuse to enter the gates of the villa, but will bring their livestock to the buticularius for the kitchen, making our work much easier. I cannot say that you are welcomed enthusiastically, but that you are no longer regarded as a baleful presence.

In spite of these encouragements, be on guard, my master, and know that these fiscs are flourishing. Surely you may find comfort in this, as I have known you to do of old. Also, I have prepared your house and stable as you have ordered, so upon your return you may be easy in your own house.

Rorthger,
camerarius to Hiernom Rakoczy

⌀

chapter nine

FRATRE BERAHTRAM SAT ON THE LIP OF THE HORSE trough in the court-yard of Paderborn Castle, his handsome face grimy from his day's labors, his usually personable expression turned to one of despair and disgust; he looked up at the sky, frowning at the dark clouds that had promised rain all day, but so far had produced nothing but grumbling thunder and occasional, distant bristles of lightning. He had been tending the wounded soldiers who had arrived the day before, and he was thoroughly sick of the thankless work; prayers availed nothing, and there was nothing he could do to ease the wounded but put a pillow over the faces of the most grievously injured; had he not been watched, he could probably have put an end to six of his charges by now. Little as he liked the idea of dispatching the men to end their suffering and stop their screams, he knew what was expected of him and did it, however grudgingly, when he was left alone; this would not advance him in the Church, and he was annoyed with Bishop Agobard for giving him such lowly tasks to do. He might as well be a nun for all the good his efforts would be. If only Bishop Agobard was not the cousin of Comes Gosbert! But since he had appealed to the Comes to aid him, he could not now turn away from what the Illustre had provided him, little though it suited his purpose. He was so lost in this unprofitable musing that he did not hear the approaching footsteps or notice anyone in the courtyard until a dark shape came between him and the late-summer sunlight that filtered through the clouds as they blundered across the sky.

"The other monks said I might find you here," said Magnatus Rakoczy, his black garments seeming to make his shadow denser. "I trust I do not intrude? If I do, tell me and I will wait for you in the dormitory." His manner was as courtly as any Illustre Fratre Berahtram had ever seen.

The reverence Fratre Berahtram made was hardly more than a gesture; he squinted up at the foreigner. "My Fratri guided you aright. Why do you seek me out?"

If he knew he had been insulted Rakoczy showed no sign of it. "I was told you are in charge of the monks dealing with soldiers whose wounds have become infected."

"I am," Fratre Berahtram admitted reluctantly. "Bishop Agobard has required it of me, and I am obedient to his Will."

"Most admirable," said Rakoczy, the irony of his tone lost on Fratre Berahtram.

Fratre Berahtram ducked his head. "I cannot say if it is, but I pray it finds favor in Heaven. If my service is valued by God, my task is a worthy one." It was what he was expected to say, and he recited the words as automatically as the Psalms of the Little Hours.

Rakoczy gave a little shake of his head. "May God be pleased," he said as good conduct required.

After a short, uncomfortable silence, Fratre Berahtram rose. "For what purpose did you seek me out?"

"I am here at the request of Karl-lo-Magne, who has been informed that I have some skill with medicaments. He has asked that I assist in caring for the wounded who have fever and infection." Rakoczy paused, aware that Fratre

Berahtram was weighing up this information. "I would deem it an honor to be able to aid the soldiers of Optime Karl."

"I see," said Fratre Berahtram. "Do you mean you can cure those who suffer?"

"No; not all of them," said Rakoczy promptly. "But I can cure some of them, and I can ease the agony of those who cannot be cured." He saw a flicker of emotion in the back of Fratre Berahtram's dust-colored eyes; it was quickly gone, but Rakoczy knew that he had glimpsed the soul of the monk, and that it was a dark and unwholesome thing, at variance with his open, regular features and well-proportioned limbs. "Let me work with you and your monks for three days. Surely that is not too long a period to ask? You may observe all that I do, and report upon it to whomever you believe you ought to. If I cannot prove my worth to you in that time, then inform Optime Karl that you would prefer I not assist you." The offer was surpassingly reasonable, and therefore impossible to refuse.

"Three days," said Fratre Berahtram, shading his eyes so he could better see Rakoczy's pleasant, irregular countenance. "This day is more than half over."

"Then let us say by prandium in three days," Rakoczy suggested. "I will abide by your decision. But I cannot refuse to try, or I will counter the Will of Optime Karl."

Fratre Berahtram sighed. "I would be more than a fool to say no to anyone coming with the King's mandate." He pointed to the dormitory that was currently serving as an infirmary. "The men with the worst fevers are at the far end of the rows of pallets. There are eleven of them just now; two died yesterday. The monks tending the others may send us one of their charges if he takes a turn for the worst. Bring your medicaments and we shall see what you can do."

"Thank you," said Rakoczy, his sincerity emphasized by a slight nod. "I will join you at your work shortly." Saying that, he turned on his heel and walked away, leaving Fratre Berahtram in the full, hazy glare of the afternoon.

Not long after Rakoczy departed, Fratre Berahtram slowly made his way back into the dormitory, thinking as he went that Abbott Rokinard had done him no favors when he had insisted that the monk learn to treat the sick and injured. But he had asked for patronage, and he had to accept what was required of him by Comes Gosbert. He hated the look of the fevered men, hated their incapacity, their delirium, hated the ruin of their bodies, hated the stench of their wounds. It was all he could do to bring himself to go to them; it took every bit of resolution he possessed not to bolt from the building. He muttered a prayer to Sant' Raffaell, asking for his support in this ordeal, and went to fetch a pail of water and a ladle to provide the suffering men with drink to relieve their thirst. He had taken care of four men when he saw the foreigner in black approaching along the aisle in the makeshift infirmary.

"What have you there?" Fratre Berahtram asked, noticing the large bag slung over Rakoczy's shoulder.

"My medicaments, or as many as I have with me," said Rakoczy, looking past the monk to the men on the pallets. "Are these the patients?"

Fratre Berahtram did his best not to breathe. "The worst of them."

"Their wounds are putrid," said Rakoczy dispassionately. "What have you been doing for them?"

"I have been bathing their injuries in basil-water," said Fratre Berahtram, trying not to gag. "And there are holy seals on their pillows."

Rakoczy nodded. "I believe I may be able to ease their hurts beyond this."

"If you do nothing diabolic, then treat them as you wish," Fratre Berahtram said, hoping that this Magnatus would be able to spare him having to deal with these dying soldiers.

"Thank you; I will," said Rakoczy, going to the nearest pallet and looking down on the man lying on it; there was a gaping wound in his side, the flesh around it red and swollen, pus crusted the length of it. The odor of infection hung around him palpably, and the man moaned with every exhalation, the sound occasionally turning to a shriek. His face was mottled and his breathing was unsteady, indicating the rot had reached his lung. "I cannot help this man to recover; I can lessen his pain."

Fratre Berahtram gritted his teeth. "Then do so."

Rakoczy shrugged his sack off his shoulder and lifted the flap that closed the sack's mouth, taking out a vial. "I will need a cup of wine to administer this," he said to Fratre Berahtram. "In fact, if you will, bring a bottle. More than one man may need this, and it would be foolish to keep you running back and forth to the pantry. Also, if you will bring olitory herbs, I would be most grateful."

"Which ones?" Fratre Berahtram asked, reluctant to raid the kitchen garden without knowing what was needed.

"Coriander, garlic, basil, for a beginning," said Rakoczy, somewhat preoccupied. "And lovage, if there is any."

Although he was suspicious of Rakoczy, Fratre Berahtram was glad for any excuse to leave the dormitory. "I will see if the buticularius will allow it."

"If there is any difficulty, ask him to send word to Great Karl," Rakoczy suggested. "As I am here at the King's behest, I will not hesitate to invoke his authority."

"That I will," said Fratre Berahtram with alacrity, and hastened away to do as he was ordered. As he stepped out of the door, he encountered Superior Leidrad, who held up his hand to stop Fratre Berahtram.

"Are you abandoning your duty?" the Superior demanded.

"I am following the instructions of Magnatus Rakoczy," said Fratre Berahtram, wanting to push past the Superior, but not daring to. He glanced up at the leaden sky as another rumble of thunder went through it.

"Why are you doing so?" Superior Leidrad persisted. "What has the Magnatus to do with your duties?"

"The King has ordered the Magnatus to help with the most badly injured men, and the Magnatus is doing so. I am going to fetch a bottle of wine for him; he has need of it for his ministrations, along with an assortment of herbs," said Fratre Berahtram.

Superior Leidrad stood aside. "Then be about your errand, for the Glory of God." He stood still while Fratre Berahtram hurried off toward the kitchens; then the Superior went into the dormitory, uneasy in his mind: much as he had been impressed with Fratre Berahtram's zeal, he had a nagging sense of apprehension about the young monk. He was relieved to see the Magnatus moving among the wounded men, as Fratre Berahtram said he would be. He went up to the black-clad man, saying, "Fratre Berahtram is doing your bidding, Magnatus."

"Very good," said Rakoczy, straightening up from his examination of a man with a severe facial wound. "I doubt I can save his eye, but I don't think he will die; he is not yet so weak that he cannot rise above his ills." He had treated worse injuries at the Temple of Imhotep, centuries ago, and had the injured recover. "If he doesn't develop sickness in his blood."

"If you think you can keep him from blindness, may the Saints guide your hand," said Superior Leidrad. "I will thank God for sparing him. Such Bellatori as this man are rare; Optime Karlus cannot spare many of them to the graveyard, and Sant' Gabraell." He made a gesture of protection, for it was considered dangerous to speak the name of the Angel of Death in the presence of the wounded or ill. "See that you employ every skill you have at your disposal, foreigner. If you are lax, the King will know of it."

"I'll do my best," said Rakoczy, his hand against the injured man's throat. "His pulse is fast and thready. He will need a great deal of rest." He would need herbs and poultices to draw out the infection as well, but that was understood by both men.

Superior Leidrad put his fingers together, relenting a bit from his previous admonitions. "If you cannot save him, save the ones you can."

Rakoczy looked at the Superior. "This man has a chance to live. Three of these men do not. I will make them more comfortable so that they need not die in unendurable pain." He saw Superior Leidrad wince. "I will not hurry their demise, but I will not force them to linger."

"Isn't that God's Will?" Superior Leidrad asked while he clutched his pectoral crucifix.

"Knowledge is God's Will as much as the hour of men's death," said Rakoczy, moving to the next pallet. "If I have it in my abilities to ease their anguish, surely it is God's Will that I use them in this cause, or I would not be here at this time."

The Superior nodded. "The Bishop would concur, and possibly the Pope as well."

"Then how can I be wrong to fulfill the King's order to treat these men?" Rakoczy said, leaning over the next man. "In the case of this soldier, God has already decided: he will not last the day. His blood is filled with sickness and nothing can stop it now."

"How can you be so certain?" the Superior asked, accompanied by drubbing thunder outside.

"I can smell it," said Rakoczy, choosing an explanation that would satisfy these Franks, and was rewarded by the approval in Superior Leidrad's demeanor. He continued on to the next pallet. "I may be able to save this man; if he does not become too weak, his wounds aren't bad enough to kill him now. I will know in a day or so if he will recover. He is not so far gone, but his blood isn't quite sound; I will need time, to see if I have a sovereign remedy for him."

"But you do have remedies?" Superior Leidrad asked, looking at the sack Rakoczy carried. "They have been tested, and you know them to be successful?"

"I have and they are," said Rakoczy. "I am honored to use them for Great Karl's benefit." He held up a jar. "This ointment can be helpful if there isn't much pus."

"There is always pus," said Superior Leidrad and swallowed hard; the stink of festering injuries was beginning to sicken him.

Rakoczy had no response to make; he went on to the last of the men, looking at the man narrowly. "This man has bleeding deep inside, and I don't know if it can be stopped. If it can be, he may live; if it cannot, he will die." He laid his hand on the man's brow. "He's far gone in fever."

"He has been readied to die," said Superior Leidrad, as if he had fulfilled all his obligations to the soldier. "His soul will go to Heaven."

"Undoubtedly a good thing," said Rakoczy. "But another ten years of life might be welcome to him, if he can come through the fever and survive his hurts." He looked back over the other ten men. "Have all of them been shriven?"

"Yes; all of them. So if they recover, the glory is due to God and the Saints, and not to any earthly deed," said the Superior, warning Rakoczy.

Rakoczy sighed. "Certainly. The glory is due to whomever you like, so long as the King is satisfied." He pulled another vial from his sack. "This is tincture of primrose. It will help some of these men, as will my sovereign remedy." He did not add that this second remedy was made from moldy bread, for that was considered corrupted matter and not fit for medicinal use.

Superior Leidrad scowled. "Do not make light of God and His Saints."

"I do not," said Rakoczy, realizing he had offended the Superior. "I am here at the pleasure of Great Karl, and I wish to render him worthy service. I must put my duty to him first, for he is master here. If God favors the King, then I do His work as well, but that is for more sagacious minds than mine to discern; I must content myself with obeying the King."

The Superior could find nothing to argue with in this and folded his hands to show submission to the King as well as to God. "Great Karlus has been given the victory, and that is God's Will."

"The Saxons haven't yet submitted, though this city has fallen," Rakoczy pointed out as he set out more vials and jars on the ledge of the small window that provided less light than the three oil-lamps that hung from the beam overhead. "It will be a while before they do."

"We are in their capital. They might as well surrender now and spare themselves more travail," said Superior Leidrad, and would have gone on, but was interrupted by the return of Fratre Berahtram.

Fratre Berahtram carried a wine-jar in one hand and a basket in the other; it was half-full of various herbs, all freshly cut. "I have done as you asked," he declared, and all but thrust these things into Rakoczy's hands. "They say there is more if you need it."

"Very good," said Rakoczy. "I will require broth before evening, preferably of goat or venison. If you will inform the kitchen of this, I would be most appreciative."

Astonished at his good fortune that would permit him to be out of the dormitory once again without shirking his responsibilities, Fratre Berahtram assured him, "I will go at once and tell them what they must prepare."

Rakoczy's quick, one-sided smile was ironic, but neither Fratre Berahtram nor Superior Leidrad saw it. "Thank you. Please tell the scullions that the broth must be twice-strained, so that it is clear of scraps and of a deep color, for that provides the greatest fortification of the body. If you would like to supervise the preparation, I believe it would make their compliance greater."

"I will," said Fratre Berahtram, and turned to leave at once.

"He is an energetic man," said Superior Leidrad after Fratre Berahtram was out of the dormitory; it was difficult to tell whether the Superior intended this as a compliment or not. "It is odd to think of him as the Fratre he is: his devotion is singular in a man so well-favored by nature. Most monks need not be troubled for comeliness, but, as you see, Fratre Berahtram is a sweet-visaged fellow, and is often tempted by those who admire his beauty. It is a great trial to him, and he often Confesses his worthlessness because of it."

"Does he," said Rakoczy, adopting the same neutral tone. He opened the wine-jar using the knife that hung from his girdle and poured a little of it into four small cups he had taken from his sack. To these he added a measure of a thick, dark liquid. "This is syrup of poppies," he told the Superior. "I will give it to those men who cannot recover. They will have less to endure as their lives ebb." He used a small glass rod to stir the contents of the cups. "I will make a less potent mixture for those who can recover, to enable them to rest. Lack of rest kills as many as putrefaction does."

"Do you truly expect seven of these soldiers to recover?" The Superior was startled at this optimism. "I would not suppose so many had a chance."

"That is what they have," said Rakoczy as he went to the most far-gone of the men, lifting his head and starting to tip the wine-and-poppy-syrup into his mouth. "A chance." The Bellatore coughed and sputtered, but was able to swallow most of the mixture. Rakoczy laid him back on the pallet and then went to the next dying man and repeated the process with the contents of the second cup.

"What if this man is destined to live?" Superior Leidrad asked.

"Then he will live," said Rakoczy, adding, "But after such a fever as he has had, I doubt he will be able to fight again." He took the third cup and went to the soldier with internal bleeding. "All this does is reduce pain and promote rest. All else is in the Hands of God."

Superior Leidrad watched with interest, doing his utmost not to give away his curiosity, for that might seem to be lack of certainty in God. "How did you come to learn these things, Magnatus?"

Rakoczy had been expecting such a question, and he answered it easily. "My travels have taken me many places. I stayed, as did the Holy Family, for some time in Egypt, learning all their priests had to teach about treating the sick, the injured, and the dying." He did not add that the priests had been pagans and that his time there had stretched for almost eight hundred years.

"You must have been a young man when you did that," said the Superior; this was punctuated by a sprink of lightning and almost at once a peal of thunder.

"I was younger than I am now," said Rakoczy, and gave the liquid in the third cup to the moaning soldier, taking the time to touch the man's distended abdomen lightly. "He will not last much longer." Another burst of lightning and a sharp clap of thunder heralded a sudden downpour. Rain came in torrents, shining like fish scales as the wind drove it across the courtyard. The smell of the storm could not penetrate the dormitory, but there was enough of an increase in the wind that the worst of the smell was mitigated. More lightning streamed over Paderborn Castle, and thunder trundled after it. "Are there more blankets?" Rakoczy asked Superior Leidrad when the echoes had dissipated.

"It is a warm day, in spite of the storm, and these men are taken in fever. What use are blankets?" The Superior turned as the bell for Sept rang. "It is the Little Hours," he said, glad of the excuse to leave.

Rakoczy was equally pleased to see him go. "Tell your monks that they need not concern themselves with these men; I will care for them."

"After Nocturnes, one of the Fratri will relieve you," said Superior Leidrad as he reached the door. "Or you may relieve Fratre Berahtram, as suits you best."

"That is good of you," said Rakoczy, aware that refusing this offer would lead to precisely the kinds of suspicions he wanted to avoid. He went to administer the fourth cup to the soldier whose thigh wound was distended and puffy, with red lines running up his body and under his camisa; the soldier muttered occasionally, but spent most of his waning energy in attempting to breathe. Rakoczy could tell the man would be dead before nightfall. Syrup of poppies would give him a modicum of succor before the end came, but nothing more.

The rain continued furiously for most of the afternoon, then tapered off, fading with the day; the thunder and lightning had ended some time before. As sunset winked through the thinning clouds Fratre Berahtram came back to the dormitory, a large iron pot hanging from an arched handle that he held with a pad of rags. He hurried up to Rakoczy, his cheeks ruddy from the heat of the kitchen and the buffing of the wind. His clothes were damp but not wholly wet.

"Here!" he exclaimed. "Venison broth, strained twice and boiled twice. The scullions were annoyed, but they did it."

"Very good," said Rakoczy. "If you'll set it down—oh, anywhere near the window." He pointed to the general area he meant. "I'll put you to work in a short while—if there is anything you would like to attend to in the meantime; the Little Hours, perhaps."

"No; I am at your service." Fratre Berahtram looked dismayed, then schooled his features to an expression of devotion. "I will do as you require, Magnatus."

Once again Rakoczy had the uneasy impression that he had glimpsed a monster within the handsome monk. He studied Fratre Berahtram for a long moment. "Very good. I will give you my instructions after Vespers or Compline, whichever you prefer."

The monk looked troubled. "Why delay?"

"Because you haven't dined, and this will be a long night. I will relieve you at Vigil—" he said, only to be interrupted.

"We keep Nocturnes here. The castle is protected by soldiers, and we monks need not patrol the grounds to ensure our safety. Here Nocturnes are sung half-way between sunset and midnight." He ducked his head to show his devotion to his Hours. "You might as well tell me now."

"Instead of Vigil at midnight," said Rakoczy. "So Bishop Wildefurt told me some days ago. I wondered—as you answer to Bishop Agobard—if this infirmary kept the same Hours as the monks on other duties. You must tend the wounded day and night."

"So we must," said Fratre Berahtram. "But Bishop Wildefurt has decided that all religious at Paderborn must follow the same Rule, clerks and servants, and Bishop Agobard is in accord with him."

Rakoczy wondered how such consensus had come about, but said only, "Then let us tend to the wounded. I will relieve you at midnight, so you will be able to rest before Matins. Dawn still comes early, and Matins comes still earlier." He indicated the herbs in the basket. "If you would, take the basil and pound it into a paste that I can use to dress the injuries that are in need of draining their putrescent humors." It was not quite as much as Rakoczy wanted to do, but he knew if he attempted more treatment than what the monks usually did, he would have to defend all his choices; it was most important that the soldiers be given his sovereign remedy, and he would delay other unusual regimens until the benefits of the remedy were apparent to all and he was considered trustworthy: these men could not endure such a wait.

Fratre Berahtram coughed discreetly. "They have already had basil to dress their wounds. What they have had should be sufficient."

"Perhaps they have had. But a newly made paste will lend more virtue than dried leaves can, and thereby increase their chance for a good recovery." He shrugged. "If you would rather, you may remain with the men and I will deal with the herbs."

"No, no," said Fratre Berahtram, slightly too quickly. "I believe it would be best for you to dispense your remedies yourself. I am unfamiliar with them, and I might not give adequate amounts, or too much." He reached for the basket. "I will prepare the herbs. What am I to do with the garlic?"

"Grind it well and combine it with this"—he took a small bottle from his sack—"and with marrow. Have the scullions get you a good measure of marrow—it strengthens the herbs."

Fratre Berahtram eyed the bottle suspiciously. "What is it?"

"Ground ginger preserved in olive oil. Use half the amount in the bottle, and make the mixture thick as porridge." He held up his hand. "Leave the coriander and the wine here."

Repeating these instructions to himself in a mutter, Fratre Berahtram made for the door, the basket clutched in his hands. "I will return after comestus, to give you what I have done."

"Very good," said Rakoczy, making this a dismissal.

Fratre Berahtram was almost to the door when he stopped to look at one of the most severely hurt—the man whose thigh wound had red lines running from it. "He is breathing more easily," he remarked in some surprise. "Your syrup of poppies has calmed him. That's something." With a nod to the Magnatus he made good his escape from the dormitory and the company of the wretched soldiers.

Rakoczy shook his head, knowing the man was near death. He went and laid his hand on the soldier's forehead, noticing that his fever had risen again. He patted the man's shoulder. "It will not last," he promised. "It will be over soon. You will not have to suffer much longer." He hoped that if the man heard him he might take some consolation from this pledge. Then he went back to mixing an unguent of willow-bark and wool-fat to dress the less grievous injuries of his patients. While he continued his preparations, he realized he would need more clean rags, and shortly, and wondered if he could persuade one of the monks at the other end of the dormitory to fetch them for him. Once again he missed Rorthger, who would have procured what he needed without causing speculation or distress. Pulling the last of his clean rags from his sack, he decided to make the best of what he had until Fratre Berahtram returned.

The soldier with the thigh wound died with the day. As the last glow of sunset faded, his breath shuddered and stopped. Rakoczy heard it, and knew the end had come. He looked up from his dressing of a mangled arm and hand and realized only one monk was in the dormitory, the others having gone for Vespers and comestus. With a slight sigh, Rakoczy went and pulled the blankets up and around the dead man, readying him for removal to the burial chapel. Then he went back to tending the ruined hand, thinking that if the soldier were not already too weak, the hand and lower arm should be amputated, for the injuries were too extreme to heal properly, and the chance for a worsening infection was very high.

When Fratre Berahtram returned, he had the herb paste in an earthenware bowl. He paused at the foot of the pallet where the dead man lay. "When?"

"At the end of sunset," said Rakoczy. "It was fast when it finally happened. He was snuffed out like a lamp, gone in a sigh, without agony or rage." He looked directly at Fratre Berahtram. "I doubt the man with the shattered shoulder will last through the night. I'll give him another dose of wine and syrup of poppies, to keep him tranquil."

It was all Fratre Berahtram could do not to gag. "If you don't think that you would be wasting them."

"No," said Rakoczy. "That's what it's for." He kept his conversation as casual as he could, wanting to mitigate his foreignness as much as possible.

"Then God will send you more if you need it," said Fratre Berahtram, "and if you are worthy."

"May it be so," said Rakoczy. "For the sake of these unfortunates, I pray it is." He studied Fratre Berahtram for a long moment, noticing how the lamplight played tricks with the monk's handsome visage. "I will dress the wounds and then leave the men in your care until midnight."

"I am expected to keep Nocturnes with the other Fratri," said Fratre Berahtram.

"I will arrange matters with Superior Liedrad," Rakoczy assured him. "I believe you will be given permission to observe Nocturnes here."

Fratre Berahtram strove to show proper humility; the thought of having to spend so much time with these men horrified him. "If there is no objection on the part of the Superior, then I will be satisfied."

"Very good," said Rakoczy, taking the earthenware bowl from Fratre Berahtram and setting to work making dressings. He worked quickly, the low light having little effect on him, for his night-seeing eyes were as keen as most men's at mid-day. As he strove to treat the men in his care, he glanced occasionally at Fratre Berahtram, trying to determine what the young monk was thinking: it was apparent that the Fratre was displeased with his duties, and it was equally apparent that he would never say so.

"I should observe Compline," Fratre Berahtram said suddenly. "It is a Little Hour, so I need not go to our chapel." He rose and went to the other end of the dormitory and knelt before the crucifix there, his arms raised in prayer, apparently shutting out all worldly considerations as he began his Psalms; two other monks joined him, leaving the men they tended to fend for themselves until Compline was over.

Rakoczy watched this with curiosity; he found it difficult to think of Fratre Berahtram as a religious man, for in spite of all he did, his eyes held secrets that had nothing to do with worship. Putting his attention to the wounded men entrusted to him, he continued to apply herbal dressings to those whose infections could respond, to make drawing poultices for those whose infections had gone deep into muscles, and to offer syrup of poppies in wine to the men riven with pain. By the time Fratre Berahtram ended his Hour, Rakoczy had all the patients ready for the night.

"What must I do?" Fratre Berahtram asked. "You have ministered to these soldiers most conscientiously." He indicated one of the men who was past saving, whose shoulder was an oozing mass of bone fragments and ruptured tissue. "What about him?"

"He's dying," said Rakoczy quietly. "When the monks come to remove the other dead man, he may well be ready to go to the chapel as well."

"They should arrive before Nocturnes," said Fratre Berahtram. "They make two visits a day for the dead—after Prime and before Nocturnes." He glanced at the other men. "Have there been any changes in them?"

"It's too soon to tell," said Rakoczy, his face revealing nothing but concern. "By morning I should be able to know more."

Fratre Berahtram folded his arms. "What am I to do, other than pray?"

"Give them water frequently; those who are truly awake are to receive the broth, and if they are hungry, give them the marrow—not much. It is in the large cup." Rakoczy pointed to the vessel.

"Very well. Anything else?" Fratre Berahtram glowered at the large cup.

"Not yet," said Rakoczy. "If there is anything that troubles you, have one of the mansionarii wake me. I will be in my chamber." He turned away, strangely uneasy about leaving his patients in this monk's care. He crossed the side yard, entered the castle through the garden door, and made his way to the narrow stairs leading up to the gallery along which rooms had been assigned by Karl-lo-Magne for his Court's use. He opened the door of his chamber and stepped inside, feeling the draw of the chest on the far side of the room containing his native earth; he did not require sleep, but he longed for the annealing presence his native earth provided. He used flint and steel to light the wick of an oil-lamp. As the little scrap of light flared in the gloom, Rakoczy took down one of his books—an ancient text in the Romanized Greek of Mediterranean merchants seven hundred years before, describing medicinal herbs—and began to read, searching for a formula to lower fever more effectively than willow bark and pansy. As he studied, he was vaguely aware that Nocturnes was being sung; in a while he would have to relieve Fratre Berahtram. He read more urgently until shortly before midnight, when he returned the book to its shelf and blew out the lamp before retracing his earlier steps to the infirmary, where Fratre Berahtram was waiting for him.

"Two more are dead. The bodies will be taken in the morning." He indicated the dead. "Lothar—the one with the shattered wrist?—he was hungry earlier." He pointed to the cup. "I fed him, as you ordered."

"Very good," said Rakoczy. "Go get some rest. The bell will sound for Matins far too soon."

Fratre Berahtram managed to make a sound like a muffled laugh, although there was no humor in it. "So it will. I will return after Prime." He turned around and hurried out of the infirmary.

Rakoczy waited until Fratre Berahtram was gone before he went to examine the corpses, finding that one of the dead men had been hurried out of this life, for the whites of his eyes were suffused with red, a condition that he had not observed earlier. Rakoczy took a long, slow breath. "He needn't have bothered; you couldn't have survived," he said as if in apology to the body. He stepped back, closing the Bellatore's eyes with care before going to tend to the living.

TEXT OF A LETTER FROM BISHOP ISO OF SANT' AUDOENUS TO BISHOP AGOBARD AT AACHEN, CARRIED BY CHURCH COURIERS.

To the most puissant, most Sublime Bishop Agobard, the greetings in Christ of Bishop Iso of Sant' Audoenus on this, the Feast of the Apostle Sant' Luchas, and a fortnight before the Feast of Toutti Santi, with the prayers that God has looked upon you with favor and given you peace and plenty in these great times. In your capacity as Bishop to Karl-lo-Magne, I seek your wisdom and assistance in coming to a most difficult conclusion, as well as your endorsement of what I must do in order to serve God and King aright.

Now that Great Karl and his Court have returned to Aachen for the winter, I make bold to approach you regarding certain matters that are needful of your immediate attention, for as great as my faith may be, I am convinced that there are considerations here that I have not sufficient wisdom to address without inspiration of the Holy Spirit, which, although I have prayed for such, has not yet come to me. So I seek to avail myself of the advice of my fellow-Sublimi, and I pray that you will not begrudge me your thoughts and prayers.

I have in my charge at Sant' Audoenus a most perplexing woman. She is not mad, but she is not free of contamination, or so it appears to me. She was entrusted to my care by Abba Sunifred of Santa Albegunda, who had received her from her parents and from Abba Serilda of Nerithe of Sant' Osmer. No one has yet determined the appropriate manner in which this woman is to be treated. I must inform you that her skin is pale as wax, her hair equally white, and that the pupils of her eyes are red as garnets. This is distressing enough, but there is more to the problem she presents, for her hands bleed as if from points being driven through them, which wounds have not been made by any mortal hand. I can affirm this because I have appointed my own attendant, Sorra Celinde, to watch over her, and to ascertain if this young woman is in some way doing herself injury in order to present the appearance of one who has been stricken by the Will of God, or the power of the Devil. According to what Sorra Celinde tells me, the young woman does nothing to promote these wounds.

This young woman is called Gynethe Mehaut, and I implore you to grant me leave to bring her to Aachen while the full Court is there, as well as the most learned Alcuin of York, who has left Sant' Martin at Tours to wait upon the King in Aachen. With such Sublimi as you and Alcuin, it must be that God will finally show His Will in all of this strangeness. I ask you to permit me the opportunity to submit her to your scrutiny and your judgment, for I have no guidance, either from prayer or dream, that can reveal to me all that I must know before I consign this young woman to a penitent's cell or cast her out upon the world as a creature devoid of Grace, or consign her to death as a messenger of Hell. Among you, and your brother-Sublimi, there must be some means of achieving a decision that will be pleasing in God's eyes. If you cannot decide, I can always bring her back to Sant' Audoenus, until such time as God shall reveal His intention to me, and I may do as He commands me.

If this is suitable to your purposes, send me word of it with the courier who brings this message. I want to be on the road before the dark of the year is full upon us, when travel becomes more arduous and the hazards are so many that no man may be prepared for them all. I have prepared a carpentum to carry the young woman, and I have demanded of the regional Potente an escort of five armed men, with horses and mules to bear them and their supplies. The oxen to draw the carpentum will come from Sant' Audoenus, and we will carry fodder for them along with foodstuffs for ourselves so that we will not be a burden to any Abbott or Abba who opens doors to us in our travels, or any hobu who extends hospitality to us.

May God guide you in your considerations, even as I ask Him to guide mine, and by Whose Hand I have been moved to ask this of you.

Amen

Bishop Iso of Sant' Audoenus,
Santisimus Salvator Mondi,
Santi Agnelli,
and Sant' Fokas

ᕭ

chapter ten

ECHOES RESOUNDED ALONG THE VAULT above the large Roman swimming pool, the shouts of Illustri, Optime, Potenti, and Bellatori creating the cacophony, augmented by the splashes of the swimmers; to join Karl-lo-Magne in his pool was a coveted honor, and most courtiers were eager to make the most of such an opportunity. Today the pool was more crowded than usual, and the men in it more rambunctious, stimulated by warmth and rivalry. Steam rose from the surface of the water, making the large room misty, and in spite of the huge fire in the broad fireplace, the air was chill, touched by the first, early snow that was falling on Aachen, beyond the thick stone walls of the swimming pool.

Karl-lo-Magne sloshed energetically as he swam the length of the pool, well ahead of his courtiers. It pleased him to send a fine spray with every stroke of his powerful arms. Reaching the end of the pool, he stood up, the water coming half-way up his chest, and laughed. "More! You men, try harder! Swim, damn your eyes! Swim!" Then he laughed again at the efforts the rest made. He leaned back against the marble sides of the pool and smiled, thoroughly enjoying himself.

His kinsman, Einhard, reached him slightly ahead of the rest and grabbed hold of the lip of the pool; he was much shorter than his cousin, and when he stood on his feet, his head was almost completely underwater. "You carry the day."

"Of course," said Karl-lo-Magne, not quite as smug as he would have been a decade ago, but still satisfied that he could best the others. "We've raced enough for now. I have duties I must attend to, as much as I prefer to spend the afternoon swimming." He glanced at the fire. "The bath will be warm for a while yet. If you would like to remain here, do so. I must be about my work." With a sigh, he pulled himself out of the pool and stood up, water streaming from his body; a slave hurried over with a linen drying sheet that had been kept warm near the fire. Wrapping himself in the cloth, Karl-lo-Magne sighed again. "A man my size needs two lengths of cloth to cover everything that should be covered. God save the weaver who gives short shrift in Franksland."

Einhard was bold enough to smile. "So there is an advantage to being smaller. I confess I hadn't thought it so until now."

Five other men were gathered at the end of the pool now, and another three were continuing to swim as if their race were not yet over. The steam in the room was getting a bit thicker as the water in the pool continued to get warmer. The slaves tending the fireplace poked carefully at the lower levels of burning logs that augmented the natural warmth of the water that flowed into the pool; one of them added a thick section of branch to the fire, and the other used a long iron staff to shove it down deep into the furnace.

"I will expect you all to attend on me at prandium," said Karl-lo-Magne as he rubbed himself dry. "There is goat and geese tonight, I am told." He thrust his drying sheet at his slave and received his camisa in its stead; the garment was made of fine wool, intended for winter wear. This he pulled over his head and tied at the neck, then reached for his clout and secured it around his loins before drawing on his leather femoralia. "That's better," he declared, and took his heavy woolen gonelle dyed a dark, dull-russet shade, pulled it on over his head, girdled it, then went to sit on the bench across from the fireplace to pull on his tibialia and then secure his brodequins over them. Fully dressed but for his small gold diadem, he got to his feet, and casting a last, reluctant look at his swimming pool, he turned away toward the corridor leading out of the bath complex and into the light, blowing snow. His damp hair clung to his head in a clammy embrace, chilling him as much as the warmth of the swimming pool had heated him. He ignored the slight discomfort, keeping up his brisk pace until he entered the main part of the castle, where he bellowed for his camerarius. "Roberht!"

The middle-aged man rushed up to Karl-lo-Magne, the diadem held reverently in his scarred hands. "Optime!" He reverenced the King.

Karl-lo-Magne clicked his tongue impatiently. "Yes, yes. Enough of this. I'll put that on when my hair's dry." He looked about him, noticing that there was a group of nine Burgundians standing near his reception room, their wide pleated britches identifying them as much as their outlandish accents. "What do they want?"

"I wish they would tell me. They say they have to speak to you, no one else. It is most grave, and they will give no more information than that." He handed the narrow band of gold with the three small, blunt crosses worked into its simple design to the King and was secretly distressed when Karl-lo-Magne slipped it negligently onto his arm.

"I'll hear them. Open the doors. And bring beer and bread for them. I will have spiced hot wine and pickled fruit. Where is the senescalus? The Burgundians will need a meal when they have finished. Use the room on the west side of the reception room. That will show them dignity, but I will not have to spend more time with them. Tell Bishop Iso and Bishop Agobard I will see them when I have finished with the Burgundians." He clapped once to send Roberht on his way, then took the side corridor to his private entrance to the reception room. As he approached his door, he signaled two of his Guards to accompany him. "Just spears. These are not dangerous men. Speak firmly and they will comply without force."

"As you say, Optime," said the Bellatore nearest him.

Pulling the door open by himself, Karl-lo-Magne went to his polished wood sedes where it stood two steps above the rest of the room and sat down, resting his arms on the broad, carved arms of the sedes. He coughed, spat, and nodded to his Bellatori. "Let them in. Keep them at least ten steps back from me: they are not my invited guests." He took his diadem and set it in place on his brow.

The taller of the two Bellatori went and opened the reception room door with a bang and had the satisfaction of seeing the Burgundians jump. "Attend and give all honor and heedfulness to Karlus Magnus, King of the Franks and all Franksland, Guardian of the Holy Catholic Church of Roma, who will hear you. Which of you shall speak?"

A man with a white beard and hunched shoulder said, "I will. I am Eutado, the Majore of our region."

"Majore, are you?" challenged the Bellatore.

"I am," said the old man firmly. "And have been since my old father died these twelve years gone; he was Majore after his father. I am also the carpenter." This line of inherited authority was impressive enough to demand the Bellatore's attention. "We have been true to Karl-lo-Magne as those who should be have not."

"That must be what you wish to say to the King," said the Bellatore. "Come and approach him, and when I tell you to halt, reverence him."

Eutado nodded to show his understanding. "If there were others, less exalted, we would have gone to them," he said as he kept up with the Bellatore, making his way across the floor in a painful limp toward the enormous man with the small golden diadem circling his head who sat on the huge formal sedes. When the Bellatore held out his spear to halt the Burgundians, Eutado led the others in reverencing the King.

"Very well," said Karl-lo-Magne. "Tell me what you seek from me."

Apparently the King's high, harsh voice took the Burgundians by surprise, for Eutado hesitated before beginning to speak. "We are from Sant' Yrieix, which has been in the fiscs of Ansegisus of Solignac." When he saw no sign of recognition in the King's blue eyes, he explained. "Sant' Yrieix is an isolated place, and we have been depending upon your missi dominici to carry word to and from our village to our Potente, which Ansegisus has ordered us to do." He paused, looking toward the man nearest him. "Ansegisus saw in a dream that he would die in Sant' Yrieix, and so will not come to our village."

Karl-lo-Magne nodded. "I have heard this." He gave an impatient gesture to indicate he wanted them not to dawdle over details. "You rely on my missi dominici."

"Yes. Fratre Cuvhild and Irmold of Chur have been the men to come to us in your name and the name of Ansegisus. They have said that they are conducting themselves in accordance with your Will, Optime." Eutado stood still while the others mumbled their agreement.

"Where is the difficulty?" Karl-lo-Magne demanded. "I see nothing distressing in what you describe. It is thus in many parts of Franksland. That is the purpose of the missi dominici."

"Yes," said Eutado, his voice dropping and becoming unsure. "But do you give them rights to order men killed and women taken for their pleasure, and wealth seized, for the purpose of paying taxes they say we owe you, Optime?" He managed a touch of defiance. "All this they do in your name, and because of that we come to you to say that we do not believe that your honor is vindicated by what they have done."

"Whom have they killed?" asked Karl-lo-Magne, making no effort to hide his doubts.

"They have killed my daughter's son Marbettou, for one," said Eutado, "and Riesina, the miller, and Dobando, the potter. They took Grasaneau, the joiner, away and we have not seen him again." His voice became thick with emotion. "I myself saw these things."

"Why were these men killed?" Karl-lo-Magne demanded.

"The missi dominici said it was your law they upheld," said Eutado.

Karl-lo-Magne's patience was wearing thin. "Which law was that?"

One of the other men—somewhat younger than Eutado, but still a man of mature years, with grizzled hair and beard—answered, his manner respectful but with an underlying dissatisfaction. "They said it was because we did not always speak Frankish or Latin. They took all the money these men had, and left their families with only their empty houses—no food, no firewood, no beds. How are their families to live? The men are killed or gone and the monastery will not take them for fear that the Bishop will punish the monks if they do. Some of the people in the town have given them what they can spare, but it is very little. We are in a harsh place and we still suffer from the famine of three years ago." He stopped abruptly.

"I have banned all tongues but Frankish and Latin," said Karl-lo-Magne, "but I did not mandate death as punishment, except when such use is an act of defiance, and therefore against my rule."

"This was no such case. It has been our intention to abide by your law, when we can. We have not had much instruction in Latin or Frankish, the monks at the monastery using our language as often as the rest of us," said Eutado. "They pray in Latin."

"Still, they should be more obedient to my laws. Yet you are not to blame for the monks' failure to teach you as they ought." He frowned at the Burgundians. "You say these killings were done with my authority, by my missi dominici?"

"That is true," said the younger man. "I saw all, and I will swear on God's Altar that this is what happened."

The King stared into the middle distance. "How were the men killed?"

"They were beheaded with Frankish axes," said Eutado. "In the market-square. Two on the same day, the other half a year earlier. Soldiers were sent by Ansegisus to do the killing, both times the same number. There were six of them, all mounted, armed and spurred."

"You," Karl-lo-Magne said, pointing to the younger man who had spoken. "Who are you?"

"I am Nonateo. I am the cow-herd. I own sixty-two head." He stood a bit straighter. "I am among the Elders of Sant' Yrieix, and I am a man of respect, which is why I have been doubly troubled by the disgrace that has been visited upon my family: my sister was taken by the missi dominici to warm their beds, though she said she had no wish to do so."

"What did she say when it was over?" Karl-lo-Magne asked, smiling slightly.

"I don't know. I wish I did, for my sake as well as hers. They took her with them and we haven't seen her again. Her name was Fellmeris, a pleasant girl with red hair and a winning smile, and she had hoped to be the woman of the master mason next year. The missi dominici were drawn to her, and they demanded she lie with them in spite of the master mason: he would not have her now, no matter what has become of her." Nonateo's color heightened, and he could not look at the King directly.

"You say there were other women taken," Karl-lo-Magne reminded them.

"Other than Fellmeris, there were sisters hardly women at all, though they were comely. Two of them, no older than twelve, and they, too, have not been seen since the missi dominici summoned them to their beds. They were called in the night and by dawn, the missi dominici and the sisters were gone." Nonateo went pale as he spoke. "And there was a woman who had often served the men who gathered at the brewer's house. No one begrudged the missi dominici her use, for that was her worth."

"You have seen nothing of these women? Have none of them sent word to you? Has no one seen any of them?" From the way the King asked he was far from troubled by the information.

"No. We have learned nothing," said Eutado. He looked to the men with him for their concurrence and was rewarded by their immediate nods.

Karl-lo-Magne took a long breath while he thought. "And you came all this way to make this report because you supposed I would punish my men?"

"We want justice for our kinsmen and our women," said Eutado. "We know Ansegisus will do nothing, for he will not come to our village, and the Bishop will not hear us, for he leaves all to the Patre. Besides, the missi dominici are your men, and their acts account to you."

"They are my eyes and ears and good right arm; they are my voice to my people, and my promise to all of them of my regard," Karl-lo-Magne agreed.

"They bring disgrace to your name, and they dishonor the Bishop, who also is Bishop in Solignac and is rarely in our village," said Eutado.

"He has three bishoprics," said Karl-lo-Magne. "The third is Sant' Leonhard of Noblac near Nevers. It is a most important monastery in its region." He pulled slowly at his beard. "It is no great crime for a man to use a woman."

"But it is a crime to sell them to brothels," Eutado said, daring to speak.

Karl-lo-Magne fixed the old man with a stare. "Do you know this is what they did? How do you know? What report did you receive?"

"Patre Drasius, who serves our village and three others, said he was told that one of the women had gone to a brothel in Arles," said Nonateo. "He could not accompany us to speak to you: he has many other duties and his wife is about to give him another child."

"You have a monastery and a priest?" Karl-lo-Magne exclaimed. "How does this happen?"

"Bishop Ambrosius does not often come to Sant' Yrieix. He prefers Solignac and so appointed a priest for us and Sant' Ianuarius the village and the nunnery, Cometou Gudi, Lacosasse, and the hermitage of Sant' Damasus." Eutado folded his arms and avoided the King's gaze.

Karl-lo-Magne cocked his head. "This is not satisfactory. The Pope cannot have approved it."

"I am told the Archbishop at Arles permitted it," said Nonateo. "Fratre Cuvhild said something of it the last time he and Irmold were in Sant' Yrieix, or so the brewer informed me. The missi dominici stay at his house when they are in our village."

"Is the brewer with you?" Karl-lo-Magne asked, his tone higher and sharper than before.

"No. He is serving as Majore in my absence," said Eutado.

"It could be that more than my missi dominici have been lax," the King said as he considered the problem. "I may have to appoint a more diligent Bishop."

"I ask you to do that," said Eutado at once, holding up clasped hands in the gesture of petition.

"I will look into it," said Karl-lo-Magne. "You, in the meantime, will go to the room just beyond this and you will dine at my table, on food from my kitchens. You will have beer from my barrels and my own mansionarii and slaves will wait upon you." He rose. "I will send for you in the morning. Do not go far from the main gate."

"No, Optime," said Eutado for them all.

Karl-lo-Magne signaled to his two Guards. "Escort them to their comestus and be sure all their wants are satisfied."

The Guards gave their Frankish salute and moved to the Burgundians, indicating with a motion of their spears that the men from Sant' Yrieix were to proceed to the dining chamber.

"This is a troubling report, if it is true," Karl-lo-Magne said to Bishop Agobard, who waited just outside the King's private door to the reception room. "They have complaint against my missi dominici and Bishop Ambrosius as well." He then summarized what the Burgundians had told him.

"A bad business, if it is true," said Bishop Agobard, his attention on Karl-lo-Magne.

"So I think. My missi have many privileges, but it is not fitting that they should exceed their authority, for it smirches me and mine if they do. I do not like to think that they would carry out executions without confirming them with me." He was strolling down the corridor, keeping his pace slow so that the Bishop would not have to rush. "What do you think? Should I summon Archbishop Heuges from Arles to tell me why he made such an arrangement with Bishop Ambrosius?"

"If he knew anything of this. It is an easy thing to say that the Archbishop has agreed when he may know nothing of it." Bishop Agobard shrugged. "On the other hand, he may have done so for excellent reason. It might be better to summon Bishop Ambrosius and Potente Ansegisus to discover what they have done. I will decide what is best before comestus tomorrow."

"And while you are considering summons, do not forget Irmold of Chur and Fratre Cuvhild—I have not. It is not fitting for men of my household to act against my wishes, if, indeed, they have done. I will not condemn them out of hand. They must have some explanation for their actions. They should present them to my face." Karl-lo-Magne paused at the head of a flight of stairs leading up toward the cubicula where most of the Court not closely related to the King were housed. "In the meantime, I want you to consider which man might serve Sant' Yrieix better than Bishop Ambrosius has done. I will take your recommendation as soon as you decide upon a candidate. I do not want to leave the Burgundians in disorder."

"You will take the bishopric from Ambrosius?" Bishop Agobard cried, appalled at such a notion.

"Not all of his bishoprics, just the one he is not willing to administer," said Karl-lo-Magne. "Your conclave may review my decision, as soon as all the Bishops arrive. This early snow will not bring them any faster." He held up his hand. "The men from Sant' Yrieix deserve our attention, for whatever else may have troubled the people of the village, if the Bishop has appointed a priest for the village and four others, he is not doing his duty. Another man will be willing to serve the Church—and me—in that place." He wanted no argument and held up his hand to forestall one.

"What about your sons? Couldn't one of them be sent there as your deputy, to—" Bishop Agobard got no farther.

"I have had one son rebel already. I will not provide incentive for another to do so." Karl-lo-Magne shot a hard look at the Bishop. "If my missi dominici have failed me, that is for me to redress, not one of those ungrateful whelps of mine." He stalked off up the stairs, his mind on the Burgundians and their disturbing accounts; he wanted to put his mind on other matters, and decided where he could manage that. He found Magnatus Rakoczy alone in his cubiculum, busy reading a leather-bound tome by the low light of an oil-lamp.

At the sound of his door opening, Rakoczy rose. "Optime. You should have sent for me."

"And been waylaid by courtiers at every step?" Karl-lo-Magne said bluntly. "No, I would prefer not. This suits me very well."

"As you choose," said Rakoczy, and indicated the single chair. "If you would like?"

"Walk with me. There are not many in the gallery just now. We will not be disturbed." As genially as he said this, it was an order, and Rakoczy complied at once, setting his book aside and pinching out his oil-lamp.

"I am at your disposal, Optime." He pulled his door closed behind him as they stepped out into the gallery.

Karl-lo-Magne walked a short distance in silence. "You did not join us swimming," he said finally.

"Alas, no. I swim very poorly," said Rakoczy with simple honesty. "You would not enjoy my company if I should get into your pool." Had it been lined with his native earth he would have been wholly comfortable, but that was impossible at Aachen.

"Still," said Karl-lo-Magne. "If you made an effort, you would improve, and that would please me."

Rakoczy considered his answer carefully. "Optime, I have a dread of drowning, as intense as any living man's fear of death. The thought of dying in the water is unbearable to me." This was less than the truth, for he could not drown, though he could lie immobilized by water and continue in his un-dead state until creatures of the water devoured him; the speculation alone made him queasy— what the reality would do was too horrendous to contemplate.

Seeing his expression, Karl-lo-Magne said, "I see you do. Well." He clapped his hands together. "I shall not subject you to such terrors, then. Have you dreamed of drowning, or have you come close to drowning in your youth?"

"I would say drowning is more of a nightmare to me," said Rakoczy, knowing it was as reasonable an explanation as any.

"I understand you, and I know what it is to have such dread that it sickens. After my second marriage, I had just such a horror of closed rooms; it lasted for more than a year, and only the holy seals I wore alleviated it. So. I will not ask you swimming again," said Karl-lo-Magne. He continued to walk, his head lowered in thought, clearly preoccupied; Rakoczy kept half-a-step behind him, content to wait until the King spoke. They went the length of the gallery together; at the end of the gallery, Karl-lo-Magne turned and went back the way he had come. "I am told, Magnatus," he said suddenly, "that you have particularly strong iron in your weapons and horseshoes."

"I use a method I learned in Damascus," said Rakoczy.

"From the impious followers of the False Prophet," said Karl-lo-Magne, affronted. "Who among them would teach a foreigner like you?"

"I learned from master metal-workers, whose blades are truer than any I have found in other places," Rakoczy replied candidly.

The King considered this answer, his back stiff and his shoulders rigid. "How could you go among such Godless men?"

"I wished to learn from them—not their religion, their methods with metal," said Rakoczy, and again waited while Karl-lo-Magne thought this over.

"Why would you do that?" he demanded of the black-clad foreigner.

Rakoczy was ready with an answer. "Do you know, Optime, I thought that if I might have to face the Prophet's men in battle, I should have swords and spears to equal theirs. I see no reason to give them an advantage because their faith is not mine." He did not add that he was no more a follower of Christ than he was of Mohammed.

This seemed to satisfy Karl-lo-Magne, for he gave a single snort of laughter and declared, "I like you, Magnatus. You're no fool. You do not let yourself stray from the purpose." He walked more quickly to the end of the gallery, then turned and went back the other way.

"And what is that purpose, Optime?" Rakoczy asked, keeping up with the much taller man without effort.

"I have a few items that would be improved by superior iron." He looked over his shoulder as if he expected to be overheard.

"And what might these items be?" Rakoczy asked. "I cannot produce Damascus steel in large quantities, nor can I make it without special equipment. I have some ingots of the metal with me, but I cannot produce more than three swords or four sets of horseshoes with them. You are welcome to them, of course. It will honor me to use them in your service." He gave the King an opportunity to speak; when he did not, Rakoczy went on, "I have begun making a proper hearth at the villa you granted me, and I can produce more ingots there, if I can secure iron and a few other components."

"I have one thing I want, as a kind of trial. I will show you what is required and you will execute a pair in your iron." This was not open to question, or to any negotiation.

"What is it you seek?" Rakoczy asked, hoping he had enough metal to fulfill the commission.

"Ice skates," said Karl-lo-Magne, grinning at Rakoczy's startled expression. "So that my couriers may use the frozen rivers to carry messages. It is much faster than trying to get over the roads in heavy snow. But in the cold, the skates often snap, and my smiths tell me that a stronger iron is needed. As you have such iron, I order you to make ice skates for my couriers." He grinned, anticipating success already.

Rakoczy was surprised, although he grasped at once the usefulness of ice skates for couriers in winter, when frozen rivers were far more reliable than snow-clogged roads. "If you will procure me a pair of the skates you have used before, I will strive to produce what you ask." He showed more caution than the King did, aware that he might not be able to do what Karl-lo-Magne wanted; it was never wise to disappoint such a man as the King of the Franks.

"I shall give you until the day after Holy Sabbath," said Karl-lo-Magne. "You may use any smithy that suits your purpose, so long as it is here at Aachen. If you do well, then, in spring, you may return to your villa until I have need of you again."

"As you wish, Optime," said Rakoczy, and dared to make one request. "But I ask that I be allowed to keep to myself in my labors: I would rather work alone, and not only to preserve my methods, which require great concentration—I do not want to have a dozen smiths gathered about me, or slaves attendant upon me, who may or may not understand what I do and why, and may interfere with the accomplishment of the task. You know how demanding work with hot metal can be." He paused, letting the King assess the problems he faced. "If you are pleased with the result of my efforts, I will teach two of your master smiths how to do the work. If what I do does not please you, then you will not have to turn your own smiths away from what they have seen."

Karl-lo-Magne nodded slowly. "It is a prudent thing. I will do as you suggest." He laid his big hand on Rakoczy's shoulder. "I am right to like you, Magnatus, foreign though you are." He chuckled. "You're a canny one, and also uncanny."

"I will regard your comments as high praise, Optime," said Rakoczy, keeping a wary eye on Karl-lo-Magne, for he could not anticipate his response.

"It is good of you to do so," said the King, unaware of any ironic note in Rakoczy's voice. "I depend upon you to do your utmost for me."

"I will certainly try," said Rakoczy. "God alone will decide if I am to succeed." He reverenced the King.

"That is so, but I know God favors my efforts, and so He must give you the strength you need, and the will, to fulfill my order. I have no doubt that you will do as I ask you." Behind his genial demeanor, Karl-lo-Magne was utterly deter-mined, and both he and Rakoczy knew it; the two men looked steadily at each other. "I will extend every assistance you require, but I must tell you that I do not look kindly on those who disappoint me in such important matters."

"I understand that, Optime," said Rakoczy. "I will do all I am capable of doing to bring your desires to fruition."

Again Karl-lo-Magne laughed, this time a bit more forcedly than before. "Good, good," he approved. "I will send word to the smithy that you will com-mence tomorrow—"

Rakoczy interrupted him. "Optime, if you do not object, I would prefer to work at night. Not only will it lessen the chance of being observed, it will allow me to work alone without giving rise to the speculation neither of us would like." He saw that this notion sat well with the King, and so only added, "I am often awake long into the night. Those of my blood have great affinity with the night."

"I cannot order you to do this," said Karl-lo-Magne as he thought over what Rakoczy proposed, "but I will make the smithy available to you through the night."

"Thank you, Optime," said Rakoczy.

"You may thank me when your task is complete," said Karl-lo-Magne. He looked away from Rakoczy toward the small, distant windows. "If you can have the ice skates ready by the time the Bishops all gather here, I will reward you doubly, for I must be prepared to send couriers to all missi dominici on the deci-sions of the Bishops."

"In winter," Rakoczy observed.

"Just so; I do not wish to have to wait until spring; the roads are too muddy for speed until the planting is almost complete," said Karl-lo-Magne. "The Bishops will be here for fourteen nights, and their retinues must be housed here, servants, slaves, horses, mules, and oxen. The kitchens will be strained to burst-ing, and the haylofts will be depleted. I have ordered my provisioners to collect oats and hay from a day's ride around Aachen. I have already commandeered all the eggs laid in all of Aachen. We will have to hunt every other day to keep the larder stocked for so great a company."

Rakoczy looked at the cubicula along the gallery. "You will have to put two or three in each chamber, I fear."

Karl-lo-Magne nodded. "To say nothing of slaves and camerarii." He paused to bless himself. "Not that I hold anything against the Church and her sons. The Church has supported me as I have stood by her, and it is entirely fitting that the Bishops should meet under my roof. I own myself fortunate to be able to serve the Church in these turbulent times."

"And, of course, you do not despise the Church's gratitude," said Rakoczy lightly, and noticed the corners of Karl-lo-Magne's mouth turn down. "For as devout a follower as you are, you are also a King with all of Franksland to consider."

The tightness went out of Karl-lo-Magne's expression. "Yes. You have the sense of it, Magnatus." He coughed and changed the subject abruptly. "So you will begin in the smithy tonight."

"If it is satisfactory to you," said Rakoczy.

"Most satisfactory." He looked down at the man in the black woolen gonelle. "What will you need?"

"A forge, properly heated; an anvil; two good hammers to work the metal; farrier's nippers; and the iron ice skates that have failed." He ticked off the items on his extended fingers.

"I will so inform Utto. He is master of the smithy, a most practiced craftsman." He scrutinized Rakoczy for a long moment, then turned away. "Present yourself at the smithy at the beginning of Compline, Magnatus. The forge will be ready, and the ice skates will be waiting for you. I will want to have your first report as soon as I have broken my fast in the morning." He had already begun to descend the stairs when he looked back over his shoulder. "I will have one of my slaves carry word to Odile that she will be alone tonight. It will save you having to deal with her discontent."

"Optime is gracious," said Rakoczy, who had not planned to visit Odile that night.

"I know how jealous women can be," said Karl-lo-Magne, a reckless lift to one heavy eyebrow. "You do not need to waste an hour placating a petulant mistress."

"As you say," Rakoczy agreed, watching the King as he continued on down the stairs. Then he went back to his cubiculum to gather the materials he would need and to change his clothes for the sooty night ahead. He set aside his gonelle and camisa and pulled on a sleeveless, old-fashioned tunica; he took a leather apron from his clothes-chest, and draped it over his arm; he would don it later, in the smithy.

There was roistering in the main hall when Rakoczy made his way from his cubiculum to the courtyard and from there to the smithy behind the stables. There he found Utto, who regarded the foreigner with open skepticism.

"Karl-lo-Magne has asked me—" Rakoczy began.

"I know what the King wants," said Utto, his accent indicating he came from the northwest part of Karl-lo-Magne's empire. He regarded Rakoczy as if the foreigner were a minion of Hell, but he went on trying to do as the King required.

"The skate is there, on the cooling table. I have set out nippers, as you asked, and I've provided two hammers and a mallet." He pointed to the supplies as he described them, as if Rakoczy might not recognize them otherwise.

"You have been very good to me, and I thank you for complying so fully with what the King has ordered," said Rakoczy, trying to calm the smith, who was striving mightily to conceal his dudgeon. "Many another man would have found an excuse not to comply."

"Karl-lo-Magne is the King of the Franks, and I am faithful to him," Utto protested, his indignation increasing. "You cannot compromise me, much as you try."

Rakoczy knew there was no point in protesting that Utto had misunderstood him, for that would only make the smith more recalcitrant. Instead he went to inspect the forge, showing his approval. "This is excellent. As good as any I have seen."

In spite of himself, Utto warmed to this praise. "Truly?"

Answering obliquely, Rakoczy was spared the burden of mendacity. "The stones are well-placed and the draw for the fire is all any man could wish. I know it holds heat and that the heat is steady, which is necessary to what I am to do for Karl-lo-Magnus." He opened his wallet that hung from his girdle and took out the first of two ingots. "I am going to heat this so that I may work with it. I see your tongs have long handles." He also saw that they were metal and would likely burn his hands unless he donned gloves. "They are well-made."

"So I think," said Utto, begrudging even this little civility to a foreigner.

"I will use them with care, good smith," Rakoczy assured him.

"You had better. I want no damage to come to them." He directed a frown at Rakoczy. "How does it happen that a hobu knows how to use a forge?"

"In my homeland I had to lead men in battle; I discovered that smithing was necessary to victory, and so I determined to learn the skill." This was accurate as far as it went; he did not add that he had acquired the trade almost a thousand years after his family had been defeated and he himself was far away from his native mountains. He began to work the bellows, heating the forge still hotter.

The smith laughed once, harshly, and flung up his hands. "What is that?" He pointed to a small ceramic vessel that Rakoczy had set beside the ingots.

"A crucible for the iron. It helps increase the heat." Rakoczy was becoming preoccupied with his work, and when he spoke he sounded distant. "It will help keep your tools from damage."

Utto thought this over for a long moment, then said, "Very well. I'll leave you to it. See you do the forge no harm."

Rakoczy gestured his compliance as Utto reluctantly turned and left. The

Magnatus went on working the bellows until the smithy was as hot as the Holy Land at midsummer; but strain as he did at the stifling forge, no sweat shone on any part of his body, or darkened the clothes he wore, as he labored through the night.

TEXT OF A LETTER FROM NOVICE FRATRE LOTHAR AT SANT' ZENO THE AFRICAN TO FRATRE BERAHTRAM AT PADERBORN, CARRIED BY TERTIARY BROTHERS OF THE MONASTERY.

Amen, and the Peace of God upon you, good Fratre Berahtram, for your many charities and good care that spared my life for God's work.

I have entered my novitiate here near Langres at the monastery of Sant' Zeno the African. Bishop Lemhaerht is master here, and of Sant' Agabus the Prophet. He is a man of great zeal, wholly dedicated to the Word and to the preservation of the faith. It is said that before he entered the Church he fought against the Saracens and the Basques for Great Karlus, and was accounted a hero. With such great deeds to recommend him, I am determined to model myself upon him. Not that I anticipate achieving his position—it is far from my intention to do so—but I am eager to devote myself to God as he has done, and to hope to rise in virtue for it. It is frightening to face so enormous a task as the one that lies before me now, and I ask for your prayers to help keep me steadfast in my purpose.

You need have no such fears as I, for you have done more to advance the cause of God than many I have ever encountered. Your unstinting care of me has earned my gratitude until my death, and a place in my prayers from now until the dead are summoned to Judgment. I am certain that your reward at that glorious time will be great indeed, as God is just and repays each man according to his worth. In this regard, you will wear a crown as bright as any martyr's.

My hand is still crabbed, and so this is being written by Fratre Estinnius, who is the senior scribe at Sant' Zeno. He has been willing to do this for me in return for me serving as his guide about the corridors and rooms, for although he sees well enough close at hand, he cannot distinguish features or objects that are more than a pace away. In this partnership of adversities we have come to be truly friends, and I am grateful to him for all he has done to aid me as I accustom myself to this life.

How well you serve me as an example in that endeavor. I have struggled to keep myself patiently, to be obedient to the Rule, and to observe the Hours of the Canon in a manner worthy of such a monk as you are. I have been given no task more important than tending beehives, which is not the same as saving lives, but I strive to do it as if it were as significant as the work you have done, particularly when you brought me back from the brink of death.

My Abbott insists that I tell you that when I first began to improve, I wanted to curse you, and that foreigner who assisted you, for saving me. I could not think of myself as anything but a soldier, and a soldier whose right hand is shattered is useful to no one. But you showed me by your fine example, that a man might retire from the world and not be a coward for doing it, and that a vocation could be won as well as given. I thank you for all you have done, first to preserve my body, and then to preserve my soul. Few men in Orders have been able to demonstrate the meaning of service as you have done for me. It may be wrong to set my sights beyond the gift of vocation, but if ever God should grant that to me, then I pray He also makes it possible for me to extend my expression to succoring the hurt and ill, so that I may also provide an example for others as you did for me.

In humility and gratitude, on the Pope's Good Friday, in his year 798, my supplication to God to bless you for all you have done for me,

Fratre Lothar
by the hand of Fratre Estinnius

∼

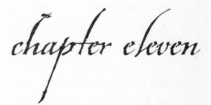

chapter eleven

ODILE STRETCHED OUT HER ARM in languorous invitation; she lay on a low bed piled with furs and rough-woven blankets, her stolla open at the throat, her dark hair, unbraided, fanned out around her; she had anointed her body with oil of lavender-and-rosemary, and the scent was like a nimbus around her. "I've missed you, Magnatus; I've missed what you do to me," she said softly as Rakoczy approached her. Although a fire burned in the hearth, the room was chilly; truant drafts skittered about the room.

"And I you. It has been ten days," he said, his voice low and musical. He came nearer still, so that he stood over her, a faint smile on his attractive, irregular features.

"I didn't think you'd keep track, being gone so long from my bed and still here at Aachen," she said, her manner flirtatious and petulant at once. "Men usually don't bother with such things."

"But you did," said Rakoczy, making this observation a caress.

"It is right that I should, being your mistress; the King expects it of me," she told him as if he were unaware of a basic truth. "I was afraid you were bored with me."

"No, Odile; not bored," he said as he sank down beside her, one knee tucked under him, the other straight so he could rest his foot on the floor.

"You're ready to fly," she said, noticing his posture. "And you say you aren't bored."

"Hardly that. Rather I hope to keep from falling off, amid all this fur," he said, amusement lending light to his dark eyes.

"Oh, don't," she protested playfully. "How could that possibly happen?"

"Do you tell me you have never slid on fur?" Rakoczy inquired as he fingered a tendril of dark hair that lay against her cheek.

"No," she said, "not off the bed, in any case."

"Well," said Rakoczy, "it is possible." He had a quick, sad recollection of Nicoris and the night they had spent in the Hunnish tent in the snow.

"I suppose I must believe you," said Odile, letting her hand fall against his neck, using all her art to engage him. "You have been gone too long, Magnatus. I have yearned for you."

Rakoczy opened the neck of her stolla more widely and bent to kiss her throat. "As I have for you," he whispered, and felt a pang of regret, for as much as he had awakened her body, he had never reached her heart, or her soul, and that left him with a quiet desolation of spirit that he was determined to conceal from her.

With a deep sigh, Odile took hold of his hair, pulling him closer to her, murmuring, "Then why did you wait so long? We are no longer free to do all that we might wish. It is the Lenten season, and the Bishops forbid sexual union between husband and wife." She was amorous and fretful by turns, and just at present her vexation was stronger than her desire.

"That means nothing to you and me," said Rakoczy, touching the slight cleft in her chin. "We are not married, and we do not practice what they forbid. We are always within the limits of their limitations, be it Lent or any other penitential feast." He pushed back from her a little. "The Bishops themselves are lax in obeying their own strictures. Let us follow their example, for how can they be wrong?"

"So I think, too," said Odile, giggling but unwilling to relinquish her grip on him. "Optime does not stint in his dalliances for Lent."

"And were this Passion Sunday, still, you and I have never done anything that violates their ban," Rakoczy reminded her.

"For your goodness, no, you haven't," she said, a bit wistfully.

"For my nature, you mean," he said, and touched her mouth with his, lightly but with the promise of passion to come.

It was some little time before she could speak again, her whole attention on the feel and texture of his lips, and when she did, she was a bit breathless. "Your nature. Yes. You told me about your nature."

"You knew from the first that I would not be as other men have been to you," he said gently. "Nothing has changed, for any reason. Not Lent, not the orders of Karl-lo-Magne, nor the hosts of Heaven can change what I have with you. Nor can anything change what I am. Since I came to be what I am, there has been no hope of returning to what I was."

She managed to smile. "Do you think I would mind? If you wanted me as other men would."

"I think you would have much more to lose if I were as other men are," he said kindly but with a direct, pragmatic note in his tone. "Your husband's brothers have said you would be cast out and compelled to enter a nunnery if you became pregnant by any man but your husband, and you have said you will abide by all they demand of you. The King allowed you to undertake this liaison for his own purposes, and your husband's family has acquiesced in it, but they will not accept a child, so it would be an unkindness to give you one, even if I could," he said, reminding her of what she had told him from their first evening together.

"And my husband is dead, and most of my children, so I have little solace in this world but what you and the King begrudge me, the King most of all," said Odile, her mien an unreadable mask. "You swore that you could not impregnate me, but men have said this many times to women, and still they bear children, either as a miracle of God's Grace, or a sign of men's lies. You, though—I never thought it would be . . ." Her words trailed off, and she began again in a more rallying voice. "I don't care, Magnatus. It may be that this is for the best. I am pleased to have you with me, and I will be glad of what you offer me. Who knows what may become of us? Life is short and uncertain, as my husband and children learned."

Genuinely puzzled, Rakoczy looked deeply into her ice-blue eyes. "If you know having another child is so dangerous for you, why do you want to take the risk?"

"I want something that is my own. My son isn't mine anymore, and my husband's relations will permit me no consolation, no matter what I may promise, and only seek to use me to increase their position at the King's Court." She stared deep into his eyes. "Though they take it from me, I wish I had a child."

"Because you are lonely," said Rakoczy, comprehending at last.

She nodded. "I want something all my own," she repeated, her face setting into stubborn lines. "I will give the baby to the Church, if I must, but I want to bear a child, just one more time. Can you understand?"

He could feel her yearning as he felt the heat from the fireplace; he hoped to comfort her. "Yes, I can understand loneliness. Still, how can you want to risk having a child by me, or any man? You tell me you would be sent into Holy Orders and any child you birth would become a foundling. How could you seek that for yourself or your infant?" Rakoczy found her emotions difficult to sort out and strove to clarify her intentions. "Unless you have a calling to such a life, I cannot believe it would be honorable of me to put you in such a position where that would be imposed upon you." He had a sharp, unhappy recollection of Csimenae and Aulutis and reminded himself that for some women, the protection of children excused any excess.

"It would not be," said Odile. "I have had a dream that shows me that I could go to my cousin, who would take me into his household. It would not be an easy way to live, but I could keep my child for as long as God let me have him." She tried to smile again and very nearly succeeded. "So, if you want more of me than you have had thus far, I will not deny you."

Rakoczy cupped her face in his hands. "I am more grateful to you than I can say, but I cannot do more than I already have. And after tonight, it may be too much." He knew he would have to describe her peril from him, and doubted she would be much inclined to listen, not with such longing in her.

She laughed, a wariness making the sound edgier than she had intended. "How can what you have done be too much? You have given me pleasure and taken none for yourself."

"Ah, there, Odile, you are wrong," said Rakoczy with a knowing look in his eyes. "Every pleasure you have had, I have shared. Your satisfaction has been mine, and I am more grateful than I can tell you that you have allowed me to know this with you." He bent and kissed her, savoring her lips, continuing a little ruefully when he could speak again. "But what we have done has a danger all its own, and you are not safe from it. I don't wish to bring you any harm, if I can prevent it—"

"What harm could you do me?" she asked, becoming coquettish again. "You have awakened me to more pleasure than I have ever known before."

"That pleasure is part of the danger," he said, kissing the corners of her mouth.

"Do you impregnate with kisses? It is said that some men are potent enough to do it." Her face was eager, and she gave him her full attention. "Is that what you have done with me?"

"No, Odile. No man is that potent, no matter what tales you hear," said Rakoczy.

"Fastrada's servant Angilberhta said that she was got with child by a kiss, and surely she delivered a girl," said Odile, her shoulders growing tense with indignation. "You say it cannot be possible, but you have not seen everything. Angilberhta—"

Rakoczy knew better than to continue the debate. "If there are such men, *I* am not one of them."

Odile sighed. "And you will not do the act to give me a child?"

"No, Odile, I will not, because I cannot." His voice was low and steady, without chagrin, for he had long ago become accustomed to his nature. "None of my blood can."

She laughed. "But they must. Or your line would die out."

It was tempting to say that that was precisely what had happened, but he held his tongue; anything he said to Odile would be reported to Karl-lo-Magne and Bishop Agobard. "Well," he admitted, "our numbers are few, and we are scattered about the world like so much chaff."

"Then give me a child and there will be more," said Odile enthusiastically. "You need not fear for his safety, Magnatus. My cousin will protect us from all mishap."

"You have his assurance," Rakoczy said, his irony completely lost on Odile.

"Yes, of course. My dream made that very clear. He will provide us with everything we need if you cannot do so." She laughed. "Tell me you will consider it, for my sake. I am getting old, and who can say how many days each of us has appointed to our lives? If I had another child, I would feel less as if I am cut adrift in the world. You would give me a great gift, Magnatus."

"Then I am doubly sorry I am unable to accommodate you, but what you ask is beyond my capabilities to provide," said Rakoczy as gently as he could. "I take great delight in you, Odile. I am beholden to you for your kindness to me. But I regret that I cannot furnish you with a child." He kissed her forehead. "If this is too hard for you, then send me away."

She grabbed his sleeves, bunching the cloth in her fists. "No. No."

He made no move to break her hold on him, saying only, "If you want me to stay, I will be graced by you again."

"Do not go," she said, and strained upward to kiss him. "I want you here, with me."

He returned her kiss, but with more tenderness than need. When they drew apart, she was calmer, but the destitution in her eyes was troubling. He would have suggested she ask the King for another approved lover, but he was keenly aware that she would interpret this as a rejection of her and her longing for a child, and so he said only, "Then I will remain."

Odile laughed a little. "You try to frighten me, Magnatus, saying you will leave me." The admonishing finger she held up was shaking a bit. "Not even my husband did that, for all his mistresses."

"I have no desire to frighten you," he said, kissing her brow and then her eyelids, his lips light as down on her skin. "But I would rather do that than bring you into danger for any reason."

"Do you think you would? You are a stranger at this Court." She licked his face along his jaw. "You tread more carefully than a Moor in a monastery."

"It is a prudent thing to do," said Rakoczy, and lay down next to her. "You may laugh at such cautions: you can afford to. But I cannot."

"You tell me so many things you cannot do," she chided him fondly. "I must be content with what you can do." Twisting so that she faced him on the bed, she kissed him urgently. "I am waiting for you, Magnatus," she whispered, and pulled another of the lacings loose from the front of her stolla, exposing her breasts.

Rakoczy touched her almost reverently, his hands revealing how much he treasured what she offered him. "How soft your skin is," he marveled as he fondled the ample curve of flesh. He bent and touched her nipple with his tongue, slowly and lightly; Odile shivered luxuriously and opened another lacing of her garment.

"This is what I want from you," she whispered, her voice low and promising. "You find excitation in me that no one else has ever found, certainly not my late husband. I will have this from you, at least." Her fingers locked in his hair again. "Do not end too soon, Magnatus."

"I have no reason to hurry you," said Rakoczy, his hands beginning to evoke more and more passionate responses from her.

"How is it you know where to find such pleasure?" She tugged on his hair, almost too sharply. "Have you been among the voluptuous Arabs? Or the luxurious Byzantines? Or have you been to distant lands and learned secrets no man in Franksland knows?"

Rakoczy thought of the Emir's son and struggled not to scoff. "I know something of the Arabs, yes, but not this. This I learned in other ways," Rakoczy murmured to her slightly rounded belly, a token of the children she had borne.

"However it was, I am grateful." She inhaled sharply, and her back arched in response to what he was doing. "Oh, yes. That's right."

He continued his exploration of her body, sliding his hands between her legs just as she unlaced all the front of her stolla. There was no question of her arousal now; he stroked her inner thighs, easing her need to allow for a more intense experience of her appetite. "Be happy in all we do, Odile," he said softly, lowering his head to the soft tuft of hair.

She whimpered with gathering fervency, pushing him down onto her, her hands tight with anticipation. "Do it, do it, do it," she insisted.

Rakoczy tantalized her with his fingers and mouth, bringing her to the verge of fulfillment three times before he moved up her body and with an adroit movement of his fingers, brought her to a culmination of the frenzy that had been building within her. His lips on her neck were as evocative as his fingers, and it seemed to Odile that her pleasure fused into a whole delicious welling that suspended everything but the savor of her flesh.

Gradually, reluctantly, she came back to herself as the deep spasms faded; her face was softened by what she had just experienced, and for the moment she was profoundly fond of Rakoczy. "You are a magician, most certainly." The smile she offered was happily lazy.

"Do not say so, or the Church will not like it," he said, only half in jest.

"You know so much more than . . ." She gazed over his shoulder as if she had forgot what she was saying.

Rakoczy put his finger against her lips. "There is no contest in these matters, Odile. Some are more attuned than others to what is wanted." He did not add that his vampirism had sensitized him to the desires of his partners long, long ago, for his gratification depended utterly on theirs.

"Then you are a master harper, as well," she said, turning slightly. "You see? You didn't slip on the fur."

"So I didn't," he agreed, his hand on her hair. "What now, Odile? It is very late—Nocturnes is over and the Guards will soon change watch—and you are sleepy."

"Optime knows you lie with me. You can remain here until morning, if you like," she said, a slight down-turn of her mouth making this seem unlikely.

"But you would prefer to sleep alone," he said, considering the cramped quarters of the cubiculum. "I understand; I, too, prefer my own bed." It was narrow and hard as a monk's, but it was made on a chest filled with his native earth and the rest it provided was sweeter than down and fur could ever be. "You will slumber more deeply if I am gone."

She would not admit it, but by looking away from him, she conveyed her answer. "You are very good to me, giving me so much pleasure." Then she looked away from him. "This isn't much, but it is mine while I serve the King, and I will remain here. You have two chambers assigned to you. There is no reason for you to remain with me."

"You're right, of course," he said without rancor as he rose and stood contemplating her features in the dim light of the room. "But you and I must talk, and soon—before I come to you again."

Now Odile's annoyance was returning. "If you say we must, we must. I shall come to choose something to read after Prime, and you can tell me then whatever you must." She stretched. "You did well by me tonight," said Odile, and pulled a bearskin around her.

Aware that this was a dismissal, Rakoczy reverenced her and stepped back toward the door. He slipped into the corridor and made his way to the stairs leading down. There he noticed that a monk was walking back and forth in front of the narrow staircase, his tonsured head catching the light from the torch in the sconce next to the stairwell. Rakoczy checked his descent, then continued on down to the foot of the flight. "God give you a good night, Fratre," he said, and saw the monk's hand go to the hilt of his dagger. "I am Magnatus Rakoczy," he added, as if he were not aware of the Fratre's intention.

"God give you good night, Magnatus," said the monk. "I know who you are."

Rakoczy was unsure how to respond, so he only ducked his head and prepared to pass on.

The monk stopped him. "Optime has need of you."

If Rakoczy thought it odd of Karl-lo-Magne to use a monk to summon him, he did not allow the thought to change his demeanor. "So late? It must be urgent."

"He is closeted with Sublime Alcuin," said the monk, indicating the Royal Residence across the courtyard.

"Ah, yes. Alcuin arrived here yesterday." Rakoczy fell in beside the monk.

"And since Nocturnes, Optime and the Sublime have been deep in discussion. Optime has asked for you to come as soon as you left Widow Odile."

The monk did not see Rakoczy's sardonic smile. "I must thank you for your patience," he said as the two of them entered the Royal Residence.

"They are in the King's library," said the monk, pointing the way.

"Thank you. I know where it is," said Rakoczy, lengthening his stride and swiftly moving ahead of the monk. The corridor was torch-lit—one of the torches produced more smoke than light—and manned by Guards with their swords out of the scabbards. Rakoczy passed the Guards, ducking his head to each of them. When he reached the library door, he found two Guards in front of the door. "I am Rakoczy. The King sent for me. If you would allow me to enter?"

The Guards opened the door and stood aside, then pulled the door closed again, leaving the three men in the room alone.

Karl-lo-Magne and Alcuin were bent over two vast maps, their full attention on what was drawn there; the King only looked up when the sharp rap of Rakoczy's heels on the stone flooring demanded notice. "There you are," he approved. "Come, Magnatus. Come." He motioned the foreigner to approach.

Rakoczy did as he was ordered. "What am I to see, Optime?" He reverenced the King, and then the Bishop before looking down at the two maps.

Slapping his hand down on the larger of the maps, Karl-lo-Magne said, "Look at this! I want to build a canal to cross Franksland so that goods may be taken to more distant markets without the many difficulties of overland travel." This sounded like an often-expressed desire, coming automatically and with habitual force. "In times of famine, food could be carried to the afflicted regions, and in time of war, supplies could be shipped more quickly by canal than carried in carpenta."

"And more easily sunk," said Alcuin. "To say nothing of the possibility of war breaking out in places the canal wouldn't reach. What use is a canal in Francia or Neustria, or Austrasia if the war is in Longobardia, or Gasconia, or Carinthia?"

"It could still be useful," Karl-lo-Magne insisted.

"Ever since he learned of Uffa's Wall in Mercia, he has been determined to exceed it," said Alcuin fatalistically. "This would make Uffa's accomplishment seem paltry."

"Is that the breastwork dyke between Mercia and Wales?" Rakoczy knew it was, but realized he should not appear to have heard of it.

"That is it," said Karl-lo-Magne. "My canal would be far longer, and much more useful." The angle of his chin made it clear that he wanted no opposition to this.

Rakoczy looked carefully at the map. "A most ingenious plan, Optime," he said cautiously, "and yet, with so many war-like peoples on your borders, I wonder if undertaking so vast a project just now might not leave you vulnerable to attack, because of the men you would have to divert from guarding your frontiers." He looked the King steadily in the eye. "If you conscript peasants to build this, you risk famine."

"That may be true, but in plentiful years, when grain and livestock flourish, we may provide against lean years, and so put men to work on the canal without famine."

Rakoczy studied the map while trying to shape his answer. "To find myself between two great men, as I do now," he began deferentially, "I wonder that you should consider anything I say."

"You are a most knowledgeable man," said Karl-lo-Magne. "You have traveled more widely than either of us, and must have seen many wonders. Therefore you are the very man to help me decide. You are not a Frank, and you do not seek to advance yourself through courtly favor. So. Peruse the map, consider the plan, and let me have your opinion."

There was no way to back out of this readily, and Rakoczy said, "I will." He pretended to be engrossed in the map, finally saying, "It is a tremendous enterprise. It will take time, many men, and money, to see it done. The expense may be greater than you wish to pay."

"Then you agree with Alcuin, that this should not be done?" The King's high voice rose a little, the challenge clear.

"I think that it can be done, but not while you have so many enemies around you," said Rakoczy, determined not to make his position unfavorable. "Once your borders are secure, I would think a pair of canals might be desirable, one here, where you have drawn it, and another crossing it at right angles, to open the way for the rest of your Kingdom. You will have less disappointment among your people if you do that, and you will ensure plenty for all Franks." He rocked back on his heels. "You plan to build a very long way, and that means the work must be done over many years, for such work cannot be done in winter."

"No, but in winter, with your superior ice skates, my messengers will use the canals more efficiently than the rivers," said Karl-lo-Magne, as if this were a clinching factor.

"Optime, I am gratified to know the skates I made have been all you hoped for, but to undertake so much for a winter road is perhaps more trouble than its benefits would be." Rakoczy took a step back from the table. "I should think you might find more worth in sledges that could be dragged along the frozen canals much as barges would be in the rest of the year."

Karl-lo-Magne looked disgruntled. "You have a point there, Magnatus." He tapped his fingers together, then contemplated the map once more. "As you say, two canals would be the wiser plan."

"But a much more costly one, for all that," said Alcuin, shooting a sharp look at Rakoczy from under his tufted eyebrows. "I see the Magnatus' purpose, and I believe it is a point well-taken, but, Optime, it would take much longer and the cost would be enormous."

"So it might be," said Karl-lo-Magne. "But nothing can be accomplished in this world without some cost—in labor, in days, or in money—accruing to it."

"Just what I wanted to convey," said Rakoczy. "So great an undertaking will require the dedication of many men for several years, and during that time, it will be difficult for you to put your armies into the field—not only for numbers, but because so much of your men and matériel will be committed to the work on canals." He shook his head. "I would be a poor guest, indeed, if I failed to warn you of the many costs such an undertaking demands. If you were to try to build the canals and then were forced to abandon them before completion, you would be derided for your inability to bring the project to completion."

Karl-lo-Magne's cheeks were flushed, and his blue eyes sizzled. "No man will laugh at me!"

"Certainly not," said Alcuin quickly. "But Rakoczy's observations are well-intended. It would be held as a failure in you if you should begin the canal—or canals—and then be forced to abandon them. It would appear that you had extended yourself too far, and that, in turn, would make you seem weakened. You know how much contempt the Longobardians had for Desiderius for his inability to complete his fortifications at Pavia. How could the Franks be less concerned than the Longobardians?"

"His men were stopped by the mal aria," said Karl-lo-Magne.

"It doesn't matter the cause," said Alcuin. "In the end he did not do the thing he vowed to do, and his people turned away from him and favored you." This was not as accurate a statement as either the King or the Bishop thought it was, but it proved to be persuasive.

"I had best work on these plans a little longer, so that when work begins on the canals, it will be finished in accordance with my orders," said Karl-lo-Magne, and addressed Rakoczy. "You are a perspicacious fellow, Magnatus. Your abilities are endless." The speculative light in the King's eyes now made Rakoczy more uneasy than his previous ire had done.

"Hardly endless, Optime," said Rakoczy. "But any poor skills I have are yours to command."

Karl-lo-Magne continued to tap his fingers. "Yes. Yes," he said as he measured Rakoczy with a piercing gaze.

"You have come from far away, and you've learned many things." Alcuin tapped Karl-lo-Magne on the sleeve. "Do not put the Magnatus at any more of a disadvantage than you already have."

"How can my favor be a disadvantage?" said Karl-lo-Magne with exaggerated innocence.

"You know better than that," said Alcuin, glancing at Rakoczy. "There are courtiers who are jealous of the Magnatus, and you know it."

"They are jealous of one another, too," said Karl-lo-Magne mulishly.

"All the more reason to be circumspect," said Alcuin. "You do not want to give them any more reason to become rivals. You are able to keep the worst of them in check, but it is still no easy matter to control them all. Do not tell me otherwise, for I have eyes and ears, Optime, and I know what transpires in Franksland."

"If Rakoczy had kin to support him, things might be different," said Karl-lo-Magne, unwilling to admit that Alcuin was right.

"But I do not," said Rakoczy, breaking in to their wrangling. "Nor will I have."

"True," said Alcuin. "No Bishop would give you leave to marry, your land being in the hands of our enemies, though you are exiled from it." He did his best to appear sympathetic, but this did not come readily to him. "You have great value, no doubt, but you are also one who must go about the world unbound by convention and blood."

"Do you think so?" Rakoczy could not keep himself from asking. "It may seem so to you, but I have great loyalty to those of my blood still in the world."

"Whom you admit are scattered and few," said Alcuin.

"That's so," Rakoczy agreed, "and all the more reason for us to honor our bonds."

"There you are right," said Karl-lo-Magne. "A man's first loyalty must always be to his blood, or all else fails. You can trust no one if you cannot trust blood."

"Then there is no more to be said," Alcuin conceded, looking away from the King.

"That woman—Odile?—is she still to your liking?" Karl-lo-Magne asked Rakoczy with a grin.

"She is a delightful creature," said Rakoczy carefully. "It was most generous of you to arrange matters for me in regard to her."

"She will be no trouble to you. If you should have any complaint, inform me and it will be tended to." His tone was final. "You must not cling to anyone you do not want."

"I would not," said Rakoczy, wondering what this was all about.

"Hathumod is a fairly dull companion, once her initial youth and sweetness palls," said Karl-lo-Magne. "In time, all women are boring, aren't they?"

So Karl-lo-Magne was shifting his interest to Odile, Rakoczy realized. "I will keep this in mind," he said to the King, and added to Alcuin, "I trust, Sublime, that I do not offend you."

"I have known Great Karlus for many years. If I were going to be offended, it would have happened long ago." He smiled wearily. "But I am grateful for your concern, Magnatus."

Karl-lo-Magne scowled. "I am only concerned that Rakoczy not be poorly rewarded for his service to me. I have nothing to be ashamed of. I Confess my sins and I accept the forgiveness of God and His Bishops. There is nothing I need repent that I have not—"

Alcuin held up his hand. "Yes, Optime. There is no reason to question your devotion to the Church and her teaching." He glanced at Rakoczy. "Optime is no monk, and no one expects him to act as if he were one."

"Of course not," said Rakoczy, and took another step back, hoping that Odile would be pleased to know that she had finally caught the King's eye. "Is there anything more?"

"Yes, there is," said Karl-lo-Magne. "I am very pleased with all you have done for me, yet there are still a few matters for which I must ask your assistance." He gave a direct look to Alcuin and went on forcefully. "I know your reservations, and I do not begrudge you a single one of them, but you and I must not be caught up in this dispute unless it is absolutely necessary. This cannot become a cause of the Church, either, for it is too divisive. If Rakoczy will make an evaluation, then neither you nor I need be required to accept this as our final decision, and it can be removed from the direct concerns of the Church. That is all to the good, for us and for the Pale Woman as well."

"If only Bishop Freculf hadn't insisted on a decision; he and Bishop Iso are at loggerheads, and many others have begun to take an interest in their dispute," said Alcuin. "There are those who believe she is the Anti-Christ, because of her hands."

"She should have been content to remain at Sant' Audoenus, among the mad and crippled. No one would have questioned keeping her there," said Karl-lo-Magne.

Rakoczy remembered the albino woman he had met on the road to Aachen. "Who is this Pale Woman, and what do you want me to decide?"

Alcuin answered. "Two Bishops are in dispute about her, and it must be resolved before the controversy spreads. This is not a time for division in the Church, or in Franksland."

"I am not a religious, and I am not . . ." Rakoczy faltered, not knowing how to continue without putting himself in a compromised position. "Surely one of your kinsman would be a better choice?"

"If the Bishops would agree, very likely," said Karl-lo-Magne. "But they will not accept any kinsman of mine, and other Illustri or Potenti are unacceptable for similar reasons. So it must be you, or someone like you. I intend to present your name to the Bishops for their approval."

"And I will support his request, for you are not affiliated with any of the Bishops, or their kin," said Alcuin. "Then the Church may be sure that there has been no slight."

Rakoczy nodded, knowing he could not refuse. "Very well; I am at your service. When do I see this Pale Woman?"

"As soon as the Bishops can agree on a time." Karl-lo-Magne grinned. "There is a conclave soon, and I will see that some arrangement for your inspection of her is made before it concludes, if it can be done. If not on this occasion, then at the next conclave." His glance toward Alcuin was eloquent, making it clear that the Bishops were not yet inclined to hear the matter.

"Then it will not be at once," said Rakoczy, relieved.

"It will not be much before the end of the year," said Alcuin, "if then."

Rakoczy managed to smile. "If I might have a month to return to my fiscs to supervise the work being done? My camerarius has been in charge, but there are many problems developing, and it is fitting that I resolve them before the next harvest."

It was a trade, and Karl-lo-Magne recognized it. "You may have a month at the end of spring." Satisfied with his night's work, he waved Rakoczy away and went back to dealing with his maps and debating with Alcuin. As Rakoczy reverenced him from the door, Karl-lo-Magne looked up at him. "See you serve me well, Magnatus. What you have done so far is excellent, but you cannot rely on past glories."

Rakoczy knew that this was more than a warning; he offered a second reverence, saying, "I understand you, Optime," as the door was pulled closed in his face.

TEXT OF A LETTER FROM FRATRE GRIMHOLD IN ROMA TO BISHOP FRECULF, CARRIED BY CHURCH COURIERS, WAYLAID AND KILLED BEFORE THE LETTER COULD BE DELIVERED.

To my most excellent master, Sublime Freculf, the respectful greetings of Fratre Grimhold at the beginning of summer in the Pope's year 798.

The Byzantine faction is gaining power. Already it is rumored that three of the Curia have embraced their cause and made common cause with the Patriarch of Constantinople, in anticipation of great rewards when Roma submits to Byzantium at last. This is a very dangerous turn of events, and many of the Archbishops are reluctant to remain in Roma while the danger exists. Four have left already, to return to their own Archbishoprics with the intention of waiting out the peril. They have taken their monks and priests with them, planning to maintain the Church away from Roma, should it fall. Many of them depend upon Karlus Rex to protect them and preserve the True Church if there is trouble.

In this difficult period, any gesture of support you might make to aid the Archbishops and other high Churchmen will redound to your benefit when Roma triumphs. This is a very good time to devote yourself to the goals of the Church and to ally yourself with the great men who aid the Pope. It will not only advance the Church for you to do this, it will also make it possible for you to advance your own position within the Church, and that must be part of your considerations, for there is no shame in following your own cause while defending the True Church.

The mal aria has already come to Roma, and the fevers are everywhere. Pope Leo has offered daily Masses for the preservation of the people and for Heaven's willingness to heal those already afflicted. The Pope has ordered that a mass grave be dug in anticipation of more deaths. He has blessed the ground so that anyone who dies of this malady may be assured of Heaven's blessing, whether the dead perished shriven or not. There are many churches in Roma that have elected to keep Hours all through the night, both Nocturnes and Vigil, so that the dead need not lie in the streets where dogs and swine will gorge upon their flesh.

It is a terrible thing, to see this city under so many ills, and some see it as a sign that the Church is failing. It is truly a hard thing to hear their fears spoken in whispers. Others say that this is the final test of faith before God comes in Glory to judge the world. It may be that the End of Times is upon us. I cannot help but wonder how Christ would see His Church in this perilous time, and how He, Who suffered so much for us all, would view those who have turned away from the Church when a little adversity is put upon it. For this reason, unless you order me to leave, I will remain here, in Sant' Pier's See, for the purpose of supporting the Pope as you have ordered me to do, and I will advance you within the Church for as long as I have breath in my body to do God's Will.

Be certain that I will send you word when the fevers have passed, or when the Byzantines have committed some indignity that exceeds what they have done thus far. In that regard, you may have heard that Empress Irene has assumed the control of the Eastern Empire; her son, Constantininus, has been blinded and imprisoned on her order and his place wholly usurped by her. I have had it confirmed that this is truly what happened, and that the Empress Irene is determined to hold the Empire within her command with the help of the army. With all of this upheaval, it would be dangerous to rely too much on any promises made by the Byzantines, and so I advise you to be circumspect about them. If Great Karlus should seek your opinion, keep in mind all I have told you. It could save you and the King many difficulties.

In every assurance of my devotion and continuing loyalty to you and the Church, I ask your blessing and prayers for deliverance from the mal aria.

Fratre Grimhold

～

chapter twelve

TWO OF THE BISHOPS HAD GOT INTO A CLUMSY FISTFIGHT, both of them drubbing at one another ineffectively, for they were too drunk to do any real harm to anyone; they scuffled and tottered about the space between the dining tables, oblivious to their fellow Sublimi, each trying to remain upright. Most of the rest of the company was in a similar condition, and a few of them egged on the hostilities. The two long tables at which the nineteen Bishops sat were spattered with the remnants of the huge meal that had been served and was almost finished; now the scullions were trying to keep the Bishops' cups filled with wine or beer.

Bishop Iso swayed on his bench and reached for the last meat clinging to the boar's ribs sticking up like an unfinished bridge in the middle of the table; he was tipsier than he had intended to be, but not so inebriated that he was behaving as badly as some of the others. Pulling a scrap of meat from the bone, he popped it into his mouth, chewed quickly, and swallowed, washing the lump of pork down with another generous amount of beer. Watching the fight degenerate into occasional shoves, he laughed, taking consolation in the certainty that in the morning none of them would remember the battle or its cause. He licked his fingers and then wiped his mouth on his silken sleeve. At least, he thought, he was not sitting anywhere near that arrogant fool, Bishop Freculf. Plenty of time to deal with him in the morning, he decided. For now he would make the most of the evening. While a scullion refilled his cup, he helped himself to the honied fruit that the mansionarii were bringing out from the kitchen.

"Sublime," said Bishop Dagoberht, slurring the title; he sat on Bishop Iso's left, his dalmatica stained all down the front, and the alb smirched with grease and a red stain from the Longobardian wine he preferred. "Sublime, how can you suppose that those two will be able to settle anything, carrying on like that?" His censure was ruined by a belch.

"They won't," said Bishop Iso, letting the honey on the pears he had chosen dribble all over the last of his wheaten trencher.

"It has been a fine banquet. Archbishop Reginhalt has done himself proud." He pointed to the High Table, where three Archbishops sat together in all their splendid regalia; they, too, were drunk, and they had reached the point of not caring that they were. "I doubt the Pope dines so well as we have."

"Not in these days, certainly," said Bishop Iso. "Archbishop Ebroin and Archbishop Sigiberht are also pleased with themselves, and will no doubt be claiming credit for the whole occasion."

Bishop Dagoberht yawned suddenly and hugely. "We'll all sleep well tonight. Thanks be to God."

"And Bacchus," said Bishop Iso, and drank another mouthful of beer. "Even Roman Emperors could not achieve what we have done."

"And with God's blessing, not His curse," said Bishop Dagoberht. "But you are not drinking as much as the rest of us. Don't tell me you've take a vow of soberness."

"No, but I have a cause to plead before the Archbishops in the morning, and I would not like my head to be ringing." He managed a dry smile. "Let Bishop Freculf drown himself in strong drink, I will not be so lax."

"It will be a chore to arise at Matins," Bishop Dagoberht muttered, and drank the last of his wine, then gestured to a scullion to refill his cup. "But with three Archbishops in attendance, and one bound for Roma in four days, we must be diligent in our observations of the Hours."

"And the sooner this evening is repented, the sooner we can banquet again," said Bishop Iso, biting into the honied wedge of pear. "This is very good. Optime's orchards have been bountiful."

"Thanks be to God. Optime has tried to keep the bounty of Franksland in Franksland against another famine. It is a most prudent thing, making stores of food. He doesn't want his people to starve again." He watched the scullion pour him more wine.

Bishop Gerbergius gave a wild punch at Bishop Worad and both staggered and fell, Bishop Gerbergius striking his head on the edge of the dais as he dropped. Around him the other Bishops laughed and pointed as their fellows lay, cursing futilely, between their double rows of tables.

"They will have a hard morning," said Bishop Iso as if pleased with that certainty.

"They will," said Bishop Dagoberht.

More fruits were being brought out, a few of them fresh, but most preserved in honey or spices; the dried plums in pepper were especially popular and the Bishops grabbed for them unashamedly. The aroma of plums, pears, apples, and quinces was intense, cutting through the odor of grilled meats. The scullions looked around to see who needed more food. The banquet was concluding, and the fire in the open fireplace was dying; on the dais Archbishop Sigiberht was nodding, almost asleep, and his two companions were weaving as they moved in their high-backed chairs. Slowly two Bishops rose, reverenced the Archbishops on the dais, and unsteadily tottered toward the door at the rear of the dining hall. One of them called out, "Thanks be to our hosts, to God, and Karl-lo-Magne for the opulence of our feast."

"Amen," said Archbishop Ebroin for all three of them.

Gradually the other Bishops began to struggle to their feet and take their leave of the Archbishops; four of the Bishops went to kiss the Archiepiscopal rings of their hosts, but most were content to reel out of the room to their various chilly cubicula and suites set aside for them at the Royal Residence of Attigny.

Bishop Iso rose slowly, glad he had abstained from carousing as much as the rest; he could tell that even with his reservations he was going to have an aching head in the morning, and he cursed himself for being foolish. He saw Bishop Freculf swagger from the dining hall and told himself that tomorrow he would be less confident and would feel less well than Bishop Iso would. As he reverenced the Archbishops, Bishop Iso hoped they would remember his conduct when they sat after Prime to hear the debate about the Pale Woman. But first there were the prayers of Nocturnes to recite and then a few hours for sleep before Matins. He intended to observe all the Hours no matter what the other Bishops might do.

When he reached his cubiculum, Bishop Iso found Sorra Celinde waiting for him, a hint of impatience in her manner as she greeted him. "I said we would be late," he told her bluntly.

"So you did. But it is after Nocturnes, and the Guards have changed. That is later than I anticipated." She sat on his bed, her arms folded and a determined expression in her soft features. "I could hear the roistering all the way from the dining hall."

"Hardly surprising," said Bishop Iso, tugging off his alb and looking at it; even in the poor light he could see it was smeared with grease from the meat and butter as well as honey from the fruit. "This will have to be washed. It's too stained to wear as it is." He fingered the messy silk. "A pity we must all wear fine clothes for these occasions. But we could not refuse. The Archbishops demand it." His tone revealed his contempt for such excess. "The Archbishops may command us anything—more than the King does. And now this fabric is no better than a rag."

"Then you ought to be more dainty in your eating," said Sorra Celinde as she inspected the garment in the dim light. "You will never get this stain out."

"Very likely not," said the Bishop as he knelt at the foot of his bed facing the crucifix that hung on the opposite wall. He began the Nocturnes prayers, reciting the words by rote, rushing through them impatiently. "Are you ready for bed?" he asked between Psalms.

"In a moment," said Sorra Celinde and pulled off her stolla, then pulled down her loose underdrawers. Naked, she slipped under the blanket. "There. As soon as you are done."

"That will not be long," he promised and went back to praying, paying no attention to her as he spoke the verses from memory.

Sorra Celinde lay in bed watching him, the sputtering lamplight making him seem to appear and disappear. She smiled contentedly, thinking that for a fisherman's third daughter of four she had done very well for herself—certainly better than her other three sisters, all of them burdened with families and husbands. She, at least, had a powerful lover, and the assurance of a place to live until her dying day. The Bishop could be difficult, but so could all men; she had known that from early childhood. She echoed his "Amen" and lifted the blanket for him as he came back to the bed and tugged his dalmatica over his head. His breechclout came off quickly; he pinched out the last lamp and got in beside her.

"I need sleep tonight," he said as she reached for him.

"As you wish," she said, disappointed but accepting. She snuggled up to the Moorish pillow, preparing to fall asleep.

"Gynethe Mehaut," said Bishop Iso suddenly. "What do you make of her now?"

"I think she is a very puzzling woman; I can understand why there is confusion about her," said Sorra Celinde cautiously. "I have watched her as you asked, but if she has cut her hands herself, I have not seen her do it, or even so much as touch a knife but to eat."

"Bishop Freculf does not accept that this woman is the Anti-Christ, or his messenger," said Bishop Iso. "It is a test of our faith, putting her in our midst. God will judge us as we judge her."

"No doubt you are right," said Sorra Celinde, yawning.

"Bleeding at the hands. What clearer sign could there be than that? Isn't it obvious that she is the opposite of Christ? She has nothing to claim as her kingdom. She has no disciples. She has no chrism. Yet her hands bleed, and she is female. Man came to grief through Eve; it must not happen again, or we will no longer deserve salvation, or Christ's Sacrifice." He stared up into the darkness. "Surely the Archbishops will see that she must be cast out."

"You will explain it all," murmured Sorra Celinde.

"As I must. But that idiot Bishop Freculf will dispute all this. He believes she is a messenger of Grace, and that her white skin and bleeding hands are signs of her gift." He could feel his body tensing, and he ground his teeth. "How can he not *see*?"

"He hasn't your knowledge, Sublime," said Sorra Celinde.

"But he is a Bishop. Karl-lo-Magne chose him as much for his piety as his kinsmen." He reached for her suddenly, rolling onto her and forcing her legs open. He was fully aroused, and he was determined to fulfill his need. "This may bring catastrophe upon us all."

Sorra Celinde pretended her desire was as swift as his own, sighing and scratching at his back, but she was almost indifferent to his bucking and grasping. She was relieved when it was over, but she held him as if reluctant to be apart from him.

"How good of God to provide you to me," said Bishop Iso as he got off her.

"I will serve you always, Sublime," she said with complete sincerity.

Bishop Iso patted her shoulder. "Of course you will."

When the first chime of Matins sounded, Bishop Iso stirred but did not open his eyes; beside him Sorra Celinde woke and sat up. The second chime rang, and this time the Bishop responded, sitting up and blinking. "My camisa—where is it?" he muttered.

"In the chest, on top, with your gonelle." Sorra Celinde was already out of the bed reaching for her stolla. "If you hurry you will be among the first into the chapel."

"And thus show my devotion," said Bishop Iso. "You're a clever woman, thanks to God for it." He put on his breechclout and stumbled to the chest to take out his camisa. As soon as he had this in hand, he pulled it over his head, struggling with the sleeves, and then felt for his gonelle. "My pectoral crucifix—the silver one with the pearls. Where is it?"

"Under the lamp." Sorra Celinde was almost dressed. She kissed her rosary and secured it around her waist. "After Prime I will wait upon Gynethe Mehaut. Where shall I take her?"

"See she is fed, and keep her in readiness in case the Archbishops wish to see her. Be aware of everything she does and remember everything she says, in case they should wish you to report on any aspect of her behavior." Bishop Iso finished dressing and went toward the door of the cubiculum. "If you have to impose your will on her, do not strike her. She should have no other wounds than those in her hands, and no bruises to cast doubts upon the bleeding."

"I will do as you ask, Sublime," said Sorra Celinde, preparing to leave as well. She would go to the smaller chapel with the other nuns, and she would break her fast with them. It was not part of the day she looked forward to, since the nuns were jealous of her and could often be spiteful to her. As she hurried down the corridor, she passed the cubiculum where Gynethe Mehaut was quartered; she paused, knowing the Pale Woman was still in the nuns' chapel, and after a short hesitation, she entered the chamber. Telling herself that this was for Bishop Iso's benefit, she conducted a quick search of the bed, the chest, and the windowsill, but found nothing other than a small crucifix and clothes. Whispering a few derisive phrases under her breath, she hurried away to answer the strident summons of the third Matins bell.

When the ten nuns entered the smaller chapel, they found Gynethe Mehaut prostrate before the altar, her pale gonella almost matching her white skin. Most of the nuns ignored her, but Sorra Celinde could not. She approached the prone young woman while the Sorrae intoned the opening prayers of Matins, and reached out to touch her shoulder. "Gynethe Mehaut," she said, ignoring the scowl of the Priora, "I will escort you to the Archbishops after Prime. They expect you to arrive before Sept. They will hear Bishop Iso and Bishop Freculf plead your case."

"Thank you," said Gynethe Mehaut, interrupting her prayers long enough to address Sorra Celinde. "I will be ready. I ask you to provide me some protection from the sun when you take me to the Archbishops."

"I will do that," said Sorra Celinde, wondering briefly what that protection might be; this was late August, and the heat of the day struck early and lay over the land well past Vespers, enervating and demanding. A winter mantellum would protect her, or a capa, but both would leave her sweltering in short order. She went to her place in the chapel and joined the prayers of the rest of the nuns.

At the conclusion of Lauds the Sorrae formed a double line and went off to the refectory; the first pale smear of dawn lay on the eastern horizon, announced by birds and cockerels. As the nuns reached their refectory, there was a flurry of activity as the scullions tried to serve both the Bishops in the smaller dining hall and the nuns in the refectory as well as the Guards who had a dining hall adjoining their dormitory. Noise from the kitchen was constant, and the odor of fresh-baked bread hung on the still morning air, stirring hunger everywhere in Attigny.

"Pray for the salvation of all mankind and the triumph of our faith," the Abba intoned.

"Amen," said the nuns, and bowed their heads.

At the conclusion of breakfast, Sorra Celinde went to collect the bread and cheese from the kitchen that would be Gynethe Mehaut's morning meal. Impulsively, she added a cup of goat's milk to the fare, hoping it would incline the Pale Woman to think well of her. As she hurried to Gynethe Mehaut's cubiculum, she told herself that this was a good, Christian act, one that would be well-regarded by the Bishops no matter what the Archbishops decided.

"When must I be ready?" Gynethe Mehaut asked as she drank the milk; there was a look of fatigue about her, an air of exhaustion that went beyond the body to the spirit. "I am ready whenever the Archbishops command me to attend their inquiry."

Sorra Celinde did her best to appear compliant and pious in her manner and spoke in a low tone. "When Prime is finished, I will come for you. I will bring a capa to cover you with; you may wear the hood up when we are in the sunlight." She studied the Pale Woman attentively, trying to discern what the Prelates might see in her; Sorra Celinde did not care whether Gynethe Mehaut was the herald of Heaven or Hell—her only concern was what effect the decision would have on Bishop Iso, so she regarded the Pale Woman with true indifference. "Will you be ready?"

"I will," said Gynethe Mehaut, and pronounced a simple blessing on the bread and cheese before she began to eat.

Sorra Celinde hurried off, bound for the little oratory near the stairs, where she knew she would find other nuns who would share her devotions. When the ritual was concluded, she went along to the Guards' station and asked to be loaned a capa.

"It is summer. Why would you want such a garment?" The Guard was a sturdy fellow with a patch over one eye and a jagged scar along his neck.

"The Bishop has asked for one." This was not quite a lie, and she felt no shame in the assertion.

The Guard shrugged. "Strange creatures, Bishops," he observed as he went to the dressing room and retrieved a capa from its depths. "Return it when the Bishop has done with it."

"I shall," said Sorra Celinde, and took the heavy woolen garment in her arms. She paid no attention to the chuckle that followed her out of the Guards' station.

Gynethe Mehaut had donned a simple honey-colored gonella over her stolla; both were linen and washed in saffron-water. Her girdle was embroidered leather worked in a design of interlocking crosses. Bands of colored fabric plaited into her pale hair were her only adornment. "I am ready," she told Sorra Celinde.

"Very good. Then follow me," said Sorra Celinde, handing Gynethe Mehaut the capa and stepping back into the corridor. "We must go to the reception hall." She led the way at a good pace, doing her best to ignore the stares of the nuns they encountered along the way. As they crossed the open courtyard, she walked beside Gynethe Mehaut, helping her to keep the hood of the capa in place to protect her face from the hot sunlight.

A monk met them at the door to the reception hall. "The Archbishops are waiting," he said. "They have taken their places."

"And Bishop Iso?" Sorra Celinde asked.

"He is with Bishop Freculf. You will see them directly." The monk turned away, indicating the women should come with him. "The Bishop's slave, Conwoin, will escort you into the presence of the Archbishops," he said.

"Very well," said Sorra Celinde, who disliked Conwoin intensely.

"When you go before these august men, prostrate yourselves and do not look at them unless they order you to do so. If you must direct your gaze at them, do not look in their eyes—choose a place over their shoulders. They are not for the scrutiny of such as you and me." The monk made a gesture of humility and pointed to the door. "That is the antechamber. Conwoin will meet you there."

"We will pray," said Sorra Celinde as she took the capa from around Gynethe Mehaut's shoulders. "May God reward you for your true service."

"Amen," said the monk, and hurried away, pointedly avoiding looking at Gynethe Mehaut.

"Well," said Sorra Celinde, "are you ready?"

"I must be," said Gynethe Mehaut, none of her apprehension showing in her calm demeanor. She was glad she could keep her hands in her sleeves, not only to conceal her bandages, but so that no one could see how badly they were shaking. She entered the antechamber and at once sank onto the bench near the inner door.

Sorra Celinde came up to her. "They will summon you at their pleasure."

"No doubt," said Gynethe Mehaut, and fell silent, her nerves jumping.

"You mustn't worry. They will decide what is best." Sorra Celinde kept her voice low, not wanting to be overheard.

"I pray they will," said Gynethe Mehaut automatically; her attention was on the closed door.

Sorra Celinde could think of nothing to say. She began to pace the antechamber, wishing it were large enough to allow her some room to move. When the inner door opened, she started. "Conwoin?"

"Yes, Sorra Celinde," said the slave, a faint note of condescension in his voice. "Bishop Iso has summoned you and the Pale Woman into the presence of the Archbishops." He reverenced her, but so profoundly that she was insulted by his action.

"You are too proud, Conwoin," she said as she went over to Gynethe Mehaut. "Come. They are waiting."

Gynethe Mehaut got to her feet as if she were girded in ice. She went to the open door, moving as if sleepwalking. Beyond she could see the hanging lamps and high bench of the reception room, and saw the three Archbishops, one of whom seemed half-asleep, seated there. In front of the bench stood Bishop Freculf and Bishop Iso, the former flushed, the latter pale.

"Gynethe Mehaut, Sublimi, and Sorra Celinde," said Conwoin, reverencing each Churchman in turn. "Where shall the Pale Woman stand?"

"There," said Archbishop Ebroin, pinching the bridge of his aquiline nose and squinting; he had a throbbing headache that the morning's debate had not alleviated. "Go there. Opposite the Bishops." He watched in silence as she went where he had indicated.

"It is done," said Conwoin, and guided Gynethe Mehaut to a petitioners' box. "Do not enter it; lie prone before it."

Gynethe Mehaut knelt and bowed her head before prostrating herself. She turned her head away from the Bishops as she lay on the polished stone floor.

"Sorra Celinde may sit at the rear of the hall," said Conwoin, not quite smirking.

The nun wanted to protest this casual insult, but knew it would be held against her; she did as he told her, promising herself there would be a time when Conwoin would answer for his insolence.

From the high bench, Archbishop Reginhalt leaned forward, his vision blurred more than usual. "You may speak, Pale Woman," he said, "when we ask you questions directly. Do not answer any questions from either Bishop. Do you understand?"

"I do, Sublime," she murmured.

"Very good," said Archbishop Ebroin. "How long have you been pale?"

"I am told I was born this way," Gynethe Mehaut answered, her voice clear and distinct. "I cannot recall a time when I was not pale."

"And your eyes? Have they always been red?" Archbishop Ebroin went on.

"As far as I know, Sublime," said Gynethe Mehaut.

"You had no illness? There was no malediction laid upon your mother? She was no handmaiden of the Devil? Or sworn to ancient gods whom Christ has cast down into Hell?" Archbishop Reginhalt's questions came too quickly to be answered. "Well?" he demanded.

"If I had an illness, I was never told of it. The priest in our village said my mother was a good woman, and helped her." Gynethe Mehaut took a deep breath. "If anyone worshiped ancient gods, they did it away from our village. I was entrusted to the Church when I was quite young, and I cannot speak for what others in our village may have done." She could feel tears well in her eyes, and she hated herself for such a display of weakness.

"Do you suppose there is anyone who would Confess to making sacrifice to the old gods?" Archbishop Ebroin asked; beside him Archbishop Sigiberht let out a rolling snore. Archbishop Ebroin sighed and did his best to carry on. "Why would anyone be so foolish?"

"I know of no one who would," said Gynethe Mehaut carefully.

"Then you *do* have contact with those who keep to the old ways," said Bishop Iso, turning toward Gynethe Mehaut. "You can't claim to be unaware of—"

"I know of these things because monks and priests speak of them, and preach of the evils of such practices. I wouldn't—" Gynethe Mehaut was interrupted by Bishop Freculf.

"That is why I am certain this woman is a messenger of God. It would be a poor messenger who didn't know the wiles of the enemies of God," he declared, looking at Bishop Iso. "You can't claim that she wouldn't know about the followers of the old gods."

"But who is to say that this is an example of God's Mercy?" asked Archbishop Ebroin. "Perhaps Bishop Iso is right, and she is a snare." He looked at her. "Woman. Hold up your hands."

Gynethe Mehaut half-raised from her position on the floor and strove to comply. "I need help to unwrap them," she said at last.

"Sorra Celinde," said Archbishop Reginhalt, "go to the Pale Woman's aid."

Little as she wanted to obey, Sorra Celinde did as the Archbishop ordered, doing her best to appear pleased to comply. "May she rise?"

"Yes; she may kneel instead of lying," said Archbishop Ebroin.

Gynethe Mehaut got to her knees and held up her bandaged hands. "I want you to be careful so that you can swear there is nothing in the bandages that could cut into my skin."

"Of course," said Sorra Celinde, her pretty mouth turning down at the corners as she set to work; she disliked this chore intensely, but took pains to conceal her repugnance. Carefully she unfastened the knots that held the linen bands in place and began to unwrap the Pale Woman's left hand. "There isn't anything in this bandage," she told the Bishops and the Archbishops as she held up the blood-stained cloth.

"Very strange," said Archbishop Ebroin, his hand to his head.

Sorra Celinde unwrapped Gynethe Mehaut's right hand and repeated what she had done with the left, with the same results. "There is nothing sharp concealed in this one, either. She has done nothing to damage her palms. But, as you see, her hand bleeds."

"Is it truly blood?" asked Archbishop Reginhalt. He blinked, trying to make out the red discoloration he thought he saw on her hands.

"Has anyone tasted it?" Archbishop Ebroin asked of the Bishops. "How else can we know it is blood if no one will taste it?"

At this suggestion, Sorra Celinde blanched. "I couldn't do such a thing, Sublimes. I will obey you in almost everything, but I won't do that."

"I'm not afraid to taste of blood so blessed," said Bishop Freculf with a hint of a swagger as he approached the high bench. "If you require it, I'll lick her wounds and tell you what I taste. I am not afraid harm will come to me through her blood."

"No," said Bishop Iso. "You mustn't. You would be damned by so perverse an act."

Archbishop Sigiberht leaned precariously on his chair, snoring boldly.

Archbishop Reginhalt shook his head, but whether at Archbishop Sigiberht or Bishop Freculf's offer was impossible to tell. He contemplated Gynethe Mehaut. "How long have your hands bled, Pale Woman?"

"As I recall, Sublime, I was in my ninth or tenth year when it first occurred. I tried to keep it secret and it soon stopped. But it happened again, and again, and I couldn't continue to conceal it," she said, and pressed her white lips together.

"Why did you conceal it?" Archbishop Ebroin asked sharply. "Were you ashamed?"

"No," said Gynethe Mehaut. "Not then. I was confused and troubled. I couldn't think what this was, or what it might portend. When the Abba first saw it, she beat me for profaning Christ."

"Did she?" said Archbishop Ebroin. "Did you not protest such usage?"

"No," said Gynethe Mehaut simply. "She was doing what she thought best, and for a while the bleeding stopped, so I was content, and she was satisfied."

"Did she continue to beat you?" Archbishop Reginhalt asked.

"Until she returned me to my parents, saying she could do no more with me. One of the Sorrae said I had summoned a demon who got her with child. My father kept me for a time, but soon grew afraid and sent me to the nuns at Santa Albegunda, where I remained until Bishop Freculf decided I should go to Sant' Audoenus." Gynethe Mehaut reported all this with little show of emotion, though she was filled with turmoil.

"Did you summon the demon?" Bishop Iso asked, a look of certainty indicating he was already convinced of her guilt.

"No; I have no knowledge of how it is done," she replied.

"Oh, come," said Bishop Iso. "A drop of the blood would bring a demon."

Gynethe Mehaut laughed unhappily. "If I could do that, I should have done it long since, and asked him to take this from me, and make my skin like that of other people's."

"There is wisdom in her answer," said Archbishop Ebroin, nodding and feeling his headache worsen.

"Or guile," said Bishop Iso, visibly sneering.

"Why do you believe she would not want this for herself?" Bishop Freculf asked. "She is humble, she prays all through the night and tends the night-blooming garden for the benefit of those who guard the places dedicated to Christ and the Glory of God. This isn't the work of a demon, or of someone who seeks to bring down the True Faith."

"She corrupts it by her existence. If she is permitted to remain among Christians, she will distort all that is good and worthy and put debauchery in their place." Bishop Iso's cheeks reddened with indignation.

"How can you look upon her and yet accuse her?" Bishop Freculf countered. "I am not so proud as to claim that I can discern all of God's Will in this, but since I first saw her, I have learned nothing of her but good, and I am reminded that we are obliged to look beyond the body to the soul. In this case what more should I do than what the Scriptures tell me, and see the soul in the deeds and demeanor of Gynethe Mehaut?"

"How better to bring down our faith, than from within the Church, with the Church's consent?" Bishop Iso's voice was rising.

Archbishop Ebroin held up his hand. "Sublimi, what is the purpose of this rancor?" He felt his stomach lurch, and he put his hand to his mouth; the Bishops interpreted this as an admonition to silence and stopped speaking.

In the stillness Archbishop Reginhalt sat back, his arms folded. "Gynethe Mehaut," he said, addressing the white-skinned young woman. "I don't know what to make of you. I haven't the time to make a study of your case, or to converse with everyone who has ever dealt with you, which is what I should do before arriving at a final judgment in your regard. You may be what Bishop Iso believes you to be, in which case, you are too dangerous and everything you say is a snare, and you put our souls at risk by being in your presence. Or you may be what Bishop Freculf believes, in which case you are to be revered and you are among the Saints. Or you may be neither, in which case you are to be pitied. But I cannot determine yet which it may be, and so I wish to lay your case before the Pope. If Archbishop Ebroin will agree, we will arrange for you to be sent to Karl-lo-Magne's Court where more learned men may confer about your condition, and add their opinions to your case to assist Leo to gain the knowledge of God."

Archbishop Ebroin was glad to do anything that would bring this wretched morning to an end; he made a blessing and clamped his jaw shut to keep nausea from rising; he did not trust himself to speak.

"Archbishop Sigiberht will agree, I'm sure," said Archbishop Reginhalt with a sideways glance at his sleeping colleague.

"Therefore, when the Paschal season comes, you, Bishop Iso, and you, Bishop Freculf, will come to the King's Court, and put yourself before the Bishops and Archbishops of Franksland—" Archbishop Ebroin intoned.

Archbishop Reginhalt interjected. "The case will be put before His Holiness, Leo III, in Roma this winter, and he will give us the benefit of his meditations on the Pale Woman's condition, and that will direct our decisions."

"Amen," said Archbishop Ebroin. "We will be able to arrive at a decision then."

Bishop Freculf reverenced the Archbishops. "Then this Pale Woman will be vindicated, for the Pope is a man of great sanctity and he will know her for what she is."

"So I hope," said Bishop Iso stingingly, and reverenced the three men on the high bench; then he turned on his heel and left the reception hall, signaling to Sorra Celinde to follow him; she hesitated, then rushed after him, her face averted from the curious stare of Bishop Freculf.

"Enough of this," said Archbishop Reginhalt, and reached out to shake Archbishop Sigiberht awake; the old prelate snorted suddenly and blinked.

"What? How?" Archbishop Sigiberht exclaimed, sawing at the air with his right arm.

"It is time we went for Sept," said Archbishop Ebroin. "Our morning audience is finished."

"Oh. Sept," said Archbishop Sigiberht as he managed to get to his feet and accompany his two peers off the high bench and out the private door to the reception hall.

Bishop Freculf approached Gynethe Mehaut where she knelt on the stones. "If you will allow me to assist you to rise?" He held out his hands to her.

She could not speak; drawing her hands back automatically, she tried to thrust them into her sleeves, but they left smears of blood on the heavy linen of her gonella and she looked about, dismayed. "Sublime . . . I am not worthy. . . ."

He took her fingers as if unafraid of the perplexing wounds in her hands. "I will summon a slave to bind your hands again. You need not fear that you will take any hurt from me." He lifted her to her feet and stepped back from her. "I thank you for permitting me to assist you."

Gynethe Mehaut could think of nothing to say in response. She reverenced Bishop Freculf to cover her confusion. "Sublime honors me beyond my station."

"How much like a Saint you are," said Bishop Freculf, and ducked his head before turning away and leaving Gynethe Mehaut by herself, her palms pressed together, letting the blood run down her arms and drip slowly onto the stone floor.

TEXT OF A LETTER FROM COMES ZWENTIBOLD IN CARINTHIA TO FRATRE BERAHTRAM AT PADERBORN, CARRIED BY MISSI DOMINICI AND DELIVERED AT THE BEGINNING OF THE SEASON OF THE NATIVITY.

To the most devoted and loyal Fratre Berahtram, the greetings of the Comes Zwentibold currently in the citadel at Reicsnau in Carinthia, in October of the Pope's year 798.

Good Fratre, I send this to implore you to come to Reicsnau for the purpose of tending our wounded. Your reputation as a healer has spread through

Karl-lo-Magne's lands, and it reveals that you are a most blessed monk, with skills exceeding those of even the Jewish physicians. I have sent a petition to the King, as well, asking that he authorize you a military escort to this place where you may attend the soldiers wounded in Great Karl's cause. It is my hope that he will grant what I ask, for the sake of my men who suffer and die with only nuns to wipe their brows as fever claims them and bears them to the Gates of Heaven as martyrs.

It is my hope that you will be able to bring other monks with you, but if this is not to be, then I must rely upon you alone to see to the men here. Surely you can save these men and restore them to strength and health. I pray you will come before the end of winter, but if you must wait until spring, I must warn you that more of my men will be dead or crippled for lack of your care.

My own officers will escort you if the King will not send his own soldiers with you, so great is our need for you. I am told that a number of suffering men have been restored by what you did for them. If God has given you the knowledge to heal, it is fitting that you spend your time in the service of the King, who is the sword and strength of the Holy Church, and the champion of the Pope.

It is right that I seek your help, and right that you give it, for it preserves the frontiers of all Franksland, and thereby brings greater strength and glory to the Church through the conquests of Karl-lo-Magne, who will deliver all Christendom from the toils of the pagans and the servants of the Patriarch in Constantinople, whose agents seek to enter Franksland along this border. In defending our land and our faith, we have a high cost levied upon us by our enemies. Let you not aid them by refusing to come to our succor, which is the obligation of every man in Orders and every subject of Great Karl, no matter how high or low his birth, or what his station in life. You cannot doubt that it is God's Will that you marshal your powers and come to bring us to the victory we seek for our King and our faith.

The certainty of your coming will lend purpose to my soldiers, and fortify them for our hard days ahead. With your prayers, we will be heartened. With your unguents, seals, tinctures, and salves, we will be proof against all damage and injury.

Comes Zwentibold
by the hand of Fratre Othmar

～

chapter thirteen

IN THE ORCHARD ON THE FAR SIDE of the fields there was a group of young men and women tossing fruit and seeds into the air; a few of them were singing, and the women embraced the trees, straddling the trunks as if they were their lovers. Leaves drifted on the ground, and the air was chill as the afternoon drew to a close; but the peasants continued their celebration, their ritual of inspiring the trees demanding that they remain in the orchard until every tree had been given their attention. The air smelled of wood-smoke, old fruit, and fungus; the wind slithered through the bare branches and across the stubbled fields.

Rorthger was riding beside Rakoczy as they completed his tour about his fiscs. "There will be a bonfire in the village of Monasten tonight, to celebrate the last of the harvest. It is the custom: there will be new beer and new wine, so you know how it will end. It is the last feast until the Nativity, and the villagers make the most of it." He chuckled. "They have killed two pigs and a goat for the feast. You will be expected; they all want to see you, and it would cause much offense if you were not to attend."

"Then I will do so, until it becomes too . . . confused," said Rakoczy, nodding at the peasants in the orchard. "I'm sorry I've been gone so long, old friend; it was not my intent," he went on in the Persian tongue. "You've had to contend with more than you should have had to."

"At least you were still in Franksland, and free," said Rorthger, recalling more than one time in the past when Rakoczy's absence had been far more ominous.

"And you are safe, as well," said Rakoczy, as if sensing Rorthger's memories; he and Rorthger were past the orchard now and let their horses canter along the damp road. They kept to the verge, where there were no ruts and footing was safer for their mounts. "In another month, nothing will move on these tracks; they will be mires and bogs."

"Only the old Roman roads will be usable," Rorthger agreed.

"Which Karl-lo-Magne is prudent enough to maintain, after a fashion," said Rakoczy. "He uses the old roads for his troops."

"They are safer for mounted men than any other lane or byway," Rorthger commented. "And faster, as well. If he had military barges, such as they have in China, he might use the rivers to speed his soldiers."

"When the rivers freeze, some sledges will travel on them, but not very far;

his couriers use ice skates and stay off the mired roads," said Rakoczy, adding, "He was pleased with the skates I made him for that purpose; it was one of the reasons he let me leave Court for a time." As he tugged his grey mare to a walk he shifted the direction of their conversation. "How many foals will we have in spring, do you think?"

"Well, nine mares have settled, and allowing for the loss of one, eight should be born," Rorthger said, moving ahead of Rakoczy as the verge narrowed.

"And how many were bred to Olivia's stallion?" Rakoczy asked. "He's a good size, and the King will be pleased if the foals are large."

"Olivia believes, based on his performance at her estate, that he is prepotent," said Rorthger, passing on what Olivia's mariscalcus told him. "If this is so, his get should be like their sire."

"We can hope that this proves the case," said Rakoczy. "It would be wise to present Karl-lo-Magne with a pair of large colt-foals; they are what he values personally the most, after women."

"A man of his heft, I should think so. We shall see what the six mares in foal to Livius produce. That is the stallion's name, according to the mariscalcus, and so we call him; Olivia probably intended it as a joke. Come spring, we'll have more mares for him to cover; I have purchased seven from estates in the region, and two more from Sant' Cyricus. I have already offered his services to the Potenti in the region." Rorthger pointed to a stand of berry-vines. "I will bring the goats to eat this back."

"Better have one of the local peasants do it—with my goats. Otherwise there may be complaint that I am taking away their summer berries at the cost of the road, or that I am showing favor to one village more than another." He followed Rorthger into the cover of a copse of beech, oak, and larch, becoming almost invisible in the dim, mottled light; only his grey horse stood out in the gloom, unlike Rorthger and his mouse-dun, who blended with the shadows.

"If that were the worst of it," Rorthger said with a worried expression.

"I haven't been here enough, I know," Rakoczy said quietly. "The villagers do not trust me, and anything I do is regarded as suspicious."

"That is only a part of it," said Rorthger, guiding his horse through the trees with the ease of experience; Rakoczy fell back and followed him. "There are other problems, I fear."

"Of course there are," said Rakoczy with a sigh. "I am foreign, and that makes everything I do highly questionable."

"That's the heart of it," Rorthger agreed. "There are secondary issues, but that's all they are: secondary." They crossed a small bridge and continued on toward a cluster of thatched-roof buildings.

Rakoczy reined in for a moment. "Who is the headman here?"

"Vulfoald. He's a woodsman, and the village butcher," said Rorthger. "He has two wives, although he only claims to have one, to keep the monks at Sant' Cyricus from interfering in the village."

"Vulfoald," said Rakoczy, memorizing it. "What else can you tell me about him?"

Rorthger was ready with an answer. "He is a strong man who thinks that he is wise rather than stubborn. The villagers are half-afraid of him. Be direct with him, or he will not extend himself at all; he is a hard man, and a bully." He started his mouse-dun moving again.

"Many village leaders are. Their lives make them so." Rakoczy looked around, noticing half-a-dozen men driving sheep and pigs into the pens at the edge of the village. He kneed his grey mare to begin her walking once more.

"They have two ponies for the hard work," said Rorthger. "One is quite old and they will need a second one eventually."

"Then I must see that they have one; it is my responsibility to provide them with a means of doing the work the fisc requires, as Karl-lo-Magne reminded me before he let me leave Aachen," said Rakoczy, thinking back to that short interview conducted while the King pored over maps of Carinthia and ordered his horse for the morning hunt. "Who breeds the best ponies in the region?"

"Hosfurt at Stavelot is reckoned to breed the best ponies, or so I have been told," Rorthger said, turning around in his saddle to speak directly to Rakoczy.

"Then let us make arrangements with this Hosfurt to purchase a stallion for this village; so that they may breed more for themselves and will not need to ask for another pony in ten years," said Rakoczy, lowering his voice so he could not easily be overheard.

"If you don't mind, my master, I will purchase several ponies, to provide all the villages in your fiscs with at least one. Given the tenor of these people and their rivalries, it would not be sound dealing to have it appear that you favor one village over another."

Rakoczy nodded. "Yes. I agree. Well, I shall make more gold for you this winter, and come spring, you may buy a whole herd of ponies for the villages of my fiscs."

Rorthger signaled his assent to this plan. "I shall attend to it, my master." He paused, going on carefully, "I realize we should not discuss this where your mansionarii can hear, and this may be the most advantageous time."

"What is it, old friend?" Rakoczy asked, hearing the unease in Rorthger's voice. He switched to the Mongol tongue. "It won't matter who overhears."

"The peasants don't like to be reminded you're foreign," Rorthger said in the same language, then sighed. "Will you be bringing your mistress to your villa? You invited her a month since, and I will have to make some preparation if you are anticipating her arri—"

"No," said Rakoczy. "She will not come here; I have it in a note from Optime himself. Karl-lo-Magne is pleased to send her to me when I am at his Court, but he will not permit her to venture beyond it; I may turn her from her purpose of watching me for him, and I may offend her husband's kinsmen, which would lead to trouble for the King."

"But the King arranged your liaison," said Rorthger.

"So he did, and he will support it as long as it suits his purpose. When Odile can no longer provide what he wants, he will present her with a new lover." There was a bleak expression at the back of his dark eyes. "And she will acquiesce in his commands, for otherwise she would be entirely at the mercy of her husband's family."

"It doesn't sound very satisfying," Rorthger remarked.

"Oh, she is a willing-enough lover, and she doesn't mind what I require of her—or not too much. She is loyal to the King, as she must be, for he will protect her from her husband's kin. Accepting the lovers he approves is a small price to pay for this. And with me, serving him is not unpleasant." He laughed once, the sound melancholy. When he spoke again, it was in Frankish. "She has so little that is her own."

Three ragged children emerged from the brush at the side of the track and, pointing at the newcomers, ran toward the village, yelling something in the local dialect that neither Rakoczy nor Rorthger could understand.

Rakoczy looked toward the center of the village, and then at the fading sky overhead. "It is getting late. The monks will be singing Vespers shortly. We should return to the villa when we're through here. What do they call this place?"

"Cnared Oert." He pronounced the strange syllables with care. "The monks call it Sant' Trinitas, to keep the ban on the old regional tongue." Rorthger dropped his voice. "There has been trouble about that."

"This is not the only place with such trouble." Rakoczy drew in his grey and swung out of the saddle, then stood, holding the mare's reins, while he waited for the peasants to respond to his presence.

Rorthger dismounted and approached Rakoczy with a great display of respect. "Let me hold your mare, Magnatus," he said in Frankish, and went to take the reins from Rakoczy.

A man in a discolored, double-woolen tunica came out of a wooden shed, a long, thick staff of wood in his hand. "Who is this?" he growled, not looking directly at Rakoczy.

Rorthger answered. "This is Magnatus Rakoczy, Comes Sant' Germainius, friend of Karl-lo-Magne, and hobu of four fiscs, master of this place." He spoke it loudly enough to be heard all through the village. "Come forward to greet him."

The children, who had reached the center of the place ahead of them, were shouting and pointing; the youngest was pale with fear, the older two posturing their bravery. A woman in the regional costume came rushing out of one of the houses and grabbed the children, hustling them away from the open center of the village. Other men and women began to gather at the far end of the open center, their demeanors wary and their glances hostile. Rakoczy noticed that all the young women were sent into the houses as soon as they appeared in the village center, and he wondered again how Comes Udofrid had used these people when he had title to the fiscs.

Finally a big man almost as tall as Rakoczy, with a brutish, bearded face and wearing a tunica of rough-cured leather over his banded trews, shouldered his way through the assembled people and stood facing Rakoczy, his arms folded, his bearing as pugnacious as he dared to be. "I am Vulfoald. I am headman here."

"This is Magnatus Rakoczy," said Rorthger. "He is hobu of this fisc."

"So we have heard." His accent was so thick it was hard to make out what he was saying, but Rakoczy listened intently. "Why is he here?"

"I am here," said Rakoczy, surprising all the villagers by addressing Vulfoald directly instead of using Rorthger as his speaker as was the custom, "because as hobu and representative of the King, it is my duty to hear your grievances and do what I can to redress them."

"What is he saying?" Vulfoald asked Rorthger, who obligingly repeated what Rakoczy had said in the local tongue. "All very well, to make such an assertion; we have heard them before, and know their worth. But what is his true intent here?"

"My intent is to perform those tasks that I am required to, in accordance with the responsibilities the King has laid upon me," Rakoczy said, pitching his musical voice to carry to everyone listening; he spoke slowly and clearly, hoping to help their comprehension.

"And what will you take in return for your help?" Vulfoald asked, daring to be sarcastic. "Our flocks? Our women? Our children to be your slaves?"

Rakoczy listened quietly, then said, "None of those things. The King has charged me to keep his law in these fiscs and I am obliged to do it, for his sake. If I take anything from you, then I do the King dishonor, and I should suffer for it."

Vulfoald turned his head and spat. "So we have heard, time and again. It is what every Potente and Primore says he will do. And yet nine of our women grew large with the Comes Udofrid's seed, and thirteen of our children were taken to serve him as his slaves, and we were left to make our laws in the old way. He, too, was King Karl's friend, and upheld his laws."

"Perhaps the King was not deceived by the Comes, and saw what mischief he did: you know he has been sent far away and his lands seized, and the Magnatus has been granted his fiscs in his place," said Rorthger, motioning to Rakoczy to remain silent. "Whatever the case, Magnatus Rakoczy is no part of Comes Udofrid or his kin, and is answerable only to Great Karl. He will hear you with fairness and will administer justice as the King charges shall be done."

"That may be," said Vulfoald. "But I have not seen it, and no one says—"

Rakoczy cut him off. "If you are to judge me, then do so when I have done something that you may decide upon. Do not accept rumor and the bad acts of others to weigh with you." There was silence; in a moment, he went on. "Tell me what wrongs demand justice and I will do my utmost to address them and dispense such remedies as I am permitted to give."

"You will tell us anything, and then you will leave, and your soldiers will come and our children will vanish, and then our women, and all will be the same as it was when Udofrid ruled," said Vulfoald. His big hands knotted into fists.

"I swear before the God of Christ and the monks of Sant' Cyricus that I will not prey upon your people," said Rakoczy.

"No one hears you but us, and that means nothing. A Magnatus, even a foreign one, may say anything to peasants and it is as if it was nothing more than a cry on the wind, to be denied without dishonor," said Vulfoald contemptuously. He motioned to three men standing a little apart from him and said, "It is time to light the evening fire. Do it."

"Yes, Headman," said the largest of the three men, and went to fetch the village torch that always hung in the iron cleat over the brazier that was kept lit day and night, year after year. It was protected by a stone enclosure that resembled a shrine—as it had once been.

Rakoczy laid his hand on the hilt of his Byzantine long-sword. "I offer an oath on this blade," he said; he had seen soldiers make such pledges and knew they were bound by them.

Vulfoald lifted his head and glared directly at Rakoczy. "Hold Court and take an oath with monks and many people to hear you, and I may believe what you say."

This insolence shocked most of the villagers, who drew back, not quite cowering, and looked from Vulfoald to Rakoczy and back again as if expecting some terrible retaliation from the black-clad Magnatus; a few of the men slipped away, bolting for their houses as if to escape from terrible danger. The very air seemed to crackle with the kindling of the bonfire, emphasizing the tension that increased with every breath. The light from the new fire cast shifting illumination on them all, accentuating their movements.

"I will hold Court," said Rakoczy. "On the Feast of the Dead." He pointed to Vulfoald. "You must bring your people to my villa then, or you will receive no justice from me."

Vulfoald slapped his palms together. "On the Feast of the Dead, we will come. If there is treachery, the curse of the old gods will fall upon you."

"If there is treachery, I shall deserve no less," said Rakoczy, and took his reins from Rorthger, preparing to remount. "Those children of Comes Udofrid: what became of them?"

"They were exposed, as all foreign infants are. The old gods and their beasts took them," said Vulfoald as if the answer must be obvious. "Did you want them for slaves?"

"No," said Rakoczy, and swung up into the saddle. "Until the Feast of the Dead."

"Until then," said Vulfoald, and turned away before Rakoczy and Rorthger rode out of the village, this studied insult making more than one of the men around Vulfoald shudder at the enormity of their headman's affront.

As they took the path that led most directly to the villa, Rakoczy said to Rorthger, "I'm sorry, old friend, but I must ask you to ride tomorrow to all the villages and monasteries in my fiscs to inform them of the Court. See that they all know about it. Anything less would lead to trouble among these people, and I fear there has been more than enough of that already." He looked ahead into the gloom of dusk. "How did Comes Udofrid do so much to their detriment? And why?"

"I cannot say," Rorthger responded. "But from what little I have been able to discover, Comes Udofrid was a rapacious, tyrannical coward who made himself loathed everywhere in his fiscs. Not even the Superior of Sant' Cyricus—who was supported by the Comes—has spoken well of him."

Rakoczy thought this over; they continued on into the gathering darkness, letting their horses find their way back to the stable. As they passed the outer walls of Santa Julitta, Rakoczy asked, "Did Comes Udofrid do anything to the nuns?"

"The rumors say he made whores of them," said Rorthger.

"Was this known? What did the Bishop have to say?" Rakoczy asked.

"The Bishop was the one who finally persuaded Karl-lo-Magne to remove Comes Udofrid from his position, for the sake of the nuns, if nothing else. The Church insisted that something be done, and Great Karl finally complied, and bore the brunt of Udofrid's kinsmen's displeasure at his ignominy." Rorthger considered his next remark. "Not that his reputation wasn't earned: his debauchery seems to have been common gossip, but nothing was said officially, which was the same as relegating it all to oblivion. If the Church hadn't stepped in, and his killer, Comes Udofrid might well be here still, continuing his old amusements at the cost of all those around him. Even with his discredit, the damage he did lingers. The nuns have done nothing untoward since the Comes left, yet the rumors remain. I have not spoken to any at Santa Julitta but the Priora, and she said nothing of it."

"Not that she would; the Sorrae would be disgraced," Rakoczy observed; the nunnery was lost to view as they went around the soft rise of the hill and into the trees once more. "Well. I have much to rectify, it appears, and the sooner I make an effort, the better for all of us. I have no wish to awaken more suspicions than I already have. It would probably behoove me to ready myself: if there are any records at the villa, I should review them before Court, so I will be prepared for the complaints." He shifted in the saddle, listening. "There is someone behind us." He waited. "More than one, I think."

"Mounted?" Rorthger asked as he reached for the short-sword in the saddle-scabbard.

"Yes. Unshod horses." Rakoczy drew his Byzantine long-sword and swung it to limber his arm against its weight.

"How many?" Rorthger asked, swinging his mouse-dun into position against Rakoczy's grey, noses to tails, flanks almost touching.

"Four, I think. Yes. Four." Rakoczy studied their surroundings and decided their position was defensible; the trees had thinned, and they were in a meadow with a brook on the far side. In the cold-scoured sky overhead the first stars were beginning to shine; the waning moon would not rise until after Compline. "This is as good a place as any to face them."

"Do you think this could be something other than an attack?" Rorthger wondered. "Couldn't this be couriers or missi dominici?"

"At this hour, in this place?" Rakoczy shook his head.

"Do you suppose there will be a fight?" Rorthger took a swipe at the air with his short-sword.

"If they are very foolish, there will be," said Rakoczy, so calmly that Rorthger knew it was certain that Rakoczy was prepared for battle.

The sound of the approaching hoofbeats got louder, and there were shouts, harsh and abrupt, that drove out all notion of cordiality; the riders were hunting Rakoczy and Rorthger.

"They'll be on us," said Rakoczy, cocking his head to indicate the curve of the road as it came out of the trees. "Be ready."

"I am," said Rorthger. "I'm only sorry I don't have a maul with me."

"They may well have one," said Rakoczy, and directed his gaze toward the track behind them. "Be careful of blows."

The first of the followers emerged from the trees at the trot, then slapped his pony into the canter; his men behind him did so as well. The leader checked his mount as he caught sight of Rakoczy and Rorthger up ahead; then he urged his pony to gallop, yelling as he closed with Rakoczy, a heavy cudgel raised above his head, ready to strike.

The impact went awry as Rakoczy swung his sword back-handed, bringing the blade up and under the leader's arm; its steel bit deeply into his flesh. The cudgel fell from his hand, striking the on-side forecannon-bone of Rakoczy's grey; the horse screamed and reared, which kept Rakoczy from killing the attackers' leader with his first slam of his blade. Rakoczy held his grey with his legs, making the horse drop back onto her front legs; she minced in place, squealing with hurt.

Two of the men had swept around to strike at Rorthger; the attack faltered as Rorthger jabbed at the nearer of the two men, missed, and thrust his short-sword deep into the pony's neck. Blood erupted from the wound as the animal went down, hooves thrashing; his rider was pinned beneath him, screaming that his arm was broken; his voice was rising in anguish. The second man pulled back and drew a short spear from a scabbard on his saddle; he prepared to rush at Rorthger, and put his pony into the gallop, only to find that Rorthger had brought his mouse-dun around to charge him.

The fourth man reined in, hesitating at the edge of the trees. Then he wheeled about and fled, leaving his companions to face Rakoczy and Rorthger alone. The man riding at Rorthger saw this and sheered off, following the fourth man toward the woods.

The single remaining mounted man shouted loudly and made an effort to take another swipe at Rakoczy, using a long knife; he reeled in the saddle, and were it not for his hardy, sure-footed pony, he would have fallen; as it was, the man clung to the high pommel as the pony wheeled on his back legs, then bore his rider off in the direction the other two men had taken.

As soon as he was sure that the other men had gone, Rakoczy swung out of his saddle and knelt to examine his mare's leg. His night-seeing eyes could clearly discern the ruin of her leg, and he knew she could not be saved; he patted her shoulder, his heart heavy. Getting to his feet, he began to unbuckle the girth of the grey's saddle while Rorthger dismounted and used the dropped cudgel to end the wounded pony's suffering; the man pinned beneath was unconscious.

"I'll carry the tack," said Rakoczy as he set the saddle on its pommel-end and prepared to swing his long-sword.

"Is it necessary?" Rorthger asked.

"Her leg is broken. She can die quickly or slowly, but she cannot survive," said Rakoczy flatly. In the next moment he had severed her neck cleanly and moved back as the mare collapsed. "The wolves will feed well tonight."

"A pity," said Rorthger, knowing that it was difficult for Rakoczy to perform this kind of duty, no matter how merciful it was. "The pony is dead, too."

"Just as well, with such a wound. He would never get to his feet again, not with such a loss of blood." Rakoczy went over and looked down. "The rider's still alive."

There was a long silence. "Are you going to remove him?"

"I suppose I must," said Rakoczy, and bent to shift the pony's body in order to lift the injured attacker. "I'm going to sling him across the back of your horse," he said to Rorthger just before he did.

"And what about you?" Rorthger asked as he prepared to remount. "Do you want to ride my horse?"

"I can walk. The villa is less than two Roman leagues away. No one will see us at this hour, so I'll carry my saddle. Where are your lashes? He'll have to be tied on." Rakoczy helped to secure the unconscious man to the cantle of Rorthger's saddle, then swung the saddle he had taken off his grey up to his shoulder. "This is an inconvenient shape," he remarked as he tried to settle it comfortably. "We'd best get out of here: the three may well make a second attempt on us."

"Two of them, possibly," Rorthger agreed. "The third is too badly injured."

"If blood loss doesn't exhaust him, he is likely to take an infection," Rakoczy said, setting out in the direction of his villa. "Who were they, do you think?"

Rorthger considered the question. "There are stories about Comes Udofrid's Guards; they shared his disgrace but had no kinsmen to protect them from penury, and so they . . . they had to fend for themselves."

Shaking his head, Rakoczy remarked, "Those were not soldiers. They didn't fight like soldiers; if they had we would have found it much more difficult to get free of them. Remember the Avars at Pityus." Although they had fought the Avars there more than 250 years ago, the event remained sharp in their memories.

"They were desperate," Rorthger reminded him as he glanced back toward the line of trees.

"So were these men, I should think," said Rakoczy, lengthening his stride. "But though the Avars were near to starvation, they fought more effectively than these four."

"Then do you have a suspicion about them?" He let Rakoczy take the lead, keeping his mouse-dun to a steady walk.

"Hardly so much as a suspicion, more of a sense," said Rakoczy. "Say rather that I cannot reconcile these attackers with the skill and behavior of trained soldiers. Four trained fighters would not make the mistakes these men did." He thought a moment. "And the ponies were more like those used by the peasants than the horses soldiers ride."

"A man must use what he can find," said Rorthger. They topped a rise and could just make out the torches burning at the front gate of Rakoczy's villa on the brow of the next low hill.

"So he must," said Rakoczy. "I fear we will arrive later than the villagers of Monasten would like." He nodded in the direction of the lume of a great fire off to their right.

"If you are there before they are all too drunk to notice, all will be well," said Rorthger, echoing the light irony in Rakoczy's voice.

"Then perhaps we should hasten," said Rakoczy. He continued to walk at a brisk clip, covering ground at a speed that would have alarmed anyone but Rorthger, had he been seen. Maintaining his celerity until they had almost reached the outer wall of the villa, Rakoczy was reasonably satisfied when he came up to the squat, massive wooden doors that were the entrance to the villa's grounds. He used the bell-chain to summon the warder and looked up at Rorthger. "How is your charge doing?"

"He is clammy to the touch and his breathing is shallow," said Rorthger. "He will have to be helped soon, or he may die in spite of anything you do."

"Then take him to my study and I will come shortly to tend to him." He put down his saddle and said to the warder as the gate opened, "Take the saddle to the stable if you would. And summon Amolon for me. He may find me in my study."

The warder ducked his head. "I will, Magnatus."

"Very good," said Rakoczy, and strode across the courtyard to the main house, leaving Rorthger to provide an account of their difficulties to the warder. He went directly to his private apartments, peeling off his gonelle as he went and loosening the ties on his black linen camisa. Once in his outer room, he paused to strike steel to flint to light the lamp hanging from the center beam; the light did not penetrate the gloom very well, but it was sufficient for Rakoczy to find the tunica he sought in one of his three chests of clothing. He pulled this on quickly, then went to the basin of water that he always ordered kept in his chambers. Washing his hands, he made sure his fingernails were clean before he left his apartments and headed for his study. There he found Amolon and Rorthger waiting for him, the semi-conscious attacker laid out on the trestle table, a stained cloth over him. Three branched lamps had been lit, giving the room enough light to treat the man.

"Magnatus," said Amolon, reverencing him.

"Amolon," Rakoczy responded. "I thank you for coming here promptly."

"I am here to serve you," said the buticularius.

"Very good," Rakoczy said as he pulled back the cloth over the supine man. "I am going to hold Court on the Feast of the Dead. Can you tell me what I must do?" He bent over the man, inspecting his wounds. "Rorthger, I will need two splints and many strips of linen; and syrup of poppies for the pain. Also a vial of my sovereign remedy, against fever from his hurts."

"I'll fetch them," said Rorthger, and left the study at once.

Puzzled and a bit nonplussed, Amolon could not think what to answer. Finally he said, "The Court is to be here."

"Yes." Rakoczy pulled his knife from the sheath at his knee and cut open the man's clothing. "His arm is broken in two places. He's fortunate it's no worse than that."

"A broken arm can be a man's death," said Amolon.

"So it can," said Rakoczy. "But I will do my utmost to be sure this man isn't among them."

Curious now, Amolon took a step closer. "Rorthger says that this man attacked you, with three others. Why are you caring for him?"

"Because otherwise he would die, very likely in agony, and I would learn nothing from him," said Rakoczy.

Amolon nodded. "Then you intend to torture him."

Rakoczy straightened up. "No. I intend to set his bones and treat him with remedies so that he can recover. Then he will tell me what he knows."

"From gratitude?" Amolon scoffed. "He will lie and work against you."

Rakoczy went back to his task. "Do you think so?"

"He was one of four who tried to kill you. You know nothing of him, or of his kin. They are your enemies, and you are reckless to— You might as well bring a wolf into the villa and let it run wild." Amolon shook his head violently. "You are being foolish, Magnatus."

"Well, perhaps I am," said Rakoczy. "But still, I must do it."

Amolon stood still, shocked disbelief making it impossible for him to move. "If he tries to kill you again, Magnatus—"

"I will remember you warned me," said Rakoczy.

With a cough, Amolon went on. "You said you intend to hold Court on the Feast of the Dead. You will have to feed all who come, and feed them well. Also they must have drink, and in quantity. You must have soldiers to maintain order, and monks to be clerks for the Court."

"All of which I expected. Shall all this be indoors or in the courtyard?" Rakoczy continued to study the bruises, swellings, and discoloration of the man on the table. "He has been badly beaten in the past; you can see scars on his shoulders and chest. Four of his ribs have been broken, and healed badly. It is a wonder he could ride at all, let alone fight."

Amolon ignored Rakoczy's remarks about the man he was treating. "Late in the year, it would be best to have Court indoors, for who knows what the weather may be? If you require the peasants to stand in the rain, they will become ill and unable to work."

"Indoors it shall be, then. Do I speak to the monks at Sant' Cyricus for clerks?" He stood up again. "This is going to be a bit disagreeable; you may want to wait in the corridor." As he spoke, he was positioning himself to set the man's broken arm.

After a single scratch on the door, Rorthger came in with a basket in his hands. "Everything you asked for, my master."

"Excellent," Rakoczy approved. "Perhaps we should begin with syrup of poppies—if you would hand me the jar?" He held out his hand for it.

"The man may need more than one dose," Rorthger said, giving Rakoczy the jar.

"Yes; I agree," said Rakoczy; he removed the seal on the mouth of the jar and tipped a dollop of the thick, amber-colored syrup between the man's lips. "It should begin to take effect shortly."

Amolon rushed to the door. "I will come back directly," he assured Rakoczy as he stepped outside.

"If you will help me," said Rakoczy to Rorthger. "I'll align the bones and if you will put the splints in place?"

"I'll be ready as soon as you wish," said Rorthger, taking the wooden batons from the basket. "He may struggle."

"He may. I'm ready if he does," said Rakoczy. "The syrup will take hold shortly." He put his hand on the man's forehead. "No fever yet. That isn't necessarily a good sign, for his hurt-chill is as dangerous as fever."

Rorthger studied the man's face. "He's not a peasant, is he?"

"I doubt it," said Rakoczy. "Or if he is, he isn't from Franksland." He checked the man's breathing. "The syrup of poppies has almost done its work."

"I am ready. You have only to tell me," said Rorthger, adding, "I trust you don't expect gratitude from this miscreant."

"No," said Rakoczy. "But I would like some information from him." He gave a fleeting, one-sided smile. "He may feel some obligation to me for his life—assuming he lives."

"He may," Rorthger said skeptically. "You may also earn his ire."

Rakoczy shrugged. "If he dies, it will hardly matter," he said. "The first thing is to bring him through this; the rest can be dealt with later." He put himself in position to set the man's broken bones. "Hold him." Using his knee to keep the man from sliding on the table, Rakoczy took hold of the man's hand and slowly tugged it out until the arm was straight; he exerted himself—the man began to moan—and carefully eased the bones into their proper position. "Splint the upper arm first," he said to Rorthger.

"At once," said Rorthger, putting the short batons into place on either side of his upper arm. He wrapped the batons into place with linen bands and tied them off. "The lower arm?"

"I will hold it. This one is trickier—only one of the two bones is broken, and it has to be maintained at an angle or it could slip again." He moved his knee and used his hip to keep the man where he had to be. "Quickly."

Rorthger did as he was told, and in very short order he had splinted and wrapped the lower arm as well. "There."

"Find a cubiculum for him and set one of the mansionarii to watch him while I go to the bonfire. I will announce the Court there, and listen to the reports of the people." He shrugged his shoulders. "Who could think that so much would be required?"

"No one would think it odd if all you did was hunt and accept your rents." Rorthger knew most Potenti lived that way on their fiscs, and thought it somewhat odd that Rakoczy was so determined not to follow their example.

"The peasants would dislike it more than if I were a Frank," said Rakoczy. "And the time may yet come when I will have need of their good-will." He laid his hand on the injured man's neck. "His pulse is strong. Be sure he has water frequently, and another portion of syrup of poppies by the end of Compline. He should be able to sleep through the night. I will examine him again at Matins."

"You'll be back before then?" Rorthger asked.

"Long before. I must begin to make gold and jewels again if I am to live as Karl-lo-Magne expects me." He looked down at his patient one last time before he left the study. "I wonder who he is?"

TEXT OF A LETTER FROM POPE LEO III IN ROMA TO KARL-LO-MAGNE AT AACHEN, CARRIED BY CLANDESTINE MESSENGER.

To the most puissant Christian King, Karl-lo-Magne of the Franks, the greetings of Pope Leo III on this, the commencement of the Nativity Season, in Christ's Year 798, with the prayers that God has continued to show you His Grace and made His Face to shine upon you.

As you must undoubtedly be aware, my enemies have struck at me upon many occasions in the last year, smirching my name with slanders and attempting to attack me as they would any criminal. Much of this originates with Empress Irene of Byzantium, who seeks to bring her power, and with it

the Greek Church, here to Roma, with the purpose of supplanting the tempo-
ral powers bestowed by your father and continued by you, and, in addition,
to bring down the Holy Catholic Church so that the Greek Church may
become the one voice in Christendom. Well we know what disaster that
could bring upon the souls of all who have faith in God's Word.

I am sending this to you with Fratre Maurizius, who has my utmost trust
and confidence. He will impart to you certain things I have learned that may
have bearing upon your actions in the world. Some have said that you might
consider an alliance with the Empress, taking her to wife for the purpose of
securing power in the East by which you could protect the West. In another
time this might succeed, but given that Irene has had her own son most cruelly killed, it may well be that she would not hesitate to undertake to have
you murdered, or worse. It would be most dangerous to pursue any such
arrangement with so treacherous a woman as she is known to be, for there is
real danger that in spite of all your plans, Franksland could fall into her
hands, and the Church would be destroyed along with your Kingdom. I
advise you to cling to your present wife and think no more of undertaking
any treaty with Empress Irene.

I am also asking you to further the terms of your father's Donation by
agreeing to be my safe-haven if Roma becomes too hazardous a place for me.
If you are willing to receive me at your Court as your Pope, I will rest far
more comfortably than if I must face the world, knowing that at any hour I
may become a fugitive.

I know of your desire to become Emperor, and I have heard the outcry
from the Byzantines, who declare there can be only one Emperor—or
Empress—of the Roman Empire. If you are willing to pledge me the support I
seek, I will do my utmost to ensure that you are made Emperor in the West,
which the Byzantines should accept, no matter how gracelessly. But to ensure
such a position, you must be willing to extend all your might to protecting
me, in Roma and away from her. You comprehend the stakes of this game we
must all play, and for that reason alone, I beg you to consider all that you
may achieve in granting what I ask. It is a pact that will exist privately
between us, and I swear on the Blood of Christ that I will honor my obligation to you so long as you remain steadfast in your devotion to the Church
and to me, as the Pope. Both of us have much to lose if you are unwilling to
vouchsafe me the assurances I seek.

Give my messenger your answer and he will bring it to me as secretly as
he came. No one will question a pilgrim, or seek to rob him. He is not part of

my Roman Court, and therefore no one will know him for what he is, providing safety for you and for me. I am grateful to you for all you have done
for the Church in the past and I am prepared to be more grateful still, in the
fullness of time.
  Amen

Leo III

Bishop of Roma

chapter fourteen

GYNETHE MEHAUT STOOD OVER THE FLOWER BED with a wedge-trowel
in her hand. She had left Sorra Celinde in the cubiculum to which they had
been assigned; the nun was about to visit Bishop Iso. This time in the garden
seemed to be an escape, at least for a short while, from all the scrutiny and inves-
tigation that eddied like water around her; there was more to come, and she
wanted to muster her self-possession before facing new interrogation. She bent
down over the new buds, noticing the faint aroma. It was pleasant to pass the time
before the end of Compline and the beginning of Nocturnes, at the conclusion
of which she would have to go to the chapel for her night-time penitential prayers;
the moon was almost full, no clouds to lessen the soft light that was kind to
Gynethe Mehaut's red eyes. Her hands felt stiff in their new bandages, but she
continued to work the earth, loosening it and turning it, glad that winter had finally released its hold on the ground. She looked up as an owl drifted across the
sky, something dangling from its beak; she watched it fly, thinking it was a failing in her that she did not hate owls as most did, but instead admired them;
perhaps this was another sign of her damnation. With that to comfort her, she
went back to her work, doing her best to concentrate on her simple task rather
than any considerations related to the state of her soul.

Although his step could be nearly as silent as the owl's wings, Rakoczy made
a point of treading loudly, in order to announce his coming; he did not want to
startle her, for that would hamper his purpose: he had been enjoined to question
the Pale Woman, and he had complied promptly, for he was aware that Karl-lo-

Magne was growing impatient with the Bishops who continued to quarrel over this young woman. Before she was moved from Attigny, the King wanted answers; all this fuss over a woman—however unusual—was unseemly. Alcuin had endorsed the suggestion that an outside opinion might provide an answer the Bishops could accept, which inclined the King to require a response from Rakoczy as quickly as possible. He saw her, pale as wax, kneeling beside a plot of night-blooming milk-flowers, her attention finally claimed by the noise of his approach. "Gynethe Mehaut," he said, his voice low and the tone mellifluous. He stopped still, letting her take stock of him.

From her place by the night-blooming bed, she studied him, taking time to consider his face in the rime of moonlight. There was a dawning recognition in her ruby eyes. "I have seen you before, haven't I?" she asked as he came up to her. "You are familiar to me."

"We met on the road to Aachen, very briefly, a few years since; I am honored you remembered. It was such a minor meeting," said Rakoczy, surprised.

"It wasn't minor, not as I saw it," said Gynethe Mehaut. "You were kind to me."

Rakoczy felt a moment of pity that so brief an encounter should have meant so much to her. "You were bound for a monastery, as I recall."

"With Priora Iditha," said Gynethe Mehaut. "She has since returned to Santa Albegunda. I think of her often." She put down her trowel and accepted his hand to assist her to her feet. "I have been told I must speak with you, and answer your questions. I will do so."

This blunt acknowledgment of his purpose was slightly disconcerting, but Rakoczy quickly recovered his aplomb. "Do you ever have news from Santa Albegunda?" he asked, choosing a matter that would not probe too painfully.

"No. No one there has sent anything to me, not letters, or stories from couriers; or if they have, I haven't received them. I have news of very little. But there isn't much I want to know, so it may be just as well. Sorra Celinde occasionally tells me what is being whispered at Court or among the Bishops, but in general, I don't converse with anyone; they leave me to myself. I am thought to be too dangerous, and so desire I remain ignorant, for my safety." She sounded more saddened than angry, but there was a hardness to her mouth that hid an abiding anguish.

"I am sorry to learn this," Rakoczy said with genuine feeling. "Come. Let us find a bench where we can talk."

"We can talk anywhere, sitting or walking," she said, her pale garments and white skin providing a stark contrast to his black clothing and dark hair. "If we sit, we may be more easily overheard. If we walk, anyone watching us will have to expose himself eventually."

"Do you expect to be spied upon?" Rakoczy said, beginning to make his way along the narrow paths between the various beds of herbs and flowers.

"Anyone who lives in such a place as this should do," she said, no emotion in her voice. "The mansionarii make themselves useful in many ways, some of them through reporting all they hear. The slaves are as bad, or worse."

Rakoczy was aware of these problems, and he said, "I, too, have noticed the attention they give. No wonder you are so cautious."

"I would say more sensible than cautious," she corrected in the same detached tone.

"Do you think you are more closely watched than some?" Rakoczy inquired, knowing the answer.

"Certainly the monks and nuns look after me, as they must," she answered, a suggestion of resentment beneath her calm manner.

"Does that trouble you?"

"I have tried to conduct myself so there would be nothing held against me," said Gynethe Mehaut. "I say my prayers, I tend my garden, and I keep to myself as much as I can. You see, I am being candid with you; any one of a dozen nuns and monks can confirm these things. Sorra Celinde is perhaps the best informed on my doings; she watches me for Bishop Iso, and tells him everything."

"Do you think she is watching you now?" He lowered his voice to ask.

"No, not now. Now you and I are as unobserved as we are ever likely to be." She offered him a hint of a smile. "I am used to being questioned. It is the only time I am likely to speak with anyone but Sorra Celinde."

"And where is she—Sorra Celinde—just now?" Rakoczy wondered.

"She is with the Bishop. She is his woman as well as his handmaiden." She walked several steps in silence. "She will come for me when he has left her, but that won't be too soon. We have some time to be undisturbed."

"How long, do you think?" The time would not be exact, but would give him a frame of reference by which to gauge their conversation.

"Until near the end of Nocturnes," she replied. "The Bishop has already attended to his evening devotions to God and now gives himself to the flesh."

"And what will she do when she is finished with the Bishop? Isn't it time for her to sleep? Surely she won't attend on you until morning." Rakoczy's sympathy for the young woman was increasing; he knew the burden isolation imposed, and the suspicions that the unfamiliar generated in those unused to it. Willing as she appeared to be to speak with him, and no matter how direct her answers to his questions, there was a great reticence within her, an impregnability that he could not breach.

"She must escort me to the chapel tonight, so I may begin my prayers after Nocturnes," said Gynethe Mehaut. "She goes with me almost everywhere."

"But surely you can go to the chapel by yourself; Attigny may be large, but not so huge that you would be lost," said Rakoczy, perplexed by the conditions imposed on her. "Why should you need an escort?"

"I suppose I could go alone, but then there would be those who would claim I had not performed my devotions, that I had shirked my duties to the Church; that would leave me open to punishment for apostasy. With her attentions, Sorra Celinde may bear true witness to my compliance," she said, no note of complaint in her voice and only a tightening in her shoulders revealing her opinion. "I am housed and cared for, and in exchange, I must keep the Hours given to me, much as a peasant must plant the Potente's crops and share his harvest to keep his children fed and housed." They had reached a branch in the path, and after a glance at Rakoczy, she turned to the right.

"You keep your Hours at night," he said.

"As I must." Gyenthe Mehaut tipped her head back to study the night sky. "I am made for nighttime as much as those flowers are. My skin cannot endure the sun, and I must stay away from it as much as I can. You said the same to me that day on the road to Sant' Audoenus. I heeded your words then, and I have benefited from them. Night is my day; I live in reverse to the nuns. While the sun is shining, I rest and sleep, which offends many of the truly industrious Sorrae and Fratri, for they see my restrictions as sloth, and rightfully condemn it. I, too, occasionally fear I am shirking my duties." She extended her arms toward him, her flesh as pale as the linen strips wrapped around her hands. "You said, on the road, that I cannot abide the sun, and you were right. I have accepted the burden this imposes on me. When the Sorrae tend the flocks and the gardens, I must remain indoors, and so I keep my Hours at night, as a penitent. This makes me more acceptable to most of the nuns, but not all." Pulling her sleeves down, she resumed walking.

"Does it seem just to you that you should be required to do this—worship all night long?" Rakoczy stayed half a step behind her, for the way was narrow and a water-worn channel ran down the center of the track.

"It is what I must do, and I am willing to do it," she answered, her posture very straight and the sound of her voice formal. "I pray as I am told, and I am spared the hard life of beggary or whoredom."

There was nothing Rakoczy could say that would negate her assumption; he nodded once. "I suppose you are constrained, then, to do as the Church instructs perforce."

"Oh, yes. I should die very quickly if I were to be left to the kindness of the laity. But I am not yet ready to enter the next world, so I do as I am commanded." She paused and turned back to look at him. "You may not have heard this: I am told my mother wanted to expose me when I was born, and perhaps she was right. It may have been a better thing than how I have had to live. My father would not permit it, for I was their only child born alive, and he thought I would acquire color as I grew older. He insisted that I be swaddled and nursed. My mother knew better. She had had a white brother; he died when she was still a child, and he remained pale to the end. My father didn't believe her. He said God would restore me." Abruptly she stopped talking.

Rakoczy had listened closely, and when she said nothing more, he told her, "It must have caused your parents much discord, to have to find a place for you."

"I know they wanted me to . . . to become as others; they gave me to the Church, thinking that this would hurry my healing. At least I didn't bring them notoriety in the town any longer, so they hoped the worst had ended. Instead my hands began to bleed, and that frightened them, I think. My father didn't want to look at me, and my mother wept." She stared down at the ground.

Rakoczy laid his hand gently on her shoulder. "And what do they say now? Have they become reconciled to your condition, as you have?"

She shook her head. "It is all of a piece: I have heard nothing of my parents for more than four years now. I don't even know if they are alive."

"Would you like to find out?" Rakoczy inquired, seeing injury in her posture that she had been able to keep out of her words.

She shrugged, dislodging his hand. "If they live, I would be glad to know of it, and if they are dead I will pray for them. But I no longer fear for them as I did after they stopped coming to see me. Santa Albegunda was a three-day journey from their town, where my father is a tanner and a seller of leather, and when he travels—as he must—it is to procure skins or sell his wares, not to visit a nunnery. My mother must keep his house for him, and tend to selling and trading hides on market-day. Neither of them can be gone from his work for long, and he only has a donkey to carry hides for him, so they travel slowly. And I think they are relieved to have me out of their lives, for I had become a detriment to them." Looking at him, a flicker of defiance in her red eyes, she said, "They have left me, and so the Church is my only kin now. As they intended. My stay at Santa Albegunda was the second time I was sent to a convent; I spent most of my young years at Sant' Osmer. I was returned to my parents shortly after my hands started to bleed."

"Did they—your parents—want to keep you with them?" Rakoczy could see that this question disturbed her, although she sounded tranquil when she answered.

"I don't know. When I was returned to their care, the priest beat me regularly, and for a time that sufficed. But the bleeding continued, and he said Santa Albegunda had waters that would cure me, so I was sent there, in the hope that the Saint might work a miracle. I think my parents were relieved to be rid of me. The rest of the town was growing nervous, and some of the neighbors had already asked that my father take his family somewhere else. He could not do so, of course, the Potente wanting to keep a tanner in his fisc." She stared toward the distant wall, seeing far beyond it. "I was tired of the beatings, and being spat upon in the street, so I consented to go to the convent at once. Perhaps I thought Santa Albegunda would cure me—I don't know—but most of the nuns weren't too much afraid, and that was a wonderful thing." As she glanced back at him, she said, "You cannot know how hard a thing it is to be despised."

"There you are wrong, Gynethe Mehaut," said Rakoczy, and there was something in the way he said it that held her attention. "I have been despised."

"For being foreign," she said.

"Among other things." He looked down into her face, his penetrating gaze as compassionate as it was enigmatic. "I know what you have endured."

She shook her head. "It's kind of you to say it, but you don't know—you can't. You are free to go your own way, which I dare not do. You have position and wealth and the high opinion of the King. At best I am a curiosity, and am fast becoming an inconvenience." With a little sigh she turned away from him, no longer able to abide the benignity she read in his dark eyes. "I believe you mean well, but you have no notion of what my life must be."

Rakoczy regarded her with deep compassion. "I may know better than you suppose," he said, "but I won't debate the question with you. You have much to bear and you have done so with more grace than anyone could expect of you."

At this, she swung back to scrutinize his face. "Your regard is unfeigned," she said after a long moment of consideration. "If you report that I am not as dangerous as many suppose, I may be given more freedom rather than increased constraint."

"Do you anticipate more restrictions?" Rakoczy asked, and anticipated her answer.

"Yes. It would reassure those who fear I am a messenger of the Anti-Christ. They want to remove me from the world." She sighed.

"Do you mean they want you dead?" Rakoczy was troubled that she would be put in such an untenable position. "How could they dare have you killed?"

"Being killed would not be as dreadful as other things." She swallowed hard. "You give me reason to hope I might be spared immurement."

"Immurement?" he echoed. "What makes you think you will be immured?"

"Sorra Celinde tells me that if there is any question regarding my . . . condition, that I will become an anchorite in a great convent or monastery, to perfect my penitence, and to give strength to the walls through my prayers." There was a tightness in her voice that she had held at bay until now. "That way, if my wounds are blessed, my sacrifice will be welcome to Heaven without bringing God's Wrath upon those who killed me. It will be a martyrdom, one the Church can revere."

"Penitence for what? Why should you be a martyr? What sin have you committed, that the Church should be willing to wall you up for it?" He felt a surge of indignation that he could not conceal. "The Church cannot expect you to do this."

"Why not? If Bishop Iso is right, my hands are an affront to God and Christ, blasphemous and . . . and profane. I carry the sign of the Anti-Christ, and no true Christian should have to endure my presence, or so says Bishop Iso. Bishop Freculf thought the same at first, but he has come to think that this is a sign of the favor of Heaven. He wouldn't protest making me an anchorite because the sanctity of my wounds would significantly strengthen the walls of any convent or monastery. But Bishop Freculf would not compel me to accept such a life, as Bishop Iso would. Bishop Freculf wants a willing sacrifice, not a capitulation." She held up her hands. "I don't know why I have these wounds. I don't know what they mean. I have no more understanding of them than any other person. I have never sought to be one with Christ, for that is not for women to achieve. I have never tried to reach beyond the vows of nuns for my deliverance, nor have I become a Sorra for fear that I might contaminate the others in the convent, if my hands are truly diabolical. I do not think they are, but Satan is the Father of Lies, and so I might not understand the damnation they bring. In all the years I lived with the Sorrae at Sant' Osmer, we were told of the purity of Christ's Blood and our salvation because of it, and for that, I revere His Wounds and know I am not worthy of them myself."

"Blood is the heart of it, isn't it?" he asked in a rush of tenderness.

"It is life, for the living and the holy dead," Gynethe Mehaut agreed, and signed a blessing. "It is the very center of Christian faith."

"And many others," Rakoczy said, remembering the chalices of blood in the mountains of Spain; he regarded her with increased appreciation, saying, "I will have to tell the King something regarding this night's conversation: what would you like that to be?"

Her expression was startled. "Do you ask me?"

"Those are your hands," Rakoczy pointed out. "Surely you are the one to say—"

She made a sudden gesture of refusal. "No. I will say nothing that will bring me any greater notice from the King."

"But how you live may depend upon what the King decides," Rakoczy told her patiently.

"So it might," she snapped. "But he will not listen to me."

"He will to me," Rakoczy said, his whole being offering kindness. "Tell me what you want him to hear."

This time when she searched his face, there was a penetration in her gaze that had been less apparent before. Finally she took a step back. "I hardly know what to say," she admitted. "No one has asked me such a question." She walked on a short way into the shadow of the garden wall. "I haven't knowledge enough to decide what is right for me in this."

"Possibly not," he said, "but you know what you experience and no one else does." He felt increasing rapport with this white-skinned woman, and a presentiment of peril to come. "Surely you must have some inclinations about what is to happen to you."

She considered her answer carefully. "I want my case to be put before the Pope as it will be for His Holiness to decide. If he truly speaks for God on earth, then he will know what should be done with me, for the good of my soul and the benefit of all faithful Christians."

Rakoczy heard her out, a coldness closing a fist within him, as if some unknown but inexorable force had been put in motion; nothing of his apprehension was reflected in his demeanor. He reverenced her. "If that is what you want," he said, "it is what I will do."

"Do you dare?" Gynethe Mehaut asked in astonishment.

"It is hardly a dare: the King has asked me to question you, which I have done, and he has asked me to make a recommendation, and that I will do. It is my commission; there is no impropriety in laying your case before the King, with my recommendation." He tried to give her an encouraging smile. "It is my intention to convey your desires as that recommendation."

She shook her head in disbelief. "If you will do this, I will be forever in your debt, no matter what the Pope decides."

"No, Gynethe Mehaut. You will owe me nothing," he said, his voice low and soft. "I am only a messenger, and that deserves no gratitude. If I can fulfill the task given to me, I will be rewarded enough." He took a step back from her, though he kept his voice low as he said, "I do understand much of your plight, little as you may think it possible: believe this."

Watching him, she realized she did believe him, and that troubled her as doubt never could. "If I am grateful, it is my decision. You cannot insist I not be so."

He inclined his head. "I am rightly rebuked," he told her, his tone light, his eyes somber.

"I haven't rebuked you," she said, chagrined that he might think she would so forget herself.

"It is just as well that you do," said Rakoczy quickly, seeing her distress. "I intended no correction, Gynethe Mehaut."

"You might," she said.

"It isn't my place to correct you," he said, wishing she would accept some gesture of affection, but certain she would not. "I intended only raillery; we are two strangers in this place: if we cannot laugh together, then we are truly lost."

She thought about this for a long moment, then gestured her comprehension. "I'll grant you so much, Magnatus. I haven't laughed in a long time; I hope I haven't forgot how."

"And I," said Rakoczy, relieved that she had not been completely put off by his attempt to amuse her.

"Why should laughter be so important? Those who laugh mock God and the King," said Gynethe Mehaut. "How can I laugh?"

"Great Karl laughs; other men laugh; the Bishops laugh." Rakoczy would have liked to touch her, to give her reassurance with an orectic embrace, but he was fully sensitized to her now and knew that she would not want it, that it would be an imposition, so he remained still. "Why shouldn't you? God shouldn't mind a little mirth in the world."

"That isn't what I've been taught," she declared, as if this would settle the matter.

"Then I am sorry for you, for to have faith without joy, you deprive yourself of its greatest gift," said Rakoczy intently. "Still," he went on more easily, "if it causes you dismay I won't do it any longer."

She was unused to such consideration, and it took her a long moment to be sure he was sincere. "You puzzle me, Magnatus."

"And why is that?" He wanted to see her walk out of the shadow, so that he could see her more fully.

"You aren't like the Bishops, or the hobu, and you aren't like the courtiers, and certainly you aren't like a peasant or a monk, so you puzzle me." As if responding to his desire, she came into the moonlight, looking him directly in the face. "You are foreign, but I suspect it is more than that."

"Why?" He took a step closer to her.

"Because you aren't afraid of me," she answered. "My skin doesn't frighten you, nor my hands. I might be any woman, and well-born at that."

"No, Gynethe Mehaut, I am not afraid of you. There is nothing in you to fear," he said, and took a step back from her. "I would be honored to be your friend, for I think you are in need of friends."

She looked away from him. "How can that be?"

"You have suffered much: I will do what I can to alleviate your affliction if you will permit me." He ducked his head to show respect. "I am not the ally a Frank would be, but I assure you that my Word is good, and I will abide by it no matter what may come."

"You do not know what may come," she countered.

"No, but I won't rescind my pledge," he told her, and gave her an opportunity to respond.

"I wish I knew why you do this," she said, and waved him to silence before he could speak. "You can say nothing that will incline me in your favor. I have no desire for the life beyond the convent."

"I was not asking for you carnally, or with any intent to seduce you," said Rakoczy, disquieted that she would think his offer of support had such an expectation. "I was hoping you would accept my assistance in any capacity I am able to provide it."

"Is this because we are both strangers, in our way? I could abide that." She did not quite smile, but a little of the resistance left her.

"Then let it be on that account," said Rakoczy; he remembered the aloofness he had first encountered in Nicoris, and how long it had taken her to trust him.

"As strangers, then, who are among strangers," she said, and turned away from him. "Sorra Celinde will come soon and I haven't finished my work in the garden."

"Among the night-blooming flowers," said Rakoczy, and waited for her to speak again.

"Yes. I want to make the most of the moonlight," she said, moving past him and hurrying back along the narrow path toward the plot where she had been working.

He followed her part of the way, saying, "I will inform you of anything the King tells me about his decision."

She nodded, indicating she had heard him. "I'll thank you, for the sake of friendship," she said over her shoulder as she fled.

Rakoczy watched her for a long moment, then turned and made his way back into the collegium of Attigny. As he walked, he thought over all that had passed between him and Gynethe Mehaut, as well as what had not. It had been an encounter that had left him restive; he was troubled by her request to ask the King to put her case before the Pope, but he would abide by his Word. He had been hoping he might be allowed to examine the wounds on her hands; but Bishop Iso had protested, and so he would have to wait for another time. Reaching the massive inner door, Rakoczy pulled on the bell-chain to summon the warder-Fratre who kept watch over the books and manuscripts within.

Fratre Gaugolf answered the summons reluctantly; he yawned as he pulled the door open and peered out at the man in the black gonelle. "It is late," he said bluntly.

"I am charged to write to the King tonight." Rakoczy waited patiently while Fratre Gaugolf opened the door.

"There is only one set of lamps lit. You will find it too dark to write," Fratre Gaugolf declared.

"Let me determine that, Fratre, if you would," said Rakoczy, his night-seeing eyes well-adjusted to the dimness of the collegium. "If you are right, I won't linger. But I must discharge my obligation to the King as handily as I may."

Grudgingly, Fratre Gaugolf stood aside and let Rakoczy enter the large chamber. "There are writing desks at the—"

"—far end of the room; yes, I know," said Rakoczy, controlling his impatience with this officious monk. "And sheets of vellum and parchment in the shelves behind them. The ink-cakes are on the desks, and the quills are in a box next to them—do I have it right?"

"Yes, you do," said Fratre Gaugolf. "Go, then, and try to write your letter." He stumped back to the bench near the fireplace; the two logs had almost burned through and now showed only sullen red embers amid the blackened wood. While Rakoczy made his way to the tall writing desks, Fratre Gaugolf took another log from the stack near the hearth and laid it on the dying fire; a shower of sparks heralded his efforts.

Rakoczy glanced at the monk, noting that Fratre Gaugolf was very sleepy and dragging his feet a bit as he went about this routine chore. He thought it likely that the monk would be dozing shortly; satisfied that he was not under surveillance, he chose a sheet of parchment, noticing that it had been used previously and the old text washed and scraped off, leaving only very faint impressions on the thin sheepskin. He carried this to the writing desk nearest the set of lit lamps, climbed onto the tall stool, and opened the box of quills to select the one he would use to write. He chose a sturdy goose-wing feather—the nib had already been pared—and set it in the groove at the top of the slanted desk-top, then took the ink-cake, moistened it with a little water from the small jar beside it, and using the rubbing stone, began to make fresh ink. While he worked, he did his best to compose his letter in his mind, so that he would be able to finish quickly.

"How long will you require?" Fratre Gaugolf asked suddenly, as if aware of Rakoczy's thoughts.

"I should be gone by midnight," said Rakoczy, thinking that he would then have the opportunity to visit Liuthilda in her sleep; the second wife of Comes Eggihard of Attigny, she was often left by herself for months on end, with nothing to do but supervise the Comes' bastards. Rakoczy would never approach her directly, but he had found that in dreams she would accept him with fervor that bordered on frenzy, and that suited them both. He dipped his nib into the ink and began to write:

> *To the most exalted, the most powerful Karl-lo-Magne, King of the Franks and all of Franksland, champion of the Church of Roma and the Pope, and Lord of Carinthia, Longobardia and the Marches of Hispania, the obedient greetings of Hiernom Rakoczy, Comes Sant' Germainius, on this, the beginning of April in the Pope's year 799.*
>
> *Optime, I have done as you requested regarding the Pale Woman Gynethe Mehaut, and I must inform you that her case is beyond my capabilities to evaluate, although I am persuaded that her condition is one of nature and not miraculous. This does not answer any of the questions you, and the Bishops, have about her. It is my recommendation that you submit her to the Pope, for his inspired opinion must be more profound than anything I, or your Bishops, may propose. I believe she would be amenable to such a resolution, no matter what the outcome may be; I offer myself as her escort to Roma, if it should be your decision to send her there.*
>
>

In all duty I sign myself
H. Rakoczy
(his sigil, the eclipse, and his name-sigil)

>

He read it over, pleased that his small, neat hand did not take up much more than half the sheet; that would allow others to use the parchment without having to scrape off his message. He was satisfied that there was nothing in the letter that would alarm the monk who would read it for the King. Then he sanded the page and waited for it to dry before rolling it neatly. This done, he wrapped the roll in a linen band and sealed the knot with wax. He returned the feather to the quill-box and closed it again, used a rag to dry off the ink-cake, and wiped the desk-top with his sleeve. Getting down from the stool, he walked to Fratre Gaugolf and handed him the rolled scroll. "For the courier."

Fratre Gaugolf blinked up at him. "The courier," he said as if he were unfamiliar with the word. "This scroll."

"For the King," Rakoczy persisted, thinking that Fratre Gaugolf was more than half-asleep. "He is expecting it. You must put it into the courier's hands."

The monk shook himself enough to be rid of the most obvious signs of sleepiness. "I will," he said, taking the rolled parchment and kissing the linen that held it closed.

"Very good," said Rakoczy. "Optime requires our compliance with his orders."

Fratre Gaugolf took a deep breath, fear in his eyes. "I will comply."

"I am sure of that," said Rakoczy, and turned toward the door. "If you will let me out?"

"At once," said Fratre Gaugolf, but took a short while to rise. "Will you be staying here at Attigny much longer?"

"No; I am returning to my fiscs in the morning." Rakoczy suspected that this information would be passed among the residents of Attigny before he was in the stable. "I may be gone before the courier departs."

"Then God keep you safe on the road, Magnatus." He made a sign of protection. "The courier will have this as soon as he has broken his fast. A pity this couldn't wait for the missi dominici, but they will not be here again for a month."

"Optime wants this letter before that," Rakoczy said as he opened the door. "May God keep you in good health, Fratre Gaugolf. May you do honor to your Church and patron Saint." He pulled the door closed and waited until he heard the bolt shoved into position on the far side of the door. Then he went down the corridor and out into the courtyard. He saw a line of monks coming from the chapel and going toward the entrance to the dormitory; he supposed they had finished Nocturnes. He stood, undecided, at the walkway leading to the residential part of the Royal Residence; it was possible that Liuthilda was not yet fully asleep, and it would be dangerous to visit her while he might waken her. When the monks were gone, Rakoczy considered going to the chapel, to speak with Gynethe Mehaut again. But she would be at prayers and Sorra Celinde might be with her; Rakoczy turned away from the chapel and strode toward the residential wing, hoping he would find Liuthilda caught in her dreams and ready to receive him.

TEXT OF A LETTER FROM ATTA OLIVIA CLEMENS IN ROMA TO HIERNOM RAKOCZY IN FRANKSLAND, CARRIED BY PAPAL COURIER.

To the distinguished Magnatus Rakoczy Sant' Germainius, sometimes called Sanct' Germain, currently at an estate near Stavelot and Sant' Cyricus in Franksland, the greetings of Olivia at the end of April in the Pope's year, 799.

You may have heard more rumors that the Pope has been attacked, very much the same as all the others over the last years: this time, the rumors are true—Leo was waylaid by a gang of street fighters, probably in the pay of the Byzantines. They tried to blind the Pope, cut out his tongue, and make a eunuch of him, but he escaped, and apparently has fled Roma. Some say he is in Hispania, some say he has gone to throw himself on the mercy of the Patriarch in Constantinople, and some say he has died and been secretly entombed. It is agreed everywhere that it is more likely that he has gone north, into Franksland, in the hope Karl-lo-Magne will protect him. If the

Pope is still alive a month from now, and in the care of the Franks, he will maintain his position, provided he has not lost his sight, his tongue, or his manhood, in which case his efforts would be for naught: he will have to resign the Papacy if he is not a whole man, which many say he cannot be. A few claim he has been delivered by God's Grace from all his enemies, in which case I must suppose he has gone to the Blessed Isles of the Saints, which no navigator has yet to find, let alone make landfall. All these possibilities are fueling more speculation in Roma, and the city is lively as a hive. You would be well-advised to stay away until the Papacy is once again secure, one way or another. Had I not only just begun an expansion of my estate, I would go to Ravenna for a year or so, but that would look most suspicious, and so I will remain where I am.

So much for the most recent upheavals. Now on to the more mundane purposes for this letter. I am pleased to know the stallion I sent to you has turned out so well. May he continue to provide you with foals of a quality that meets your standards for horseflesh. I am grateful to you for your offer of one of his colt-foals, but I won't ask for him just yet. Get a second generation of his line, and then I will be delighted to receive one of your foals, with enough new blood to give strength to the foals to come.

My own herds are doing fairly well, but there has been a spate of hoof disease. I have had to destroy eleven of my stock, and that saddens me. I am determined to restore my herd in the next year, and to find something to treat the hoof disease so that it cannot harm my animals again. My horses are my wealth in these days, and I will not see them all come to nothing. I have asked Niklos Aulirios to review all the material we have on treating diseases of the hoof in the hope that there may be something we can turn to good purpose. If among your various medicinal substances you have a treatment for peeling hooves, I would be grateful to know of it. I have moved most of my sound horses to Villa Ragoczy, with the intention of keeping the disease from spreading, and if it is in the ground, to keep it from passing on to the rest of my horses.

You will wish to know that Villa Ragoczy has been partially repaired, but I fear the old stables have fallen to ruin: there are now only stalls enough for fifty-six horses and not the four hundred that you boasted when the Villa was new. The second atrium is still in disrepair, but the larger one has been made secure and I have installed two mansionarii at the Villa to guard it and to supervise the mariscalcus and his grooms. It has very little of the luxury it had when I first saw it, when Vespasianus was Caesar, although it is no longer as battered as it was when last you saw it. But then, Roma is much less than it was when I was a breathing woman. You haven't seen your Villa in more than two centuries; the whole of Roma is like Villa Ragoczy, and you may find it a disappointing place when next you come here.

I have recently turned away from the attentions of Ermanaricus, a personable young man who is somewhat of a functionary of the Papal Court. It would probably be unkind to call him a spy. He has been a courier and has performed other services for Leo, which is why I have so much information about the attack on His Holiness. He has been a lovely dalliance, full of passion and invention, but I do not want to bring him into our life; he is under too much scrutiny and it is difficult enough to manage as a vampire in this world as a breeder of horses: to try to maintain the position of a Papal servant would be impossible and would expose all of us to precisely the kind of notice we seek to avoid. So I have bid him farewell, and that has left me in an unfortunate frame of mind, bouts of loneliness and a sense of being ancient vying for my attention.

So I hope you will come to Roma. There is nothing like a month in your company to restore me to a sense of the world once more. I know you are still attached to Great Karl's Court, but it may be that you can persuade him that you can best serve him in Roma. At least do not turn from such an opportunity, should it present itself. I am thankful that at least you are no longer in Hispania, or those remote Wendish marshes where you have vanished from all contact but the Bond of Blood. Come to Roma, Sanct' Germain. You and I could recall our long years, together and apart, and indulge in nostomania for a while, until memories becoming boring and we look to the future again.

There. I have done with my spasm of wistfulness. I will not impose on you any longer, but I will send this off with Fratre Modestinus so that it will be in your hands within a month if all goes well and his donkey doesn't founder. He is bound north in two days and will go to three monasteries before he reaches your region. Luckily the spring has not been a wet one and I understand the roads are dry enough for travelers to get through all but the highest passes without bogging down on the road; it is a reassuring thought that few outlaws bother with monks.

Be sure that this comes to you with all my love, and a little nostalgia as well—the love is by far the stronger.

Olivia

chapter fifteen

EO III, POPE OF THE ROMAN CATHOLIC CHURCH, was haggard, still unable to stand upright but considerably more alert and active than he had been a month ago when he had arrived at Paderborn in the bed of a carrucum, concealed by a load of cabbages and sweet grass and protected by monks from Longobardia. The cuts on his face were a raw-looking liver shade and were going to remain as a constant reminder of the attack that had nearly killed him. This morning he leaned on the arm of Fratre Berahtram, saying, "I believe I can walk a short distance on my own, Fratre. I thank you for supporting me all this way."

Fratre Berahtram looked out into the neglected garden just beyond the door, and he hesitated. "Holiness, I think it is my duty to stay near you."

"I understand," said Leo, sighing a little; he sighed often these days. "And in this time and place, I am sure I should avail myself of your care. You are a most devoted assistant. I am very grateful." He coughed once and winced at the pain it caused.

"Exactly," said Fratre Berahtram. "I would not forgive myself if any harm were to come to you, Holiness. I have sworn to the King that I would guard you from now until you return to Roma."

"In a garden in the castle controlled by Karl-lo-Magne, how could I not be safe?" As he spoke, Leo flinched. "You may stay near-by, but permit me to walk in the garden on my own, if you will. You have given me excellent care, Fratre Berahtram, and you may be sure of my gratitude."

It was less than Fratre Berahtram had wanted, but enough that he was satisfied. "As pleases you, Holiness," he said, and released his hold on the fragile Pontiff.

Leo took a short while to steady himself, then started forward, his step uncertain but determined. He made his way slowly toward the rear of the garden, looking up into the summer sky as if expecting to see Heaven itself suspended high over Paderborn. His sight was still cloudy from the attempt to blind him, and although his vision was improving, he could not make out sharp details and used his sense of smell as much as his eyes to guide him down the beds of fragrant herbs and opening flowers. He made a slow circuit of the beds of flowers and vegetables, to the night garden, where a few plants still remained, their petals closed for the day; his face was drawn, and even so mild an exertion as this had left him short of breath and faintly sweating in the early August heat. So that he would not appear as weakened as he was, he went to the wall where pear trees

were espaliered; the first of their fruits were ripening. There he paused, his breathing strained, for his broken ribs were not yet fully knit. Much as he wanted to,
he could not summon the words to pray, which troubled him: if anyone should
pray, it was he, not just because prayers were required of the Pope, but because
he had such good reason to be thankful for his life and deliverance. He lingered
at this corner of the garden for some little while, contemplating his salvation on
earth as much as Heaven.

Fratre Berahtram came up to him. "I was worried, Holiness," he said, excus-
ing his behavior.

"Ah, Fratre. Truly they say you are a great healer. You have brought me out
of the jaws of death." He fingered the long, livid line on his chin and chuckled.
"I shall remember you in my prayers every day of my life." The Little Hour of
None was fast approaching, and he would have familiar words to recite, and the
opportunity to recommend those who helped him for celestial favor.

"Thank you, Holiness," said Fratre Berahtram, trying to sound humble and
pleased at once, though he was neither.

"When all of this problem is sorted out, and I am once again in Sant' Pier's
Seat, I shall reward you more appropriately," the Pope went on, his fingers moving nervously in the folds of his long dalmatica. "You have a talent for tending
those afflicted in their bodies, no doubt. Your patron Saint must be a powerful
advocate for you before God."

This kind of pronouncement did little to end Fratre Berahtram's frustration.
He wanted to say it was the potions and unguents Magnatus Rakoczy had given
him that had healed him, not any patron Saint, but he could not admit that the
responsibility—and therefore Pope Leo's gratitude—belonged to another. After
all, he, Fratre Berahtram, had tended the injured man; and it had been he, Fratre
Berahtram, who had been summoned to Paderborn, not Magnatus Rakoczy.
Surely God intended that he should receive the esteem reserved for the man who
had saved the Pope, not the man who had made the medicaments that he had
used. "You are all charity, Holiness," he said, hoping his silence would be taken
as awe instead of the calculation it was.

"Yes, yes," said the Pope ruminatively. "You are an example that more religious
should follow. I will let the King know of my high regard for you, and between
us we should arrive at some suitable recognition for you." He looked up at the
sky. "So few clouds today."

"May God be thanked," said Fratre Berahtram, uncertain what was expected
of him. His stomach growled, missing the prandium that was just concluding;
Pope Leo had not been hungry, and so he, too, had to fast.

"Truly. Every day. I hadn't realized until I was spirited out of Roma, how thankful I could be." He smiled a little, one scar pulling down a corner of his mouth. "It has been a most instructive experience, surviving to come here. I have a new understanding of the Power of God." He coughed. "And I am every day reminded of the Power of Karl-lo-Magne," he added.

So Pope Leo was in one of his cheeky moods again, thought Fratre Berahtram, frowning at this realization. He had yet to gauge a proper response to these Pontifical sallies. "As the Saxons are learning," said Fratre Berahtram.

"I am grateful, also, that he has sent his couriers to Roma to inform the Cardinal Archbishops that I am alive and whole, and in his care," said the Pope. "It will cause the Byzantine faction some disquiet."

"No doubt," said the Fratre. He was grateful when the bell sounded for None. "Holiness?"

"Yes. If you will walk beside me as far as the chapel, you will increase my obligation to you." He did not hurry, knowing it would be folly to arrive at the chapel out of breath; better to be late than seem to be ailing. "I am told the Saxons have burned another monastery and killed all the monks."

"That is what the courier said," Fratre Berahtram murmured.

"A great tragedy, not only for the monks, but for those pagans, if only they realized it. They are the ones who have suffered the most. They sin against the True Faith and will suffer for it when Christ comes to reign in Glory." They were almost to the garden gate. "The courier reported much fighting. Do you think anything will happen to Great Karlus?"

"God has preserved him so far, and he has sons to carry on his work," said Fratre Berahtram as he opened the gate.

"Yes. So he does." Pope Leo went through the gate and along the wall toward the chapel. "We must pray for him, asking that God's Strength and Mercy be upon him. Without him, the Church would surely be in Byzantine hands by now, and the promise of salvation lost forever."

Being able to think of nothing else to say, Fratre Berahtram cried, "Amen."

"Truly. Amen." The Pope was flagging a bit, his steps growing shorter and slower. "Do not rush, Fratre Berahtram. They will wait for me." He lifted his hand to the Bishop who stood in the chapel door waiting for him. "There, you see? They haven't started yet."

"They wait upon you, Holiness," said Fratre Berahtram, knowing what was a proper response, "out of respect."

"Bishop Agobard is a most prudent man," said Pope Leo, smiling slightly; the cicatrices across his face felt like hot wire. "Karl-lo-Magne is fortunate to have him as an advisor, just as he is fortunate that God sent him Sublime Alcuin." He almost stumbled but caught himself before Fratre Berahtram had to steady him. "Don't fret, good Fratre. You have brought me back to the world and I intend to stay here until God is finished with me."

"May God be praised," said Fratre Berahtram, feeling a bit foolish.

"Perhaps," said the Pope, "Bishop Agobard could name you his successor. Would you like that, or would you prefer to remain among the sick and injured, to do cardinal Acts of Charity?"

Somehow Fratre Berahtram managed not to grin or whoop. Finally to get away from stinking infirmaries, from the howls and demands of the dying! His stock of medicaments was running precariously low, and he dared not approach Magnatus Rakoczy for more, knowing he would be exposed if this became known. He pretended to consider the matter. "God called me to tend the afflicted, and now, through you, He calls me to other work. I will do as you wish, Holiness, certain that you speak for God in the world."

Pope Leo cocked his head to look at Fratre Berahtram. "Very well," he said at last. "When the King returns, I will speak with him and Bishop Agobard about changing your station." He patted the Fratre's arm. "If you will escort me back to my apartments when None is finished, you will have until Vespers for your own."

"You are very good, Holiness," said Fratre Berahtram, reverencing the Pope. He hoped he could find some meat left in the kitchens; probably most of the scullions would have devoured anything not eaten in the dining hall, but they were supposed to set aside a portion for charity, which, if anyone deserved, it was he.

The chapel was cool and dark; the monks, priests, and Bishops sat on benches according to their rank; they rose for the Pope and reverenced him, then, when he had taken the sedes before the altar, sat again and began their devotions in near-silence. The men in the chapel all tried to demonstrate their piety so that the Pope would look upon them with favor and remember them when he returned to Roma.

In his place toward the rear of the chapel, Fratre Berahtram exulted, praying to express his gratitude for the advancement that the Pope had promised him, for promise such a pledge must be. He asked God to return Karl-lo-Magne quickly and safely, not for the King's benefit, but so that he, Fratre Berahtram, might finally be given the advancement he had so truly earned.

It was three days later when Karl-lo-Magne clattered through the stockade gates of Paderborn just after mid-day, accompanied by a dozen Bellatori, a trio of Potenti, and a Comes to announce that he had beaten back the Saxons and exacted revenge for the murder of the monks. He was grimy, sweaty, and his knuckles were skinned, but he grinned hugely as he got down off his horse and roared for a cup of honey-wine. "We must drink to celebrate our triumph!"

Immediately the soldiers garrisoning the castle gathered around him, shouting their approval and demanding to know more. One Primore took advantage of his advanced rank and pushed through the milling crowd to the King's side. "What has happened?" he bellowed.

Karl-lo-Magne, standing head and shoulders above almost all of the men, laughed immensely. "We caught the greatest part of their hosts unaware—men and women, the aged and the young—and we surrounded them. We had the advantage in surprise and weapons and we made the most of it; we surrounded their camp and charged from all four sides. They tried to fight, but we over-whelmed them, killing those who lifted arms against us, taking prisoners and slaves from the rest; it was over in less than half a day. A hundred of the men will be made into eunuchs and sold to the Moors, who always want fair-haired eunuchs. They will not stand against me again, and they will have no sons to oppose me." He clapped his hands, and the men around him rollicked. "We have brought back women, young women, for the delight of you—my trusted soldiers. You may make wives or concubines or whores of them. That is up to you. But I will not have them giving birth to any but Franks, so that we will finally have an end to this infernal rebellion."

A mansionarius hurried up, a large pitcher in his hands. "Honey-wine, Optime. Honey-wine. My deputies will bring cups in a moment."

Karl-lo-Magne stretched out and seized the pitcher. "Bring a second one for my men," he ordered. "This is mine!" He raised the pitcher and drank from its lip, swallowing eagerly until the pitcher was half-empty. "A worthy beginning to what must be a feast!"

The mansionarius beat a hasty retreat to comply with the King's orders and to alert the kitchen that they would have to make ready for a major celebration. Behind him he heard Karl-lo-Magne shout, "Day after tomorrow! I want all my Bellatori here, and all the Bishops who can get here! Send couriers at once!"

There was a sudden flurry as the couriers detached themselves from the crowd around the King and hastened off to the stables, an under-senescalus in their midst, issuing assignments to the couriers as they went.

Comes Godefrid, who had ridden in immediately behind Karl-lo-Magne, yelled, his roughened voice not as easily heard as Karl-lo-Magne's strident cries. "We captured over three hundred horses, almost all of them sound. And we have yet to count the swords and spears, or the shields and axes and daggers."

This, too, was excellent news, and the men hooted and clamored enthusias-tically. The Bellatori had dismounted, and now the Potenti joined them, thrusting their reins at grooms who stood at the edge of the throng, hands outstretched. Gradually the grooms were able to extricate the horses from the crush and lead them away toward the stables.

Karl-lo-Magne was taking another drink, his face beaming. "We will celebrate our victory and the victory of the Pope!" he announced. There was a brief silence as the men recalled that the Pope was a resident of the castle, but it quickly gave way to more hearty demonstrations as the mansionarius returned with two large pitchers and a parade of scullions behind him carrying trays of cups. The confusion increased in the frenzy to be first to drink with the King, and a few times men exchanged blows before Karl-lo-Magne called them all to order again. "We must thank God that the Saxons have paid for their desecration of our monasteries. It is good that the Pope is here to see the men who have delivered his Church from defilement." He held up his pitcher, which was now almost empty. "Where are my daughters? Let them come to share my joy! Where is my wife?"

The mansionarius looked about in dismay. "They must know you have come, Optime," he said uneasily. "Your daughter Gisela is at prayers."

"She's an Abba. She ought to pray," said the King, dismissing this. "Where are the others? Gisela may join us after—what Hour is it?—None?"

"Yes, Optime," said the senescalus as he came back from the stables. "Your couriers will be away shortly. I have dispatched nine of them."

"Good," Karl-lo-Magne approved. "Very good." He drank a little more; his pitcher was almost empty. Seeing this, the mansionarius signaled one of his scullions to go and fetch another two pitchers. "What is there to eat now? It is late for prandium, but there must be something they can put on a spit for us."

"Of course, Optime," said the mansionarius, looking helplessly at the senescalus.

The senescalus of Paderborn took over. "There are geese and ducks that can be prepared quickly. And two stags are hanging, dressed, in the slaughter-house. They will take longer to prepare, but if you will be content to have the birds first, you need not be famished for long."

"Excellent, Recho," Karl-lo-Magne shouted. "Be about it at once. You!" He pointed to the mansionarius. "You go and tell the cooks to ready the geese. We'll need at least twenty of them. And more than that number of ducks. Don't dawdle, fellow. Go!" He did not wait to see if he would be obeyed; he swung around, still relishing his success. "The rest of our army will be here in time to banquet in two days. Make sure that Catulf and Gersvind are summoned to attend: they will have much to do between now and then, and their service should be reward-ed, along with Fratre Berahtram's." The mention of the two most respected Jewish physicians in Paderborn brought cheers from the men, most of whom had been treated by them at one time or another. "I wish that foreigner Rakoczy were here; he would be useful."

"Your missi dominici could fetch him in . . . perhaps twenty days, if the weather holds and they ride hard," said Recho, preparing to dispatch the pair currently at Paderborn.

"No, no," said Karl-lo-Magne before he drank the last of his honey-wine and held out the pitcher to trade for another. "In twenty days I may be ready to return to Aachen, and then he would have been summoned for nothing. No, let him remain at his fiscs for the time being." He moved through his men. "I would like to have a swim. A shame we haven't a pool here."

"There is the river," Comes Godefrid reminded him.

"Not the same. The river would have to be guarded, and that spoils the sport." He drank from the second pitcher, but less eagerly than he had from the first. Wiping his mouth with the back of his hand, he gestured to Recho to come nearer. "Put the kitchen to work. We're all hungry and if we don't eat something soon, the men will be wild as Avars."

"At once, Optime," said Recho, reverencing the King before rushing off to speed activity in the kitchen.

Karl-lo-Magne raised his free hand and motioned his men to follow him. "To the dining hall. There will be bread, at least, and new butter." All but crowing he led the surge into the central building, going directly to the dining hall. He took his place on the dais in the center chair and signaled to Comes Godefrid to sit on his left. "The Pope should join us. He may have my right hand. The other chairs are for my daughters and my wife."

Comes Godefrid reverenced the King and hastened up to the High Table, saying, "You show me much honor, Optime."

"You fought well, Comes," said Karl-lo-Magne. "It is fitting that you, being near-kin to me, should have this favor." He slapped his big hands on the table, the loud thump signaling for silence where the men were jostling for places to sit on the benches at the three long tables. "Do not fret about your ranks. Seat yourselves among your comrades and enjoy their company."

Another troop of scullions—Saxon slaves—appeared bearing pails of beer and large baskets of round loaves of bread. They struggled to distribute these among the men while a mansionarius served the King and his second cousin once removed. The commotion had died down a little when Bertrada and Rotruda came into the dining hall, shouting out greetings to their father and hurrying toward him as if they were still children. Karl-lo-Magne slewed around in his chair and opened his arms to receive them.

"It's so *good* to have you back again!" Rotruda exclaimed, and kissed his hand, giving attention to his skinned knuckles.

Karl-lo-Magne bussed her cheeks, saying, "Where is my wife?" between kisses.

"She'll be with you soon," said Bertrada. "She's been keeping Hours with

Gisela, in the hope that she will finally conceive." She glanced at the mansion-arius. "I'll have wine. The red from Tuscany if you have any."

"There may be some, Illustra. I'll have to look," said the mansionarius, apprehension in every line of his body; he knew that his disappointment of this powerful woman would mean a beating.

"Do so, and quickly," said Bertrada.

"You'd best bring two bottles or more. Gisela likes Tuscan wine, too," said Rotruda. "I'll have honey-wine, from my father's pitcher." She favored him with a winsome look.

More slaves came from the kitchen, bearing wheels of cheese and tubs of butter; they were welcomed with cheers and eager gestures as they made their way along the three tables. In the middle of this, the bell that signaled the end of None rang, and the men paused to sketch a cross in the air in front of them before resuming their scramble for food.

"Gisela and Luitgard will be here shortly," said Rotruda, sinking into a chair beside Comes Godefrid. "How was the fighting, cousin?"

"It was fierce, but good," he said, reaching for his drink.

"Has my wife been good company for you?" Karl-lo-Magne asked Bertrada. "She has not always liked coming on campaign, but it would be folly to leave her behind, unprotected. Who knows what might befall her on my account?" He patted his daughter's hand.

"Luitgard is sensible in her way," said Bertrada. "She knows she must stay with you, but you cannot blame her if she dislikes the conditions this imposes."

"She's not like you, is she? She has no taste for the rigors of campaign, though she must endure them," he asked fondly, brushing his hand over her long braids. "You've been at my side since you were out of swaddling bands."

"As have we all," said Bertrada, and looked up as Leo III appeared at the far end of the dining hall. She rose and reverenced him; gradually the room went quiet as the rest of the company followed her example, except her father, who remained seated until the Pope reached the dais and came up to him.

"Most Holy Leo," Karl-lo-Magne said, rising and embracing the Pope. "You honor my table. Sit and dine with us."

Pope Leo nodded, acknowledging the reverence the King offered. "I am thankful to you, Karl-lo-Magne."

"God has given us a victory, Holiness," Karl-lo-Magne went on, making sure he spoke loudly enough so that everyone in the dining hall could hear. "Your prayers and presence brought us strength and took will from our Saxon enemies."

"Then let us praise God for His Goodness," said Pope Leo, holding his hands up in prayer before taking the seat the King indicated at his right. "It is always a worthy victory when the Church is vindicated." He reached for the silver cup the mansionarius had just placed before him. "I am grateful to you for doing God's Will."

"Amen, Holiness, amen," said Karl-lo-Magne, and heard this echoed throughout the dining hall.

More bread and cheese were carried in, to be grabbed and gobbled by the men on the benches; the under-mansionarius came to the High Table with silver trays of bread still warm from the oven, and cheese in waxen rinds. He reverenced the estimable figures before him as best he could, then served the food as if this were a banquet instead of an impromptu meal.

As Pope Leo broke the loaf he had been offered, Gisela and Luitgard entered the dining hall and made their way past the long table to the High Table. They reverenced the King and the Pope, then took their places, accepting the cups the mansionarius had managed to fill with red Tuscan wine.

"You look tired," Gisela said to the King. "Was it a hard fight?"

"It was. The Saxons are purposeful foes, but they could not stand against us." Karl-lo-Magne turned from his daughter to his wife. "Have you been busy here at Paderborn?"

"Oh, yes," she answered. "I have been teaching your children—the ones who haven't learned already—how to do sums."

"How good of you," said Karl-lo-Magne, and looked back to Gisela. "What more have you done in the last weeks?"

"I have read a great deal. Odile has shared two of Magnatus Rakoczy's books with me, and I have found them most interesting." She took a long draft of wine.

"Ah. Odile," Karl-lo-Magne said with a slight smile. "Is she well?"

"She is very well," said Gisela with a knowing look at her father. "She is here at your pleasure, Optime. As are we all."

Karl-lo-Magne gave a single nod, then gave his attention to the Pope. "There are many things we must discuss, Holiness."

"I agree, Optime," said Leo. He drank a little more wine to fortify himself. "Now that I am nearly recovered, I must return to Roma."

"You must, it is true, but that need not be at once," said Karl-lo-Magne. "Best wait until you are fully restored to health."

"That may mean traveling in winter, which is more hazardous than taking to the road now. Once the rains come, and the snows, I may be unable to move until spring, which would give my enemies many months to prepare for my return. I would prefer not to give them such an advantage." The Pope turned in his chair to look directly at Karl-lo-Magne. "You must be aware that the longer I am gone, the weaker my supporters become."

"Your enemies know you are with me, and that ought to give them pause," said

Karl-lo-Magne, and was cut short by the stamping of the men's feet in welcome to the first spit of geese, sizzling and smoking from the fire. He waited while these were portioned out, then went on. "Anyone who acts against you acts against me."

"A most laudable sentiment," said Pope Leo, "but permit me to say that it may not be as true as you want to believe. In this time, there are many demands on the members of the Papal Court, because I am not there to hold the Church on course. Too many of the Cardinal Archbishops are inclined to listen to the Byzantines, and to lend them support. If I were in Roma most of them would hesitate before undertaking any alliance with the Patriarch, for they would know I"—he stopped while a kitchen slave cut wings and legs from the largest goose and laid them on a tray, then split the body in half, putting one section before Karl-lo-Magne and one before the Pope—"they know I will punish such sedition with severity. No one can force their compliance as I can."

The King had picked up his section of goose in his hands and was tearing at the skin with his big, yellow teeth. He stopped, chewed, and said, "If you are going to indulge in a contest of wills, Holiness, you would be well-advised to wait until you know that you can carry the day. If you remain here, all my Bishops will be summoned to vow their continuing allegiance to you, and that will make them eager to accompany you on your return, which will increase your strength beyond your present supporters."

Pope Leo thought this over while he used his knife to cut away a section of breast. "You have a very good point, but it isn't persuasive enough to convince me that it is worthwhile to be gone longer than I must be."

"I would never feel I had done my duty to you if I should allow you to leave before you have had the opportunity to solidify your position with the Bishops of Franksland," Karl-lo-Magne said with feeling. "They will be your staunch defenders if you need them."

More fowl was brought in on spits—ducks this time—and they were distributed among the men, a special spit being brought to the High Table. Each person there was given a duck apiece and another tub of butter to rub on the blackened skins.

When he had drunk more wine, Pope Leo said, "In regard to your Frankish Bishops, I have a request to make."

"What would that be?" Karl-lo-Magne asked through a mouthful of hot duck.

"Fratre Berahtram. He has done me excellent service and I would like to reward him for it, not only because he is deserving, but because he makes a fine example to all the rest of them." He finished his wine and was nonplussed when Gisela refilled it for him.

"Oh, yes. He is a most worthy man with a fine reputation. He deserves a bishopric of his own." The King scowled. "Though Christ alone knows where I shall find one without giving offense to one or another of my Court; they have to defend their—" He broke off. "Wait a moment." He picked up his honey-wine and drank it down as if it would speed his thoughts. "Wait. There is a place . . . part of a bishopric, but neglected. The Majore of the central village came to . . ." He thumped his forehead with the heel of his greasy hand. "What is the *name* of that place?"

"What were you planning?" the Pope asked, alarmed at this display.

"I will split this portion of the bishopric off from the other; they're far enough apart that it won't rile the other Bishops. The Bishop rarely goes there, if the peasants were correct in their complaint, and I would think Fratre Berahtram wouldn't mind traveling a bit for his reward. The Comes doesn't go there, either, and so I can advance one of the men who have supported me against the Saxons with fiscs that do not encroach on another's." He smiled wolfishly and took another bite of duck. "Ambrosius of Solignac has the bishopric, that much I recall. He will not mind giving it up if I advance that bastard of his to a Magnatus. He understands these things."

"Is there a monastery for his sedes?" Pope Leo asked, pulling a strip of meat off the duck and popping it into his mouth. "It is hardly a bishopric if he has no sedes."

"Oh, yes. It's proper. It has four villages, as I recall, and at least a monastery." He drank again; his cup was refilled by the mansionarius. "There's a nunnery, too, as I—*Sant' Yrieix!*" he shouted, a spray of wine and half-chewed duck heralding the village. "That's the place! Sant' Yrieix. And the others are Cometou Gudi, Sant' Ianuarius, Sant' Damasus, and . . . and . . . Lacosasse." He pounded the table with his fist; all those around him stopped eating and stared at him. He shook his head. "It's nothing to do with you. Go back to your meal!"

The Pope was at once relieved and dismayed. "Optime, you have frightened your daughters."

Karl-lo-Magne laughed, a great rumbling guffaw. "My daughters don't frighten, Holiness. They have been on campaign with me for all their lives. They have seen the worst and the best of me, and they are not troubled by minor outbursts. Are you?" He looked from Rotruda to Gisela and then to Bertrada. "Well?"

"You haven't frightened us since you returned safely," said Rotruda. "It is your absences that frighten us, not your presence."

"There, Holiness, you see? Even my wife knows not to fear me." He reached out and tweaked her chin, leaving a smear of grease where his thumb had been.

"It seems to me that some of your fighting men were startled," said Pope Leo, determined to make his point.

"That's because they're on their mettle with me," said Karl-lo-Magne proudly. He raised his fist and was answered with shouts and drumming hands. "They are ready to follow me into the mouth of Hell, if that should be what must be."

The Pope took another drink of wine. "Then you are more blessed than any King has ever been."

"That I am; don't think I don't know it," said Karl-lo-Magne with a trace of smugness. "I thank God in all my prayers for all the good things He has heaped upon me, and I vow to serve Him as His vassal on earth, as I expect to be served by my vassals." He drank most of his cupful of wine, and then said, "Now. About Sant' Yrieix. Bishop Ambrosius appointed a priest there, and I would think that as soon as I notify Ambrosius of his change of enrollment, I should send missi dominici to the priest and the Majore, to inform them that they will have a new Bishop, a man of good character who has earned his advancement." He winked at the Pope. "This is what the villagers wanted, and you know how obdurate peasants can be. I have punished the missi dominici who abused my trust, but I will now be able to make it possible for these peasants to have what they wanted."

Pope Leo heard this out with conflicting emotions: he certainly wanted Fratre Berahtram to have a real benefit from all he had done to treat him, but he was wary about the King's decision being so relentlessly pragmatic; there was no concern for the souls of the peasants and monks and nuns, only a regard for their governance. He lifted his cup. "God will reward you for your labors as they are deserved."

Karl-lo-Magne raised his cup in agreement. "Amen, Holiness. May God hear you and answer you with Majesty." He finished his honey-wine and signaled for more. "All in all, this has been an excellent day, Holiness. Yes. An excellent day."

"And say we all Amen," said the Pope, and as he lifted his cup, he wondered how he would explain his coming change of circumstances to Fratre Berahtram. The one thing he decided he must do was perform the celebration of the monk's elevation to Bishop before he departed for Roma. But that, he reminded himself, was for later. Now he wanted only to help Great Karlus applaud the latest defeat of the Saxons.

TEXT OF A LETTER FROM ODILE AT AACHEN TO MAGNATUS RAKOCZY AT HIS FISCS.

To the most esteemed Magnatus Hiernom Rakoczy on the full moon called the Woodman's Moon, in the Pope's year 799, my most sincere greetings.

The missi dominici who carry this to you also return the books you were kind enough to loan to me in those days when we were lying together. You will agree that I would be in error to keep them now that I have the King's child growing in my womb. I am so joyous I can hardly find words to express it. I will have another child before I die. And I will not lose all my late husband bestowed upon me. This is the one father my late husband's family must accept, and receive with pleasure and favor, or risk losing their position of respect at Court. They have been promised that the King will do my son honor, and if I give him a daughter, he will arrange a suitable marriage for her, or find a convent where she may be Abba, so that she will not be a burden on me or on my late husband's kin.

I am grateful to you for the time we spent together, for through your attention, my worth became apparent to Great Karl. I am also thankful that you did not leave me with child, or I would not be able to present the King with another child. For this and your many considerations you will remain in my prayers for at least two years.

You must not grieve that I am no longer your mistress; you yourself said that we would not remain together for many years, and you know that I am resigned to our separation, as you must also be.

Odile

part two

HIERNOM RAKOCZY, COMES SANT' GERMAINIUS

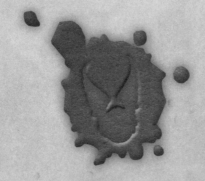

To the most excellent Magnatus, Hiernom Rakoczy, on this, the last day of January in the Pope's year of 800, the greetings of Alcuin of York, Bishop of Sant' Martin at Tours, of Sant' Josse, Sant' Loup, Flavigny, Sens, Ferrieres, and Cormery, with the prayers that this finds you in good health and enjoying the continued favor of Karl-lo-Magne.

Magnatus, I have taken the liberty of writing to you in order to prepare you for the changes that may soon come upon you. I know Optime is not inclined to allow his people time to prepare for the work he intends for them. I think you would be better served knowing what has recently passed between the King and me in regard to you and your many skills.

Well do I know that you have been more devoted than most of those Franks who are his kinsmen, and that you have received more envy than thanks for all you have done. Therefore I am going to tell you what the King wishes you next to do: he will send you to Roma, in advance of his going there. He has certain unfinished business with his Holiness which must be smoothed unofficially, and that is the task he intends to wish upon you. At another time he might have sent me on such a mission, but he is now trying to keep the Church from any appearance of dispute as well as giving Pope Leo every opportunity to show his own power so that it will not be assumed that the Pope has become a Frankish puppet and not a Byzantine one, as some of the Cardinal Archbishops continue to hope.

Since Optime is aware that I am not in favor of his efforts to make himself Emperor, he has permitted me to remove myself from the contention in Roma, which I am grateful to him for granting me to do. The Bishops of Franksland are divided enough for many reasons; I have no desire to provide them with an excuse to be more alienated one from another. So some of my burden will fall on your shoulders. You, as a foreigner, need not uphold the honor of any kin, and this gives you opportunities most of Great Karlus' Court do not, and cannot have. You may not think this a reason for rejoicing, but I must tell you that you perform a true service when you undertake this mission.

In addition to all the rest, the King will ask you to escort the Pale Woman, Gynethe Mehaut, to Roma so that the Pope may make a decision in her regard. As you may have been told, after due consideration, it was thought too dangerous to bring her to him while he was still recovering from his wounds, in case her bleeding hands are truly a sign of the Anti-Christ, and therefore sure to be harmful to Pope Leo. In Roma, surrounded by Cardinal Archbishops, the Pope will have fewer reasons to fear Satanic strength than he would have in Paderborn, where he lacks the support of the Cardinal Archbishops. If you are not troubled by her—and I have been informed you are not—then you would spare many clerics, and the young woman as well, the risks that many feel she represents. I hope you will pray on this, and meditate on all she may represent before you agree to escort her, for once she is in your care, you will not be able to walk away from her until she is in Roma, and by then, you may be damned. That would be poor recompense for all you have done, and an unworthy end to your service to the King and Church. If you decide you can endure her company, then God will surely bless your endeavor unless you succumb to the lures of diabolical forces.

Bear in mind, if you will, that this woman is not like others, and though she appears similar to most, she is apart from humanity, as much as she would be if she were an ape. Do not be deceived. You will have to protect yourself from any malign influences she may have, and it will be your duty to be sure that others are likewise protected. Your escort cannot be snared by her seeming helplessness, or you will not be able to travel safely. If it should be revealed that these wounds and her pale skin are signs of God's Favor, then all who guide her may count themselves most blessed for the honor of being in her presence for so long as it takes you to escort her.

The King will provide escort of his own soldiers, which will vouchsafe his protection through all his realm. For that reason, you will not be needing your manservant, who may remain on your fiscs in order to act in your stead as he has done before. The soldiers will not tend to your wants beyond their mandate, but you do not need a servant to look after you at all times as some of the effete Romans do. Be sure to take such belongings as you will need in Roma, including a full ceremonial dalmatica for the coronation Optime is planning for himself. If you would prefer to purchase such garments in Roma, then be sure you take sufficient sums to pay for them; as much as Karl-lo-Magne shuns display in his general life, he insists upon it for ceremonial occasions, and no one is exempt from his requirements, no matter how great the cost may be.

I hope you will receive this in the spirit in which I intend it, for you have been a most exemplary Magnatus and therefore, in my opinion, deserving of a chance to prepare for the journey you will have to make. You are an experi-

enced traveler, and that is to your credit. I pray that you will find the roads passable and free of bandits and other rogues, but that is in God's Hands, is it not?

Alcuin of York, Bishop
By my own hand

∽

chapter one

RORTHGER SECURED THE STRAP around the second trunk filled with Rakoczy's native earth and tested it to be sure it would hold. "How soon must you depart?"

"The escort will be here tomorrow or the day after, if we have no more rain." He looked around his upper room, the small windows ajar, his athanor still cooling from his night's work. "There will be gold enough for the both of us for more than a year as soon as I can remove the crucible."

"That is all to the good," said Rorthger. "You will make another tour of the fiscs before you leave?"

"A cursory one, yes. I'm afraid I have to ask you to come with me, so that the villagers understand that your authority is my authority while I am gone." He sat on the tall stool and opened an alabaster jar set on the table in front of him. "This is for all manner of stings, bites, and burns. Use it sparingly. And remember, it is no help against the bite of a mad dog." He stared into the middle distance. "Almost nothing is."

Because he had heard these instructions many times, Rorthger asked no questions; he watched his master, doing his best to read his state of mind in his behavior. "No. Almost nothing is." He glanced toward the largest window, indicating the cloudy sky. "This is a wet spring."

"Yes," Rakoczy agreed. "And the water will be high, for a wet spring here brings an early thaw in the mountains." He looked down at his Persian boots of black, embossed leather; the thick soles and heels were atypical for the design, but only Rakoczy and Rorthger knew that. "The earth in my soles should be replaced tonight."

"I'll attend to it," Rorthger promised. "Will you see Waifar? His arm is fully healed and he is becoming unreliable."

"Is he stealing?" Rakoczy asked.

"I think so. He's also snooping about the villa. One of the women in Sant' Fleur complained that he had tried to waylay her when she went to drive the sheep into the meadows." Rorthger shook his head. "He has no gratitude to you, and no obligation."

"I didn't set his arm with that anticipation," said Rakoczy, and went to his old, red-lacquer chest. "You know where I keep the sovereign remedy and the lotion for pustules. The drawing-paste is in the yellow jar, and the tincture for wheezing and coughs is in the tall bottle. The syrup of poppies is in the stoneware container. Linen strips are in the drawers. What am I forgetting?"

"It hardly matters, my master," said Rorthger with a faint smile. "I know where you keep all your medicaments. The green box has the herbs to ease childbirth, and the covered scyphus has the liquor for bathing open wounds." He approached Rakoczy and closed the doors of the chest. "How long do you suppose you will be gone?"

"I hope less than a year," Rakoczy told him. "The King won't travel south until he has spent much of the summer and fall on campaign. Then, when winter stops the fighting, he will come to Roma for his coronation, or so I understand from what the missi dominici said before they left yesterday." He rubbed his face and encountered stubble. "You'd best shave me and trim my hair before I leave, as well; with no reflection, I can hardly trust myself with a razor or shears."

"At least mirrors are few," said Rorthger, determined to shake off the first intimations of melancholy that were encroaching on Rakoczy. "I will tend to that when I have done your boots and your brodequins. Will you visit any women before you go?"

"You think I should, don't you?" Rakoczy said. "I may. Will you be content to leave it at that?"

Although it was not the answer he hoped for, Rorthger nodded. "You have a long way to go, and in sunlight. It would be prudent to fortify yourself."

"I don't disagree," Rakoczy said. "But with Waifar on the prowl, it might be wiser to find a woman at some other estate on my travels."

"You will go from here to Attigny?" Rorthger asked.

"Yes, to get the Pale Woman. Then we'll go south to Luxeuil, through Burgundy to Tarantaise, then east across the mountains to Lake Como." He ticked these destinations off on his fingers.

"To your villa there?" Rorthger asked, supposing it would be his destination as a break on his journey.

"Yes, if there is no trouble with it. I have a Will from my supposed uncle, bestowing it on me. It will match with the copy at Sant' Chrysogonus, and that should be enough for the local Potente to permit me to take possession of it; he does not know me. My native earth is in the foundation and it will certainly strengthen me." He shook his head. "Old friend, please believe that I will not put myself in any danger that I can avoid."

Rorthger was not convinced, but he said, "Of course," and let the matter drop. "When did you want to make your rounds of the villages?"

"Soon, I should think. Have Hradbert saddle our horses—none of those I am taking with me; they need a day of rest and feeding—and we'll set out as soon as I have a word with Bufilio." At the mention of this mansionarius, Rakoczy saw Rorthger frown. "What is it?"

"He has gone to his uncle's house. He left last night, a short while before sunset. He said there was something his uncle required of him, but I don't know what it is." Rorthger swore under his breath. "I think Waifar followed him."

"To do him mischief?" Rakoczy asked sharply.

"I can't say, but I worry. I should have mentioned it, but with all the activity of yesterday, I didn't remember noticing until just now." His scowl hid his chagrin.

"You needn't castigate yourself," Rakoczy told him. "I might not have noticed such an event at all." He got off his stool. "So. Inform Hradbert that we will ride out shortly. I trust all is well with the horses; he has said nothing about any trouble."

"All is well," said Rorthger, relieved that he could offer Rakoczy some welcome information. "Livius' new foals are thriving. We have three so far. You saw the two colts; there is also a filly." He inclined his head. "I'll go find Hradbert at once."

"Fine," said Rakoczy. "I'll finish with my medicaments I'll carry in my sack, and then I'll come to the stable."

"Shall I wait for you there?" Rorthger paused on the second stair beyond the door.

"Unless I am delayed too long." He gestured toward the windows. "I'll go get my leather mantellum, in case of rain."

By the time they met again in the stable, Rakoczy had donned his black leather mantellum and had pulled on black gloves from Verona; these were very likely among the most impressive items of clothing he owned, for gloves were a luxury in Franksland, and simply wearing them would awe the villagers and peasants he would see. "I know," he said to forestall the remark he could sense Rorthger longed to make, "but it is more effective than shouting or ordering beatings would be."

"So it would," said Rorthger as he climbed onto a big-shouldered bay gelding. "And much less trouble."

Rakoczy gave a crack of laughter. "Am I so obvious?" His grey gelding minced and sidled as Rakoczy swung his leg over the high cantel.

Hradbert stood by the wide stable doors, shaking his head. "You only use those blunted rowels. You'll never get any real speed from your horses without sharpened rowels."

"That hasn't been my experience," said Rakoczy, and used his calves to urge his grey into a trot; the horse was fresh and wanted to respond, his forward action slightly exaggerated. "He'll calm down in a bit." Gathering the reins, Rakoczy started his horse toward the villa gate; as he passed out of the villa, he saw Waifar loitering around the corner of the wall and wondered briefly what the man was doing there. Then Rorthger caught up with him and they set off at a canter for the village of Monasten, keeping to the narrow roads rather than cutting across the newly planted fields.

The village was in the middle of a ring of fields, woods flanking the fences defining the two tilled plantations just now beginning to bristle with new growth of barley and rye, and the fallow land that for this year would be pasture where sheep, goats, and cattle grazed. Smaller fields contained the last of the winter cabbages, and the rest of the meadow was kept for hay. There were sounds of trees being felled, and nearer to the cluster of houses, a chorus of children's voices was raised in determined protest. As Rakoczy and Rorthger rode into the center of the village a large, thick-coated dog began to bawl. Almost at once a number of people came stumbling and running from all directions; young, old, and in-between, the peasants turned out to hail their Magnatus into their midsts. Most of the peasants were glad to see him, but a few had the sullen, reserved stares that indicated discontent, and not one of them would have welcomed the Magnatus inside his house; generous and just Rakoczy might be, but foreign he certainly was, and that outweighed all other considerations.

Nirold, the Majore of Monasten, came in from his work on repairing the creamery roof; he was covered in flakes of sawdust, and he was sweating freely. He managed to appear welcoming in spite of his obvious and immediate labors. "Magnatus," he said, ducking his head. "It is a pleasure to look upon you."

"Thank you, Nirold," said Rakoczy, stopping his grey near the well. "It is a pleasure to be here. If someone will draw up a bucket for my horse, I will be grateful."

Nirold snapped his fingers and gestured to a pair of lads about nine years of age. "This is not the usual time for your inspection. What brings you to our village, Magnatus? You aren't bringing us another pony, are you?"

"Not if you don't need one," said Rakoczy with enough of a smile to indicate that he found the request amusing. "I should hope you will make do with the one you already have."

"No, we don't need another, not so long as we have mares enough for your gift," said Nirold. "The stallion you brought to us has done his work with a will. We will have two more ponies by the end of spring. In time we may be able to sell our ponies at market. That will be a great day for all of us." He stood with his chest thrust out, knowing that it would be a real distinction for the village.

"That means the breeder gave good value," said Rakoczy. "See you treat his get well, and make sure you keep the best of the mares to be your dams."

"We will do," said Nirold. He looked about, unprepared to report and trying to find some other sign of their improvement. Finally he declared, "And we will have more goats this spring. There are fourteen lambs so far, and we will only use eight of them for food before the first market." He stared up at Rakoczy. "Will you be here, to attend our first market of the year?"

One of the nine-year-olds brought a pail of water to Rakoczy's horse; the other child did the same for Rorthger's bay gelding.

"A very good number," said Rakoczy, doing his best to sound approving. "May all your nannies and ewes bring forth healthy young, and may you have a good summer. And may you have a rich harvest." He waited a moment, knowing they would not like what he had to tell them. "I regret that I will be gone from my fiscs for some months and won't be able to—"

There was a mutter of protest, and Nirold barked an order to quiet his people. "Why are you going?"

"I go on the order of Great Karl himself, and I will see the Pope in Roma," said Rakoczy, knowing this would quiet most of the villagers. "While I am gone, Rorthger will assume my rights and authority, as he has done in the past. You will address your complaints and requests to him and I will uphold his decisions."

"Do you plan to become a monk?" one of the men asked.

"No; I won't do that," said Rakoczy. "The King wouldn't like it, and, as I am a foreigner, most Orders would probably not be willing to accept me." He dismissed the idea with a gesture of his beautiful, gloved hand. "The fiscs will still be mine, and while they are, you will be treated as I have done from the first. Let Rorthger hear you, and it will be as if I had."

The sound of a falling tree held the attention of them all, and then, when the cracking moan had been replaced by a scraping slap, one man burst out, "How can he? He is only a servant. He cannot do more than servants are permitted to do."

"And I am only a Magnatus, the King is only a King, the Pope only a Pope," said Rakoczy. "It is not the position, but the man, that matters. His service includes being my deputy, a duty he has discharged excellently in the past." That past stretched back more than a thousand years, but Rakoczy did not mention that. He reached into the pouch that hung from his girdle and brought a handful of silver coins. "This is so that you may rebuild the houses that burned last year. If any is left over, build another house." He handed the coins to Nirold.

Nirold took the coins and counted them carefully, staring in astonishment. "So many? Magnatus, there is a coin for every soul in the village."

"Not quite that," said Rakoczy. "But there are fifty of them, which should serve you in good stead; your village has seventy-nine people in it, if no one has been born or died in the last ten days. These fifty coins are yours. See that you spend them wisely. This is not the time to hoard them against a later need: you have houses that must be repaired or their families will spend another winter jammed into the houses of others. And you need to expand the village a little."

"We can exchange labor for that," said Nirold, his manner cautious.

"Perhaps you can, but you will need coins to buy iron for the cooking pots and spits in the fireplace, and you will have to purchase certain other supplies, such as iron for the smithy and clay for the potters. All the village will benefit from such purchases. And, of course, you will have donations to make to the monks and nuns." Rakoczy held up his hand. "Do as I bid you, Nirold. It will bring you no harm, and you will find that it is most useful to your purposes."

Nirold sighed. "As you say, Magnatus."

"Take your harvest to market and earn coins for yourselves; you will not need many of them to improve the lot of your village," he recommended. "You should have enough of a surplus to do that."

"We like to keep our surplus," said Nirold.

"For those things you can store, a very good idea," said Rakoczy, and paused before going on. "But for those things you cannot store, that will only rot if you try, those you should carry to market to make the most of them so that if you have a shortfall, you can purchase what you need. That would make you better prepared for hard times than trying to keep things that decay." Knowing that he could persuade this group of villagers with this, he added, "It is what the Romans of old did."

Nirold folded his arms. "Then we shall do it. If your servant will not take our earnings as his own."

"He will not," Rakoczy said.

"So you say. But while you are in Roma, he may decide that he can add to his own wealth while you are gone—for who is to say you will ever return? If Roma itself does not hold you, there are dangers on the road that could prevent your coming back. You might be held for ransom, or killed by brigands, or be maimed in an avalanche." Nirold made a gesture against bad fortune, and many of the men did the same. "You plan to return, but who is to say what will happen once you are gone?"

"No one knows what lies ahead," Rakoczy agreed. "But we must plan as best we may, and trust to God to guide us aright."

"So the Abbott says." Nirold did not quite sneer, but he showed his uncertainty by pinching his left shoulder, to rid himself of sinister influences.

"You should listen to your Abbott," said Rakoczy, and prepared to swing his grey around. "I am giving Rorthger the right to hold Court if it becomes necessary. I am giving him the authority to collect the revenues of the fisc at the same rate of last year, and not a jot more. I am ordering him to do all repairs and improvements that I have begun, and to maintain the schedule I established. All this is done according to the Rule of Karl-lo-Magne, King of the Franks and ruler of all Franksland."

Nirold frowned. "We shall abide by the Rule, unless it is found to be in error," he said grudgingly, and motioned to his people to stand back.

"That is all I can ask," said Rakoczy.

One of the boys holding pails shouted, "God favor our Magnatus!"

A few of the villagers echoed this sentiment, but Nirold glared at the child. "That's not suitable, Roewion."

Rakoczy leaned down in his saddle. "Still, it was high tribute, and I thank you for it," he said, and slipped a copper coin into the boy's hand. As he straightened up, he pulled his grey around and started toward the edge of the village; the peasants fell back, opening the way for him.

When they reached the outer limits of the village, Rorthger said, "His father will take that coin from him. And he may be beaten."

"He may be beaten in any case," Rakoczy said. "This way, he has something of his own the whole village knows—my gratitude."

Rorthger nodded. "In a week, all this will have been changed in retelling, in any case." He indicated the narrow path leading into the trees. "The woodmen went that way. Do you wish to speak with them?"

"I suppose the others in the village will tell them what transpired," Rakoczy said. "I think it is best to visit the Abbott of Sant' Cyricus next; he will want that courtesy, and he is in a position to make things awkward for Monasten if he feels slighted."

"As you say, my master," Rorthger affirmed, and set his bay trotting behind Rakoczy's grey.

Abbott Hroccolf received Rakoczy and Rorthger in the central courtyard of the monastery. He leaned heavily on a stick and made no attempt to reverence the Magnatus. "How does it happen that you have come here just now?"

Rakoczy explained his reason for the visit, and ended by saying, "If it is possible, I will advance the name of this monastery with Pope Leo; I may not have the opportunity, but if I do, I will. I can promise nothing more than that, but that much I do assure you I will do."

"As a man of your position should," said Abbott Hroccolf. "We will pray for your safe journey." He raised his head to meet Rakoczy's steady gaze. "If you do not speak for us, we will curse you."

"I understand," said Rakoczy, a wry light in his dark eyes. "I will bear that in mind."

"See that you do. Roma is a most seductive place; many men with high purpose have been undone there."

"I have been there before," said Rakoczy.

"Still," said the Abbott. "Don't forget that Roma is as dangerous as it is holy."

"I will keep that in mind, good Abbott," said Rakoczy, and signaled Rorthger that they should depart. He offered the Abbott a half-reverence from the saddle.

"One more thing, Magnatus," said Abbott Hroccolf.

"Yes?" Rakoczy held his grey in place.

"If your servant should disgrace you, we will tell the peasants to disobey him, and we will offer them sanctuary from him." The Abbott pointed to Rorthger. "We have seen the treacheries of servants before, and we will do all we must to contain it."

"If I can repose perfect trust in Rorthger, Abbott, you should have no difficulty in doing so." Rakoczy began to ride toward the gate.

"No one can have so much trust in a servant," the Abbott insisted in a louder voice.

"Perhaps among the Franks," said Rakoczy, stung to a sharp reply. "Among those of my blood, we have no such uncertainties."

Beside him, Rorthger said quietly, "Don't anger him, my master. He will not take it well."

"Why is he so adamant in his distrust of servants, I wonder," said Rakoczy as he urged his horse through the gates of Sant' Cyricus and out into the road that led to Stavelot.

"He need have no reason; most of the Potenti and Magnati distrust their servants." Rorthger pointed back at the gates of Sant' Cyricus. "All of them. The Abbott is no different."

"He's a bitter man, that is a difference," said Rakoczy. "Be careful of him."

"I will do," said Rorthger.

They had visited Santa Julitta and four villages by the time the sun dropped low in the west. "There is one more village on this road," Rorthger told Rakoczy.

"Yes. I remember," said Rakoczy. "Vulfoald's village. Cnared Oert."

"Sant' Trinitas," Rorthger added.

"Shall we go there? They will be about to eat." Rakoczy checked his grey. "Well?"

"Do you want to leave them out? They might take it badly," Rorthger warned.

"And they will take an interruption of their meal badly, too, so either way we may cause them distress," Rakoczy observed, then shook his head once. "But best to inform them, or they will assume the worst: that they have lost favor and will be singled out for punishment." He started his gelding down the road.

Following him, Rorthger said, "They will remember your kindness to them."

"Do you think so?" Rakoczy countered. They rode for some distance without speaking, watching the sunset arrive and fade from the sky, until they were guided by the large communal fire at the center of the village, and they could hear the buzz of conversation.

"Shall I ride ahead and announce you?" Rorthger asked.

"No; that would only alarm them," said Rakoczy. "We'll just ride in together." In the nearest pasture, the sheep began to mill and baa nervously. "We're announced, after all."

Torches flared to life as four men lit them and hurried toward the track that led into the village. The people gathered around the fire moved back from it, seeking haven in the shadows.

"It is Magnatus Rakoczy," Rorthger called out. "You have nothing to fear. He comes only with his servant. There are no soldiers." He moved ahead of Rakoczy and into the circle of light. "You know me. And you know my master."

Rakoczy pushed forward. "I am no stranger here."

"Yet you are a foreigner," Vulfoald reminded him as he came up to Rakoczy's horse and ducked his head. "But you are welcome here."

"Thank you," said Rakoczy, and began to explain his coming absence. "It is an honor to do the work of the King," he said as he saw the men exchanging uneasy glances.

"It could be putting you into danger in the King's stead," said Vulfoald. "Why else would he send a foreigner to Roma?"

"Perhaps because I know the Roman Court," said Rakoczy, and continued his account. "You will find justice and succor at my villa, in the person of my servant Rorthger, who has been my deputy in the past."

"He's also a foreigner," said Vulfoald. "But we know him."

"That you do," Rakoczy agreed at once. "Until I return, you may rely upon him."

Vulfoald held up his hands. "We will. But only if we cannot deal with our own, or if we must face outsiders." He indicated the coins Rakoczy had given him. "We will use this at market, but only for those things we cannot trade to get."

"That is all I ask," said Rakoczy, and continued telling the villagers how long he supposed he would be gone.

Vulfoald ducked his head as soon as Rakoczy finished. "We'll do as you say, when our needs are beyond the village." He coughed. "We caught an outlaw, some months back. He was injured. He and his companions had been plundering small crofts about here. We killed him for what he had done."

Rakoczy considered his response carefully. "In future, it would be better if you bring such criminals to my Court. If you have transgressors within your village, you may deal with them, but if they are from beyond, it is more suitable to allow my Court to—"

"Those outlaws have money enough to bribe any judge. We have suffered the injury, and we will be avenged." Vulfoald folded his arms. "In other things, we will honor your order, but in this, we must have vengeance, or we will be left to endure more impositions."

"I would rather you do not do so, but as I will not be here . . ." He looked over at Rorthger. "What do you think?"

"I think that if I hear of vengeance being claimed here that I will have to demand someone answer for it." Rorthger directed his gaze at Vulfoald. "And if I learn that a killing was concealed, I must report it to the King, and you know what Great Karl will demand."

"All the men of the village will be taken as slaves, and all the women as whores. The children will be sold for slaves, and our stock will be given to the Magnatus," said Vulfoald, and spat into the fire.

"Yes. And if I do not uphold the King's Law, I will have to answer for it," said Rakoczy, "as will my servant."

"You can stay in Roma if you don't want to answer to the King. The Pope will shield you," said Vulfoald.

"Not this Pope," Rorthger countered. "This Pope owes his life to Great Karl."

Rakoczy kept silent, knowing he could not say anything that would be acceptable. Finally he raised his hand. "I will come back, so long as I am . . . alive."

Vulfoald studied him. "I am inclined to believe you, for now. You have kept your vows before," he conceded.

"And I will do so again," Rakoczy told him.

Again Vulfoald studied him. "All right. We will do as you tell us, foreigner."

"Magnatus," Rorthger corrected.

"Magnatus," Vulfoald repeated. He lowered his head. "It was good of you to give us silver."

Rakoczy nodded his acknowledgment and said, "Resume your meal. I rely upon you to hold to your Word as I will to mine." With that, he rode out of the village, knowing Rorthger was close behind him.

"Vulfoald does not trust you," Rorthger remarked once they were past the limits of the fenced land.

"No, he does not; I doubt he trusts anyone," Rakoczy said, putting his grey on the narrow road back to his villa.

"He could betray you to outlaws," Rorthger added.

"He could, but he won't—it would wound his pride," Rakoczy responded.

"He may have done it before," Rorthger said. "Someone told those outlaws we were on the road, and where we were going."

"Yes, but it didn't have to be Vulfoald," Rakoczy said.

"You're inclined to give him the benefit of the doubt," Rorthger said in a tone that suggested his disapproval.

"Perhaps that's because I would like him to do the same for me," Rakoczy said, and went on in a steady manner, "He may be a scoundrel, and he may have parlayed with outlaws, but he has taken my coin, and that changes things."

"Yes. It makes him want more from you," Rorthger warned, and was content to ride the rest of the way in silence.

They reached the villa some time after dark, their only incident being a brief encounter with a flock of sheep that had escaped from their fold. They were met by Bufilio and Amolon, who were keeping watch at the gate for the Magnatus' return.

"We must have a word with you, Magnatus," said Amolon as he reverenced Rakoczy.

"Can't it wait? My horse needs a good brushing and a measure of oats for his work today." Rakoczy dismounted and started to walk toward the stables, his pace brisk as if he had not been riding all day, his grey gelding walked slowly behind him, his pace slowed by fatigue.

Bufilio was clearly nervous, tugging at his cuculla and camisa as if he were a child caught in mischief. He coughed. "Magnatus, you must hear us. It is urgent."

Rakoczy stopped and turned to his mansionarius. "What is it, Bufilio?"

"Amolon discovered the theft; I saw the thief flee. We knew you had to be told." He shook his head as if unwilling to impart any more bad news without permission.

"Told what?" Rorthger demanded as he dismounted. "What is so wrong that you meet us at the gate with your tidings?"

Rakoczy held up his hand and shouted for Hradbert. "Mariscalcus! Come get these horses!" He led his grey around the well in the courtyard, saying, "Until he is groomed, he needs to be kept moving."

Rorthger followed after him, leading his bay at a brisk walk. "This gelding needs to have his shoes checked; his on-side rear shoe is clicking." He turned to Rakoczy. "If Hradbert is at comestus, then I'll walk the horses until they are claimed for grooming. You go with Amolon and Bufilio."

"Whatever they have to say, you should hear with me," said Rakoczy, unwilling to relinquish his reins. "I'll wait until you can be with me."

"You may not want Rorthger to know—" Amolon began, only to be cut off.

"Rorthger will have to serve in my stead. He must know everything I do," said Rakoczy. "If you cannot tell him, then you must not tell me."

Amolon ducked his head. "Very well." He was about to withdraw when Hradbert came bustling up, wiping his hands on a square of cloth. "I didn't realize you were back, Magnatus," he said to Rakoczy. "I ask your pardon. I should have met you at the gate when you arrived." He held out his hands for the reins.

"A moment," Rorthger said, and told Hradbert about the loose shoe. "They must have oats tonight, and be given a day in pasture so that they may rest."

"I will do so," said Hradbert, taking the horses and leading them away.

"Now," said Rakoczy to Bufilio, "what did you need to say to me?"

"Here? In the courtyard?" Bufilio looked shocked at the very idea.

"Yes. In the courtyard. No one can approach us without being seen," Rakoczy said. "In the house, it is possible for any person to listen, if he isn't noisy. Tell me what troubles you."

"It is Waifar," said Amolon, dropping his voice to a whisper.

"What about Waifar?" Rakoczy asked.

"He is gone," said Bufilio. "I saw him leave. He had a sack slung over his shoulder, and he went out by the gate by the kitchen, where no one was watching."

"You were watching," Rakoczy pointed out.

"But I was there because I had been talking to my uncle. I was not stationed there as a guard," he said. "I saw him go, and it struck me as odd that he would leave in such a manner."

"And what manner was that?" Rakoczy asked, noticing how apprehensive Bufilio had become.

"Furtive," said the mansionarius. "He slipped away as if he feared pursuit."

"That may be his habit," Rakoczy said. "He has been an outlaw and must have studied how to move stealthily."

"Then it is well-learned," said Amolon. "I found that your small chest in your book room—the carved one that contained your jewels?—was empty. The mansionarius for the ground floor told me that Waifar had been in your book room only a short time before."

Rorthger whispered a curse in Latin. "That is how he thanks you for saving his life."

"I never expected thanks," said Rakoczy, a sardonic lift to his fine brows.

"Just as well," said Rorthger, who knew of how genially obdurate Rakoczy could be. "Are you sure he is the one who took the jewels? Are you certain they are gone?"

"Yes," said Amolon, cowering in expectation of a beating. "I would have stopped him had I known what he had done."

"I am certain you would," said Rakoczy. "I'm not holding you responsible, nor you, Bufilio. If anyone is to blame, it is I, myself." He glanced at Rorthger and saw his disapproving expression. "You cautioned me, and I didn't heed you."

"But your jewels are your fortune," said Amolon, daring to speak in spite of his fear.

Rakoczy nodded. "That they are. And a man in my position must have some wealth of his own beyond what the King grants him." He took a deep breath. "So I suppose I will have to make more of them." He managed a quick, enigmatic smile.

"What do you mean?" Amolon gasped; he looked about guiltily.

"Well, it is one of the things that is whispered about me among the servants, is it not? That I make jewels?" Rakoczy asked, his manner becoming remote. With Bufilio and Amolon staring at him, he went into the house, leaving Rorthger to explain his remark.

TEXT OF A LETTER FROM BISHOP ISO AT SANT' STEPHEN PROMARTYR IN TRIER TO BISHOP FRECULF AT THE ROYAL RESIDENCE OF QUIERZY, CARRIED BY MISSI DOMINICI.

Amen

To the Sublime Bishop Freculf currently residing at Quierzy at the behest of Great Karlus, King of the Franks, the earnest greetings of Bishop Iso at the church of Sant' Stephen Promartyr in Trier on this, the beginning of the Paschal Season in the Pope's year 800.

Good Bishop, surely you must see that your continuing defense of the Pale Woman Gynethe Mehaut is proving to be a most contemptible stance for so worthy a Churchman as you have shown yourself to be in years past. I can only conclude that this creature has bewitched you with the power gained by her bleeding hands and her red eyes. You seem unaware of the risk she imposes upon you, and for that reason, if no other, I am inclined to pray for your deliverance from her influence; I have dreamed again of her malignity, and the disaster she is capable of bringing to all Christendom through her most reprehensible blasphemies, which you mistake for blessings.

How is it that I cannot persuade you to turn away from her and make it plain to all good Christians that she is a snare and a deception? How else is it possible for a woman—the instrument of Adam's Fall—to bear the wounds of Christ but that she intends to pervert the Sacrifice Our Savior made for us? Say whatever you will, this woman is clearly the agent of the Anti-Christ, if not, in fact, the Anti-Christ herself. How could she be anything benign with such eyes?

I implore you to abandon your defense of her, or if you will not, that you will remain in Franksland and not follow the Court to Roma. Without your advocacy, the Pope is certain to find that she is the demonic presence I know her to be. If you insist on pursuing your ill-conceived apology for her, you may yet throw the Church into disorder that will serve no purpose but to further weaken the position of the Pope and the Roman Church, which may well lead to the capitulation to the Byzantines and the end of Salvation.

If you cannot concede that your course may lead to debauchery, ruin, and unspeakable sin, then it can only be that the evil of that Pale Woman has overtaken you, and when it is shown that she is a snare to all the faithful, you may have to share her fate. Before you put yourself into any greater danger, I beg you to think on these possibilities and pray for the guidance you have not had thus far. As it is the Paschal Season, I urge you to remember His Death and His Resurrection, and in such contemplation, I trust that God will give you His Light to lead you from the darkness you have embraced in this Pale Woman. If you cannot learn from the Passion of Christ, then you must truly be lost to our faith. If that should be the case, then I will supplicate for your removal and excommunication, which are abhorrent to me.

In the Name of God and His Son, forsake the cause you have made of this woman before you are the first and most lamentable of her victims. Her penitence is a ruse, and her worship contaminates everything she touches. Renounce your adherence to her and leave her to the Pope—so I pray.

Iso,
Bishop and Brother in Christ

⌒

chapter two

AMONG THE SIX SOLDIERS WHO ARRIVED with their leader at Rakoczy's villa to escort him were his own patroned men: Usuard, son of Ansgar, and Theubert of Sant' Cyricus brought up the rear of the armed men who would accompany Rakoczy and Gynethe Mehaut to Roma; this was intended as a compliment to Rakoczy, for the King rarely permitted his Court to be guarded by patroned soldiers, for fear of creating a potential insurrection. The soldiers rode in at mid-afternoon and were greeted by Rorthger, who ordered beer and bread for them, along with rounds of cheese. "In the dining hall, as proper guests." It was the only proper way to greet men of rank who had been on the road, and Rorthger had been prepared to give them the expected reception for the last two days.

"A handsome offering," said the escort leader Einshere, for once meaning it rather than simply following the forms demanded by custom; his fourteen years of soldiering had taught him to appreciate true hospitality. He signaled his men to dismount and permit their horses to be led away to the barn for a grooming and oats. "We will leave at dawn tomorrow," he shouted to Hradbert and the grooms. "See they are fed again at Matins. You must hear the bell at Sant' Cyricus. Rise with it, and give oats with hay."

Rorthger did his best to look pleased with this high-handed demand. "Good Bellatore, we know that you must rise early. We will also take every care to see that your horses are ready for the journey. Your tack will be cleaned and any necessary repairs made, and your mounts will be groomed. Their legs and hooves will be inspected, and we will do the same for the mules that will carry the matériel needed for the long days ahead. You may leave here certain that your animals are sound and you have enough food, for yourselves and your horses and mules." He was pleased to see the mansionarii emerge from the house with pails of beer and a tray of large drinking cups. "See, Bellatori? Here is your first libation of welcome to this villa. Drink in the name of my master and Great Karl."

Einshere took the first cup offered and watched impatiently while it was filled. Then he shouted, "All honor to King Karl-lo-Magne!" and drank down the whole contents and held out his cup for more. "Is your well sweet?" he asked, adding, "So many are not. Water is a chancy thing."

"In that we are fortunate here," said Rorthger. "This well is pure and runs the year around. It's true that many other villas are not so fortunate as we are."

"And your master?" Einshere demanded in an abrupt change of subject. "Where is he?"

"He is completing the packing of his garments and readying his chests for travel," Rorthger answered as if this were the most usual thing in the world.

"He does not use his servants for such work? Where are his slaves—in the fields?" Einshere was half-finished with his second cup of beer. "This is very good."

"My master, being a foreigner, keeps no slaves. And he has traveled much in his life, and has oftentimes packed his own chests." Rorthger could see that Einshere was becoming flushed already, his fair skin turning ruddy on his cheeks and forehead. "Let him suit himself. Your bread and cheese await you in the dining hall. I fear it is not a grand chamber, such as you find in Royal Residences, but it is sufficient to handle your numbers." He indicated the door and graciously led the Bellatore toward it. "There will be comestus come Vespers. You will be well-fed then. They are already busy in the kitchen, turning two lambs and a shoat on spits for you, and making a porridge of lentils and onions."

"Fine fare!" Einshere held his cup so that he left a dribbled trail of beer for the others to follow. "I am hungry. Three days in the saddle and I am a wolf at table."

"As any man would be," said Rorthger at once, doing his best to be cordial. "Well, come in and have your bread and cheese. There is no new butter—the day has been too wet for that—but there is clotted cream, and that should serve in its place."

Behind Einshere, Usuard and Notrold, a burly soldier from Mainz whose father had been Archbishop there, shouldered his way, forcing the others to move aside; Notrold looked about as he entered the house, saying as he did, "Your patron does well for himself. Look at those hangings. Such rare things they are." He pointed to two lengths of embroidered silk that had come from China more than two centuries ago. "Those are treasures the King would not despise."

"Yes," said Usuard, awed by the hangings and the fine Spanish hanging lamps. "Yes, he does."

The dining hall was only large enough to accommodate forty men, but the two tables were of fine polished wood, and the benches had low backs on them, a touch that had Notrold's immediate approval. "Very wise. No man will fall over and take the whole row with him. Someone in this household is clever." He went and took a seat near the fireplace, thumping his fists as he sat; his cup rang like an ill-tuned bell. "Sit, sit," he said to Usuard. "The scullions won't bring us our bread and cheese until we're all seated. That's how it is in grand houses like this one."

"And you know this, do you?" Einshere muttered.

Usuard did as he was ordered, taking the place opposite Notrold. A moment later, Theubert of Sant' Cyricus sat beside him. "Did you know our patron was so well-off? He is grand as a Comes, they say," he whispered. "The servants are well-fed and their clothing is new."

"I noticed this," Usuard admitted. A moment later, the rest of the escort took places at the table.

Rorthger went to the door leading to the kitchen and called for the scullions to attend at once. "You have the bread and cheese ready. Bring it here."

The six men thumped the table in anticipation and were shortly rewarded by the arrival of loaves of new bread and a wheel of cheese as well as a tub of clotted cream; their leader did his best to maintain an air of decorum, but failed. The men at the table fell to as if they had not eaten in days.

"Is all well?" Amolon asked Rorthger from the corridor.

"Thus far," Rorthger replied. "And you?"

"Yes. I have informed the Magnatus that the escort has arrived."

Rorthger smiled slightly. "I must suppose he heard the commotion." He cocked his head. "I'm sure the monks of Sant' Cyricus know you have arrived."

"That's so. Our master has many things to do before he departs with them, and must finish before he can greet them properly. He said he will not present himself until the soldiers have had their bread." Amolon tugged at his beard. "They will probably be drunk soon."

"Probably," Rorthger seconded this. "But when they have slept it off, they will be better company." He turned back to stop one of the scullions going back to the kitchens for more bread. "Cut the loaves in half, or they will stuff themselves and they won't waken for comestus."

The scullion nodded and hurried on.

"You!" Notrold shouted, pointing at Rorthger. "Come here!"

Rorthger obeyed stiffly. "What is it, Bellatore?" he asked with as much propriety as he could summon up in front of these men. He glanced at Einshere to see what the leader of these soldiers would say; Einshere remained silent, staring down into his cup.

"Who held these fiscs before your master?" Notrold demanded.

"I am told it was Comes Udofrid," Rorthger answered.

"No kin of your master?" Notrold went on.

"No. My master is from distant mountains. None of his blood, save he himself, live in Franksland." Rorthger paused. "And the King knows all this."

"There! You see?" Notrold half-lunged at Usuard and Theubert. "Your patron has no connections to support you if he should fall from favor. Better to ally yourself with kinsmen of the King than rely upon this Magnatus."

"Under whose roof you now eat," Rorthger reminded Notrold more sharply than he had intended.

Notrold waved this away. "If he is a sensible man, the Magnatus understands these things, and he will help you two in finding patrons more worthy of your skills."

"The Magnatus is obliged to maintain two soldiers for the King," Rorthger said with a quick glance at Theubert and Usuard. "These are the two he has undertaken to patronize."

"Well and good for the Magnatus, but a disadvantage for these soldiers." Notrold was becoming pugnacious, leaning on his elbows and holding his half-devoured loaf of bread between his hands like a dog with a bone. "You have accepted patronage, but it is good to use it to advance in the world. You needn't rely on what I say: anyone would tell you the same if you bothered to ask." He wolfed down another mouthful of bread and followed it up with more beer.

"We cannot spurn our patron, especially not in his house," said Theubert. "I have a great obligation to him. His patronage has already advanced me beyond my expectations. I was a guard at the monastery of Sant' Cyricus, two German leagues from here, and I never thought I would be more than that; without a patron I could not have advanced beyond that position. Magnatus Rakoczy changed my life, and I am in his debt for all he has done."

"Which only goes to show that he is clever. Many foreigners are, of necessity and to make a place in the world." Notrold shook his head emphatically. "He is not in a position to do any more than he has for you; others will hoise you, not Rakoczy. It is correct that you show him regard, but it is time you looked about to improve your lot. Ask our leader; he'll tell you the same."

"Not while we are guests here," said Einshere, and occupied himself in slathering clotted cream on his loaf of bread.

Rorthger, who had listened to Notrold with amused indignation, interrupted the debate by saying, "Your cubicula are ready for you, if you would like to rest before comestus. If you would finish up your bread and cheese, I will have Amolon, the buticularius, escort you there."

"You want to get rid of us, do you?" Notrold challenged.

"No, good Bellatore," said Rorthger, his manner now once again deferential. "I wish to do as my master has bid me, and see that you are fully rested for your long journey that you will start tomorrow."

"Humph," said Notrold, but began to eat with more determination. "Shortly. We will be ready shortly. If our leader will release us."

"You may do as you wish," said Einshere.

Anshelm took the tub of cream and used his knife to scoop out a generous portion; he spread this on his loaf and began to consume it in large gulps as if he expected the bread to be snatched from his hands. His grin was enhanced by a sheen of grease; he continued to bolt his loaf. He said as he chewed, "Will there be bread to take with us?"

"Some hard, dark bread," Rorthger told him. "Not this good white, which does not last long. It isn't prudent to take it on journeys. You will not be deprived; you will have several wheels of cheese, and many strings of sausages." He reverenced the soldiers at the table. "There is food in plenty being readied for your travels. You need not fret."

Just this recitation made Anshelm's eyes glaze in anticipation. "It sounds wonderful," he said, and avoided the glare Notrold directed at him. "The Magnatus is very generous."

Notrold snorted. "The Magnatus is seeing to his own tastes."

Rorthger was tempted to deny this, but kept his thoughts to himself; there would be nothing gained in wrangling with Notrold, who clearly flourished on such disputes. "If he is, who can blame him? The journey is long, and you will not always be able to find shelter and food for the night, or a bed to sleep in. This way, you can be assured of a meal, at least, and a blanket to wrap yourself in. There should be enough to sustain you to Lake Como and my master's villa there."

Notrold looked shocked. "He has property in Longobardia?"

"And in other places," Rorthger said, deliberately vague.

"Does the King know of this?" Notrold asked cholerically.

"Notrold," Einshere admonished him without looking up from his food.

"I must suppose he does, for he has ordered my master to break his journey there so that you will not all arrive in Roma worn out from the road. He has horses there, and orchards, and vineyards. You may pass pleasant days there."

As much as this pleased the other soldiers, it displeased Notrold, who scowled ferociously. "He may be in league with the Longobards, and working to their benefit. His villa may be a trap, set for all of us, to keep us from the tasks set for us." He rocked back as far as the stay on the bench would allow. "You say the King has approved this?"

"So much so that he has said he will dispatch his missi dominici to that villa with any new orders he may have, as your leader must know." Rorthger signaled the mansionarius to pour more beer for Notrold. "You should have been informed of this before you left the Royal Residence of Herstal."

Notrold finished the last of his bread. "I was told the missi dominici would be sent. Einshere said that they would visit us before we reached Roma. I was not told where we would wait for them; only our leader knows, and probably the

Magnatus, as well. Yet I gave it some thought and I supposed it must be Milan." He shot an angry look at Einshere as if to blame their leader for his own embarrassment.

"No," said Rorthger. "Nor Pavia. You will go to the villa and you will receive the missi dominici there." He watched while Notrold took another long draft of beer. "My master can show you the orders from Karl-lo-Magne."

"No," said Notrold, who could not read. "But if I think we have waited too long, I will order us to go on to Roma."

"As you think best," Rorthger murmured.

"You said there will be comestus this evening?" Pepin asked as he reached for a half-loaf of bread.

"Yes. You will have a good meal," said Rorthger. "This is only to relieve the fast of travel." He indicated the scullion with the basket of bread. "There will be trenchers tonight. You may take bread with you, if you like."

"You will be . . . you are willing to feed us twice in one day?" Pepin wondered aloud. "This would be sufficient." The others glared at him, and he fell silent.

"You are soldiers of Karl-lo-Magne, and my master is his willing vassal. We are honored to have you here." Rorthger reverenced the soldiers.

Notrold drank down the last of his beer. "Well," he said as he surged to his feet, "I would be glad of a rest. So would you all, I should think."

"Oh, yes," said Anshelm, and nudged Sulpicius. "What do you say?"

"A rest is welcome." He colored to his scalp. "The senescalus is right."

Rorthger accepted this designation. "Amolon will escort you. When you are ready," he added as he watched Notrold reel down the dining hall toward the corridor.

"We must be ready for comestus," Notrold blustered. "A nap will help."

Anshelm got to his feet. "I'll go with him," he said, and left the table. Einshere watched them without saying a word.

Amolon looked to Rorthger for his recommendation; Rorthger nodded, and Amolon said, "If you soldiers will come with me?" and started off toward the stairs to the second floor. "Along the gallery there are cubicula," he said. "They have two beds to a room. The first three cubicula are set aside for you." He pointed to the doors as they approached them.

"We'll take the nearest to the stairs," Notrold declared.

"As you like," said Amolon, and opened the door for them. When the two soldiers had gone in, he closed the door and returned to the ground floor and the dining hall, where the other soldiers were now waiting to be taken to their cubicula.

When all the soldiers had retired to rest, Rorthger climbed to Rakoczy's room at the top of the house, where he found the Magnatus sorting through a handful of unpolished jewels. "Just in time," Rakoczy said. "Well, how are they?"

"The Bellatore Notrold is likely to try to force his authority, and take the place of the leader, a fellow named Einshere, who keeps to himself, or tries not to argue with Notrold; I don't know which," said Rorthger. "Einshere is probably trustworthy, but he isn't of an emphatic disposition. Notrold has the inclinations of a tyrant, and though Einshere is the leader, he isn't inclined to stop him. The men are not much minded to oppose him, though they may be pushed too far by Notrold's despotism. Einshere isn't apt to insist on any change in behavior."

"I shall keep that in mind." Rakoczy took a small leather bag and counted fourteen gems into it. "The rest will stay here with you," he said to Rorthger. "Keep them where Waifar cannot find them, in case he returns for another harvest."

"Do you suppose he will?" Rorthger asked. "I would have thought he would flee."

"Perhaps," said Rakoczy. "But if he has kinsmen here, he may prefer to remain with them than to forge his way alone."

"It's possible," said Rorthger dubiously.

"If I am wrong, where is the harm in being prepared? Nothing will be wasted, no matter what Waifar may do, wouldn't you concur?" Rakoczy asked gently. "Think, old friend. I will be gone for many months, and that may lead some to believe that this place is undefended, which you and I know is not the case, but those who have lived here for generations may not comprehend. It is fitting that you should be prepared to deal with any number of impositions."

"All right. I'll put the jewels in an unlikely place for safe-keeping." He scooped them up and dropped them into his wallet. "For the time being, I'll keep them here."

"Very good. Make sure, if you must sell them, to offer them to the King first, and then to the local Bishop. Karl-lo-Magne may not want them, but he would want to have the opportunity to purchase them ahead of all others." He touched the tips of his fingers together. "With his coronation coming, he may want to array himself for the occasion. Sheepskin is all very well for hunting bison, but it will hardly do for a celebration at Sant' Pier's."

"Truly," said Rorthger, and patted the wallet. "I will tell the mansionarii to refuse Waifar access to the villa."

"Do so," Rakoczy said, "but remember that we are the foreigners here and we need not be obeyed as those who have been here for generation upon generation."

"Do you mean you think someone may let Waifar into the villa against specific orders? That is a very dangerous thing to do. A servant's betrayal of a master is punishable by execution." Rorthger nodded before Rakoczy spoke. "Of course that could happen in spite of the possible consequences, if there are familial reasons. You're right, my master. I will keep that uppermost in my thoughts."

Rakoczy looked around his upper room, at the various vessels and measuring devices, at gleaming basins of gold and beakers of glass, at his athanor. "I don't like having to leave," he admitted.

"You could tell the King you are unable to travel. Say you were warned in a dream not to go beyond your fiscs until autumn." Rorthger wasn't entirely serious, but there was a suggestion of sincere purpose in what he said. "Great Karl puts much stock in dreams."

"Yes, he does," Rakoczy agreed. "But if I refuse him this, he may not trust me again, and that would be far more perilous than going to Roma. Karl-lo-Magne is a loyal friend—when he believes he has the fealty of his ally. When he suspects, or imagines, falseness, he is quick to requite the wrong. If I were his kin, he might allow me some leeway, but as I am not even a Frank . . ." Shrugging, he reached for a silver pectoral chain studded with rubies and clasped by an ornament in the shape of his eclipse device; he put this into a silken bag and put it into the saddle-pack that lay on the floor at his feet. "I will send you word along the way, so that you needn't be left to wonder what has become of me."

"How will you get your messages back to me? You dare not give them to the missi dominici; Great Karl would not approve of it," said Rorthger.

"No, he would not," said Rakoczy. "But I can engage Fratri who are going to shrines and monasteries, to carry a letter for me. If I make a donation to the monastery, and give the Fratre a small token to aid him in his travels, you will receive my letters safely enough."

"If that is acceptable to you, I will receive every monk who comes this way," said Rorthger, a trace of amusement in his tone. "The Abbott at Sant' Cyricus may not approve."

"Why would he not?" Rakoczy asked, puzzled.

"He is a man who knows his own importance," said Rorthger. "Abbott Hroccolf will feel slighted if I do not send some of the peregrines to him. He may even hold it against the fiscs, which I will have to address somehow. I may provide him with more bread; that should lessen his affront."

Rakoczy nodded once. "Yes. You're right." He set two pair of Persian boots aside. "These will go in with my clothing in the saddle-pack."

"Do you suppose your goods will be gone through?" Rorthger asked.

"It's possible. It may be also that we will be robbed or our goods seized." Rakoczy gave Rorthger a long, steady look. "You know that as well as I."

"But it seems you don't trust your escort, either," said Rorthger.

"No, I don't," said Rakoczy.

Rorthger shook his head in exasperation. "All right. I won't question you any more, but you mustn't reprehend me for having misgivings about this whole venture."

"I would not do that, old friend," said Rakoczy with an elusive smile.

"Will you send for me if you decide not to return to Franksland when your stay in Roma is over?" He asked in the language of western China, afraid they might be overheard.

Rakoczy answered in the same tongue. "Of course. I don't want you to have to search half of Europe to find me." He finished loading his saddle-pack. "This is ready, and my sack of medicaments. They should go on my saddle. The rest should be carried by the mules; four for pack and one to draw the Pale Woman's wagon. I'll want eight changes of horses—one for each of us—so that we'll not be stranded if something happens to any of our mounts. Get the long leads, so the remounts can be ponied."

"Of course," said Rorthger. "And I'll supervise the loading of food and drink on the second mule."

"Very good," Rakoczy said, and prepared to leave his upper room. "I'm going to miss this place."

"As much as your house in Spain?" Rorthger said.

"They aren't comparable," said Rakoczy. "The Spanish house is lost to me for now and I may never see it again; this villa is still mine, or as much mine as the King will allow." He went to a chest near the stairs and retrieved two swords and a dagger. "I wish I had one of those little throwing axes the Franks use: the francisca. Perhaps when I return I'll make a few of them."

"What will Great Karl think?" Rorthger was doing his best to make light of the matter.

"If I approach him properly, he may well be flattered," Rakoczy said seriously. "Remember that Chian Dju?"

Rorthger nodded, his visage more austere than ever. "He wanted to kill you for using his weapons."

"It may be that Karl-lo-Magne is very like Chian Dju, afraid that a weapon will change its loyalty if used by another." Rakoczy picked up his saddle-packs and handed them to Rorthger. "If you will tend to these?"

Rorthger took the two packs. "Do you want to carry your medicaments yourself?"

"It might be wiser that I do it," said Rakoczy, slinging the strap over his shoulder. "It's prudent to let the soldiers see this and know what it is."

Rorthger held open the door so Rakoczy could leave the upper room. "Shall I lock this room, my master?"

"No; it would only inspire the mansionarii to try to get into it. Close it, and be sure to check it once a day," Rakoczy said as he stepped onto the stairs. "Have the soldiers gone to rest? I would rather not encounter them until after comestus," said Rakoczy, descending the narrow flight two steps ahead of Rorthger.

"Do you think they'll find that odd?" Rorthger asked.

"They may; but I want them to get used to the notion that I won't eat with them. If I keep away during their meals here, they won't be too surprised when I . . . dine in private while we're traveling." He reached the floor below. "Are they in the cubicula along the gallery?"

"Yes, they are." Rorthger came down beside him. "I'm going to the stable. Where will you be?"

"In my study; I plan to keep a record of our travels for Karl-lo-Magne's itineraries. They have descriptions of the roads into Roma, but if I can show them very accurate accounts of what they know, they may be more willing to accept my representations of places they don't know." Rakoczy glanced toward the gallery. "I don't expect that any of the soldiers will want to see my study."

"Very likely not," said Rorthger, and moved toward the second flight of stairs that led down to the ground floor. "I will tell the soldiers you are still busy if they ask where you are at comestus."

"Thank you." When he reached his study, Rakoczy slipped inside and shut the door behind him. He did not bother to strike flint-and-steel to light the oil-lamps; he saw well enough in the gloom. Going to his chest of books, he opened a drawer in the bottom of the cabinet and pulled out eight sheets of parchment; he rolled these tightly, then went to get an ink-cake, which he put into a small sandalwood box. These he put in the sack with his medicaments, reminding himself quills could be found on his travels, and water. Then he took down a book from the shelves and opened it; the text was in Latinized Greek, a compendium from the time of Nerva of wild plants of the Italian peninsula and their virtues. Finding his leather-upholstered Moorish chair, he dropped into it and began to read. Only when he heard the bell for the end of Vespers at Sant' Cyricus did he close the volume once again and return it to its place on the shelf before leaving his study for the dining hall and his first meeting with the soldiers who would escort him to Roma.

TEXT OF A LETTER FROM BISHOP BERAHTRAM TO ARCHBISHOP REGINHALT OF VIENNE, CARRIED BY CHURCH MESSENGER AND DELIVERED FIVE WEEKS AFTER BEING DISPATCHED.

To the most exalted Archbishop of Vienne, Reginhalt, son of the late Bishop Childeric of Osnabruk, the greetings and prayerful devotion of Bishop Berahtram on the eve of his departure for Sant' Yrieix and its related See, on the Feast of the Martyr, Sabas the Goth in the Pope's year 800.

Primore, I make bold to send this to you in the hope it will lead you to be willing to hear me when I am in need of council and blessing in my new post. I have been a Fratre for twelve yars, and I know that ever since his Holiness, Pope Leo III, elevated me to my new position, I have wondered if I am deserving of such an advancement, and I have prayed for guidance, that I may serve God and the Church in the capacity I have been given in a manner that would add to the prestige of the Saints.

If you will consider being willing to instruct and guide me, I will enter my duties with far more certitude than I have found within myself thus far. You have had many years of experience and you know the region to which I am sent far better than I do. If only you are willing to impart your wisdom, I know I shall be able to perform as the Pope bade me.

I am also moved to tell you of a certain rumor that has reached my ears and caused me much dismay: it is said that the healing I have been allowed by God to impart to Bellatori and religious alike was not a sign of Heavenly Favor, but the result of unguents and other medicaments provided me by the foreigner Rakoczy. There are those who claim that this foreigner has knowledge of medicinals that none of our physicians—Christian or Jew—can claim, and that it is those medicaments that have brought healing to the wounded. I am loath to call any man liar, but we will all answer before God for our lives, and this troubles me more than I can say. I have no wish to attack the reputation of this foreigner, for he has Great Karlus' confidence, and it would not be a Christian deed to cause trouble for the King. Yet I am appalled that many people believe it. Fratre Lothar, whose hand was shattered when he was still a Bellatore, will testify to my work among the injured, but I fear to ask him to do so, in that it could lead to the kind of animosity that could lead to bloodshed, a result that would smirch my reputation.

You are more experienced in these matters; I know you can recommend how I might best conduct myself in this situation, not only for the honor of the Church, but to preserve my own. I have no desire to detract from another man's virtues, so long as they are his to own. But I cannot remain silent while there are lies and boasts made that take Glory from God, Who has done the work of saving these men through His Mercy imparted through my undeserving hands. You will know the repercussion I may expect if I should dispute this calumny, and what may result from my silence. I will most gratefully accept any advice you can give me, and I promise you, I will praise you for your sapience to the world, or as much of it as I am able to reach.

Great Primore, you know, far better than I, that the Church is always in danger from without and within. I have sworn to advance our faith, and I will do my utmost to fulfill my oath, but I also know it is not for all men to champion God; I must find my way, and I ask you to be willing to shepherd me to the true path of Christ if I should wander from it. As we both are ser-vants before God, I implore your aid in shouldering the burden the Pope has put upon me in the Name of Christ, Who has borne the sins of the world, and Who is Glorious and Merciful to all men.

Amen

Bishop Berahtram
of Sant' Yrieix, Sant' Damasus, Sant' Ianuarius, Cometou Gudi, and Lacosasse

chapter three

RAIN WISPED DOWN FROM TATTERED CLOUDS, cloaking all the town clus-tered around the walls of the Royal Residence of Attigny in a moist embrace. The day was cool, but windless, so there was no edge in the chill, and the party that left through the main gate wore leather capae with hoods up, not the heavier mantella reserved for penetrating cold. There was little activity in the town, most of the people remaining indoors; only a gang of Wendish slaves were working on restoring a roof of a weavery, and they paid no attention as the eight mounted men, eight horses on leads, four laden pack-mules, also on leads, and the mule-drawn plausterum clattered by in the slate-paved street below them.

At the gates of the town, the road became a muddy morass, keeping the trav-elers to a slow, messy walk; the mule pulling the plausterum labored to drag the wagon through the paste-like ruts. Mud spread up the animals' legs and onto their bellies and flanks, leaving smears on the tibialia and brodequins of the men, and on the heavy cloth covering the plausterum. As they slogged toward the south, they could see Attigny behind them for almost half the morning before they had gone far enough to have it sink below the horizon.

By mid-day they were into the forest and the rain had got heavier, dripping sullenly through the leaves and puddling in the long grooves made by other wagons bound for the Rhone Valley.

"I don't think it's going to let up," said Magnatus Rakoczy from his place in the middle of the soldiers and immediately ahead of the covered plausterum.

"Of course not," Notrold jeered. "What else would you think?" He gave the leader a contemptuous glance.

"I think," said Rakoczy with a firm nod, "that we would do well to find shelter and prepare prandium for all you. Otherwise you will be too hungry to keep on." It was less than the truth, but he knew the men would agree to such exaggerated apprehension.

"I could do with some cold vension," said Sulpicius, looking to his comrade for support. "You're hungry, aren't you?"

"Who isn't?" Notrold interjected.

"I am," Anshelm said, but he looked around in growing disgruntlement at the road and the damp. "Where can we stop?"

"There is a chapel ahead on this road, or there was two years ago," said Einshere. "It has a small chamber attached to the chapel; we could eat in it. No monks maintain it, but unless something has happened, it should be shelter."

"Does it have a fireplace?" Rakoczy asked. "You could make a rich stew in the cauldron."

Usuard sneezed. "It would be good to be out of the rain."

"I don't recall a fireplace, but we could lay a fire in the shelter of the roof," said Einshere.

"A foolish notion," said Notrold. "Best to go along to the next monastery or nunnery. There must be one up ahead. This is an important road, and there must be places for travelers all the way down its length."

"Certainly there must be," said Pepin of Corbie, "but where?" He gestured at the road ahead. "Nothing but trees as far as we can see."

"And any respite could be a trap," said Anshelm, as if he anticipated such an eventuality.

"So it could," said Einshere, sounding very tired. He looked at Notrold, then turned away.

Rakoczy thought to the many times he had traveled and the men in whose company he had been; these six were no worse than most and better than some, just as the road, while difficult to use, was an improvement on a host of others he had journeyed upon since the Romans stopped building and maintaining their roads, more than five hundred years since. They would have to cross rivers, and that bothered him more than the pathways through the forest did, just as the rain gave him a special discomfort that none of the rest had to endure; at least the running rainwater was not as uncomfortable as a river was. Still, he remind-ed himself, it was preferable to intense sunlight.

"Something troubling you, Magnatus?" Theubert asked; he was riding on Rakoczy's left and had made a point of trying to engage his patron's interest. "Are you worried about what may lie ahead?"

"No," said Rakoczy. "Only I find the rain a bit . . . dreary. Weather of this sort wears on me." He raised his head and settled more squarely into the saddle.

"It has been a wet spring," Notrold said in an accusing tone.

"That it has," Rakoczy said at his most bland.

Usuard did his best to be part of the discussion. "The farmers will be glad of the rain; it makes their crops grow well."

"If the rain continues," said Notrold. "If it ceases we may still lose crops."

Theubert glared at Notrold. "All this is possible, but so far the signs are very good."

Einshere held up his hand. "Halt," he said.

The company did as he ordered, going silent as well. As if responding to Einshere, the woods around them quieted, too; only the leaves of the trees wor-ried together, as if apprehensive about what was happening beneath them. The silence increased, the soft patter of the rain sounding louder than a downpour.

Then the mule drawing the plausterum let out a stentorian bray; the pack-mules joined in while the horses whinnied and piaffed nervously; birds took noisy flight in all directions, and ahead on the track, a small herd of bison appeared, shaggy heads lowered as if weighted down by curving horns.

"They have young with them," whispered Sulpicius.

"Yes; that makes them doubly dangerous," said Rakoczy in an undervoice.

"We should get into the trees. They can reach us too easily on the road." Einshere looked around as if hoping to see a path away from the road.

"If we move, the bison may charge," said Rakoczy.

"That's so," said Pepin, and jobbed the reins anxiously in a sign of disquiet; his dun, unable to wheel and run, flung up his head and took a step back, into the side of the mule pulling the plausterum, in an effort to get away from the bison up ahead. The mule laid back his long ears and bit the dun on the rump; the dun lashed out with his rear hooves, catching the mule just above the breast-collar. The mule swung around as far as his lead would allow and tried to rear, slipping in the mud. Pepin struggled to hold his horse, trying to keep him from sidling into one of the remounts. Usuard, who held the mule's lead, struggled to keep hold of the braided leather rope while the mule thrashed, half-fallen and held up by his harness and the lead.

"What is going on?" Einshere looked from the bison to the trouble among his company. He was frightened by this sudden eruption of chaos.

Farther down the road, the bison, alarmed by the upheaval among the men and their mounts, prepared to defend their young. The adult males turned to face the disruption, their cows and calves behind them. One of the larger bulls began to paw, leaving gouges in the thick mud; he bellowed a challenge.

Four of the horses were shifting around, bouncing on the uneven footing, the remount horses pulling on their leads in an effort to get away from the confusion. One of the pack-mules was trying to shake off his load and bolt; Rakoczy took the lead from Pepin and maneuvered his grey in close to the mule so that he could shorten the lead enough that the mule could not turn or toss his head. The mule pulled back but managed to scramble to his feet, more incensed than afraid, and let out another bray, echoed by three lesser squeals from the other pack-mules. This was too much for the bison; the lead male rushed at the mounted party, snorting and trying to run in the mud; his efforts would have been comical had not his intention been so deadly.

"Get off the road!" Notrold shouted as the men and horses made for the narrow verge and a safe retreat into the trees.

The mule pulling the plausterum would not budge. He spread his legs and almost sat down like a dog to keep from being dragged away to safety; his neck stiffened as the lead grew taut. Rakoczy reached for his sword and used the flat of the blade to smack the recalcitrant creature on the rump; the mule kicked out at the wagon and brayed again.

The bison scrambled, floundered, and fell, landing hard on his side and thrashing; he bellowed in ire and frustration as he struggled futilely to rise. Pepin, seeing this and feeling a desire to make up for his earlier mishap, released the leads he held and, pulling his spear from its sheath, rode toward the volutating bull, preparing to dispatch the bison in a single thrust. He paid no attention to the warning shouts of his comrades, putting the whole of his concentration on the thrashing bison. "I will take care of—" His confident beginning ended with a shriek as the bison wallowed toward Pepin, catching his horse on his horn and opening up a huge rent in the gelding's chest. The horse screamed and dropped down onto his knees, flinging Pepin out of the saddle and into the path of the bison's horns. Now the bison had got onto his rear legs and began to lever himself up from the mud, slipping on the fountaining blood from the dying horse.

The bison snorted, shook his head, and bent to gash Pepin a second time. Farther down the road, the rest of the bison herd moved on, seeking to protect their new calves from the upheaval.

Pepin howled briefly, then gasped as the sharp front hooves scraped into his side.

Rakoczy raised his sword, then leaned down in the saddle to speak to the woman in the covered plausterum. "I'm going to hand you the lead for your mule. Hold it firmly. The worst that will happen is that you will turn in circles." He lifted the front flap and handed the lead to the white hand that she held out. "And I'm giving you the lead on my remount. Tie it to the rear of the plausterum."

"I will," she said, and took the second lead. A moment later the flap dropped.

The bison was pawing at Pepin's chest, the sound of splintering ribs unnaturally loud; Pepin's gored horse finally collapsed, his neck landing on Pepin's legs, pinning him in front of the bison. Pepin moaned, the sound bubbling, as steam rose from the pink, foamy rents in his side.

Rakoczy swung his horse around and holding the grey gelding with his legs, he started the grey down the road toward the bison. He readied his sword and began to shout. He was distantly aware of the men of the escort back in the trees and realized he could not rely on them to take any needed action, so he swung his sword and howled loudly, holding his horse firmly on course at a slow trot toward the bison. As he neared the big animal, he shouted more loudly and swung his sword in a circle over his head. The bison shook his head, pawed nervously, then turned and ambled after the rest of his herd. Rakoczy drew in his grey and swung out of the saddle, sheathing his sword as he hurried toward Pepin and the dead horse.

Pepin sighed, blood running from his mouth. His eyes fluttered as Rakoczy dropped to his knee beside him. "It's . . ."

"No," said Rakoczy. "Don't talk." He could tell from the man's blood that he would not last much longer, and given the extent of his injuries, survival would not be possible.

Pepin managed a faltering sigh, and his eyes rolled back, the wounds in his side ceasing to bubble.

Rakoczy got to his feet slowly, pulling the horse's head off Pepin's legs before lifting him into his arms and carrying him back to the plausterum, leading his grey as he tried to make his way through the ruts. There was blood on his tibialia and femoralia, and the hem of his capa, and his hands were red.

There was a cry of a bird, and it was answered by another.

Usuard was the first to emerge from the trees, his horse still held on her lead, and a pack-mule close behind, although the lead was broken. "Magnatus?" he said uncertainly as he came up to Rakoczy.

"We should carry this man to a chapel or monastery. He'll need proper burial." Rakoczy went to the rear of the plausterum, calling out as he did, "Gynethe Mehaut, will you allow me to put this man in with you? He's dead. He won't harm you."

"But he is bloody," she said uneasily.

"Blood is a living thing; this man isn't alive. You have nothing to fear from him. Just let him lie in the rear of your plausterum." Rakoczy looked directly at her as he lifted the covering of the rear of the wagon. "You understand how important even a small act of compassion can be."

Her red eyes met his dark ones. "Very well. Put him in the rear, there." She indicated the place at the back of the plausterum where there was a stabilizing board. "I will use a belt to secure him on the board. Until he is given to monks for Christian burial, I will let him have the protection of my plausterum."

"Very good, Gynethe Mehaut," said Rakoczy, and lifted Pepin as if he weighed no more than a saddle or a sack of grain into the position Gynethe Mehaut had indicated.

Einshere rode out of the woods, his spear clutched in his raised hand. "Is he—"

"Dead," said Rakoczy. "Gored by the bison."

"He died trying to protect us all," said Einshere, and raised his voice. "The rest of you! Reassemble on the road at once!"

His orders were obeyed slowly, three of the soldiers unwilling to look at the body stowed on the back of the plausterum. There was a mutter of plans while the men reassembled in their places with their remounts in tow. One of the horses was missing, and Anshelm looked embarrassed as he confessed his remount had got away from him.

"Then it is just as well that we have Pepin's remount with us still," said Rakoczy, giving a long, hard stare to Anshelm. "If you will be careful of this horse, you will have a second—"

Einshere did the unthinkable and interrupted Rakoczy. "We must move on. The bison may circle back, and we have already lost one of our number to them."

"And we're not half-a-day from Attigny," muttered Notrold, staring at the rear of the plausterum.

"What do you mean by that?" Einshere demanded. "You! Tell me."

"Only that this trouble came after we began our escort of the Pale Woman; nothing more than that," said Notrold resentfully. "You can't deny that this was more than an accident."

"No; Pepin was reckless enough to attack an angry bull. How could he have been so foolish?" Einshere said in a tone that dared the other to challenge him. "If he had been content to withdraw into the trees and let the herd pass by, he would not be lying in the back of the plausterum, waiting for the grave."

"So *you* say," Notrold mumbled, glancing toward the plausterum again.

"You saw what happened," said Einshere as forcefully as he could; he glanced at Rakoczy. "You have done much for us this day, Magnatus."

Sulpicius did his best to ease the growing tension. "Let us all thank God that nothing worse happened than what we have endured."

"Amen," said Theubert, making a sign to ward off all evil.

"You don't have to worry about that, about protection from malice," said Notrold. "It's this mission. You should keep in mind who rides in the plausterum. The Pale Woman, with her hands wrapped in linen. No one can doubt that she has brought this—"

Rakoczy interrupted him. "No. You don't know that she has done anything. That is for the Pope to decide. You look at Pepin dead and you assume it was worse than what could have befallen us, but you cannot be certain: it may be that she has saved us from worse than the loss we have had. Without her presence, we might have had far more destruction to deal with. If the herd had charged us, more than Pepin and his horse could have been lost."

"If not for her, we wouldn't be here," said Anshelm, siding with Notrold.

The men exchanged uneasy glances. "That's so," said Usuard, glancing restively at his patron. "But I would be glad to be out of this part of the forest."

"Then let us move on," said Rakoczy, starting his horse walking. "Come."

Einshere echoed this order and rode up to Rakoczy's left hand. "The bison haven't gone far, not with calves." He laid his hand on the hilt of his spear. "I will be ready if I must be."

"Very good," Rakoczy said, and wondered what Gynethe Mehaut was thinking, for she must have heard Notrold's accusation.

"How many more of us will die before we reach Roma?" Notrold persisted, glaring at Einshere.

"That is in God's Hands," said Theubert.

"You have monk's answers because you guarded a monastery," said Notrold, dismissing Theubert's pious sentiments. "There is more to the world than that."

"I have a monk's answer because it is the answer the King accepts," Theubert countered.

"The King isn't here," Notrold pointed out, his chin jutting angrily.

"But his Will is here. We are going to Roma for his Will," said Theubert, and deliberately fell back behind the plausterum.

Notrold sat on his horse visibly seething. He looked about as if trying to find someone to fight with, but Einshere made a gesture with his dagger that warned him to hold his peace. Thwarted, Notrold rode a little ahead of the party, hoping for trouble.

He hoped in vain. The party arrived at Santa Radegund the Queen convent just after the monks and nuns had finished None. They invited the escort and Gynethe Mehaut to have a meal in their refectory; this turned out to be a vegetable gruel with bits of fish mixed into it.

"I don't blame the Magnatus for not eating," muttered Notrold as he poked at the mess in his wheaten trencher with his knife.

"Be glad you don't have to cook it; the monks and nuns have spared us that labor," said Usuard. "If we were on the road, you would probably have cold cheese and dry bread."

"You're right, but this is sorry fare," said Notrold, wholly unrepentant.

Einshere slapped his hand on the table. "They prefer silence here."

Notrold glared but said nothing more as he ate his meal and drank down his yeasty beer with the rest of the men while Gynethe Mehaut ate alone in an alcove between the kitchen and the dining hall; Rakoczy used the time to make arrangements for Pepin's burial, drafting an account of his death to be given to the next pair of missi dominici to come to the convent and moving saddles and bridles to the remount horses so that they could leave as soon as their meal was over. They departed at mid-afternoon with instructions on where they could spend the night. The rain had let up and the sky was mottled with clouds; a breeze had sprung up making the air brisk and the promise of spring seem counterfeit. They went along at a sober walk, wanting not to tire their animals.

That night they slept around a campfire, and the next night they occupied an old stone house that was missing its roof. By the third night they had reached the old Roman road and their pace improved, first to seven Roman leagues, and then, after a night at a Potente's villa, they covered ten Roman leagues in a single day and spent the night at Luxeuil, where they were given spitted meats and red wine to revive them: Gynethe Mehaut was whisked away with the women of the monastery, most of whom were slaves. After most had retired to bed, she took her usual turn about the gardens.

"You cannot imagine how they look at me," Gynethe Mehaut said to Rakoczy as they came to the bed of night-blooming flowers.

"I think perhaps I can," said Rakoczy. "They are ignorant and frightened."

"They hate me," she said. "No matter how I try, I cannot accustom myself to it."

"Do not try." Rakoczy laid his hand on her shoulder very briefly, wanting to comfort her.

"But I must. If I cannot, how am I to live, but in an anchorite's cell, away from the world?" She stopped and looked up at him. "Why is it that you are awake so late into the night?"

"Those of my blood sleep little," he said, an enigmatic smile on his mouth.

She pressed her lips together, thinking. Finally she spoke. "Aren't you worried about what they might say about you—believe about you—for how you live?"

"Whether I worry or not, it will not change what they think," said Rakoczy, hoping to ease her apprehension.

"But don't you want them to think well of you, to guard your good name from any smirch?" She put her wrapped hand to her eyes. "What of your family honor—don't you protect it? Any man of character must."

"I may have done, when I was younger," he told her. "But no more."

"How did you—" she began and stopped herself. "No. I won't ask."

He studied her face. "When you want to know, whatever your question may be, ask me."

"Will you tell me?" She folded her bandaged hands together.

"Yes," he said. "My Word on it."

Gynethe Mehaut nodded once. "I will believe you." She resumed her walk. "I'm tired. Travel wears on me; I can't sleep in the plausterum, not on these roads, and I need to pray at night."

"No night-time prayers while we journey," said Rakoczy. "Surely you can't be expected to pass the night on the floor before the altar."

"Oh, yes. If I don't pray, someone will tell the Bishops that I have been lax and it will go against me when the Pope finally sees me." She frowned. "Do you think he will see me?"

"Why would he not?" Rakoczy asked.

"He didn't while he was at Paderborn; it would have been an easy thing to send for me," said Gynethe Mehaut. "In Roma he might delay and delay, and in the end send me away." She sighed once, a hard sound. "What will become of me then?"

"If it happens, you will decide then," Rakoczy said.

"Do you think so? Shouldn't I prepare for the worst, as soldiers do?" She stared at him with her red eyes.

"It is wise to realize that something may have to be done, but not to assume it must come," said Rakoczy. "You know there is danger, but it doesn't always have to be realized."

"Is that why you make a point of walking with me, as you're doing now? Don't you assume I will need your protection?" She had not changed the tone of her voice, but she spoke more sharply, with greater precision.

"I walk with you because we are both about after dark, and I enjoy your company," he said so unreservedly that she was almost convinced of his sincerity.

Gynethe Mehaut stepped back from him. "You trouble me, Magnatus."

"I?" Rakoczy shook his head. "I am chagrined to hear it. Why do I trouble you?"

"You were uncomfortable crossing the river today, weren't you?" She caught her lower lip in her teeth as if she were bothered by admitting she had noticed this.

"Is that what troubles you?" Rakoczy asked her.

She did not answer at once. "You . . . you cause doubts to grow in me," she admitted.

"What doubts?" Rakoczy asked gently.

"If I knew them, they would not trouble me," she said, and walked away from him.

Rakoczy followed after her, keeping his distance but remaining near enough to guard her.

The next day found them farther down the river, the day warm and fragrant. All of the party but Rakoczy were pleased with this improvement in the weather, and they kept up their pace longer than they had intended, so that by evening they were almost twelve Roman leagues from where they had begun their day; the road had been rising steadily toward high peaks that loomed ahead of them, white, distant, and grand. They camped for the night at the edge of a vineyard that was part of an estate of the Grav of Bensancon and did not find it an imposition to be outdoors, and all they had to fear were wolves; for once they were glad that Rakoczy was willing to keep watch all night long. The road grew steeper the next day, and mud once again slowed their progress, so they covered less than six Roman leagues before stopping for the night at a small monastery dedicated to the Holy Spirit and manned by monks all of whom had been soldiers; it was late in the afternoon, and long, purple shadows stretched down from the high peaks, sending the slopes into early twilight.

The Abbott, a one-handed veteran named Chlodis, greeted the party with cautious enthusiasm, asking after the Potenti Hilduin and Werinbert with a kind of nostalgia that revealed he had not left his military life entirely behind him; he was saddened to learn that Werinbert had died the previous autumn. "Well, we will pray for his soul, and trust that God has given him a hero's welcome in Paradise," he said as he led the visitors into the courtyard. "You may stable your horses and mules there."

"I will tend the animals," said Rakoczy, and began to gather leads and reins; now that the sun was setting, he was feeling more vital and more hungry. The greater energy was welcome, but his hunger was not; he would have to find some source of sustenance in the next few days, or he would begin to suffer for it. "And I will guard the woman we escort." He indicated the plausterum. "If you have a women's cubiculum, then she should go there after Vigil; she has prayed all day while we traveled, and now needs rest." He glanced around at the thick walls. "I assume you keep Vigil here, and not Nocturnes."

"Yes; we keep Vigil," said Abbott Chlodis.

Einshere looked about as if he had wakened from a dream. "This is a sacred place," he announced.

"That it is," said Abbott Chlodis. "The Holy Spirit is present here. That is the reason we name it Sant' Spiritu." He held up his hands in an attitude of prayer, extended to the sides. "We are thankful for it."

"I will pray here," Einshere stated as if there had been some question of it.

"Our chapel has a Penitent's Stone," Abbott Chlodis said. "All our Fratri begin there."

Einshere shook his head. "I am not one of them."

"Are you certain? Have you no sin to expiate?" Abbott Chlodis asked, and without waiting for an answer, started toward the dormitory. "The woman will be led by Fratre Grado; he is a eunuch and so no sin may be visited upon him." The Abbott pointed toward the refectory. "You may take cold meats with us before prayers, but we will begin Vespers shortly."

Einshere fell in behind the Abbott, seeming thoughtful and subdued. He motioned to his men to come with him. "Leave the Magnatus to his work and the woman to the Fratre."

"Must we pray?" Notrold demanded. "I'm tired and I want to sleep."

"You will, but in good time, after we have eaten and done our duty to God." Einshere was not willing to discuss this.

Notrold glared at Einshere. "If we must be away at dawn, then I will need to sleep long."

"We all sleep long," said Abbott Chlodis. "When God calls us." He had led them across the courtyard to the refectory. "There will be meat here when Vespers are done. Pray with us if you like, or remain here and drink wine."

Notrold laughed. "I'll drink wine and remember the Blood of Christ."

"You shall not speak so in this place," Einshere said abruptly, and rounded on Notrold. "You will spend the night in the chapel praying for your redemption."

Usuard made a gesture of protection, and the other men did the same. "I will pray with you."

"And I," said Theubert, and was seconded by Sulpicius.

"The next leg of your climb is demanding," said Abbott Chlodis. "You would do well to take your rest where you can. God will understand if you sleep instead of praying."

"No," said Einshere with more force than he had shown previously. "You will all lie before the altar from Vigil to Matins, and pray for our journey and the cleansing of sin." He met the Abbott's questioning gaze. "The woman we escort has prayed for us all day long; now we will show our piety."

"What of tomorrow?" Sulpicius asked.

"Pray for strength," said Einshere at his most blunt, and bowed his head.

Rakoczy, leading their horses and mules to the stable, frowned as he watched the men walk away, and he weighed his observations carefully before speaking to Gynethe Mehaut, who was still in the plausterum. "Be careful here."

"Why here? Aren't we safe?" She opened the front flap of the cover and looked over the mule's head to his troubled eyes.

"I can't say," he answered. "We are protected, but . . ." His words trailed away.

"You don't trust these monks?" She barely whispered this, fright making her breathless.

"No; not the monks," he admitted reluctantly. "There may be some trouble between the men."

She let out her breath slowly. "So. You believe our soldiers may turn against me."

"Not among them, between them. I wish I knew what it was." They were inside the cavernous stable now, and he came to help her out of the plausterum. "I should change your bandages."

"You haven't told me what you fear, Magnatus," she reminded him.

"No; I haven't," he agreed, and reached for his sack of medicaments to pull out another roll of linen strips with which to wrap her bleeding hands.

TEXT OF A LETTER FROM PRIORA IDITHA TO BISHOP FRECULF, CARRIED BY A SLAVE FROM SANTA ALBEGUNDA TO SANT' TEILO, AND DELIVERED ON MAY 2, 800.·

> To the most Sublime Bishop Freculf at his spring sedes, Sant' Teilo, the respectful greetings of Priora Iditha of Santa Albegunda, written on this twelfth day of April in the Pope's year 800, in response to the letter from the Sublime Freculf which was delivered here by episcopal courier on April ninth.
>
> Amen. May God witness that I have writ the truth, as I shall answer for all I say at the Last Judgment which will bring us all before the Mercy Seat.
>
> I share your concern for the welfare of Gynethe Mehaut and I am thankful to know that you have taken it upon yourself to gather accounts of her that may be sent to His Holiness, Pope Leo, for him to consult in his consideration of her state. I have been told that Bishop Iso has been making a record of all things derogatory to her interests with the intention of presenting them when he accompanies Great Karlus to Roma. We have also received an inquiry from Bishop Berahtram of Sant' Yrieix, who has allied his interests with Bishop Iso's, and who, therefore, was seeking accounts that would show Gynethe Mehaut in an unfavorable light. I believe that Abba Sunifred has sent some message to him—I cannot tell you what it may contain.

While Gynethe Mehaut lived among us here at Santa Albegunda, she was a model of piety and humility that has put many of the Sorrae to shame. She accepted her penitential prayers without rancor, and fulfilled every item of her given Office. I do not suppose she would have balked at any devotion asked of her. In the time she was living at our convent, she was always acquiescent in our Rule, and made every effort to live in a blameless way, to draw no attention to her afflictions, and to uphold the honor of our Santa Albegunda in all her conduct. Would that more of our Sorrae were as diligent. I can pray for her without fear that I have succumbed to the powers of Satan. I regret to say that many of our Sorrae have been less than charitable toward this woman, something Gynethe Mehaut knows, but has always forgiven without reservation, again an exemplary demonstration of Christian faith that ought to inspire emulation, not wrath, from our other Sorrae. I have seen few nuns who are as willing to accept what God has laid upon them than Gynethe Mehaut has been.

Let me also state that I have no reason to suppose that she has done anything to her hands to bring about her bleeding. I have kept watch over her and I have set other Sorrae to do the same, with the result that none of us can account for this perturbing continued bleeding. If she is doing anything to her hands, I cannot determine what it may be. There are those who say this is the mark of the Anti-Christ on her, and if it is, she has borne it in a way that should redeem her, for God has raised up far more grievous sinners than Gynethe Mehaut, and brought them to Glory. If these marks originated with Satan, Gynethe Mehaut has done all that mortal could to put herself beyond the touch of damnation, and in that she serves as a most wonderful example of the triumph of faith over the wiles of Satan and all his minions.

I ask you to use this in any way that will be to Gynethe Mehaut's benefit and the support of our Church.

Amen.

Iditha,
Priora Santa Albegunda.
by my own hand

chapter four

I N THE ANCIENT VILLAGE OF LECCO the fishermen were cleaning their boats, much as they had done since before the Caesars ruled; few of them paid any attention to the soldiers and the plausterum that clattered by on their way to the large villa that occupied a low promontory that brooded over Lake Como. The warm breeze carried the odor of orchards and pasture, as well as the hint of pine trees from the higher peaks, lending the afternoon a sweetness that took the sinister out of the shadows and lent a beauty to even the most ordinary sights.

"You say this villa is in your family?" Notrold asked skeptically as they neared the gates of the expansive holding with its fine stone walls extending almost half-a-league around the estate.

"Yes. Since the time Pliny came here," said Rakoczy, thinking back to those discussions they had shared that lasted long into the night and the long correspondence that had resulted from it.

"Who is that?" Theubert asked.

"A Roman maker of descriptiones and itineraries," said Rakoczy, finding it difficult to reconcile himself to the loss of Pliny from the world of memory.

"A useful sort of man," said Sulpicius. "He must have been a monk."

"No. He was a scholar," said Rakoczy, knowing such a distinction was meaningless to these men. He took the lead as they neared the gates, calling out, "Ombrosius! Senescalus! Open the gates! It is Sant' Germainius!"

There was a bustle of excitement inside the walls, and finally a badger-grey head appeared in the warder gate and an elderly servant gaped out at them, his tunicae a bit askew and belted haphazardly. He studied the men and horses, hesitating to act. Rakoczy, who had donned his silver-link collar with the eclipse clasp, rode up next to the gate. "Let us in, Ombrosius. You know me and you recognize my sigil. You had my letter saying to expect me. Well, I have come at last."

The old man nodded several times and added something under his breath, then went on in his regional dialect that had more Latin in it than Frankish. "That you have. Goodness, look! It is Comes Sant' Germainius. With a party of armed men. Saints save me!" He ducked back behind the door and slammed it shut as if to keep the soldiers out.

"They are welcome here, Ombrosius," said Rakoczy patiently, adding to Einshere, "He is cautious, and that is a good thing, to my mind."

"As you say," Einshere said distantly; he had been preoccupied since they left Sant' Spiritu to continue their long trek over the high passes into the warmer climate of Longobardia. Einshere had taken to reciting the Hours as they rode and was now readying himself for Vespers.

"It looks to be a good place: easy to defend, at least these inner buildings. That wall would need a full company of soldiers to hold," said Notrold, giving Einshere a look of veiled contempt.

"I gather it has been manned by a century of Legionaries, in the past," said Rakoczy.

"Stout walls and a fine position," Notrold enlarged his praise. "How large is the villa? With all the grounds?"

"It is smaller than it was," said Rakoczy, remembering how much of the estate he had had to sacrifice in the last six hundred years; originally it had extended for a full Roman league along the lake, and had taken in all the land for half that distance from the shore. "But at its present size, it houses a staff of thirty-four and employs more than fifty peasants and artisans. There is room for twenty guests, with stalls for fifty horses."

"How many slaves?" Sulpicius asked.

"I keep no slaves," said Rakoczy. "Not in Franksland, not here, not in Wendish territory." He could see the men exchanging glances at this oddity of character. "Foreigners are often deprived of property, and slaves are more spies than servants for most foreigners. Servants are more dedicated."

"As long as they are kept well," said Notrold.

"That's so," Usuard said as the gates were pushed open and Ombrosius came bustling out, bowing and reverencing all the men.

"May you all be glad, Bellatori, and Magnatus, for coming here. It is a fine day when the Comes returns to us, one which we will celebrate. We have fresh fish to cook for our comestus, and tomorrow a proper feast shall make you truly welcome." He looked up at Rakoczy. "Shall I heat the caladarium? Or let more water into the tepidarium? Do your men want to swim?"

"They may want to tomorrow," said Rakoczy, anticipating this Roman luxury for himself. "I will be glad of some time in the caladarium. Can you heat it for me so that I may bathe while they dine?" He dismounted and shouted, "Avitus!" for his mariscalcus. "Bring your grooms. We have horses in need of grooming and food."

"Avitus is not here," said Ombrosius, and stared off at the northern peaks on the far side of the lake.

"Not here?" Rakoczy was surprised to hear this. "Where is he?"

"In Heaven, so I trust," said Ombrosius, and made a gesture of protection. "He took a fever in winter, and it turned into a putrid cough. He died of it."

"That saddens me; I trust his family has not suffered because of it," said Rakoczy.

"We have followed your instructions, Comes," said Ombrosius. "They are still housed and fed in his name."

Rakoczy made a gesture of approval. "Who is mariscalcus in his place?"

"Heraclius, his nephew, has done his work." Ombrosius looked over his shoulder in the direction of the stable. "Shall I summon him?"

"Of course," said Rakoczy, and turned to the men with him. "Dismount. My mariscalcus will take your horses and tend to them directly. In the meantime, Ombrosius, send for mansionarii to show my guests to their quarters. See that they are comfortable, that their property is respected, and that they have no reason to complain of their treatment. And summon one of the kitchen women or laundresses to wait upon the woman who rides in the plausterum." He saw the excitement in the old senescalus' eyes, and said, "No, I do not bring you a lady to be chatelaine here, though she is worthy enough. She is summoned to Roma in answer to the Pope, and we escort her at the Will of Karl-lo-Magne."

"The Pope summons a woman?" Ombrosius exclaimed, and was stopped from further observations by the arrival of Heraclius, who reverenced Rakoczy and nodded to Ombrosius.

"Comes Sant' Germainius," he said. "I had the honor to see you once when I was a little child. It is a most welcome thing to greet you again."

Rakoczy, who had in the past years left Hispania and gone east into Wendish territory, had made two short journeys into Italy to procure horses from Olivia; he supposed he must have seen the young man on the more recent of the two, when he had remained at this villa through most of the winter. "I am pleased to see you grown, and I am sorry to hear that your uncle has died. He served me long and well." He watched Heraclius reverence him and wondered how long this too-plausible young man had practiced it.

"As, I hope, I will," said Heraclius, holding out his hand for the reins and leads Rakoczy held. "Your orders before were for sweet hay, two measures of oats, an apple or a handful of grapes, and oil of turpentine on the hooves. Have you changed any of your preferences?"

"Comb their manes and tails, and rub them with wool-fat, then brush their coats," said Rakoczy. "And when they are cool, give them fresh water to drink. We will be here for a few days, and for that time, the horses are to be in the pasture during the day and stalled at night."

"As you wish, Comes," he said, and signaled for the grooms to take the other horses.

"Hold the mule drawing the plausterum," said Rakoczy, and went to assist

Gynethe Mehaut to get down. He paid no attention to the gasps of his servants, but showed her all the deference courtesy demanded. "She will need a woman to serve her."

Ombrosius all but goggled at his first sight of Gynethe Mehaut. "A ghost!" he cried out, and retreated half a dozen steps, his face averted. "Look away! Look away!" The mansionarii who had come hurrying out of the central building stopped in their tracks and stared, shocked by the appearance of the white-skinned woman with the red eyes.

"No, she is no ghost, no matter how pale her skin. This is Gynethe Mehaut," said Rakoczy as if his servants were behaving well. "She is called by His Holiness, Pope Leo, to wait upon him in Roma. You will show her all respect while she is here."

As the men of the escort surrendered their horses and remounts, a few of the mansionarii came forward to take the chests from the mules before the grooms could lead them away. This simple task broke the spell that seemed to have fallen over everyone in the courtyard.

"I have a cousin. She is called Zenevra, a most excellent, sensible woman, not given to fancies or frights," said Ombrosius, making a recovery at last. "She has three living children, all grown. She lives with my brother and tends to his family. She will come here and wait upon your . . . guest. If you will permit me to send for her, she will remain with . . . her, and—"

"Fine," said Rakoczy. "Send one of the mansionarii who knows her. I will see your family is rewarded for this service to me."

Relieved that he had nothing more to do to show his remorse for his earlier dismay, Ombrosius bustled about, his head bobbing as he gave crisp orders to the various servants. "Luculian, see the soldiers to the dining hall, and Rouanius, build up a fire in the caladarium. Merusian, go to the bakery and fetch the new bread and tell the cook to ready more." In a short time, everyone had gone about their assigned tasks, and Rakoczy was left alone with Gynethe Mehaut standing next to the pile of chests and packs that still had to be taken to cubicula of the soldiers and his own apartments.

"They are willing," said Gynethe Mehaut. "You are fortunate in that."

"So I am," Rakoczy agreed. "And the people of Lecco have been faithful to those of my blood for many generations."

"How long have your kinsmen held this place?" Gynethe Mehaut was staring at the fine old stonework left over from the time when the villa was new.

"For centuries," said Rakoczy. "I am going to assign you to apartments instead of a cubiculum. You will be able to rest there and not worry about the sun." They had been built for Olivia, but the precautions that would support a vampire would also serve an albino well.

"Won't that cause talk? If you have a chapel here, I might—"

"You have been praying every day since we left Attigny. You may rest a little from your observances," said Rakoczy, and indicated a young mansionarius who was making for the warder-gate. "He will bring you Ombrosius' cousin Zenevra, and she will tend you."

"But if I don't keep the Office," Gynethe Mehaut protested, "will it not be held against you?"

"If you wish to continue with the Hours, I would never stop you, but I would also not require it of you. I haven't the authority." Rakoczy started toward the main building.

"I'm afraid we'll be watched—one of the Bellatori, or your servants—" She looked over her shoulder as if anticipating the discovery of a lurking spy.

"You aren't under surveillance here unless you should wish to be. I give you my Word." He stopped, aware that he had not allayed her fears. "Come with me, Gynethe Mehaut. I will be pleased to guide you."

"That could make it appear I am your mistress," she said, her face showing confusion more than distress.

"What would be the harm in that? It would mean you are under my protection, which is accurate. I am master here, and you are my guest. And my servants will not press their advantage, or gossip more than most of them do." Rakoczy watched her while she thought about this. "The servants would be most attentive if they assumed you were my woman."

"They're afraid of me," said Gynethe Mehaut.

"They're startled by anything new; some of them are wary of me," said Rakoczy. "You might prefer to keep to your apartments while you are here, or you may use any part of the villa inside the walls. There are baths—old Roman baths—and two gardens and a small orchard you may visit safely." They had entered the vestibule, and Rakoczy pointed to the three corridors that converged there. "The atrium has become a garden, a small one," he went on. "The reception hall, dining hall, and withdrawing rooms are down there, to the right, the private apartments are to the left, on the upper floor. The cubicula are on the ground floor."

"This is a very fine place. Not at all like the Frankish villas." She went toward the wall ahead of her, staring at the faded murals there. "What Saint does this depict?"

"Not a Saint," said Rakoczy. "The painting is too old for that. It shows the adventures of Gaius Julius Caesar. You see? There he is in Gaul, that part of Franksland where Attigny stands."

She contemplated the figures Rakoczy indicated. "Was he a pious man, do you know?"

Rakoczy thought of the Latin definition of that word, meaning affectionate devotion, and said, "Yes, he was, for those he called his friends."

"And was he martyred?" she asked, pointing to the last illustration, showing him falling under the daggers of Brutus and the others.

"Some might say so," Rakoczy answered.

"What would you say?" She tried to read his face as he answered.

Considering his answer carefully, Rakoczy said, "He dedicated his life to Roma, and all that he believed it stood for. His enemies killed him for it. So, yes, he made himself a martyr, not to God, but to Roma." He perused the mural, and said, "The portrait isn't very good. It misses the wryness of his features. For an ambitious man, he had a rich appreciation of the absurdities of life—not that that stopped him from pursuing his objectives."

"You speak as if you knew him," said Gynethe Mehaut.

"Do I." He turned away from the wall. "I'll show you your apartments."

She followed him obediently, climbing the stairs two steps behind him. "This gallery—does it go all the way around the . . . the . . ." She pointed down into the atrium.

"No," he said. "It goes along two sides of the atrium, as you'll see in a moment. Just keep to the left at the top of the stairs."

"To the left," she said. "I will."

"Your apartments will overlook the atrium. Mine are at the corner and over-look the lake." He stopped at the top of the stairs. "There." He pointed along the gallery. "You see? There is a door at the start of the corridor. That is where you will stay. There is a bedchamber and a parlor, and a cubiculum for a servant. You may arrange it to your taste." As he said this he felt a sudden pang, missing Rorthger. "If Ombrosius' cousin is willing to remain here, then there will be a place for her in the cubiculum."

Gynethe Mehaut had stopped and was leaning against the gallery railing. "Look. There's a fountain in the atrium. It's flowing."

"Yes," said Rakoczy. "This villa is Roman, and it has the Roman way with moving water: it is piped in from the lake. Most of it goes through the holo-caust, to heat the caladarium and the water in the kitchens, but some is used for this fountain, and the tepidarium. That's in the next building. You can see its roof just over there." He pointed.

"Is it all for the tepidarium? How big is it?" Gynethe Mehaut was astonished. "It must be bigger than Great Karl's swimming pool at Aachen."

"It is," Rakoczy admitted. "But there are many, much larger, ones in Roma—or there were." He gave a little shake to his head and smiled at her. "You will see for yourself when we go there."

She shook her head. "I won't see them. I cannot go about the city."

"But you can, you know." Rakoczy resumed walking, passing through a narrow, brilliant band of light where the setting sun found a notch in the roofline. "Be careful," he warned her.

She winced as she walked through the bar of luminous gold. "I wouldn't like to be exposed to that for very long."

"You're safe enough here," he said, wishing she, too, could line the soles of her footgear with her native earth to protect her from the depredations of light. "There are only three places along this gallery where you can be hit by direct sunlight, at any time of day, or season of the year."

"What a fortunate thing," she said, "that you came upon such a place as this."

He wanted to tell her it had been built to his specifications, but that would have required him to admit to having lived far beyond the usual human limits, and he was worried about her reaction to such knowledge, so he only said, "Yes; it was." He had visited a pilgrim woman in her dreams three nights ago and so was no longer famished, but he still missed the intimacy of acceptance that such dream-visits never afforded. Nearing the door to her apartments, he said, "If there is anything you need, you have only to tell me and I will have it done for you."

She managed a sad smile. "Can you put my skin to rights, or my eyes? Can you keep my hands from bleeding?"

"No," he told her. "But I can attend to your comfort, and provide you with food and drink to please you."

"You are a gracious host," she said. "And you have been kind to me as no one else has."

"It isn't kindness, Gynethe Mehaut," he said, and stopped himself from going on. With a flourish, he opened the door for her. "There. You see, you have a chest for your clothes, and your bed should be made up for you." He supposed that Ombrosius would see to that if he had not done so already.

Gynethe Mehaut looked about the sitting room with its two couches and three chairs, all provided with silken pillows. There was a writing table with an ink-cake and a box of quills waiting to be used, and a tree of oil-lamps waiting to be lit. "This is . . . splendid."

"Hardly," said Rakoczy, who had seen real splendor many times in his long, long life and realized that while this was more comfortable than what she was accustomed to, it was far from luxurious. "If it gives you a pleasant stay, then I am well-satisfied." Again this was less than the truth, but it was no deception.

"I will be comfortable here," she said, "more than comfortable." She smoothed her hand over the lovely pine-green silk of the nearest cushion, her fingers lingering on the glistening fabric. "I wish I could . . ." She stopped.

"You wish you could what?" he prompted, coming half a dozen steps into the room.

"I wish I could wear such grand material. No one would pay any attention to my skin if I dressed in jewels of cloth." She sounded wistful.

"I shall order a gonella and a stolla made for you of whichever color you would like. It will be my gift for you, for your stay in Roma." His smile was meant to reassure her.

She moved away from him, her bandaged palms folded. "If you can assure me that no blame would come for such opulence, I will accept, although I should not."

"You are my guest, Gynethe Mehaut," said Rakoczy, sensing that she wanted time to herself. "It is my privilege to offer such things to you. The Pope doesn't expect you to come before him as a lost soul, with nothing to recommend you but the calluses on your knees and the wrappings on your hands. He has a Court, and the Cardinal Archbishops are as grand as any Comes of Great Karl's. You would do well to dress in silks and gems, so that you will not seem someone who can be overlooked or dismissed."

"Harlots dress in silks and jewels," she said brusquely.

"And Queens," said Rakoczy.

Gynethe Mehaut was very still, then made a gesture of dismissal. "I am tired, Magnatus."

"Then you must rest," said Rakoczy. "If you need anything, pull the chain by the door and someone will come to you."

"And where will you be?" she asked as if to keep him with her.

"I'll go to the caladarium. It's at the south end of the tepidarium, in a small stone building with two tall chimneys at the north end. When comestus is over, I should be finished. If you would like to bathe in warm water, I will tell the servants to keep a fire in the holocaust."

"I . . . I may," she said. "Where should I dine? I cannot sit down with the soldiers, not even here."

"Have Ombrosius bring your food to your rooms," Rakoczy suggested.

"I am no invalid," she reminded him.

"No; but you may dine alone in any case. I have had guests who prefer to keep to themselves," he said, faintly amused. "Those of my blood also take nourishment in private. Ombrosius is used to such requests."

She turned away from him. "I would be glad of a hot bath."

"Then you shall have it," said Rakoczy. "Would you prefer to go before me?"

"No," she said, shaking her head emphatically. "No."

"Very well," he said, reverencing her. "I'll have a servant escort you to the caladarium when I have left it."

She nodded. "Yes. Fine."

Rakoczy stepped back to the door. "Summon Ombrosius. He'll assist you."

"Are you sure he will come, and not some other?" She held up her hand as if to keep him from leaving, but then motioned him away.

"Yes." He swung the door closed, then continued down the corridor to his own apartments. Once inside his sitting room, he pulled off his gonelle, tossing it aside. He then shed his black linen camisa and unfastened the ties of his femoralia, pulled off his tooled-leather Persian boots and tugged off his tibialia, leaving them all in a heap. Wearing only his breechclout, he reached into one of the two chests in the room and drew out a drying sheet of dark-dyed cotton. He wrapped this around his shoulders and looked for a pair of sandals. The earth in them had not been changed in years, but he donned them as much out of habit as need and prepared to go to the rear stairs that led down to the caladarium and tepidarium. Pulling the ends of the drying sheet across the wide band of scar tissue that covered his torso from the base of his ribs to the top of his pubis, he opened the door and slipped out into the corridor. He glanced in the direction of Gynethe Mehaut's apartments and was both relieved and saddened to see the door closed; he moved quickly toward the rear stairs and went out into the evening, where the intense odor of broiling fish wafted toward him, with a second aroma of baking bread.

Outside the caladarium there were two torches fixed in sconces, their flames making dazzling flags in the encroaching dusk. Rakoczy took one of the torches and went into the smaller outer room, where he used the torch to light a stand of oil-lamps before going into the central room where the heat enveloped him. The pool itself, fifteen hands deep, was twice as long as it was wide, and long enough for a man half again as tall as Rakoczy to stretch out full length, which would accommodate even Karl-lo-Magne easily. After he dropped the drying sheet, Rakoczy got into the water, the heat settling into him with such clarity that he felt it as if it were metal and not water at all. He was uncomfortable for a short while, but then grew accustomed to the heat and lay back, half-floating, letting the tension and the grime of the days crossing the mountains fade from his body. He let his thoughts wander, remembering the two years during which this villa had been built. Roma had been slightly past its zenith, but was still dynamic, safe and fairly prosperous. He had chosen this place for his villa after a journey to his homeland had detoured along Lake Como; he had been taken with the beauty and tranquility of the location and had paid the full price demanded for it, in gold. All the buildings sat on foundations filled with his native Carpathian earth, and not even the water in the tepidarium could cause him discomfort. The villa became his retreat: when politics in Roma became dangerous, Rakoczy often came to this villa to keep from being caught up in the chaos that was increasingly the style of the Senate in its dealings with the Emperor and the Legions.

"Have I done wrong?" Her voice was so tentative that at first Rakoczy supposed he had imagined it. "If I have, I will go."

Rakoczy opened his eyes and stared into the steamy half-light. "Gynethe Mehaut," he said, standing upright in the hot water.

"I only thought you wouldn't mind if I came . . . you said I could use this caladarium. I wanted not to be alone here. So I have come." She took a few more steps toward the pool. "If you don't want me here, I will go."

"No; I am pleased to have you here." He pointed to his drying sheet. "Put your stolla there, and your sandals."

She hesitated. "Is it wrong? Should I not be here?"

"Bathing in hot water?" he asked, knowing she did not mean that. "No, it isn't wrong. You may find it a bit too warm, but if it is, I will open a spigot from the tepidarium and cool it off." He moved to the edge of the pool and indicated the place where there was a shelf in the pool. "You can step on that until you become accustomed to the heat."

Taking uncertain steps, she came up to where he leaned on the side of the pool; she loosened her girdle and dropped it on the heavy tiles. "Oh. I will have to wear this wet when we are done." Next she took the stolla off in an impulsive hurry, standing awkwardly once she was nude. "What about my hands?"

"You should leave your bandages in place, I think; the heat is likely to increase the bleeding and you'll want to know if it becomes serious." He wondered if he should hide his scars, but he had no notion how he could, and he was sure his efforts would only draw attention to them.

"I think you should turn your back while I get in," she said, trying to conceal her breasts and her loins.

He did as she requested. "You needn't worry, Gynethe Mehaut. I won't importune you."

"Only Fratre Nordhold at Sant' Audoenus ever has. And even he only tried when he was drunk." She sighed. "I don't want to have to endure that again, but I would like someone to look upon me as something other than loathsome." She put her linen-wrapped hands to her face. "I am too strange for any man to want me; I have known that for many years. That may save my virginity, but it is not because of my virtue."

Rakoczy shook his head. "I don't find you too strange—you are no stranger than I am. In some ways I am stranger than you are." He remained standing with his back to her; he remembered more than seven hundred years ago, how he had spent an evening in his caladarium at Villa Ragoczy outside of Roma; it was much larger than this pool was, and decorated with mosaics. Tishtry had joined him there, and they had made love in the hot water. He made himself put such recollections behind him.

"You are kind to me, Magnatus, and I believe you are sincere, but I don't—" Gynethe Mehaut sat down on the side of the pool and eased her legs into the water. "This is very hot."

"It's supposed to be." He moved away from her so that she would have more room to herself. "Get in slowly until you get used to it."

"It is . . . not unpleasant," she said, the sloshing of the water telling him she had lowered herself still farther into the water.

"In time you will come to like it," he said, going to the far side of the caldarium. "Choose where you would prefer to stand, or lean back and float."

"I can't do that," said Gynethe Mehaut. "Standing is all I can manage."

Rakoczy laughed softly. "If you would like to try floating, I will help you, if you like."

There was a long silence between them while Gynethe Mehaut settled into the pool. Finally she said, "If you would like to turn around, all you will see is my head."

Rakoczy swung about, stretching out toward her, half-floating. "If you will let the water carry you, you will find the heat restful."

"I may try, but not just yet." She considered what he had said. "If you will show me?"

"Of course; this is how it's done," said Rakoczy and lowered his feet to the bottom of the pool, then gradually lay back, letting the water support him until he was on his back, his scarred abdomen almost completely exposed.

"Your injuries must have been . . . dreadful," Gynethe Mehaut said, moving toward him as if impelled by the heat of the pool.

"They were, but that was a long time ago," said Rakoczy.

Gynethe Mehaut stared at him. "No wonder you said you understood. . . . I thought you had dreamed or imagined . . . But this is . . ."

"And it is more than you see," he said, his voice dropping to just above a whisper.

"How?" She came up close to him. "What did that?"

"Broad knives and hooks, for the most part," said Rakoczy; they had been made of bronze, and tended to dull quickly, so that the edges of his scars were jagged, a reminder of those bronze knives. He resisted the urge to turn away or stand upright again. The day of his death, more than twenty-eight centuries ago, remained vivid in his mind, though it no longer repelled him as it had once.

"God and the Saints," she marveled. "Do you never fear that people may become upset by those scars?"

"Yes; that is why I rarely show them. Unlike you, I can conceal my differences. But they are very real, nonetheless." He held out his hand to her. "Let me see how you're managing."

She reached for him. "This is very nice. But my hands feel odd. They tingle."

"The heat is probably—" He lifted her hands. "You are bleeding, but not alarmingly." The nearness of her blood was intoxicating, reminding him of the satisfaction that he had missed for so long, that after his most recent encounter with Csimenae, he could not believe he deserved.

"Shall I remove the wraps?" She was staring into his face as if she had sensed something of his need.

"No. Not yet. Not until you are ready to get out." He let go of her and took a step back.

"Why? Are you afraid the water will harm me?" She held up her hands. "What am I to do? If this blood is a sign of perfidy, as Bishop Iso has said, won't you need a priest to bless this water, whether I keep my bandages on or not?"

"No," said Rakoczy. "But I will put a little oil of primrose in the water, against contamination, as I do every time I use this caladarium." He smiled at her, his own misgivings fading. "So long as the water is clear and hot, it cannot do you harm."

She made a complicated little sigh. "So I pray."

"Do you have any reason to doubt?" he asked, trying to understand her anxiety.

". . . No." She raised her arms and splashed them down. "No! I have nothing to doubt!" Her burst of laughter echoed eerily in the steamy room. "I may come to a bad end, or a good one, but just now, I will enjoy myself."

"That would give me great honor," said Rakoczy. "I thank you for—"

She put her hand to his mouth; he had to stop himself from licking her bandages. "No. Say nothing. Help me to enjoy this, but don't explain it to me." She ran her hand down his chest to the scars. "I will accept all you do here. You know what suffering can be, and you will not use that against me."

Little as he liked having his scars touched, he let her explore the white swath; he made no effort to stop her, nor did he say anything. It was an odd experience for him, having his fatal injuries so thoroughly scrutinized, and he struggled to maintain his composure, thinking that Gynethe Mehaut had to endure much worse every day of her life. Finally he said, "It was all done long ago." He waited while she considered this, then added, "After this, I was an exile."

"Then your enemies did this," she said.

"The enemies of my people," he said. "They killed most of my family and made me a slave. Eventually they punished me." He said nothing about his success in battle that had so frightened his captors that they dared not leave him alive to rally others around him.

"They used you cruelly," she said.

"So I think," Rakoczy agreed. "But it was a long time ago."

She shuddered in spite of the heat and took shelter in his arms. "For this lit-tle while, will you pretend that I am just like any other woman, and you like any other man?"

He stroked her neck. "Yes, Gynethe Mehaut. I'll pretend." And saying that, he bent to kiss her.

TEXT OF A DISPATCH FROM KARL-LO-MAGNE AT STRASBOURG IN ALEMANNIA TO HIERNOM RAKOCZY AT LECCO, LAKE COMO IN LONGOBARDIA, CARRIED BY AN OFFICIAL KING'S COURIER AND DELIV-ERED ONE WEEK AFTER RAKOCZY AND HIS BAND LEFT FOR ROMA; FROM THERE, CARRIED BY CHURCH MESSENGER FROM SANT' CHRYSOGONUS TO BOBBIO IN LONGOBARDIA AND FINALLY DELIVERED FIVE WEEKS AFTER IT WAS WRITTEN.

To the most excellent Magnatus, the foreigner Hiernom Rakoczy, Comes Sant' Germainius, the greetings of Karl-lo-Magne, King of all Franksland, on this, the beginning of May by the Pope's calendar in his year 800.

Magnatus, it is my intention to extend your right of paravareda, so that you may requisition horses and lodging as you need them in your journey through Longobardia, where my Will is recognized by all as being the equal to any Longobardian King, and therefore as binding on the Longobardians as it is upon the Franks and all the people of Franksland.

I am relying upon you to arrive in Roma as soon as you may, and to establish yourself there within the walls, so that you may always be reached quickly if the Pope's staff should require that you present the Pale Woman to the Papal Court. You are not to leave her unguarded at any time, nor are you to permit her to travel abroad without your escort to ensure no mishap befalls her. It is still my intention to arrive in Roma by the end of October, but if I cannot make good time, or if my enemies keep me here for months more than I have anticipated, then perhaps it will be up to you to reassure Leo's Court that I will indeed arrive in time for the ceremony we have arranged. The Pope's own difficulties we may have hit upon a way to relieve, but I will consult my Bishops and Archbishops before I consider the matter settled. When I have had the full benefit of religious council, I will inform you of how we will progress. I will not ask you to take an active role in this unless it becomes necessary, in which case, I will dispatch men to help you maintain the Pope's authority, should that flag in his absence. If you should hear of anything that may compromise the Pope more than has been the case thus far, I ask you to send me word of it with all haste. Use an episcopal courier from one of the Frankish Bishops or Archbishops, for only they may be relied upon to bring me a full and true account of your concerns.

If you cannot find the means to maintain a proper household within the city walls, then I instruct you to put yourself in the protection of Archbishop Hesengarius, who will house you until I come. I would prefer that you keep your own establishment, but the Pope may not permit this, for he may feel the need of keen ears in Roma upon which he can repose confidence. You will be expected to do your utmost to act in Leo's interests so long as it also coincides with mine. However you must carry on, I want you to strive for independence; the climate of Roma is rife with politics as it is with the mal aria. It is not an environment that I would like you to become entrapped in, let alone participate in. Leave that to the good Bishops and Cardinal Archbishops of the Church.

It is being arranged for Leo and I to meet north of Roma and to enter the city together, which suits me very well. I am convinced that this show of unity will tend to persuade the Byzantines that the Church of Roma will stand any upheavals, and that all of Europe will band together for the sake of the Church. The Pope will be absent from Roma until I may accompany him there, although many of his Cardinal Archbishops will visit him at Spoleto to settle matters that need the Pope's attention, and cannot wait against my arrival. Leo is an apt pupil of the affairs of state that impinge upon the Church, and for that reason he is keeping abreast of all that transpires in Roma during his absence.

I am grateful to you for your undertaking this mission. There is no one in my Court on whom I can rely more than on you, at least in this situation. You can do more for me by being apart from my Court, and you are skilled enough to know how perilous Roma is. I ask you not to lose sight of this, no matter what blandishments might be offered to you. Keep your head, and think of the difficulties that the Pale Woman faces, for she, more than you, could suffer for being caught up in the maneuvering of the Church. Also, you comprehend the subtlety of the Byzantines, and you do not underestimate their capacity for intrigue. Nowhere in the West is that more apparent than in Roma.

The Pope is concluding negotiations with Constantinople regarding the matter of my title in a most secret manner, for the Byzantines have not been willing to consider any of our requests. They have resisted allowing me Emperor and Augustus, but Leo is a clever man, and more tenacious than any

of the Greeks know. I am confident this will be settled long before I leave
Franksland to journey to Roma. If Leo should call upon you in this capacity,
then I will release you from your assurances that you will remain aloof from
such dealings. If you are required to venture to Spoleto, inform me of it before
you leave, so that I may know at what stage these processes are. I am certain
that you, being a foreigner, may move about the Papal Court more readily
than the Frankish Archbishops, who surely are being watched by the Greeks.
So, allowing for the exigencies of circumstances, I give you leave to decide
what is best: you can put yourself in Pope Leo's service for this, and this alone.

The matter of my title rankles. I have no wish to war with the Byzantines
over it, but I also have no desire to capitulate to their demands. The Pope has
suggested that I unite with him by being Emperor of the Church, which is
Universal, thereby expanding my realm beyond being King of the Franks
and the Longobards. We are agreed on Most Serene Augustus, Crowned by
God, Great, Peace-giving Emperor. The Pope wants the addition of Imperial
Governor of all the Romans, and I suppose I must comply, for that would
clearly make me Emperor in the West, by virtue of the lands included, but it
falls short of making me a Roman Emperor, one with the Caesars and therefore heir to their Emperor. But I know that the Pope is right, and the Greeks
would not accept such a sweeping title without a battle, so I will leave it to
my successors to reclaim the Roman Empire on behalf of the Church. When
that dream is finally realized, all Europe will rejoice. If I were twenty years
younger, I might still take on the Greeks over this title, but I have wars
enough to last me until I die, and I do not wish to vitiate my armies with yet
another campaign. Leo may confer this upon me and I will accept it without
cavil, and say we all Amen.

Be stalwart in your purpose. Do not yield in your dedication to my cause.
I will reward your fealty just as I will punish any lapses on your part. You
are my secret advantage in Roma, and I require you to uphold that obligation or face confiscation, imprisonment, and death. Earn my high opinion,
Magnatus, and the world will know of your trustworthiness.

Karl-lo-Magne
King of all Franksland
by the hand of Fratre Perquitus

⌒

chapter five

B Y TERCE ROMA WAS ALREADY HOT, the morning light shining off the top-pled marble stones that marked the old Forum and the ancient, tumbled temples to old gods no longer honored in this city. The sun was a brassy smear half-way up the high-clouded sky, lending a glare to the morning even while it robbed the shadows of their sharpest edges. A number of little chapels were open to the many pilgrims who wandered the Roman streets, a number of them with small crucifixes sewn onto their shoulders to show their penitence to the world. Gangs of slaves moved through the avenues with wooden sledges, collecting tumbled blocks from old buildings; these were being used to repair the three largest breaches in the walls as well as to rid the city of rubble.

To the rear of the Pantheon, a party of Frankish monks were reciting their prayers, the great dome with its central opening drawing their eyes toward Heaven. The odor of incense hung in the air like dust motes, almost covering the sweaty presence of the monks. There was almost no one about but the Franks; one of them, a maimed, blunt-featured fellow named Lothar, kept his attention on the glowing aperture, his face suffused with rapture. The others with him prayed, too, but without the ecstatic delight Fratre Lothar felt. Beside him, Fratre Egicaberht droned the prayers of the Little Hour, doing his best to disregard Fratre Lothar's excesses. When the Office was finished, all the monks but Fratre Lothar prepared to leave the venerable building.

"Fratre," said Prior Ricimar, touching Fratre Lothar on the sleeve of his white Roman dalmatica. "Terce is over."

Fratre Lothar blinked. "What?" He frowned. "Oh. I was preoccupied. This church—"

"—began as a pagan temple, and reminds us that we must be diligent in our service to Christ, or the pagans will once again claim the earth for their false gods, even here in Roma, where Christ reigns triumphant. It is the lapse and error we must see, not the victory," Prior Ricimar said bluntly, his glance raking over the eight monks who waited around him in their linen dalmaticae, presenting a much more uniform appearance than they usually did at home. "We have two more churches to visit before prandium and None," he reminded the monk with the ruined hand. "You cannot remain here, lost in praying, while we have a duty to do here in Roma."

"I ask your pardon, Prior," said Fratre Lothar, lowering his eyes to show his humility. "I should have been more alert."

Standing slightly behind him, Fratre Smaragdus said nothing, only watched with hooded eyes.

"Yes; you should," said Prior Ricimar, and turned to leave the Pantheon.

"You will get us all into trouble," Fratre Egicaberht hissed to Fratre Lothar; Fratre Smaragdus nodded. "Keep your thoughts to yourself."

"It is just that I have never seen such holy places, and it is as if nothing I have ever seen before has had any meaning, no matter how grand," Fratre Lothar said with intense emotion. "This is a culmination of my calling, to worship here. Since I came to my vocation, I have longed for the opportunity to see the churches and basilicas of Roma."

Fratre Chunfrid, who was almost deaf, clung to Fratre Fustel's sleeve and struggled to understand what was happening.

"You have been to Aachen and seen the Royal Chapel there, and you have been to Paderborn," Fratre Egicaberht reminded him.

"When I was a Bellatore, I saw those places. That was another life, and I another man. I thought nothing of worship then. Aachen was Aachen, a Royal Residence. Paderborn was the capital of the Saxons. And they were not this city, which is the heart of our faith." The blazing sunlight made him blink, and he stared about as if he were uncertain of where he was. "The sun dazzles here in Roma."

"So it seems," said Fratre Egicaberht, motioning his companion to silence.

They followed Prior Ricimar through the confusion of streets that led toward the Tiber and the rambling brick house that was used by Franks in Roma. The streets were noisy, and everyone appeared to be busy, trying to get their morning work completed before prandium and their mid-day nap that let them slumber through the heat of the afternoon. Twice they passed small parties of monks carrying bodies in winding-sheets, a grim reminder that the summer fevers had come early this year.

"This is an important day," said Prior Ricimar as they reached the steps of Sant' Ioannes Laterano. "The Cardinal Archbishop Brunehaut of Marmoutier, a fellow Frank, will show us this church; he will point out its most holy possessions and show us the names recorded in the Pope's Book of Martyrs." He indicated a book to Fratre Chunfrid and hoped the monk would understand.

"To die for the true faith!" Fratre Lothar exclaimed. "How blessed they are."

"If God will accept me among them," said Fratre Gondehold.

"Amen," said Fratre Smaragdus.

"So you may think now, in the splendor of Roma with the might of the Church all around you," said Prior Ricimar. "But few have the stalwart purpose to endure what God sends them. Fratre Lothar, think: you have been a soldier, and you have faced the foe and death, yet I wonder if you would be willing to accept a martyr's crown, for all your prayers?"

"If God would think me worthy, I would embrace such an honorable death," said Fratre Lothar, and looked around at his comrades in the hope they would endorse his enthusiasm.

"For God's sake, be quiet," said Fratre Egicaberht. "You embarrass us all."

"How can I?" Fratre Lothar asked. "Are we not all dedicated to God and the work of His Church?"

"We're monks," said Fratre Fustel, as if it was explanation enough. He patted Fratre Chunfrid's hand.

"And therefore we are soldiers of God," said Fratre Lothar.

"And therefore we are monks," said Fratre Fustel. "It is nothing more than that. To aspire to more is a failure of devotion. We have our Office and our Order and that is enough for God." He glanced at Prior Ricimar, expecting a reprimand.

"True enough," said the Prior. "You should seek to live as a monk, in simplicity and acceptance of what God provides you, and not hanker after advancement, even within your Order. All monks must give their Will over to the Will of God, and acquiesce in His design. You haven't surrendered to God, yet, though you think you have, because you have accepted God as you would a Dux of the army. The Church isn't the army, Fratre Lothar. If there is advancement to be gained it will be for your modesty and virtue, not your enterprise. You have no patron to sponsor you, and all God asks is that you abide by the Rule, and keep the sacraments holy. If you seek after more, you compromise your devotion. Do the simple things that are required of us with a glad heart, and abide in trust in God and the Salvation promised us." He was getting nervous; he paced the steps, peering into the crowd as if expecting to find the Cardinal Archbishop there. "Anything else smacks of Pride, and that is the Cardinal Sin, above all others."

Fratre Lothar looked down at his feet. "I hope I may live without sin."

"More Pride," Prior Ricimar declared. "No man is sinless but Christ, Who was not a man, but was made flesh."

"Amen," said Fratre Ildebald, and glowered at Fratre Lothar.

"How long are we going to wait?" piped the white-haired, half-foolish Fratre Sigisteus. "I'm getting hungry."

"We'll wait until the Cardinal Archbishop Brunehaut comes for us," said Prior Ricimar. He folded his hands and tried to stand still.

Half-a-dozen pilgrims entered the church, one of them stopping at every step to prostrate himself and recite prayers. The monks got out of the way, and Fratre Chunfrid sketched a gesture of blessing in the direction of the prone man.

There was a flurry of excitement inside the church, and then Cardinal Archbishop Brunehaut came out onto the steps and said, "Prior Ricimar? I welcome you to Roma and Sant' Ioannes Laterano. I am glad you're here." He indicated the door.

"Come, Fratri," said Prior Ricimar. "I want you to be with me for prandium, and the nap afterward, so when we have completed seeing the church, we may depart and be ready for our meal and our prayers."

"Yes," the Cardinal Archbishop said. "You keep your observations, and when they are over, and the afternoon nap is finished, there are some matters we must discuss." He motioned to the monks.

"We are at your service, Primore." Prior Ricimar lowered his head and waited for a sign to go on.

"Yes. You are." He stepped back into the narthex and pointed toward the altar. "There is where the Pope says Mass, when he is in Roma. While he is gone, each of us Cardinal Archbishops says Mass, one of us each day."

"Have you said Mass recently, Primore?" asked Fratre Sigisteus.

"Yes; three days ago," said the Cardinal Archbishop. He stared at the monks as if trying to make up his mind about them. "If you wish to see the chapels, I will take you around the nave." He coughed gently and went toward the side of the church, where small alcoves served as chapels for those wishing to pray privately in this large building. "The Popes have dedicated chapels to each of the Apostles, and, as you can see, there are ten chapels to Our Lady. Many pilgrims pray at each one of them, reciting the 'Ave' ten times in each." He walked slowly enough to allow the monks to look into each of the chapels, but quickly enough that they could not linger. As they neared the choir, he pointed to a cluster of chapels behind the benches. "These are dedicated to the early Martyrs and Saints. You can see their stories in mosaics on the walls of each chapel." Again he let the monks glance in, but kept them moving. "Come this way," he said, taking the monks behind the High Altar to the Penitents' Chapels; these were closed cells with barred and locked doors, where single lamps burned to illuminate the occupants of the cells, who spent their days and nights in constant prayer for the remission of sin.

One of the penitents laughed as he prayed, his voice high and sing-song as he recited Psalms in Avar-accented Latin. As the monks passed his door, he stopped and called out, "You should all be ashamed. You are lazy, and that is a Deadly Sin. You should be praying every hour of every day. Anything less will bring ruin on Roma."

Fratre Ildebald was shocked; Fratre Fustel was frightened, which served to alarm Fratre Chunfrid; Fratre Lothar was transfixed by this unexpected accusation. The three monks stood by the iron door, wary and upset. Fratre Smaragdus listened closely to the muttered Psalms of the occupant of the cell.

"Pay no attention," said Prior Ricimar. "This is the fate of those who are too zealous in their devotion. Let him be a warning to you all."

"A warning?" Fratre Lothar exclaimed. "An example, rather. How could you think this man is a warning when his piety is so complete? This penitent is willing to show us the way. Our dedication is not genuine if we are unwilling to make his sacrifice." He looked to the Cardinal Archbishop. "Primore Brunehaut, what do you say? Surely this monk is more worthy than we are."

"He is more rigorous," said Cardinal Archbishop Brunehaut. "He could not be were it not for Fratri like you who are willing to do the daily labor that supports him and the other penitents in their prayers. Without monks like you, these men would starve, and their cells would become tombs."

Prior Ricimar made a sign of agreement. "Listen to him, Fratre Lothar. You are still new to monastic life and you are like a suitor in the first flush of courtship, all ardor and fine intentions. Yet a monk is not a husband but a servant, and he must accept the nature of his calling or fail God. You have been a soldier, and you have known what it is to submit to the rule of a leader, even in the heat of battle. So must you submit to God's commands now you are a monk."

"Well-said," approved the Cardinal Archbishop. "The Church has need of monks who are willing to consecrate their calling to the most simple tasks—farming, baking, weaving, cheese-making, tending the sick and injured, providing shelter for travelers, and all the other Christian acts that show God our desire to be like Christ in our humility."

"The penitents in these cells have more to answer for than you do, and more to repent than most men," said Cardinal Archbishop Brunehaut, raising his voice a little as if to remind the penitents of their purpose. "They have all committed some great crime or affronted God in some way that is beyond what most men do." He motioned to the monks to hurry, and led them out the west door into a small cloister. "Here. You may join us for Sept. The bell will sound shortly." He shaded his eyes with his hands and looked up at the sky. "The clouds are thickening. There will be rain by evening, thanks be to God."

The monks all made gestures imploring deliverance, and Fratre Egicaberht chanted the "Pater Noster," his hands raised in worship. Fratre Smaragdus folded his hands as if to disassociate himself with such excesses. Cardinal Archbishop Brunehaut hesitated a moment, then joined Fratre Egicaberht in his recitation.

"You are staying at the House of the Franks, aren't you? With the others from Franksland?" The Cardinal Archbishop was most business-like as he asked, all his pietistic manner gone. "A messenger will find you there, won't he?"

"We are bidden to the infirmary at Holy Martyrs to help care for the ill, as part of our service," said Prior Ricimar. "But this evening at Vespers most of us will return to the House of the Franks."

"Very good," approved the Cardinal Archbishop. "Who among you is doing night duty at Holy Martyrs?"

Fratre Gondehold and Fratre Lothar signaled that they were to undertake that duty. After a moment, so did Fratre Smaragdus.

"They are the first. Tomorrow night two or three others will serve," said Prior Ricimar in a tone that brooked no discussion, although a few of the monks were unhappy about this. "Those who will not tend the sick and injured may clean latrines."

"Very good," Cardinal Archbishop Brunehaut repeated. "My messengers will find you."

"Amen," said Fratre Gondehold, his face shining. "I will be most eager to aid you in any way you wish. You have only to state what you require."

Cardinal Archbishop Brunehaut coughed once. "For that I am grateful." He indicated a distant gate in the cloister enclosure. "That is the Pope's Walkway. It leads to his quarters; they are not so fine as Karl-lo-Magne's, but they are worthy of His Holiness." In fact, the Papal quarters were little more than a dormitory with a few small reception rooms and three private chapels, but the Cardinal Archbishop knew better than to admit this.

"Will the Pope reside there when he returns?" Fratre Sigisteus asked.

"It is expected he will, but that isn't for me to say: Leo must decide where he is to live, and who is to be housed with him." A shadow crossed the Cardinal Archbishop's face, as if a cloud had more completely blotted out the sun. "He is a cautious man, and it has served him well in this world."

"May God protect him," said Prior Ricimar, and heard his monks echo this sentiment.

"That is as He Wills," said Cardinal Archbishop Brunehaut.

"We are all in His Hands," said Fratre Ildebald.

"No doubt," said the Cardinal Archbishop dryly. "Although God has been aided by Great Karlus."

"That, also, is God's Will," said Prior Ricimar, puzzled by the Cardinal Archbishop's demeanor. He waited a long moment, then added, "May our Roman Church be preserved from her enemies, and may we help her to survive and prosper."

"That will need God's diligence," said the Cardinal Archbishop, "for her enemies are legion." A circumspect silence settled over the monks as they watched the Cardinal Archbishop raise his hand to bless them all. "May you do God's Will in all things, and may He make His Face to look upon you with favor." It was a signal that their audience with him had ended. He nodded in the direction of the main gate of the cloister. "You may return to the street there. You will have enough time to see the Basilica of Sant' Bartolomeo before prandium and None."

"Then we must make haste," said Prior Ricimar, and pointed the way to his Fratri. "We are grateful to you, Primore."

"Yes; yes," said Cardinal Archbishop Brunehaut, and headed away from the group of monks.

"That was . . . Christian of him," said Fratre Sigisteus as the Cardinal Archbishop left them to their own devices.

"He has many responsibilities. God has given him much to do," said Prior Ricimar, but without the conviction he felt he ought to have. He made another attempt to account for the Primore's odd behavior. "With the Pope away, the Cardinal Archbishops have many more duties."

The monks seconded this notion with nods; Fratre Lothar seemed about to speak, and then thought better of it. A Laterano slave who served as warder opened the gates for them, let them out into the hectic street, and closed the door behind them immediately.

"I believe Sant' Bartolomeo is that way," said Fratre Smaragdus, pointing toward the northeast; a train of well-laden donkeys went by him, the two peasants leading them in the middle of a heated argument in the local dialect. "Follow those donkeys."

"I think, rather, it is down that street," said Fratre Gondehold, indicating the way that led to the largest break in Roma's walls.

"We will go that way," Prior Ricimar insisted, starting out toward the street he had chosen. He had to stop to permit four armed men to ride past, and then he almost tripped over a pile of broken bricks that had fallen from one of the sledges being dragged through the city; the Frankish monks were close behind him, walking carefully through the confusion, meticulously avoiding the groups of too-pretty boys in short tunicae with soot on their lashes who loitered outside the Laterano.

"I don't think this is the way," Fratre Sigisteus said when they had gone a short distance. They were now in a small square that was dominated by an old Roman building with an imposing but neglected front; a group of larger-than-life statues of men in antique armor were tumbled in front of its wide steps as if they had been struck down in battle. All but one of their pediments were missing, and the remaining one was cracked; no inscriptions remained, just gouged marble where writing had been. No one was in the square but a pair of young women with painted faces in gauzy stollae, who gazed at the monks then smiled behind raised hands.

"That isn't Sant' Bartolomeo," Fratre Lothar said. "This is a pagan temple. And those women are whores."

"They have the look," admitted Prior Ricimar. "Perhaps we should go." He glanced about the square uneasily, then noticed the front of a large house in surprisingly good repair. Desperately he went up to it, afraid that he was approaching a brothel or worse. He pulled the chain to summon the warder, and was startled when a handsome man with dark hair answered the summons. "Your pardon, Roman," said the Prior in his best attempt at the city's patois, "but how may I find Sant' Bartolomeo's Basilica?"

The man answered him in excellent classical Latin. "You go up that street," he said, pointing to the way they had come, "and at the square with the chapel to Santa Svinthtude, turn to the left and go down the Street of the Coopers. Sant' Bartolomeo's is two squares beyond."

"You are a most gracious Roman," said Prior Ricimar.

"I'm not a Roman, I'm Greek," said the man, and saw the Frankish monks recoil. "Not Byzantine," he added. "I have lived in Roma for many years. I tend this house for my mistress."

"Then you are a slave?" Fratre Ildebald asked.

"You wear no collar," said Fratre Sigisteus, as if this made everything he said suspicious.

"I am a bondsman," said the handsome Greek, preparing to close the door.

"What manner of house is this?" Fratre Smaragdus demanded suddenly.

"It belongs to Domina Clemens, a respectable Roman widow," said the bondsman with great formality. "Those women in the square have their establishment in the Temple of Hercules, where the statues are overturned. They are not associated with my mistress." He gave the monks a brusque nod. "May God guard you here in Roma, good Fratri," he said, and closed the door.

"What kind of woman would put herself in a place like this?" asked Fratre Egicaberht. "So near vice."

"She may have her reasons for being here," said the Prior dubiously, and sidled away from the stout iron door of the widow's house. "We must go back the way we came."

"Vice is everywhere in Roma," said Fratre Lothar. "Those youths near Sant' Ioannes Laterano . . ." His voice dropped away.

Fratre Fustel tugged on Fratre Chunfrid's sleeve, encouraging him to keep up with the rest of the monks.

"All the more reason for the Church to remain here," said Fratre Gondehold. "There is much for her to do."

"Constantinople is no better, and very likely worse," said Fratre Fustel. "No one can hide from vice in this world."

The monks nodded among themselves and moved more quickly along the narrow street. The bondsman's directions proved correct, and they came to the

Basilica of Sant' Bartolomeo in good time. The square in front of the column-fronted church was filled with an impromptu market: bee-keepers were selling honey-combs, and wine merchants offered sealed jars from all over Italy; hawkers of nostrums proclaimed the virtues of their concoctions, while a man with a bladder-pipe played tunes for coins or food. On the west side of the square a building had been demolished some time ago; young shrubs were already growing out of the ruin. Sant' Bartolomeo was being added onto, and the sounds of workers added to the cacophony in the square.

Inside the Basilica the air was thick with dust from the construction going on at the back of the building. The noise of saws and hammers mixed with shouted instructions and the occasional slap of a whip. In the center of the building, half of a fine new altar was in place, and slaves struggled with another section of polished stone. An alabaster screen was being fitted into the aperture of a window in the lantern of the small dome. Half a dozen Fratri gathered around a small altar behind the larger, new one.

"Perhaps this isn't the best day to be here," shouted Fratre Sigisteus, hoping to be heard.

"They will work every day except Friday and Sunday," Fratre Egicaberht reminded them all. "There are Masses all day on Sunday."

"And Friday is a day of Observation for all of us," Fratre Lothar reminded them all needlessly. "We must fast and pray all day."

"Yes, Fratre Lothar. We know." Fratre Sigisteus was mildly annoyed by the fervent new monk. "I have lived by the Rule for twenty-nine years."

The others nodded. A moment later they were horrified by the sound of a shriek and a thud; the silence that gripped the Basilica for four heartbeats afterward was more frightening than the scream had been. Then there was a burst of exclamations and curses and men poured into the apse from all directions, hurrying toward the still workman lying in a widening pool of blood.

"We must help," shouted Prior Ricimar, and gestured to his monks to assist the workmen. "Make sure he is blessed."

"He died working on a holy building," said Fratre Ildebald. "He is already in Heaven."

"Amen," said Fratri Egicaberht and Gondehold at once.

The crush of workers and monks around them grew greater, and it was soon apparent that there was a mystery about the dead man; the overseer of the men working on the lantern did not know the man, had never seen him in his gang. No other overseer recognized him, either. The men who had come so quickly to care for the fallen man now withdrew with equal rapidity, leaving the Frankish monks to deal with the unknown corpse.

"How did he come to fall, do you think?" whispered Fratre Fustel as he made a blessing over the man.

"Pushed," said Fratre Smaragdus. "He'll be buried with the other workmen and slaves who die during this construction. No one will know who he is, or how he came to die."

"Do you mean he is murdered?" Fratre Gondehold was so disturbed that he could barely speak. "In this Basilica?"

"It seems so," said Fratre Lothar, and bent over the body. "See?" he said, turning the shattered head to one side. "There is another wound, here; in the side of the skull. It isn't like the other side of his head. This is like the blow of a battle-ax." He raised his head. "I have been a soldier. I know these wounds." He rose to his feet. "This man was dead before he fell."

"Then who screamed when he fell?" asked Fratre Egicaberht.

"If he was murdered, the man who killed him may have done this to cover his actions," said Fratre Fustel, and coughed.

"Why should anyone kill him?" Fratre Sigisteus wondered.

"Why kill a workman? Surely he is a workman—look at him," said Fratre Egicaberht in his most reasonable manner. "His clothes, his—"

Fratre Lothar lifted one of the dead man's hands, tipping the wrist back to expose the palm. "His clothes are unimportant. No workman has hands like these. See? There are hardly any calluses. He is someone who doesn't labor." He put the dead man's hand down. "These clothes are misleading. What is more urgent is knowing why he was wearing them at all." He slipped his hand inside the tunica. "He's warm enough: he hasn't been dead long."

"True enough," said Fratre Ildebald.

Prior Ricimar, who had been watching Fratre Lothar with revulsion, now said, "We must take this body to the cemetery and see him interred as a Christian. At once." He straightened up and shoved Fratre Gondehold in the shoulder. "You. Take his feet."

Fratre Gondehold did as the Prior told him, glad he had something to do. In a moment Fratre Smaragdus bent and tried to lift the man's shoulders; Fratre Ildebald leaned over to help Fratre Smaragdus. No one in the Basilica paid any attention to their efforts, even when the monks raised the dead man to carry him out of the building into the side-yard where there was a makeshift graveyard. There were slaves busy in one corner of the yard, but they continued their work without looking up as Prior Ricimar ordered his monks to bear the body to the nearest open grave. They took their positions to release the dead man, Fratre Sigisteus reciting the Penitential Psalms, Prior Ricimar pronouncing the benediction, and were about to consign the corpse to eternal repose when a priest of mature years with a pock-marked face and rust-colored hair came running up.

"No, no, good Fratri," the priest yelled. "No!"

Prior Ricimar looked up sharply and gestured his monks to halt. "Patre," he said.

"This is not permissible," the priest said anxiously. "This is wrong."

"Burying a man with Christian rites is wrong?" Fratre Lothar asked, his indignation increasing with every word.

"No. But this man . . . This is very complicated," the priest dithered.

"Who is this man? You must know," said Fratre Lothar.

The priest averted his eyes, then looked at the dead man. "Yes. Yes. It is as I feared. This is Patre Servatus, one of the Pope's secretaries; he was also a courier for His Holiness."

"Are you sure of this?" asked Prior Ricimar, worried about the dead man.

"How do you know?" Fratre Lothar asked at the same moment.

"I know because I, too, am a secretary to Pope Leo," said the priest. "I am Patre Ariolfus. The Archbishop of Arles sent me to Roma eight years ago." He stared down at Patre Servatus. "Poor man. That he should be killed, and in the Pope's name."

"How, in the Pope's name?" Fratre Lothar asked.

"He was one who helped the Pope flee Roma after he was attacked," said Patre Ariolfus.

"What do you think we should do?" Prior Ricimar was decidedly uncomfortable asking.

"I think you ought to leave this to the Abbott of Sant' Bartolomeo; the monastery is near-by. He will make such arrangements as are appropriate for Patre Servatus. The builders should be willing to lend you a sledge to bear Patre Servatus' body out of here." He looked around and pointed to one of the overseers. "Speak with him. He'll help you."

"That I will," said Prior Ricimar, and stumped off to the muscular man with the whip; his monks watched as he made a bargain with the overseer, then signaled to Fratri Egicaberht and Ildebald to come fetch the sledge the overseer had selected for their use. The monks hastened to obey, and in short order they had the sledge and had loaded Patre Servatus' carcase aboard it. They went out the side door and entered a narrow way that connected the Basilica with the monastery, which was housed in three stone buildings that stood around a large courtyard.

"It will soon be time for prandium," said Fratre Sigisteus, sounding quarrelsome.

"We have a duty to this priest," said Fratre Fustel rather loudly; he ducked his head apologetically, but repeated, "We have our duty."

"So we do," agreed Fratre Gondehold. "One of us must find the Abbott, then we will know what's what."

"I'll go," said Fratre Smaragdus, and almost sprinted toward the nearest entrance to one of the buildings.

"What do you suppose they will say?" asked Fratre Sigisteus as he watched Fratre Smaragdus rush into the building.

"It is not ours to guess," said Prior Ricimar. "This priest deserves the full protection of the Church, and if we fail to secure it for him, we will answer before God for it."

The monks exchanged glances, afraid of more earthly consequences, but finally there was a commotion in the doorway where Fratre Smaragdus had gone, and a moment later, two priests appeared with the monk and made for the Franks standing around the sledge.

"God be with us!" cried the first. "It *is* Patre Servatus! Saints and Angels!" He dropped to his knees beside the sledge and gingerly touched the dead man's battered head. "How dreadful." He looked up. "Who has done this?"

"We don't know," said Prior Ricimar. "We were told by Patre Ariolfus to bring him to you. He would have been buried in a workman's grave had he not spoken."

"Patre Ariolfus?" repeated the priest on the ground. "Who is that?"

Prior Ricimar frowned. "He spoke as if he supposed you would know him."

"Red hair, pock-marked face and neck, about thirty or thirty-five," said Fratre Lothar. "A little under height, but with strong arms and a broad back."

The other monks nodded, although most of them had not noted so much about the priest.

The second priest shook his head. "No. I don't recall such a man in Orders."

"He told us to bring him here. He gave us directions," said Fratre Gondehold.

"It may be God sent an Angel to care for His priest," said Fratre Fustel. "Or a Saint."

The kneeling priest nodded. "Yes. That must be how it was." He rose and met the eyes of the monks, each one in turn. "Then we must all give thanks to God for preserving Patre Servatus for our care."

"Amen," said Prior Ricimar.

Only Fratre Lothar seemed unconvinced. "He might have been sending you a warning," he said suddenly. "This was not an act of Christian charity, but one soldier challenging another." He folded his arms. "It is what I would have done if I had killed a man by stealth and I sought to have it understood what I had done."

"The man was a priest, not a soldier," said Fratre Sigisteus. "Didn't you see?"

"I did see," said Fratre Lothar stubbornly. "And I cannot forget that the Pope was attacked in Roma. If his enemies would not stop at trying to murder him, surely they wouldn't hesitate to kill a priest." He shook his head. "He was probably the murderer, making sure his deed was known, so that others would know the threat."

"Fratre Lothar, you are still too much a soldier," chided Prior Ricimar. "This is Roma, the holy city. You said so yourself."

"And it is," said Fratre Lothar. "But where there are Angels, there are Devils, too." He glanced over his shoulder and made a sign to ward off the Evil Eye.

The two priests had been whispering between themselves, and finally one said, "We will take him into our chapel and make him ready for burial. May God show you Grace for what you have done."

Realizing that he and his monks were being dismissed, Prior Ricimar moved aside, allowing the priests to pick up the body. "May God grant Patre Servatus glory in Heaven."

"Amen," said the priests as they bore the body away, leaving the Frankish monks to stare after them.

TEXT OF A LETTER FROM RORTHGER IN FRANKSLAND TO HIERNOM RAKOCZY IN ROMA, CARRIED TO THE HOUSE OF ATTA OLIVIA CLEMENS IN ROMA BY HIRED COURIER.

To the Magnatus Hiernom Rakoczy in Roma, consigned to the care of the Widow Clemens in the Square of the Temple of Hercules, the greetings of Rorthger from Rakoczy's fiscs in Franksland, near Sant' Cyricus on the Stavelot road, at the end of May in the Pope's year 800.

Magnatus, this is to inform you of what has transpired here since you left and to ask for your instructions in regard to them. I trust this will find you well, and the duties of the King not lying too heavily upon you.

To begin: shortly after your departure there were a number of robberies on the roads in this region. There are those who believe it is Waifar's doing, for the robbers appear to be well-informed as to the activities of villagers and travelers. I cannot say if this is so, but I must warn you that the villagers of your fiscs fully intend to kill Waifar if ever he should be caught. I have engaged two men-at-arms to provide escorts to villagers bound to market, and travelers on the roads with valuable goods and stock.

The mariscalcus, Hradbert, has succumbed to the Bending Fever, which came upon him after he cut his leg on a harrow, and has been buried by the monks at Sant' Cyricus; I have promoted Grandefus to his position. If you are willing, I will make this a permanent post for the young man. I have also provided housing for Hradbert's family, and I will continue to see them fed and housed unless you tell me that I must not, or the missi dominici bring such orders from the King.

I have paid the taxes to the Grav and the King, and I will tithe to Sant' Cyricus and Santa Julitta when the harvest is in. I have also provided a small stipend to both the monks and nuns for their maintenance and I have paid for masons to provide stones for stouter walls. The nunnery is also in need of a new barn, which I will authorize men to build unless you tell me this is not acceptable.

The orchards are coming into heavy fruit, although it is a little late for this; the late spring rains slowed the development of the fruit, and this has led to worry among the peasants, who are apprehensive that this may mean a hard winter. I see no signs of this, but nothing I say is given any credence, for I am a foreigner. I believe there will be a fine harvest and that the yield of the orchards will be bountiful, and so I shall plan. I will preserve as much of the surplus as I can, through drying or sealing in honey, and store this against leaner times.

One colt-foal died soon after birth, and his dam with him, but otherwise all mares have delivered sound foals—six fillies and five colts. Livius has another nine mares in foal and I will still breed him to mares until high summer. Incidentally, that catch-colt is showing promise, and I would recommend not gelding him quite yet; he may still be a good sire for smallish, strenghty horses suitable for travelers if not soldiers. I will select the most promising yearling colts and send three of them to Aachen to the Royal Stables, as you told me to do. I think the dark bay and the tall sorrel would be welcome additions to Karl-lo-Magne's stud. For the third, I am inclined to send the chestnut, although he isn't as broad as the other two, he is tallest of the three, and that should make him useful to the King's enduring search for bigger horses.

I am going to authorize the villagers of Sant' Trinitas to cut more trees; that will allow them to till more land as well as undertake to provide their own barrels. I have already given permission to Vulfoald to establish a cooperage, so that his village may prosper more than it has done. I hope you will concur with this decision, for Vulfoald is suspicious enough of all we do without reason—if you give him one, he will be truculent beyond anything he has been thus far.

My next report will be at the end of July, unless there is some disruption that demands a more immediate decision.

Rorthger

Post Scriptum to Atta Olivia Clemens,

I rely upon you to give this to my master when he arrives in Roma. I hope you are thriving and that Niklos Aulirios is well. And I thank you for your enduring friendship, both for me and the Magnatus, which has never wavered through so many, many years.

chapter six

FIVE DAYS AFTER THEY LEFT LECCO, the travelers reached Bobbio; the monastery was a hive of activity, and the town that stood around it also thrummed with industry, all this in spite of sodden July heat that made for an enervating atmosphere. Rakoczy, astride his grey, was at the head of their train as they entered the town shortly after the end of None, when the town would ordinarily be resting; preparations for the coming festival kept the workers busy through the heat of the day and the Little Hour of Sext, striving to be ready by sundown. Beside the Magnatus, Einshere rode in preoccupied silence, his attention on some inner disturbance that had increasingly demanded his concentration. In the plausterum, Gynethe Mehaut was caught up in private thoughts as well; since her first evening in the bath with Rakoczy, she had been aware of a fascination that was more than gratitude or respect. She peeked out of the cloth covering, hoping to see Bobbio as a town before they reached their destination; she wanted something new to think about.

"So," Rakoczy said as he turned off the road leading to the monastery onto a broad street paved with stones in the old Roman fashion, although the houses showed fine fronts and new construction. "It is just as well that I have secured a house for the night. The monks are in the midst of celebrating the Feast of Santa Maria Fructens; we would not be welcome inside their walls."

"You mean they would be drunk," said Sulpicius, doing his best to sound worldly.

"Among other things," said Rakoczy, and pointed to a street where a number of tall houses stood, their fronts blank but for wooden plaques that indicated their function.

"Do you mean there might be fighting?" asked Anshelm, as if he would welcome a brawl.

"It's possible," said Rakoczy. "It's happened before."

"Where are we going?" Notrold was surly and spoiling for an argument.

"To a house I mentioned." Rakoczy pointed ahead. "I sent a messenger ahead, ten days ago, to make arrangements. It is the House of Tullius."

"Just after we arrived at Lake Como?" Anshelm sounded surprised. "Did you know then when we would be here? Did you send your messenger with such certainty?"

"I have traveled much in my life," said Rakoczy. "I thought it prudent to leave nothing to chance."

"Do you truly expect the house to be waiting for you?" asked Theubert, staring around him skeptically. "These houses are fine."

"I am a Magnatus and I am traveling at the behest of Great Karl," Rakoczy reminded him. "Who can deny me with such bona fides?"

"As if that matters in Bobbio," said Notrold.

"I have paid for the house already," Rakoczy said, keeping his voice level, "and received a letter of accommodation. It will be sufficient."

"More fool you, then," said Notrold.

They drew in as a group of tanners went by, carts laden with hides stinking in the heat. There were two young children amid the tanners, apprentices most likely, their hands already darkened with the work for which they were being trained.

"They're as rank as a battlefield," said Einshere, the stench penetrating his reverie. "What kind of man is content to tan hides all his life?"

"The man born to it," said Usuard, and added, "Without patronage, all men follow their fathers, or God." He looked at Rakoczy. "How many of those tanners could find a patron?"

"Some may become religious," said Rakoczy quietly, and started his grey forward. "The house we seek has brass shutters and a Virgin over the door."

"I'll watch," said Sulpicius, making a show of watching for the house.

At the next curve of the street they came upon the house they were seeking. Rakoczy dismounted and pulled the bell-chain, waiting for the mansionarius to answer his summons; the man who came to the side-door was an angular man in a dull-green tunica with a border of keys in brown. He folded his arms. "My master is not here."

"I am Magnatus Hiernom Rakoczy, bound from Franksland to Roma on the business of Karl-lo-Magne. I have a letter from your master Tullius, with his sigil, that will permit me and those with me to enter this house as his guests. I will produce the letter if you require it." He indicated the collar he wore. "This should be recognizable to you. You will have a copy of it so that it may be identified."

The mansionarius scowled. "You weren't expected for two more days—after the Feast of Santa Maria Fructens. How is it you come today?" His accent was comprehensible, but just odd enough to be difficult to follow, a more liquid version of the Franks' tongue, and pronounced more softly, with emphases on syllables that sounded wrong to the soldiers.

"We made good time through the mountains, with the weather so fine and our horses rested. It is good to be in so fine a town as Bobbio," said Rakoczy, shifting his speech to match the cadences of the mansionarius; he took a step back. "Are our chambers ready?"

"I think most of them are, for which you can thank the buticularius," said the mansionarius. "The others can be made ready by Vespers, the chambers for the soldiers." He moved to lift the bolt from the main door. "The stables are at the rear of the courtyard."

"Is there someone who will arrange for the paddock? Before Vespers?" Rakoczy asked as the big, metal-fronted doors swung open. "Go in, Einshere."

"Very well," said Einshere, and signaled to the others to follow him.

The courtyard was similar to those of Franksland, but with more flowering plants and a fountain splashing into a marble pool that had been part of the original Roman building seven hundred years ago. The second story had been added when the fortifications were put in place, and the third floor on the east and south side of the house was less than a century old.

"What does Tullius do?" Notrold asked as he went through the gate. "He must be wealthy to live like a landed Potente in this town. This is as fine as any Illustre's house in Franksland." In spite of himself, he was impressed by what he saw.

"He trades in spices and dyes; he supplies them to the monastery here and to the Pope, so he keeps a house in Roma, where he has gone just at present," said the mansionarius still in the Bobbio dialect; the men accompanying Rakoczy barely understood him.

"A good line of work for a merchant; there are always those who want spices and dyes, and they are costly," said Usuard; he had been paying attention to the travelers on the road and had begun to understand about the success of the various merchants they had encountered.

"That he is, a good trader," said the mansionarius. He clapped his hands, and half-a-dozen slaves swarmed forward, some to take the horses, some to remove the crates and chests from the mules, some to offer cups of honied wine to the travelers.

"Are you the buticularius?" Rakoczy asked as he handed his reins and his lead to the slave waiting for them.

"No. He is out, arranging for our master's donation to the evening's celebration," said the mansionarius. "I am his deputy while he is gone."

"Santa Maria Fructens," Rakoczy said, remembering the old pagan celebrations in honor of Pomona and Ceres that used to be held at this time of year.

"The monks will revel tonight," said the mansionarius.

"Just as well that we arrived when we did. I have seen this Feast in Pavia. After sunset we might not have been able to get through the streets," said Anshelm, dropping down from his big-shouldered copper-dun. "You know what they say about the licentiousness of monks. Santa Maria Fructens is the worst of all the Feasts for wildness." He grinned suddenly.

"Do you want to attend it?" Einshere asked; he sounded worn to the bone, and he dismounted as if his bones were made of iron.

Anshelm chuckled. "It's been a long, hard ride, even with the days at Lecco. I would like to go out onto the street for a while, after dark."

"So would I," said Theubert. "I've heard about these occasions, but I have never seen one for myself. The monks at Sant' Cyricus didn't have such celebrations."

"And I suppose the rest of you would like to, as well?" Einshere seemed faintly disgusted. "If you must go, go together, and return before Vigil is over, or face reprimands and a beating." Belatedly he glanced at Rakoczy. "If you don't mind, Magnatus."

"You are leader of these men. It is for you to decide," Rakoczy answered as he prepared to help Gynethe Mehaut get out of the plausterum. "But I will not allow you to beat them—not for such an infraction." Any response this might have aroused was stopped by Gynethe Mehaut's emergence from the plausterum.

The mansionarius gasped at the sight of her and made a sign of protection. He could not bring himself to speak, but the panic in his eyes was apparent. All the slaves in the courtyard had gone still, waiting to see what the mansionarius would do; two of them turned away and refused to look at her once they realized what she was; the others watched in amazement.

"Yes," said Rakoczy calmly. "Well may you stare. This is a most remarkable woman, summoned by the Pope himself to Roma." He regarded the mansionarius with a steady gaze. "She must be taken to her rooms at once, and a woman sent to attend upon her. She is an honored lay-Sorra, known for her piety; you are fortunate to have her stop here."

The mansionarius goggled, nodded, and clapped his hands fussily to keep the slaves working. "On this day, of all days, to have a tertiary nun in this house," he muttered, and reverenced Gynethe Mehaut. "If you, and the Magnatus, will come with me?"

Gynethe Mehaut had donned a wide-brimmed hat made of straw that Rakoczy had given her at Lecco, and so the sunlight did not fall directly on her pale skin, but it could not stop the relentless heat; sweat stood out on her face, its shine making her look even paler than she was. "I would be glad of a glass of lemon-water," she said, her voice low.

"Lemon-water for the lady," the mansionarius shouted, then said to Rakoczy in a lower voice, "Our master took his wife and her servants with him to Roma. I can ask only one attire-woman to look after her."

"That will suffice," said Rakoczy. "So long as you quarter her as she deserves."

"In the eldest daughter's apartments," said the mansionarius. "I didn't understand who would use it, but the daughter married two years ago and the chambers are empty, but as suitable as any in the house." His nervous chatter was louder as he led Rakoczy and Gynethe Mehaut into the main hall. "We will take the stairs, and I'll show you the way. Your quarters are next to hers, if this is satisfactory?" He gave Rakoczy no opportunity to speak as he began his climb up the stairs. "I didn't know what to expect, you see. I had your name and a copy of your sigil—well, Enzius, the buticularius, did, but he showed it to me—but I hadn't been told about the lady. This can be hard, because of the festival." He tried to keep his voice low, resorting to a dramatic whisper. "If anyone should find out about her . . ."

"The slaves know, and so I will assume all of Bobbio will by sunset," said Rakoczy, no ire in his tone. "It is, as you say, unfortunate that you keep festival today, but so long as we remain within doors, I can see no reason for her to encounter any—"

"Misfortune," said the mansionarius. "Yes. But many will be out, including your soldiers, and it may be difficult to keep—"

Rakoczy reached up and laid his hand on the mansionarius' shoulder. "It is an easy matter to have everyone come and go through the rear door, and keep the front bolted. Also, I will order one of the soldiers to remain here to stand guard."

"A sensible plan," said the mansionarius in a skeptical voice. "It may be enough. If it isn't, you cannot put the responsibility on me."

"No; the responsibility is mine," Rakoczy soothed him. "You know your town better than I, but certainly a guard will help."

"I must ask Enzius when he returns," said the mansionarius, babbling on in an effort to conceal his nervousness. "But if he is willing to have it so, I am content. It is fitting that your lady be kept safe." He pointed across the corridor. "That door opens on the lady's rooms. She will find all in order, I believe, and may repose her confidence in the slaves and servants; Tullius has us trained and maintains us handsomely, each with a cubiculum of our own and two new camisae a year, and brodequins every two years. We are fed from his table, and we are allowed to take food to our families on Sunday. He even gives us coins at the Nativity, to put by for our families. I, myself, have three brothers and two sisters to—" He paused, abashed at having said so much. "Well. Enough of that. Why should you want to know about Tullius' household? I will send the attire-woman up to her shortly." He moved quickly, as if to get beyond any influence that Gynethe Mehaut might have about her person. "Your door is the next one along, Magnatus. I am going down to supervise prandium. Your soldiers must surely be hungry, and you will want—"

Rakoczy held up his hand. "Thank you, but I dine alone and will fend for myself; if you will send food up to Gynethe Mehaut, she need not disturb the household again, and those who are permitted to join the festivities may do so without a thought to our arrival."

The mansionarius nodded repeatedly. "Just as well. Yes. Just as well. They wouldn't like having to remain indoors tonight, I will tell you." He watched while she entered the apartments assigned to her, then pulled open the door to Rakoczy's quarters. "There is a door between the . . . you understand it was assumed the woman with you . . . It can be locked."

"I will take care of it," said Rakoczy. "She will keep to herself."

"Not that any man would try anything with such a . . . but it would be safer for her if she . . . Tell her to keep the bolt shot on her door," he finally managed to get out before he bolted from the room, leaving Rakoczy to take stock of it.

There was a small couch in the Moorish fashion, and next to it, a chest where a stand of oil-lamps was placed beneath a simple crucifix. An X-shaped chair completed the furnishings. In the bedchamber, a large, enclosed bed was opposite the shuttered windows, its hangings turning the bed into a closet. The only other item in the room was a night-stool with a chamber-pot set under it. Rakoczy flung back the bed-curtains, considering having a nap, but stopped almost as soon as he had considered it. If he could not find a sleeping woman to visit in dreams tonight, he would have to rest on a chest of his native earth or be exhausted in the morning. Next he made a careful inspection of the walls and finally discovered a peep-hole next to the bed; he would have to be careful what he did in that room, for it could all be reported to Tullius or the Abbott of Bobbio. He left the bedroom and went back to the withdrawing room, going to the inner door between his apartments and Gynethe Mehaut's. For a long moment he leaned against the iron-strapped wood, wanting to sort out his complicated response to her, and decided he could not delay speaking with her. He tapped on the door.

She came to answer the summons. "Thank the Saints," she said. "I am afraid to move in this place. Look at it!" There were Moorish hangings behind a divan, and two chests and a table on which was a small casket banded in brass. Five branches of oil-lamps hung from the beams. On the wall, four paintings depicted the life of Santa Felicita, with emphasis on her Martyr-sons. The bedroom beyond was equally grand, with shining silk around the bed, the nearest side pulled back to reveal the tall bed with three large pillows and two woolen coverlets atop the puffy mattress. Gynethe Mehaut flung out her hand, staring at the lavish display. "I don't know if I should sleep in such a bed."

"Of course you should," said Rakoczy. "Your penitence won't be compromised by a down-filled mattress. Not for two nights."

"But these rooms," she said, trying to mask her astonishment. "My hands . . . If I should bleed on the bed, it would be a shameful thing."

"Then I will wrap your palms with double-bands." Rakoczy was able not to laugh at this concern, no matter how unlikely he thought it was.

"I still can't bring myself to wear the stollae or gonellae you gave me; I don't want to bleed on them, either," she said. "Especially the silken ones."

"They are meant to be worn, Gynethe Mehaut, just as these pieces of furniture are meant to be used." He did his best to reassure her. "Enjoy this while you can. It may be the finest bed you will ever sleep in."

"No; this is very grand, but it isn't the finest bed: that was at Lake Como," said Gynethe Mehaut, her ivory skin suffusing with color. "No bed is sweeter than that one. I slept as if in Heaven, and dreamed of such wonderful things."

Rakoczy tried to respond without revealing the intense desire that surged within him. "You do me honor, Gynethe Mehaut." He tried to persuade himself that he was glad that he had not gone to her in her sleep, to visit her dreams.

"You guarded me from all evil, and you made my comfort your business. You did not scorn the way I am forced to live, and you never once made me feel—" She sighed unsteadily. "This is more luxurious, but it isn't as comfortable."

"If you will rest, you will find it is—" He was interrupted by an outbreak of cursing and a loud clatter as if something had fallen on the stairs. "Well, you may want to wait until your chest is brought to you, but it is so hot, you will be better for a nap."

She shook her head. "I'm afraid to lie down. The coverlets are so white."

"The coverlet on my bed is black wool. Would you like me to bring it in to you and take yours away?" Rakoczy offered, sensing her emotions, her ambivalence and her isolation; he wanted to take her in his arms to reassure her, but knew that would only stimulate his need of her, so he contented himself with taking her hand in his.

"No," she said, then, "Yes. Will you?" She smiled eagerly. "Yes. That will be very good, if you will do it."

"Perhaps I should wait until your prandium is brought up to you, and the attire-woman waits upon you. That way no one will see the change and remark upon it." He led her toward the divans. "In the meantime, you can recline on these."

"But they are Moorish," she protested.

"They are as much old Roman as they are Moorish; the old Romans reclined on such couches to dine. They had luxurious habits of their own; the Moors are not alone in that," Rakoczy said. "Think of the Caesars when you lie on one, and you'll feel much more appropriate."

She managed a bit of a smile. "I will." For a long moment she was silent, her hand lying in his. "I don't know what else to ask. You have anticipated everything."

"Anything you like," he said, and let her hand go.

"Perhaps later this evening you would spend a short while with me? I cannot go into the streets, but the festival should be exciting." Her expression was wistful.

"Frenzied, more likely," he said with a quick, wry smile. "When monks celebrate, they are apt to be fractious."

Gynethe Mehaut shook her head. "And the town? Will the people be fractious as well?"

"It's possible," said Rakoczy, who expected frenetic activity in the streets once Vespers ended. "Just as well to be indoors on such a night."

"Did you know that they would be keeping festival when we arrived?" There was a doubtful look in her eyes. "Do you want to celebrate with the people?"

"I know that Bobbio keeps the Feast of Santa Maria Fructens in July, but I don't know their calendar," said Rakoczy candidly.

"Surely it is the Pope's calendar," said Gynethe Mehaut.

"More or less. The Feasts are often kept at different times in various regions, as suits the way that their crops increase." Rakoczy shrugged. "I hoped the Feast was over; it was in Lecco. They keep it much more quietly."

"Was that when the priest went and blessed the trees and the villagers drank most of the old wine?" she asked. "I don't remember any Feast like it in Franksland."

"There are Midsummer Feasts, but they're not quite the same," said Rakoczy, wanting to add that the old gods of the Italian peninsula were unlike those of the Franks, but he decided not to add to her confusion. As much as he wanted to linger with her, he knew he ought to leave her before the attire-woman came and found them together, for this would create gossip that would follow them all the way to Roma, making Gynethe Mehaut's circumstances even more precarious than they already were.

"No, they're not," she said, and turned away, as if aware of his thoughts. "When the attire-woman is gone, will you come again?"

"After you have eaten, I will," he said, and went to the door. "Make sure you set the bolt in place. The attire-woman will notice."

"Are you certain?" She shook her head. "Yes, you are. We are constantly watched, you and I, and I cannot hide what I am."

"Then we must continue to be careful in all we do."

By sundown the whole town was alive with monks reveling. Most of them had fasted from dawn to sunset and drunk half-a-dozen chalices of wine after Vespers. Bawdy songs echoed in the streets as groups of men staggered from chapel to chapel to drink Communion wine and dance to the tunes on a bladder-pipe.

Gynethe Mehaut admitted Rakoczy to her rooms when the night was fully dark and Tullius' house was very quiet, most of the servants and half of the slaves having gone into the streets with the Frankish soldiers—all but Einshere, who was keeping guard over the rear gate—to roister until Matins. She had donned her lightest stolla, one of white linen washed with oil of lavender and decorated with embroidery of leaves at the neck and sleeves. One of the shutters was open, and Gynethe explained at once, a bit shamefacedly, "I hoped for a breeze, to cool the room. It is still hot, and I wanted some air."

"And you wanted to hear the merrymaking," said Rakoczy, smiling gently at her.

"Yes," she admitted. "Although I should be praying."

"If the monks can abandon their Office for one night, you ought to be allowed to follow their example," said Rakoczy, reverencing her before approaching her.

"I would like to; I'd like to sing and dance, as well," she confessed. "They sound so jolly, the singing and laughter."

Rakoczy suspected this would soon give way to rougher amusements, but he kept this to himself. "It is a fine festival. But few women attend it," he added.

"Women would be attacked by the men is what you mean? I suppose the women who do join in are light women, whores and entertainers?" She cocked her head. "Probably even they aren't very safe during this festival."

"No, they're not," said Rakoczy, remembering the three ravished and slaughtered women he had found in an alley in Tergeste almost five centuries ago, the hapless victims of religious delirium that had been the culmination of four days of public demonstrations. The women, who had been sold to brothels as children, had become the target of the riots because they were obvious and part of the people of the city who were against the austerities of the Paulist Christians. He suspected that even in her white stolla and with her crucifix hanging on a thong around her neck, Gynethe Mehaut would fare no better in the streets of Bobbio than those three women had in Tergeste.

She sat on the nearer divan. "You were right. This is very comfortable. It was here I ate prandium, and I was very much at ease. I didn't recline, but the couch was still easy." Her fingers pleated the folds of her stolla and she looked up at him. "Will you sit down, please?"

He chose the other divan and sank down onto it. For an instant, he remembered the Emir's son and the time he had spent in his service, as well as his escape from it; San-Ragoz had been forced to travel by night and to hide from the world, as did all runaway slaves. But that was eighty years behind him. He offered an enigmatic smile to Gynethe Mehaut and remarked, "Yes, this is very nice."

"You speak as if you thought it would be," she said.

There was a spurt of noise and a shouted exchange from the street below, then a loud report of breaking crockery and a crash of metal.

"Of course," said Rakoczy. "I have known couches like this of old."

She contemplated his face for a short while, the flickering oil-lamps changing his features with shifting light and dark. "I don't know what to make of you," she said at last. "I want to understand why you are so willing to see me as someone like others."

"Why should you make anything of me?" he countered, but deferentially so that she felt no challenge in his question.

"You are kind to me. You do not fear me, or shun me for my afflictions." She had been rehearsing this in her mind, and she spoke now with the directness of practice. "You tell me you understand, and I have come to think that perhaps you do. Why is that?"

Rakoczy contemplated his hands while he thought. "Those of my blood," he said at last, "have limitations imposed upon them, very severe limitations, in many ways not unlike yours. They shape all that I do, and have since I was a very young man. Over time I have learned to accommodate them, but I can't ignore them. That's why I am able to understand; my limitations may not be as obvious as those you have, but that is in part because I know what I must do in order not to appear more foreign than I am."

"Is that why you dine alone?" She was openly curious now, as if his explanation had given her the opportunity she sought.

"It is . . . related," he answered. "For those of my blood, taking nourishment is a very private act, and so we keep to ourselves when we do it."

She thought over what he said. "Can you tell me any of the things you do? Or what your blood imposes on you?"

He contemplated her face, perusing her features for any sign of apprehension or duplicity. Finding none, he decided to be candid with her, at least on this point. "Like you, I must avoid the sun, unless I take steps to protect myself first," he told her. "If I do not prepare, sunlight will burn me as surely as hot metal, and I will have to remain in the dark for some time in order to recover."

"But you aren't white," she said, pulling back her sleeve and extending her pallid arm.

"No," he agreed, "but in this I might as well be."

"Then what do you do?" The plaintive note in her question brought a pang to his soul that made it difficult for him to answer.

"I fear what protects me will not protect you," he told her. "My native earth is proof against all but the most extreme sun. So the soles of my boots and brodequins are lined with my native earth. So are my carpenta and plaustera, and my saddles."

Gynethe Mehaut stifled a laugh. "What a fine device! How did you come to think of it?"

"I happened upon it long ago," he said, not wanting to admit how many centuries had passed since he had come upon this stratagem. "It has served me well," he said.

"It must. You don't appear to suffer at all," she marveled.

"This isn't the only imposition my nature makes on me," he went on, almost eager to speak. "It is the one I have been most able to correct."

"Are all foreigners like you?" Gynethe Mehaut inquired. "The few I have known were not so hampered as you say you are."

"No. No, those of my blood are few and we are scattered far over the earth," he said.

"That's sad," she said. "But at least you have others like you."

Another eruption of noise reminded them that the celebration was growing more tumultuous; the songs had begun to degenerate into howls and shouting.

"Yes," he said, and smiled at her. "I've seen those like you, as well."

She studied him, her red eyes shining like good wine in the lamp-light. "Where? What were they like?"

"I saw three in Egypt," he said, recalling the white-skinned children brought to the Temple of Imhotep, two of whom had been so badly burned that they died quickly; the third was an infant, abandoned by her parents and at last given to Pharaoh as a concubine and raised with the children of other royal concubines. "I saw two in the western lands of the Great Khan, and two in Tunis."

"I hope this is true. I am so weary of being told that no one has ever been like me before," she said in a rush. "I know my uncle was said to be like me—white of skin and red-eyed, but he didn't bleed and he died long before I was born, so I have no sense of him beyond the tales the family told." She sighed, holding up her arm and pulling back her sleeve. "You say you saw those like me?"

"None of them bled from the hands," he said, and saw the animation leave her face. "They were white, as white as you, though."

"Yet they aren't *truly* like me, are they?" She sounded so forlorn, so alone, that Rakoczy slipped off his divan and sat at her feet. "This damned blood!" she muttered, making her hands into fists as if that would put a stop to the wounds.

"Oh, no," Rakoczy said, taking her hands and opening them carefully. "Blood is never damned. It is the one thing that is completely and utterly yours, and for that it is sacred. These wounds may not be welcome to you, but do not accuse your blood, or despise it: value it, and know that it is truly yours, the vessel of your soul."

Gynethe Mehaut stared at him. "Does it seem so to you?"

"It is so," he answered, keeping her hands, his compelling eyes on hers. Very slowly and very deliberately he began to unwrap the bandages. "This is a gift that is greater than any other, to know someone in blood, as those of my kind can do."

She watched, fascinated; as he hesitated, she laid her right hand on his hair. "Do what you will."

"If it is what you wish, as well. If I impose my desires on you, it would not serve you or me. It must be what you seek; otherwise there is no virtue in it, and of no use to either of us." He set the linen wraps aside and stroked her skin gently, avoiding the central wound. "Tell me: what do you long for?"

Her breath trembled. "I hardly know."

In the street sudden loud shouts silenced the bladder-pipe player, and a flute began a quick melody; cries of approval greeted the tune, and some of the men began a ragged, rollicking chorus.

"What would you like to try?" He touched her again, so gently that tears welled in her eyes.

"That is . . . lovely," she murmured. "If the blood doesn't bother you."

"No; it doesn't bother me." He lifted her palm to his lips; a smear of blood left on his mouth marked where he kissed her.

Gynethe Mehaut was unable to speak for several heartbeats, and when she did, her voice was hushed, as if she was afraid to be overheard. "What can you do?"

"Tell me what you like," said Rakoczy, sensing her passion, but unaware of what she sought, he was reluctant to go on.

"I haven't known anything of men's nature but what was forced upon me. I don't want that," she said, her hands shaking as she admitted this.

"All right." He kissed her hand again, and the taste of her blood lingered on his lips. "How can I give you pleasure?"

"Do you want to give me pleasure?" She was genuinely surprised.

"Yes, because then when we touch each other, it will not be in the flesh alone. That contact is the very heart of pleasure, the essential core that gives joy to intimacy." He looked directly into her eyes. "I want to do all that will delight you."

"I don't know what that could be," she said quietly. "To be in your company is a delight. I cannot imagine anything more satisfying."

"Then you're frightened," said Rakoczy, feeling her hesitancy. "You have no cause to be."

"That is what I was told before," she said. "And then he accused me of tempting him from Grace." As she pulled her hands away, she looked mournful.

Rakoczy was quiet, his perceptions a tangle of her eagerness and dread and his own yearning. He remained on his knee beside her divan, and finally he said in a tranquil voice, "It seems to me that you bestow Grace, not compromise it."

Someone in the street screamed, and this was answered with angry bellows as well as the scrape of metal as weapons were drawn. There were a series of excited shouts, accompanied by the slap of iron on iron, and then someone wailed in pain, and there was a clumsy scamper of retreat.

"Do you truly believe that?" Gynethe Mehaut asked, breathing more quickly.

"Yes; with all my heart," said Rakoczy, and took her offered hands again.

"What do you want of me?" Her words were hushed.

"I would like us to touch one another so that we know each other to the limits of our souls," he said; the blood on her palms was as heady as wine, and he could not conceal his desire for her.

"May we have this always and always?" she asked, renewed eagerness lending her energy.

"No, not always," said Rakoczy quietly. "Those of my blood may love knowingly no more than six times; after that, there is a change."

"What change?" she breathed.

This was going to be difficult, and Rakoczy did not speak at once. "After six times, there is certainty that when you die, you will become what I am, and those of my blood are. And once that change has occurred what is between us now will be over." There was a long silence between them.

"Would I still be white?" Gynethe Mehaut asked at last.

"Yes," Rakoczy said, and kissed the palm of her unwrapped hand. The nearness of her blood was tantalizing, but he kept from doing anything more until she accepted him.

"Would I still bleed?" Her voice was almost inaudible.

How difficult it was to answer her! "I don't know."

"So. There will be no more than six times that we can have our intimacy." She looked at him. "Is that what we will have?"

"If it is what you want," said Rakoczy, new hope gathering in him.

"Wouldn't it be better to lie in bed?" she asked, getting to her feet and motioning to him to rise.

He did, and caught her up in his arms; he was startled by how little she weighed, and thought it had to be on account of her frequent fasting. As he bore her into the bedchamber, she reached up and put her hand behind his head to draw him down to kiss her. "So," he said as he laid her on the black wool coverlet, her pale skin and stolla seeming to glow against the darkness, "now we know where to begin to awaken your exultation."

"You mean with kisses?" she murmured, red eyes sanguine as rubies.

"For a start," he said, and began a slow, ineffable exploration of her body with lips and hands, evoking gratification and rapture from every part of her flesh until she quivered like a wind-blown reed, clinging to him as she discovered her own passion and felt his as if they had fused, and for an eternal moment, she comprehended their shared nature and, at the culmination of her ardor, his esurience for blood.

Text of a letter from Fratre Grimhold in Roma to Bishop Freculf at his principal seat, Sant' Pothinus of Lyons, in Franksland, written in coded Latin, carried by hired courier, and finally delivered in late August, 800.

To the Sublime Bishop Freculf in Franksland, the greetings of his agent in Roma, Fratre Grimhold, with the continuing assurances of his devotion to the Bishop's cause, and the Pope, on this, the 19th day of July in the Pope's year 800.

Sublime, I have done as you ordered me. Not only Patre Servatus, but Fratre Eugenius are dead, both paying the price for betraying His Holiness, Pope Leo, and the Roman Church. I did not employ the Patre Ariolfus disguise to deal with Fratre Eugenius, for that was too hazardous, as it turns out: the Frankish monks who helped me to see Patre Servatus blessed and buried have described Patre Ariolfus to the Laterano Guard, so I took a capa, such as those worn by the street gangs of Roma, and I put a bandage around one eye so that it would be thought I was half-blind, then I found a remote corner near the place that Fratre Eugenius meets with the Byzantines to give information to them and to collect their promises of advancement when Constantinople rules in Roma. Fratre Eugenius expected to become Metropolitan of Roma for his treachery, but that is not the case any longer; he has left this earth for whichever destination best pleases God.

This is how I accomplished my ends: I sat on a fallen column, the way the organized beggars do, and Fratre Eugenius ignored me, just as Patre Servatus paid no heed to a fellow priest entering the Basilica of Sant' Bartolomeo. I was able to overhear everything the Byzantines said, and I thought Fratre Eugenius was a fool to believe the Greeks, for I am certain that had I not killed him for the Pope, the Byzantines would not allow him to live, what with all the secrets he knew about them and their activities in Roma. His dreams of elevation were not visions of what was to come, but of his own greed for achievement in the world, for the Church has become a worldly prize, when not so long ago, it was only a promise of Salvation. He was even so foolish as to drink the cup of wine the Greeks gave him—I would have refused, for everyone knows how adept the Greeks are with poisons. Fratre Eugenius' hubris was so great that he never so much as questioned this gesture, but I thought him a fool.

You may rest assured that when the body is finally discovered, it will be assumed that Fratre Eugenius was waylaid by thieves, for I put a thief's knife in his ribs, one that has a gang-marking in the horn handle, and this will remove any suspicions that he was killed because of his dealings with the Greeks. This will serve your purpose well, for an accident such as being way-laid by outlaws is not nearly so dangerous a development as a monk being killed for dealing with the Patriarch's servants. I was at pains to put him out of the way, in an old tunnel; it may be that he will not be found until he is bones, for I disposed of him in an empty quarter of the city, where the few buildings standing are ruins, and only beggars and outlaws live there, another reason for it to be assumed that he was set-upon by criminals. The Guard rarely goes into that part of the city, and only in armed companies, for they are often attacked and repelled by those who live there. The tunnels in that quarter are not often inspected, and no one who lives there will report this killing. So it may be that Fratre Eugenius will simply vanish, and no matter how much people may wonder about him, it is possible that his fate will be unknown.

I did take the time to say the prayers for the dead over him, so that God may be aware of his dying, even if only you and I are the only men who know of it. I have also added his name to those I remember at Nocturnes, so that he will not be completely forgotten, though it may be no more than what he deserves.

I am prepared to do your bidding again, but I must warn you that I am becoming uneasy about the killing. I understand why Patre Servatus and Fratre Eugenius were dangerous and needed to be disposed of, but I confess I do not understand your most recent order—to do away with the foreigner Magnatus Hiernom Rakoczy because he escorts a white woman to Roma. You tell me that so foreign a man as he must give strength to those who oppose her and seek to condemn her. You are afraid that distrust of him will increase the opposition to her, and work against her in the Papal Court. I can comprehend how this might happen, but I don't see the use in killing him. I would not like to have to Confess to his death as I have had to do for Patre Servatus and Fratre Eugenius. The priest who has heard my Confession is one who supports all you do, but I may not be able to persuade him of the need for this death. If you will provide more information, so that I need not fear having to spend the rest of my life in penitence, I will increase my grati-tude to you in all my prayers.

If you insist upon the plan being carried out, I ask only that you provide access to this Rakoczy for Patre Ariolfus, so that I may have a creditable rea-son to seek him out without creating doubts in his mind, or in the minds of those around him. I should warn you that I have had a dream that reveals that this foreigner could be more dangerous than either you or I believe he is, and I have heeded my dreams in the past, and will do so now. We must be very careful in any attempt on this man, or we will both come to grief. If I must approach him as a street-tough, I will need to have men around me, for you tell me that he comes to Roma with an escort of soldiers, and with the promise of protection from Great Karl himself, in which case he isn't likely to go about the streets unattended. Inform me of your wishes in this regard as soon as you may. I am ready to do your bidding, but not if it exposes us both to the wrath of Leo or Great Karl, for surely that would be a foretaste of the Wrath of God.

Word has it from the slaves of the Cardinal Archbishops who are known to the couriers that Bishop Iso and his retinue are approaching Roma and are expected to arrive here in two or three days. There will be ten with him, including his Sorra Celinde, who is supposed to report to the Cardinal Archbishops on what she observed while caring for Gynethe Mehaut. I could more readily understand a desire to do away with Bishop Iso than the foreigner Rakoczy, but you must do as you know best, God no doubt guides you in all things, and this is just another sign of His Will. For the honor of our family and the preservation of the Church, you may be sure that I will continue to work on behalf of both until I am summoned to answer before the Mercy Seat.

Fratre Grimhold
by my own hand

～

chapter seven

THEY CROSSED THE HILLS and reached the Aurelian Road at the site of the old Roman town of Luna, where the port continued to flourish although the community had shrunk to less than a third of its former size. They spent that night at a hostel for travelers and in the morning discovered that Sulpicius had been robbed sometime between midnight and dawn.

"Should we report it to the town leaders?" asked Einshere.

"They probably receive a portion of the booty," said Notrold. "It happens often, when there's loot involved."

"Perhaps the Abbott at Santa Cruce should be told," said Rakoczy. "He may be able to record the event, at least, though who knows what can be done. Or will be done." He added the last as he handed a short-sword taken from his own chest of weapons to Sulpicius. "You can carry this for now. At Roma I'll see you have a new sword. And for now I will provide you with two of Great Karl's silver coins, in case you must pay for something directly. You cannot go about this part of the world without something to spend." He glanced around at the others of his company. "You all have coins from me to use to that end. Do not begrudge Sulpicius these. I would do the same for you, were any of you robbed as he has been."

"Next time, we all sleep in the same cubiculum or dormitory," said Theubert. "It was a mistake to allow him to lie down with strangers."

"Comrades might do the same, if the rewards were great enough," said Notrold with a snide expression that was supposed to be a smile, "and the Bellatori were lax enough to let it happen."

"He's lucky he wasn't killed," said Usuard. "They could as easily have stabbed him as taken his sword and coins."

The soldiers knew this was true; they exchanged uneasy nods and waited for their horses to be led out, along with the pack-mules, their remounts, and the plausterum. It was a shining morning, and the wind off the sea promised relief from the heat they had encountered inland.

"The White Woman," Anshelm ventured. "Is she well? The heat has been fierce, and she—" He stopped.

"She is doing well," said Rakoczy calmly. "And travel will be easier now we have the Via Aurelia to go on." He used the old Roman name deliberately, as a reminder of the superior roads they had made.

"The coast is cooler," said Notrold. "And there are towns along the way used to travelers. No more sleeping in barns." They had done just that for two nights on the road from Bobbio and Notrold had complained mightily, for he felt it slighted him to share a stall with an ox.

"And the road is better," Einshere said, reiterating Rakoczy's point. "We should make good time now—perhaps fifteen or sixteen leagues a day."

"Those are Frankish leagues, I suppose, not Roman," said Rakoczy. "For Roman leagues we will do well to cover eight or nine in a day." He thought back to the time of Vespasianus, when couriers routinely covered twenty-eight Roman leagues a day in all seasons but winter, a distance that now seemed fabulous.

"Yes, Frankish," said Einshere, a bit offended that he should be asked such a question.

"In Longobardia most reckon in Roman leagues, not Frankish," said Theubert, and added as the soldiers turned toward him, "The priest at Sant' Chrysogonus explained it to me before we left Lecco."

"That was good of him," said Rakoczy, and took a copper coin from his wallet to hand to the groom leading out his horse and remount; the slave stared at this unexpected largesse and doubled over at the waist in gratitude.

"You shouldn't do this," said Einshere to Rakoczy. "Slaves are slaves for God's Will, and they need nothing more than the rewards of Heaven. To give them money corrupts their service."

"In their place, I would be glad of a copper or two." He had been a slave more than once and was keenly aware of the limitations such a condition imposed. "Two coppers are hardly extreme wealth. It won't buy him much more than a pair of wooden-soled brodequins to keep his feet dry in the winter." Rakoczy checked the girth and, satisfied it was firm, swung up into the saddle and gathered up the reins and the lead-rope.

"That's for his master to do," said Einshere. "Or the monks."

"Then consider it an act of charity," said Rakoczy, refusing to be drawn into an altercation.

Einshere took his blood-bay in hand, mounted up, and reached for the lead on the mouse-dun. He stared off between his horse's ears as if trying to disassociate himself from the party in the hostel courtyard. Only when Anshelm spoke to him did he recall himself from his reverie. "What did you say?"

"I asked if we should carry our spears at the ready or in their sheaths. Should we carry our swords, or keep them in their scabbards?" Anshelm looked annoyed.

"In their sheaths, at least for now. Swords in scabbards." He looked at the sun as it hung over the distant eastern hills. "When we stop for prandium, ask me again."

Anshelm shrugged. "As you say." He reached for his horse and mounted up without checking the girth, saying to the slave at his stirrup as he did, "If this slides, I'll have the skin off your shoulders."

"It will not slide," said the slave, his face turned away in a show of respect.

Gynethe Mehaut came out of the women's side of the hostel, her face protected by a fine veil, a gift from Rakoczy that she had finally consented to wear. She stood in the shelter of the narrow porch, waiting for the plausterum, her freshly bandaged hands folded in front of her to show her modesty.

Rakoczy rode over to her. "I hope you slept well."

She looked up at him. "I slept," she said. "The baker's wife snored."

"That's unfortunate," said Rakoczy, wishing he could show her more attention than he did, but keenly aware that this would be unwise.

"I spent the time praying," she said, wrapping her arms across her body and grabbing her elbows. "I maintained my penitence."

Rakoczy would have liked to say something to comfort her, but Einshere called to him. "We'll talk later," he promised her, and bent down to reverence her as much as the saddle would allow. "May you travel peacefully and as comfortably as the road will allow."

"If such a thing is possible, Magnatus, I will." She nodded to show her readiness.

Now Theubert and Usuard were mounted and had their remount leads in hand; at last a slave led out the plausterum, one of the mules harnessed to it. He handed the lead to Rakoczy and ducked his head, accepting the copper coin he was handed with a great show of thankfulness.

Bells were ringing the end of Prime as the little party went out of the gates of Luna and onto the Aurelian Road, bound to the south along the coast. The Roman paving was intact in most places; where it was broken the patching was clumsy and slowed down their travel, for they had to be particularly careful not to wreck the wheels of the plausterum or to damage their horses' legs and hooves. As the day wore on the travelers became more testy. The mules slowed to a walk and would not be rushed over bad stretches of road. The first day on the Aurelian Road they covered eight Roman leagues and spent the night at the monastery of Sant' Erunicus. The next day they went another eight Roman leagues and arrived at a small market town. The soldiers bought new squashes and beans and had the hostel-keeper add them to the stew he made for them that night. The day after they managed only six Roman leagues and had to put up at a monastery with a smithy where Rakoczy worked through the night repairing and strapping the plausterum's wheels.

They reached Pisa and found a travelers' house on the south side of the city. Rakoczy suggested that they spend a day there, letting their horses rest and buying more supplies for the road. No one wanted to give up an opportunity to rest, and none of them were inclined to challenge this decision; Rakoczy arranged for two nights' lodging and paid for a private chamber for Gynethe Mehaut.

That night, Gynethe Mehaut came to Rakoczy after comestus and sat in the chair beside his in the small reception room. "I miss you," she said. "At night."

"And I you," he told her.

"Then perhaps . . ." She took his hand and lifted it to her lips.

"I would like to hold you," he said in an undervoice.

She shook her head. "You needn't."

"Why?" he asked, aware that she still had the capacity to surprise him.

"I am not used to embraces," she admitted after a brief silence. "Not even my mother wanted to touch me, or hold me; she was too frightened—and such demonstrations are not encouraged among the Sorrae." She turned to look at him. "Most people are unwilling to touch me."

"The white will not come off," said Rakoczy, with a swift, ironic smile.

"If it did, I could be rid of it and have embraces every day." She put her bandaged hand to her mouth, shocked by her own admission. "I wish we could spend more time alone together."

"On the road it wouldn't be wise," said Rakoczy, lifting his finger to his lips. "And certainly not in a place like this."

"Then when can we . . . where can we—?" Gynethe Mehaut whispered.

"In Roma, where we will be alone," he said, turning her hand and kissing the bandage that wrapped her palm.

She laughed unhappily. "How can we? It will be worse: in Roma we shall be watched and scrutinized and spied upon."

"As you are now," he reminded her as kindly as he could.

"It will be worse in Roma," she predicted, staring down at the floor.

"Not if we go to a safe place," said Rakoczy. "I have an . . . associate in Roma who will be our hostess. She is expecting us. It is all arranged."

"Then her slaves will observe what we do and tell anyone who will pay them," said Gynethe Mehaut. "Slaves are always watching."

"Not at Olivia's house," said Rakoczy. "She knows what she must do to be safe, and keeps only loyal servants around her—no slaves."

"You keep no slaves, either," she said.

"For similar reasons," he told her with a quick glance at the door.

Gynethe Mehaut considered this. "Is she like you?"

"She is of my blood," Rakoczy admitted.

"Then she will do what is necessary, for her own sake, and the sake of your family," said Gynethe Mehaut, then thought of something more worrisome. "Will the Church allow this?"

"Certainly," said Rakoczy. "Olivia is well-known to the Papal Court, and her character is beyond question, even in Roma, where everything can be corrupted."

She listened to this, then rose and moved away from him. "I must wait."

"It won't be too long," Rakoczy said. "If there is a chance before then, you have only to tell me and I will exult."

"If it is possible," she said pensively.

"In Roma," said Rakoczy as a slave came in to announce that the lamps would be extinguished shortly.

"In Roma," she said as if trying to encourage herself.

After Pisa they made fairly good progress, covering seven to eight Roman leagues on most days, and encountering only two delays before they got to Alsium; the ancient town was being rebuilt, for it had been sacked thirty years before and was at last beginning to make a real recovery. There was also a new monastery being built on the outskirts of the town, its fortifications nearly complete, laborers gathered in the shadow of the walls for their mid-day rest. The heat of early afternoon penetrated everything, sapping strength and encouraging sleep; the sun glared down from an empty sky. For once there was no breeze off the sea. Only insects droned around them in annoying shoals.

"Shall we stay here?" asked Gynethe Mehaut from her plausterum; the mule hitched to it was restive, tossing his head and pulling at his bridle. Few of the pack-mules had the vigor to do more than sulk; the remount horses fidgeted on their leads, stamping and slapping the air with their tails.

"None isn't over yet," said Rakoczy, squinting up toward the sun. "We can cover another two leagues or more before Vespers. Then we can reach Roma tomorrow by day's end."

Einshere interrupted, declaring, "This is a good place to stop. The air is heavy, and that means it is filled with infection. It is better to rest than to move in such air. If we need an extra day to get to Roma, so be it." He swung around in the saddle to see what the soldiers felt; all but Sulpicius nodded.

"This is a most difficult decision," said Theubert. "We are obliged to travel swiftly, but if we do, we may risk sleeping in a barn or by the side of the road."

"True enough," said Notrold, giving Einshere an uncertain glance. "But so near Roma, it would be wise to make haste, so it may be reported that we didn't dawdle."

The soldiers shifted uncomfortably in their saddles, their faces deliberately blank. At last Anshelm said, "We'd best go on. No one will report us laggards if we do."

"And there is infection everywhere, all kinds of infection," said Notrold.

"The sun will be bright for some time yet," said Sulpicius. "If we continue on, we'll have daylight."

"At least until Vespers," said Theubert, sighing.

"But why not take advantage of the day? We have had prandium, and comestus will come at Compline; none of us can complain of hunger," said Einshere with a brusque assertion of authority that surprised them all. "We can go on, if we must." This was so abrupt a transition that the five soldiers were more troubled than they had been at his first suggestion that they halt for the day. "Let us go forward." They continued slowly along the road, the torpid heat of the afternoon taking a toll on all of them.

"There is a convent not quite four Roman leagues ahead," said Rakoczy. "If we press, we should arrive there at Vespers."

"A convent. Which convent?" asked Einshere, his tone almost angry. "Tell me."

"Sant' Xystus the Second; there is a monks' portion and a nuns' portion at the convent; it is small but it is safe enough. The patron has a fine reputation, and the convent is prestigious because of it," said Rakoczy. "He was a Pope and martyr to the faith," he added for the benefit of the soldiers.

"A hero, in other words," said Einshere, his face brightening. "They will admit us."

"We have the paravareda from Great Karl himself. They can't refuse us," said Notrold harshly, and laughed.

"They have dormitories for travelers," said Rakoczy carefully. "Unless they have no room, or there is fever in the convent, they will accommodate us."

"What shall we do if there is no room?" Notrold demanded. "I don't wish to sleep in a barn again. The fleas are still with me from the last time."

"Would you want to stay near fever?" Usuard asked. "A barn is preferable to an early grave."

"It is the time of the mal aria," said Anshelm, and made a sign to protect himself from the dangers of the illness. "I have holy seals to wear."

"And I," said Usuard. "Pray God it is enough."

"Then let us keep on," said Notrold dryly. "If we debate, we lose light." He clapped his heels to his red roan's sides; the mare bounded forward, overtaking Rakoczy and Einshere in the lead; his remount neighed in distress at this treatment.

"Rush your horse and you will lose time; and your remount will be too tired to ride," said Rakoczy. "On such a day as this, we must walk or the horses will suffer."

"So you say," Notrold blustered.

"So I do: and they're my horses," Rakoczy said curtly. He was aware of the resentment simmering within Notrold and was careful not to challenge him, for the soldier longed for an excuse to rebel.

"Fall in line, Notrold," Einshere said as if heartily bored.

The soldiers waited to see what Notrold would do next and were not surprised when Notrold drew his sword, dropped the remount-lead, and pulled his horse around to charge Einshere, shouting as he did, "You said we should stop, now you say go on! Where is your courage? You disgrace us all!"

Rakoczy moved to put his horse between Notrold and Einshere, but the grey balked, half-rearing and neighing as Notrold lifted his sword; Einshere swung his spear from its sheath and held it as Notrold rode into it and screamed in outrage as the iron point penetrated just below his ribs, half-lifting him out of the saddle.

Einshere let go of the spear abruptly and looked away from Notrold, who was reeling in the saddle, his side pulsing blood as he pulled the iron point out of his flesh. Notrold's roan sidled, tossing the wounded soldier onto the ground before she ran off a short way, then stopped, flanks heaving, sweat on her withers. Rakoczy rode after her, leaving the soldiers to care for Notrold; such a wound was quickly fatal—not even syrup of poppies was quick enough to spare him pain. He quieted the roan and led her back to the company, relieved to see that Sulpicius had the remount in hand.

Anshelm and Theubert had dismounted and were kneeling beside Notrold, who had turned an ashen hue; sweat stood out on his face and his breathing was ragged. Theubert was praying, reciting prayers for the dying, tears running down his face.

Einshere remained rigid in the saddle, looking straight ahead, his eyes like pebbles. "How long?" he asked flatly as Rakoczy rode up.

"He's going quickly," Rakoczy said, and studied Einshere.

"It was easy to kill him; it is right he should die. He should have fought the bison, not Pepin. Then this need not have happened," said Einshere remotely. "His family and mine have fought for generations, so this was inevitable. No one could have prevented it, though both of us promised the King we would abandon our feud in his service. Notrold swore a blood oath against us when he first learned to fight. So did I. It is more binding than any promise, even one given to a King: Great Karl should never have made us part of this escort, not both of us."

Rakoczy heard him out without comment; he handed the leads and reins to Einshere, then dismounted to go to Notrold; the man was pasty, his breath shallow, and his eyes had rolled up so only a sliver of blue showed at the edge of the lid. He gestured to Theubert, signaling him to continue his prayers, and he bent down to touch Notrold's neck. "He will be gone shortly."

"Then I suppose we will remain here for tonight," said Anshelm in a soft, stricken voice.

"I think we must." Usuard made a sign of protection. "He has to be given to the monks or a priest, so he may be buried as a Christian."

"Karl-lo-Magne has said that his soldiers must be accorded a good burial." Anshelm stared at Notrold. "All that blood. To lose it so quickly."

"His breath is stopping," said Theubert.

"It will be quick," said Sulpicius, making a sign of protection.

Rakoczy went to the plausterum and stood near the rear opening, saying quietly, "There has been a misfortune."

"I know," said Gynethe Mehaut very quietly. "They will blame me for it." In spite of the heat, she crossed her arms and took hold of them as if making a barricade against the world.

"How?" Rakoczy asked, trying to keep his voice level; even as he asked, he realized she was right.

"They will dream, they will decide it was so, one way or another they will find a reason that I caused this fight." She sounded frightened.

"Einshere says their families are feuding," Rakoczy pointed out. "That has nothing to do with you."

"Still," she said. "They will tell the Pope's Court, and I will be condemned as the Anti-Christ."

"No. That won't happen," he said with more determination than confidence.

"Because you won't allow it?" She waited. "You're a foreigner. How can you change what they want to do?"

"I can speak with Great Karl, and if he listens, he will make the Pope listen." He was whispering now, hoping to keep this between them.

"Why would Great Karl do anything that could cause dissension among his subjects? You are not a Frank, or even a Longobard." She said nothing more; Rakoczy saw Theubert drop his head, and he went from the plausterum to the fallen body of Notrold.

"He's dead," Anshelm announced grimly. "It's over." He rose, rubbing his hands on his femoralia to rid them of blood.

Theubert stayed where he was, his hands lifted to his shoulders in an attitude of prayer. He continued to recite Psalms in a monotonous tone. Finally he reached the end of the verses and stopped talking; his face was stark as he got to his feet. "We must find a church or monastery."

"At this time of day, they'll be at devotions or prandium," said Sulpicius, looking about as if expecting to find the world dramatically changed.

"We'll have to carry him, or put him in the plausterum," said Einshere.

"Put him in the plausterum," said Theubert. "He deserves to be sheltered."

Rakoczy could see that these men were poised for violence; he hoped that Gynethe Mehaut would understand why they would have to use her plausterum to carry a body once again. "If you will lift him, I'll open the rear of the—"

Theubert nodded. "Yes. In this heat, he mustn't lie in the sun."

Anshelm bent to take Notrold's shoulders in his hands; blood had pooled around him in the road, and it hung off his body in long, stringy globs that no one dared touch. As Theubert lifted Notrold's feet, he almost dropped them as he saw Notrold's wound clearly for the first time. He uttered an oath and the flush that heat had imparted vanished, leaving him pale and shaken.

"You've seen wounds before," said Anshelm, deliberately blunt.

"Yes," Theubert said, and swallowed. "This is different."

"Because we have served together? Because we kneel to the same King?" Anshelm scoffed. "And if there should be a new war tomorrow, and your family compels you to one side and I must fight for the other, what do you suppose would happen? Do you tell me you would refuse to take up arms against me? Would you hesitate to kill me? For I wouldn't hesitate to kill you." They managed to get the body into the rear of the plausterum, both taking pains not to look at Gynethe Mehaut.

"I wouldn't kill you," said Theubert. "It would disgrace the King." He pulled the cloth into place, shutting the dead man in with the White Woman.

"Better to disgrace the King than the family," said Anshelm, and made a sign to ward off evil. "If you fail the family, all honor is gone."

"Best not to fight at all," said Rakoczy pointedly. He was grateful now that this had occurred during the heat of the day, when all those who could rested indoors; there were few witnesses to the fight, and there should be no conflicting accounts that might delay their travel.

"I will stay with Notrold and see him properly buried," said Sulpicius. "I'll come along as soon as it's done."

"No," said Einshere. "I should remain behind. You go on without me." He swatted mosquitoes from his forehead, leaving a smear of blood behind. "I will arrange for Masses for his soul, commission a proper stone, and follow you to Roma if I am permitted to do so. It should take no more than five days."

The soldiers said nothing, aware there was little they could say. Finally Anshelm found words for them all. "We will pray for you."

"That is kind of you," said Einshere distantly. "Which turning will take us to a church?"

"The next on your left," said Rakoczy. "Half-a-league from the road, I'd guess. You can see the bell-tower through the trees," he said, pointing. "There."

"So it is," said Einshere. "Then we shall go there." He lowered his head. "I will accept any penance bestowed upon me: for the honor of my family, and the honor of the King."

Sulpicius, who was leading Notrold's remount, said, "See that the monks write it down. Make sure there is a record of what happened."

"Yes. I must." He continued to stare at a vacant place ahead of him. "It is a pity, but honor must be vindicated."

"What had he done that was so reprehensible?" Rakoczy asked, and realized at once he had erred. "You need not tell me."

"Notrold did not do it himself, and there have been any number of things that have passed between our families over the generations, though the most recent touched me closely," said Einshere; he told the story in a colorless voice, as if reciting an ancient lesson. "His father's brother took the wife of my grandfather away from him and kept her as his concubine. When my grandfather appealed to the Bishop, who was Notrold's father, he ordered the wife returned, as the King required, but she and Notrold's uncle caused his death instead."

"You mean they murdered him?" Sulpicius asked, appalled.

"Worse. They performed rites that struck him down. He was a blighted man. He could not speak and his limbs were blighted, and at last, he suffered a fall, and that ended his life." Einshere blinked as if fighting off sleep. "They had ensorcelled him. The Bishop agreed, and the woman was hacked to pieces. It was only one of many wrongs they have done us."

Rakoczy said nothing this time, for there was no observation he could make that would change any of these tragedies. He kept his grey moving steadily and wondered what would happen to Einshere.

"What happened to the man?" Usuard finally had the courage to ask.

"Three of his fiscs were confiscated and given to the Church," said Einshere; he was drawn and tired now.

"And now you have reclaimed the honor of your family," said Theubert sadly.

"Thanks be to God," said Einshere. He achieved a smile. "I hope you will forgive me for not going into Roma with you, Magnatus."

"I'll have to explain it to the Frankish Bishops," said Rakoczy.

"We'll make an account," said Anshelm. "To our own people. The Romans would not understand, being sots and laggards, all of them."

"Except the Pope," said Suplicius.

"Yes, of course: except the Pope," Anshelm agreed. "The Franks know how these matters are."

"No doubt," said Rakoczy dryly. "And I will make my report, too." He felt dismay at the turn events had taken.

"As you must," said Einshere. "And you will tell the truth, since you have no family involved in this." He smiled slightly. "You must tell me if you want me to pray for you, too, as part of my penance."

Rakoczy shook his head. "You must decide that for yourself."

"Then I shall," Einshere said. He stopped talking, his whole attention focused on the road ahead until they reached the door of Sant' Salvator and summoned the priests with a tug on the bell-chain; a young woman with a mass of brown hair under an untidy veil and in the last months of pregnancy answered the summons, saying, "My husband will be with you shortly. He is finishing None. As soon as he is done, he will come out to you." She gave the party a guarded look, as if expecting the worst of them.

"God give you good day, Priest's Wife," Theubert said, and managed a moderate sort of reverence from the saddle.

"And so He has, but I fear you men are about to end it," she said, putting a hand to her back. "If you are on the road when most men are praying or sleeping, you must have urgent business."

"And so we do," said Rakoczy. "I regret that we must disturb your husband with this, but we must entrust a fallen soldier to the Church for the burial of his body."

"As well as the preservation of his soul," said Einshere, and dismounted, handing his reins and lead to Rakoczy. "I thank you, Magnatus. You have done more than was asked of you, and for that I am grateful to you. When I have made my account, I will have it carried to Roma for your sigil for its authenticity. If you will do that for me, I will count myself a fortunate man." He turned to the priest's wife. "Is there a penitent's cell here?"

"Yes; two," she said, more puzzled than ever.

"Good. I will enter one of them once I have finished my Confession to your husband." He lifted his hands in an attitude of prayer. "May God hear me with Mercy."

"Amen," said the priest's wife apprehensively.

Anshelm and Theubert dismounted and went to the back of the plausterum; they moved slowly, reluctant to do the work that had to be done. They retrieved Notrold's body and bore it to the entrance to the little church.

"How long has this man been dead?" she asked, going pale.

"Not long," said Einshere. "I killed him."

Now the woman was upset. "Why do you bring him here?" She held up her hand in a gesture to keep away misfortune.

"He is a true Bellatore and worthy of burial as a Christian," said Einshere. "I will entrust him to you and enter your penitent's cell to expiate my sins."

"Nothing more?" the priest's wife challenged. "You are all armed. Is that all you want?"

"What more is there?" Sulpicius asked her.

"Nothing," she said quickly. "God preserve us all."

"Amen," said all of them in ragged chorus.

"I will gladly make a donation toward Masses for the dead man's soul," said Rakoczy, and reached for the wallet on his girdle.

The priest's wife smiled, her expression showing intense allayment of anxiety. "That would be welcome, and a charitable act."

Rakoczy handed the woman two silver coins. "This should suffice for twenty Masses."

She took the money. "Yes. Twenty Masses."

A bell sounded inside the church and a moment later, the priest emerged, his alb still in place. "In God's Name," he exclaimed as he looked down at the body.

Both Einshere and Anshelm began to explain; while they were trying to make themselves heard, Sulpicius leaned over toward Rakoczy and whispered, "What more can happen? So near to Roma, surely this is the end of our misadventures."

Rakoczy nodded to show he had heard, but kept his thoughts to himself.

TEXT OF A LETTER FROM CARDINAL ARCHBISHOP PAULINUS EVITUS IN ROMA TO PATRIARCH PETROS OF ANTIOCH IN CONSTANTINOPLE, WRITTEN IN GREEK CODE AND CARRIED BY A CLANDESTINE MESSENGER.

To the most excellent Patriarch Petros of Antioch, the submissive greeting of Cardinal Archbishop Paulinus Evitus, with the assurance of his continued fealty and affection, in anticipation of the Pope's return to Roma in one or two months.

Now that summer is ending, there is increasing certainty that Leo will be back in Roma before the season of the Nativity, and in the company of that Frankish barbarian, Karl who is called Great by his people. It is unfortunate that we must receive him as if in triumph, but failure to do so is likely to bring about more bloodshed and destruction than we will suffer for the presence of the Franks in this city. If the Cardinal Archbishops do not take it upon themselves to refuse the Pope entrance to the city, then we may not be able to keep him from reclaiming Sant' Pier's Seat. This would be a tragedy for Christians everywhere, and I am troubled by the lack of resolve I have found among my fellow Cardinal Archbishops.

That does not mean all is lost. There have been so many rumors about the misconduct of Leo that he may find such accusations impossible to refute, and therefore he may yet have to resign the Papacy in order to preserve the Church, which will make it possible for us to put our candidate forward. Once he wears the tiara, he will be able to subsume the Roman Church to the Orthodox Church, and thereby bring all Christians to the true Church. I pray day and night for that joyous day.

I do not fear the Franks, mighty in war though they are. I am certain that devotion to God is greater than any allegiance to a worldly lord. This buffoon imagines that he is heir to the Caesars! The temerity of the man! Yet many Cardinal Archbishops tremble at his name and profess themselves ready to recognize him as governor of all the Romans. It would be an insult if it were not so absurd. I cannot conceive of any circumstances that would render Karl worthy of the high regard he demands, and which Leo, the fool, provides him. It would be a dreadful thing to join the Church to such a one as he.

You have warned me that there are fewer Cardinal Archbishops favoring the Orthodox Church than there were a year ago, and that is probably so, but I am confident that those of us who still adhere to your Church are more committed to the victory of the faith than those who have wavered in their duty. It is imperative that all of us cleave to the Orthodox Church of Constantinople. To that end I dedicate my soul.

Cardinal Archbishop Paulinus Evitus
by my own hand

⟶

chapter eight

T HIS IS ROMA?" Gynethe Mehaut asked, her voice hushed, as they made their way past the gate newly built in the ruined city walls. She had pulled the covering of her plausterum aside in order to look at this most renowned of all cities in Karl-lo-Magne's domain. What she saw appalled her: a dead horse lay between the shafts of an abandoned cart in the curve of the old, collapsed wall; the flies and other insects had had the greater part of a day to feast upon it as the stultifying heat sped bloating; already the taint of putrefaction was on the air around the animal, cloying and metallic. Within the shadows of a dilapidated emporium beggars watched the horse, as if hoping for an opportunity to butcher it before it became too rotten to be of use.

"It is." Rakoczy almost added *now*; this was not Roma as he had first seen it, in the time of Julius Caesar, and later, when Nero and Vespasianus ruled. The city had been bursting then, with a much larger population, its walls intact, its buildings new.

Sulpicius shook his head, half in awe, half in disappointment. "What happened here?"

"It was sacked," said Rakoczy. "Repeatedly."

Gynethe Mehaut stared up at the ruins of the Circus Maximus, looming behind a row of two-story brick buildings. She made a sign to protect herself. "What have they done? Why is it like this? How did it come to be so . . . so wretched?"

"Romans have been taking its marble facing for four centuries," said Rakoczy, "and the bricks have been used by everyone."

They went farther into the city, passing deserted buildings with plants growing out of the cracks in their stone fronts, over an old bridge that had once been graceful and sturdy, with statues of gods at both ends; now it was patched with wooden beams, and the road-bed had a few holes worn through, where the Tiber could be seen, all green and white. After crossing the bridge they went toward the House of the Franks, keeping to the streets that were fairly clear of rubble; it was a dismaying vision of fallen splendor. Yet Roma was not devoid of beauty: the afternoon glowed a buttery gold, and the first aroma of the grape harvest— which had just begun—made the air vibrant with promise. The old stones, amber and aureate, were impressive in the waning day, vivid as living flesh, yet would soon fade to lunar canescence in the intense blue of twilight.

"I don't think it is wise for you to go about the city, just you and the White Woman, not so late in the day," said Usuard. "You cannot be sure of your way and mischief could happen."

"It is true that Roma has changed since I was here last and I might not find the most direct route to the house we seek," Rakoczy conceded, "but you don't know your way at all. I can find the old Temple of Hercules, and the square before it, which is all I need to know this evening. Let me offer you this: if I believe we are in danger, I will return here. You may repose confidence in me—I will defend Gynethe Mehaut to my death, should it come to that." He held out three of the six leads he had gathered in his hand. "You may keep these horses for your use. I will have remounts aplenty from my hostess." He smiled slightly. "I will pay for their feed."

"You are very generous, Magnatus," said Theubert. "When I tender my report, I will say you have done this for us, as well as your other good acts."

"That is very welcome," said Rakoczy, who knew all beneficial reports about him were given limited credibility by most of those who read them. He ducked his head in respect, then swung his grey around, and with his single remount behind him and three mules on a lead, including the one drawing Gynethe Mehaut's plausterum, he looked about the square before the House of the Franks, aware of the attention they had attracted.

Usuard was the only one of the soldiers who reverenced Rakoczy, and he stopped half-way through the gesture, looking shamefaced.

Rakoczy made his way through the gathering purple shadows, picking his way around the various abandoned buildings and damaged paving. He called out to Gynethe Mehaut. "We're not far from the place now."

As if to punctuate his assertion, a near-by carillon began the Vespers' chimes and was soon joined by a chorus of bells in that quarter of the city. There was a last flurry of activity on the streets, and a closing of shutters and doors.

"It is getting dark," said Gynethe Mehaut.

"We're almost at the Temple of Hercules," said Rakoczy.

Gynethe Mehaut said, "How dangerous is it at night? Not the temple, the city itself."

Rakoczy laughed sadly. "It isn't safe for anyone after dark. Gangs of criminals roam the streets. They attack anyone hapless enough to be abroad at night, and they war with one another. The Guards permit it because they're unable to stop it, and they would rather the gangs fight one another than join together against the Guard." He turned a corner into the dusk of long shadows, although the sky above glowed lilac and apricot with the afterglow of sunset. "Almost there. The Temple of Hercules is right ahead."

Three painted women in vivid-hued silken stollae hurried past them, rushing toward the steps of the massive building; Gynethe Mehaut watched them and felt her face grow hot. "You are taking me to a brothel?"

"No; no," said Rakoczy. "But you will find that there are brothels all over Roma, unlike it was during the time of the Caesars, when the prostitutes had their own district. It was called the Lupanar." He did not add that in those long-ago days, the women in that profession were not despised, and the fortunes they made were their own. He turned toward the blank-fronted building across from the Temple of Hercules and dismounted before it. As he pulled the bell-chain, he tried to recall how this square had looked when he had first seen it; his thoughts were interrupted by the door being pulled open by a handsome Greek, who reverenced Rakoczy with a flourish and then offered him an old Roman salute.

"Sanct' Germain," he said, standing aside to admit them all. "Welcome to Olivia's house." Beyond the door was a large courtyard in excellent repair, a two-story Roman house, and a stable, all fronted in marble. The courtyard stones were a vast mosaic, hard to make out in the fading light, but extensive and expertly done, with a complex pattern of horses and verdure against a pale-ochre background. Torches were burning from a dozen wall sconces, whipping like brilliant silks in the evening breeze and giving a ragged brightness to the descending dark. "There are paddocks behind, if you need them. There is a caladarium through that arch, and a small tepidarium. The caladarium can be heated in a short while, and the tepidarium is cleaned and ready for use. You don't need to do anything more. The grooms will take care of your horses and mules, brushing them down and stalling them for the night; your chests and satchels will be taken to the chambers assigned to you." His accent was excellent, very Roman, if a bit old-fashioned, and his smile was easy and wide. "It is good to see you again, Sanct' Germain, and it is an honor to have you a guest in this house."

"Efficient and effusive as always, Niklos," said Rakoczy with an approving nod. "You have anticipated almost every question."

"To assume two more," said Niklos with a wicked grin accompanying his slight bow of acknowledgment, "your suite is on the ground floor; I am sure you will find it comfortable. The woman you escort has her choice of apartments; I have rooms ready for her on the floor above you, if you will permit me to discharge my duty as major domo. You may wait for Bonna Dama Clemens if you like: my mistress is with her mariscalcus; she will join you directly."

Rakoczy gestured his satisfaction. "I am left with nothing to ask, then, but how you are, and how life is here in Roma." He went to the rear of the plausterum as he spoke and pulled back the cover. "Gynethe Mehaut, come down. We are arrived."

Gynethe Mehaut answered the summons, stepping down carefully to the narrow platform and then to the stones of the courtyard; she looked around, her eyes widening as she took in all she saw. "This is a fine villa, surely. How lovely it all is."

"Not quite a villa, but I thank you in any case," said Niklos Aulirios. "Illustra, I welcome you in my mistress' name." His Frankish was tolerably good, but he returned to the Roman dialect at once. He clapped his hands. "Wine and water for our guest."

As if materializing out of the evening air, four mansionarii came up, drink on one tray, a basin of water and a drying cloth on another; the remaining two without apparent purpose reverenced her without any impression of surprise.

Gynethe Mehaut turned to Niklos. "I . . . I am not used to being received so well." She stared at the magnificence around her. "This is . . . very grand."

"Hardly," said Niklos. "But for now it will have to do." He pointed to the mansionarius with the basin. "Cyrillus, help our guest rid herself of the grime of the road."

Another barrage of chimes sounded, and chanted prayers began to drone in the dusk. The mansionarii paid little heed to this, continuing instead with the rites of welcome. Grooms came to take their animals away, and a man who was probably the buticularius brought out a brazier that burned wood for light and branches of rosemary for aroma.

"How near is that?" Rakoczy asked while Gynethe Mehaut puzzled over how best to use the basin of water without getting her hands wet.

"There is a church in the next street—very old, or so they claim. The building is old in any case, but it hasn't always housed priests. These days they keep the Hours meticulously. And four blocks away there is a monastery," Niklos answered. "And there are chapels everywhere; you must have noticed. Every thermopolium and tratorium has become a chapel, dispensing blessings instead of food. There are over ten in the blocks around us, and many more in the lanes beyond. During the day, the streets are thick with pilgrims, and the women in the Temple are kept busy."

Rakoczy gave a single crack of laughter. "No doubt." He noticed Gynethe Mehaut's dilemma and went to her at once. "What is the matter, my confidant?"

"This," she said in a burst of exasperation, holding up her bandaged hands and feeling suddenly helpless. "Should I wash or—"

Rakoczy took the drying cloth and dipped one end in the water, wrung it out, and handed it to her, ducking his head respectfully. "This should suffice for now. You may want to use the caladarium later, to ease you."

Gynethe Mehaut took the cloth and wiped her face and neck; the tension in her face lessened, and she nodded. "Oh. Yes, please. I think so. Yes. That would gladden me very much." She wanted to conceal her nervousness, but could not think of how to do it, so instead she babbled on. "Your welcome is generous, and grand enough for a Dux or the King's sons. How can I show you my appreciation?"

"By taking advantage of what we offer: you'll want comestus first, I should think," said Niklos. "You've had a long journey, Bonna Dama." This Roman title came easily to him, but it sounded unexpected to her.

"I suppose I must answer to that," she said thoughtfully. "Is that what the Papal Court will call me?"

"I hope so," said Rakoczy with strong feeling.

Niklos Aulirios reverenced her, this time not more extravagantly than good manner required. "I trust you will prevail." He signaled to the mansionarii. "Well, Zelotius, are you going to pour water and wine, or not? And Crispernus, bring a torch and a mirror so that she may—"

"Oh, no, no mirror," said Gynethe Mehaut, shaking her head. "It isn't right. The Sorrae never allowed it, and I admit that I dislike seeing myself."

"That's unfortunate," said Niklos. "But as you wish." He motioned one of the mansionarii away. "At least tell me you will drink. The wine is reputed to be very good—will you have some?"

"Yes, and gladly," said Gynethe Mehaut, accepting the alabaster goblet she was offered; the wine within it was lit through the thin, pale stone, and glowed red as a jewel. "This is excellent," she said, and took the silver cup half-filled with water and drank that, too.

"For comestus we have spitted hens and rabbits stewed with sweet onions and summer pears." Niklos watched to see if this would interest her. "Nothing very elegant, but tasty in its way."

"Niklos, stop apologizing to our guests," said a voice from the archway leading to the stables. The woman was of middle height with a mass of fawn-brown hair done up in a disorderly knot. She wore a palla of bronze-colored linen girdled and bloused, and Persian boots. Her clothes were dusty but her hazel eyes shone. "Sanct' Germain!" Without bothering to reverence him, she ran across the courtyard and flung herself into his arms. "How like you, to arrive at the last minute."

"I apologize, Olivia," said Rakoczy, kissing her forehead and embracing her heartily.

She beamed up at him. "I'd given up on seeing you today."

"And yet, here I am," he said lightly, then caught her hand. "I thank you for permitting us to stay with you. If I must stay within the walls, I can think of no place better than this house."

She shook her head. "You've done as much—and more—for me." She started toward Gynethe Mehaut, pausing just long enough to reverence her. "You are welcome here, Bonna Dama."

"I've already said that," Niklos remarked.

"Pay him no heed," she recommended. "He's always watching after me, for which I am very grateful, when I am not nettled by his solicitous manner. He has no concept of subordination, which is just as well." She glanced back over her shoulder as if to be certain that she was still dragging Rakoczy after her. "You're quite a remarkable woman, that's apparent. I'd imagine most of the Church officials are terrified of you."

"They think I may be the Anti-Christ," said Gynethe Mehaut, shocked at how bitter she sounded. "Bishop Iso especially thinks so."

"They think you're *different*," Olivia corrected her. "That is enough to make anyone—particularly any woman—the Anti-Christ. The Church is inclined to blame women for anything that troubles the men who run it. When the Caesars ruled, that wouldn't have happened. The Vestal Virgins might not have held office, but they were the equal of the Senate and the Emperor. That power made a difference for all women in Roma. Now . . . Well, you don't need to be reminded, do you?" She came up to Gynethe Mehaut and put an arm around her, apparently unaware of how unused Gynethe Mehaut was to such treatment. "These *men*! What can be done about them?" Seeing the shock in Gynethe Mehaut's face, she went on, "Oh, not *these* men"—she waved toward Rakoczy and Niklos Aulirios—"but men in general, and prelates particularly. I've seen your Bishop Iso, incidentally, and what a self-important mass of smugness he is—worse than most of them, I'd venture."

"They are the servants of God," said Gynethe Mehaut, wondering what this eccentric woman would say next.

"Another man, and a bad-tempered one at that," Olivia said, dismissing the whole issue. "It doesn't matter. Come in, come in, and be comfortable. There is food for you, and a proper couch for your meal."

"Don't overwhelm her, Olivia," Rakoczy recommended. "She's had a long, difficult journey, and she has much ahead of her."

"All the more reason to relax now, while she can," said Olivia, adding inconsequently, "I liked the city better before." She let go of Rakoczy and Gynethe Mehaut and took several long strides toward the central entrance to her house. "But enough of that. The river of time flows only one way; hardly original, but true."

"Anything else would be too perplexing," said Niklos, following after them. "One moment you would be facing Hannibal, then you would be listening to Marcus Aurelius, then you would be seeing Cleopatra enter Roma, then you would have to run not to be crushed by Alaric's charge—"

Olivia giggled. "Don't. I am losing all gravitas."

"If you ever had any," said Niklos.

Her response was somber. "Oh, I did. Ask Sanct' Germain." She looped her arm through his, saying to Gynethe Mehaut, "You must excuse me. I haven't seen my old friend for years; it's a bit heady having him here at last. I don't quite believe it. Lend him to me while you eat, for kindness. I promise I won't keep him away from you for very long."

Gynethe Mehaut was unable to answer, afraid of offending this most unlikely widow. She went into the house and saw a rosewood iconostasis at the door to the nearest reception room; portraits hung on it, most in the clothing of past centuries, and there was an elaborate Greek crucifix in the center of the portrait, which Gynethe Mehaut supposed must be of Saints and Martyrs. "Are you a follower of the Greek Church?" she asked, feeling suddenly cold. "I thought you were attached to the Pope."

"I am. In Roma, to be anything else is reckless. This screen is more than two centuries old, and it was a gift. I don't follow the Greek Church, not here in Roma, in any case; perhaps I would if I were in Byzantium." She had acquired the iconostasis in Constantinople; she had thought it lost when she left the city, for she had escaped with little more than her skin. At the time she was happy to be rid of it, since it reminded her of those unhappy years in Justinian's Empire, but over the years she had come to miss it; Niklos had reclaimed it for her two decades ago, and now she felt it was a memento of a difficult period in her long life.

"Why do you keep it?" Gynethe Mehaut stared at it, horrified and transfixed at once.

"I cannot easily explain it," said Olivia, and went into the atrium, which now contained a vast array of plants in tubs and pots of almost every description. "I warned you about this; I might as well put down soil and farm," she said to Rakoczy, then turned to her pale-skinned guest. "Comestus should be ready. The dining hall is through that door. Do you want me to escort you?"

"Are you going to eat? Or are you like the Magnatus?" It was a daring question for Gynethe Mehaut, and she anticipated a reprimand.

"She shares my nature," said Rakoczy steadily. "I hope you're not offended."

This was still bewildering to Gynethe Mehaut, and she hung back. "What are you going to do?" Her question was directed to Olivia.

"I'm going to show Sanct' Germain my horses while you dine. Would you rather see my herd with us and eat later? It will take some time." Olivia waited, so confident that Gynethe Mehaut wanted to flee. "Tomorrow I'll have them parade for you, if you'd prefer."

"I don't know much about horses," said Gynethe Mehaut, an irrational stab of jealousy going through her so vividly that she knew she would have to Confess it as soon as possible.

"What would you like instead?" Olivia asked. "You have only to ask me."

That made it worse; Gynethe Mehaut felt upset at her own dismay. "Thank you," she said stiffly. "I am more in your debt."

"Nothing of the sort," said Olivia. "Put yourself in Niklos' hands. Have some food and a little more wine, then take a long soak in the caladarium until you are ready to retire. Sanct' Germain can knead the knots out of your muscles as if you were an athlete."

Rakoczy came to her and took her hands in his; she pulled them away as he spoke to her. "You have nothing to fear: Olivia and I are of the same blood, and I haven't seen her for many years."

"It's not that," said Gynethe Mehaut, but could not say anything more.

"You and I will meet in the caladarium later," he promised her. "If that is what you want."

"I ought to pray instead. Perhaps tomorrow," she said in a small voice, refusing to meet his gaze.

"As you wish," said Rakoczy. "If you change your mind, I will be delighted."

Gynethe Mehaut broke away from him, and trying her best not to weep, she ran toward the dining hall, wanting time to herself. She hoped there were no other guests in the house, for she doubted she could endure meeting anyone else. The dining hall proved to be a beautiful chamber with fresco murals and a single couch set out for her, a carved rosewood table set before it. A chalice of wine waited for her, and a ewer of water with a filled cup beside it.

"You'll be served directly, Bonna Dama," said Niklos Aulirios, coming from the far end of the dining hall. As he reached her, he spoke more softly. "Don't let it bother you; there is nothing to worry you. They see each other so rarely that they become a little giddy when they do." He reverenced her and put a silken pillow on the couch. "Please. Recline. I'll have figs stuffed with soft cheese brought to you, and other tidbits to tempt your appetite."

To her consternation, Gynethe Mehaut burst into tears. She kept trying to speak but could not stop crying. Finally she sank onto the couch and dropped her head into her hands, using her bandages to wipe away her tears. "I . . . this is . . . how can you . . ."

Niklos put his hand on her shoulder; Gynethe Mehaut went rigid at this unanticipated familiarity. "Listen to me, Bonna Dama. You have no reason to think ill of them. They don't mean to offend you, or to cause you pain. You have no reason to fret. Yes, they are very close—exiles of the same blood often are. They have endured long separation, and will again. You can understand loneliness: then think how they are—they're each alone in the world, and their bond is often all they have."

Gynethe Mehaut tried to smile and failed dreadfully. "I should . . . understand."

"In time, you may," said Niklos. He stepped back and summoned the mansionarii. "This Bonna Dama is the guest of our mistress. See that she is given all that she wants. Attend to her as you would to one of the Papal Court."

This was more than Gynethe Mehaut could bear. She started to rise, wanting to get away, but was stopped by the appearance of a scullion bearing a platter on which artichoke hearts chopped with walnuts in olive oil in a Moorish bowl lay next to a dish of grated lettuce and a plate of figs stuffed with cheese. Very slowly she sat down again, licking her lips without being aware of it.

"You'll be glad of a meal," said Niklos, and offered the chalice of wine to her. "You're worn out from traveling, as who would not be?"

Gynethe Mehaut took a long sip of wine. "I *am* a bit fatigued," she said. "And I am hungry."

"Then let us feed you." He took the platter and set it down on the rosewood table. "I think you will like the artichokes. They are a bit past their best, but they are still quite good." He offered her a moistened linen cloth. "For your h—" he said without thinking, managed an abashed smile, and added, "Well your fingers. You will find it useful."

She took it and wiped her mouth. "The wine is very good." It was beyo... question the best she had ever had, superior even to the wine she had drunk in the courtyard, but she was reluctant to be too lavish in her praise. "I'll enjoy it."

"Splendid," said Niklos. "When you have had as much of that as you like, summon a scullion or a mansionarius, and ask for your next dish, or let me do it for you, as you prefer."

"Is there bread?" She was surprised not to have seen any.

"Yes, but it hasn't finished baking." Niklos ducked his head. "The household had prandium at mid-afternoon and our comestus will not be ready until after Compline. This is for your reception; you may decide how you will savor it."

Now Gynethe Mehaut was more distressed than before. "I didn't think . . . Should I wait?"

"Not at all. You're a guest in this house and you may command anything within our power to provide." He pressed his lips together. "My mistress is a Roman of the old school, and you will find that she—"

"You said she is an exile," Gynethe Mehaut exclaimed, suddenly suspicious.

"Yes, she is, although this is where she was born and where her family is buried— and her husband. But for her, to be a widow is to be an exile, even here in Roma." Niklos poured more wine into her chalice. "Drink. It invigorates the palate."

"But Rakoczy isn't Roman, is he?" Gynethe Mehaut persisted as she drank another generous sip. "He told me he came from mountains in the east."

"No, he isn't Roman, but that changes nothing," said Niklos smoothly. "Please." He pointed to her chalice.

Not wishing to appear ungrateful, Gynethe Mehaut drank down almost half the chalice of wine; it really was delicious. She began to feel restored. "Thank you."

Niklos waved the compliment away. "My mistress has an estate a short distance outside the city walls; it has been producing wines since—long before I became her major domo." He took a turn around the beautiful room. "I should leave you to eat in peace."

"No. No, stay," said Gynethe Mehaut, realizing she was glad of new company, especially such a good-looking man as Niklos Aulirios was; he was also willing to overlook her white skin and red eyes and treat her as if she were as other women, and one worthy of regard. Another sin to Confess, she thought: Envy first and now Vanity, and very possibly Gluttony as well. She drank more wine to cover her disconcertion.

"That's most courteous of you, Bonna Dama." Niklos summoned the scullions again. "Bring bread and oil as soon as you may."

Gynethe Mehaut was devouring the lettuce, noticing it had a tangy vinegar on it. She lay back, reminding herself that this was a Roman house, a very grand Roman house, and that those who lived here were not like the Franks. She had another sip of wine and decided to eat more in order to remain sober; the figs and cheese were an unfamiliar flavor, but she was taken with it. After she had chewed well enough to be able to speak, she remarked to Niklos, "I thought Roma would be different—grander."

"It has been," said Niklos.

"So the Magnatus told me," she said. "I didn't understand what he meant until we came through the gates."

Niklos shook his head. "A pity you must see it this way. But it can't be what it was."

She shook her head vigorously. "But it can," she told Niklos with a burst of passion. "Great Karl will make it better than it was. You'll see: Roma will be restored to her place in the world. The King has said so. The Pope has agreed."

"Not even those two men can repair four centuries of war and neglect," Niklos said matter-of-factly. "But if the city is improved, it will benefit us all."

A scullion brought a small pitcher of olive oil and a basket of bread still warm from the oven; the aroma was as exhilarating as the wine. He set these down on the rosewood table and withdrew; Gynethe Mehaut tore off a piece of bread, and said, "This is almost as white as I am." She had not seen such pale bread before, not eaten any as fine. It was all she could do to swallow.

"The fields produce good wheat, and the millers know to grind well," Niklos said. "I have seen Frankish bread in Neustria; it is darker and coarser than this Roman bread."

"Yes," said Gynethe Mehaut, drinking more of the wine as she ate another gobbet of bread. "At Sant' Audoenus, we had bread that was as brown as ale, with soaked grains baked in the dough. It was supposed to be restorative, or so we were told."

"Did you eat anything more substantial, or was that your food?" Niklos was curious and made no excuse for it.

"On the Lord's Day, we had bread and fish, as the monks said was right. Other days we had cheese and fowl when it was available. The Potente occasionally brought us deer or boar, but that was infrequent." She finished the wine and drank water instead; Niklos refilled her chalice. "Our wine wasn't like this, though some was brought up from the south, and was better than what we grew in our region."

"The north makes better beer than wine; most agree this is so." Niklos glanced up as another scullion arrived carrying a spit on which two hens smoked, smelling of herbs as well as fowl. "Both of these are suitable; choose which one you would like, and the portion that would please you."

"So much!" Gynethe Mehaut marveled. "For not a Feast day."

"My mistress keeps—"

"The Roman traditions; yes, you've said so," Gynethe Mehaut finished for him. "But to have fowl and rabbit and all the rest. It is extravagant, perhaps too extravagant."

"It is fitting," said Niklos, and refilled the chalice.

"I am getting drunk," Gynethe Mehaut announced, but took the chalice.

"Where is the harm in that?" Niklos asked. "You are in the house of a friend and we have no lack of bottles in the cellar. You have no reason to fear ill-will, and you are in need of repose. If you drink wine, it will come more fully and more quickly."

"This is . . . unseemly for me," she said, and put her hand to her mouth.

Niklos smiled a little. "Let the scullion know which hen you want."

"I will," said Gynethe Mehaut; she studied the two hens: both were plump and smelled of bacon-fat and garlic. "The one on the left is a bit browner. I believe that will be better."

"Philetus, serve the one the Bonna Dama wishes." Niklos watched while the scullion did what he was told, cutting the meat from the bone with a shiny, narrow knife that he wielded expertly.

This fascinated Gynethe Mehaut; she leaned forward, bracing herself on the couch with the silk-covered cushion Niklos had given her. "I haven't seen anyone carve so well. We take the birds off the spit and pull them apart at the joints."

"Many do; the Romans of old expected more art in their food than we do today."

"Wonderful," said Gynethe Mehaut, drinking a little more wine. "How was he taught?"

"Carefully," said Niklos, and smiled to show he intended this to be amusing. "The cooks here teach the most promising of the scullions how to carve along with all the other kitchen skills."

Gynethe Mehaut heard him out, listening intently. "You apprentice scullions?"

"Yes," said Niklos. "Our cooks are expected to do this. If they refuse, they leave the famiglia."

"It's not done that way in Franksland," said Gynethe Mehaut; she had some difficulty speaking clearly, and that bothered her. She put the chalice down, gingerly picked up a wedge of hot thigh, and began to eat the sliced chicken.

Niklos dismissed the scullion and said quietly, "If you drink more water you won't have a headache in the morning."

Obediently Gynethe Mehaut reached for the water and drank eagerly, then picked up another slice of chicken. "This is very good," she said, no longer surprised.

"It had better be," said Niklos, more amused than autocratic. He summoned another scullion. "Prepare a bowl of the rabbit stew and bring another round of bread."

"What else will you bring me?" She almost dropped the slice of chicken she was eating. "I didn't mean that. I meant that I want to know if there is any more food planned for this meal. I don't expect any more. Indeed, I don't expect this much—"

Niklos cut her short with a raised hand. "If you want berries in honey, you have only to ask for it."

Gynethe Mehaut shook her head. "No. I have indulged more than I—" She stopped herself for a moment. "It is the wine and the food and all the—"

"You're worn out and in need of rest," said Niklos. "Finish your meal and I will escort you to your apartments."

"There was a dead horse lying just inside the gates," she said suddenly.

This remark did not distress Niklos; he gave a single nod. "There has been much worse," he admitted. "But I'm sorry you had to see that on your first day here."

Feeling confused, Gynethe Mehaut ate hurriedly. She was grateful for a chance to gather her thoughts, but discovered that she could not hold them long enough to deal with them. "You're right," she said unsteadily. "I am tired."

"As soon as you're done eating, you can rest." Niklos put more water in her cup.

"I wanted to bathe, but not tonight," said Gynethe Mehaut. "Will it be possible tomorrow? At the nunnery we bathed before the Lord's Day; oftener was called Vanity."

"You may bathe when you wish, for as long as you wish," said Niklos, and stood aside so that another scullion could offer Gynethe Mehaut a dish of stew.

She broke off the last of her bread and put it into the stew, then picked up a bit of the well-flavored meat. "This is very good, too."

"Rabbit may be common, but there's no reason it has to be plain," said Niklos, and retired to a corner of the magnificent room to wait for Gynethe Mehaut to finish her meal.

"I am done," she said a short while later, licking her fingers. "I'm going to need new wrappings for my palms." Looking down at the floor, she saw there were more mosaics.

Niklos noticed how her attention had shifted. "There are mosaics everywhere on the ground floor," he told her. "Tomorrow, when it is light, you may look at them as much as you like. The smaller reception room has the most interesting ones, I think; it shows the seasons of the year in fruit and flowers."

She rose, swaying a bit, and put her hand to her pectoral crucifix. "I should probably sleep now," she said, color suffusing her cheeks and neck. "I'm ready for my bed."

Obediently Niklos led her out of the dining hall to the nearest stairs. "Your rooms are at the end of the corridor. The door is painted russet and there is a brazier just outside. I can send you a maid to attend you: my mistress has four of them and she has put one at your disposal." He paused. "Would you rather I escort you?"

It was what she wanted, but she dared not ask for it. "No. I'll find my way," she said, and began to climb the stairs, her steps a little unsteady. "What is the name of the maid?" she remembered to ask when she was almost to the top.

"Dysis. She's Greek," said Niklos. "As I am."

Gynethe Mehaut repeated the name twice to fix it in her mind, then resumed her climb; below her, Niklos watched until she was through the door to her rooms; then he went off in search of Sanct' Germain and Olivia to tell them his impressions of their remarkable guest.

TEXT OF A LETTER FROM RORTHGER IN FRANKSLAND TO HIERNOM RAKOCZY IN ROMA, WRITTEN IN ARCHAIC LATIN AND CARRIED BY HIRED MESSENGER AND DELIVERED IN MID-SEPTEMBER.

To my most excellent master, the Magnatus Hiernom Rakoczy on this, the end of July in the Pope's year 800, at the house of Atta Olivia Clemens in Roma, the greetings of Rorthger from the Magnatus fiscs near Sant' Cyricus on the Stavelot Road.

I am sorry to have to tell you that another complaint has been brought against Waifar, this one more serious than some of the previous ones: it is said that he raped and murdered a ten-year-old girl. The child is certainly dead, but I cannot yet determine who has done it. The villagers are convinced that Waifar is guilty, and nothing I have done has changed their minds. I have warned Vulfoald that if he tries to manage Waifar's punishment himself, I will have to inform the King's Court of this, and it is likely that their village will be razed and the population dispersed throughout Great Karl's Empire: it has happened to other villages before now, and I do not doubt it will happen again. Vulfoald has said that he intends to have revenge on the criminal who has done this, and to that end has vowed before God to see Waifar suffer for what he has done. I have implored the monks of Sant' Cyricus to speak with him and his villagers, to admonish them to leave this matter to you, but I have no confidence that this will be possible; revenge is so important to these people that threats mean nothing.

On happier subjects: the foals are all doing well; Livius has two more since I last wrote to you, and they are doing well, although I have had to put one on to the speckled mare, for his dam is not thriving, and has been unable to produce enough milk . The yearlings are being worked as you have ordered, and I am pleased to say that the chestnut is showing real promise. I know you will be pleased to see him when you return.

I have purchased a donkey and given it to the monks of Sant' Cyricus. It seemed the prudent thing to do, given how testy they have been of late; their orchards have been blighted, and the fruit is shriveling before it can be harvested, which is a disappointment to the monks, as well as to the villagers, whose fruit trees have also fared badly. With poor yield from the orchards, the hives are not doing well, either, and so I am arranging a trade with the villagers of Santa Famiglia, which is distant enough that their orchards have thus far been spared: for their fruit and honey, your fiscs will supply them with cut wood and tanned hides, both of which they lack. I trust this meets with your approval, and that you will continue the trade as long as it is needed.

Barley and oats are doing well, wheat a little less so; the end of next month should tell the tale for grains, but I see nothing to worry me in that regard. I have told Vulfoald that the new cooperage had better be ready to have barrels for flour, and soon, for once the harvest has gone to the miller, it will be wise to store it in barrels rather than sacks; rats find it harder to get into barrels. There are peas in plenty this year and they can be dried and stored for the winter; I have already set that in motion.

Swine fever has struck the nuns at Santa Julitta and seven Sorrae have died. I have sent over two vials of your sovereign remedy, but the Superiora has declined to use it, saying it betrays her nuns' faith in God to protect and

preserve them in their hour of need. I have told her that she may avail herself
of this offer at any time, but that it is important that she keep the Sorrae—all
of them—within the convent walls until the fever passes. I have also told
them not to take in travelers, for swine fever spreads easily, as you and I
have seen many times before. I was not too adamant about your remedy
because I don't want it said that you lack dedication to Christ: that could
work against you when next you must deal with the Bishops of the region.

I have received a requisition from Karl-lo-Magne, brought by special
courier, not his missi dominici, requiring nine horses from your stable for his
journey to Roma. I have complied without cavil, as you instructed, and chosen the largest of the younger horses for the King's use. I have also, without
his order, sent three mules to him; from what you have said, he will need
them crossing the mountains. He has campaigned in Longobardia often
enough to value mules on such a trek.

I have authorized three market-days for your fiscs to be held at the end of
August; this has been well-received, although the Abba at Santa Julitta has
asked that they include a morning fast with prayers for her Sorrae. I will
arrange something with her that will not be too encumbering for the villagers. This is not the time to impose prayers on them, no matter what the
Abba may think. I am trying to maintain cordiality throughout this region,
my master, but it is a complex task. I will write to you again at the conclusion of the market-days. I will probably have to hold the letter until spring,
or send it with the King's troops, for once Karl-lo-Magne and his soldiers
take to the road, no merchant will want to, and no private courier would be
willing to carry messages. So, until the end of August, may you enjoy the
favor of all the gods, and the high opinion of the King.

Rorthger
by my own hand

chapter nine

LATE SEPTEMBER HAD TURNED BLUSTERY, with sharp-tempered squalls blowing up the Tiber from the sea. All through Roma tree-limbs broke and fell, slates crashed from roofs, and parchment window-coverings were torn off their frames. Men and women seemed to catch the spirit of the wind, for arguments flared over nothing, extending farther and doing more damage than was usually the case. Even horses and dogs became disgruntled, striking out at humans in displays of unprovoked pugnacity that brought immediate and heavy-handed repercussion. The morning was overcast, layered, frayed veils of clouds sweeping across the sky ahead of the increasing winds that promised a storm by the next day.

In her plant-filled atrium, Olivia held up the parchment that Niklos Aulirios had just carried to her, waving it at Rakoczy. "Sending out messengers on a morning like this! What was he thinking? The poor monk might be swept up into Heaven on such a day. Who is this Bishop Iso that he should make such demands? And by what right does he summon you to the Lateranus?" She put her hands on her hips. "The Pope is still at Spoleto. Why should you have to obey this upstart Frank?"

"I probably don't have to," said Rakoczy as he packed earth around the roots of a young hissop sprout. "But it would be advisable."

"Nothing of the sort," Olivia scoffed. "From what Gynethe Mehaut has said, the Bishop is trying to condemn her. Why should you help him?"

"Because if it appears I am not willing to cooperate, it could result in added suspicions about Gynethe Mehaut. It would be very bad for her if it's decided that she is not doing all she can to make herself available to the Church, all the more so because Bishop Iso is one who is convinced she is damned. I would rather not give him any more reasons to think ill of her; or of me, for that matter. He's as vindictive as a cobra." Rakoczy walked across the mosaic tiles, his attention on the parchment Olivia still held. "Tell me, when does the Bishop want to see us? How soon?"

"According to this, this afternoon, between prandium and Vespers. At least that's what I suppose he is saying." She continued to read. "His Latin is atrocious—he has no elegance and he uses words like a bored student, with no regard for correct grammar, or form. And he assigns endings all anyhow."

"They all do," said Rakoczy. "It is one of the many things that have been lost in the last five centuries, particularly in the north." He picked up another small plant from its rough ceramic tray and carried it to a waiting pot.

Olivia relented. "The Church isn't much better." She held out the parchment. "What are you going to do about—?"

Rakoczy sighed. "I suppose I'll have to inform Gynethe Mehaut of this—"

"This what?" she asked from the door. She was dressed in a green stolla and bronze gonella, with a golden crucifix hanging from a chain around her neck. In the weeks since they had arrived in Roma, she had spent most of her time inside Olivia's metal-gated house, seeking to avoid the kind of observation she had come to dread.

"Summons—to the Lateranus," said Rakoczy, and deferred to Olivia with a gracious nod.

"So the impertinent Bishop Iso has ordered that you—" She broke off as she saw the expression on Gynethe Mehaut's face.

"He has . . . spoken with me before. He sent Priora Iditha away and set his Sorra to watch me." She went to a shadowed bench and sat down, dismay growing within her. "If he is in Roma, she must be here, too. He wouldn't leave her behind."

Rakoczy put the plant into its pot and wiped his hands on a cotton square. "If she travels with him, as she did in Franksland, I should suppose she is."

"I don't want to see her," said Gynethe Mehaut bluntly. "She pretends to have high regard for me, she watches me, she accompanies me everywhere, engaging me in conversation, and then tells the Bishop all he wants to hear. I don't trust her. She's dangerous." She put her hands to her eyes. "I thought she liked me, but it was sham."

Olivia gave a harsh laugh. "Churchmen, and their women, rarely like anyone but those who can advance them in the Church, and even then, liking isn't necessary: think how many of the Cardinal Archbishops despise Leo. He, at least, is discreet in his private tastes, which is more than you can say of most of them." She rubbed her arms through her woolen sleeves. "What can you do about it? Is that woman apt to—"

"The Bishop will insist that she remain with me," said Gynethe Mehaut miserably. "I can do nothing more than comply, or face greater reprobation."

"But you are my guest, and I haven't invited her into my house. I doubt the Bishop is so lost to propriety that he would foist his spy upon us," said Olivia, trying to mitigate Gynethe Mehaut's disquiet. "After all, I am a well-reputed Roman widow, my prestige is high in the Papal Court. To send a nun here would impugn my reputation. I will speak to the Cardinal Archbishops: Urbinus and Donatus will listen to me—and they're Romans, so will uphold my honor, no matter what Franks may say."

"But Bishop Iso might—" Gynethe Mehaut attempted to protest.

"Let him try," said Olivia, a martial light in her hazel eyes. "Urbinus has ruled the Cardinal Archbishops—unofficially, of course—for more than a decade. And Cardinal Archbishop Urbinus has been my good friend for years. Your Bishop Iso will be at a disadvantage without Cardinal Archbishop Urbinus' support, and I shall exert my influence to ensure your safety."

Gynethe Mehaut wanted to believe her; she took a deep breath. "I pray you are right, but I know what Bishop Iso has done before." She rose. "When must we leave here?"

"After prandium," said Rakoczy. "We'll go by biga, if Olivia will spare us one."

"Certainly," said Olivia. "I have a fondness for those old, open chariots, myself. Besides, getting through the streets is easier in a biga than in a carpentum or carruca." She pointed to a small tree in need of transplanting. "You can deal with that one next."

"With pleasure. Where does it come from?" Rakoczy studied the handsome evergreen.

"Somewhere in Hind, or so the ship's Captain told me; I haven't seen one before," said Olivia. "I like its smell—don't you?"

"It is pleasant," said Rakoczy, and looked about for a sufficiently large tub to hold the little tree. "How large will this grow?"

"I'm informed it will be as high as the second story." She shrugged. "I haven't actually seen one at full size."

"All right, then I'll err on the side of growth. That tub with the lion's head on it should do." He carried the little tree to the tub and dropped a dead fish from a small wooden cask into the earth in the tub before setting the plant in place.

"Why did you do that?" Gynethe Mehaut asked, coming closer.

"It feeds the plant," said Rakoczy, and explained. "They do this in parts of the East, and their plants flourish."

Gynethe Mehaut shook her head. "How can a . . . oh, as a symbol of Christ and life everlasting!" She held up her hands in an attitude of prayer. "That must be its virtue."

Olivia bit back a retort, and only said, "You may look at it that way if you like."

Rakoczy completed his work and saluted Olivia in the old Roman manner. "If you will order a biga, I will change into garments more fitting than these for the Lateranus."

"Of course," said Olivia, and called out to Niklos, "Have the larger biga hitched up for Sanct' Germain." Then she studied the clothes Gynethe Mehaut wore, her head cocked and her lips slightly pursed in thought. "You'll do well enough, though I would advise you to put clean bandages on your hands. You don't want to draw attention to them."

"No, I don't," said Gynethe Mehaut, hiding them behind her back and ducking her head.

"Not that you should be ashamed of them, either," said Olivia, shooting a cutting glance at Rakoczy. "But you want to present a good appearance. This is all that is left of the old Imperial Court of the Caesars and the Cardinal Archbishops know it; they live like Princes, at least as much like them as they can with the world so changed from those times. You will do well to keep this in mind. Slovenliness may be very well for hermits and holy fools, but for handsome young women, it will not do, not in Roma, not at the Lateranus." She went over to Gynethe Mehaut and laid her hand on the pale woman's shoulder. "You want to give them as few reasons as possible to question you about what has happened to you. If you go among those vipers—meaning the Cardinal Archbishops—as if you are guilty, they will be glad to assume you are. But if you carry yourself as one blameless, they will respect you."

"They will say I am Prideful," said Gynethe Mehaut, remembering all she had been taught.

"Then they will be wrong," Olivia countered. "I have seen enough evil in the world to know you are no part of it." She gestured to Rakoczy. "Sanct' Germain, go make yourself ready. Gynethe Mehaut will have something to eat—"

"I'm not hungry," said Gynethe Mehaut.

"All the more reason to eat," Olivia exclaimed in ruthless geniality. "You will not be faint when this upstart Bishop Iso talks to you." She almost shoved Gynethe Mehaut to her feet and pointed her in the direction of the smaller withdrawing room. "Nothing fancy, just enough to keep you from getting light-headed by Vespers."

"You had better go with her," Rakoczy recommended with a wry smile. "It's easier than resisting her: believe this."

"Oh, I do," said Gynethe Mehaut, her demeanor showing more anxiety than amusement. "I will do as you insist," she said to Olivia, and went off with her.

Rakoczy met the two women again at the vestibule of the house; he was very grand in a dalmatica of heavy black silk shot with silver thread and girdled with embossed black leather. His Persian boots were deep red, with thick black piping and thicker soles. A silver collar clasped with his eclipse sigil hung around his neck, gleaming against the silk. He reverenced the two women, and asked Olivia, "We're almost ready to leave. Do you have a veil you can spare for Gynethe Mehaut?"

"I have a full measure of sea-green silk that will serve; I've sent my attire-woman to fetch it," she answered; it was apparent that she had decided upon this well before Rakoczy asked about it, and was glad to offer it to her guest. "It will reach almost to your knees, and that will cover your hands."

"Thank you," Gynethe Mehaut murmured. "I don't know why you should be so kind to me."

"Is there any reason I shouldn't be?" Olivia asked, and when Gynethe Mehaut could not answer, she went on briskly, "Well, then, you will please me if you do this."

"The biga?" Rakoczy asked.

"Niklos went to the stable to order it when you went to change your clothes," Olivia answered. "It should be waiting. I've had my blue roans harnessed to it. They'll certainly create a stir; they're quite striking. Full brothers, both geldings; you'll like them."

"I have no doubt," said Rakoczy, and started into the courtyard. "I always like your horses."

"That's because you taught me all I know about them," said Olivia candidly.

Before he could answer her, the attire-woman hurried up, a full length of blue-green silk in her hands. She reverenced Olivia and then Rakoczy, and finally Gynethe Mehaut, saying as she did, "Here is the silk, Bonna Dama."

Olivia took the material and opened it, then lifted it over Gynethe Mehaut's head, pulling at the fabric to make it drape evenly. "You'll become accustomed to it, and it won't impair your vision very much. Just keep hold of the corners, or the wind may carry it away."

Gynethe Mehaut stroked the shining cloth. "This is so very fine," she said, her voice hushed.

"As well it should be, for what it cost," Olivia responded. "Go on, now. And don't be flummoxed by the Bishop. His authority may be great in Franksland, but here in Roma he is just another Churchman, and there are many greater than he."

They had reached the courtyard, and the biga was waiting for them, a handsome if old-fashioned two-horse chariot, well-made and beautifully ornamented with carving and paint. The blue roans hitched to it were glossy, their manes and tails combed, their harness newly waxed; they were alert without being jumpy, needing only one groom to hold their heads.

"As fine as any you have ever bred, no matter what I did or did not teach you about horses," said Rakoczy as he stepped into the biga and gathered up the reins. Adjusting his stance for balance slightly behind the wheels, he said, "This is very well-sprung."

"I'll tell Niklos—he designed the system," said Olivia.

"Do that, and thank you." He reached out to help Gynethe Mehaut step into the chariot beside him. "Be of good cheer, Olivia."

"Of course," she said, and took a step back, but could not resist adding, "Keep to the main streets and don't challenge the Lateranus Guard: they are on their mettle, and look for excuses to fight. It won't help either of you to give them a reason. I will expect you before Vespers unless you send a messenger to say you are delayed. And if you are, hire an escort to protect you. Not even you should be abroad after dark without protection." She signaled her mansionarii to open the gates and watched as Rakoczy put the team in motion and headed out into the square of the Temple of Hercules.

"Are the streets busy?" Gynethe Mehaut asked, trying to see the confusion in the street through the thick veil of silk.

"Fairly so," said Rakoczy, expertly guiding the biga through the throng of men, horses, donkeys, dogs, geese, and ducks that filled the roadway. "There has been worse."

"But it is so noisy," she remarked, hanging on to the side-rail as tightly as her bandaged hands would allow.

"And apt to be more so before we reach the Lateranus," said Rakoczy, using the end of his whip to keep a dog from straying into the path of his pair. "In Constantinople, there would be camels and asses as well as everything we have here."

She resisted the temptation to lift the corner of her veil, not wanting to reveal herself to the crowd. "How long will it take us to get there?"

"Not long," said Rakoczy. "About half as long as the prayers of None, if there are no delays."

"So little time," she whispered, and quivered.

"We don't want the Bishop to have any reason to complain." Rakoczy turned his team along a broad avenue lined with chapels and small stalls providing food and drink to those on the streets. "If we are not prompt, he will say it's because you are afraid, and that will not do you any good before the Cardinal Archbishops. No matter what the Church says, the Cardinal Archbishops are the men who must concern you now. The Pope may make the final decision, but the Cardinal Archbishops are as powerful as he, and he is at Spoleto." He checked the horses, noticing confusion ahead of them.

"What is it?" Gynethe Mehaut stared ahead, seeing only running men and a massive shape blocking their passage.

"A carpentum has overturned, by the look of it; it's blocking the way. They're trying to unyoke the oxen now," said Rakoczy. "If we don't want to be trapped here by the wagons and horses behind us, we'll have to go down one of the side-streets."

"But Bonna Dama Clemens said we shouldn't—" Gynethe Mehaut protested.

"If she were with us, she would do the same," said Rakoczy, clucking to the horses to get them to back up. "We would be in more danger immobilized in this crush than going around it, I assure you."

"Very well," she said, and hung on as Rakoczy pulled the biga around and started down a narrow street lined with two-story buildings with blank fronts facing the road. There were only a few interruptions in these stone fronts; heavy, wrought-iron gates gave fragments of views of courtyards and atria, but nothing suggested access until they reached the end of the block where the side-street ended and a small chapel marked the convergence of two alleys. "Now which way?"

"To the north," Rakoczy declared, and swung the team into the narrow passage. He kept the horses moving at a steady trot, and a short while later entered another broad boulevard that gave onto a jumble of broken buildings and a stagnant fountain. "It isn't far to the Lateranus," he said to reassure Gynethe Mehaut.

She glanced about restively, and blurted out, "Someone is following us."

"Very likely," said Rakoczy. "We can't be the only ones trying to get around that jamb." He spoke steadily enough, but he, also, felt a twinge of apprehension.

"There are gangs who live in the ruins, or so Bonna Dama Clemens—"

"Yes, Gynethe Mehaut. I know about the gangs," said Rakoczy, trying not to be too brusque.

"Yes; of course you do," she said, and stared straight ahead as he drove toward the bulk of Sant' Ioannes Lateranus, the spires of which could be seen above the roofs of the buildings around it; it seemed near and distant at once, as if she could reach out and touch it, all the while despairing of ever getting to it. She began to grow anxious. "How much farther?"

"About six or seven blocks, as I remember," said Rakoczy. He urged the team to a faster trot, paying no attention to the way in which the biga jounced over the paving-stones.

They had almost reached a sizeable square when a pair of men in rough capae and banded tibialia came rushing out of the wreckage of an old house and into the path of the biga; both were carrying small brass shields, and they used them to flash light in the horses' eyes, throwing the pair into disorder.

"Hold on!" Rakoczy ordered Gynethe Mehaut as he reached for the sword that was usually kept in the scabbard of the biga; the weapon was missing. He cursed in his native tongue and took hold of the lash of the whip; wrapping the long, braided-leather thong around his arm and using the stiffened handle as a long staff, he tried to drive off the two men, only to discover that there were two more behind him. He veered around, swung the whip-handle, and had the satisfaction of hearing it crack on bone; one of the men behind them put his hands to his jaw and began to wail in pain. While the others faltered, Rakoczy used the whip-handle again to thump into the chest of the second man behind them; he kept the reins short so that instead of running, the blue roans reared, lashing out with their iron-shod hooves, neighing in distress.

"Get the White Woman!" one of the men shouted, reaching out for the biga.

The man whose chest had been hit by the whip-handle coughed repeatedly but gamely tried to grab her arm; he missed his chance and staggered back, winded.

"They're going to kill us," Gynethe Mehaut cried, clinging to the rail and struggling to remain standing.

"No, they're not," Rakoczy said as he pulled the reins on his team to turn them toward the nearer attacker in front; the on-side horse came down on all four feet, narrowly missing the rough-clad man's shoulder, and the off-side roan almost fell over; he scrambled, pulling at the bit, and kicked back at the front of the biga, leaving a clear impression of his hoof in the carved wood. Rakoczy raised his hand holding the reins as high as he could, keeping the horses' heads up so they would not fall.

The man on the off-side rushed forward, a long dagger raised as he went for the off-side horse; he was intent upon crippling the animal and incapacitating the biga altogether; he reckoned without Rakoczy's whip-handle, which came down on his shoulder, cracking his clavicle upon impact. The man screamed and fell backward, rolling into a ball.

"If I were you," Rakoczy said to the man on the on-side front, "I'd run while I still could." He swung the whip suggestively.

The man threw a wad of ox-dung at Rakoczy, shouting, "Fucker of swine! Get of a she-camel!" even as he bolted and ran.

Two of the remaining men were badly hurt, and one was dizzy from the blow to his jaw. He staggered to the nearest of his fallen comrades and tried to lift him, only to go down on his knees beside him. "You're a devil!" he shouted at Rakoczy.

"All the more reason to beware me," said Rakoczy as he unwound the whip-lash from his arm and took the handle once again. "Tell whoever sent you what happened here."

"Sent us?" The man with the bruised jaw was finding it painful to talk, but the flush in his face came from more than pain.

"Do not suppose I am stupid," Rakoczy said cordially. "You followed us from the overturned carpentum. That means you intended to waylay us and no others. Did you arrange for the accident on the road, or was that just a happy circumstance you used to your advantage?" He steadied his horses. "Move aside, Bellatori, or I will be forced to drive over you."

The three men scrambled to the sides of the roadway, pressing back against the stones as the biga went on down the street—the horses at a rapid but controlled trot—and turned at the corner.

"Did they follow us?" Gynethe Mehaut asked, fascinated.

"Judging from the response we had, I assume they did," Rakoczy said dryly.

"They called you the White Woman, although you're completely veiled, so they must have been told to waylay us specifically. They knew who you are."

"Then you didn't see them follow us?" She was surprised by his remark.

"No, but it seemed a useful ploy, and so I—" He gestured to show how quickly he had acted.

"I was frightened. I thought you'd be killed," she admitted. "Four evil men . . . but you stopped them."

"It takes more than those men to kill me," Rakoczy said grimly. "Fire will do it, and beheading, or anything that breaks my spine above my heart. But those men?" His laugh had no humor in it. "They have no notion how to fight me, let alone kill me. So long as I have my native earth in my shoes, sunlight cannot burn me, and I had the advantage of this biga and two fast horses. If we had had to flee, they could not have caught us." He knew there were any number of ways the four men might have disabled the geldings, or damaged the biga, but they had made the mistake of supposing their attack would be easy because there were four of them against a single man and a woman. He maneuvered the biga around a group of artisans pulling carts of their goods and supplies, then added, "Olivia did well to warn us."

"Oh, yes," Gynethe Mehaut agreed, wiping her brow with the linen around her hands. "I must remember her kindness in my prayers."

Rakoczy shook his head. "I wouldn't mention that to her." They were almost to the square in front of Sant' Ioannes Lateranus; Rakoczy pulled the roans to a walk and made his way around the side of the building to the gate that led to the Pope's living quarters. He saluted the Lateranus Guards in the old Roman manner and said, "I bring Gynethe Mehaut to answer the summons of Bishop Iso."

The nearest Guard looked narrowly at Rakoczy, mentally taking stock of his appearance and manner. He shifted his lance to his left hand and said, "A groom will look after your chariot."

"See they have water, if you will," Rakoczy requested.

"Yes," said the nearest Guard automatically. "And you are—"

"Hiernom Rakoczy, Comes Sant' Germainius, in Roma at the behest of Karl-lo-Magne, King of the Franks and the Longobards." He stepped down from the biga and held his hand out to assist Gynethe Mehaut. "I am appointed her escort by the King himself."

The Guards were grudgingly impressed; the shortest of them jutted his chin and studied the blue roans. "Handsome team you've got."

"It is, isn't it?" Rakoczy said affably as he put his hand on Gynethe Mehaut's shoulder to guide her through the gate. "Be good to them in our absence."

The nearest Guard opened the gate. "The door is on your left."

Rakoczy deliberately reverenced Gynethe Mehaut again as she passed through the door. "It is my honor to attend you."

She glanced at him, their gazes meeting through the veil. "Must you be so courteous?"

"We are at the Papal Court. This demands good conduct," Rakoczy reminded her, and looked at the peeling frescos on the side of the Lateranus; the building was far from elegant and seemed woefully small to be the Papal residence. Slaves, mansionarii, monks, priests, Archbishops, Cardinal Archbishops, and a few nuns thronged the courtyard between the residence and the side entrance of Sant' Ioannes Lateranus. A group of pilgrims with crosses sewn on their shoulders were huddled together on the far side of the courtyard, attempting to sing Psalms in the confusion. "The door on the left." He pointed to a squat-arched entryway. "There must be someone who can direct us—"

"There is," said Gynethe Mehaut deploringly; she recognized the figure of Sorra Celinde standing just inside the entrance.

"That nun?" Rakoczy asked.

"She is Bishop Iso's woman. She must be our guide." She sighed. "I cannot trust her."

"I should think not," said Rakoczy, but continued to walk toward her.

Gynethe Mehaut faltered. "What do you think? Shall we go or stay? I don't want to speak to her; she twists my words and seeks to compromise me."

"Then don't turn away, or she'll assume the worst," Rakoczy advised as he went directly to Sorra Celinde and half-reverenced her.

The nun almost jumped. "I didn't realize it was you," she said, recovering herself and attempting to smile. "I'm sorry. You did startle me. That veil . . ."

For the first time Gynethe Mehaut was glad that she was still wearing it. "Bishop Iso summoned us."

"So that he may question you before the Pope returns." Sorra Celinde was attempting to regain her authority. "I will show you to his apartments. They are rather small, but it is because so many other Bishops are in Roma just now." She started up the steep flight of stairs.

"The Pope will be back before the Mass of Christ," said Rakoczy. "No wonder so many of them want to be here." He reverenced the nun to take the sting out of his observation.

Sorra Celinde glared at him. "I know about you, Magnatus. I didn't realize you would be with Gynethe Mehaut."

"Surely you didn't expect her to walk the streets alone," Rakoczy said.

"We were attacked by roughians on our way here," Gynethe Mehaut blurted out, stopping on the narrow tread. "If not for Rakoczy, I should never have lived to reach this place."

Sorra Celinde looked at Rakoczy. "You fought them off?"

"There were four of them," said Gynethe Mehaut. "They followed us." She stopped talking suddenly, as if she had realized she was saying too much.

"Four men attacked you?" Sorra Celinde asked Rakoczy, continuing to climb.

"Yes," he said.

"And you escaped them?" The nun looked dismayed.

"In a manner of speaking," said Rakoczy, helping Gynethe Mehaut to continue up the stairs.

"He fought them," said Gynethe Mehaut, feeling compelled by an external force.

"Four against one?" Sorra Celinde was skeptical and surprised at once.

"We were in a biga," said Rakoczy, as if that explained his victory.

They were at the top of the stairs now and making their way along a narrow, ill-lit corridor. Distant chanting filled the air, although it was not the time of devotions. A dozen monks came down the hallway, large scrolls in their hands; they argued in the dialect of Carinthia, paying no attention to Sorra Celinde, Gynethe Mehaut, or Rakoczy.

"Bishop Iso requires a short while to prepare himself for this interview," said the nun as she pointed to a door. "If you will wait there, he will call upon you shortly."

By which, Rakoczy thought, the Bishop needs time to put a spy at a watch-hole to observe them. "We are here at the Bishop's pleasure," he said smoothly, and guided Gynethe Mehaut into the reception room, which was little more than a cubiculum.

"Why are we—?" Gynethe Mehaut asked, only to go silent at a gesture from Rakoczy.

"Sit down, Bonna Dama," said Rakoczy, maintaining a formality that no one could fault. "I hope they will send a slave with water and wine; if we must wait, it would be appropriate to let us be comfortable."

"I don't care what they provide," said Gynethe Mehaut. "And why should you?"

"If we are guests here, the Pope owes us courtesy, or his Court does." Rakoczy sounded indignant, and he took a turn about the room as if annoyed. When he came back to Gynethe Mehaut's side, he leaned down and whispered, "There are two peep-holes."

Gynethe Mehaut's hands clenched. "This is maddening."

"Then we shall complain to Great Karl, when he comes to Roma." Rakoczy continued to pace. "It is grossly insulting to be detained like slaves."

"It may be the Bishop wishes to allow me to compose myself in prayer. Better that I should recite the Psalms than regale myself with the Pope's wine." She looked up at him. "This is a most imposing place."

Rakoczy thought of how grand Roma had been before, and the other splendid places he had seen over the centuries, from the Temple of Imhotep to the palaces of Peiking: the Lateranus was far less than the others. "It was intended to be."

Gynethe Mehaut stared at the door. "How long will we have to wait?"

"That is up to the Bishop," said Rakoczy, and kept on pacing and covertly scrutinizing the peep-holes, where the flicker of eye movement glinted.

TEXT OF A LETTER FROM PATRE MAXIMUS OF SANT' SALVATOR ON THE VIA AURELIA TO HIERNOM RAKOCZY AT THE HOUSE OF ATTA OLIVIA CLEMENS ON THE SQUARE OF THE TEMPLE OF HERCULES IN ROMA, CARRIED BY A BURGUNDIAN PILGRIM AND DELIVERED TWO DAYS AFTER IT WAS WRITTEN.

To the distinguished Magnatus, Hiernom Rakoczy, courtier to Karl-lo-Magnus, the Emperor of the Franks and Longobards and protector of the Pope, the humble salutation of Patre Maximus, and the fulfillment of a pledge to a dying man on this, the Eve of Toutti Santi in the Pope's year 800. Amen.

My Bonna Dama, Ina, who had the felicity to speak to you when you came here to consign the earthly remains of your comrade to my care and the prayers and Masses for the dead, told me that you were the one responsible for all these arrangements, and I commend you for your charity as well as your generosity.

It is a doubly sad thing, then, that I must write to you with distressing news: the Bellatore Einshere, who came here to do penance for his revenge-killing of the Bellatore Notrold, took the mal aria and died of the fever that possessed him. He said before he died that as he had exacted vengeance on Notrold, so God would exact vengeance upon him. He was content to have it so, but he implored me to send word to you, with the desire that his family be informed of what became of him, and that he achieved the restoration of the family honor. I do so now with the hope that you will accept this duty as suits a man of your rank and standing in the Emperor's Court.

May God bless and guard you in the trying days ahead, and may you always maintain the conduct worthy of your estate.

Patre Maximus
by the hand of Fratre Fortunatus

chapter ten

IN SPITE OF THE RAIN the streets of Roma were filled and had been since dawn, for Prime had been set aside in favor of this momentous occasion; monks and pilgrims lined the streets holding crosses and palm-fronds, singing *Alleluia* and reciting the prayers of thanksgiving. The blare of buccinae from the Tomb of Hadrian announced that the party escorting the Pope to Roma had been sighted, along with the lances and banners of Karl-lo-Magne's hosts. A cheer rose in answer to the brazen cry of the buccinae, and a few of the monks began to dance, turning in slow circles while reciting the *Gloria* over and over, their faces filled with ecstasy. While the joyous excitement increased, pick-pockets made their way through the crowd, taking what they could, while a number of Fratri worked with the Guard to maintain order.

"You'd think it was Titus returning, and not poor old Leo," Olivia said as she stood on her upper balcony, a hooded mantellum of boiled wool protecting her from the weather as she watched the excitement; her palla beneath the mantellum was a beautiful shade of sea-green silk edged in a design of Persian gryphons. "Are you going down into that?"

"Eventually I'll have to," said Rakoczy, and glanced at the veiled figure of Gynethe Mehaut. "I'll take you to Karl-lo-Magne later, when the streets are clearer." He was in a black silken dalmatica, a long capa of black-dyed goat-leather over it; he had not bothered to raise the hood.

"So tell me, when will all this nonsense be over?" Olivia asked. "They might as well bring back the Games; the people would be better occupied than they are now."

"But this is a holy occasion," said Gynethe Mehaut, and pulled nervously at her veil.

"It is, for a small number of all those people. But for most Romans it is a festival, and for a few, it is a political contest." Olivia turned to Gynethe Mehaut and smiled. "I'm past redemption, I fear."

"You say it so . . . so merrily," said Gynethe Mehaut.

"Well," said Olivia, "I am of the same nature as Sanct' Germain, and I've seen more than I'd like over the years. That is the difficulty with long life: you see too much." She smiled slightly and then tried to take the sting out of what she had said. "When I was a breathing woman, the women of Roma were protected by laws that gave us property and inheritance. I was unable to use all the law provided me, but that was not the law's fault. In that time women were not beholden to men for everything, and we were more than chattel. All that we had has eroded away, and it troubles me."

Gynethe Mehaut stared at her. "How is it possible that you would know—" She stopped and ducked her head. "I was assuming you were much younger than the Magnatus."

"I *am* much younger than he," said Olivia. "Ask him yourself if you doubt me." Rakoczy nodded. "Yes. She is many centuries younger than I am."

"How many?" Gynethe Mehaut demanded, then fell silent, dreading the answer.

"Not quite twenty-one, as I recall," said Rakoczy as if none of this interested him. "She came to my life when Vespasianus ruled."

Although she was unsure how long ago that was, Gynethe Mehaut shivered. "A long time."

"Yes." Olivia raised her head as another blast from the buccinae filled the morning. "They must be nearing the gates."

"Let's hope so," said Rakoczy, moving forward on the balcony and shading his eyes against the suffused glare of the shrouded sun. "I can see nothing yet."

"It must be vexing," said Olivia a bit later as their waiting drew out; below in the streets the crowd was growing restive. "Your own Villa Ragoczy is three thousand paces beyond the walls, and you aren't permitted to live there. Not that it is in the best repair, but it is walled and most of the villa is standing. You could be more comfortable there than here in Roma."

"It seems foolish, but I understand why Great Karl required it." Rakoczy cocked his head toward Gynethe Mehaut. "He wants her to be within the Church's beck and call. If she is outside the walls, then she might be able to decide for herself when she accommodates the summons of the Church."

"I would never defy the Church; for the Church has protected me all my life," said Gynethe Mehaut.

"Ah, but the Churchmen don't know how loyal you are," said Rakoczy as kindly as he could. "They assume that they must keep close guard on you, which is why I am with you. Had you come with pilgrims, who knows what might become of you here in Roma or on the way. You might not have arrived at all, and there would be no one to blame for it."

"And even Karl-lo-Magne is not such a barbarian as to order you to travel with his army," said Olivia.

"Why not?" Gynethe Mehaut challenged. "His daughters do."

Olivia shook her head. "They are different. It is prudent for him to keep them near him. And only a fool would make demands on the King's daughters. It would not be the same for you."

Gynethe Mehaut set her jaw firmly. "Great Karl would protect any woman in his company."

Olivia laughed aloud. "That must be why he has so many bastards." Then she regained her self-control. "I don't mean to insult you, Gynethe Mehaut. I understand you far better than you know. But Great Karl is not the paragon you want to make him: no one who rules can afford to be, not in this world. I will give him credit for ambition and rigorous campaigning."

Rakoczy held up his hands. "You will neither of you change your minds," he said.

"I won't," Gynethe Mehaut declared. "And Great Karl is here. From today he rules in Roma, and all Romans are subject to him."

"He's lucky he got his army through the high passes before the snows came," Olivia remarked. "Leo would have had to stay in Spoleto until spring, and that would have given his enemies more time to close ranks against him. They certainly have tried to, in his absence."

Gynethe Mehaut sighed. "It's terrible that the Pope should be so besieged," she said, and made a sign of protection.

"It's his own doing—or his predecessor's," Olivia said, dismissing Leo's misfortunes. "When the Church allied itself with the Franks, it opened itself to the corruption of worldly gain, and all that accompanies it. It has already happened in Byzantium. Roma is following that example, unfortunately, and eventually all of the Roman Church will pay the price for this folly." She turned her head suddenly, calling out, "Niklos! Bring my guest bread and wine. And a bowl of soup; there must be some in the cauldron in the kitchen." This was as close to an apology as she was prepared to offer.

From the floor below Niklos Aulirios answered, "I will directly, Bonna Dama."

The buccinae sounded again, long and more enthusiastically; the shouts and chanting in the streets became louder, and slightly more coherent.

"I wonder who entered the gates first?" Olivia mused.

"If Karl-lo-Magne hasn't forgotten himself entirely, he would allow the Pope to enter ahead of him. Anything else could be seen as a slight, which would be unwise in this place: this is the Church's city, and the Donation of Pepin makes it the Pontiff's. As Pepin's son, Karl-lo-Magne should uphold his father's acts." Rakoczy folded his arms under his capa. "The avenue to the Lateranus must be impossible. There will be people everywhere. How could his army get through?"

"Will he go there, to the Lateranus, first, or to Sant' Pier's?" Gynethe Mehaut inquired uneasily. "It would show the Byzantines that he means to hold the Roman Church apart from theirs, if he goes to Sant' Pier's."

"Let us hope that he chooses wisely, wherever he goes," said Olivia. "Roma is still recovering from the last sacking she had."

"You don't think it would come to that, surely?" Gynethe Mehaut protested. "This is Roma, not Aachen or Paderborn, or Pavia."

"That has never stopped anyone before," said Olivia brusquely. "In fact, the city has become something of a prize, though I sometimes wonder why: it is not what it was."

Rakoczy put his hand on her shoulder. "Nothing is," he told her.

"So you say," she answered, then made a quick dismissing gesture. "And on such a day as this, why be cast into gloom? Look. You can see the first of the Bellatori. Down there." She pointed to a gap in the high roofs; a procession of armed men rode by on barded horses, lances raised, axes displayed. "They're impressive," she conceded. "For barbarians."

"The men of Franksland aren't barbarians," Gynethe Mehaut declared, scowling at Olivia. "They are great warriors and faithful monks."

"You can say that, after the way you've been treated?" Olivia asked.

"Do you tell me the Romans would behave any better?" Gynethe Mehaut countered her question with a sharper one. "The Franks are not barbarians."

"They seem so to me," Olivia responded without apology. "And I have seen more than my share." She looked around as Niklos came onto the balcony carrying a small table bearing a loaf of bread, a bowl of steaming pork-and-lentil soup, and a cup of wine. "Good. Just what I had in mind. Set it down where Gynethe Mehaut can enjoy it."

"You're most generous, Bonna Dama," said Gynethe Mehaut, lifting her veil enough to eat. She whispered prayers before she took her knife from her girdle and cut the bread.

"You are my guest, though sometimes I treat you woefully," said Olivia, and returned her attention to the activity in the street. "Everyone is saying Karl-lo-Magne is a giant. Is he?"

"Well, he is head and shoulders taller than I am," Rakoczy said. "He stands roughly nineteen hands. I have seen taller men, but not many."

"Nineteen hands! What is he—a camel?" Olivia shook her head. "It can't be possible. You are what—sixteen-two? And you are above average."

"Not as much as I used to be," said Rakoczy. He pointed to the gap where they could see the procession. "A carpentum. That must be Leo; the cloth over it is purple."

"Then Karl-lo-Magne is being sensible," Olivia approved. "What do you say, Gynethe Mehaut?"

Interrupted in mid-bite, Gynethe Mehaut swallowed too quickly, coughed twice, and answered, "I say that the King will support and uphold the Pope in all he does."

"If you will pardon me for doubting it," Olivia said, "I will agree that it appears so."

"Olivia," Rakoczy chided gently.

"I don't mind," said Gynethe Mehaut, half-reverencing the carpentum as it slid from view.

"I meant not only for you," said Rakoczy. "This is a precarious time in Roma and anyone speaking so takes a great chance."

"When isn't it a precarious time in Roma?" Olivia said, expecting no answer. "Is the soup to your liking? Would you like something else?"

"This is very good. You keep a fine kitchen, Bonna Dama," said Gynethe Mehaut, and resumed her meal.

It was mid-afternoon before all of Karl-lo-Magne's soldiers had entered Roma, and the noise from the crowd had become deafening; Rakoczy, Olivia, and Gynethe Mehaut had gone in from the balcony some time before as the parade became repetitious. By then, the squall of the morning had passed and turned to scattered clouds riding a brisk wind, and the festivities in the street had become more frenetic than they had been earlier in the day. About half the populace was drunk, and the rest were so excited that they needed neither wine nor beer to stimulate their celebrating.

"Must you go out?" Gynethe Mehaut asked as she stood by the saddled grey in the courtyard. "It could be dangerous."

Rakoczy touched her face through her veil. "I am charged to present myself to the Emperor upon his arrival. You have nothing to fear: we were only attacked once, in all the eight times Bishop Iso summoned us. I don't think I have reason for apprehension, not with Great Karl here in Roma. I have my long-sword with me, and my francisca." He patted the weapon that lay along the small of his back under his girdle. "I must present myself at the Emperor's Court or risk his displeasure; that is far more dangerous than anything in the streets."

"But if there were many of them . . ." She held up her hands joined as a sign of petition. "Take Niklos with you."

"He's needed here," Rakoczy reminded her. "Particularly now, with so many strangers in the city." He took the reins from the groom standing at the mare's head. "Look for me before midnight, though I may return earlier, if the King orders it."

"Tell me you'll have an escort when you return," said Gynethe Mehaut.

"I guess that the women in the Temple of Hercules would rather I didn't. They'll get little sleep tonight." He took hold of the saddle and vaulted up.

"I'll pray for your safety," she vowed.

Earlier in his life Rakoczy might have asked her not to bother, but now he said, "If you want to do so, I thank you." He rode out of the gate and had the satisfaction of hearing it clang shut behind him. He kept his horse to a walk, picking his way through the alleys and lanes, away from the main avenues where the greatest roistering was going on. Even then, he encountered bands of men in pilgrim's weeds, wandering the streets, half-drunk, celebrating. Once he made a wrong turn and ended up in a cul-de-sac where half-a-dozen ragged children played, two of them with scarred faces. As they cowered in trepidation, Rakoczy backed his grey out of the closed way and turned off to the west; the faces of the children haunted him as he rode.

At last he reached the House of the Franks and was confronted by such activity and confusion that he could hardly move his horse through the milling mass of soldiers and monks. He looked over the bustle for a senescalus or buticularius who could take him into the King's presence without delays that would last well past sunset. Dismounting, he led his horse to the stable and handed the reins to a mariscalcus, asking as he did, "Can you tell me where I might find a mansionarius?"

The mariscalcus laughed harshly. "In the streets, with the other sots," he said, then pointed to a narrow passageway. "Someone will find you if you go through there."

Rakoczy gave him a silver coin. "For your trouble."

"No trouble at all; an honor to serve the hobu," said the mariscalcus. "I'll have your grey in the third stall on the left, with the two bays. I'll provide water and grain."

"Very good," said Rakoczy, and strode off toward the opening the mariscalcus had indicated.

The crowding was as bad inside as out: mansionarii busied themselves fetching and carrying everything from mantella to messages to casks of wine and beer. The babble of voices echoed so that it became a tide of noise in the stone building. Rakoczy followed the corridor until it reached a reception hall where a group of Bellatori and Comesei stood around a table littered with the remains of an impromptu meal. All of them were drinking, and one of them—Rakoczy recognized Comes Haganric—was holding up a map of Roma, pointing at it and insisting that the others look. In the next room along the corridor fourteen women were seated at a table, wholly occupied in eating: these were Karl-lo-Magne's daughters and current concubines. Rakoczy glanced in, wondering if he would find Odile among them, but she was missing from their number. As he reached the main hall, he heard the sound of a lituus and a bladder-pipe played together, the merry tune accompanied by clapping and stomping. On impulse, Rakoczy went toward the music and found Karl-lo-Magne sprawled in a large, carved chair, three Bishops sitting near him, with Cardinal Archbishop Paulinus Evitus at the King's elbow, three Potenti a bit farther off on the opposite side. A group of mansionarii hovered behind the group, anxiously waiting for any order that the King might issue.

Tapping his toe in time with the rollicking melody, Karl-lo-Magne was saying, "—and the Declaration of Innocence should end any calumny clinging to Leo's name. Anyone who would question him after he makes the Declaration will do so at his peril. Pope Leo will make the Declaration before all the Cardinal Archbishops, and it will provide incontrovertible proof that the Pope has done nothing immoral or illegal. Such an oath is as binding in Heaven as it is on earth." He slammed his hand down on the arm of the chair. "Then we'll have my coronation, and the whole will be settled. I'll be Emperor."

"Do you expect that this will be acceptable to the Byzantines?" asked the Cardinal Archbishop. "Shouldn't you tell them what you are planning?"

"Why should their opinion concern me?" Karl-lo-Magne asked. "This isn't their territory. They have no reason to concern themselves with what happens here."

"Do you want to send word to them? As a courtesy?" The Potente who asked was unfamiliar to Rakoczy; the man was almost bald, and he leaned on a stick; his accent was Longobardian. "Shall we dispatch messengers?"

"When it is done," said Karl-lo-Magne. "There will be plenty of time to have them know what has happened here in Roma. There is nothing they can do to change it, in any case. Why should I tantalize them with an announcement before the deed is done?" He motioned to the musicians. "Get a tabor. I want to hear the beat without having to provide it myself." Then he saw Rakoczy standing at the edge of the men. "Magnatus! I was beginning to wonder what had become of you."

"I came as quickly as I could. The streets are not easily traversed at present." He reverenced the King and moved in a little nearer.

"You have the White Woman with you?" Karl-lo-Magne asked.

"Here in Roma, yes, but not in my company just now. I didn't think it would be wise to expose her to the celebrations. She is with a distinguished Roman widow who has been our hostess since we arrived here. Your Bishop Iso can confirm this." Rakoczy kept his manner carefully deferential.

"I have no doubt that you have followed my orders to the limit," said Karl-lo-Magne, but with a slight hesitation that was eloquent of uncertainty.

"I gave you my Word that I would," said Rakoczy, aware that he had become the object of curiosity. "I have fulfilled my Word."

"And I am mindful of your service, and your reliability in its execution," said Karl-lo-Magne, stifling a huge yawn. "It has been a long journey, and I will not have much chance to rest. There is a great deal to do before the Mass of Christ."

A third musician carrying a tabor came up to the other two; they whispered among themselves and then began a quick tune, the tabor pounding out the beat emphatically. The men around Karl-lo-Magne paid little attention to this, although the King began to snap his fingers along with the tabor and occasionally hum along.

Rakoczy ducked his head. "I have escorted Gynethe Mehaut to Sant' Ioannes

Lateranus eight times, at his request. I will continue to provide her that duty as long as you require it."

"Yes," said Karl-lo-Magne, drawing out the word. "About that. Now that I am in Roma, there are many to give the White Woman the escort she requires. Once the Mass of Christ is over, the Pope will hear her case. As soon as that is done, I want you to return to Franksland. Go to your fiscs and wait there for my orders. I don't want the Cardinal Archbishops saying that I am giving preference to an outlander at this time." He glanced at Rakoczy from under his tufted eyebrows.

"I am at your service, Optime," said Rakoczy, reverencing him again; inwardly he was filled with dismay. He had assumed that he would have another two or three months in Roma to keep the Church at bay and work to improve Gynethe Mehaut's position.

"If only you were kin of mine, I would be able to distinguish you more. Still, Magnatus, you have provided a good example for my men. I will acknowledge it." He pointed to Rakoczy. "Look upon this Magnatus," he said to the others. "Take him as your example if you would serve me."

"Optime is kind," said Rakoczy, once again feeling uneasy, the result of the intense gazes of the men around the King.

"I expect you to continue to obey me. By Epiphany, I want you to depart from this city, so that you will be at the foot of the mountains when the passes open. You will return to Franksland." Karl-lo-Magne clapped his hands. "Slaves! Where is our wine?"

Three mansionarii hurried off to find slaves who could answer the King's command, and one of the Bishops fidgeted in his chair. The musicians reached the end of their tune and, after a brief consultation, began another, this one a bit slower of pace, the melody wistful.

"These Roman musicians, so eager and proud," said Cardinal Archbishop Paulinus Evitus. "These three are better than most."

"With a tabor to keep the beat they are very good," said Karl-lo-Magne. "No dirges," he warned them. "Nothing so very glum. This is an occasion for rejoicing; I will have glad music only, to reflect the delight that the Pope's return must engender in all Romans. Tune your instruments to that." With a glance at Rakoczy, he said, "I have been told you play well."

"I play—the hydraulis, the kythera, the Egyptian harp, the psaltery, among others," said Rakoczy. "How well is a matter for others to decide, not me."

"You are too modest," Karl-lo-Magne protested. "According to Odile, you are as accomplished as any clan harper." He gazed into the middle distance. "A pity about her."

"A pity?" Rakoczy repeated.

"Yes. She had a daughter and contracted a fever shortly afterward. She succumbed to it when her child was, oh, five or six months old, and the girl has been put to a wet-nurse. I'll make some arrangement for her if she lives long enough. The Church will always receive her if I cannot find a man of rank to marry her. In any case, she will not be cast upon the world without means." He looked directly at Rakoczy. "You must have known Odile wasn't strong. She miscarried four times when her husband lived. She served me well while we were together, but God claimed her as His own." With a gesture of protection, he put an end to the subject. "How many men will you need for an escort north?"

"I don't quite know yet," Rakoczy said, still trying to comprehend the death of Odile; he forced himself to respond to the King's question. "To be candid, I hadn't thought I would have to leave quite so soon. Coming here I lost three of the men of my escort, and I cannot suppose I will get to Franksland unscathed, but I cannot guess how many men I will need for my travel." He ducked his head. "If I may have a few days to consider the matter?"

"Certainly. You may wait until shortly before the Feast of the Nativity. I would rather you tell me sooner, but with all you must do for the White Woman, you may need more time. You will have to escort her to the Pope when he requires it." Karl-lo-Magne saw a dozen slaves approaching with large ewers of wine; he pulled out his dagger and slapped the nearest one on the shoulder with the flat of the blade. "About time, you dogs. Do not be so lax again or you will be beaten for laziness." He pointed to the Bishops and the Cardinal Archbishop with the dagger. "Serve them from your knees."

The slaves rushed to obey; the man in front of Rakoczy held up a goblet and a jar.

"I'm sorry; I do not drink wine," said Rakoczy, and motioned to the slave to rise.

"Give that to the Potente Luchandus," Karl-lo-Magne ordered. "You're too lenient, Magnatus. The cur deserved a kick."

"He is not my slave," said Rakoczy, dodging the issue. "If I were a Frank, it might be otherwise, but as I am a foreigner, I am in no position to reprimand slaves of the Franks."

"An apt point," Karl-lo-Magne admitted. "I must give it my consideration." He took a goblet of wine and drank a little. "I must join my women. Since my wife died, they have more need of my company."

"I was sorry to learn of your Queen's death," said Rakoczy.

"Yes. It is unfortunate. She never gave me a child, and I have nothing to remember her by." He sat up. "I will speak with you all tomorrow. Potenti, you know what information I must have to be ready for the coronation. See that it is done, and in good time. I have authorized each of you to spend one hundred pieces of silver."

"So great an amount," said Potente Rodolf, reverencing Karl-lo-Magne.

"Do you say it is too much?" Karl-lo-Magne asked, not quite rising from his chair.

"No," Potente Rodolf said hastily. "But it is a very large amount of money. How can you spend so much at this time? Shouldn't you hold some back, in case there is trouble? If you have to hire mercenaries, you will need all the silver you can find—and more."

"Why should I hire mercenaries with eight thousand Frankish troops in Roma?" Karl-lo-Magne asked.

"Well, the Byzantines have a vast army, and if they should bring it—"

"That is my concern," said Karl-lo-Magne, rising to his full height. "They could not get here before the Mass of Christ if they set out today, and by then it will be too late."

"But if they have started out already?" Potente Rodolf asked nervously.

"They haven't," Karl-lo-Magne stated. "Do you think the Greeks are the only ones with spies? I have been receiving dispatches regularly."

Rakoczy listened uneasily, aware that the Potente was not the only Frank with apprehensions about the coronation. "It is winter. The Byzantines will not want to put to sea until the storms are less frequent."

"Listen to the Magnatus," Karl-lo-Magne advised, and turned on his heel.

"He is good to his women," said Potente Hincmar, not entirely approving of this.

"It was a vow to his mother," said Bishop Aelischer, as if the King's behavior needed some explanation. "It is to his credit he has honored it for so many years."

"He has taken his women with him for many years," said Cardinal Archbishop Paulinus Evitus.

The Potenti nodded, and Rodolf said, "He wishes them to be safe and believes they can only be so with him or with the Church. Three of his bastard daughters are Abbas, and one of the legitimate ones."

Potente Luchandus shook his head. "He gives them too much, and they become demanding."

"Because Optime would not allow you to woo his daughter for marriage, you speak ill of his affection for his women," said Bishop Aelischer, his remark serving as an end of their discussion.

Rakoczy took advantage of the moment to reverence the company as he prepared to depart. "Potenti, Bishops, Cardinal Archbishop, may your enterprise flourish here in Roma."

"And you, Magnatus," said Cardinal Archbishop Paulinus Evitus. "We will look to you for guidance."

Taking this as a warning, Rakoczy lowered his head as he threaded his way from the reception room, through the brimming corridors to the stable. He found his grey in the stall, led the horse out into the courtyard, swung into the saddle, and holding the gelding to a walk, started back through the streets. Vespers were sounding all over the city, and the clamor of the bells was almost drowned out by the rollicking populace; no one stopped rejoicing to observe the Hour. Small parades had sprung up, soldiers and monks occupying the streets in groups, drinking and singing together, and occasionally giving way to ineffective battles among the carousers.

The square in front of the Temple of Hercules was crowded: soldiers waited in lines that led into the temple. A few men, already finished with the women inside, lounged on the steps, sharing skins of wine and tossing dice. An old woman made her way down the lines, asking the men what their preferences were and how much they could pay.

Rakoczy summoned Niklos with a tug on the bell-chain and was surprised when it took more than three clangs to bring the major domo to the door. "Trouble?" he asked when the door was finally opened.

"Nothing I didn't expect," said Niklos as he set the bolt in place. "The men occasionally ring this bell, which is why I didn't answer at once. Earlier three Bellatori tried to get in, and I was forced to repel them. Fortunately, they were drunk, and a single blow with a cudgel was enough to discourage them."

"I should think they would be," said Rakoczy, leading his grey toward the stable.

"The women are in the atrium; they gave up any hope of sleeping until late tonight, if then." Niklos looked toward the entrance to the house. "I'll escort you in shortly. I'm afraid the grooms and the mariscalcus have been given the night to join the festivities; so have all but two of the mansionarii."

"Probably a wise decision," said Rakoczy, and took his grey into the stable and began to remove the tack; then he brushed down the gelding and led him into a stall before going to fetch a flake of hay to put in the manger. When he had cleaned his saddle, girth, and bridle, he went to the house, going directly to the torch-lit atrium.

Olivia was clipping the dried heads off the last of the autumn flowers, dropping the faded petals into a pail. Gynethe Mehaut sat near the fountain, her veil pulled around her shoulders, her head uncovered. The two looked up at the same time, both of them showing their individual kinds of relief.

Rakoczy reverenced them both. "I hope you haven't found the day too difficult," he said.

"Noisy more than difficult," said Olivia, making a gesture with her shears to indicate the clamor that still filled the air. "If it keeps up all night, then it might be difficult."

"You had planned to go out?" Rakoczy asked.

"Later; there will be many men sleeping in the street; I hope to meet them in their dreams, which can be so sweet." She smiled and glanced at Gynethe Mehaut. "I've been telling her about the way my life has been, how I have lived and what I have endured—not to boast, mind you, but to let her know what could lie ahead of her if she decides to come to our life: why it would be especially dangerous for her, and why it is precarious to have two vampires in a city this size."

Gynethe Mehaut managed a ghost of a smile. "It is true. She has told me about her life and how much it is like mine. But she can hide her nature, and I cannot hide mine." She sighed. "Yet both of us must fear the sun, as you have said, and both of us are feared. Olivia says it is ignorance. It seems otherwise to me, but both of you have told me the same thing." She looked up at the clear, November sky, at the brilliant stars. "I have tended the night-blooming flowers since I was a child. I know the stars as if they're Saints. I see them from season to season, and I watch the moon."

"And what have you learned?" asked Rakoczy.

"I've realized that all things come as God Wills," she said, and looked at Olivia. "I know you see it otherwise, and I suppose the Magnatus does, as well."

"You must forgive us," said Olivia. "It is our nature." She put her shears in the pail and left off all semblance of tending her garden. "The longer you delay telling us what happened, the worse we will assume it is."

Rakoczy lowered his eyes. "I know. And I'm sorry to hesitate."

"Then it isn't good," said Gynethe Mehaut fatalistically.

"No, it isn't. But it could be worse," Rakoczy said, wanting to offer some mitigation. "The King has ordered me to start for the north after Epiphany. He wants me to be in Franksland as soon as the passes are open. It would be folly to disobey him."

"Particularly now," said Olivia. "Yes. Great Karl would not take well to his authority being compromised, and by a foreigner."

"You do understand," said Rakoczy; he turned to Gynethe Mehaut. "Until then I am to remain your escort and you will be allowed to reside here. What will happen after that, I cannot say."

Gynethe Mehaut folded her arms across her chest. "It is in the Hands of God."

Olivia shook her head. "No. Unfortunately it is in the hands of men." She saw Rakoczy nod in agreement as he went to Gynethe Mehaut, holding out his hand to her.

She looked away. "I am not . . . There is no reason to . . ." Huddling into the folds of her veil, she wrapped herself in misery, refusing all sympathy and comfort as she considered her future.

TEXT OF A LETTER FROM FRATRE GRIMHOLD IN ROMA TO BISHOP FRECULF IN FRANKSLAND, CARRIED BY ROYAL COURIER AND DELIVERED TWO WEEKS AFTER EASTER.

To the most excellent, Sublime Freculf, Bishop and servant to the Emperor, whom God save, on this, the Feast of the Circumcision, the first day of the year 801 by the Pope's calendar. Amen

This is to inform you of all that has happened since Karl-lo-Magne and Pope Leo entered this city in triumph toward the end of last November. It is most regrettable that you were not able to come here to see these fine events for yourself. May God, Who seeth all things, impart to you the wisdom to know His Will in this time of so many glorious victories and so many griefs.

The celebrations of the Pope's return lasted for three days, and the people spent every waking hour in the streets, although on the third day there was a terrible storm, and some of those celebrating took ill and some died of putrid lungs. I cannot tell you what excesses were committed in the name of this sacred occasion, but I must tell you that a goodly number of prostitutes are exhausted but richer than they were before the Pope came back to the city. The meetings at the Lateranus were ongoing from the time of the Pope's return, and the Churchmen and Karl-lo-Magne's Court had many things to work out among them so that the coronation might proceed without challenge or incident.

The first matter was the Pope's Declaration of Innocency, which was given before all the Bishops and Cardinal Archbishops in Roma; now anyone doubting the Pope's virtue must have proof to present that is incontrovertible, or that person will become a criminal. Rumors may continue, but their damage has been curtailed, and the Pope has made himself all but impervious to any slander, which in turn ensures his authority and ascendancy in the Church. I have seen the Cardinal Archbishops debate among themselves what is to become of the Pope if the Byzantines should press their advantage at the beginning of the new year, but it is generally agreed that with his Declaration the Pope has removed himself from all but the most egregious attacks, and those can be dismissed as spite. The Byzantines must take all this into account if they are to move on Roma or the Church.

On the day of the Mass of Christ, the men of the Church all gathered as our faith compels us, at Sant' Pier's Basilica. Among them were all the Potenti and Bellatori of the Franks, including the King, all of whom attended the Mass with all respect and reverence, their conduct worthy of all Christians. Karl-lo-Magne wore a white dalmatica of fine wool and a mantellum of green edged in silver, as if he were a Roman patrician and not a

Frank. The entire Basilica glowed with new silver brought by the Franks and hammered into foil by the artisans of Roma. All 1,365 candles in the candelabrum were lit, so the entire interior was bright as day. When the Pope himself had celebrated the Mass with Cardinal Archbishops to assist him in the Mass, he summoned Karl-lo-Magne to the tomb of Sant' Pier, where Great Karl knelt to read the Gospels and there Leo crowned him Emperor of the Franks and Longobards and Imperial Governor of All the Romans in the West. The Emperor's praises were sung, and the litanies of exultation recited. Then, to the astonishment of many—and the fury of some—the Pope knelt to Karl-lo-Magne and did him obedience as would any lord in the world, or the Byzantines would do to their Emperor. All the congregation were required to adore him, nobles and clerics alike. Karl-lo-Magne accepted this and pledged to guard and protect the Church as he would his own lands.

There was a great feast that night, greater than the Feast of the Nativity on the previous night, for this one was to honor the Franks as well as Our Lord. Some of the Cardinal Archbishops were displeased, and were heard to complain loudly that the Pope had betrayed the Church by making himself subject to the Emperor. Others said that in spite of his Declaration, Leo III was no longer worthy to hold his exalted position and should resign for the good of the Church and all Christendom. This was quickly silenced by the Frankish Churchmen, and many of the Bishops who had accompanied the Emperor to Roma were loud in their condemnation of these Cardinal Archbishops. Many of these discussions quickly grew acrimonious, and by morning there were many with blackened eyes and other injuries to serve as tokens of their disagreements. I did not attend the great feasts, for monks and priests were not included among those invited to the Lateranus for the splendid meal. I attended the meal served at the House of the Franks, which, while plentiful and of good quality, was not the equal of what the Pope could command for his guests.

I have been informed that Gynethe Mehaut will be summoned before the Pope in three days, where testimony will be given in regard to her and all she has done. The hope is that the examination may be kept private so that more scandal will not be visited upon the Church just now. Nonetheless, she will have to listen to praise and accusation and answer any questions the Pope may choose to address to her. Based on what he hears, he will decide what is to become of her. I should warn you that Bishop Iso has been busy trying to find those who will speak against the White Woman, saying she is an agent of the Anti-Christ, and demonstrating how she has shown this over the years; his woman, Sorra Celinde, has been commanded to tell all that she knows.

Because of this, and because so much of what she does has been under scrutiny, I have decided not to attempt to do away with Hiernom Rakoczy, at least not until the decision in regard to Gynethe Mehaut has been made. Any action taken against him is likely to attract Papal attention, and that, in turn, might lead to many questions. If, after the examination of Gynethe Mehaut is complete, it is decided that Magnatus Rakoczy has contributed to her corruption, I shall follow your orders and see him killed. But I must warn you, it may be that in so doing I will bring your part in all this to light, and if that happens, your victory may be short-lived, and Gynethe Mehaut may be the one to pay the price for your attempts to save her from the intrusions of the world. I know you believe she carries the marks of crucifixion as a sign of blessing and favor, and you wish to eliminate anything that might serve to blight her recognition, but I am also convinced that there is good reason for you to guard yourself in this, for you may have to answer for your efforts on her behalf. You may wish to know that the Emperor has ordered Rakoczy to return to his fiscs as soon as possible: he is to leave Roma at Epiphany, in the company of nine soldiers, or so a slave in the Emperor's train has told me. I thanked him with a woolen blanket and a dagger through his side, for which I have Confessed and received Absolution.

Although this may seem like defiance, I am still your servant, and I am as devoted to you as I am to the Church. You may repose trust in me from now until God summons me to His Throne, to judge me and all men.

Fratre Grimhold
by my own hand

～

chapter eleven

"WE ARE HERE AT THE PLEASURE of Pope Leo the Third," said Rakoczy to the Lateranus Guard who held his spear up to halt the foreigner wrapped in a black mantellum of boiled wool, riding a grey horse and leading a plausterum drawn by a pair of liver-colored ponies with flaxen manes and tails.

"I am Hiernom Rakoczy and I have the honor to escort Gynethe Mehaut." Although it was mid-morning frost still glistened on the road and roofs of the city, and a biting wind whipped out of the north, sending debris flying and chilling everything it met.

The Lateranus Guard cocked his head. "At what hour were you summoned?" He made a point of exchanging glances with the other Guards on duty at the gate. It was four days since the Mass of Christ, and Roma in the wake of such grand celebration had sunk into lethargy. The streets were half-empty, the chapels had closed their doors, and even the beggars remained inside, waiting for the day to improve before venturing out.

"At Terce," said Rakoczy. "There should be someone to escort us to His Holiness."

"There should be," said the Lateranus Guard. He leaned back against the closed gates. "I haven't seen anyone yet this morning who could admit you."

"There will be a priest or a monk come for us," said Rakoczy confidently.

"I can't open the gate until I have the authorization," said the Guard.

"Of course not," said Rakoczy, as the bells of Sant' Ioannes Lateranus began to toll for Terce. "And I expect our usher will be here directly."

His calmness was troubling to the Guard, who was more used to bluster or subservience. "We all serve the Pope."

"And the Emperor," said Rakoczy as an old priest appeared in the warder-door. Reverencing the priest from the saddle, Rakoczy said, "Unless I am mistaken, our usher is here."

The Guard gestured to his comrades. "Find out whom the priest wants."

"The White Woman and her Magnatus escort," said the old priest, smoothing his beard. He shifted his weight from foot to foot as if trying to keep warm.

"We are at your service," said Rakoczy, tugging the ponies' lead to bring the plausterum up to the gates; they swung open with complaints from the massive hinges that clashed with the sounds of the bells. The Guard stood aside and made a hint of a reverence as Rakoczy brought the plausterum through into the court-yard where a pair of grooms stood, trying to appear alert.

The priest came up to Rakoczy's horse. "You will go to the chapel to Santa Viviana the Martyr, where the Pope will receive you. He and the Court of those who are to judge the White Woman are assembled there now. The chapel is on the far side of the High Altar." He ducked his head respectfully.

"You aren't going to come with us?" Rakoczy asked as he dismounted.

"No. His Holiness has said you are to bring her alone." He touched his hands together in a sign of petition. "I must do the Pope's bidding."

"And so must we," said Rakoczy, handing his grey to a groom who bustled forward. "Loosen the girth and see that he has water. The same for the ponies." He held out the leads to the groom. "Do not unhitch the plausterum."

The groom lowered his head. "I'll stall them together."

"Very good," said Rakoczy, and gave the groom a silver coin before he went to the back of the plausterum to help Gynethe Mehaut to descend; she was wrapped in an ankle-length capa, a long veil over her head and hanging almost to her knees. Rakoczy reverenced her and pointed toward the side entrance to Sant' Ioannes.

"I am ready." She managed to speak without a tremor in her voice and took an absurd moment of pride in this. Under the veil she folded her freshly band-aged hands and began to walk. "I'm glad they're all at prayers," she said quietly to Rakoczy. "I wouldn't want them to stare at me."

"Then it is as well that he summoned us when he did," said Rakoczy, going through a narrow doorway and looking into the dimness. Far ahead he saw the shine of light from the low dome lantern four stories above, long bars of muted illumination suffusing the area around the High Altar. "The chapel of Santa Viviana is on the far side." Ambrosian chants echoed and rang along the stone vault, making harmony of plainsong.

"Yes. I know what the priest said. I may be white, and too much light may blind me, but I hear well enough." She held her hands together, putting a bit more distance between her and Rakoczy, a subtle reminder that she had no wish to be touched. "Lead the way, Rakoczy."

They stopped to reverence the High Altar and continued on through the incense-scented gloom, looking for the chapel of Santa Viviana, neither speaking. At last, among a line of chapels, they found a grated door standing open, and the glow of many candles from within. A fresco on the wall showed a young woman holding an olive branch in one hand and a cross in the other. Benches were set out in an octagon before the altar; Pope Leo occupied the center bench all by him-self; Bishops and Cardinal Archbishops flanked him, and behind them stood the witnesses, including Sorra Celinde, who kept her gaze directed at Bishop Iso.

Rakoczy paused in the door to reverence the august gathering within. He stood aside and allowed Gynethe Mehaut to enter the chapel; she was trembling, but she was able to maintain her composure as she reverenced the Bishops and Cardinal Archbishops, then knelt to the Pope, remaining on her knees after she had kissed the Fisherman's Ring.

"You may leave us," said Pope Leo, dismissing Rakoczy with a motion of his hand. The scars on his face were still faintly pink and distorted his speech a little.

"Alas, Holiness, I fear I must refuse," Rakoczy said as respectfully as he could. "The Emperor has made me Gynethe Mehaut's escort: I have been with her from the Royal Residence at Attigny to Roma, and until you have decided her fate, I am bound to stay with her or fail in my duty to Great Karl."

The Cardinal Archbishops began to mutter among themselves, and one of them spat to show his opinion of the situation. The Frankish Bishops seemed confused, for they had no wish to abrogate the Emperor's commands. They were on the verge of serious debate when the venerable Roman aristocrat Cardinal Archbishop Ittalus spoke up. "This foreigner is right. If he is her escort mandated to accompany the White Woman by the Emperor, he is obliged to remain." This silenced all objection, for Cardinal Archbishop Ittalus was known to be more knowledgeable on matters of vassalage and fealty than any other Churchman in Roma.

Pope Leo made a nod of concession and summoned a slave with a small, brass bell. "The Magnatus must sit. Find him a chair." The slave hurried to obey, returning shortly with an old-fashioned Roman chair that he placed apart from the others. Once he was gone, the Pope continued. "We are here today on the matter of the woman, Gynethe Mehaut, to determine if she bears a sign of Godly favor or is a harbinger of the Anti-Christ. All of us are enjoined to listen to all she says, and to contemplate carefully what the witnesses say. While we engage in this task, we will observe no Hours, nor will we take food or water; our devotion to the right must be complete or we will not deserve this task God has set for us. All our questions and testimony must conclude by sunset; we will then all celebrate Vespers and prepare for an evening of meditation and prayer. You, White Woman"—he addressed her directly for the first time—"remove your veil."

Very slowly Gynethe Mehaut complied, handing the lovely silk to Rakoczy as she listened to the whispers and oaths that accompanied her exposure. She found that she was remembering her days at Santa Albegunda, and for a moment she missed the convent with an intensity that bordered on despair.

"Now remove the bandages from your hands," Pope Leo ordered her.

She obeyed, carefully rolling the linen strips so that she could use them again. When both her palms were bare, she extended her hands toward the Pontiff. The puncture wounds were easily seen in the candlelight; they were bleeding sluggishly today, so it took a short while for a drop of blood to fall to the stone floor.

This time the whispers were alarmed, even frightened. Cardinal Archbishop Paulinus Evitus made a sign of protection; Bishop Gondebaud covered his eyes and turned away.

"How come you by those wounds, White Woman?" Pope Leo demanded, obviously shaken by what he had seen.

"I cannot say," Gynethe Mehaut answered softly.

"What do you do to get them?" Cardinal Archbishop Iovinus asked, repelled and fascinated at once.

"I cannot say," Gynethe Mehaut repeated.

"But you must do *something*," the Pope exclaimed. "Wounds like that do not simply appear."

"These do," said Gynethe Mehaut; she sounded tired already.

"How?" Cardinal Archbishop Ittalus asked, his tone carefully neutral.

"I don't know, Sublime." She pressed her lips together.

"Actually, I am properly called Primore," Cardinal Archbishop Ittalus said.

"I don't know, Primore; I wish I did," Gynethe Mehaut corrected herself. "It began when I was young. No one knew what the cause was. I never sought them. I did what I could to be rid of them. My parents, too, wanted them gone: they did all they knew to heal the wounds, but, as you see, nothing could make them close." She had a brief, vivid recollection of some of the treatments, and her stomach tightened.

"Were the wounds not cauterized with hot irons?" asked Cardinal Archbishop Rufinus Colonnus.

"Four times," said Gynethe Mehaut, feeling a bit faint; she reminded herself that the inquiry was just beginning and that she had much more to deal with before the day was over.

"And still your hands bleed!" Bishop Didier marveled.

"As you see," said Gynethe Mehaut, wishing she could lower her hands, but not daring to.

"Does it never stop?" Cardinal Archbishop Iovinus inquired, doing his best to keep the perturbation out of his voice.

"Not that I have been aware of," said Gynethe Mehaut.

"Have you repented your sins?" Cardinal Archbishop Rufinus Colonnus asked her, his temper barely in check. "How dare you have such wounds."

"Exactly what I have maintained from my first sight of her," said Bishop Iso, springing to his feet. "She is the embodiment of the Anti-Christ! Look at her!"

"Sit down, Sublime Iso," said Pope Leo, and waited until he was obeyed. "You may tell us what you saw and how you regarded it when you are called to bear witness. Until then, keep your peace."

"Yes, Holiness," he said with the appearance of contrition, although his eyes shone with anger.

Pope Leo saw Bishop Iso's distress. "My son in Christ," he said placatingly, "learn to bear all with Patience, which is a Cardinal Virtue. Address your prayers to that end."

"I will," said Bishop Iso. "But is it not incumbent upon me, as a Christian, to denounce Satan's Work wherever I see it?"

"It is, and you shall, but in the right time," said Pope Leo. He rubbed his jaw along the jagged scar, then went on. "You have already demonstrated your position, and I am well-aware of it. You needn't worry that I will lose sight of all you have told me." He made a sign for protection. "May God keep us from harm."

"Amen," said everyone in the chapel.

The Pope gave his attention to Gynethe Mehaut again. "You have done penance for these . . . these injuries, haven't you?"

"And my skin, and my eyes," said Gynethe Mehaut tonelessly.

"Yet you are still pale as whey," Pope Leo said, shaking his head. "How is it God could so afflict you, were it not that you have done some wrong deserving of punishment?"

"I don't know, Holiness, nor do I know why." She lowered her head and her hands. "If I have done anything against God's Law, I cannot think what it could be. I have been guided by the Church since I was a child, and all I have done has been scrutinized."

Watching this, Rakoczy wanted to explain to the Churchmen that occasionally infants came into the world in this way, that it was not a failure of faith, but an accident of birth; he held his tongue, for this argument would mean nothing to the clerics, and might serve to put Gynethe Mehaut in more danger than she already was. He hoped he would be given the opportunity to speak on her behalf, but knew better than to expect such a concession, even from Pope Leo, who was so much beholden to Karl-lo-Magne that he might as well be one of the Emperor's vassals. He put his hands on his knees and listened closely to all that was going on.

"—because of your parents?" Bishop Didier was asking.

"How could they have done this? What act of theirs would visit itself upon my flesh in this way?" Gynethe Mehaut asked. "It was a dreadful burden for them, heavier than most have to bear. My father sometimes said he had been cursed and I was proof of it."

"Some beasts have red eyes. If your mother had congress with such an animal, one with a white coat, surely you might bear the mark of it," said Bishop Gondebaud.

"My mother would not do such a despicable act," said Gynethe Mehaut with a little heat in her words. "If she had, she would have Confessed and they would have drowned her for it, and I would never have been born."

"Your father, then? Could he have been possessed by a demon when you were conceived, or a demon taken his form planted you in your mother's womb?" Bishop Gondebaud pursued.

"I cannot say if a demon possessed my father," Gynethe Mehaut said. "But he said that God had marked me to some purpose, and that I must bear it or bring more shame upon my family."

"A wise man, no doubt, and one who may have enemies capable of blighting his child before birth," said Pope Leo. "Yet that may be the knowledge of experience, of one who has caused ill to others and has been made, through this woman, to pay the price. What might he have done that would bring this upon his child?"

"I suspect the father may have been a priest of the old gods, and gave his daughter to their use," said Bishop Gondebaud. "Many simple people still try to follow the old ways, forsaking their salvation."

"Sublime Gondebaud is right," said Cardinal Archbishop Paulinus Evitus. "Even here in Italy, the old ways still have adherents."

Rakoczy wondered what Olivia would think of this condemnation, with her lares still on display on the iconostasis, presented as Saints instead of household gods and ancestors. How many others, he asked himself, used similar devices to keep up the traditions of Imperial Roma?

"You can see her eyes are red," said Bishop Didier. "Surely this can't be a sign of Heavenly favor." He had got to his feet and began to pace.

"No, indeed," said Cardinal Archbishop Ittalus. "God requires that we be vigilant."

"We are doing so," said Pope Leo. "We are here to do His work." He leaned forward. "White Woman, do you recall anything your father might have said that would account for your condition? Remember you are in God's Court here."

"I have always been dedicated to God and His Good," said Gynethe Mehaut, beginning to feel as if all this was futile.

Cardinal Archbishop Iovinus regarded her narrowly; he rose and approached her, looming above her so that his shadow fell across her. "It is a simple thing to say, but how can we know it is anything more than sophistry?"

"If Bishop Freculf were here—" Gynethe Mehaut began, then stopped herself: Bishop Freculf was in Franksland, and anything he might have said on her behalf was of no consequence here. "I have spent many years doing penance; I have kept the night-blooming gardens at convents where I have lived, because I cannot easily endure the light of day without hurting my eyes and burning my skin. I have prayed in my cubiculum, keeping all the Hours, and I have lain before the altar from Vigil to Matins, reciting the Psalms."

"Very commendable, if the prayers you say are to the Glory of God, and not the worship of Satan," said Cardinal Archbishop Ittalus.

"I have prayed as the Priora and the Abba, and the Bishop, have instructed me, remembering always that Christ suffered to take our sins away and to redeem us." She had to fight back tears; they weren't listening to her, they were deciding among themselves already, and she could not change their minds. She saw two more drops of blood on the floor and wished she could rewrap her hands.

"That is worthy conduct," said Bishop Gondebaud dubiously. "But if you have been so devoted, how is it that you are still white and your hands bleed?"

"I cannot say," Gynethe Mehaut told him.

Pope Leo clapped his hands. "We have witnesses," he reminded the Bishops and Cardinal Archbishops. "It is fitting that we let them speak." The men were immediately silent: they resumed their seats and became decorous once more; the Pope cleared his throat. "I will hear the first witness. Come forward and give your testimony."

One of the witnesses came around the end of the benches and knelt before the Pope; he was an old man, with gnarled fingers and a bent spine, his eyes rheumy and moist. "May God save you, Holiness."

"Amen," said Pope Leo. "Who are you and what is your testimony in this matter?"

"I am Foudu. I am a mendicant, and have been since I escaped from slavery in Carinthia. I was despised because I am a Christian, and I prayed when they said I should work. When I escaped, I came here to Roma as a pilgrim and have remained, a tertiary monk and mendicant." He rubbed his knotted fingers together. "I have begged in Roma for four years. I saw this White Woman arrive in Roma; she came surrounded by a flock of black ravens, and they swept about her in a cloud. She spoke to them in their tongue and they did her homage. She pointed to men in the street and they fell dead, the ravens alighting to feed upon them."

Rakoczy got to his feet. "Holiness, may I question this man? I escorted Gynethe Mehaut to Roma, and I saw nothing of this."

"You may ask him three things," said Pope Leo. "But remember that God gives special sight to those who suffer in His Name."

"I won't question his devotion," Rakoczy said, and turned to the kneeling mendicant. "Tell me, Foudu, what time of year was it that you saw this portent?"

"I saw it as Holy December was beginning, and the churches set out their lights for Sant' Ioseppi and Santa Maria." He made a sign of protection.

"And what time of day was this? What Hour was being sung?" Rakoczy inquired.

"Sept was sounding," said Foudu. "I had knelt to recite the Psalms."

"Very good," said Rakoczy. "And other than ravens, what companions did she have?"

"A hunchback with one empty eye and the other white as hoar," said the mendicant.

Rakoczy turned to face Pope Leo. "Holiness," he said, "I swear before you, and your God, and by the trust reposed upon me by the Emperor Karlus Magnus, that I and three armed men escorted Gynethe Mehaut into Roma in September.

She rode in a plausterum, covered, and drawn by a mule. If this man saw us arrive, he did not see the things he has described. I do not say that this man has not had a vision, but he has not seen Gynethe Mehaut in it. The soldiers of the escort are still in Roma; I can summon them to testify before you. If you wish to hear these men, I will go to the House of Franks and bring them to you before Sept. I can ask our hostess to tell you how long we have been guests at her house, and in what state we arrived."

"You are with Bonna Dama Clemens, aren't you?" asked Cardinal Archbishop Rufinus Colonnus. "A most useful woman, beyond all doubt."

"Yes. We are guests of that widow," said Rakoczy.

"I will send a messenger to her, a monk, so that she may swear to her account," said Cardinal Archbishop Rufinus Colonnus. "If it will suit your purpose, Holiness."

"Oh, yes. By all means see it is done," said Pope Leo. He contemplated the mendicant. "Do you say it was this woman you saw? This woman, and no other." He pointed to Gynethe Mehaut. "By your soul. Bearing false witness is a grave sin."

"The woman I saw had skin like milk and eyes like embers, young and of a hideous beauty. It had to be her," said Foudu.

"There, you see?" Bishop Iso demanded, pointing to Foudu. "He knows her for what she is."

"The Anti-Christ is not a woman accompanied by ravens, no matter what color her skin and eyes may be," Rakoczy said. "*The Apocalypse* has no such avatar in it. The Whore of Babylon rides on a many-headed beast, and has no ravens." He stared over at Bishop Iso. "You've read the signs, haven't you, as Sant' Ioannes saw them, and wrote them in his book?"

"Yes," said Bishop Iso. "And I know Satan is filled with wiles and has as many disguises as there are stars in the sky."

"Why should Satan, if he can disguise his demons, send one into the world so obvious as this?" Rakoczy asked, and glanced at Cardinal Archbishop Ittalus. "You are said to be learned. What would be the point of having such a woman as this be the agent of Satan? Wouldn't it be more in keeping with the trials God gives to those who might achieve sainthood?"

"Blasphemy!" shouted Bishop Iso.

"Possibly not," said Cardinal Archbishop Rufinus Colonnus, studying Gynethe Mehaut as if seeing her for the first time. "But if Satan wished to deceive mankind, he might present us with the model of sanctity but in such a way that all eyes would be on her, and her example, by appearing virtuous, would lead others to emulate her and thus fall from Grace."

"But that would only be if she were considered deserving of emulation. If that were the case, this Court would not be sitting," Rakoczy said, speaking directly to the Pope. "She has lived withdrawn from the world, doing humble work and praying. What more can she do to prove her merit?"

Pope Leo shook his head. "This is one of the matters we must consider, with all the rest. Let us hear another witness." He gestured to the gathering behind the benches. "Fratre Lothar. Come forward."

The monk with the ruined hand came and knelt before the Pope. He ignored Foudu, as if he were afraid of contagion. "I am your humble servant, Holiness."

"Amen," said Pope Leo. "Give us your testimony, Fratre, and may God give you to know the Right. We will attend to your words and your manner."

"So I pray," said Fratre Lothar. "I tell you this in all duty, in humility and devotion. To this end, I tell you that I have been in Roma more than a year. I came from Franksland with my Fratri, and have resided in the monastery attached to the House of the Franks, Sant' Ioannes. But before I was a monk, I was a soldier, and because of that, I sometimes talk with Frankish soldiers, to learn what has become of my old comrades. This is not uncommon; many monks who were soldiers do the same. In that habit, I had reason to dine with the remainder of Gynethe Mehaut's soldiers, those who accompanied her from Franksland to Roma. These men are known to Magnatus Rakoczy and the Emperor." He stopped to take a deep breath. "I spoke with these men—they told me of their travels with this White Woman, and what became of them in their travels."

"What did they tell you?" the Pope inquired.

"They said that they had lost three men—almost half their number—coming here. The first was killed in Franksland by a bison. This was a terrible misfortune, or so they all supposed. What else could such a death be? They said at the time, that they thought nothing more of it, and that in their journey over the mountains nothing more worrisome occurred." Fratre Lothar made a sign of protection. "So they were safe enough for some of their journey, but then two of the men quarreled for reasons that had not troubled them earlier, and Einshere, the leader of the escort, killed Notrold, and, I have learned, succumbed himself to fever in a penitent's cell. All this could have happened by God's Will without any intervention of the White Woman, but the soldiers who rode beside her to guard her are certain that their misfortunes were caused by her presence, and they hold her responsible for the loss of Pepin, Notrold, and Einshere."

"How did you come to learn of this?" Bishop Gondebaud asked. "You say you have been a soldier. Is that why they would impart such things to you?"

"Of course, and Sulpicius is my kinsman, although a distant one," said Fratre Lothar.

"Why have their Confessors told us nothing?" asked Cardinal Archbishop Rufinus Colonnus.

"I don't know what they have Confessed. I am only a monk, and I hear nothing under the Confessional Seal." Fratre Lothar lowered his eyes. "I can't tell you what their Confessors know."

"May I speak to this witness, Holiness?" Rakoczy asked.

The Pope paused for a moment. "All right. But you may not question this monk's character or his veracity—that has already been established to my satisfaction."

Rakoczy contemplated Fratre Lothar. "When you had your discussions with the soldiers, where did they take place?"

"In the House of the Franks," said Fratre Lothar. "I thought that was plain."

"But where in the House of the Franks? The building is large and has many halls and chambers for any number of purposes. Where were you when you talked with these soldiers?"

"With the other soldiers, of course. In their dining hall." He shrugged as if the answer were obvious. "They would not come to the monastery, and if they did, they would not come for talk, but for worship."

"Yes," said Rakoczy. "That is my point. They welcomed you to the soldiers' dining hall. The men eat and drink there, do they not?"

"Of course. All men dine in dining halls," said Fratre Lothar. He considered Rakoczy narrowly. "They said you were a very capable soldier in your way."

"That was good of them," said Rakoczy, refusing to be distracted. "Is it possible that the stories they told were improved, made more exciting, more boastful?" He held up his hands. "No. Don't tell me that never happens; we both know how soldiers love to tell of their adventures. So it could be that some of their tales were meant to entertain the listeners as much as impart the truth." He bent down to look into Fratre Lothar's eyes.

"Soldiers do like to boast," said Fratre Lothar.

"And some soldiers are wary of signs, so that they see them in everything from clouds to cheese." He let Fratre Lothar think about this. "Do you tell me you have never seen this?"

Fratre Lothar shrugged. "I knew a Bellatore who would not attack if the opposing leader rode a spotted horse."

"Exactly," said Rakoczy, and was about to go on when the Pope lifted his hand.

"I take your meaning, Magnatus. Stand back. Cardinal Archbishop Rufinus Colonnus, you may question this monk on behalf of all the Cardinal Archbishops. If others have questions, let them wait until Cardinal Archbishop Rufinus Colonnus has finished, and then inform me of what they wish to ask." He sat back, his hand on his jaw as if to support it.

"Tell me, Fratre," said the Cardinal Archbishop, "since you have been studying all the accounts of the White Woman for three months, what indications has she given that she was one of Satan's hosts?"

"There were deaths among those who escorted her," said Fratre Lothar.

"Is there anything that made them suppose—at the time—that she was the cause of the deaths, or did that only come to them later?" Cardinal Archbishop Rufinus Colonnus kept his voice calm.

"I cannot know. I only spoke to them after they arrived here in Roma," said Fratre Lothar. He bent forward and touched his forehead to the floor.

"But this is what they told you," prompted the Cardinal Archbishop.

"Yes. That is what I was told. On my honor as a soldier and my vows as a monk." He sat up again, looking directly at the Pope. "And so I swear."

Pope Leo nodded. "You were right to come forward. Rise and go to your prayers, Fratre." He waited while Fratre Lothar got to his feet, reverenced the Pope, the Cardinal Archbishops, and the Bishops, then hastened out of the chapel without looking again at Gynethe Mehaut. "Who is the next witness?"

Sorra Celinde stepped forward, her head lowered and her whole manner subdued. "I am, if you will permit me to speak, though I am a woman."

Bishop Iso rose. "This nun has served me for many years. You may repose trust in her. She will put herself in the service to the Church by giving her testimony if you will permit it."

"You have told me so already," said Pope Leo, and turned to Sorra Celinde. "It is fitting, since a woman is at the center of this inquiry, that a woman should speak as a witness." He gestured to the nun. "Kneel; give your testimony."

Sorra Celinde did as the Pope instructed her. "May God support me in this hour, and aid me in this difficult time," she said, making a gesture of protection.

"Amen," said the Pope, indicating that she should speak.

"As Bishop Iso has said," Sorra Celinde began, just above a whisper, "I have served him for many years, and I am devoted to him as the embodiment of the Church in Franksland, and the source of God's Wisdom for all in the world." She turned her gaze on Bishop Iso as if she adored him. "This is a rigorous matter, and I cannot easily speak of what I have seen and what I have suspected." She glanced at Gynethe Mehaut. "In Franksland, I saw her when she was brought for examination into the bishopric of Bishop Iso. Her former guardian, Priora Iditha of Santa Albegunda, could no longer fulfill her duties to this woman, who was then entrusted to me on behalf of Bishop Iso. I accepted this responsibility because Bishop Iso required it. I shared a cubiculum with the White Woman, and I was able to observe her for many days. She prayed as she was required to do, and she tended the night-blooming gardens, as she has stated. She rested indoors for much of the day, and read holy texts."

"All admirable acts," said Pope Leo.

"When they are sincere and devoted," agreed Sorra Celinde, with a hint of doubt in her face. "But anyone can mimic piety."

"Yes," said Cardinal Archbishop Ittalus. "So one can." He put his hands together in supplication. "May we be preserved from such deception."

"In all things," said Sorra Celinde, and waited for a signal from Pope Leo to continue. "I was charged with following this woman in order to see what she did, that she kept the Hours as she was required to do. I was also told to determine what caused the bleeding in her hands. I thought she must have a needle somewhere about her clothing, and that she must use it to prick her palms in order to keep bleeding. I never actually saw her do such a thing, but I am certain she must do something." She sighed heavily. "It must be that she wounds herself, or she is truly a messenger from Hell, and been given the blood as a sign of her perfidy."

"Is there anything more?" Pope Leo asked when Sorra Celinde stopped talking.

"Yes, Holiness," she murmured. "I have watched her in the night-blooming garden, and seen her dance to the moon. She has made wreaths of night flowers and worn them in her white hair, in the manner of the ancient pagans. She has summoned a lover out of the darkness and embraced him. I saw it. I heard her cry aloud in passion."

Gynethe Mehaut put her hands to her face. "I never did that!" she protested.

"You did," said Sorra Celinde, swinging around to face her. "You don't think anyone can see what you are, and you believe that if you pose and posture, you will deceive the Church and all good Christians. But I know you for the monster you are. I have seen you when you thought you weren't watched, and you cannot tell me that you didn't summon a lover, and engage in the lewd acts of carnality."

"No. No!" Gynethe Mehaut cried. "You have spied upon me, and now I know why: you planned to betray me from the first. You have sworn to see me condemned, and all to please your Bishop. If Bishop Freculf had come here, Bishop Iso would not dare to let you do this!"

Sorra Celinde scrambled to her feet and moved out of Gynethe Mehaut's reach. "Unspeakable!" she shrieked as she backed away.

"You have nothing to fear," the Pope admonished her. "You are in a holy church, and everyone here will protect you." He motioned her to move to his side. "Now you cannot doubt that you are safe."

"She is the handmaiden of Satan." She made a sign of protection. "My God keep you from her many stratagems."

"You speak as if she has worked them upon you," said Cardinal Archbishop Paulinus Evitus.

"Of course she has. I began by wanting to protect her, but when I discerned her purpose, the scales were lifted from my eyes." She pointed at Gynethe Mehaut. "Let her say what she likes, she is the heart of evil."

Rakoczy listened with a sinking sensation in his chest. "May I ask the witness a question?"

"No!" Sorra Celinde shouted. "He is in her thrall!"

Pope Leo smiled sadly. "It would not be right." He motioned Rakoczy into silence and looked back at Sorra Celinde. "You see? You have nothing to fear."

"But who will speak for me?" Gynethe Mehaut asked desperately.

"God will defend you, if you are virtuous. If you are not, then you will know that Satan has forsaken you," said the Pope.

Listening to this, Rakoczy felt a fatalistic gloom settle over him; Sorra Celinde continued to rail against Gynethe Mehaut, and no one was willing to stop or question her. He wondered what he could do to protect Gynethe Mehaut now, and tried to think of some way to comfort the pale woman kneeling near enough for him to touch, and yet as far away as if he were in the land of the Great Khan and she at the ends of Hispania.

TEXT OF AN ORDER OF REQUISITION SUBMITTED TO THE EMPEROR KARL-LO-MAGNE FOR HIS APPROVAL ON JANUARY 4, 801.

For the north-bound journey of Magnatus Rakoczy, ordered by Karl-lo-Magne, the Emperor, the following men and supplies are requisitioned:

Men:	*Willigond*
	Ulfila
	Constantinus of Rheims
	Gradovic son of Baldegard
	Freieus
	Beneventus
	Odobald
	Latifundus
Horses:	*these are to be provided, mounts and remounts, by Magnatus Rakoczy*
Mules:	*the same as horses*
Food:	*of cheese, 6 rounds*
	of beer, two full kegs
	of wine, two full kegs
	of oil, one cask
	of bread, six hard loaves

> *of sausage, nine in casings*
> *of dried cod, one full fish*
> *of honey, one comb*
> *of onions, three strings*
> *of beans, one full sack*
> *of smoked meat, one haunch of venison and one ham*
> **Feed:** *of oats, three sacks*
> *of dried apples, one sack*
> **Weapons:** *to be supplied by the Magnatus*
> **Others:** *twelve unshaped horseshoes*
> *two cooking spits*
> *one cauldron*
>
> *All these are ready to pack in chests and put on mules on the day after Epiphany, if there is no rain.*
>
> *Approved by the Emperor*
> **Karl-lo-Magne**
> *prepared to the order of the Potente Edelfus*
>
> ∽

chapter twelve

A T OLIVIA'S HOUSE, the torches and oil-lamps gleamed long into the night, shining off the snowflakes that drifted over the city, turning everything pale as marble. In Gynethe Mehaut's apartments the window, made of small, costly sections of glass, turned the falling snow to many-faced crystals. It was cold, but the heating channels in the walls from the floor below kept the rooms fairly warm, so that Gynethe Mehaut was wrapped only in her stolla and gonella as she sat in a chair lined in marten-fur, her pale face lit by a stand of oil-lamps.

Rakoczy sat at her feet, holding her bandaged hand in his. "I'm sorry I must leave," he said for the third time that evening.

"It is the order of the King . . . the Emperor," she corrected herself. "You are his vassal."

"His vassal? In some respects," said Rakoczy, "I am. In others, as I am a foreigner, I am not." While this was true, he was aware it made no difference in the orders he had been given; it was only an admission of his diminished protection.

"But you won't stay here," she said, touching his hair with the tips of her fingers.

"It wouldn't be safe for any of us if I did," said Rakoczy with a rueful smile. "Not you, not Olivia, and not I would be able to avoid scrutiny and condemnation."

"You're certain of that," she said, wanting to be persuaded otherwise.

"So are you," he pointed out. "And if I were to remain in Roma, I would have to leave this house, or bring the Church and Karl-lo-Magne's men down upon you. No, I must leave."

Gynethe Mehaut sighed. "I'll miss you."

"And I you," said Rakoczy, already feeling her pull away from him, though she did not move.

"I'm sad," Gynethe Mehaut said a short time later. "I shouldn't be, but I am."

Rakoczy rose on his knees and put his arms around her. "If you are sad, then it is what you should be."

She shook her head. "It is giving way to sin. God sends us what He wishes us to have, and to be sad denies His Goodness. It is the sin of Indolence."

"Who taught you that?" Rakoczy asked, knowing the answer.

"The Sorrae," Gynethe Mehaut said.

"You have a right to your sorrow; it isn't Indolence, it is mourning," said Rakoczy. "If you cannot honor your grief, you lose much of your love."

"Love is for God and the Emperor's Will, for children who live, and for those who protect us." She spoke dreamily, as if far away from him. "That of men and women is mere Lust, and a sin."

"More of the nuns' lessons," said Rakoczy. "You need not accept those things—"

"I don't want to talk about such matters." She pulled her hand away from him. "You speak so . . . I can't believe . . . It isn't as if I . . . I can't tell you; you'll be angry."

"No, I will not," said Rakoczy quietly. "Tell me: I will listen."

"So you say," she murmured. "But you will grow angry with me, and then—"

"I won't be angry—I may be disappointed, and that more for myself than on your account—but never angry. I have tasted your blood and you are part of me. How could I be angry with you?" He turned her face toward him with a light touch of his fingers. "You have my Word, Gynethe Mehaut—I will not be angry."

She studied his eyes as if seeking deceit. She finally mustered her thoughts, took a deep breath, and said, "I never thought anyone would be as kind to me as you have been. But you put questions to me that I cannot answer. No one has ever touched me, but you, without disgust and fear. Yet it has to end. You said, yourself, that you cannot lie with me again after tonight or I will become what you are when I die, and I want no part of such a life. I am what God made me, and to Him I shall return. I will not be compelled to be what you are, no matter how benign you may be." She put her bandaged hand to her brow in an attitude of supplication. "I will accept my life because it is what God has given me. But to rise into a life that isn't His, that would make a true blasphemy of my skin and my eyes, and show that I am what I have been accused of being. I would become what I have been called so unjustly: I would truly be the demon they think I am now."

"You are no demon, and could never be," he said as gently as he could.

"It hardly matters, if Bishop Iso has his way. I will have to endure the fate of all demons, and burn for it." She sighed. "Pope Leo has suffered, and I think he may not condemn me utterly. He knows what it is to have the world against him."

Rakoczy pulled her closer to him. "He is frightened, and that makes him dangerous."

"You tell me so, but I don't know that it's true," she said to him, disengaging herself from his arms.

"Then what do you want of me, Gynethe Mehaut?" he asked, his voice low.

She considered her answer carefully. "I want to lie with you again, this last time. You said it is still safe for us to . . . to comfort our bodies. I want to have your touch to remember. If I must be a martyr to the Church, I will be, but I will have some delight for myself, if only to liven my Confession." She eluded his hands. "Don't press me, or engulf me so. I don't like such embraces."

"As you wish," said Rakoczy, and rose to his feet, holding out his hand to her. "Come. You will choose where we are to lie, and you will tell me what would pleasure you most."

"I don't want to demand more of you than you wish," said Gynethe Mehaut. "You may not intend to give more to me than you have, but there is much I haven't found yet."

"That is why I implore you to tell me what you seek," said Rakoczy, indicating the private room attached to the parlor where he and Gynethe Mehaut had sat for a good part of the evening.

"This is going to be an interesting farewell," said Gynethe Mehaut, as if she had determined to enjoy herself at any cost.

"What do you suppose would please you?" Rakoczy asked as he opened the door. "The bed is made with linen and good fur. You can be comfortable and warm."

She nodded. "This is good," she said, and smiled. "The room is warm; it is much more agreeable to be warm." Glancing nervously in his direction, she said, "I don't know what I should do now; can you tell me what would be best to do?"

"Choose what most gratifies you and that will satisfy us both," said Rakoczy as he went to the side of the bed. "The coverlet on or off?"

"On," she said. "I will lie atop it." She unfastened her girdle and tossed it aside. "Take off my gonella."

Rakoczy moved to her side and slowly lifted the soft woolen garment. "And your stolla?"

"I don't know yet," she said, shivering a little either from cold or anticipation. "Just don't press me," she said again.

"No. I won't." He went to her clothes-tree and took down the largest of the three silken veils Olivia had given her. "This has a touch a breeze could envy," he told her as he ran the sea-foam fabric through his hands. "You may not think so now, but I will show you."

She stood watching him. "You will not bind me?"

"No, I will not," he said, trying to find some way to reassure her. "My Word on—"

"Yes, yes," she said impatiently. "Well, no doubt I will see for myself." She sat on the edge of the bed and stared off toward the lamps hanging near the head of it. "Compline is over and we have until Matins."

"They will ring Vigil," Rakoczy reminded her, puzzled by her state of mind.

"So they will." She lay back. "May God forgive me for my happiness tonight."

"Why should you need forgiveness?" Rakoczy asked, coming a step nearer.

"I should spend the night in penance, as I have done so often. While we traveled, it wasn't possible, but I have been lax since I arrived here. God may not look kindly on my neglect of Him." She held up her bandaged hands. "He could exact contrition."

"You make God sound like a petulant parent, jealous of His own children, and Christ a rebellious youth," said Rakoczy, who had often thought that the understanding of God had shifted from the original teaching of the founder of the Christian faith.

"Don't say that. It is blasphemous," said Gynethe Mehaut distantly. "I don't want to have to repent for listening to you."

"Then perhaps I should be silent," he suggested, coming close to her and letting the edge of the veil drift over her.

She caught the end of the veil in her fingers, letting it trail slowly. "It is so soft."

"It is," Rakoczy agreed, and came to the bed, putting one knee on it and moving the veil so that it fluttered over her.

"It is like a butterfly," she whispered. She pulled her stolla up, exposing her thigh and waiting for him to do more. "Where will you land, lovely butterfly?"

Rakoczy flicked the silk, letting it brush her skin without lingering too long in any one place, flirting it along her body, across her stolla to her hands, and over the bindings that covered the wounds in her palms. Then he floated the silk down her exposed legs, a languid progress that eased her thighs open and brought her nipples erect, honing her senses to a keenness she had not experienced before; every part of her had come alive and was now yearning for greater stimulation. Although he could see the changes coming over Gynethe Mehaut, Rakoczy continued his tantalizing ministrations, using the silk to dally along her legs until she wriggled completely out of her stolla.

"Is this all?" she sighed, her body moving to follow the caresses of the veil.

"For a while yet," Rakoczy said, aware of her increasing arousal. "Doesn't it give you pleasure?"

"Oh, yes," she breathed.

"Good. Then I'll continue," he said, and danced the veil up her taut belly to her small, high breasts.

Her breath hissed into her, and she shivered but not from cold; the sensitivities possessing her brought her to a pitch of excitement that astonished her. That a single piece of silk could work such marvels! She felt its caresses as if they were kisses, and she opened herself to them as she had seen the night-blooming flowers open to the darkness. So caught up was she in the sweet delirium of her body that she hardly noticed when Rakoczy set the silk aside and slowly, exquisitely, stretched out between her legs, gently lowering himself so that his head rested just under her chin. Slowly his hands repeated the lambency of the silk, their touch so light that it was almost as if the air caressed her. Her body responded to him, and she felt a gathering of heat within her that surprised and gladdened her. Gradually she moved to accommodate him, ecstacy putting all her fears to flight while his hands and lips discovered new raptures. Finally she was shaken by a sudden spasm that alarmed her with its intensity, and she pushed against his shoulders.

He moved immediately, lying beside her, his hand resting just beneath her breasts where he could feel her heartbeat, and her breathing. "Gynethe Mehaut," he whispered.

She was panting still, and she took a short time to answer. "Before you . . . The other times . . . This time you didn't . . ."

"It will come," said Rakoczy.

"Aren't you finished?" she asked, her eyes growing wide.

"No; you aren't," he said, a hint of amusement in his dark eyes. "You have only started to learn what your body can give you."

"But—" She stopped herself, not wanting to name the sin she had committed.

"All your life, your body has been your adversary, a necessary vessel for your soul, but not an ally. You resent it, and it isn't surprising that you do." He stroked the line of her ribs. "It dispirits me to see you so blighted. If I can give you nothing else, at least let me have this chance to help you accept your body as a confederate and not an opponent."

"You didn't do this before," she said, suddenly suspicious.

"No; you had no desire for that experience, but you do now." He raised himself on his elbow, the black of his gonelle lying like a shadow along her white skin.

"Why do you say that? How can you know?" She wanted to pull away from him, but her limbs would not obey her will.

"I know that because I know you." He moved his hand up, lightly cupping her breast.

She started to move his hand away and then stopped, unwilling to give up the rapturous sensation that was welling within her once again. "How can you?" she repeated.

"I told you: when I tasted your blood, some of you became part of me." He fingered her nipple, gently, gently, then grazed a kiss on it.

Gynethe Mehaut shuddered deliciously and felt herself lapse again into that apolaustic state that must surely demand repentance at a later time. For now, this was all the world and everything she could desire, and not even the joys of Heaven could lure her from the fervor he awakened in her. She closed her eyes and gave herself up to the ardor and the rapture that Rakoczy evoked in her, a glorification of her living body that she had not expected to find except before the Throne of God. When his lips brushed her neck, the culmination of her passion carried them both far beyond happiness to the fulfillment of joy. After what seemed to be half the night, Gynethe Mehaut opened her eyes and stared at Rakoczy lying beside her. "What was that? I've never experienced anything like it. What happened to me?"

"You found intimacy," he said simply, and carried her hand to his lips to kiss the bandage. "We touched one another, and you touched yourself."

"It was more than that," she said.

"There is no more than that," he told her, and brushed her pale wisps of hair back from her face. "And many people live all their lives without ever knowing what you have known."

"But this is the flesh," said Gynethe Mehaut, a sudden wave of anxiety taking hold of her. "How can it be more than the meeting of skins and the making of children?"

"Because," Rakoczy said softly, "our bodies have touched, and through that, our souls."

"That cannot be true. You drink my blood." She flung the accusation at him as if to barricade herself against the emotions welling within her.

"As you drink wine as the Blood of Christ, to achieve union with the Saints," he reminded her, no trace of blame in his words.

"The Saints abhor the flesh," she said forcefully.

"Some of them do," he conceded.

"The only union for Christians to desire is union with God," Gynethe Mehaut charged him.

"Whose kingdom is within, according to Scripture," Rakoczy reminded her. He moved back, then reached for the blanket of fox-fur that lay atop the chest near the wall. "Here. You'll get cold. Wrap this around you and stay warm."

Gynethe Mehaut huddled into the soft pelts, not entirely to keep warm, but to protect herself from his nearness. She was shivering again, this time for reasons she could not define. "When Vigil sounds, I should go and pray. It will ring shortly, I expect."

"If you think you must, then do," said Rakoczy without any indication of dismay.

She watched him as he rose and gathered up her clothes. "You puzzle me, Magnatus."

The use of his title made him flinch. "Why is that, Gynethe Mehaut?"

"You offer me this gratification as if it were the gift of Angels, and not a sign of the sins of the flesh," she said, trying not to think about the shame that threatened to overcome her.

He began to fold her stolla. "Why cannot you have both?"

She could hardly believe he had spoken. "Impossible. The flesh is the realm of the Devil. All sins lie in the flesh."

He put the stolla down on the chest and picked up the gonella. "Is that why you have come to dread all touching—because you fear the sins of the flesh?"

"As all Christians must," she said as she did her best to make a gesture of protection. "We must turn away from the body to be worthy of Heaven."

He remained very still, profoundly aware of her growing conflict. Watching her, he longed for the means to help her accept her delectation, and recognized the impossibility of it. As he set her clothing aside, he wanted to speak of something that would ease the alienation that had arisen between them so quickly. "When I first came to this life, I was the demon some would have you think I am. But that was almost three thousand years ago, and in time I have learned that the brevity of life is what makes it most precious, and that time itself makes demands upon us. If Heaven has more to demand of us than life does, it is too remote for the living."

She listened to him attentively. "You don't want me to say you have caused me to change my mind, do you?"

"No. I was hoping to show you that I understand why you wouldn't." He came to the foot of the bed and stretched out his hand.

"Then not all your women have become like you," she said, a suggestion of doubt in her tone.

"No; most of them have not," he said, and had a momentary recollection of Csimenae, and another of Nicoris.

Something must have shown in his face, for she said, "Does that trouble you?"

"No; no, it doesn't." He touched her ankle. "If you don't want the life I live, then don't enter it. You are not in danger of it now."

"But it worries you that I would choose not to have it," she persisted. "That's what you expect, isn't it? For me to change my mind and become like you."

"No," he said. "I was remembering someone who should have refused and didn't."

She was immediately curious. "How did that happen? When?"

"It was a long time ago," he said. "Not everyone is ready to live as we do. Not everyone was ready to outlive all children, friends, enemies, and their grand-children, and great-grandchildren until you are gone from memory. Only legend might survive."

She shook her head. "I will never have children." She pulled the fox-fur up to her chin. "I don't know what it would be like to have friends as others do."

Rakoczy said nothing for a short while, and then he said, "I'm sorry you haven't had friendship. You have an aptitude for it."

Gynethe Mehaut laughed once. "I suppose you expect me to cling to you, as my friend if not my lover. You want me to demand your devotion so that I will have to be one with you."

"No," said Rakoczy. "I would never compel anyone to come to my life."

"Wouldn't you?" She waited for him to argue with her.

"I wish I weren't leaving as much as you wish it," said Rakoczy as levelly as he could. "If it were my decision to make, I would remain here at Roma, in my old villa outside the walls."

"Though you say you would not come to my bed again, in case I should end up a vampire," she said bluntly. "You are glad you're leaving."

"No. No, I'm not glad." He came to her side and laid his hand on her shoulder. "If I could remain here without putting you in danger, I would, but if I defy Great Karl, I expose you to his anger, and that might incline the Pope to agree with Bishop Iso. So, as much as I would rather stay, I will leave you in Olivia's care and hope that Pope Leo is more sensible than he has shown himself to be thus far." He bent and kissed her brow. "Whether I am in Roma lying beside you or on the plains of Asia, I will love you and value you until the True Death claims me, and nothing you do will alter that."

She looked up at him, struck by his remark. "How did you know?"

"That you want to drive me away?" He smiled at her, his enigmatic gaze lingering on her. "When will you believe that I know you?"

Very slowly she lowered the fox-fur to beneath her shoulders. "I don't understand you, Magnatus."

"If you were to share blood with me, you would be able to know me better," said Rakoczy. "And I don't say that to persuade you to accept my life, only to tell you what you might gain."

She stood up, the fox-fur blanket wrapped around her. "I want to hear nothing more of it." She took a few careful steps toward the door.

"Of course," he said, wondering where she might be intending to go. "Are you planning to pray?"

"Not yet. I would like to go down to the Bonna Dama's garden. I haven't tended a night garden in months." She achieved an acceptable smile. "Come with me, if that would please you."

"It would please me to be in your company while I may," he said, falling in slightly behind her.

"In spite of Bonna Dama Clemens?" This last was a challenge.

"Why should Olivia have anything to do with us?" Rakoczy asked, continuing before she could answer. "Yes. She was my lover when she lived, and my comrade and friend since she came to my life. She isn't jealous of you, and you have no reason to be jealous of her."

"So you say," she said, walking more quickly, a portion of the fox-fur blanket trailing behind her.

"If you doubt me, speak to Olivia herself. I haven't been jealous of the men she has loved since she and I were lovers and she a breathing woman." He reached the outer door and added, "Once she came to my life we could no longer be lovers. No vampire can love another, not as you and I have loved tonight."

She stopped and turned to him. "Why not?"

"Because we must seek life, and once we change from living to undead we have none to offer each other," he said, and waited for her response.

She stopped walking and turned around to look at him. "Are you sure?"

"Oh, yes," he said with a slight, sad chuckle.

"But—" She stopped herself.

He came up to her and took her hand. "Those of my blood cannot afford jealousy."

Her red eyes were full of doubt. "But surely . . . there must be . . ." She pulled the fox-fur blanket more tightly around her.

"What would be the purpose of jealousy?" Rakoczy asked. "We must seek the living or we starve and raven." He winced at his recollections of those times. "Love isn't measured out in dribs and drabs for fear of exhausting its supply—it expands to enfold all it touches, and grows by usage. It is fragile only if you make it so, for, like the silk, its lightness is its strength." His compelling, dark eyes met her red ones. "If you learn nothing else from our time together, I implore you, learn this."

She stared at him, fascinated and a bit apprehensive. Finally she blinked. "I'll . . . I'll try to bear what you say in mind."

"I can't ask you for much more," Rakoczy said, accepting her pledge.

"You tell me that now, and in the morning, you will leave," she said, and continued toward the stairs that led down to the atrium, her fox-fur blanket swinging with every step. When she reached the foot of the stairs, she turned to see if he was following her. "How can you remain with me tonight when you depart at Prime?"

"Would you prefer I leave you to yourself?" he asked.

"No. But surely you have tasks awaiting you." She cocked her head. "Do you tell me you do not? If you are delayed in the morning, you will hold me accountable for it."

"I won't, you know," he said. "I have traveled more times and gone farther than you can imagine. If I cannot tend to my readying by now, I am truly beyond all hope." He came up to her. "It is snowing. Would you like me to fetch your slippers?"

"Those leather ones from Egypt that Bonna Dama Clemens gave to me?" Gynethe Mehaut asked, and realized that her feet were cold. "If you are willing . . . I would like . . ."

"Certainly. And if you would like other clothing?" He indicated the fox-fur blanket.

"No. This will serve me very well," she said, and turned to the pots on shelves under the overhanging eaves.

Rakoczy went to fetch her slippers and encountered Niklos Aulirios in the upper gallery. "Is all well?" the handsome Greek major domo asked.

"As much as can be expected," said Rakoczy, holding up the slippers.

Niklos nodded. "Your chests have all been carried down to the stable and will be loaded onto your mules before dawn. That's when your escort is supposed to arrive, isn't it?"

"So the Emperor's messenger informed me," said Rakoczy with a wry twist of his mouth.

"It is most difficult to travel in winter; you've done it enough to know how risky it is," said Niklos with a look that encouraged comment.

"So it is," Rakoczy agreed. "But I am to cross the mountains as soon as the passes are open, so I will do my utmost to reach Lecco. I can stay there until word comes that it is safe to travel."

"It seems to me," said Niklos in Alexandrian Greek, "that there are those who want you away from Roma when Gynethe Mehaut's case is decided."

"It seems so to me, as well," said Rakoczy, and went past Niklos toward the stairs, where he paused to ask, "Is Olivia—"

"Out. She should be back between Vigil and Matins." He sketched a reverence in Rakoczy's direction. "I'll order bread and cheese for your soldiers first thing in the morning."

"And a keg of beer. They'll want something to help them keep warm." Rakoczy hastened down the stairs and found Gynethe Mehaut bending over a small fern. He knelt next to her to hold her slippers for her.

"You're being very kind to me," she said as she donned them.

"I am showing you courtesy," Rakoczy said, and thought that the Court of the Emperor was hardly the place to look for such gestures.

"It is good of you," she said, and moved away from him. "This atrium will be filled with flowers by the Paschal Mass."

"Very likely," said Rakoczy.

She continued around the atrium, staying under the eaves but clearly trying to take in the whole of the garden. "I wish I could see it," she admitted a bit later. "All in flowers and filled with sweet odors. But that won't be possible, will it?"

"Probably not," said Rakoczy, wishing he could offer her greater solace than that.

There was a long silence between them, one that only ended when Vigil sounded from the monastery three streets away. "You would think, in this city, they would observe Nocturnes and not Vigil," she said inconsequently. "But Roma has been sacked, so it may be that they wish to have guards all through the night."

"Or their Abbott wishes it so," said Rakoczy.

"Whatever their reason, they call me to prayer," she said, and started toward the corridor leading to the small room that had been transformed four centuries ago from a private temple to the Magna Mater to one dedicated to Virgine Maria. "I will keep my Hours."

"Do you require anything of me?" Rakoczy asked, knowing that he had failed her.

"No. Only your prayers." Saying that, she vanished into the dark of the corridor, leaving Rakoczy alone in the atrium.

It was there that Olivia found him some while later. "Sanct' Germain!" she exclaimed, startled.

"Olivia," he said, reverencing her.

She looked around, tossing back the hood of her mantellum and letting the snow fall onto her fawn-brown hair. "And Gynethe Mehaut?"

"She is in your chapel, reciting her Offices," he answered.

"I would have thought she might forego that tonight," Olivia remarked, arching her brows in speculation.

"We had from Compline to Vigil," Rakoczy said, and shook his head.

"I am sorry," Olivia said.

"She is facing the Pope's decision. I understand why she wants to keep all her devotions." He came up to Olivia. "And so do you."

"Of course. But you must forgive me a little indignation on her behalf, and yours." She put her hand on his arm. "I hate to see you go."

"But I must," said Rakoczy.

"I know." She stepped back from him and turned her face up into the falling snow. "It is a cruel beauty."

"But it is beautiful," Rakoczy agreed.

Olivia turned slowly, arms extended, the light of the garden torches making a dance of her movements. "Tonight all Roma glows, but tomorrow there will be dead beggars and pilgrims from here to Ostia. The monasteries will pile the bodies in their crypts until the ground is soft enough to bury them."

"You saw bodies when you went out earlier," said Rakoczy with a knowing half-smile.

"Exactly. More than a dozen by the Circus Maximus—what's left of it. I passed it on my way to a most willing young pilgrim; at least he won't freeze tonight." She tugged her fur-lined mantellum closed. "It is sad to see what has become of Roma."

"Yes, it is," Rakoczy told her.

"And the streets so empty," she went on.

"If they truly are empty," Rakoczy said. "It would be wise to be careful: there are more than the usual number of spies about."

"That there are," she said. "Lurking like rats in the corners. I've had to pension off four mansionarii for selling information to the Lateranus Guards." Her expression showed the extent of her disgust.

"When was this?" Rakoczy asked, doing his best not to show the alarm he felt.

"Since summer." She could see his dismay. "Don't suppose it was on your account, Sanct' Germain, or not wholly so."

"But to have treachery in your own house—"

She put her hand on his. "It is nothing new. From time to time I must dismiss those who seek to carry tales. You have done the same."

"Yes," he said, still disliking the notion.

"It began with the attack on the Pope; everyone was frightened and no one knows where to turn," said Olivia. "It has grown worse since Karl-lo-Magne came here. Still," she added, "it would have been worse had Leo's enemies prevailed."

Rakoczy realized she was right. "If you will, do what you can for Gynethe Mehaut."

"Certainly," she said promptly. "And I will inform you when I can what has transpired here. It may be difficult, given the cost of reliable couriers. But, Sanct' Germain, when have I failed you, but in the Years of the Cold Sun?"

"That was hardly your doing," Rakoczy said, and started toward the stairs. "Will you see me off at dawn?"

"How can you doubt it?" She came up to him. "And I'll do all that I can to protect Gynethe Mehaut. I will pray that the matter is settled by spring, not drag on for the greater part of a year; I should be able to do that."

Rakoczy reverenced her as the most stringent of his worries finally lessened. "Thank you, Olivia."

TEXT OF A LETTER FROM ALCUIN OF YORK TO THE MAGNATUS HIERNOM RAKOCZY, CARRIED BY CHURCH COURIER.

To the most respected foreigner, and confidant of the Emperor Karl-lo-Magne, the Magnatus Hiernom Rakoczy, Comes Sant' Germainius, at his fiscs near Sant' Cyricus, the greetings of Alcuin, Bishop of Sant' Martin at Tours, at the end of March in the Pope's year 801.

Amen.

I have received from Roma today the first dispatch of spring, which contains material that will interest you, and I have taken it upon myself to inform you of what it contained, for it is unlikely that the missi dominici will bring you this news. Upon reviewing the report, I am inclined to impart to you all the appropriate information that has been vouchsafed me. It has to do with the Pope's decision in regard to Gynethe Mehaut, and the manner in which it will be carried out.

His Holiness has deliberated upon the condition of Gynethe Mehaut and has announced that he will send her to Bishop Berahtram of Sant' Yrieix, to become an anchorite at the convent of his bishopric. This way, if she is a manifestation of the Anti-Christ, she will be guarded so that she cannot damage, malign, or damn any Christian, and if she is a messenger from God, she will increase the sanctity of the nunnery of Sant' Ianuarius through her prayers and her presence. This is a wise decision, one that both Bishops Freculf and Iso can accept, and one that will bring Bishop Berahtram to the notice and gratitude of Pope Leo, which can only strengthen the Church in Franksland. You may be pleased to know that your concern on her behalf mitigated the severity of the Pope's resolution, which might have been more restricted than an anchorite's cell.

The woman is to be escorted to Sant' Ianuarius in May, when troops will come north from Roma and will provide the guards she requires. Word will be sent to the Emperor as soon as she is installed at Sant' Ianuarius, and as soon as I receive confirmation, I will inform you with the understanding that you will do nothing to attempt to bring her out of her immurement, for that would only serve to show that she is a servant of the Anti-Christ. Let her do the penance the Pope demands of her, and thank him for his mercy.

I must thank you for the maps you have sent to us. If half of what you show us is true and accurate, the lands of the Great Khan are vast indeed. I shall put them among our itineraries and descriptiones, with gratitude for your knowledge. I pray that in time God will send us other travelers to confirm what you have shown us. I have informed the Emperor of your gift to us, and asked that he honor your donation even as we have done.

In the conviction that I have not acted against God or the Emperor in sending this to you, I send you my blessing and my prayers for your loyalty and long life.

Alcuin,
Bishop and Abbott, Sant' Martin at Tours,
Ferrieres, Cormery, Sens, Sant' Loup, Flavigny,
and Sant' Josse
by my own hand and under seal

chapter thirteen

VULFOALD STOOD WITH HIS ARMS CROSSED and his expression set in stern lines; before him three villagers grasped Waifar, forcing him down onto his knees, his arms held behind him with knotted thongs, a trail of blood running down his face from an ugly bruise above his left eye. "So," he said as he glowered at the captive. "You weren't content to rape and kill one of our women—you must try for two."

Waifar spat out a tooth and stared defiantly at Vulfoald; he muttered something in the patois of his own village, words that were unintelligible to Vulfoald and his people, although his intent was plain. Finally he glowered. "They're both wanton. The first sought me out. The second was . . . She lured me," he said at last. "It is *her* doing!"

No women or girls were among those gathered in front of the village well, all of them having been sent to their houses, although a few pale faces could be seen in the narrow doorways, listening.

The largest captor gave Waifar a sharp jab in the abdomen, grinning with satisfaction at the painful grunt this elicited; he smiled as Vulfoald signaled his approval. "Say nothing against our women," he recommended, holding Waifar more tightly. "Else I'll do worse to you."

"She tempted me," Waifar muttered.

"She was milking goats," said one of the villagers, disgusted.

"She *sought* me!" Waifar insisted.

"This is a lie. We have heard her testimony, and we have seen her injuries. She said how you knocked her over and tried to take her maidenhead by force, how you struck her with your hands and tried to choke her. The proof is on her face, and her neck, and shoulders. You held a knife to her throat, and she has the wounds to prove it; she was spared defilement when she hit you on your head with her pail. She lost all the milk, but preserved herself, as the nuns have said she must. She swore this was true—and that you were the one who attempted to violate her—before the altar at Santa Julitta, the very day it happened. The Sorrae heard her and found her truthful." He motioned to his nephews. "Bring me my skinning knives. There is work to do."

"I am not the one who hurt her, if she is hurt," said Waifar, his voice rising. He huffed as another sharp blow went into his belly.

"Summon her," said Vulfoald. "Have her point this man out as the assaulter. We shall have the right to us before we kill him."

A boy of seven or eight whooped and ran off to one of the huts, shouting "Bleide, Bleide, come out!"

There was a long moment of silence, and then a young woman with a badly bruised countenance that was just turning from purple to green and yellow, with a number of half-healed nicks on her neck and jaw and a clump of hair pulled from her head, came painfully out of her family's hut and walked slowly toward the well. She went up to Waifar, stared at him for several heartbeats, then screamed and kicked at him, catching him on the shoulder and the ribs.

"This is the man?" Vulfoald asked.

"Yes," she said, her face growing red with fury. "Yes!"

"And you swear before God and on the honor of Great Karl that he forced you?" Vulfoald pursued.

"I swear. May my eyes rot in my skull if I speak lies," she said, and kicked

Waifar one last time, then turned away and walked back toward her family's house.

"So," said Vulfoald. "Does anyone doubt Bleide?" He looked around for any possible protest, expecting none. "Very well. We are all agreed this man must pay."

"Shouldn't we turn him over to the monks at Sant' Cyricus?" asked one young man known to have weak eyes, and therefore destined for the monastery to serve the Fratri.

"What would they do? They have cells where they could keep him, but nothing more than that; they cannot mete out punishment, and they cannot give him escort to the King's Court. They can only imprison him, and if his comrades come, they would give him up to them. Monks have no reason to fight the brigands." Vulfoald let this sink in, and then added, "The disgrace is upon us and our village. It is for us to make him answer. Where are my knives?"

"We may have to appear before the King's Potente to—" one of the men began and fell silent under Vulfoald's ferocious gaze.

"No doubt there will be questions about what we do; we must expect it. The monks, at least, will need to be told at Confession, and they may have to inform the Magnatus. We will answer anyone when they come. But we must not allow this disgrace to remain, or we will be unworthy of any aid from the King or any hope of Heaven." He pointed at Waifar. "You killed the woman Ratrame after you ravished her. For that alone you deserve death. But you attempted another such act, and that has put you beyond all redemption in this world and the next." He looked up as his nephews approached, carrying his two skinning knives. "Hone them for me. Do it carefully."

Waifar muttered another curse and glared up at Vulfoald. "You will be made a slave for this. They will make all your women their whores."

"Better a slave than a Majore who failed his people," said Vulfoald.

There were murmurs of agreement from the villagers, and one of the older men called out, "Let me make the first cut: Ratrame was my daughter."

"You may cut, Gottmar, but not the first time; when the time comes, you may be avenged on him," said Vulfoald, and turned slowly to face every man, one after the other, fixing them each with a hard stare. "Now, I will act for all the village."

A few men shouted their disappointment, but most agreed with Vulfoald's decision. "Not too quickly," one of the men recommended. "Let him know what he has done."

"Our women suffered, and so shall he," said Vulfoald, and motioned to the men holding Waifar. "Tie him to a beam. Hands and feet. Where we slaughter the goats." He saw Waifar blanch. "You deserve nothing better. If it could be done, I would see you had worse."

Waifar cursed, and tried to kick; one of his captors pulled his bound arms up behind him until he screamed, and then he said, "Try that again, and we will put a cord around your neck, just tight enough to keep you docile."

"Urthan," Vulfoald admonished him. "Don't let him trick you. He may try to have you kill him by accident, so he will spare himself the fruits of his crimes."

"No rope around the neck, then," said Urthan. He maneuvered his knee into the small of Waifar's back, bending the outlaw forward so that his face was almost in the dirt. "It will be as you say, Majore."

Vulfoald's nephews continued to work the whetstones over the knives, the one holding the heavier, longer blade making the iron ring as he stropped the stone along its edge. "See you give a good edge," Vulfoald encouraged them.

"You will die for this!" Waifar shouted. "The Magnatus will order you hanged."

"What will it matter to you, if you are dead already?" said Vulfoald.

"The Magnatus took me into his house," Waifar reminded the villagers.

"And you repaid him with treachery," said Vulfoald. "It is known everywhere in his fiscs. You have no call upon him, either for obligation or kinship. The Magnatus may even set aside the law in our favor." He raised his hands. "When you are dead we will put your body into the midden. It may never be discovered. It is where you belong."

"You will all die because of this," Waifar shrieked, becoming more desperate with every breath.

"Only after you have died," Vulfoald reminded him, glancing up as his older nephew brought him his larger knife. He took the knife and held it up. "Make him ready," he said with finality.

Waifar struggled, twisting in the grasp of the men who held him and spitting curses at them all; he wriggled and kicked as he was dragged upright, but in spite of all his efforts and his shouting, he was relentlessly dragged to the slaughtering beam near the goat-pen, where, in spite of all his efforts to prevent it, his wrists were bound to the beam, and the beam hoisted up until he dangled a short distance off the ground. Waifar kicked and squirmed, but his feet were confined and tied to tall stakes driven into the earth beneath the frame. The men pressed more closely around him, leaving only enough room for Vulfoald to work.

"Bring salt," Vulfoald ordered. "And mix it with dung."

Three of the younger men went off to do the Majore's bidding, one of them shouting, "He will pay!"

Slowly and deliberately, Vulfoald cut the sleeve of Waifar's camisa, then, just as deliberately, sliced off a long, thin sliver of flesh and muscle from Waifar's right forearm; Waifar screeched, straining against his bonds, blood running down to his shoulder and over his chest.

The men of the village cheered even as Waifar panted oaths.

"Now the other arm," said Vulfoald, and repeated his actions on the left, leaving Waifar keening and increasingly pale. "Put the salt and dung on his wounds and leave him until the next Hour sounds." He motioned to the men of the village. "Go about your work and come back when you hear the bells."

The men obeyed even as Vulfoald's younger nephew gave him his smaller, sharper knife. "It is as sharp as I can make it," he said as if expecting criticism.

Vulfoald tested the blade with his thumb. "It will do," he said, and put his hand on the boy's head. "Pay attention to this. It is important for you to know what happens to those who transgress."

The boy turned shocked eyes on his uncle. "Will they punish us for this?"

"They may. But that means nothing," said Vulfoald. "If we don't hold him to account, we will forfeit our right to Heaven and the protection of our own Saints."

"And the old gods—what of them?" The boy lowered his head.

"They are our Saints; if you call them that, the Fratri won't mind. If you call them gods, the Fratri will be angry." Vulfoald looked up as three men went up to Waifar with a tub of dung mixed with salt. He motioned to them to do their task.

Waifar whimpered and fainted as the noxious mess was smeared on his open wounds. The three men stepped back and moved the tub a short distance away.

"What are you going to do now, Uncle?" asked his nephew.

"I will go attend to the ewes with new lambs," he answered. "And then I shall help notch the ears of the goats." It was a simple means of identification and one the villagers had used for centuries; the chore was one all villagers did every spring.

"When None sounds?" The boy shifted from one foot to the other, suddenly uneasy.

"Then we will have two more slices from that criminal, and he will have time to consider his errors." Vulfoald spoke bluntly and without emotion.

The boy nodded and bolted for the creamery, where the new cheeses waited for turning.

Vulfoald walked over to Waifar. "I will return at None. Think of your sins while I am gone."

Through the warm mid-day, the village kept to the routines of spring, making preparations for the second market of the year as well as going about the daily chores; the women kept to their houses, only occasionally looking out to the man on the slaughter-frame. By the time None sounded, the villagers had completed most of the work they expected to do in that time. The men put aside their tools and went to the well, gathering around Vulfoald as he returned from the goat-pen, wiping his shears on his sleeve. No one spoke as Vulfoald took his larger knife and approached Waifar, who began to scream, a steady, high sound coming out with every breath.

"You brought this on yourself," said Vulfoald, and sliced open the hanging man's femoralia, exposing his thigh. This time it was more difficult to cut the muscle from the front of his thigh; Waifar shook with pain before he lost consciousness. Vulfoald took his time on the second leg, tossing the flesh to the midden when he had severed it completely. "Salt and dung. Do it."

At Vespers, Gottmar castrated Waifar and fed his penis and testicles to the hogs; by morning, the outlaw was dead. The villagers cut him down and shoved his body into the midden, pushing it deep into the steaming heart of the dung-heap; only then did the women and girls emerge from the houses, and they went to the midden, as if to assure themselves that Waifar was gone. Bleide emptied the slops onto Waifar's exposed foot and then burst into furious tears. The villagers left her alone, knowing she was tainted and undeserving of consolation.

For the next four days the villagers went on as usual: the pigs were driven into the forest to forage for acorns; the goats and sheep were turned out into the fallow fields; the four ponies were harnessed to sledges to pull cut logs from the forest into the village where the sawyers could ready them for market. The women baked, made cheese, and worked their looms. Everything was as it had been, and the villagers were as content as they had ever been. Then, on the fifth day, the Magnatus Rakoczy rode into the village with his foreign servant right behind him. Most of the villagers came into the center of the village reluctantly; only Vulfoald greeted him, and with as little respect as he dared, hardly reverencing him at all and standing defiantly before the well.

"God give you good day, Vulfoald," said Rakoczy. He was in a severely cut gonelle of black wool with a high neck and a broad, black leather girdle. His femoralia and tibialia were black as well. His silver collar was held with a tibia in the shape of his sigil, the eclipse.

"Why are you in this village?" the Majore demanded.

Rakoczy remained on his big-shouldered grey gelding. "Surely you know the reason: I have been told that this village has broken the law. I am required to find out the truth of it. I have to hear all sides of the events before I submit my report to the Emperor's Court." He seemed very tired as he spoke.

"What law do you mean?" Vulfoald asked.

"The law of Great Karl, Emperor of the Franks and Longobards, that forbids unofficial Courts of Law to be held, and unofficial sentences to be carried out. It has been declaimed everywhere in Franksland." Rakoczy considered the men standing in the square in front of the well. "It is said that you condemned and killed the brigand Waifar."

"We have not done anything wrong," called one of the older men.

"No, we haven't. He murdered Ratrame after he raped her, and he attempted to rape Bleide." Vulfoald stared at Rakoczy defiantly. "How can we do wrong to avenge our women?"

"You should have brought your complaint to me, or to the Abbott at Sant' Cyricus," said Rakoczy, his voice strong enough to carry in spite of his fatigue.

"The affront was to us, not to you or the Abbott," said Vulfoald. "We have done what had to be done."

"And it was right of us to do it," said Gottmar.

"It may have been right, but you have exacted your revenge at great cost to yourselves," said Rakoczy, his expression somber. "Tell me what transpired and I may be able to lessen your—"

"None of us ask for that," said Vulfoald, interrupting Rakoczy without apology.

"I trust you don't intend to let all your village answer for the acts of a few." Rakoczy tried to offer a means of reducing the impact on Sant' Trinitas. "If those who helped in the execution will own it, perhaps I can convince the Emperor to exact his sentence on those men only."

"All of us were part of it," Gottmar shouted. "For my daughter and for Bleide."

Rakoczy shook his head slowly. "If you tell me this, I can do little to soften the blow that will fall upon you." He directed his steady gaze at Vulfoald. "You must know that this has heavy consequences for you all."

"Only if the King hears of it," said Vulfoald.

"If I have heard of it, the Emperor will hear of it eventually, and then you and I will have to answer for it." He studied the men. "Why didn't you trust me to uphold your women?"

"A Magnatus defend peasant women? You haven't summoned any of our women for your use, but you have been gone. How can we expect you to give any attention to our women's misfortunes?" Vulfoald scoffed. "You must think we're all fools."

Rakoczy acknowledged the truth of what he said. "Yes. Many hobu would be willing to overlook the abuse of peasant women, or even abuse them himself, but I am not one such, and Karl-lo-Magne has said he is not such an Emperor. The protection of all his subjects is important to him, from the highest to the most common. If you will not allow him to see justice done, then you compromise everything he hopes to accomplish."

"Fine words," said Vulfoald, making no effort to conceal his contempt. "But the Potenti have used our women for their pleasure—"

"Have I ever done so?" Rakoczy cut him off.

"Not that I have heard of," Vulfoald allowed. "But you have been away. Who knows what mischief you might have done had you remained here." He took a step forward. "Either way, if we do not protect our women, they will all suffer."

"And so will you," said Rakoczy, glancing at Rorthger. "I am required to report this. I could have done so when I was first informed of it, without learning anything from you about the incident, but I wanted to give you an opportunity to protect your village. You have a chance to minimize the suffering imposed on your people; I hope you will make the most of it."

"So you say," Gottmar shouted, and was echoed by cries from a few of the men.

Rakoczy did his best to keep his voice level. "Your protection of your women will end if you are all sold into slavery for breaking the Emperor's Law. Why should your children be forced to pay for your actions?" He waited, letting the men consider this. "You will be separated from your women and your children; you'll never know what becomes of them, nor they of you."

"It doesn't need to happen," said Vulfoald.

"No, but it is likely it will," said Rakoczy, wishing he could find some way to convince the villagers of the danger in which they stood.

"Not if you tell the King nothing," said Vulfoald, his voice heavy with meaning. "You could leave here and say nothing. Or you could not leave here."

Rakoczy heard him out without a qualm. "It's bad enough that you have killed a criminal, but now you propose to kill me and my manservant—you do realize you would have to kill him, too, don't you?—and then whom?"

Vulfoald gave a lupine smile. "We would know nothing of it—you would simply disappear. There are outlaws in these woods, and who is to say that they wouldn't kill you? Waifar was an outlaw who preyed upon travelers, as you know. Other outlaws could attack you. We wouldn't have to know anything about it." He looked around at the men behind him, one or two were faltering, the others seemed belligerent. "We've dealt with one man who wanted to bring disgrace upon us—what is to stop us doing the same with the two of you?"

"My mansionarii know where we are and they have heard rumors about our errand; so have the soldiers who guard my villa. The Abbott of Sant' Cyricus knows what you have done, and he would report it to the missi dominici. Think," Rakoczy implored Vulfoald. "You have already put yourself in danger, and now you compound your error."

"Only if it is discovered," Vulfoald insisted, but with less impetus than before. "Men disappear from time to time, and no one but God knows why."

"I wouldn't be one of those." Rakoczy held up his hand. "I have a sworn duty to the Emperor, just as you do. But I have no desire to see all of this place razed and the people scattered. Give me the opportunity to act on your behalf. It is better to lose four or five men than to be completely dispersed."

"You cannot do that," Vulfoald challenged him. "You are a foreigner, no matter what privileges the King gives you, and you have little say in what becomes of us."

"Without your help, I can do nothing about what becomes of you," said Rakoczy. "Believe this: if you will not give me an account of Waifar's trespasses, then you will have to take the brunt of the Emperor's Law."

"And if we tell you all he did, how can we know that you will report it aright?" Vulfoald demanded, his hands on his hips.

"You have my Word," said Rakoczy simply.

"Is that all?" Vulfoald asked.

"Do you need anything more?" Rakoczy countered, watching the villagers narrowly.

Vulfoald lowered his head in thought. "How would you present our actions?" he asked at last.

"I have parchment, water, nibs, and an ink-cake with me. I will write down what you say as you say it, and that will be included with the report I am obligated to prepare." Rakoczy saw the villagers staring at him. "I am no cleric, but I can read and write."

"So you say," Vulfoald repeated. "You might do anything and call it writing, and who are we to question you?"

"Fetch a monk from Sant' Cyricus if you doubt me," said Rakoczy, beginning to lose patience with these stiff-necked men.

"What monk would question a Magnatus?" Gottmar asked, looking to Vulfoald for support.

"An honest one," said Rakoczy, and waited with such a calm demeanor that the villagers began to back off from him, unnerved by his composure. "If you need to have the assurance of the Church, choose any monk or priest you prefer to witness what I write. I will wait until the monk can be brought, if you insist upon it, and I will permit the monk to write down all he hears."

Vulfoald shook his head. "Fetch Fratre Larius from Sant' Cyricus. He will watch all you write and attest to its accuracy."

"That is satisfactory to me," said Rakoczy, and motioned to his companion. "If you will carry one of the villagers to the monastery, we can begin to take down the account of Waifar's activities and the manner in which you addressed it."

Vulfoald shook his head. "Our man will ride one of our ponies." If he recalled that the ponies originally came from Rakoczy, he gave no indication. "It will be better for him to ride separately, in case they should be pursued."

"As you wish. But if the Fratre is to be fetched tonight, it would be wise for my man and yours to leave shortly." Rakoczy was growing weary of the resistance he found in this small village. "Rorthger, help them to saddle a pony."

"I will have Gohewin ride with you," said Vulfoald, and pointed to the young man with a scraggly beginning of a beard. "He is my cousin and he will act for me."

Rakoczy nodded. "As you wish." He finally dismounted and walked up to Vulfoald; the Magnatus was half-a-head taller than the Majore, and he lifted the well-bucket. "My horse is thirsty."

"Let him drink," said Vulfoald, aware his permission was not needed.

"Thank you," said Rakoczy, and dropped the bucket, listening to it splash into the water.

"If you would like to drink, there is beer and some new wine," said Vulfoald angrily.

"It is very generous of you," said Rakoczy. "But it is unnecessary. I would rather you give some of the wine and beer to your people." He began to draw up the bucket.

Vulfoald was torn between feeling insulted that the Magnatus would not accept his hospitality and satisfaction that the people of the village would be allowed more celebration. "What can we do to show you honor?"

"Give me a full account of your dealing with Waifar and I will be satisfied. I would like that better than food or drink." Rakoczy also thought that if the men were slightly tipsy they might be more candid in their reports than if they were wholly sober and resentful.

Vulfoald glared at him, suspecting subterfuge. "We have work yet to do before sundown," he said.

"Then do it. While my man and yours go to Sant' Cyricus, you may complete your daily labors. I will accompany you into the forest to see how your clearing of trees is coming, that I may include your industry in my report to the Emperor." Rakoczy hoped that this would serve to put the villagers more at ease; he put the bucket under his grey's nose and held it while the horse drank.

Vulfoald frowned. "If it is your wish, it is our duty to accommodate you."

Gohewin reverenced Rakoczy. "Magnatus. I must go fetch one of the ponies."

"Yes. Do it," Rakoczy said, and watched the young peasant hasten away.

"You are determined to stay here until the Fratre is brought," said Vulfoald, making it an accusation.

"Yes. The Emperor requires it of me when I have discovered a possible crime. I must remain where it was said to occur to make sure any of those who could have participated do not flee." He met Vulfoald's irate gaze with a look that bordered on sympathy. "As you have your duty to me, so I have mine to the Emperor. I wish you could comprehend that."

Vulfoald laughed angrily. "A fine excuse. What does the King know of us, and why should he care what happens here, particularly to a man who rapes and murders?"

"Great Karl has set rules for his empire, and if any portion of his rule fails, it all fails," said Rakoczy.

"You sound like the Abbott and all his high-flown praises of the Bishop." Vulfoald made a sudden gesture of frustration. "You pretend that what we do is watched by the great ones, the Potenti and Optime himself, but they do not care what we do so long as they have their revenue."

Rakoczy agreed with Vulfoald but he said, "It has been thus, but Great Karl is trying to return to the ways of the Romans, putting law above men." He set the bucket back on the rim of the well.

"No man does that, so long as he has relatives and obligations to his family." Vulfoald turned as the clop of hooves heralded Gohewin's return, a small speckled mare on a lead. "The saddle is in the barn."

"I'll attend to it, Majore." He handed the lead to Vulfoald and rushed off to get the one riding saddle the village owned.

"When he brings the Fratre, we'll be ready to tell you all we know," said Vulfoald. He held up the lead to Rorthger and walked away without waiting for Rakoczy to give him permission. "Everyone return to your work. Don't be lax because the Magnatus is waiting here. Be back at sundown. We will eat and drink to the King's honor, and the Magnatus' good fortune." The villagers hurried to obey him, moving out of the square quickly, as if ashamed to be seen there now.

Rorthger, still mounted on his copper-dun, looked down at Rakoczy. "What do you think will happen to these people?" he asked in Greek.

Rakoczy answered in the same language. "You know as well as I do: at best the men will be made slaves; at the worst, all of them will. Nothing I say can stop that. The Emperor will declare that justice has been done, and this land will be given to peasants from other parts of Franksland."

"Then why must you—" Rorthger began, then stopped. "Of course. They will Confess it, and the monks will report the incident, and then their punishment will be worse."

"Exactly," said Rakoczy. "This way, I should be able to persuade Karl-lo-Magne to be lenient on the women. It will be hard for them to manage without their men, but at least they will have their children and a place to support them. It isn't much, but I cannot do more."

"Do you think the Emperor will take your advice in this matter?" Rorthger inquired. "How can you be sure he will listen to your plea?"

"I hope he will. He has declared himself beholden to me for my service to him. I will make my request for mercy contingent upon my past service, and he may decide to honor my recommendation." A slight frown flicked over his face.

"This is a hard thing to do—asking Great Karl to show these villagers the same considerations that he grants to the hobu."

"Do you think you will succeed?" Rorthger asked, then said, in the Frankish of the region, "So, you are ready to depart?"

Gohewin put the saddle on the mare's back and tightened the girth in a quick jerk. "I am, almost." He had a bridle hanging from his shoulder, and he put this on over the rope halter the mare wore. "Now. I am ready," he announced, and climbed into the saddle, pulling the reins in and reaching out to claim the lead from Rorthger.

"We will return as quickly as possible," said Rorthger to Rakoczy.

"I will be waiting for you," said Rakoczy.

"Are you certain you stand in no danger?" Rorthger asked in Greek.

"No; but it is not so great that I am afraid," said Rakoczy in the same language, then added in Frankish, "The Emperor will welcome anything I can tell him about the nature of this place, and how the villagers have done so much to make the most of the land."

Rorthger turned his gelding's head toward the narrow track that led to Sant' Cyricus. He signaled to Gohewin, saying, "Walk out." As the two of them moved off, Rorthger drew his sword, holding it at the ready.

From across the square Vulfoald spoke up loudly. "Your man has nothing to fear from Gohewin."

"But you, yourself, reminded him that the woods are dangerous," Rakoczy said, and swung up onto his grey. "Let me see how your men are faring in the forest. The more I can tell the Emperor that is to your credit, the more likely he is to be willing to issue a lenient decision."

Vulfoald sighed. "If you insist."

"It is in your best interest," Rakoczy told him.

"So you say," Vulfoald responded. "Well, come this way," he went on, dropping his voice. "The King forbade us to use our language and put us under the authority of the monks, and hobu like you, and he expects we will accept his dictates without question?"

Rakoczy could not dispute any of this, so he said, "He is the one whose decision will leave its mark on your village for generations to come. It is fitting that you do everything you can to show your worth to the Emperor." He could tell from the set of Vulfoald's shoulders that he believed none of this, and as he followed him toward the edge of the trees, he wondered if anything he said would prevail with the determined Majore.

TEXT OF A LETTER FROM FRATRE LOTHAR IN ROMA TO CARDINAL
ARCHBISHOP BRUNEHAUT OF MARMOUTIER CURRENTLY RESIDING IN ROMA,
DELIVERED BY HAND TO THE CARDINAL ARCHBISHOP BY FRATRE LOTHAR.

*To the most illustrious Primore, the Cardinal Archbishop Brunehaut of
Marmoutier at the Basilica of Santi Sergius and Bacchus the Martyrs at the
Viminalis Gate at Roma, the most submissive greetings of Fratre Lothar,
monk and pilgrim currently residing at the monastery of Sant' Ioannes the
Frank, on the first day of May in the Pope's year 801.*

*Primore, I send this to you with the full and certain belief that it is my
duty to serve you and the Church before the Emperor as it was my duty to
serve the Emperor before the Church when I was still a soldier. It is fitting
that I should address you, for you are the most powerful Churchman I have
had the honor of meeting. I kneel at your feet and trust you will make use of
everything I impart to you for the glory of God and His Church.*

*It happened fourteen nights ago that I went to Mass at Santa Maria
Gloriosa and there encountered a number of Frankish monks who reside
here in Roma. As men will do, we repaired to the refectory after Mass and
drank new wine from Compline until Vigil, for at Santa Maria Gloriosa
Vigil is kept in addition to Nocturnes. As wine loosened our tongues, many
of us spoke of what our lives had been before we entered the Church. Most of
the accounts were not unusual—much the same for many of us. One had been
a butcher and still slaughtered for his Fratri, one had been a merchant, one
had been a fisherman, one had been a notary, one a farrier, one a cooper,
another a smith, and other such trades.*

*There was one monk, however, a Fratre Grimhold, who became quite
drunk. and in that state, talked about his present labors here in Roma on
behalf of a certain Frankish Bishop whose name he did not speak, but whose
agent he has been for some years. I must report what he said, for if even half
of it is true, he is doing things contrary to the conduct demanded of monks
by Pope Leo. I shall give you all the information this monk imparted in his
drunken state, and I pray that you may determine the truth of it.*

*I have prayed about what I heard and I have asked my Abbott if I should
do this, and I have followed his counsel in preparing this for your consideration. If you doubt any particular in what I say here, I will present myself to
you to answer any questions you may have, and swear on the altar of God
that I have told you what was said to me. It is my intention to say everything that I was told, to keep nothing back and to add nothing.*

The monk, Fratre Grimhold, said he had done much to advance the cause of the Church by ridding it of its enemies within. All of us in Orders are bound to do this, within the framework of our vows, and any monk failing to act in this manner is aiding our foes as much as if he foreswore his vocation in favor of advancement among our opponents. We are pledged to maintain the True Church at all costs. This is a laudable goal, and one that any devout Christian must support. But it is also true that there are acts that monks should eschew. From what Fratre Grimhold said that night, he has not allowed the Commandments to limit his zeal. The Frankish Bishop who has given orders to Fratre Grimhold has gone well beyond the restrictions monks should observe. I have taken some time to try to verify his claims, and I will include what I have learned in this account, so that you may decide for yourself how much credence to lend to these accounts.

This Fratre Grimhold said he had killed Churchmen who were employed by the Greek Church and the Patriarch who are supposed to do their utmost to turn the Roman Church to serve Greek ends. He swore that the deaths were justified, and that he had refused to carry out one killing because he was uncertain about the man's importance in the course of the Roman Church. And it is the killing he has done that troubles me. He has killed four men, three of them Churchmen, and he has not been apprehended for these acts, nor has he been called before any Court, Royal or Papal, to answer for what he has done. The first Churchman he killed was a priest from Neapolis who had sheltered many Greek religious who had come to that city to aid in keeping the Greek churches established during the time of Belisarius and Narses open and receiving souls into them. He said this killing was necessary, and one that anyone would support who put his faith in the Pope. The second killing was of a courier who had accepted bribes from Greek prelates for showing them the texts of the messages he carried on behalf of the Pope and the Cardinal Archbishops. This was the most laudable killing, and one that I learned did take place in the manner he described. There was another Churchman killed, and he claimed to have killed a Carinthian Bishop who had gone over to the Patriarch. I cannot find confirmation for that death, but I believe it can be found. Fratre Grimhold said he had put the man into a well, where he could not escape and would vanish utterly; I cannot find any references to a missing Carinthian Bishop, but if the killing was so clandestine, there may be an account of one disappearing and it may provide an explanation for his being gone.

The man he said he could not kill was a foreigner sent here with the White Woman, the one who is now an anchorite, because his Bishop thought the presence of this foreigner compromised her holiness, and it may be so, but Fratre Grimhold was not convinced that his death was required, and for that reason, if no other, he was certain that he could not, in good conscience, kill the foreigner. The foreigner has gone from Roma some months since and if his going has enhanced the White Woman's reputation, there is no indication of it, so Fratre Grimhold may have been right in his hesitancy.

I listened to all this monk said, and I cannot help but think that he is a dangerous man to have here in Roma. I implore you, Primore, to call this man before you and ascertain the true extent of his activities, and see he is properly disciplined for all he has done.

This is submitted to you with a humble heart and the whole devotion of my soul. If I have erred in any way, I ask you to correct my faults and show me the means to contrition for my sins. May God and Christ show you Their Will and give you wisdom to judge this matter so that the Church is vindicated and the Emperor upheld. I am certain that God will reveal all things to His servants if He is satisfied that we have made ourselves worthy of His Mercy and the Glory of Heaven. I pray that the Church may be preserved from all evil, and the Pope be delivered from iniquity.

Amen

Fratre Grimhold
by the hand of Fratre Nicetius

⟳

chapter fourteen

AS VESPERS SOUNDED, Bishop Berahtram made his way toward the anchorites' chapel at Sant' Ianuarius, determination in his stride and stern purpose in his face; his task was clear and he would not fail, not for himself, but for the honor of Sant' Ianuarius and the Church. In this remote place God would give him victory over the Anti-Christ, and the Pope would be saved from the evil he had been commanded to guard; it would be shown that this manifestation of the wounds of Christ was the work of Satan, and would be known for the temptation to Pride it was. That revelation could only occur away from the Courts and cities of the Emperor and the Pope, and no place was more suitable than Sant' Ianuarius: the convent, perched on the edge of a cliff high above an unapproachable valley, constantly moaned with wind, a continuing reminder of the ignominy of humankind and all the works of the world. Bishop Berahtram thought the convent a particularly suitable one for the sixty-seven women who lived in it, for their withdrawal from the world was reinforced by the isolation of Sant' Ianuarius itself. Not even the eighty-nine slaves who served the nuns had much contact with the rest of his bishopric, or the villages farther down the mountain.

The nuns in the main chapel had begun chanting their prayers when Bishop Berahtram opened the fourth anchorite's cell and addressed the white-skinned woman who stood swaying slightly near the single, high window that provided the only light in the cubiculum. She stared at the Bishop, and finally said, "Sublime," in a harsh, soft voice.

"You may come to your chapel for Vespers," Bishop Berahtram said to Gynethe Mehaut. "I will hear you Confess."

Gynethe Mehaut blinked, steadying herself against the wall. For the last four days she had survived on a half-loaf of bread and a skin of water; during that time she had prayed without ceasing, chanting the Psalms over and over until her voice was now almost gone, hardly more than a hushed whisper; the chanting had long since become a rasp. After five nights without sleep, she found it difficult to concentrate. She blinked again, keeping her eyes closed a bit longer than before.

"You will not rest!" Bishop Berahtram ordered her. "Not until you have made a complete Confession of all your sins."

"No," she muttered. "I will not." She put her bandaged hands to her face.

"You must remain awake," said Bishop Berahtram, his voice taking on a harsh edge. "If you cannot do what God requires of you here, you must be sent to another nunnery where the Rule is more strictly enforced. The Pope commands it."

Gynethe Mehaut nodded several times and tried to focus her attention on the Bishop, but she found it difficult to do, for this man seemed to be a vision or a dream, one moment as real a presence as the stones around her, the next as elusive as a specter.

"You have a duty to perform, Sorra," said the Bishop, his manner as demanding as any Potente's.

Gynethe Mehaut concentrated on what the Bishop said, and forced her tongue to respond. "I am devoted to the Church and the God we serve." It came out singsong and with little meaning to her, but it was enough to satisfy him for the moment.

"The chapel is waiting. You must recite Vespers. Then I will hear your Confession, and *then* begin your night devotions." He stood a little straighter.

"You are sworn to make this a holier place than it is now. If you fail, you will show that you are the handmaiden of Satan, as Bishop Iso believes, and many others fear. For the sake of your salvation, keep your vows."

"It is my duty," said Gynethe Mehaut, as she had said twice a day since she arrived at the convent three weeks ago. She took a faltering step toward the door, feeling dizzy from the effort. As the light from the torch in the corridor struck her, she turned her face away, flinching at the sudden brightness; her head throbbed, and there was a steady ache of hunger gripping her.

"How can you be so lax?" Bishop Berahtram demanded as he followed after her. "You wobble with every step. Are you so afraid of the altar that you cannot reach the chapel without losing your way? Does the presence of God so distress you?"

"I am . . . weak," she said, trying to moisten her cracked lips, and finding her tongue dry.

"You are unable to do what you have been ordered to do?" he challenged. "You say you're not capable of doing the penance expected of you?"

"I . . . pray for strength," she murmured, stumbling a little on the uneven floor.

"As well you might," said Bishop Berahtram. He pointed to the chapel door. "You know what you must do."

"I know, Sublime, and I am grateful," she said, and winced at the high trill of laughter that came from the nearest anchorite's cell.

"Pay no heed to Sorra Riccardis Vigia," Bishop Berahtram warned her. "She is possessed by demons when night falls."

"Hers is a terrible laugh," said Gynethe Mehaut. She thought it sounded like the howls of wolves that often filled the winter's nights at Santa Albegunda; her memory grew stronger as she knelt at the door of the chapel and began to make her way on her knees toward the altar.

"It is always so with demons," said Bishop Berahtram, coming to stand over her. "Begin your Office, and remember to include the penitential prayers at the end."

"Yes." Gynethe Mehaut stretched out facedown before the altar as she had done so many times before, in this convent and in others, although tonight they all seemed fused into one, an unbroken stream of devotion that had brought her to a pervasive torpor of spirit. She wondered vaguely if Priora Iditha, or Sorra Celinde, would come to take her back to her cubiculum when she was finished. But no, she remembered. Not here. Here she was in the care of Abba Dympna and Bishop Berahtram. Her thready voice sounded through the chapel, as monotonous as anything she had ever heard, except the droning of bees. The words made little sense to her, although she felt shame that she paid so little attention to them.

"You repeated the same verse three times," Bishop Berahtram said, cutting into her drifting thoughts. "The same words: '*He has given redemption to His people: He has made His covenant with them for eternity: holy and glorious is His Name.*'"

"It has meaning for me," she said, because it was the one statement he would not dispute. "How could saying it more than once be an error?"

"God knows what it is. You needn't repeat it for His benefit," he told her.

"I repeat it for my benefit, for the consolation of my soul," she said, wishing she could close her eyes and rest. Her body ached for sleep, but she knew that to succumb would prove the worst suspicions of her. Forcing herself to stay awake, she resumed her Psalm, starting it from the beginning. "*Let all praise the Lord; I will praise Him wholeheartedly in the assembly of the devout, and to humble worshipers . . .*" She continued to the ninth verse, which she again repeated, much to Bishop Berahtram's consternation.

"You must not do that," he ordered. "You are to say them as they are written."

"But . . ." She rubbed her face with one hand, hoping the rough texture of the cloth around her wounds would bring about more clarity of thought. "*He has given redemption to His people: He has made His covenant with them for eternity: holy and glorious is His Name.* How is there error in saying that many times? Isn't it true? Doesn't it praise God, as we must do, as good Christians?" She felt so desperate, so alone.

"Do not argue! Go on to the next verse." He could not stop himself from kicking her shoulder. "You test the patience of the Pope."

"No, Sublime. I . . ." She could not bring herself to admit that she was so exhausted that she could not think of what came next, for that would surely confirm his worst apprehension.

"Go on!" He kicked her again, this time harder. "And offer up this punishment for your errors."

"Amen," she whispered, and made herself go on. At the next Psalm, she stumbled over the phrase *For the devout, their faith is as a light in the darkness,* and she cringed in anticipation of another sharp kick, which did not come—not yet.

"Go on," said Bishop Berahtram, his breath coming quickly.

Gynethe Mehaut continued with the Psalms, completing them at last, and then began the prayers that had been added to her Office. These were harder to remember, and so she said them more slowly, occasionally tripping over a word or two; when Bishop Berahtram kicked her, she did her best to pay no attention to what he had done, and instead concentrated on the words she was expected to recite. Finally she was through; the other nuns were observing Compline, which Psalms Gynethe Mehaut would have to wait until she was in her cubiculum to recount, if she could bring all the prayers to mind; she was so worn that keeping anything whole in her memory was becoming harder than speaking with her ruined voice.

For a moment she even forgot where she was and had to fight a surge of panic that coursed through her. Regaining her inward composure, she got to her knees and said, "Good Bishop, in the Name of Christ, hear my Confession."

Bishop Berahtram knelt beside her. "I will, Sorra Gynethe Mehaut." He made a gesture of protection. "I will hear you."

It was so difficult to know what to say first; Gynethe Mehaut felt turmoil rising within her, more troubling than her fatigue and her hunger. "I Confess that I have longed for Santa Albegunda instead of this place, preferring it to Sant' Ianuarius, although I know this is wrong, for it is God's Will that I am here, and I must accept and welcome His Will."

"The life at Santa Albegunda was lax," said Bishop Berahtram. "You were permitted liberties that are not suitable to you."

"I know; I know, and I want to repent them. I ask God to relieve me of that longing, but so far He hasn't given that peace to me. It is my fault, for if I were worthy, He must show me mercy." Her voice was little more than breath now, and her throat felt chapped.

"Who are you, to bargain with God?" Bishop Berahtram regarded her with icy contempt. "It is for God to decide what you must endure."

"I know," said Gynethe Mehaut again. "I am mindful of all God has brought upon me. I think on it every hour."

"Blasphemy!" He got to his feet and struck her with the full force of the back of his hand. "You are insolent of God!"

Gynethe Mehaut doubled over, her hands against her jaw. She could not cry out; she had not voice enough for that. Her misery was engulfing as she lay on the stones. At least she had not said the two worst things she might Confess: what she had learned from Bonna Dama Clemens about the Church and the Pope, and her yearning for Rakoczy, whose love was utter profanation of every sacred thing.

"Get back on your knees!" ordered Bishop Berahtram.

It was an effort for Gynethe Mehaut to move; her vision was wavering, and she shook with the effort he demanded of her. She feared she might fall over, so she held her hands out in front of her to break her collapse. "I don't . . ." she apologized.

"Remain where you are." Bishop Berahtram came around in front of her, his face set in a rictus that alarmed Gynethe Mehaut; he reached out and grabbed her shoulders. "You must tell me your sins. Your penance means nothing if you will not Confess."

"I will Confess," said Gynethe Mehaut. "I will tell you my sins."

"And in time you will be absolved of all your wrongdoing." Bishop Berahtram tightened his grip on her. "You have much to atone for."

"Yes; I must atone," Gynethe Mehaut croaked. She hated the sound she made, and fell silent.

"Well?" Bishop Berahtram demanded. "Well?"

She could not summon up enough sound to speak; she lowered her head, weeping. Finally she was able to mutter, "I miss . . . Roma." She stopped herself from saying more, although she wanted to explain what she meant, to get the Sublime Berahtram to understand her wish to return there, to the house of Atta Olivia Clemens where no one stared at her, and the only rules imposed upon her kept her safe and content.

"A holy city, the model of Heaven on earth," said Bishop Berahtram, who had never seen it for himself. "Any good Roman Christian must long for that place." He forced her to raise her face. "Are your tears for your soul?"

"I . . . don't know," Gynethe Mehaut admitted, horrified at her candor.

"Then how dare you cry?" Bishop Berahtram demanded. "How can you do such a reprehensible thing? Do you want to be immured?"

"No . . . No, I don't," Gynethe Mehaut said, appalled at the notion of being walled up, with only a single slot for bread and water, and a grate through which to Confess, until she died.

"It is what I must do if you cannot Confess everything and repent of all you have done to bring dishonor on your family and your Church," said Bishop Berahtram.

Gynethe Mehaut shook her head repeatedly. "I intend nothing against the Church," she whispered, and broke off, coughing.

"You must do your utmost to acknowledge your sins." He rapped out the words crisply. "Tonight you may contemplate your errors. You will not sleep. Use your meditation bell to keep yourself awake. And when you have finally numbered your sins, you will Confess them to me at None tomorrow. Then you may rest, if your Confession is complete. Otherwise, you must not have the succor of rest, for you will be prey to demons and you will end up like Sorra Riccardis Vigia, in the throes of Hell."

Gynethe Mehaut sighed deeply. She dreaded what lay ahead, but she could not turn from it. It was hard to get out a few more words. "I will thank God for His Goodness."

"You will humble yourself, White Woman," said Bishop Berahtram. "The attention you have received has corrupted you."

It was difficult for her to move, as if her limbs were weighted, or the cloth was suddenly sodden. She struggled to her feet, trying to stand without feeling dizzy. There was something she ought to say to the Bishop, but she could not bring it to mind. As she started toward the corridor, Sorra Riccardis Vigia began laughing again, a high, nervous bray that alarmed her more than she could admit. "Sublime," she said, her voice cracking.

"What?" he asked sharply, standing to block her at the entrance to the corridor.

"It is . . . my hope that . . ." She could not speak any more.

"That what? What?" Bishop Berahtram insisted, leaning toward her. "What do you mean?"

She tried to speak, but only a gagging sound came from her, for her throat was dry and as fiery as the hot wind of summer. Ducking her head, she made a gesture of abject apology and began to cough again, all the while clasping her hands together in supplication to the Bishop. The coughing continued and finally stopped, leaving her struggling to breathe.

"I will order a cup of wine for you tonight, but you must not let it lure you into sleep. Do you want a scourge to keep you awake?" Bishop Berahtram offered. "You have more prayers to recite."

"I . . . can't," she forced herself to say.

"You must," he reminded her, the hint of concession gone. "If you do not pray loud, how will anyone know you aren't sleeping? Must I order one of the Sorrae to whip you?"

As much as she wanted to scream, Gynethe Mehaut could not, and that made it seem much worse to her. She crossed her arms on her breast and tried to maintain a repentant demeanor, but it was becoming more difficult than she had first anticipated. Swallowing hard against the pain and rage that seemed to choke her, she mouthed, "Put a Sorra to watch me. For the sake of my soul."

Bishop Berahtram struck her across the face. "You insolent whore! You faithless harlot!"

With a ragged cry, Gynethe Mehaut reeled back, slamming into the wall and sliding down the rough stones to the floor. She covered her head with her hands and began to weep silently, wretchedly. Had she been less enervated, she would have tried to resist this assault, but all she could do was cower under the continuing blows and insults, and implore God to tell her what sins she had committed that deserved this extremity of chastisement and to feel the silence that was the most condemnation she would ever receive. She began to crawl along the corridor back toward her cubiculum, driven by the Bishop's kicks and blows and her distress. Twice she tried to speak, but all that came out was a breathless caw, and that increased her misery. She was vaguely aware of Sorra Riccardis Vigia laughing, and that set the seal on her utter dejection.

"I will send Abba Dympna to watch you, and to be sure you do not sleep. If you cannot remain awake, she will flog you." Bishop Berahtram felt the full strength of his zeal, and knew he was serving God and the Pope to the very limits of his devotion. "You will Confess at None, and then you shall rest."

Gynethe Mehaut nodded and made a gesture of submission, hoping this would stem the tide of abuse being heaped upon her. As another kick landed on her ribs, she curled into a ball and lay, whimpering, a few steps from the door to her cubiculum. She had never been more harrowed than she was now; her despair was so profound that it stopped her tears and bestowed upon her a black, fatalistic calm. Carefully and slowly she got to her feet and made her way into her penitent's cell, finding enough voice to say, "I await the Abba," before she pulled the door closed on herself. Aware that the Bishop was watching her, she stood very still, making herself remain upright through determination alone. Her lips moved as she began her prayers, although no sound came.

When Abba Dympna came to Gynethe Mehaut's cubiculum, she carried a tray with half a loaf of bread, a skin of water, and a small cup of wine. She let herself into the cell and put the tray down on the round stool that was usually employed for Confession. "Gynethe Mehaut," she said, noticing the blank expression on her white face.

"Good Abba," Gynethe Mehaut managed to grate out; she went back to her silent recitation of prayers.

"I have brought a flagellum with me," the Abba said, pulling it from under her stolla. The short-handled whip had six lashes, each one with a small iron star tied to the end. "The Bishop has told me I must use it to keep you awake."

"So he has told me, as well," Gynethe Mehaut breathed. Her throat was so sore it was hard for her to think of anything but surmounting the pain.

"You may have your meal," she said, indicating the bread, water, and wine. "Water first," she added.

Gynethe Mehaut was famished, but the thought of swallowing anything was appalling—she doubted even the water could go down her throat without intense agony. She ducked her head obediently and went to the stool. She lifted the skin of water and took the plug from its neck, then tried to drink. The water was sweet, and her thirst began to slake as she drank, but her throat shot new anguish through her with every gulp. When the skin was almost empty, she set it aside and reached for the bread, breaking off a bit of it and soaking it in the wine, hoping this would ease it down. She chewed carefully, trying to soften the coarse-milled grains. The pain was fierce but endurable, and she broke off more bread to soak in wine.

"Are you well, child?" Abba Dympna asked, noticing the difficulties Gynethe Mehaut was having. Her manner was careful, as wary as it was gentle.

"Sore," she said hoarsely, pointing to her neck.

"Your penance is severe," said the Abba. "If the Bishop were not here, I would modify it. There is little merit in demanding such stringent disciplines."

Gynethe Mehaut shook her head emphatically. "No," she whispered. "The Bishop has done what he has vowed to do." She wanted to scream but kept silent.

"It can't be necessary to impose so much on you." She sounded genuine but her eyes flicked from Gynethe Mehaut's face to the crucifix above the cot. "You cannot be as dangerous as they say." The doubt in her words leached the sympathy from them.

"The Bishop . . ." She stifled a cough; her whole body felt warm, and her clothing seemed scratchy.

"You don't seem well, Sorra," said Abba Dympna, taking a step back from her, as if afraid of taking contagion from her.

"I'm . . . hot," Gynethe Mehaut murmured.

"If your penance is making you ill, you are being overly austere. God does not ask us to compromise our repentance with illness. When you are well, you may resume your penance, but now you need a nurse." She sighed uneasily, keeping her distance from her charge. "Bishop Berahtram is a devout man, and full of good works. He doesn't always see that others do not have his capacity for rigor."

Coughing again, Gynethe Mehaut was hardly able to say, "I will do . . . what I must . . ."

"You are feverish," said Abba Dympna, beginning to be frightened; if disease visited the nunnery, all of the Sorrae were vulnerable to sickness. "You should be taken to the infirmary. We must tend you, and end your suffering."

It was difficult to listen to this; Gynethe Mehaut knew it was meant in kindness, but she also knew it was dangerous for her to listen to such seditious words. She busied herself with eating the wine-soaked bread and inwardly asked God's Mother to intercede for her and accept her suffering for the expiation of her sins. She was almost finished with her meal when she tottered and stumbled back, landing half-on, half-off her cot, a wail of dismay renewing the burning in her throat. Her face, flushed from wine and fever, was an alarming shade of red, almost as ruddy as her eyes.

Abba Dympna stared at her in shock. "Demons!" she shouted.

Gynethe Mehaut wanted to say no, that it was the wine—it had gone to her head, creating the color that so alarmed the Abba—and her overwhelming tiredness, not demons. She could not speak, and her attempts to breathe out the words went unheeded.

"Demons! She is being taken by demons! Look at her! There are Hell's fires in her! Oh, God, God, save me! Deliver me from this evil!" Abba Dympna used the flagellum, bringing it down hard across Gynethe Mehaut's cheeks and neck.

"Drive the demons out!" She struck again, beginning to sob with fear. "The Anti-Christ! The Anti-Christ!"

The sound of running footsteps in the corridor brought another peal of ghastly laughter from Sorra Riccardis Vigia, and a jumble of shouts and cries as Bishop Berahtram and a group of nuns rushed toward Gynethe Mehaut's cubiculum.

As he pulled open the door, Bishop Berahtram rapped out an order. "Someone go to Sant' Yrieix and bring Patre Drasius. Tell him to bring his pyx." He did not bother to notice if anyone carried out his order; he knew a slave would be riding a mule down the mountain before Vigil.

Abba Dympna was flushed and shaken as she struck at Gynethe Mehaut again, whooping in dread as she used her whip again and again. She screamed prayers and petitions to God for His intervention, then retreated to the far side of the cubiculum as the Bishop flung into the room. "See! See!" She pointed at Gynethe Mehaut, her eyes huge.

Bishop Berahtram snatched the flagellum from her and stared around at Gynethe Mehaut, who huddled, blood spattering her clothes, her face bleeding from gouges and scratches left by the Abba's attack. He came up to the White Woman and looked down at her. "So. It is known."

"No," Gynethe Mehaut whimpered. She pressed her bandaged hands to her face.

"This is the proof, isn't it?" Bishop Berahtram exclaimed; this was all he had hoped for, a vindication of what he had done to Gynethe Mehaut. "Now we are sure." He tried not to smile and almost succeeded.

"She is foul! She is corrupted!" Abba Dympna shouted, doing her best to escape from the cubiculum; she could hardly stand for shaking.

"We shall contain her," said Bishop Berahtram. "Go to your chapel and pray. Cleanse yourself, Abba." He took her elbow and all but thrust her out of the cell, shoving the other nuns aside.

The nuns who crowded in the door showed a mixture of trepidation and rapt excitement as they peered in at Gynethe Mehaut. One of them, a woman with a withered leg, said, "She is dangerous."

"Not if we keep ourselves staunch in our faith," said Bishop Berahtram, unwilling to give up his victory to such pessimism. "Pray for God's protection, and you will be proof against anything that Satan might do. Go away, all of you. Go to your chapel." He bent down and grabbed Gynethe Mehaut by her wrists and hauled her to her feet. "You are hot. It is a foretaste of Hell."

Sorra Riccardis Vigia's laughter turned to howls that were enhanced by the echoes they created.

"Anti-Christ," accused a soft-faced nun whose mouth was square with hatred.

Gynethe Mehaut cowered, struggling to master her skittering thoughts; the ache behind her eyes was sharp as fangs, and she could not overcome the hurt in her throat or the pain in her torn face. She struggled with the Bishop, trying to break free of him as she heard the door of her cubiculum slam closed, leaving her alone with him. She stole a look at him and saw the triumph shining in his face. "No," she tried to say.

"You are everything Bishop Iso said," Bishop Berahtram gloated. "You are sacrilege incarnate. You are the font of evil." He pulled her toward the cot and pushed her down upon it. "You summon up all the Deadly Sins, and you profane everything holy. You will be immured. You will be held captive here so that you cannot spread your contagion to other faithful Christians." He held her down. "Your blood is the blood of perdition. Your breath is the breath of damnation."

Gynethe Mehaut felt the sting of tears in her scored face, but she could not stop herself from weeping. Why she wept she could not determine. Was she, in fact, the pernicious thing the Bishop claimed? Was she so treacherous that she could be the vessel of all iniquity and not know it? She had heard that Satan was a subtle foe, filled with lies and preying upon the weakness of men, but how was it that she had become so vile? Her woe grew, and with it, a grief she could not name. To have endured so much and have it all come to this! She keened, the high, piercing sound stopping Sorra Riccardis Vigia's laughter at last.

"You will be exorcized," said Bishop Berahtram, his voice cutting through her wail with its icy determination. "When Patre Drasius comes, Satan will be driven out of you, and then, for your own salvation, and the salvation of all the Sorrae, you will be immured. May you be redeemed." He spat the last as he began to tie her to the cot, using his girdle to bind her wrists to the frame.

"Too tight," she muttered as the Bishop tightened the leather around her wrist.

"You must not escape," said Bishop Berahtram. "Satan is wily, and he will use you to bring down any who approach you." He used his knee to hold her body down while he tugged at the girdle. He pulled her girdle from around her waist and used it to bind her foot to the bar at the end of the cot. "You will be restrained until Patre Drasius arrives."

"But . . ." She began to cough, her body wrenching against the bonds that held her.

The Bishop pressed his knee down more firmly and worked on tying her other ankle. "You will not move! You will vomit up devils if you move!" He got off her and worked to tighten all his knots. Behind his outrage there was a hint of terror; Gynethe Mehaut sensed it and found it difficult to believe. "You will recite all the prayers of Vigil, and you will keep praying until Pater Drasius comes, and then you will Confess to him and to me. If your Confession is sufficient, and your repentance genuine, we will grant you Absolution, and—"

"Immure me?" she asked, nearly inaudibly.

"You should be thankful that God in His Mercy will let you expiate your sins, not question the means of being restored to Grace." Bishop Berahtram was panting a little, his face shining from effort and ardor. "I will watch you through the night, and if you sleep, I will see that you regret it."

"I will not sleep," Gynethe Mehaut promised in an under-voice. She knew her hands would shortly ache and then begin to lose feeling.

"No, you will not." This was a grim vow. He picked up the water-skin and sprinkled what little remained of it on her face and then used the cuff of his sleeve to wipe away the worst of the blood on her face. "You have been a trial to all of us, which the Sorrae have borne for the sake of their souls and the sanctity of the convent." He put his hand on her forehead. "You are burning."

"I . . . hurt," she strained to say.

"If you are ill, then it is God's punishment. But you will have to appeal to God for your healing," said Bishop Berahtram.

"You are supposed to be a healer," Gynethe Mehaut challenged, the sound of it like ice breaking.

"My skills are for the afflictions of the world, not the visitations of Satan or God," he said, resenting again that he no longer had the medicaments he had been given at Paderborn. Not that he would want to use such valuable substances on such as Gynethe Mehaut. Panting, he turned around and flung out of the room, leaving Gynethe Mehaut in darkness.

It was too difficult for Gynethe Mehaut to speak again, so she lay back as much as her tied ankles and wrists would allow; she was grateful that her arms and legs were pulled too tightly for her to relax for she was so worn out that if she had the least opportunity to fall asleep, she would. She stared up at the ceiling, trying to make out the various cracks and fissures that had held her attention during the long isolation of her days here. The room was too dark to see much more than the faint spill of light from the grate in the door, and she longed for a lamp, hoping that she would be provided one so that while she was watched, her guardian would not be lulled into sleep. She waited, anticipating the arrival of Abba Dympna and, after her, Patre Drasius. These two would provide an end to her uncertainty, one way or another. She recalled the time she had spent with Rakoczy, and it seemed to her to have been ages ago, so remote to her now as to be the stuff of tales. It had been sweeter than she knew to be with him, to enjoy his courtesy and his wooing. Few women were shown such high regard as he had shown her; he had been as noble a lover as anyone could wish for, no matter how he chose to love her. And how peculiar it was to think of love without addressing God or the Emperor. It was a difficult concession to admit that she wanted what she had had from him, and lying here tied as if for slaughter, she worried that she might remember the time with Rakoczy as finer than it was because her life had become so limited. Suddenly she realized she had been half-speaking her thoughts, her wrecked voice too hushed—she hoped—to be heard, but ruinous in what she said. At once she pressed her lips together and told herself that she should say nothing more, particularly when anyone could listen to her. She must not reveal anything about Rakoczy beyond what they already knew; she must never hint of their love. The word alone frightened her, and if it had that capacity, she could not bring herself to think what it would mean to admit the whole to others.

The sound of the door opening startled her; she jumped as much as she could, given her bonds.

"So you are held down," said Abba Dympna, holding up a single oil-lamp. "Just as well. Who knows what mischief you might—"

"No . . . mischief," said Gynethe Mehaut.

"Have you spent the time praying?" the Abba asked in disbelief.

Gynethe Mehaut could not bring herself to answer. She made a sound that was not a cry of protest or a cough, but something in between.

"You are bringing death to the convent," said Abba Dympna, her voice sharpened by her barely controlled dread. "You are unnatural and you're marked by sin."

It was too hard to answer, so Gynethe Mehaut shook her head repeatedly, and saw this did nothing to soften the Abba's convictions.

"You will Confess, and when you do, we will begin to rid the convent of your baleful influence. You will be walled up so you may harm no one else for the rest of your days. Then the demons may come to you as they will, and harm no one but you, who are already their servant." Abba Dympna stepped back two steps to the wall and leaned on it as if to be held up by it. "Your Confession is the only thing that will save the rest of us, so you will make it."

For a long moment, Gynethe Mehaut contemplated Abba Dympna, all the while vowing inwardly that she would do everything that she had to in order to satisfy the Abba and the Bishop, for she could not endure much more of the demands they put upon her—she would tell them everything, that was, but what had passed between her and Rakoczy: that was her one treasured secret, and she would keep it safe within her as long as she had breath left in her. As she promised this to herself, she hoped she could uphold her determination, not just for Rakoczy, but for the sake of her own soul.

T EXT OF A DISPATCH FROM K ARL-LO -M AGNE AT A ACHEN TO H IERNOM
R AKOCZY AT HIS FISCS, CARRIED BY SPECIAL I MPERIAL COURIER AND
DELIVERED A UGUST 2, 801.

*To the highly reputed and esteemed Magnatus, Hiernom Rakoczy, Comes
Sant' Germainius, at his fiscs near Sant' Cyricus, the greetings of Karl-lo-
Magne, Emperor of the Franks and Longobards and Imperial Governor of all
the Romans in the West on this, the 9*th *day of July in the Pope's year 801.*

*My dear Magnatus, loath as I am to act against you after the many services
you have rendered me and duties you have undertaken without the promise of
advancement or favor to give you the inclination to act, certain accusations
have been laid against you that demand my most attentive response. In other
circumstances I would not be moved by these various charges, for I have seen
for myself how devoted you have been to my work. But there are those who see
this dedication as subtle enmity, and are alarmed that I have been willing to
put as much reliance upon you as I have, and for that reason, I must reconsider
the favor I have extended to you and assign it elsewhere, among my own
Franks, so that no one can claim you as an enemy again.*

*It is unfortunate that these accusations should come just now, when
Bishop Iso is claiming all manner of vindication for himself regarding the
woman Gynethe Mehaut, who, as you must have heard, has admitted to
having congress with demons under the impression that they would take the
whiteness from her skin and the red from her eyes, though they told her that
marked her as their kinswoman. Had you not been her escort to Roma, few
calumnies could be made to hold against you, but as you have been in the
company of a Confessed diabolist—one who has been immured and for
whom the Mass of the Dead has been sung—you have taken her taint, for all
believe that no man can resist the lures of female demons. I cannot stand
against such certainties, as you must understand, and I am fully aware that
there are cogent reasons for the men who are afraid to have such fears, for
well we know that there are many devils and other agents of Satan loose in
the land, all determined to bring down the True Church and leave the world
in the hands of the most dreadful fiends.*

*Therefore, reluctant though I am to do it, I am rescinding my grant of fiscs
that I gave you, and I am requiring that you depart from them within ten days
of receiving this notification. My courier will inform me of the day on which
you read this, and he will remain to see for himself that you have departed. My
second cousin Magenfrid will come in September to occupy the fiscs, and he
will have my authority to imprison you if you have not left the fiscs by then.*

You may take your own belongings, of course, and as many horses and mules as you may need for your journey. I am sorry that I cannot provide you an escort to whichever border you seek, but as you know, the Great Pox has been rampant in the center of Franksland and I cannot spare soldiers, nor missi dominici, to guide you. I trust to your resourcefulness to bring you safely to the border you seek. You will be allowed to leave Franksland or Longobardia without any taxation being imposed upon you in my name, for in leaving your horses behind, you have supplied enough value to make silver an unnecessary addition to what I have already received. So long as you are gone by the time I have stipulated, you will be excused further charges against you. It is not much of a concession but it is the best I can offer you.

So that your passage will be unhampered, I am including with this a passagius, which will authorize you to traverse all Frankish and Longobardian roads without let or hindrance. The passagius will be enforced for forty days, after which time, if you are still within my territories, you will have to make what arrangements you can for your journey, and on terms that are not supported by my favor. This may seem harsh, but it is as lenient as I dare to be, given the feelings that have been aroused against you here in Aachen. It is a sad thing when I must turn away from so resolute a hobu as you have proven to be—and if you were a Frank, I would not—but these are difficult times, and, as you know yourself, I am not in a position to risk offending my own, for it is their support that has made my Empire flourish; much as I hold you in high esteem, I will not compromise all I have worked for all these years. I am sure you will show your fealty in the speed of your departure. If you do not leave in the time I have ordered, soldiers will be sent to the fiscs and you will be taken into custody in my name, and brought before my Court to answer for your defiance; I must warn you that if this should happen, your enemies will have an opportunity to strip you of everything you own and to cast you into prison for the rest of your life. As much as I would want not to condemn you, I cannot make an exception of you, a foreigner, and then impose such sentences on Franks, for that would lead to insurrection and war.

Since you will have to leave behind many horses, I will take them in change and add them to my own herds. This is as much of a tribute as I can offer to you, and to that end, I have ordered that your catch-colt—the tall one with the red coat—will be put into my stable as well, as one of my own mounts. This will show my kinsmen that I do not disdain you, and it may make it possible at some future time for you to return to Franksland and to my Court, when there is less unrest.

I pray that we will meet again, on this earth. There are many things that I should still like to learn from you, and I am certain that, in the years ahead, I will be able to make some demonstration of my good opinion once again. In the meantime, I wish you swift travel and the satisfaction of knowing you have served me well.

Karl-lo-Magne
Emperor of the Franks and Longobards and
Imperial Governor of all the Romans of the West
(his sigil by his own hand)
by the hand of Fratre Hinehild

chapter fifteen

INSECTS BUZZED IN THE WARM NIGHT, small eddies of them following the two men and nine animals who made their way along the broad ruts that led across the swath of pastureland toward the dark mass of the forest; the moon, two nights short of full, poured down its pellucid light on the fields in the last throes of summer, the brightness making all shadows blacker by contrast.

"There may be bandits in the woods," Rorthger warned; he could not forget Waifar and their first encounter with him, and all that had resulted from it. That alone made him apprehensive; he was riding behind Rakoczy, leading a horse and three well-laden mules, and the hard pace his master had set over the last ten days was beginning to tell on him as well as their animals. They were moving through Austrasia at nine leagues each day, the best time they had made since they left Sant' Cyricus.

"There probably are, but at this time of night, they will all be asleep. They only watch the roads during the day, or at twilight. No one is abroad after full dark, and the brigands know this better than anyone." Rakoczy spoke as quietly as he could and still be heard; he led a remount and two pack-mules.

Rorthger accepted this. "The moonlight won't help us when we get to the forest."

"No; we will find a place to stop before we get there. It is still many leagues distant." Rakoczy relented. "Your point is well-taken, old friend. I must not punish you or our animals for my own dismay."

"Dismay?" Rorthger said before he could stop himself; he did not want to question Rakoczy, knowing that such inquiry could send his master into a more removed state of mind than the one in which he already was. "Why should you feel dismay?"

"What else should I feel: perhaps chagrin," Rakoczy said ironically. "I, of all men, should know not to rely upon the gratitude of rulers."

This admission brought Rorthger fully alert. "Did you rely upon Great Karl?"

"Far more than I should have," Rakoczy allowed with a hint of a rueful smile. "I should have remembered that for a Frank, kinship is everything, and that I, as a stranger, would never have his complete support no matter what he promised. I knew that, but I allowed myself to be persuaded that he would not be bound by the demands of his relatives. It was foolish and I know better: nothing is more compelling than the ties of blood." He managed a single chuckle. "How could I forget such an essential thing?"

An owl flew over them on silent wings, then dove into the field, emerging with a rat in its talons.

"Great Karl doesn't uphold blood as you do, and he professes to honor merit above blood; it was an easy thing to believe, for he has advanced those not among his kin—think of Alcuin, who is no Frank," said Rorthger. He peered into the limpid distance. "There is a hamlet up ahead."

"Yes; I see it," said Rakoczy. "We'll probably hear dogs barking shortly."

"Doesn't that trouble you?" Rorthger asked; he had seen Rakoczy like this many times in the past, and always it had disquieted him—that careful courtesy and slightly reticent demeanor that served to tell Rorthger that there was deep pain and intense grief behind the self-contained facade.

"They will assume deer have come down to graze in their fields, or a bear is in their orchard. They won't expect two men and a string of horses and mules." He looked at the leads in his hands. "If they see our tracks in the morning, they'll assume merchants went by before dawn."

"You're sure of that, are you?" Rorthger challenged.

Rakoczy did not answer at once. He kept his eyes on the road ahead. At last, when they had gone another half-league, he spoke up again. "The worst they might do is throw rocks."

"And they will remember," Rorthger warned.

"Perhaps, if they actually see us," said Rakoczy. "But so far, not even one dog has barked." He urged his grey on as the road began to rise. "Do you remember the ponies we rode across the steppes? They would be useful to us just now, wouldn't they?"

"Yes, they would," said Rorthger. "And so would good Roman roads."

"True enough," said Rakoczy. "In another two months, this will be a mire, and it will be well into spring before anyone will travel on it again."

Rorthger knew it would not be possible to get Rakoczy to speak about what was vexing him, so he abandoned the attempt. He settled in for a long, silent ride on the twisting road. The moon rode overhead, sliding down toward the west as the night began to fade; they were not far from the trees now, and the first stirrings of night's end had begun, and Rorthger looked around for an isolated building to bring to Rakoczy's attention.

"There," said Rakoczy, pointing to a small stone chapel. "It is a good place to spend the day."

"If no monk or hermit lives in it," Rorthger cautioned.

"No, not now," said Rakoczy. "There is a Pox sign on the side of it. Whoever lived there died during the summer."

Rorthger knew that Rakoczy could see in relative darkness far better than he could, but this startled him. "You can see it?"

"So can you if you care to look," said Rakoczy. "It is quite large." He pointed to the side of the squat stone building. "In rust-colored pigment. The Great Pox took a high toll on this part of Franksland since May. We have seen its depredation from our crossing at Mainz. Everything to the east of the river has been blighted by it. That hamlet may have lost half its people if the outbreak was as severe in this region as it was at Mainz; they lost at least one in six in that town—that has been the pattern here for more than two centuries."

"The Great Pox is a curse to men," said Rorthger. "Anyone it touches takes its mark whether they live or die." He wanted to add something about the whiteness that marked Gynethe Mehaut, but he could not bring himself to speak of her, fearing he would worsen the pain that had Rakoczy in its grip; he bided his time and hoped that eventually Rakoczy might offer his thoughts of his own accord.

Rakoczy said nothing more until they reached the turning for the chapel, and then he said, "If you will look for a well or a spring?"

"Certainly," said Rorthger. "The horses and mules need drink."

"And it would be pleasant to wash. I feel as if I have grime everywhere," said Rakoczy; he noticed a stand of reeds. "There may be a stream."

"If there is a stream, there are surely ducks," said Rorthger, who did not want to admit how hungry he was.

"Yes," Rakoczy said, his tone still distant.

"Do you plan to go on before nightfall?" Rorthger asked, and patted the neck of his copper-dun as if to reassure the horse that their long night was almost over; his back was tired, and he hoped for a full day of rest before they rode on.

"Probably we should leave in late afternoon." Rakoczy was almost at the entrance to the chapel. "We'll have a clear night again and I hope to make the most of it while the moon is at its brightest."

"Shouldn't we go after dark? You will be able to guide us through the trees, and fewer people will see us," Rorthger suggested. "I will catch a brace of ducks."

"Just as well. We're both hungry." Rakoczy got out of the saddle and took the reins and leads, pulling the animals toward the entrance to the chapel. "Take them all inside. Give them grain from the sacks, and a palmful of oil each."

"All right," said Rorthger as he dismounted. "The peasants won't like having their chapel used as a stall."

"Will you tell them? For I won't," Rakoczy countered with a trace of amusement. "We can bed the floor and sweep it out before we leave."

This satisfied Rorthger. "I'll help you cut reeds for bedding. We have time enough before dawn." He forced open the door, pushing it back in spite of groaning hinges; the chapel was dank from disuse, the air stale. The altar was little more than a plank table under two high, barred windows.

"Close quarters," said Rakoczy, moving his animals inside and making room for Rorthger.

"Truly," said Rorthger as he came inside with his horses and mules.

"We'll make do," said Rakoczy. He tied the reins and leads to the frame of a small shrine near the door. "I'll take the sickle with me. If you'll see to the unsaddling, I'll get the first armful of reeds."

"Of course," said Rorthger, and secured his animals to the other side of the shrine. "Which Saint is this, do you suppose?"

From the door, Rakoczy laughed slightly. "I suppose it is one of the old gods who has been re-formed as a Saint. Look at the cat at her feet. One of the old goddesses rode in a chariot drawn by cats—I forget which one, but I suspect the villagers could tell me, for if they say this Saint has a connection with cats, I surmise that connection is similar to the one the old goddess had." He slipped out of the door, leaving Rorthger to his tasks. He returned a short while later with a double armload of reeds. He put them down almost as soon as he was inside and began to spread them about. "Not as good as straw, but better than branches and twigs," he said as he continued to work on the bedding.

Rorthger had stood the saddles on end and was preparing rough-leather nosebags with grain and oil for their animals. "I'll take them down to drink in a while."

"Why don't you go get more reeds and snare a pair of ducks for our comestus?" Rakoczy recommended. "I'll tend to the grooming; I'll make camphor wraps for their legs to reduce the chance of lameness." He picked up the box of brushes and began to work on his older grey. "Their manes need wool-fat. I'll treat them, and their tails."

"Very good," said Rorthger. "I'll catch the ducks—you can have the blood and I'll eat their flesh." He knew he sounded hungry, and for once, he did not care. Taking the sickle and a pair of weighted nets, he left Rakoczy to care for the horses and mules. As he stepped outside he looked up and saw that the eastern sky was beginning to lighten, a soft dove color shone over the mountains; in the west, the moon had dropped below the peaks. In the distance, a cock crowed, announcing morning, and Rorthger hurried to do his work, not wanting to be discovered by early-rising peasants. A short while later, as he snared his second duck, he heard two cows lowing; he hastened to cut an armful of reeds and carried them and the squawking ducks back to the chapel.

"I don't think it would be wise to make a fire," Rakoczy said as he saw Rorthger come inside. He was brushing down the fourth mule and had a large jar of wool-fat tucked under his arm. "Do you want me to flay the ducks for you?"

"I'll do it," said Rorthger. "When you're through."

"All right," said Rakoczy, and went on working. "I want to braid the mules' manes, to keep them from worse tangles. We'll be into the woods shortly, and they'll have brambles and branches to snare knots in their manes."

"Do you have thongs enough to tie them?" Rorthger spread the reeds he had brought; in the nets the ducks still struggled.

"I believe so." He smeared wool-fat into the mane and forelock, then used a wooden comb to spread it through the hair. "One more to go." He did the same for the jenny-mule's tail.

"All right," said Rorthger. "The peasants in the hamlet must be waking."

"I heard the cows, and the cock," said Rakoczy. "Milking will be first, and that will take a bit of time. When that's done, they'll go out into the fields. We have a little time yet." He moved on to the last mule and gave him a good brushing.

"A pity we had to leave Livius behind," said Rorthger, watching Rakoczy closely. "He would have assured us a welcome at any fisc."

"But he would be remembered and he was wanted by Great Karl, who would have begrudged our taking him." Rakoczy continued to ply his brush. "That and the catch-colt—such a sturdy horse, and sweet-tempered."

"For the Emperor's daughters to ride," said Rorthger, and before Rakoczy could say anything more, changed the subject. "We're all hungry."

Rakoczy put his brush aside and reached for the wooden comb. "As soon as I am finished with this, I'll deal with the ducks."

Rorthger nodded. "I could use a good meal."

"So could I," Rakoczy admitted candidly. "But ducks will have to suffice for now." He combed wool-fat through the jack-mule's mane. "I am sorry I couldn't do anything to mitigate what became of Gynethe Mehaut," he said in an undervoice. "I would have liked to have spared her suffering; she has had more than she should have done long before now."

"Anything you might have done would have made her situation worse," said Rorthger. "Think of Nicoris. She didn't—"

"She didn't want to live as a vampire must, and neither would Gynethe Mehaut. I know. And your point is well-taken." He stopped grooming and put the brushes and the jar of wool-fat away. "Give me the ducks. I'll do the camphor wraps while you eat."

Rorthger lifted the two nets with their protesting contents. "Here they are."

"I won't take long," Rakoczy assured him, and went to the far corner of the chapel to take what he needed as privately as he could. When he came back to Rorthger a short time later, the two ducks were silent and limp; Rorthger took them and went to work with his knife, removing the skin so that he could eat the raw flesh. When he was finished, Rakoczy had completed wrapping their animals' legs and was nearly done braiding the mules' manes. "Are you going to rest?"

"I think it would be prudent, don't you?" Rakoczy asked. "We have a long way to go to Wendish territory, and not many days to get there. The King's passagius doesn't allow us much time to reach the frontier, and I don't want to try to extend its grant of passage."

"Do you think he intended that you shouldn't get away?" Rorthger asked as he cut away his first long strip of succulent duck.

"I would like to think that he would not be so petty as that, but I cannot be certain," said Rakoczy slowly. He tied his last small braid with a short leather thong and finally put his things away. "I will be glad of a short rest, I admit."

"But you're not well-fed," said Rorthger.

"And I will not be for a while," Rakoczy agreed. "Still, I can't see any advantage in trying to find a woman to visit in her sleep—not here, and not at Fulda in the Travelers' Hall." The famous monastery was a day ahead of them. "The cubicula are watched."

"Then one of the slaves?" Rorthger suggested.

"No. I will take nothing from slaves. They have lost too much already." He frowned, remembering his time with the Emir's son.

Rorthger knew better than to argue, but he could not keep from fretting as he ate the two ducks; he paid no attention to Rakoczy when he fetched his bedroll from the pack-saddle and opened it on the rough stones of the chapel floor. "Rest well," he said as Rakoczy stretched out on the bedroll. "I'll take care of the horses and mules," he said as he finished his meal.

"Thank you," Rakoczy said, lying back on the thin layer of his native earth.

After he disposed of the duck bones and skin in a hastily dug hole, Rorthger took their pail and went out to get water for each of their animals in turn. On his fifth trip to the stream, he saw a young boy staring at him from the other side of the water, eyes wide and face showing worried astonishment. Keeping the lad in his view, Rorthger filled the pail and went back to the chapel, noticing with relief that Rakoczy had not yet fallen into the stupor that passed for sleep among vampires. "I was seen."

"By whom?" Rakoczy asked.

"A child." Rorthger held the pail for the third mule.

"Boy or girl?" Rakoczy had pushed up onto his elbow and was watching Rorthger closely.

"A boy," said Rorthger. "About six or seven."

Rakoczy frowned. "Did he speak to you?"

"No. He gaped at me, and fretted," said Rorthger. "He might have seen a haunt."

"You said nothing?" Rakoczy asked, sitting all the way up.

"Of course not. He was alarmed enough without that." Rorthger shook his head. "He was still standing there, watching me, when I came back here."

"That's something," said Rakoczy. "If he is apprehensive, it may buy us some time." He rose and began to wrap up his bedroll. "I'll help you saddle up."

"Do you mean you intend to leave?" Rorthger stared at him. "The animals haven't all been watered yet."

"We'll do it on the road," said Rakoczy. "Give the others a little of what's in that pail."

Rorthger shook his head. "They're tired."

"Then we'll go slowly." Rakoczy tied his bedroll to the pack-saddle again.

"Won't the *passagius* give you the right to rest here, if anyone questions you?" Rorthger asked.

"If there is someone in that village who knows what a *passagius* is, which I doubt, and someone who can read it, which is unlikely, then it might help us, but under the circumstances, it makes more sense to get away while we can." He took a saddle-pad and put it on the grey he had been leading. "Ride the remounts. We'll remain at Fulda for two days, to let the animals recover."

"And if the Great Pox is there?" Rorthger took the pail to the next mule. "These animals are wearied already."

"So are you, and I," said Rakoczy, hefting the saddle onto the gelding's back. "We should be away as quickly as possible."

"Why do you expect trouble?" Rorthger demanded as he set the pail aside.

"Because this place is a shrine and we are strangers. Our presence defiles this chapel, or so the peasants are likely to think. There is no church in the village, nor is a monastery or convent near-by, so this is their sacred place and if they are like most Frankish peasants, they will defend it from outsiders." He secured the girth and began to buckle on the breast-collar.

"This isn't Csimenae's land, and there are no cups of horses' blood on the altar," Rorthger pointed out. "You don't know these people will be as . . . ferocious as she has been."

"Her people aren't the only ones who guard their shrines." Rakoczy put the next saddle-pad on the jack-mule standing beside his horse. "I'll remove the wraps before we go. I want them to get as much benefit as they can from them."

"Do you think the peasants will come here?" Rorthger began to saddle his red-speckled roan. "I'll lead the copper-dun, as you like."

"It's easier on the horses." He lifted the laden pack-saddle with an ease that would have astonished anyone but Rorthger or Olivia; he settled it on the mule's back and reached under for the girth. "Are the nose-bags empty? These two are."

"Yes," said Rorthger. "They're hungry as well as tired."

"I'll see if we can purchase some apples along the way, for a treat." He tightened the girth and then the breast-collar. "I want to be away from here as soon as possible."

Rorthger kept his thoughts to himself, but he was convinced that Rakoczy was being more cautious than necessary. He kept on with his work; although he sensed Rakoczy's urgency, he did not feel the same pressure within himself. Still, his long centuries with Rakoczy had taught him to respect his master's intuitions. When he finished saddling the pack-mules, he handed a bridle to Rakoczy and kept one for himself as he removed nose-bags from all the animals. Rakoczy busied himself taking off the leg-wraps and storing them in the sack on the fourth mule's saddle while Rorthger gathered up the leads and handed three of them to Rakoczy, keeping four for himself. "Are you ready?" He swung up into the saddle as Rakoczy pushed the door open before mounting.

"Yes. And in good time," said Rakoczy. "A pity we didn't have time to sweep out the bedding, but . . ." He gathered up the reins and the leads and started toward the road. The sun was half-way up the sky, brilliant as brass in the cerulean expanse; the day was turning hot already.

They had gone less than a thousand paces when they came upon a group of peasants, many armed with pitchforks and sickles, coming toward them; four of the men in the lead had badly scarred faces and the wan look of those recovering from the Great Pox. Rakoczy pulled his horses and mules to the side of the road and allowed the people to pass. He did not expect any of the peasants to speak, for it was not acceptable for peasants to address a hobu without permission. By moving off the road he had been more generous than most Franks would be. He signaled to Rorthger to keep behind him.

When the peasants had passed, Rorthger said, "We should have left sooner."

"We went as quickly as we could," said Rakoczy. "At least we are on the road. And now, I think, it would be wise to pick up our pace for a while. The peasants will come back in a short while and we should be gone."

"Do you think they would detain a hobu and his servant?" Rorthger inquired.

"Do you think they would not? Who knows where we are?" Rakoczy pushed his gelding to a jog-trot, and reluctantly, the mules jogged after, craning their necks as the leads pulled on their halters.

Rorthger kicked his speckled roan to a jog and followed after Rakoczy and his remount and mules. By noon they were into the next valley and on a better road, leading to the monastery and town of Fulda. There were other travelers around them now, some of them showing the ravages of the Great Pox; a wagon drawn by goats held half-a-dozen children—orphans by the look of them—and behind them came a carpentum loaded with slaves bound for the monastery; a monk led the oxen.

"There's supposed to be a fair in the town," said a merchant from Longobardia, his clothes identifying him as much as his language. He had dared to speak to Rakoczy because his carrucum was laden with wine-casks bound for the table of the Bishop or the Abbott.

"Even with the Great Pox?" Rorthger said. "I would think most people wouldn't dare to enter the town." He spoke offhandedly as if he thought that would be the end of their talk, but the merchant beamed at him and fell in beside him on the road.

"You haven't lost a summer's worth of selling, as I have, and many of the peasants have, as well. They must have a market or face a hard, hard winter. After the Great Pox, who can blame them for wanting to bring what goods and wares they can, for trading and for a copper or two, or a tun of ale for a wheel of cheese. The Great Pox has taken a toll on us all. My own escort was struck, and when two men took the fever the other two refused to go on, so I was forced to journey alone or fail the Bishop." The merchant laughed with a kind of whimsy that was eloquent of years of just such troubles. "The Bishop wants his wine. That's something I may be sure of. The rest is in the hands of God and Fortune."

"And do you know this Bishop?" Rorthger asked, knowing it was expected of him.

"Of old, of old. He is Flodoard, a distant kinsman of Karl-lo-Magne himself. I have brought him wine for fourteen years, and he has never found a faulty barrel among my wares. He has even served some to the Emperor himself, and been praised for its quality. Well, he would do, with his family bond and Fulda such a prize. He has to show his gratitude." The merchant grinned. "I am Urtius, from Pavia. It's a pleasure to have someone to talk to."

"Urtius," said Rorthger. "I am the camerarius of Comes Sant' Germainius, my master." He could see the dubiety in the merchant's face but decided to ignore it.

"He doesn't look like much, black as a crow, and no jewels," said Urtius. "But what man travels in jewels if he has no soldiers to guard him?" He chuckled fulsomely. "The cloth of his gonelle is high quality, I can see that for myself, and his horses are from good lines—any fool must know it." He arched his brows speculatively, his large, fleshy features creasing into an obsequious grin.

"It is suitable to his rank," said Rorthger in a tone that would have put off most men.

But Urtius from Pavia was not easily discouraged. "A man of some influence, is he? Your master?"

"He is highly esteemed by Great Karl; he has done many things for him, and been thanked, though he isn't a Frank," said Rorthger, and in the next instant wished he had bit his tongue, for he saw Urtius' small bright eyes grow shiny.

"He is probably nothing but a faithless Bishop," said Urtius. "He has been sent away from his bishopric." He licked his lips eagerly.

"He is a Magnatus," said Rorthger, "and a man of learning."

"But not in the Church? Is he a Jew?" Urtius cocked his head. "I do business with Rindarus, the Jew. He is a great friend of the Bishop here."

"My master is faithful to the teaching of his fathers," said Rorthger.

"But you said the Comes isn't a Frank, didn't you?" Urtius feigned surprise. "He doesn't have the look of it, with dark hair and eyes. Was his mother from Hispania?"

"No, he isn't a Frank. That is why he was chosen for this errand. It would be wise for you to keep in mind that the journey we undertake is for the Emperor." Rorthger could see that Urtius was already anticipating boasting of this encounter, and perhaps enlarging upon it. "Keep in mind that secrecy is required for the task my master is charged with to succeed."

"Why would Great Karl prefer a foreigner to—" Suddenly he nodded. "Oh. Yes, indeed." He put his hand to his nose. "*Sub rosa*. Better not to use a Frank then."

"Exactly," said Rorthger, wishing he could break off this conversation. "Do you expect to have the Bishop receive you?"

This ploy failed. "How does it happen that you travel without escort?" asked Urtius, nodding toward the mules. "I would think that soldiers would—"

"Ah, but that would create more attention, and a war-like presence that would damage the mission," said Rorthger, and shot a sudden look at Rakoczy.

"So! He is more than a courier, after all." Urtius put his hand to his nose again. "Well, I will keep your council, and say nothing."

"I am grateful to you for your wisdom; if my duty is compromised it will go badly for the Emperor," said Rakoczy suddenly, and added to Rorthger in the language of the Asian steppes, "We had best avoid Fulda. We cannot suppose this man will not speak of this meeting."

"I am sorry, my master," said Rorthger in Frankish.

"Hardly your fault, old friend. These garrulous men can be tenacious. Perhaps I should have intervened before now. You had best say something that will frighten the fellow or he'll stay with us for the next two leagues, and then we'll have to turn toward Fulda or be even more conspicuous than we already are." Rakoczy changed back to Frankish. "You should ride ahead now."

"I will," said Rorthger, and nodded to the merchant. "May your friend the Bishop receive you well, and may you prosper."

"You are gracious," said Urtius, beaming at Rorthger and ducking his head in Rakoczy's direction. "I must tell you how pleased I am that we have met."

"You are very kind," said Rorthger. "And I pray you will have no reason to regret this meeting."

"And may your mission be fruitful for Great Karl," said Urtius, already anticipating the tales he would have to regale the Bishop and his company that night or the night after, whenever the banquet was held. "How could I regret this meeting?"

"The enemies of Great Karl are always alert to the failures of his messengers, and if that fate should befall my master, anyone we have spoken to stands in danger from them." He ducked his head. "I am sorry to repay you so ill for your friendliness."

Urtius went pale. "Ah. I had not considered . . . Your point is . . . I see your point."

"For your own sake, keep this meeting secret. You would not want to suffer any grief on our account." Rorthger made a gesture of protection. "May the Saints and Martyrs guard you, Urtius of Pavia. May you escape all danger."

"Amen," said Urtius, and did not protest when Rorthger moved out ahead of Rakoczy and the two took a side road rather than the main one.

They kept on all day, passing Fulda at mid-afternoon, standing below them in the valley. "The horses will need a good rest, wherever we fetch up this evening," said Rorthger, pointing out Fulda through the screen of trees. "If we had gone to the monastery we would be resting now, you and I, and our animals."

"I know," said Rakoczy. "And I have been thinking. Do you remember the ford at Sant' Wigbod? Where we crossed when we came into Franksland."

"Where the peasants brought the sledges?" Rorthger asked. "Yes. It is north of here, perhaps thirty Roman leagues."

"Yes. The road is clear between here and there. I trust we might cross at that point again," said Rakoczy. "They must take many travelers over the river at this time of year."

"But wouldn't that be folly? The Emperor would expect you to go that way, and if he wishes to stop you, he will send his soldiers there." Rorthger was troubled by this suggestion. "Why would he want to stop you? Is there some reason he might withdraw his defenses?"

"So he might. And we must be ready for that. But a handful of silver coins should buy us a day or two of protection among the peasants of this region." Rakoczy managed a quick, hard smile. "The peasants are probably willing to keep our passage a secret for a day or two if I pay them enough, if only to have a secret."

Rorthger shook his head. "It is too much of a chance."

"I don't think so," said Rakoczy. "We have good reason to go that way. It is the easiest crossing into Wendish territory away from the main roads. From there it is only three days to the frontier, which is closer than in many places. There are no battles, or any campaigns, in that region, at least not now."

"But it could be dangerous. Armed men could be waiting," Rorthger said nervously. In spite of himself, he looked back over his shoulder as if he expected to see men in pursuit.

"Armed men could be anywhere," said Rakoczy, as if knowing his apprehension. "For now, let us look for a village where we can pass a day or two. There must be some place in these hills where we can let our animals rest without attracting notice." He, too, looked over his shoulder at the road behind them. "No one has followed us this far, and that is something in our favor."

"You may be overly cautious," Rorthger reminded Rakoczy.

"I may be," he agreed. "But better too cautious and free than careless and in the hands of those who are against us." He pointed to the crest ahead. "There should be a village or a hamlet in the next valley, or the one beyond, or perhaps a monastery. Let us hope, whatever we may find, they will be able to provide us a place to stay for a day or two."

Rorthger tried to look skeptical, but had to admit that he had a strange sensation on the back of his neck. "All right. And then on to Sant' Wigbod."

"Yes," Rakoczy said, and once again took the lead on the narrow track that led into the fastness of the rugged hills.

TEXT OF A LETTER FROM BISHOP FLODOARD TO BISHOP ISO, CARRIED BY CHURCH COURIER AND DELIVERED SEVEN WEEKS AFTER IT WAS WRITTEN AND DISPATCHED.

To the most Sublime Bishop Iso, the greetings of your Brother in Christ and the Church, Bishop Flodoard at Fulda on the 22nd day of August in the Pope's year 801. May you find favor in Heaven's Eyes and advancement in this world. Amen.

The soldiers you dispatched to this monastery, after two weeks waiting here, have moved on, for the men they were seeking have not come this way. I have already dispatched word to the fortress at Erfurt, advising the Comes there that he may have to detain this Rakoczy and his servant. As much as we have done to locate the criminal, we have not been able to discover where he may have gone. It is most perplexing to have a man and one servant so completely elude you. There has been no report of them amongst the travelers stopping here, nor has anyone seen them in the village around the monastery. The wine-merchant spoke of seeing a hobu with an escort some distance from this place three weeks since, but as no one else has reported such an encounter, I put little credence in his account, for he is often moved by what he sells, and in the retelling, a flock of sheep becomes an army. Yet even if he did encounter this foreigner, he makes it no easier to find the fellow. I know this is most disappointing to you, I know, for you have been determined to call this man to answer stringent charges. I am in sympathy with your predicament, for when such miscreants as this foreigner Rakoczy and his camerarius are said to be are allowed to move about the Empire of Karl-lo-Magne, all of Franksland must be held accountable for permitting his escape. For this alone you and I will have much to answer for if the Pope should ever decide to question these events.

At least the White Woman has Confessed at last, telling Bishop Berahtram that she had congress with many devils who were summoned by Rakoczy in diabolical rites intended to harm the Pope and bring about the end of the Roman Church. She has also said she has been in the Circle of the Damned and heard curses called down upon our Emperor, and for such evil, not even the Pope can save her. It must be troubling to His Holiness that the White Woman so glamored him that he did not see Satan in her when she was sent to appear before him. He will not extend protection to her now that it has been shown that she is as a viper sent to poison the hearts and souls of good Christian Franks. Her immurement will provide her the opportunity to expiate the worst of her sins and bring sanctity to Sant' Ianuarius, as well as enhance the reputation of Bishop Berahtram, who has been able to show her for what she is, and thereby defend both the Church and the Emperor. May God grant him long years and a good death.

I must tell you that I am disheartened that I have been unable to assist your soldiers in apprehending this foreigner. I am informed that Optime has been reluctant to condemn this Magnatus because he believes that Rakoczy rendered him honorable service during his time as his courtier. I cannot express what a disappointment I have experienced since I have learned that Great Karl has refused to send more soldiers to these eastern frontiers for the purpose of seizing this foreigner and sending him back to be tried before a full Council of Archbishops.

One of the travelers who recently came here to Fulda suggested that this missing foreigner might have been killed by bandits on the road. There have been more than twenty such killings this summer, and I must agree that this is possible, and, if it has happened, we must all thank God for deliverance from the powers of Satan. It is also possible that he was struck down by the Great Pox that still lingers in this region, and has claimed many lives since summer began. If that is the case, the man lies in some nameless grave and you and I may be free of worry. I have asked various pilgrims if they have heard of any foreign hobu dying of the Great Pox while on the road. I have learned nothing so far, but I have dreamed that he succumbed in just that fashion, and if, by the Nativity, I have heard nothing more of him, I will know my dream to have been a true vision. I pray you will find the same surety that I have, so that you may inform Optime that he has no reason to fear the return of Magnatus Rakoczy. My revered colleague, Bishop Iso, I implore you, let it be as if the foreigner never existed, and God will bring us all to Grace for honoring His Might.

Flodoard,
Abbott and Bishop
Fulda, Sant' Maclovis, Santa Fabronia,
Emaerich, and Sant' Fides
by my own hand and under seal

⌒

EPILOGUE

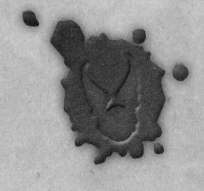

To my oldest, dearest friend, Ragoczy Fransicus, still in Kiev in the Khazar Empire, the greetings of Olivia in Venice, and a miserable place it is, too, all filled with water and the constant movement of the tides, on this, the onset of Lent in the Pope's year 815.

Not content with leaving Karl-lo-Magne's Empire, you have stayed far away from the Empire in the West. I cannot believe that you would prefer to remain in that distant city. On the other hand, I can understand why you want to be beyond the reach of the Franks. They certainly excoriated your reputation as soon as you were gone. But Karl-lo-Magne is dead now, for a bit more than a year, and his son, thus far, has not shown his father's energy the way his daughters do. How unfortunate that power had to pass to Louis and his Court of Bishops instead of Bellatori. If Gisela or Rotruda had been able to rule, things wouldn't be as precarious as they have become.

Living here in soggy Venice, I often hear from sailors and merchants of what is taking place in the broad world. The merchants from the north— some from as far away as England—say that there are Norsemen coming in long, shallow boats to plunder the western part of Franksland and the northern ports of Hispania. I have seen no proof of this for myself, and I hold such accounts in some question, but there have been enough of them and they have been consistent enough that I am willing to believe that they are true, which means that Louis will have to make some attempt to shore up his harbors against these Norsemen or lose the control of them. Can you imagine what his father would have to say about that? I fear if Louis isn't strong enough to hold his ports, it will only be the first of his misfortunes. I also understand that Frankish custom requires him to divide his lands among his sons, as Karl-lo-Magne would have done had more of them than Louis outlived him. At a time when the Empire is in peril, dividing it seems to me to be folly. But perhaps I am too much of an old Roman to see the virtue in this arrangement.

One of the many things I dislike about this horrible collection of islands is that I cannot keep my horses here. Everything is boats, boats, boats. I can see the advantages in that arrangement, but I cannot accustom myself to have my horses on the mainland, where any thief might take them, while I am

condemned to a small stone house that even Niklos Aulirios finds insuffi-
cient to our purposes. Still, it is a place where the Pope does not come, and
the Church confines itself to two islands, affording me a degree of license I
have lost in Roma. It is unfortunate that I could not mend my break with
Leo, but since matters worked out so badly for Gynethe Mehaut and she was
my guest, I was tainted in Leo's eyes, and absenting myself from the city has
been prudent. I have heard that Leo is ailing, and if it is so, I may soon be
able to return to Roma; eleven years in Venice has been an eternity of discomfort to me. I will be delighted to see the Flavian Circus and all the old
Fora once again, and love them, no matter how damaged and battered they
are. Roma is my native earth, and I honor it as the first of my lares.

It is a most dreadful thing, the loss of Gynethe Mehaut. Nothing you tell
me will convince me that Bishop Iso did not have a hand in her disgrace.
And as for Bishop Berahtram—who is now Archbishop of Arles, as you may
have heard—I am deeply troubled by all I hear of him. He is high in the ranks
of Louis' advisors and he is regarded as highly as any Grav in the Empire. I
think the man is a toad who bullied and frightened Gynethe Mehaut into
saying things that would advance him in the Church, not help her soul. It is
ironic that the people of Sant' Yrieix have begun to make shrines to her and
ask her to pray for them in times of affliction. Nothing the Church has commanded thus far has stopped them from revering her. It is scant consolation,
I know, but it should salve your wounds at least a little.

And do not waste ink telling me your wounds have healed, for I know
you better than that. You still blame yourself for what happened to her, or
you would have returned to your native mountains before now. Do you
think I am unaware of your pattern? When you are dissatisfied with yourself
you impose isolation as a kind of penance. Only when you are ready to
accept what has happened do you go to the Carpathians and restore yourself.
This time has been particularly long—you continue to be vexed by what
Csimenae has made of her vampiric life, and now you have Gynethe
Mehaut's death to add to your ledger. No wonder your exile has been so long,
and so distant. I ought to be thankful you haven't gone to China again.

Sanct' Germain, listen to me. You cannot take the world on yourself. From
what I have learned, in spite of what the Church teaches, not even Jesus did
that. You are more generous than any lover I have ever known, and have
been since we first met under the stands. You say it is your nature to extend
yourself, but you and I both know it is your kindness and not simply your
nature that makes you seek to mitigate the suffering you find. It may be use-

less to tell you that there is no need for you to seclude yourself in remote parts of the world, but I would not be content with myself if I failed to remind you of this.

Wherever you are, I hope you have found love there. I hope you have not been condemning yourself for things you could not have prevented and cannot now change. I long for the day when I see you again, whether in Roma, in China, or on the moon. And before this becomes intolerably maudlin, I will close it, with my enduring devotion and abiding affection.

Olivia

by my own hand, of course